THE RIDDLER'S GIFT

GREG HAMERTON

Eyri

WESTMILL
STORMHAVEN
SOUTHWIND
KIRONKILN
FENDWARROW
RAVENSCROFT
BRIMSTONE
RUSSEL
Amberlake
Black River
CELLARSPRING
WAXWORTH
Bairwood County
FIRST LIGHT
Winterborn Manor
ROTCOTFORD
Phantom Acres
Fynn's Tooth
Meadowmoor County

Other titles by the same author
Beyond The Invisible
The Fresh Air Site Guide

The Riddler's Gift
First published June 2007

Publishers
ETERNITY PRESS
1 Brounger Road
Constantia, 7806
Cape Town, South Africa

info@eternitypress.co.za
www.eternitypress.co.za

Printed by Thomson Press

BIC : FM

ISBN 978-0-9585118-4-1

Greg Hamerton has always been fascinated with magic and fantasy. He lives in Cape Town where he writes in an old green shed at the end of the garden, among many books and a stone dragon called Qwert. He is an outdoors enthusiast and enjoys soaring over clouds and getting lost in the mountains on his paraglider.

The Riddler's Gift is the first novel in the Lifesong cycle.

Find out more on www.eternitypress.co.za

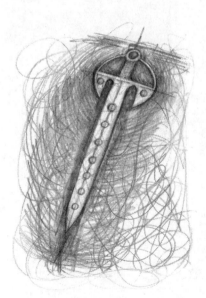

PREFACE

There is a song that drifts on the breeze through all the world. Its rhythms are echoed in our breath, the music is caught in our laughter, hidden in our language, woven through our life. Singers reach for the melody, but it is too delicate to hold and too elusive to remember. As the Ages pass, so the Lifesong retreats under the sounds of our time, its potent beauty and danger ever more a mystery.

Few know how the Lifesong has shaped our world, for those who hear its tune would rather sing than write, and to grasp its tale we must go back, far back beyond our brief and incomplete history, to when the world was changing, when Life was shadowed by a mighty legend.

In that most vital era, when the destiny of Humankind was balanced on a blade, the inhabited Earth was known as Oldenworld. Magic was a raw force then, released from the confining code that so tightly binds it today, yet to master that magic required great patience and even more wit; few apprentices became casters, fewer still became masters.

So much power in the hands of so few. Ever has it been the cause of woe. At first those gifted masters wrought works of great beauty in the rising civilisations of Oldenworld. But they became distracted by the powers they had discovered, seeking majesty, seeking mastery. Seeking might.

And so those who had first been hailed as the Wise, the wizards, now fought amongst themselves, determined to prove one lore over another, to justify one vision of magic as superior, all-encompassing and absolute.

The battle for power was fierce. Those wizards who did not fight to prove their lore, fell.

At first the wizards used principles of Dark and Light for their spells. Such an elementary form of magic came to be known as the first axis. After much study the Wise discovered a second axis, but this only intensified the conflict as those who summoned raw Energy now rallied against those who could command solid Matter. The wizards were driven by the escalating violence to find a resolution; Oldenworld could not sustain such a conflict. Their urgency led them to the third and most advanced axis, a lore of Order, a lore that promised ultimate peace.

There was a hidden price to pay. Order demanded perfection. Order demanded knowledge and structure, it demanded control. The wizards could see no danger; they eagerly developed the magic of the third axis, hoping to mold Humankind into ever greater stability. How different the world would be, if wisdom preceded action.

Too late they considered what might develop on the opposite pole of their third axis, too late they noticed the one who had mastered Chaos.

He swung the third axis like a warhammer: Ametheus, the Sorcerer, the Unbinder. The bringer of Ruin. He tore apart their ordered web of control before the wizards had even recognised their common foe; he smashed their College and their future with it. When the wizards gathered again, they numbered only twelve of thirty-three. By the time they had agreed to unify in one Gyre, they numbered only eight. And eight, they found, was too few.

They had failed to prepare for the coming of the tide, and Oldenworld began to change. The entire lowlands north of the great mountains fell to the Sorcerer's way, one realm after another corrupted by the spreading web of silvered essence, the horror named Wildfire. The people were ravaged with such change they could not recognise their own kinfolk. Beings which should have had no place in the history of Humankind walked the face of the Earth.

The Gyre fought to restore Order, they fought to save the precious networks of commerce and culture, but Ametheus severed the veins of every system and corrupted the blood of every resistant soldier. Such was his hatred for the wizards and their Order.

Those who could, retreated south, to the heartlands, where for a time the Sorcerer's power could not reach. But all things that slumber, awaken renewed. When his influence began to spread again, the Gyre suspected that Oldenworld faced its doom.

Ametheus. Some said he was mad from the first. Some began to whisper that he was the shadow of another, more ancient evil, for it was true that he reached beyond the knowledge contained in any of the wizard's lores; he drew his inspiration from a mightier source.

The wizards of the Gyre even began to fear that their own reasoning had become affected by Chaos. They trusted their perfect foundation of knowledge, but they fought amongst themselves, and had begun to serve the Sorcerer's ends in so doing. They needed a champion to resist the Sorcerer, someone with a special talent, different to their own. Yet such a champion would have to be born in a place where nothing was known of Ametheus, where no trace of his power lurked. And so they conceived of Eyri, the most secret of secrets, a realm to be sheltered from the very essence of Chaos for as long as possible. The wizards chose an unknown region in the southern mountains beyond the heartlands—the furthest territory from Ametheus which lay fertile and populated, and as yet untouched by the scourges to the north.

The Gyre wove a powerful shield around Eyri and devised a complex network of rules to ensure that the realm wasn't tainted from within. They selected a precious talisman of power and set it in place. They chose one member of their circle, the one best suited to sift gold from gravel, and they bade him farewell. Then the seven wizards departed from that precious jagged-rimmed realm.

They tried to forget what they had done, for even a secret held in mind might not be safe from the Sorcerer. They dared not think upon it, and yet they dared not forget it, because without the crucible of Eyri they would face Ametheus without hope.

The battle for Oldenworld continued, and in the years that passed, the Gyre began to understand their foe. They found ways to bring peace to places he had ravaged, they struck blows that shattered his cruel inventions, and they survived, as a pack of wolves survives when facing a bear. Yet before their eyes Oldenworld continued to crumble. So much was lost, so many lives were stamped into the mud of battlefields that should not have been trodden upon, so many people lost their lives to despair.

The wizards of the Gyre grew tired. To assert Order required continuous effort; spreading Chaos took no effort at all. Ametheus surged into the heartlands, his presence pouring in from both the west and the east. As the beleaguered Gyre fought, their fear grew, for they suspected that the Sorcerer would not stop until he had disrupted everything. He reached for powers that should remain untouched. He would bend the course of Time upon itself until it ruptured. His vision was of all Order ended, replaced by an existence so far from our natural course that nothing precious would remain, not a leaf, not a light, not even the tale of the Lifesong. The Sorcerer reached for the End, and no one could stop him.

The only hope lay in Eyri. And yet, for years, there was only silence from that mountain-rimmed realm.

1. THE GLEE OF GENESIS

"The strength of a song can be marked
by the silence that surrounds it."—*Zarost*

The shadows were long. The fading sun rested among the tall western peaks. The forests which carpetted the slopes around the high village had begun to darken, and the wind had a bite to it—a warning there would be snow before winter thawed. The scent of smoke lingered in the lee of the buildings; indoors there would be warm hearths and watchful hounds, but the people would be gone.

Tabitha quickened her pace through the empty streets, worried that she would be late. Her soft boots hardly made a sound on the cobbles, only the fabric of her dress whispered with every step. A curl of hair blew across her face, and she tucked it hurriedly behind her ear.

She knew that she shouldn't have lingered for so long to practice, but she had been determined to perfect her recital. She had tuned her familiar lyre again and again, but it wouldn't hold the notes to match her voice, as though the instrument knew of the contest tonight and shuddered under her nervous fingers. She wanted to win a place amongst the three best singers, and so earn a chance to perform in the King's Challenge. All the villagers of First Light would be at the inn, and a good many visitors besides. She should be there already.

The street held a tense air as if the neighbourhood waited for Tabitha to pass. A building moved, or its shadow shrank against a wall. Her mind was playing tricks with her. She turned away from the imaginary disturbance to take a short-cut, but just as she did so, a toddler tottered into the street up ahead.

He was a lone little figure in a hooded red coat, small between the looming buildings. The child wobbled uncertainly, then turned towards Tabitha. She recognised him, and she guessed that he had only just realised he was lost. Kip was too curious for his own good, and his mother was often too distracted to keep a constant eye on him. His expression showed that his curiosity had once again led him beyond the limit of his bravery.

A tall man rushed from a doorway beside Kip. Although his back was to Tabitha, his black robe seemed to pull the shadows in his wake. He snatched the toddler from the cobbles, and strode off toward a side alley, with Kip's head protruding from under his arm. Kip gasped like a fish, but didn't make a sound. Tabitha stared after him, too surprised to move.

A queer shiver ran down her spine; what she was seeing could not be true.

"Hey! Wait!" she shouted. The man threw an angry glance over his shoulder, and disappeared into the shadows of the alley at a run.

"Stop! Child-snatcher!" Tabitha shouted, but the street was empty of help, and the windows dark. She ran for the alley before she could consider the consequences. Her lyre bounced hard against her back on its strap, and she lost a moment securing it under her arm. The alley was gloomy, and the cobbles were slippery underfoot. The man was so fast that only the flutter of his robe showed where he ducked around the corner. He seemed to blend with the shadows.

Kip still hadn't made a sound. He should be bawling his lungs out.

Tabitha sprinted. Her foot slipped at the corner, and her dress tangled around her legs, causing her to career wide of the turn. She caught herself against the far wall of the alley. When she gathered her dress and ran again, the child-snatcher was out of sight. The street into which she emerged was empty, but for a broken-down cart which slumped against a wall, and too many shadows.

The sound of running came from her left, and she chose the first break in the buildings to dart that way. The passage opened onto another deserted street, where the last of the sunlight was fading from the roofs. Tabitha slowed to a jog. The little one had to cry out soon, and she would follow that sound.

But there was nothing to hear—only the wind moaned through the eaves.

Her stomach knotted tight. She tried to ignore her mounting dread, and peered alongside every building.

What kind of man steals a child?

A smudge of red caught her eye, but when she turned her head, there was nothing there. She tiptoed between the buildings and into a short dead-end street. A jumble of crates occupied the wedge of two converging warehouse walls.

Then she caught sight of a little face behind a latticed crate-side; a panicked prisoner within the discarded cage. Kip's face was screwed up, his body shook, but although it was clear that he was crying, he still made no sound. Tabitha looked nervously around. The doorways nearby were empty, the doors closed deep in the shadows.

The strange dark man was gone.

Relief made her legs weak. The black-robed abductor had been more than just a stranger; the way the shadows had clung to his shape, his swift movement, like a predator, stalking. He had preyed upon a child! She hoped that she would never see him again.

"Oh, Kip, it's all right, it's all right!" she called out, making her way to him. She tipped the crate aside, and reached for the little adventurer.

A sudden, cold gust crept up her skirts. The street darkened at her back, and she realised she was not alone.

"Hullo, pretty."

Something sharp pressed against her ribs, and a dry hand caught her neck. "Not a word, or you'll feel my knife in your heart. I care nothing for your life."

It was not the words which made her weak, it was the certainty in the declaration. I care nothing for your life—she knew he meant it, she could feel his ugly menacing spirit. She clutched Kip close, and tried to resist shaking. The man's touch was cold, so cold. He bent his cowled head close to her. One glance at his face and she turned quickly away. Cold, grey eyes watched her, marbled orbs with yellow-stained whites, eyes devoid of mercy. Her shivering became impossible to control.

"The Master could use you as well," he said. "Walk with me a while." It was a mocking invitation. The pressure of his knife compelled her to turn. She lifted Kip to her chest to keep ahead of their captor.

He forced a quick pace toward the outskirts of the village. He moved to her side, with an arm around her shoulder, as if to pretend there was nothing unusual about their procession. Tabitha didn't dare break from his hold, his grip was cruel, the blade was too close against her, the tip cold and sharp where it had pierced her clothes and found skin. The darkness seemed to follow them, as if the shadows thickened when they passed.

Something shot low over their heads, a dark winged shape born upon a whistle of wind. The man snaked his arm around Tabitha's throat, and brought her to such an abrupt halt that she almost lost her grip on Kip. Her lyre pressed painfully under her arm, but it was the knife she suddenly felt the worst. She tried to arch her back away from the pain. She prayed he wasn't about to sink the blade home.

A raven croaked at them from a rooftop, then heaved itself into the air. The man didn't move; he watched its flight, then cursed when it croaked again.

"You've led someone to me, bitch." He gripped Tabitha by her hair, pulled her hard against his chest. "I'll be back for you." It was not a threat, it was a statement—he believed it. Tabitha believed it. As he released her, his cloak must have brushed over her eyes, for a sudden darkness passed across her vision. Tabitha wondered if she was about to faint.

"You'll say nothing to give me away," he said, his stale breath close. "Silence!"

She gagged against a sudden cold in her chest, and coughed. The knife at her back was gone. Her vision cleared.

She didn't dare turn until she was sure of her balance, in case he was still there, in case the sound of fleeing footsteps was just a fantasy. She clutched Kip tight. He was warm, but his body still shook with his silent cries.

The footsteps came back, a pounding, heavy tread. Tabitha didn't bother to check where he was, she just ran.

"Stop!" boomed a man behind her. "Stop, in the name of the King!"

She fled down the street, but something in the commanding voice made her glance over her shoulder.

The figure who charged after her was not the black-robed man after all. A Sword, one of the King's soldiers, all muscle and burnished steel, raced up the street. Not just any Sword, she realised, as she came to an abrupt halt. The powerful man in the blue cloak of office was unmistakable. Glavenor, the Swordmaster of Eyri. She could not have imagined a more welcome sight. The highest law in the land had arrived.

The Swordmaster wasted no time in catching up to her. He halted close enough that Tabitha could smell the freshness of his oiled leather, see the reflections in his armour. His expression was fierce.

"Where are you taking that child?" he demanded. He reached for Kip, and she pulled back in reflex. She searched his face in alarm, and began to answer his question, but found that she could not speak. She formed the words; nothing came out.

The Swordmaster gripped her wrist.

"Someone called out the alarm for a child-snatcher, and here I find the child. Explain yourself, young lady."

Tabitha choked on her panic. She had lost her voice. When she cleared her throat and tried again, nothing more than a wheeze passed her lips.

"Come with me," said the Swordmaster. "I'll see this child returned to its mother. Then you and I shall have a chat."

Oh, Mercy, he thinks I'm the child-snatcher.

She shook her head violently. She held Kip with her right hand, and Glavenor had her left, so she was forced to point with her chin down the street, to where her captor had escaped. The gesture appeared idiotic, no doubt, and there was nothing for the Swordmaster to see when he finally caught her meaning. The street was empty, there was no trace of the black-robed felon, nothing within the shadows, or without.

When Glavenor turned on her again, his voice was as forgiving as an iron bar. "It'll go easier on you if you just come along, without a fuss."

The stranger will get away! she tried to say. Not even a whisper passed from her lips; she had lost her voice, and so had Kip. That was more terrifying than anything she had endured.

"The child," he said, extending his free hand. She let the Swordmaster take Kip. He placed the tearful boy high on his shoulder. She offered no resistance when Glavenor led her away.

The route the Swordmaster chose took them toward the centre of First Light. The villagers would be gathered outside the Tooth-and-Tale, the inn which was hosting this year's singing contest.

The contest! Tabitha realised with alarm. *How am I going to sing at all?* She tried to free her hand from Glavenor's grip, but he shot her a forbidding glance.

She knew Glavenor was a good man. He had brought justice to the village in the few times he had passed through. He was a hero of Eyri, young for his rank, but peerless. To be led in his hand like a bad girl was deeply embarrassing. That he might consider her to be a felon was worse, but she couldn't talk to save herself.

As they drew nearer to the people, she quailed. People from all over Meadowmoor County, some of them she didn't even know. She was supposed to stand before that crowd tonight and entertain them with her singing. She could not be led before them like this. Not by the Swordmaster.

Glavenor seemed to understand her distress, for he eased his grip on her wrist. "You try to run, I'll catch you."

Tabitha nodded, mute. The Swordmaster allowed her to walk beside him unrestrained, but he was near enough to fall upon her in an instant.

As soon as they neared the sprawling inn and joined the edge of the milling crowd outside, a stout woman cut a path towards them. Mrs Quilt brooked no nonsense, and the innkeeper's eyes were firmly locked onto her toddler.

"And where have you been?" Mrs Quilt scolded, with only a cursory nod to Glavenor to acknowledge his presence.

Glavenor handed the child over. Mrs Quilt hugged Kip close.

"Thank you, Swordmaster! And Tabitha. Where did you find him?"

Tabitha gagged on her reply, then hid her inability with a cough. The shock grew worse, every time she tried to speak. She dropped her eyes.

"This young lady was trying to escape with your child," Glavenor said, at her side.

Mrs Quilt was instantly offended. "Tabitha? A child-snatcher?" Surprised faces within the crowd turned their way. "Don't be ridiculous. He's wrong, isn't he, Tabitha?"

Tabitha shook her head, then nodded, then paddled in the air with her hands. How could she explain chasing the man in the black robe, and the horror of being caught? She gestured toward her throat, then held up an open palm.

"I take it this young lady is a mute?" asked Glavenor.

"Tabitha Serannon is our truthsayer!" Mrs Quilt said. "What's the matter, Tabitha?"

But Tabitha couldn't answer.

Glavenor's eyebrows rode upwards. "This is Trisha Serannon's daughter?" he asked. "She's changed a lot since I was last here." His expression softened, though in his disciplined features, it was hard to be sure.

Two years. He had last been in First Light two years ago. Tabitha remembered lingering wherever he was in the village, and wishing she would one day find the courage to talk to him. She was surprised Glavenor remembered her at all.

Glavenor watched her with a level gaze. "Why did you run from me, when I first saw you with the child?"

Tabitha touched her throat, and shook her head again. Dry, terrifying silence.

"Maybe she's been practising too hard for the singing tonight," suggested someone within the crowd. Tabitha pointed to the toddler, then back to herself, and mimed speech.

"What's wrong with the youngling?" someone called out.

"There's nothing wrong with my Kip!" Mrs Quilt exclaimed. She held Kip at arm's length, but it was plain for all to see that he was trying to cry, yet making no sound.

"Wait! I've seen this before," Glavenor said. His brows were gathered like storm clouds. "Be damned that it could happen here! Is there a Lightgifter in the village?"

"Only Tabitha's mother, but she's out on their farm," replied Mrs Quilt.

"Any spritesalt?" he demanded. An uncomfortable mutter passed through the crowd.

"I have some," offered a prim little lady who Tabitha knew as Fran Semple. "It's expensive," she added. That was no lie; the healing spritesalt was not something to be thrown about.

"Heavens, Fran! I'll pay for it," exclaimed Mrs Quilt.

"The King's coin will pay for it," Glavenor corrected. "If this is what I suspect, I must act fast."

Fran Semple offered the Swordmaster a small vial. The blue glass glowed with an inner light. Glavenor removed the stopper with care. Even so, a few sprites spilled to the ground. Fran Semple frowned, but said nothing. Glavenor took a pinch of spritesalt, and slipped it into the toddler's mouth. Kip pushed his tongue out at what Tabitha knew to be a sharp taste, then he swallowed.

Tabitha waited with the hushed crowd. If this didn't work -

She didn't want to think about it.

The toddler coughed once, drew a rasping breath, and howled at the top of his lungs. Despite the appreciative murmur of the crowd and the toddler's wail, Glavenor's quiet curse found Tabitha's ears.

"Shadowcaster."

She wished she had not heard that word. It made her hand quiver as she took a hasty pinch of spritesalt for herself from the vial Glavenor offered. A Shadowcaster could not have come to First Light. Their kind were only heard of in Fendwarrow, leagues to the east. She noted how Glavenor had clenched his jaw.

She recalled the stranger's predatory eyes. The way he had wrapped the gloom around him. The way he had forced cold into her throat. She had not wanted to consider the possibility, she still did not want to. She had been touched by a Shadowcaster. The sprites worked their magic, releasing the Light essence, and she coughed against their sudden warmth.

"Kip was taken by a stranger," she announced. Her voice was scratchy, as if she had sand in her throat, but it was a voice, at least. "I chased after them. I found Kip, but the man was hiding, and he came up behind me, with a knife. He was taking us both out of the village when you arrived, Swordmaster. He fled, but he said he would be back, and that I should remain silent. That's when I lost my voice. He used the Dark essence, I think. He wore a black robe. He was a Shadowcaster."

So saying, she confirmed the truth, for she was the village Truthsayer. Her skill compelled honesty, and her word was true. The man who had abducted her, here in First Light, was a Shadowcaster, no matter how chilling it was to believe.

Through the telling of her story, Glavenor had become still, though he was anything but calm. He was a cat, tensing for the hunt. A large and dangerous cat. He nodded, slowly.

"They evade the law like rats in the dark," he said. "Describe him."

"He was tall, like you, but—thinner. I didn't get to see much else but his grey eyes, the whites were all yellow."

Glavenor grunted. "Jurrum. They all use it."

"The tales of the Shadowcasters are real?" challenged Mrs Quilt.

"The casters are real, all right," the Swordmaster answered. "I have too many reports to say otherwise. But I wouldn't believe half of the tales about them. When I catch this vermin, I am sure we shall find that it squeaks."

"But what's he doing in First Light?" Mrs Quilt demanded.

Garyll shrugged. "It's always been lone farms and Lightgifters they've harassed, until now, I've not heard of them in a village, and never this far from Fendwarrow." He backed away from Tabitha and the others. "When he left you, which way did he run?"

"Toward where you came from. I thought you were the Shadowcaster, returning."

"Swordmaster! What should we do?" someone cried from within the crowd.

"Get indoors, and keep a closer eye on your children. I shall rouse the Sword and scour the village. We shall find him, or cause him to flee."

The Swordmaster caught Tabitha's eye last. His level gaze made her stand straighter. In that moment, she forgave him for arresting her. He was the Swordmaster of Eyri; he carried the weight of the sword of justice. He had to be thorough, and firm. Then he turned, and was running.

She wished she could have asked him how she had changed in his eyes, that he had not recognised her.

◆ ——————◆

The Tooth-and-Tale was crowded, even though it was enlarged for the contest night. The wall furthest from the bar had been swung back on its giant hinges, and the common-room was linked to the hall beyond, an innovation which had seen the Tooth become the place for all village gatherings, back when the Tall Hall had burned down.

A singer, on the hearth-side stage, strained to be heard over the clamour. Tabitha was kept too busy serving drinks to worry about the unfairness of the noise on contest night. She couldn't quieten the patrons—she was the one they were talking about. Her and the Shadowcaster.

As the wisdom of fermented liquids took hold, the inspired opinions became louder. More than one patron held the door with a wary eye. Any newcomer dressed in a dark cloak generated a gust of silence before the clamour returned, redoubled.

Tabitha just wished her voice would heal in time; she would have to hold a strong voice tonight to be noticed. She took a quick sip of Honeydew when she reached the bar. It soothed her throat, but not her nerves.

"Five Dwarrow, two Dew," she called out to Mrs Quilt, and set the coins on the bar. Mrs Quilt checked the payment with a tireless enthusiasm that would have made her late husband proud. Old Stamper Quilt had been very enthusiastic about money. Too much so, some said. It was gold that had led him to his untimely end—the hope of an enlarged profit from dealing direct with the winegrowers in Bentwood County. A bridge had given way. Nothing could be proved, yet they all suspected the tale had a dark side; it didn't pay for innkeepers to bypass the wagoneers and agents when acquiring wine. Almost a year now, since Old Stamper had braved the road to Fendwarrow. Mrs Quilt forged on without him now, and she didn't show signs of strain so long as she was selling wine and collecting coin. Mrs Quilt filled Tabitha's glasses with a practised·hand, set the dark reds beside the two of pale gold, and sent Tabitha on her way. It was tricky to balance the loaded tray through the crowd and reach the patrons who had ordered the wine without spilling it on the way.

Most of the orders were for the Dwarrow wine. Two barrels had arrived that day, and they stood high on the end of the bar in clear sight, the characteristic brand-mark burned in the tap-ends. The price of the Dwarrow rose with every barrel as its lusty reputation grew. A large profit could be turned by trading in such a wine.

Two men began to fight, and Tabitha backed away from the commotion, keeping her tray high. The unrest subsided as she rounded it when others pulled the men apart, yet the argument continued to simmer below the surface of tight expressions. She hoped that the bystanders were wise enough to keep those men apart all night, and to change their drinks for something milder.

Such was the cost of trading in Dwarrow. Everyone who drank it seemed to become boisterous, or angry. Yet they hollered for more, and as they demanded, so Mrs Quilt sold. At a profit.

Tabitha dispensed the drinks, and heard a new voice take up the challenge from the stage. She turned to watch Lyndall for a moment. She hoped the innkeeper's daughter made the cut for the King's Challenge. Lyndall Quilt was a good friend. The sturdy blonde was singing Fynn Fell Down, and that meant it was almost time. Tabitha would be next. A nervous thrill skittered through her stomach. She hurried back to the bar, to steal a last few sips of Honeydew before her voice would be put to the test.

A skew-toothed youth thumped away on an empty wine-casket to the beat of Lyndall's song. He kept a reasonable time, and folks began to follow his lead, clapping, or beating their tankards on the tables. The dancing began on the open floor, and Lyndall had to compete with the revelry. She was doing well, though. She had caught the crowd, and that would count in her favour.

Even little Kip was trying to clap his hands in time to his sister's song. He was sitting where he had been placed, in clear view upon the bar beside Mrs Quilt. Tabitha waved to him, and he googled and smiled, all his tears forgotten. Tabitha wished she could forget so easily; she could still feel the dry grip of silence that had held her captive.

The sweet Honeydew wine was cold and clear, as if it retained all the sunshine and freshness of Flowerton, but the glass wasn't deep enough, and Lyndall's singing seemed to end too soon after it had begun. Before Tabitha could even test her voice, she found herself approaching the stage through the waning applause for Lyndall. She collected her lyre from the corner. She plucked the strings gently to settle her stance on the stage, and to announce her readiness, though she was not ready at all. Butterflies had taken permanent residence in her belly.

The judges for Meadowmoor were seated close by—the three Elders from First Light, and one each from Russel, Cellarspring and Brimstone. Similar trials would be taking place in each county around Eyri—the town of Wright would hold Westfold's contest, Flowerton would stage Vinmorgen's, the singers in Rockroute County would be tested in Respite, and in Fendwarrow the sultry voices of Bentwood would be driving the revellers wild. Tabitha wondered just how many singers were singing that night in Eyri, and if she would be lucky enough to meet them at the King's Challenge.

"I'm to play the Glee of Genesis," she announced. "Could you set me down a glass, of your choosing?"

The elder from Russel, a spry lady with a delicate shawl about her shoulders, sat forward on her seat. "You can do that part of the song?"

"I hope so."

The placing of the glass on the edge of the stage brought a new surge of speculation from the crowd, and it was to a returning clamour that Tabitha strummed the introduction to the Glee. She abandoned herself to the music. She could do nothing about the crowd, except win their silence by singing.

It was a beautiful song, and one she loved to sing. Her mother had taught her well, and yet Tabitha had surpassed even Trisha's singing of it. There were few singers who could perform the Glee of Genesis as it was intended, and reach the high Shiver. She stroked her lyre, and gave voice to the myth of creation. Her voice held.

The Glee told of the Creator's first elements and how they warred. Air rushed through Fire, blowing the red flames high and far. The melody rose. Fire was angered so deeply it burned gentle Water, and thus set great clouds to fill the Air. The notes went higher. Water appealed to Earth, and so the rocks rose up and swallowed the Fire whole, for Earth and Water were lovers. But even the Earth could not contain the anger of Fire, and so great streaks of flame erupted from the rocks, and the surface of the ground was scorched.

The notes of the Glee climbed to the sky, and Tabitha's voice held.

The Goddess Ethea threaded music through the elements, bringing balance to their strife, weaving currents in the chaos, binding the elements into a sphere filled with the infinite patterns of life.

Tabitha followed the final melody of the Glee of Genesis, raising the notes. The crowd barely murmured. She wished there was a way to fill the gaps in the room with her sound, to touch the people with the vibration of every note. She felt the lack in her singing most keenly, she sensed there could be more to it, but tonight she had to settle for the fact that most of the village listened, and waited for the ascent, the final high note.

The wine-glass resting on the stone caught the orange light of the lamps overhead. She followed the path of the pure notes, upwards, to her limit.

The crowd was hushed. She could feel the imperfection in the glass waiting to turn her voice. She reached for the note of the Shiver.

In the legend, the sphere of the elements exploded to a million fragments upon that note. All life was set free in the Universe, bound only by the skin of time. In the Tooth-and-Tale, before the crowd and judges of the Singer's Contest, the glass shattered.

Tabitha wound the Glee of Genesis to a close with the last few words, of how the Goddess Ethea's song was now just an echo, heard by few, but the crowd had already erupted into applause, and her voice was drowned. She knew she had done well, for the stamping and whistling was louder than it had been even for Lyndall.

She guessed that the Dwarrow wine had much to do with the applause, but she still felt a surge of pride. Her throat tingled, but her voice had been true to the end. It had been her best performance. Only when she rose from a curtsey to the crowd did she notice the magnitude of what she had done. Embarrassment flared across her cheeks.

Not only the selected glass had been shattered.

All around the stage, drinks had spilled from glasses broken in hand. Mrs Quilt eyed a jumble of shards on the bar, and worst of all, the Swordmaster was there, seated amidst broken glass. Glavenor was gripping his forearm. She hadn't even seen him enter. He picked at something embedded in the flesh, and set it on the bar. A red bloom spread from his wound. He pressed a cloth to his arm, and shook the remaining glass from his lap as he stood.

The world spun around Tabitha, with the thunder of applause.

Glavenor looked up at her. His crimped smile held no anger. He joined the applause. For the first time in her life Tabitha wished she had not sung so well.

"Sorry," she said to one and all, when the clamour subsided at last. "I'm terribly sorry."

Some of the patrons laughed. Lyndall was already sweeping the floor; a girl well accustomed to accidents in the common-room.

"I saw six glasses burst, and I saw who held them," Mrs Quilt called out. "You six may come aside for another, on the house."

Tabitha left the stage feeling stunned and not a little stupid. She hadn't realised it was possible to cause so much damage with the Shiver. She had never sung the Glee with so much passion before. The spry old lady from Russel was still clapping her hands with great merriment. At least one of the judges had enjoyed the joke. She hoped the others would remember her singing, and not the accidental extra damage.

The Swordmaster bowed slightly as she approached the bar. He had quenched the bleeding on his arm.

His jaw was clean-shaved, his cheeks reflected the oil-lamp at the head of the bar. He was looking directly at her.

"Care for a drink?" he asked.

She clutched her lyre tighter. "What?"

Glavenor had deep, dark eyes. "Would you care for a drink, Miss Serannon?"

Her blush was renewed under his gaze. She could feel his attention holding her. The smile he gave her could have melted ice.

Tabitha was too startled to answer. The great Swordmaster had just been assaulted by her exploding glass. Yet his voice was deep and warm, not at all the hard command of justice heard earlier, or the harshness she still expected now.

"I'm still on duty, Master Glavenor. I'm not supposed to drink while –"

"You're off duty for a while," cut in Mrs Quilt, leaning over the bar. "You've just sung, and Lyndall's out cleaning and serving."

"Sorry about the glasses, Mrs Quilt. I'll pay for the damage."

Mrs Quilt folded her arms across her ample bosom. "No you won't. Better this, than the damage that would have been, had you not found my little Kip. A few glasses can be replaced, my child's life cannot. I'll cover the cost."

"I feel so silly about it. I sang too loudly."

"You did us proud with your singing, though I've learned something tonight. When there's a handsome man at the bar, I'll be hiding my glasses when you sing to him."

At that comment Tabitha knew she blushed rose-red. She tried not to look at Glavenor's arm, where the fresh cuts glistened as he removed the swab.

"A drink?" repeated the Swordmaster. She couldn't avoid his attention any longer.

"I'd love to. H-honeydew," she answered, taking the stool he offered. She balanced the lyre on her lap. Even the air seemed tense around Glavenor, as if he commanded that space as well.

"I'll have a touch of the same, Madam Quilt," Glavenor said.

"Not the Dwarrow?" Mrs Quilt asked. Hopeful for a higher price, if Tabitha guessed correctly.

"It has a kick it didn't have in the old days. I prefer to keep my thoughts whole."

Glavenor took the glasses, and offered Tabitha one. "I wish to apologise, for being harsh, earlier. You are a beautiful young woman. I did not recognise you for the girl I last saw here."

His aura of strength pressed against her. He smelled of leather and steel, and his tightly-bound hair glistened darkly against the light.

He eroded her composure more with every flattering comment. She had to turn the conversation. "What happened to the Shadowcaster, Swordmaster Glavenor?"

"Please, call me Garyll. You'll wear your sweet voice out if you use my title every time we speak."

She gave a little laugh, and looked away from his steady gaze, pretending to note the next performer begin on the stage. Garyll. She savoured the word, but couldn't bring herself to say it out loud. The Swordmaster must have been young when he earned the title; he was still younger than many in his service, yet he was at least fifteen years Tabitha's senior. He was a grown man.

He was still watching her. "We scoured the village," he said, keeping his voice low, "but I believe the Shadowcaster has fled. A horse was stolen from Hemsen's stable. With the traffic of the contest, it was impossible to track him in the dark further than the High Way. I'll send a patrol out in the morning, but for now the men are on guard. Which is why I am here, to see the gathering is safe."

He would make sleeping in a bear's den seem safe, were he near. He bristled with martial alertness, even while he sipped at his wine and watched her.

"You play the lyre very well," he said.

Her answer came out in a rush. "It's my mother's old lyre, the first one she had, but she's got another one carved by the crafter in Stormhaven which plays a deeper tune than mine, and has twice as many strings, so it gives a richer music, but it's more difficult to play, and I'm not good enough to pluck the deep-lyre and sing at the same time, so this one serves me best." She stopped suddenly, realising how much she had said in only one breath. Saying the first thing which came to mind was a terrible idea.

She turned the lyre in her hands, and fiddled with the end of the taut strings. *I'll bite my tongue, if I have to.*

"I've never met a woman who could stop six men drinking, all at once," he said, with an earnest expression.

When she realised he was teasing her, she glowered in mock anger.

"No, really, it was wonderful piece of singing," he said, raising his hands as if to defend himself. He smiled. "You're good. You're very good."

"Thank you." She turned quickly away before he could see how wide her smile was.

He's just being polite, stop getting all worked up about his eyes.

And yet his compliments seemed genuine, unlike the flattery she had learned to ignore from those shifty-eyed patrons who stayed too late.

A youth from Brimstone was singing on the stage, the last of the contestants. He couldn't hide all of his nervousness from his voice, but his lute-work was brilliant. The judges would have a hard time choosing, this year. She hoped she was one of the three who'd have a chance to travel to Stormhaven at Yearsend, to play before the King.

She turned to face Glavenor again. "Is Stormhaven really roofed in gold?" she asked. She regretted the vapid words as they fell from her lips. He smiled, and didn't tease her ignorance.

"In a manner of speaking. A few roofs in the Upper Quadrant have gilt capping. Of course there's the Palace, and the very tops of the battlements too, but for the most part it's stone, and the ancient stonewood. In the mornings, when the mist from the lake is thin, the gold catches the sun, and the glow fills the city. For that time, Stormhaven is the most beautiful place in all of Eyri. You can feel the history under your feet, you can feel the strength of the city walls, the order that binds all of Eyri together."

"I hope to travel there, some day," she said, wistful. Garyll's description had made her want to pack for the King's Isle that night.

"You'll surely sing in the King's Challenge this year."

"I have to be judged worthy."

"And so you will. You have the most beautiful voice," he said, a glint to his eye.

She took a breath.

"Thank you, Garyll."

It sent a thrill up her spine. Garyll. She had called him by his first name, and he didn't seem to mind. The Swordmaster of Eyri, talking to her, and she had called him Garyll.

"It's been a while since I've been in Stormhaven myself," he admitted. "Too much unrest, elsewhere. Lone farms. Lightgifters in trouble."

"Around Fendwarrow?"

He nodded, and spread his hands. He had strong hands. "There is always good in the bad, and bad in the good, but in that village, things are rather darker than most. It's as if the wildness comes with the Black River, and seeps into everything. We have to transfer the Swords in that station every year. There is more work for a Sword trying to uphold the law in that small village than there is in the entire city of Stormhaven."

He pushed an empty glass across the bar, then rose.

"Which reminds me I'd best patrol again, before I become entranced by your smile. All seems well here. It may not be so elsewhere."

Lone farms and Lightgifters. Her parents stayed on the farm. Her mother was a Lightgifter. A nasty little worry crept up her back.

"Miss Serannon, I enjoyed your company. My apologies again, for the misunderstanding." He lifted her hand to his lips, and kissed it. The gesture was acceptably polite, yet it sent shivers up her arm. "Good night," he added, letting her hand slip from his. When she only nodded, he bowed, and made his way to the door.

Tabitha couldn't make her tongue work. This time, it had nothing to do with the strange magic of the Shadowcaster.

"Thank you, and good night too," she said, at last, to his retreating back. Too late, but maybe he had heard her.

"You can call me Tabitha," she whispered.

But the door to the common-room swung open, and the Swordmaster was gone. Master Glavenor. Garyll.

She became aware of the clamour of the inn again. The Tooth

would not empty for a while yet, the judges were still deliberating, and Lyndall was weaving through the crowd with a tray held high.

Mrs Quilt leant on the bar beside Tabitha.

"Now that's a man we could afford to see far more of around these parts," she said.

"Do you think he'll stay for long?"

Mrs Quilt harrumphed. "A man like the Swordmaster travels all the time. Don't you get your heart set on him, you hear? He'll be off before the week is out, and never come back for a year. That's his duty, as Swordmaster of Eyri. He must go everywhere, see everything. He is the hand of justice, and he is needed elsewhere than in this sleepy hollow."

"Would one see more of him in Stormhaven?" said Tabitha, shifting on her stool to face the matronly innkeeper.

Mrs Quilt puckered her lips. "Forget him, girl. He was just being polite with you. Chasing him will give you nothing but a sore heart."

Tabitha nodded, but kept her thoughts to herself; Mrs Quilt was mad. You did not forget a man like Garyll Glavenor.

A bell rang from the stage, on and on, until the noise of the crowd subsided, and the judges of the singing contest could be heard. Each of the elders had their say about the wonderful quality of the singing, the fresh new talent, the importance of such events, and thanked the people for their support. The discourses only served to wind her nervousness as taut as a lyre string. At last, the spry old lady from Llury stood to the fore, to pronounce the result.

"Lyndall Quilt from First Light, Peter Prookle from Cellarspring, and Tabitha Serannon. Congratulations, you are selected for the King's Challenge."

Applause filled the common-room like the sound of heavy rain. Lyndall emerged from the crowd, and took her hand as Tabitha joined her to approach the stage. Tears fell bright on Lyndall's cheeks, but her smile was enormous. When they accepted their tokens from the senior judge, the crowd whistled, hooted, and stomped on the floor. The gilded disc suspended on Tabitha's ribbon had the King's seal stamped in the centre of the cross. The King's seal.

She couldn't wait to show her mother. Trisha Serannon would be so proud. Sunday evening suddenly seemed a long time in the future, and the farm at Phantom Acres a long way away.

2. THE RIDDLER
"A life that is free, isn't easy,
and an easy life isn't free."—*Zarost*

Twardy Zarost slipped from the crowd. A cold and blusterous night lay beyond the door, but the delivery of Dwarrow wine shouldn't wait. It was a good time to travel, a good night. The rain would pelter, thieves would shelter, and Trouble would stay in bed. A quick journey then, before the wrath of the storm. He ducked around the corner of the inn and headed for the stable.

The singing contest had been a treat, and the clear-eyed brunette the very cherry on top. She could go far if the right hands guided her—he decided that he would watch the Lightgifter's daughter. But tonight he could not get involved, not with the Swordmaster so near. Maybe another time.

When the girl had showered Great Glavenor with glass, Zarost hadn't been able to contain his laughter. If the commotion and applause hadn't been so very thunderous, he would have been picked out as a mocker. A better prank he couldn't have played on the Swordmaster, had he planned it himself.

His horse, Horse, was reluctant to leave her warm stall. A handful of sweet barley convinced her that Twardy Zarost was a good man, even if a little tricky. He paid the stable-hand a full silver for guarding the valuable cargo, and turned the loaded cart northwards upon the road.

They soon bounced over the last of the cobbles, and joined the smooth-packed earth of the High Way. Better, he thought. The wine wouldn't be jostled any more. He looked ahead, to where the trees tilted over the road as if they wanted to walk upon it themselves but couldn't get their roots to move. The forest sighed in anticipation of the coming storm. Zarost listened carefully to the symphony of hums, moans, creaks and rustles as they passed through the trees.

His favourite part of Eyri's Great Forest, this oft-bypassed tract, where the strangle-oaks threw their sheltering arms over the road, and the wind could howl over the canopy above. The night was darker than a shaftful of Shadowcasters, but it was a good night nonetheless.

Horse trusted that he was guiding her, and he trusted that Horse would follow the easy trail all on her own. He kept his pipe glowing as long as he could, even when the rain came to dance upon his hat.

They reached the ramshackle cluster of planks that called itself Brimstone just as the snow began to fall. The village innkeeper was none too pleased with being woken in the small hours, but when he recognised the brand on the wine barrels, he led the Riddler to his best rooms.

Twardy Zarost turned in for the day.

◆ ——————— ◆

The weather improved the following night. After reaching Llury and concluding his trade there, Twardy Zarost decided to push on again. The Dwarrow wine had caused a disagreement with the burly Llurian loggers about someone's paternity. That convinced him to ride with the dawn, before his remaining barrels were holed, or stolen. When he was clear of the town, he dozed, while Horse followed the descending trail. Morning became afternoon, all on its own.

The traffic increased after the junction to Tarbarn, as wagoneers bound for the High Way passed by. A cart loaded with vegetables and greens from Hillow, a loud metal-peddlar from Chink or Respite, a family of potters with their whares, probably from Kironkiln. A group of riders who parted for him, a patrol of Swords who did not. Zarost tipped his hat at every one, but didn't stop to talk.

His load was very much lighter than when he'd set out from Fendwarrow, and his purse was as fat as a feast-day hog. Sad that it was not his money. Neither was it his wine; but at least being a wagoneer took him away from Ravenscroft for a week or three. He had been too long in that dark hole, so long that he was losing faith in his own wise words. Yet every time when he completed his wagon-run, it was the same. He returned to Ravenscroft, to cast riddles in the shadows, wasted riddles for an unlikely contender. Nonetheless, it was a duty he couldn't shirk.

"If I don't stir for another year, I'll go completely mad," he announced to the mare.

Horse rolled an eye at him, as if to suggest that it was already too late, and continued drawing the cart at a plod down the trail to Stormsford. Zarost knew the mare understood more than she should. He considered flicking her rump to reward her for her cheekiness.

They came upon a broad puddle, where Horse dropped her head and snorted briefly at the water. The cart wheels sloshed through the broken reflections. The nearby willows dripped, the air was a forest of standing vapours above the sweep of the Storms River. What sunlight did touch Eyri, glistened on the jagged rim of high mountains, making them appear all the more like teeth, protecting or ensnaring the green land they contained. The bare trees away from the river cast dappled patterns across the road.

Light and Dark, dark and light. Twardy Zarost scratched his beard.

Twenty years, and still no significant change in the magic of Eyri.

The paths to wizardry were many, and yet here in Eyri, the paths seemed to go round and round, and never led anywhere. He supposed it was the council's own fault. The order which the Gyre of Wizards had created within this realm was too pure, the shield was too thick. Eyri was safe from the outside, but equally, nothing could peck the egg open from within. And so, the Order remained untainted and sterile, and the true purpose of the talisman remained undiscovered.

Horse sauntered under a tree, and a low branch tipped the hat from Twardy's head. He caught it behind his back, then flicked it up. The stripes of the racoon pelt caught the sunlight as the hat spun tip over brim. It landed atop his wiry mop. He crammed it down. The hat should stay there for another month, now that it was aired. He twitched Horse's rump for the prank this time, and she whinnied, delighted with herself.

Zarost returned to his ruminations.

The talisman was being hoarded by the Darkmaster, and so the development of magic had stagnated in Eyri. The Ring should have moved on, years ago, to someone who had more potential. Although Zarost was tempted to interfere, he knew that the course of the Ring should not be meddled with—it would only succeed under the strictest conditions of fairness. There might be other rings which could enslave their bearers, but the talisman which the Darkmaster held was made for a wiser purpose. The path it followed could not be dictated. His oath to the Gyre of Wizards bound him tighter to that requirement than the rims to the cart wheels.

Round and round, going nowhere.

The Ring was supposed to be a catalyst, and yet the essence of magic was so settled, in this realm.

"A touch of Chaos, a lick of fire from Ametheus, that's what Eyri needs," he told Horse. The Gyre would make him chew soap, for a comment like that. He pressed his lips firmly together, but grinned all the same.

An old reflex made him turn his eyes skyward. The grin slipped from his face. He reined Horse to an abrupt halt, and stared at the impossibility—a terrible falling star, high above. He was inside the Shield, he was safe, he reminded himself. It could not be; his idle words could not have summoned that kind of magic. The name of the Sorcerer held no power here.

Yet there it was. The ball of argent fire hurtled downward. Closer, closer, until Twardy was sure it had come too low. Horse shied, and tossed her head in her traces.

The essence of Chaos, the wildfire of Ametheus, like a tangle of silver snakes all fighting to be the first to find their prey. Zarost remembered when he had first seen such a mark in the sky.

Kinsfall, or Kings Meet as it was known in that time, had been a beautiful city, the centre of the gracious Three Kingdoms of Oldenworld. Set on the northern limit of the long shadow of the mighty Winterblade range, King's Meet had been a fair place to live, so mild in winter the snow never touched the smoothed brownstone streets, so mellow in summer you could smell the distant Sailor's Sea almost every afternoon as the cooling breeze swept across the golden Moral plains. Twardy Zarost had loved the place almost as soon as he had arrived as a young pilgrim from Kaskanzr. He had sought solace from the disastrous end of his family, anything to keep the visions of blood and blades from returning to his mind, and so he had traced along the strengthening network of magic, from Kaskanzr through Koraman, into Moral, and to the origin at King's Meet.

There he found what he was seeking, for not only did the respected rulers convene here for regular sessions in the Royal Halls, but so did the Wise, those men and women of the secret lore, although their meeting place was far less public. The College was where the most important decisions were made, some said it was the heart of Moral Kingdom. It was a tall cluster of artfully angled buildings that were set on the slopes of Northing Torr so as to catch the sun with their gold-veined walls. And it was here that the acolytes came from all of Oldenworld to complete their quest for knowledge, for it was written upon bound pages and sealed parchments and even engraved on the delicate chromed-steel leaf, every study and practice of the Five Lores known, and all collected in the Loreward, the learning available for those who could prove themselves worthy, those who could unriddle the riddles. Some even said the forbidden Sixth Lore, that of Chaos, was written of too, but Zarost had seen little evidence of it in his years of sneaking around the shadowed halls. Perhaps that was their failing, Zarost thought. Perhaps they really had needed the rude words of Chaos in their sacrosanct library, at least to prepare for the threat such thinking posed to their precious Order, if for nothing else. Ah, they had been ill-prepared for Chaos when it had come.

Ametheus struck like a hunter. That conflagration of silver threads fell upon the College first, and twisted through the walls as if they were made of butter and the threads were of hot steel.

Zarost was on his way to the College, he was returning a book nobody knew that he had, the book of Transformation and Restitution; he was not a block shy of the College doors. The air was sweet with the scent of summer, it had been a quiet night, a soft night, a lover's night. He still remembered it, the bright flash. The priceless book falling from his hands to the street.

A roar hammered his cheeks as it passed away from the College. The angled roofs and walls disintegrated, and Zarost knew that within its hallowed bowels, slabs of heavy stone dropped on the collected people. The tale of their defence was carried out by few survivors. A few Matter-masters bonded the blocks into new forms at once, but they could not repel the fall of loose debris. Some Energy-adepts tried to repel the momentum of ruin with an uncontrolled burst of fine essence, but they killed themselves and their colleagues in their desperation as the raw energy tore apart the bonds of everything nearby. A young novice threw up a wall of dark motes, though what she had been trying to achieve using such an elementary spell of the first axis Zarost had never guessed. Some traces of wizard's advanced Order-spells escaped from the College before the silver dust-cloud billowed out from its basement, but their efforts were wasted. Fighting alone they could not triumph. Even on that first day, Ametheus wielded power the equal of two wizards acting in unison, or even three.

The rest of the collegiates were students, not even sensitive enough to recognise the danger before it swept through them. They tasted the wildfire, it infected their lungs and bodies as it sought through the passageways and halls.

Screams rose from within the crumbling ruins. The silver magic had done more than turn stone to grey sand. Zarost cursed himself for a lily-livered coward, but his traitorous feet backed away. Only later did he learn how wise his instinct had been.

They emerged from the swelling ash like a plague. Cords of movement flickered across the first one's skin, a tattered web of Chaos feasting upon living flesh. Zarost recognised her, a pretty novice from Orenland, or she had been pretty, once. Where the Chaos touched, her body changed, bursting with the growths of a rampant cancer. Eyes formed all down her cheeks and upon her throat, lidless eyes, mucuos-rimmed and wet like a layer of fish eggs and glue within her skin. The eyes twitched, searching in conflicting ways, and the woman ran, screaming, off the raised arm of stone beside the stairs. It was a mercy that she broke her neck—she did not have to see what came behind her.

Nightmare shapes crowded through the smoke issuing from the door. A figure with a bull's horned head tore at the collar of its tunic until it had split the tight fabric from its thickening neck. Its hands grew leathery and black-nailed. It bayed, and gripped the nearest body roughly by the hair. The bull-headed freak bayed again, and bit into the throat of its captive.

One of them ran, a blurred figure, but it tripped and broke upon the upper level, and washed down the stairs as a greenish grey spill, nothing more. An old wizard, one of the founders of the College, was casting Order-spells upon himself, but to no avail. His legs joined at the knees, then at the ankles, then he seemed stuck to the ground. The bull-headed murderer closed on him, as other creatures flocked by. Zarost couldn't watch any more.

But Ametheus was not yet done with the capital of the ordered kingdoms of Oldenworld.

The second and the third wildfire strike came, and Zarost's eyes burned with the visions of King's Meet. Those beautiful buildings crumpled and fell, the fair streets became rivers of malignant ash, but the worst was to watch the people set upon, innocents and nobles, good people all, taken by the new terror, the magic that forced change, the magic that warped the living and loosened the structure of things that stood still, magic that slipped through the patterns of any known defence and left the survivors to become insane at their own transformation.

The Sorcerer had reached into the heart of a civilisation and as near as ripped out its life. The College was buried in wildfire, and no one dared to ever disturb the remains after that day. People ran, Zarost ran, feeling an awful weight of loss in his gut, for the sacred Loreward had been destroyed with the College. His chance to become Wise was gone—without the books, there was little hope for him to study any further knowledge to advance in ability. Little hope for him, or anyone else.

In that judgement alone, he had been wrong. He had learned a thing or two in the long years which had passed since then, the most important being to trust his own ability to reason things out, to unriddle the riddle.

So he sat atop his cart on that puddled road in Eyri, with Horse straining at her traces, and the willows dripping, and he watched the approaching wildfire, and he thought.

The Sorcerer had no reason to concentrate anything vigorous upon Eyri; nothing more than the random sparks that his network threw off everywhere in Oldenworld. The Gyre believed that Ametheus was still fooled by the Shield, and his attention was in his own realm, in the Lowlands. When Zarost had last seen the Gyre, they had been all aflutter about a spell far worse than wildfire. There had been rumours, from Thren Fernigan, or somewhere equally distant in the Oldenworld Lowlands, just rumours and broken accounts, of a crushing empty worm of ruin, a horror they had no name for, a fatal spell beyond the Gyre's ken which tore through earth and air and flesh alike, writhing through all life, wrangling death in its wake. Zarost hadn't shared the Gyre's concern; no spell endured forever, especially the knots woven under the erratic hand of the Sorcerer. That magical invention would run up against the vast bulwark of the Winterblade range. It didn't concern him, his task was in Eyri, and he had told them so. The Gyre had allowed him to return to the blessed realm, if only because their need for his success in Eyri was more urgent than ever.

They were wrong about the rumoured worm of ruin, Zarost thought. It would never cross the Heartlands. It would never reach Eyri.

Yet Chaos-magic streaked down at him. By the burning crow! it was too close. He clutched his hat.

The falling star exploded. An expanding ring of angry silver flame tore through the sky, heading for the horizon.

Zarost sighed with relief. Just an ordinary wildfire strike. There would be devastation, true, but the realm of Eyri was protected. The Shield had held. Outside in Oldenworld, the bright silver fire would wound the earth, the mountains, the forests and wastelands, marking a huge circle beyond the borders of the realm with the freakish touch of Chaos.

Why had the wildfire struck just then?

He had spoken the forbidden name out loud, and the Sorcerer had answered.

No, it had to be coincidence! For if it was not coincidence, there was a small breach in the Shield, a crack in the continuum. If there was such a breach, then it would be possible for something to slip in, through the crack, just as his careless words might have slipped out and summoned Chaos.

He would have to watch his tongue.

He stuck it out. The pink tip waggled at him. He put it away again.

It would be best to say nothing to the Gyre of Wizards about such undecided matters. The star had burst, just as it should, and that was the end of that.

He flicked the reins. He shouldn't have wished for wildfire in the first place.

But if the dust of Chaos ever did fall in Eyri, he would wish it to fall upon Cabal of Ravenscroft first. The Darkmaster clutched onto a wealth beyond his due; it would be fitting to see *him* turned into a horned and bitter toad.

3. THE WIZARD'S RING

"If something is used, but never owned,
can it ever be stolen?"—*Zarost*

The Darkmaster watched the circle of silver fire explode across the firmament.

He would have been within his darkened room at the Crowbar in Fendwarrow, but something had urged him to come outdoors, to squint into the bright sky. A tension lurked in the air, a feeling he knew only too well, but seldom had to endure—the sensation of being watched.

He was the one who did the watching in Eyri. He was the one who should send a chill down the spine as his Morrigán birds passed overhead. He was the one to cause men to glance nervously at their own shadows. They didn't call him the Darkmaster for nothing; he was a genius in the art of inducing fear.

"I don't wish to be watched," he said to the air, his voice a dry hiss. No doubt the lurker was one of his own Shadowcasters, experimenting with the Morrigán spell. He would find the culprit, and the discipline would be swift. Nobody was allowed to track Cabal of Ravenscroft; nobody dared.

Then he had noticed the falling star, and realised that he had been mistaken. The weight of its impending presence was the problem. A starburst always made him feel small, and he hated it. The ring of silver fire ripped across the sky. As usual, there was no threat to it, yet it unsettled him. He sneered at the bright flare in disgust, and turned on his heel.

The death of a star was pointless, especially so because he could not benefit from it. He wondered why one never saw the fragments of the explosion descend from the sky. Maybe they were too fine to be noticed.

Yet then he did see the stardust. A fine sprinkling, not more than a pinch of salt, settled on his shoulder, staining the black robe with a delicate trace of silver. He brushed the dust with his hand. It disappeared under his fingers.

Cabal was touched by something wild and weird, something—he struggled to find the right word for it. A shift of power, difference, change, a moment in another world. Then it was gone, and everything was the same as it had been before. The sky was winter blue, the day too bright.

He shrugged off the strange mood. He should not have emerged today at all.

Fendwarrens scuttled away from him along the narrow street. No one liked to encounter the Darkmaster, especially when the sun was high. If a person was visited by the Darkmaster during the day, they would die in their sleep that night. Cabal ensured that the warning was often repeated, and that it yielded results from time to time.

Fear was a wonderful armour to wear.

As Cabal reached for the door, something fell to the ground with a tinkling like a dropped coin. A small coin, a hammered blackmetal, no doubt. He didn't bother to search for it; he had enough wealth to buy the village and its people. He threw the door aside, and strode into the dimness of the inn.

The Crowbar—Fendwarrow's finest and only place of ill repute. He had a good understanding with the owner, Mukwallis. Cabal made sure the innkeeper's shady activities were kept shady, concealed in ways only his art with the Dark essence could provide. Whenever the Swords followed a trail, the things they searched for disappeared, and people didn't speak. Jurrum, stolen goods, whores and weapons— they were all here, in Fendwarrow, right under the noses of the tinpot Swords. Even the air within the Crowbar held a perfume of debauchery, thick with cheap pipe-smoke, cloying musk, and wine.

Not a few competitors had come and gone over the years, but they always found misfortune wrapping about their ankles like thorn-weed. In return, the Crowbar paid its dues. By night, people came there for one thing alone. Such folk were ripe for the picking; a taste of the Dark power was all they needed. Soon he would have claimed enough of them to complete his designs. Then the rebellion would begin.

He slipped off the main corridor into a curtained alcove. He knocked twice, then once, upon the narrow door to the Long Room. A shifty-eyed man with many jowls cracked the door open, then welcomed him into the deeper gloom. The man's mottled green robe matched his nature.

"Mukwallis," whispered Cabal, by way of greeting. "Is the Lightgifter dealing?"

The innkeeper nodded, then mimed a number with his fat fingers.

One-Ten.

Cabal raised a questioning eyebrow. Mukwallis indicated a point in the wall. The Long Room was narrow, and ran the length of the building. It had been a closely-guarded secret, but nobody kept secrets from the Darkmaster for long. From here, he could spy on every guest of the inn.

Cabal stepped quietly up to the knothole Mukwallis had indicated. The view was of a finely-trimmed bedroom. Two figures were engaged in discussion—a middle-aged Lightgifter with a pepper-brown tonsure, and Cabal's tall Shadowcaster, Kirjath Arkell.

Arkell had been showing too much ambition of late, a sign that his usefulness might be coming to an end. Cabal expected his Shadowcasters to abduct new recruits for the cause, but not in a village where the Swordmaster of Eyri was patrolling, and not where the Dark essence was so thin on the ground. Arkell had no patience, no sense of restraint—he was reckless. It was not the time to reveal themselves to the Sword. The rumours and fears of the Shadowcasters needed a while longer to spread through the realm, before the people would be ripe for conquest. Something would have to be done about Arkell.

Cabal recognised the Gifter whom Arkell dealt with as a minor Father of the Dovecote, named Onassis. It was good to know everything about everybody, especially those with a weakness. Once Onassis had tasted the intoxicating pleasures of jurrum, he had fallen very rapidly into Cabal's hands.

The Gifter commanded a hazy cloud of sprites, and produced more from his heavy travel-bag. A copious quantity of Light essence, allocated for healing the villagers of Fendwarrow, no doubt. Amazing how much essence that particular task had used up over the years.

Cabal cracked his knuckles. The missions of mercy to Fendwarrow were often a ruse. Onassis was a regular trader. The Father chanted away to his sprites, and they collected in a pool of Light on the bed. Gradually, the Gifter formed the pattern of the Turning, a twisted circle. Arkell wove a trail of motes to join the Father's sprites.

Cabal felt a surge of pride as he watched the Turning spell engage, and the sparkling sprites became cold black motes, just like Arkell's. It was a masterful design. It was his design. With the Turning, came the Dark, and with the Dark, a world of possibilities, his to exploit. The Gifter and Arkell chanted together, guiding the essence in unison from the one extreme to the other, until all was given to the Dark.

A pity he had not solved the riddle of charging the essence himself, the way the Gifters could in their Dovecote. He always had to rely on a trade—a willing Gifter, bearing the gift of fresh sprites, and a counterpart from the Dark, to work the spell of the Turning. Then the Gifter had to be paid, in whatever currency they preferred.

No matter. Willing Gifters were not as hard to find as they liked to believe. And in time, all of them would be his servants.

The Gifter collected his payment from Arkell. Cabal counted out the jurrum leaves as they were dealt to Onassis. *Fifteen.* He had given Arkell twenty, expressly for the Lightgifter.

So, the Shadowcaster was lining his own pocket. He had expected it, the way Arkell's eyes were so yellowed of late.

Cabal placed a silver into Mukwallis's sweaty palm as he left. As always, the information gained in the Long Room was worth the coin exchanged. Cabal chuckled. It was the toad's own protection money he had used to pay him with. They struck a good trade, Mukwallis and he.

Arkell's jurrum addiction could be used to Cabal's advantage. The leaves that found their way into the Shadowcaster's pocket would be especially potent in future. A man 'juiced' on jurrum could become fearless beyond reason, prepared to take a suicidal risk. He would be useful against the Lightgifters, especially against the stubborn ones who refused to be turned.

◆ ——————— ◆

Ashley Logán squinted against the glare. The training yard at the Dovecote was dazzling, more so than usual. His sprites seemed pale above the sudden fierceness of the white sand.

His attention was broken, and he shielded his eyes as he looked up. The remains of a starburst rolled towards the horizon, a perfect ring of silver; silent, sparkling. The remains of a falling star, they said, but that legend had often puzzled him. It was broad daylight, and everyone knew that stars only came out at night.

"Attend, Logán!" The sharp voice brought him back to the present—the Dovecote in Levin, and his duties as an apprentice. Lightgifter Hosanna stood before him, all regal and indignant. She wore her crisp beauty like an accusation of his mediocrity—her honeyed hair was pulled into a perfect plait, her robe was the whitest white, and the pert line of her lips always a precise curve. The knot at her waist always lay flat. She would be truly beautiful if she smiled, once in a while.

He tried to look apologetic as he weathered her tirade.

"Is this task beyond you, half-knot? Shall we move on to someone more capable? If the sprites are to be wasted, there are better uses for them."

Ashley shook his head. "It was too bright, Sister. I'll try again."

He had been attempting to link the flows of Light essence into one pattern when the starburst had upset him. The complexity of the spell boggled his mind. To command his own sprites was easy, but to join many sources into one unified spell required immense concentration.

"There can never be too much Light," Hosanna stated, "only those who don't yet have the strength to face it. The fault is not with the essence."

Ashley nodded. It did no good to disagree with a full Gifter, especially one like Hosanna when she was in a preaching mood. One rebuttal would lead to a dissertation. He flicked his gaze around the circle. Fifteen apprentices were ranged around him, the 'half-knots' of the Dovecote. Sprites swirled in readiness above their upturned palms. The two Gifters, Sister Hosanna and Sister Grace, who wore fully knotted cords around their white robes, watched him expectantly.

He sent his awareness out to all the sources of the Light essence, and tried to hold in mind the pattern that would link them all into a perfect Flicker spell, the Lightgifter's flame. He spoke the slow words of invocation. Sprites came to him from three of the apprentices, then four, five. He strained to reach the others. He was determined to prove himself better than Hosanna expected. He pushed his concentration to the limit. Six, seven sources.

Then it seemed as if somebody poured a handful of sand over his head from behind. Something trickled through his hair, and stung his scalp with a hot tingle. Silver dust collected on his shoulders, then disappeared into the fabric. The world lurched, and his spell erupted into chaos.

There were voices, confused voices, jabbering and whispering voices, all speaking at the same time. He saw a blonde youth in a white robe, standing on the sand, but the image was split, as if reflected in many mirrors, and he saw the same half-knot from different angles in the same instant. He recognised the apprentice.

That's me.

Voices, voices, voices.

Sprites left upturned hands, and combined in a pattern he had never seen before. Light rushed from the pattern like a bursting of the sun. With it came a blast of sound, so loud that Ashley was thrown to the ground. It was the crash of thunder added to the boom of breaking rock, the roar of a beast and a hammer's blow combined, a howling, shrieking, deafening sound that drove deep into his ears. The bare sand quivered where he lay. Too many sprites, too much Light released. Pain and shock swirled through the people around him, driven by the wake of the awful peal, and he knew their distress. People cursed, and their rancour scoured his mind, as if they were within his head.

He couldn't escape the ire—there was nowhere to go, they were within him.

Ashley clung to the sand, and tried to believe that it wasn't true. But it felt as if a cleaver had parted his skull, and his mind was open to the lash of every angry will around him. He cowered where he lay, twitching against the virulent thoughts that invaded his mind. Gradually, the Lightgifters and half-knots recovered from their shock, and so the animosity faded, and he came back to himself.

He was Ashley Logán. He didn't want to open his eyes until he was sure.

Gentle hands lifted him. The shade of the Dovecote building passed over him, the stone steps were cool beneath him. He kept his eyes closed. He tried to make sense of the many voices he could hear. A soft Healall spell began to work through his body, and he privately thanked Sister Grace for her kindness. Grace. He didn't look up, somehow he knew it was her. Her voice filled his head.

"Poor Ashley. Hosanna shouldn't have pushed him so hard."

Ashley lay completely still. Unspoken words, but clear in his mind.

He opened his eyes. A brown wall cut the sun from the sky. Apprentices circled close in silence. Concern aged their youthful faces. Sister Grace wove sprites over him, her grey eyes determined, her experienced hands gentle.

Something had gone wrong with his Flicker spell, or something had gone too right. Before he could decide which it was, a heavy tread approached from within the Dovecote at his back.

"What is it? What has this boy done?"

Ashley's heart sank. Rector Shamgar. There was nothing worse in the whole world than to come under the scrutiny of the leader of the Lightgifters. Nobody spoke.

"Sister Hosanna, a report. What has occurred, and what was that flash in the practice yard? What?"

"My apologies, Illumination. Apprentice Ashley lost command during a linking exercise. He could not control his Flicker. Something—strange was created."

Ashley was certain that the Rector sneered, though he couldn't see him. "Was anyone injured with this incompetent spell?"

A mutter rippled through the apprentices, but no one mentioned their pains.

"Shame on you, then, for weakness!" the Rector declared. "Hosanna, for your weak judgement in pushing a half-baked half-knot. Grace, for your succour of this fumbler. He'll not learn if you soften his failures. And shame mostly on you, Ashley Logán, for causing harm with the holy Light essence!" Ashley didn't dare turn. He could see the purple hem of the Rector's robe close behind him.

"The boy has no idea what he's wasted!"

Ashley drew a sudden breath. He had heard the Rector's voice, yet Shamgar hadn't spoken. *"If this fumbler doesn't lay apology at my feet, I shall have him scrubbing for a week!"*

Ashley turned quickly on his knees, and spoke to the Rector's robe. "I'm sorry, Illumination. I lost command. I beg forgiveness." Ashley looked up just in time to see the small, indulgent smile tucked into the corner of the Rector's fat cheek.

"As you were, then." The Rector said, waving a dismissing hand. "I have important tasks, and little time, what?" He disappeared into the Dovecote once more.

"Full of compliments, isn't he?" thought Sister Grace.

It was as near to a curse as the gentle Lightgifter could come. Ashley giggled at her sense of humour, and found that once he'd begun, he couldn't stop. He needed to laugh. He was hearing voices in his head, and he knew who spoke when they didn't speak at all. It was quite possible that he was going mad.

Sister Grace frowned, and resumed the Healall spell, touching him with a practised web of Light, humming the words that bound the sprites.

"I think his seizure has passed," she thought. *"I hope the laughter isn't a sign of damage."*

Ashley grinned at her. She had such clear, grey eyes.

"What a dashing young man. If I were younger, I would —"

Ashley jerked upright. He was definitely going mad. He concentrated on his own voice, in the hope that the others would fade away.

"Thank you, Sister Grace. I feel stronger. I'm better now."

No voices invaded his thoughts again, but the suspicion of the Sister's affection was an ember that wouldn't pale. The Lightgifter Grace! By the Creator, she's thirty years older than me! Yet the years had been kind, and she bore her beauty with carefree modesty. He couldn't deny that he had watched her, as she progressed about her work.

His ears were warm. He stood quickly, and took a position on the Sandfield. The class resumed, but he caught himself watching Sister Grace when she filled a sconce with retrieved sprites.

◆ ———————— ◆

Tabitha Serannon dreamt, as she lay in the meadow.

In her dream, a silver star burst across the sky. She heard the singing of many voices, a choral symphony, beautiful, complex. Then she was carried through the sky by the giant composition. She soared on its themes. She played wild notes on a golden lyre, following a strangely timed tune that was haunting and powerful. She sang potent words, and other voices joined her in harmony, and she felt her voice ring clear across the universe, bringing vitality where there was none, linking everything with a pulse of life, binding a million fragments into one. Then silver stardust trickled down through the boughs of an oak tree in her dream. She felt the tingle of the dust as if it had touched her forehead.

She woke to the insistent bleating of sheep.

"Come on, lazy-bones!" her father called out. "Noonday nap is over. We need a hand with the herding! Quick!"

Father. It had been a relief to see his smiling face at the inn, and to hear that all was well on the farm. Now that she was back, her fears seemed childish. Nothing was wrong on Phantom Acres; no wicked Shadowcasters had breached the peace. The sky was late-winter blue, empty and cool. The branches of the oak tree reached out in silence, overhead.

"Coming!" she called, rising to her feet and dusting her dress off. She raised a cautious hand to brush her forehead, but there was no trace of silver there. Her hair was soft, and clean.

Her parents were dipping the sheep. Only as she jogged over to them did she notice the chaos. The sheep were crowding the trough, and behaving strangely. The dripping ewes wriggled and fought to stay in the dip, and the lambs circled back after being ejected, trying to sneak around for a second try. Getting the sheep into the trough was usually the problem, but today they jostled and bleated for the honour.

Tabitha ran some of the wet sheep away with a switch, chasing them until they forgot the bath. When the sheep reached the limit of their memory, they became content to munch on the grass.

They were simple creatures. Tending them was usually tedious. Tabitha's mind drifted along a familiar path. She would become a singer in Stormhaven, or be accepted as a Lightgifter, if she were lucky enough to be chosen.

If she were a Lightgifter, she could marry a noble, live in a grand house in Levin or Stormhaven, or on an estate in the northern lands of rich Vinmorgen County. Yet her mother had left the Dovecote to work this farm. Hank Serannon was the man her mother loved, and Hank Serannon was the man she had married. Tabitha wondered if she would ever find that depth of love, something that made dipping sheep seem like a pleasure. Times could be hard on Phantom Acres, with the bitter winters, wolves and wildcats, and the yearly tithe to the landlord.

She loved her parents dearly, but they must know that one day she would want to leave. With her selection for the King's Challenge, that day might be sooner than ever.

Back at the trough, the sheep were a chaos of milling, bleating, jumping wool, some wet, some dry, all trying to get past her father's big hands and into the dip trough.

"What did you put in the water?" Tabitha shouted above the clamour. "They're all mad."

Trisha was peering into the trough herself. "The usual Healall spell, I just added something to make the wool grow thick and fleecy!" One ewe cleared Hank's arms and landed with a huge splash. Tabitha giggled at the sight of her mother the Lightgifter, scolding the wide-eyed sheep that had drenched her. The Dovecote couldn't suspect that one woman used the healing sprites to better tend her husband's sheep.

Thinking about the Dovecote reminded Tabitha of singing, and the strange dream. She approached her parents.

"Was there a starburst a while ago?" she asked her father.

"Yup, big old silver circle out across the sky. Quite a good one."

She paused, turning to her mother. "Did you hear anything?"

"They never make a sound, dear," Trisha said. "Just a ring of light. If I didn't know better I'd have said it was the starburst that unsettled the sheep. Why, what is it?"

"I was dreaming. I thought I heard singing."

"Dreaming of winning the King's Challenge?" her mother teased, though with a hint of pride.

"No, no, it was more than a wish, it was different—new. The song is still there, but as faint as a whisper."

Her mother gave her a strange look. "Then it might be more than a dream. Why don't you start preparing our supper early. When I come up to the house, you can try to play the music for me, before you forget it."

"And if there isn't a fine song, I'll know you were dodging another afternoon of being a shepherdess!" Hank warned, a good-natured smile on his broad face. "Why can't you be more like your mother? She loves sheep."

He received an elbow in his ribs for his troubles. Tabitha laughed, and ran.

"Don't forget the eggs on the way up!" came her mother's shout. Tabitha heard her, but in her mind she was already playing a golden lyre and singing a song of a hundred voices. If she could only remember it, she was sure it would be a sensation, at the King's Challenge. If she could create a new song even half as wondrous, she would become a famous singer.

She was not going to chase animals all her life. She hummed to herself as she ducked into the chicken coop. Hens scattered underfoot.

When she came upon the third broken egg, she realised there was chaos in the lay-house as well. Eggs were hiding in impossible places, tucked up underneath the roof, balanced in the corners of narrow perches. Many lay shattered on the floor, wasted among the droppings and straw.

She scolded the hens, and tucked what meagre bounty she could find into a basket. The hens continued to cluck and squawk long after she had pulled their door closed. Maybe the starburst affected them too. Maybe they heard the complexity of sounds which teased her own mind, voices coming and going like echoes in the wind.

She wanted to sing, to set it all in order. There was a pattern and structure to the music, if she could just find a place to begin.

◆ ————————— ◆

Kirjath Arkell spat a lump of jurrum onto the street.

The wrath of the Darkmaster scoured Fendwarrow like a winter storm, and Kirjath was driven to action. Children were probably wetting their beds, even in their mother's arms. The men he had seen turned away, white-faced. Only the Shadowcasters would escape retribution tonight, and only because they were inflicting the Darkmaster's fury upon others. Kirjath didn't doubt that the Darkmaster would turn his wrath on his own Shadowcasters when they failed. Cabal's anger would feed upon itself, because he had made the mistake. The Darkmaster had lost his ring.

Kirjath had never seen a ring on the Master's hand. Yet Cabal insisted that there was one, made of glass, so clear that it reflected no light at all. To find it during the day would have been difficult. To find it at night, with the moon a naked sickle in the sky, was a bitter waste of time. Yet find it they must, or they would all scream under the lash for their failure. Already the Master had sent a wave of Dark essence through the streets, bringing the cold grip of coercion to every Fendwarren. No one would dare to leave this village tonight, no one would be able to hide. The fear washed over the villagers like a hungry beast breathing down their necks, and the force of duty gripped the Shadowcasters by their throats.

Kirjath cursed under his breath. He had been taken away from a night of dealing and debauchery, and a secret trade of jurrum seed which had taken months to set up. The Darkmaster cared nothing for his plans. They were all just pawns to the Darkmaster, little pieces on a board, to be ordered this way and that. He was Kirjath Arkell! He deserved more respect. He gritted his teeth.

I am the shadow and he is my Master.

To learn the ways of the motes, to own the Darkstone, he had to follow that oath. The benefits of serving Cabal outweighed the disadvantages. But the Darkmaster pushed those who served him to the limit of their tolerance.

They spent the better part of the night scouring the streets to find the strange missing ring. Then the Darkmaster ordered them to enter the houses. Their agreement with the Fendwarrens would be breached, but Kirjath didn't care. The bond to the Master worked both ways. What he did in the Master's name was not on his conscience. He was under orders.

His boot crashed hard against the door and the lock tore from the weak wood. He stalked into the house, grinning, the motes of Dark essence swirling close in his wake. Time to work the Master's will.

A man came at him from the shadows. He was easy to see, wearing a clean night-shirt, brandishing a cudgel of sorts. Kirjath summoned the motes to cover his own body, and side-stepped the man's charge, using the cover of darkness to hide his movement. A woman screamed, and Kirjath felt the hot rush of anticipation course through his veins. He would get to the woman, in time. First, he had to teach her husband a lesson about the folly of resisting a Shadowcaster.

He had learned many spells in Ravenscroft, though they followed the same basic form. Draw the black motes to his hand with the Summoning spell. With the aid of the Darkstone at his throat, form them into the pattern of his need, and release them with the spoken word.

"Illusion, stand beside me now," he whispered, and gestured to his right. The motes wove tightly to his body, then shifted away to fill the space beside him with a figure. To the man in the night-shirt, there would suddenly be two intruders. Kirjath backed a few paces into the deeper shadows.

The man leapt to tackle the false figure. In the certain light of day, he might have seen that the figure was not quite human, made only of a shifting skin of darkness. The man's arms found air. He crashed headlong onto the floor.

Kirjath had expected the fall. He jumped forward to swing a heavy boot against the man's temple, then stamped him to the floor and stood across his shoulders. The woman screamed again. Soon, my lovely, soon. He guided a small amount of the Dark essence into the man's ears.

"Sleep," he whispered, though it was probably unnecessary. The man wouldn't wake for many hours. He might not wake at all.

"Shut up, or you'll be raped," he shouted at the screams. They stopped, and he heard only gasping breaths. Good, she had much fear in her. Let her hope that she could win her freedom by complying. The despair would be great when she learned her mistake.

"I'm looking for a ring, a talisman, a good-luck charm, shall we say," he announced. Kirjath stepped over the fallen man, and walked deeper into the darkened house. He could smell the bedroom, and the sweet stench of fear coming from the woman within it.

"It is a clear glass ring, a simple circle, but it will bring a terrible fate to anyone who holds onto it. The ring belongs to the Darkmaster." He paused for a moment. The Master hadn't told them what the ring was for, in truth. He wondered what could make such a little thing so valuable. He approached the sound of the swallowed tears. The woman sat upright in her bed, the sheets clutched tight against her chin. He allowed a tendril of the Dark essence to brush her wet cheek. He knew how cold that touch could be.

"Do you have it?"

The woman was shivering wildly, and made only strangled sounds. Fear poured off her like a mist of wild musk.

"Don't lie now, I can hear the tone of a lie."

That trick had been the first lesson in his apprenticeship. Give them a large enough taste of fear, and people will do whatever you want, believe that you mean whatever you say. He had no way to tell a truth from a lie, he wasn't a truthsayer, but she would never guess it, because she feared the possibility too much. He sent the essence curling around the back of her neck.

"We haven't got it," the woman whispered. "I promise, oh my lord I promise, we haven't got the ring, any clear thing. Nothing! Please, we have nothing!"

"Good," said Kirjath, tightening his web of Dark essence around her body, guiding the motes over her thighs, between her breasts, up to her head. "Lord, eh?"

"Here, might you have a better taste of who I am," he breathed in her ear as he completed the spell pattern of Fear. His tongue flicked over her lobe. She shook with the terror of his presence, paralysed, unable to escape. The Darkmaster had thought to deny him his pleasures. It was time to take them back.

4. THE MESSENGER

"Bad news travels faster than good."—*Zarost*

Flakes of an obstinate winter blew past the window. Tabitha was glad for the weather—it gave her good reason to curl up on a fireside chair, and play to her heart's content. It was the second day since the starburst, and the dream-song still haunted her. She plucked the basic melody from her lyre. The notes were evocative, invigorating, and best played with a light, fast touch, as she recalled it from the dream. Yet when she tried to sing the words, she lost the delicate thread of music, and the lyrics which had seemed to be on the tip of her tongue were gone. She couldn't find the powerful voice she had engaged in the dream. The best she could produce was a frustrated hum.

"Still struggling, love?" Her mother eyed her over the top of her loom, her shuttle paused in mid-air.

"I think I can hear the words, but when I try to sing them, they scatter."

"Give it time, the song will come," Trisha said gently, resuming her weaving. "It's hard to create something new. That melody—be careful with it."

"Mother?"

The shuttle wove backwards and forwards, a nimble dancer amongst the coloured threads, binding them tight with its chosen pattern.

"I recognise something in the music. I—played with something similar, a long time ago. The lyrics were like echoes of a distant voice."

That was exactly what it was like—there was a voice, singing the song, and she caught only the echoes of its sound, never clear enough to mimic. But even when she wasn't trying to recall it, the song was still there, like a theme to every moment of the day.

"Promise me something, Tee. Think about the words before you sing them, consider their meaning if they come to you. I cannot stop you discovering things, but a song can sometimes be more than it seems."

"S-sure. I promise."

Trisha didn't look up from the loom again, but Tabitha knew that her mother's attention wasn't given solely to her weaving. Tabitha repeated the instrumental, and searched for those words she had sung in her dream, those words which had resonated through the stars. But her mother's caution made her critical of every thought, and the lyrics were driven further from her reach than ever before. She wondered what could be wrong with such a beautiful song.

She gazed out the window and played the tune again. Her eyes followed the movement of the scudding clouds. The forest of alders on the hill swayed as if shaken by a giant's hands. Tabitha's father hauled wood to the shed, his cowl raised against the weather. Two men stopped him halfway across the yard. Tabitha's fingers froze on the lyre strings.

"There are some Swords with Dad." She jumped to her feet. Not just Swords. The one man was a Sword, true. The other man was Garyll Glavenor, Swordmaster of Eyri. She pressed her nose to the window.

"Whatever can they want?" Tabitha's voice misted against the glass. She wiped it away, and the Swordmaster waved back. Glavenor addressed her father. Hank Serannon nodded, and the three men approached the homestead. The Swordmaster's eye caught Tabitha before she left the window.

Heavens, he's seen me, I have nowhere to hide.

Her heart beat furiously. She caught herself.

Why should I need to hide?

She was wearing the plainest brown dress, and an oversized woolen jersey. There was nothing to do about it. She set her shoulders, and hoped her best smile would distract him from her simple garb. She turned the handle, and the three men came in with a gust of weather. Glavenor seemed to fill the whole house as soon as he entered.

Her father offered introductions. "Trisha, you know Sword Ayche from First Light, and Swordmaster Glavenor. Glavenor, my wife Trisha, and my daughter Tabitha."

"I think we all know each other, but I'm pleased to be introduced to such fine women again," Garyll said. He bowed low, including both Tabitha and her mother in his smile when he straightened. "I had the pleasure of hearing Tabitha sing, and hope to be at the King's Challenge to hear her again. You have raised an exceptional daughter."

Glavenor faced Trisha, but Tabitha could feel the warmth of his attention against her cheeks.

"Thank you, Swordmaster," said her mother, "but most of what Tabitha is, is due to her own efforts. Come, there's no need for gallantry, your haste is plain. How can we help you?"

"Forgive my urgency, but a rider came last night from Fendwarrow. The Shadowcasters passed through the village like a scourge, and too many folk witnessed their foul deeds to pass it off as a wild rumour. The rider saw things himself, and he is a Sword whose word I trust. His captain forbade him to ride, yet he rode nonetheless. He fears to return to Fendwarrow."

Somehow, the chill air from outside crept into the room, for an icy hand crept up Tabitha's back. The Shadowcaster. Eyes like grey slate.

"This is bad news, Swordmaster," said Hank, "but why do you bring it to our farm? What are we to do?"

"No threat intended, Mister Serannon. I'll be gone in a moment, and you can surely guess where I'm going, but first I wanted to ask your wife's assistance in sending a message."

"A Courier?" Trisha asked.

Garyll nodded. "Could you send word to the Dovecote?"

"What would you have me say?"

"I have searched Fendwarrow myself, and found nothing before. Yet this news is too extreme to ignore, told by one who has nothing to gain in the telling. I must find where these Shadowcasters dwell, how they hide. If I am to be successful, I believe I need the assistance of the Lightgifters."

"When do you leave?"

"Forthwith."

"You'll need the Gifters in Fendwarrow by tomorrow evening then?"

Glavenor considered, then shook his head. "Morning."

It would be a hard ride indeed, what with the foul weather and treacherous road.

"How many?" Trisha asked.

"Five should suffice. I don't need a whole host, I just need assistance to find what I am not seeing. My men will make the arrests."

"I'll do it at once," said Trisha. She backed away from them a few paces. Sprites of Light essence filtered down from the ceiling, drawn to Trisha's hand by her summoning. She touched the white orb at her throat in benediction, then whispered her spell to the Light essence.

The Light swirled closer to her hands, the delicate filaments thickened as more essence joined. A bright shape formed in Trisha's hand, and grew into the complex pattern of the Courier. Trisha was a practised Gifter—the form of the bird was nearly perfect. The white feathers glistened, the head bobbed with curiosity as it searched for guidance. She spoke gently into the dove's ear.

"Find the Rector at the Dovecote in Levin, and tell him this: the Swordmaster needs five Gifters to be in Fendwarrow in the morning, to help in the search for Shadowcasters."

She carried the dove to the door, and lofted it into the morning air.

"Go, deliver your message to Rector Shamgar."

With an eager flutter of wings, the white dove shot away.

Tabitha wished it could have been her hand that had sent the Courier skyward; she wished she could have helped Garyll in the way her mother had. But she was not yet a Lightgifter. She might never be—the Gifters might not even choose her to be an apprentice at Yearsend.

"Can I offer you both a cup of broth before you go?" she asked the men. Her mother gave her an approving glance.

"Certainly!" Garyll said, his smile broad. "If it's no trouble, that is. We must only stay a moment."

"No trouble!" said Tabitha gaily, scampering for the kitchen.

"We have the pot bubbling for the noonday meal," she heard her mother say behind her. "It's just a scoop and a scrape."

Tabitha lifted two heavy mugs from their hooks.

"What kind of crimes are we talking about here," enquired Trisha in a hused voice. Tabitha guessed that they thought her beyond earshot.

"These—Shadowcasters," Garyll answered, "went through the town and broke into every house. They searched for something, though no one knew exactly what it was. Some talisman, a glass ring of sorts. They tortured the folk with their Dark magic. It was as if a madness possessed them."

Her father muttered something she couldn't quite make out.

"That was not the worst of it. In one house, a man was beaten almost to death," Garyll added, his voice dropping to a whisper. If Tabitha had not hastily replaced the lid on the bubbling pot, she would have missed the final words. "His wife was raped."

Her hand froze on the handle. Her mother's voice was strained and slow. "Do you know who that was? Did the rider say who's house it was?"

Glavenor was silent, but Sword Ayche filled in for him. "The Trench house, he said." Tabitha lost her grip on the mugs and they crashed and broke upon the pot. In the next room, her mother stifled a cry. Lillian Trench was Tabitha's aunt, her mother's sister.

Tabitha burst into the room. Garyll was glaring at the other soldier, the Sword was looking at the floor, and Hank was holding Trisha in his arms. Tabitha joined her parents' embrace. Her mother's tears were fierce.

"Daran will need healing," her mother said, pulling suddenly away and wiping her face. "Oh Lillian! what have you done to deserve this?" She covered her mouth with shaking hands, then clenched them into fists.

"Can I ride with you, Glavenor? I must be at my sister's side."

Garyll, for once, appeared to be at a loss for words. He looked from Hank to Trisha and back. His jaw worked beneath tight lips.

Trisha whirled, and strode to the stairs at the back of the room. Hank followed her from the room, his stride angry. A door slammed.

Although her parent's bedroom was on the upper floor, the sound carried through the wooden boards. Hank's raised voice was muffled.

"You cannot go alone!"

The answer was too quiet to discern.

"How can I leave the farm?" came her father's distorted question. "Winterborn will have my neck. You know how he is these days."

Her mother's answer was too soft to hear.

"How do you know you'll be safe?"

Trisha's response was muffled.

"I know it's your duty as a Gifter. But you're still my wife! I don't want you in danger!"

The three of them stood in the main room, unsure of what to say. Glavenor looked angry, Sword Ayche looked spare, and Tabitha felt more awkward than ever. Her parents continued to argue upstairs, their voices lowered now, sounding like the buzzing of angry bees.

"Would you show me the farm a little?" Garyll asked her.

Tabitha gratefully led them from the room. The day was cold outside, but she didn't mind. They walked in silence across the yard, past the Sword's tethered horses, toward the chicken-run and pastures. It was awkward, but far less awkward than standing in the homestead.

"She'll come with you," Tabitha said, at length.

"How can you be sure?" Glavenor replied.

"She'll get her way, because it is a matter of a Lightgifter's duty. My father respects her pledge. I think it's why she loves him so much."

Tabitha slowed her steps.

"How can she travel to Fendwarrow? You only have the two horses."

Garyll was quick to answer, and certain in his words. "She has helped me, so I shall return the aid. I shall run, until I tire," he said.

♦ ———————♦

"Be careful, my love," said Hank, his face stern. And to Glavenor, "Look after her, Swordmaster. Look after her with your life."

It was as much a warning as a request, Tabitha realised, but Glavenor clasped her father's hand and held his eye. "You have my word, Hank Serannon. Trisha shall not come to harm in Fendwarrow."

Hank grunted, and released the Swordmaster from the pledging handshake. Garyll gave Tabitha one long, final look, then turned and urged the others to follow him from the yard. Trisha was surrounded by a halo of sprites. Some of the Light essence of Phantom Acres was departing with her. It was of no use to those who stayed behind, and the need in Fendwarrow would be great.

Glavenor ran at a steady lope, ahead of the trotting horses. His sword and armour had been strapped to the packs, and he moved with an easy rhythm.

"How far do you think he can run like that?" Tabitha asked her father.

"I'd bet on the horses tiring before he does."

She hoped he was right, that Garyll was that strong. The Swordmaster of Eyri was the only shield her mother would have from the Dark in Fendwarrow. The further they passed from sight, the greater her dread became.

"Come, help me stack the wood," Hank said, gruffly. "It'll do no good to dwell on the maybes."

♦ ———————♦

Ashley Logán sat in a high alcove in the west wall of the Dovecote, and considered the steep terraces of Levin below. The city clustered onto the descending slope, looking like a mongrel's coat brushed the wrong way. Sharply-pointed roofs of red-and-grey slate thrust upwards in clumps from amongst the lower districts, and even the white walls of lightning-quartz had been finished with irregular heights, so that Levin seemed to be all the more rumpled where the slope eased beside the Amberlake, far below.

He pressed his back against the curve of the high stone balcony.

It was his private place, the one part of the Dovecote where he could escape the demands of training and the watchful eyes of his mentors. The alcove had become an architectural appendage—the door at his back had long ago been reduced to a narrow, glassless window by some mason's hand. The chamber within was dark and disused. The only access to Ashley's alcove was to climb up the patterns of the Dovecote's western wall. He was hidden from those who might walk past below.

He spun the Light essence idly through his fingers, playing with the shapes he could create. A ball of sprites, a pool, a spiral.

A Courier dove winged out of the west, high over the Amberlake. It cut a direct path to the Dovecote. He followed its flight. The bird circled the Dovecote's tower, then passed out of sight at Ashley's level, aiming for where he knew the rooms of Rector Shamgar to be.

It was rare for a message to be sent to the Cote, they usually went from the Cote. Very few displaced Gifters could spare sprites on messengers. It had to be something important. No doubt they would be told of it soon.

But there was no announcement, that day. The messenger from the west went silently into the depths of the Dovecote.

The Darkmaster walked the length of Fendwarrow's main street. The street was empty. Fendwarrens learned their lessons well—even the Swords were contained in their barracks, since his 'chat' with their captain. His coercive spell was tentative, but it worked well enough on all the tinpots, for they had been in Fendwarrow a long time since the last changing of the guard. He would use their weakness to its full potential. For now, it meant moving unchallenged through the village, searching for the damned Ring.

One tall Shadowcaster was at his side—the most arrogant of his underlings, Kirjath Arkell. Cruel pride flashed in his yellowed eyes. His hunger for power had begun to bunch his shoulders, he walked like a vulture searching for prey. Arkell probably thought that the Darkmaster favoured him. The fool. It was because he could not be trusted that the Darkmaster had excluded him from the retreat to Ravenscroft. With the help of the jurrum, it would not be long before Kirjath reached for things beyond his ability to control. Such ambition made him a useful tool, to retrieve what had been lost.

"Kirjath!" Cabal rasped dryly.

"Yes, Master?"

"I put an important task in your hand." Cabal kept his voice low. Whispering always made men like Arkell think they were being offered a secret. As if he would extend his trust that far!

Kirjath gazed blankly at him and nodded for him to continue. The cheek of it!

"I shall be leaving," Cabal announced.

"And abandon the search for the ring? I thought that you valued it highly. Master." There was a hint of distaste in the second word. Answering the Darkmaster without the honorific would have earned Arkell a painful blast of essence, and he knew it. Yet the deference was always a shade too hesitant.

Cabal held Kirjath's pale eye until the Shadowcaster dropped his gaze.

"My Morrigán tell me that the King's Justice approaches. That man is too righteous to be confronted here. He cannot be turned in time."

"The Swordmaster?" Kirjath asked with a sneer.

Cabal nodded.

"How do you know he cannot be turned?"

Such insolence did not deserve an immediate answer. It deserved a long week in the torture rooms in Ravenscroft. Cabal looked off into the distance.

"You will stay here, and remain hidden. It will be your task to search for my ring, wherever that search takes you, however long it takes. I want that talisman found!"

"How will I find the ring, if you have failed here?"

"I have not failed!" shouted Cabal, turning on his underling. Kirjath didn't even have the prudence to flinch. Cabal backhanded him. He put little weight behind his bony fist, more to save his own hand than for any feeling of mercy. He considered filling Arkell with essence, freezing him on the spot, and then hitting him again with a rock.

"The ring lies in some corner of this town. When it moves, you shall know."

Kirjath pretended to be calm, but his ticking eyelid gave him away.

"How will I know? Master."

Cabal considered his answer for a moment. Kirjath's understanding of the talisman's power might bring further trouble, but that was exactly why Kirjath was so perfect for the task. He would covet the Wizard's Ring, and so would find it. If he was stupid enough to wear the Ring himself, he wouldn't have the time to use it. He would be drawn back to Ravenscroft by the Darkstone at his throat. He probably didn't realise how tightly the oath he'd made to his Master would bind him.

Cabal didn't answer the hanging question. Instead, he cast his mind back to when he'd first worn the Ring. He'd been daring, inventive and so very aware. It had been such an exciting time. Too brief, before he'd lost all that clarity. His advisor had hinted that there might be a way to regain the use of its power, but it involved releasing it from its safety-chain and leaving it untended in the sun. His advisor was wily; Cabal had never completely trusted the man. He'd kept the Ring close instead, and yet through all those frustrating years, he'd never found a way to affect it, to make it respond to him again. It had remained cold and useless. He hated the thought of someone else finding it, being able to tap its power.

"Whoever finds the talisman will probably try to sell it," he announced, somewhat hopefully. "If not, they should appear as a beacon to your senses, because they'll have a guilty conscience. The Ring won't let them lie to themselves. Everyone knows it is mine."

Kirjath didn't look convinced. "Then why don't I sense anyone now? There's nobody in this town that hasn't faced our Darkspells and none of them have confessed."

"Then the Ring is still lying hidden, or the thief has already left the village. There's another thing. If someone with talent wears it, they'll be trying all sorts of spells. New spells. Strong spells."

Kirjath considered this for a moment, and Cabal could read his thoughts as if they were spoken. If he found the Ring, he would probably try to use it. Then he'd want to keep it.

So. The cur would have to be drawn back to Ravenscroft kicking and screaming against the compulsion of his Darkstone.

Kirjath smiled with oily greed. "So I'm looking for the scent of a new spell, a sudden show of skill with the essence, someone who displays more talent than they should."

Cabal put a hand on the Shadowcaster's shoulder, and let a subtle

Domination spell seep through Kirjath's cloak. The man understood his task, and he would stick to it. Although Cabal had his reservations, Kirjath was his best chance of finding the talisman, and he could not afford to be without it when he moved against the King. More to the truth, he could not afford someone else to discover it. It was too powerful.

"Find it. Bring it back," Cabal ordered.

They parted ways then, in front of the Crowbar. Kirjath Arkell slipped into the shadows. Cabal rounded on the stables, a low-roofed hulk of a building set behind the inn, near the river's edge.

He had to leave, because the Swordmaster was coming. He was fleeing as if he was a frightened burglar! It was infuriating, but the time to face the King's minister of Justice had not yet come. Timing was everything, in war. If you did not strike the right pieces at the right moment, years of work and planning could be for naught. His plan was intricate, and he wanted to choose the moment of its commencement.

He mounted his rough-natured stallion, and it cowered underneath him, then bore him at a gallop from the grimy village, up the south-east trail for the secret pass to Ravenscroft. He let his left hand trail behind the saddle, brushing the ground with a fine touch of Dark essence. The hard-packed soil showed no trace of his passage in the gathering dusk. It would be morning before the Swordmaster reached Fendwarrow, but you could never be too careful with someone like Garyll Glavenor.

Besides, Cabal had a special place for the Swordmaster in his plans.

5. THE SEED OF POWER

"Would you recognise an acorn,
if you searched for an oak tree?"—*Zarost*

At last, Tabitha could stand it no longer. Almost a week had passed, a week of long days which never seemed to end. The unspoken question lingered in the air wherever she went.

The floors of the homestead had been scrubbed and waxed until they shone. Balls and balls of yarn had been spun for her mother's loom. The pile of chopped wood she was stacking for her father had grown to the height of the eaves. And still no news.

"Father, something's wrong. We should have heard from her by now. We must go to Fendwarrow."

Hank rested his axe on the ground, and stared off into the east, where the last light of the sun fell against the harsh peaks of the Zunskar. "I'll give her another day, but I agree with you, treasure. I can't take this waiting either. We'll go before the weekend. Madam Quilt will manage without you. Lord Winterborn be damned—I should have left the farm and gone with her in the first." Hank set another short log on the chopping block. He hefted the axe above his head.

Fendwarrow. A scourge of Shadowcasters, the messenger had said.

The axe cleaved the wood with such force that the head was buried deep into the chopping block. Tabitha placed the next log for her father.

Lone farms and Lightgifters, common targets for Shadowcasters.

Smack! The heavy axe severed a knot, leaving jagged splinters. Tabitha retrieved the halves, and set them high on the woodpile.

A rough sort, Garyll had called the Fendwarrens. She was glad her father had decided to go, but she was afraid as well. Too many things turned foul in Fendwarrow.

A sudden movement caught her eye. Figures moving in the forest, riders on horseback, coming down from the High Way. Only two.

"Father."

He followed her gaze. The riders took forever to wend their way down the few switchbacks in the trail. When they finally emerged into the meadow above the homestead, Tabitha's heart leapt with joy.

A Sword rode the lead horse, the same Sword who had departed from First Light. Behind him, rode her mother.

They ran to meet the travellers. The horses cantered to close the final distance. They met on the high meadow behind the homestead, and Hank took Trisha from the saddle in his thick arms.

"Ah, it's good to have you back," he said. "We were worried sick."

Trisha looked hard-worn and haggard. "I'm sorry that I couldn't send word, my love. I used every scrap of Light essence to heal, yet it was still not enough to right the wrong in that village. There was nothing to tell, at any rate," she ended, pulling Tabitha into the embrace as well. "There was no sign of Shadowcasters, only the aftermath of their work. There was little danger, only woe."

"I wish I was a Gifter," said Tabitha, squeezing her mother's hand. "I wish I could have helped."

"I know, dear," she said, her voice full of sympathy. "Maybe it was better that you missed this one, though. You don't need such sorrow to make you old before your time."

"Don't wish too hard for an apprenticeship at the Dovecote," Hank added. "It's a dangerous career with nothing but a few sprites in hand."

"I had more than a few sprites beside me, my love," Trisha said gently. "I was in good company."

The third member of their trio was still absent.

"Where is Garyll?" Tabitha asked.

"He's already Garyll, is he?" Her mother smiled wanly. "I'll speak more about Swordmaster Glavenor later, but he remained in Fendwarrow. He was still searching for some trace of the Shadowcasters when I left. I was little help in that regard."

"Come rest your bones while we make you supper," Hank said, turning them in his arms toward the homestead. "Sword Ayche, come on in for the evening," he invited over his shoulder. "You're surely tired and hungry."

Ayche was still in the saddle, securing a lead to the reins of Trisha's mount. "Thank you, Serannon, but I'd like to press on to First Light, truth be told. My missus will be waiting for me."

"Of course. Don't let us delay you then. Appreciate you escorting Trisha safely."

Sword Ayche gave Hank a quick salute, and swung his horse back to the trail. The second mare trotted behind him on tired hooves. They were soon lost to view in the trees and gathering dusk.

◆ ——————— ◆

The meal was a celebration. Simple bread and stew seemed to make a feast, that night. The kitchen was warm from the stove and the joy of reunion.

When Trisha had absorbed enough of the nourishment, she spoke of her news. "Lillian is a stoic woman, I'll say that for her. Daran Trench was near to death's door, and it took me three days to even get a word from him. Never once did Lillian weep for their situation, or ask for sprites for her own pain. She said his pain was greater, and wouldn't hear any of my sympathies. But she's clenched so tight, in anger or fear, she won't speak of that night."

"Are they going to stay in Fendwarrow?" Tabitha asked.

"I tried to get them to move, come and join us on the farm while they search for a new life, but Daran says the ageing of the Dwarrow wine is what he knows, and it's what he shall do. It was almost as if they were afraid of retribution, should they leave. There is so much fear in that place, dread of the Shadowcasters and the one they call the Darkmaster."

"They should leave that place," said Hank.

"The other villagers were none too friendly, even when I brought them healing. They seemed to think it would get them into trouble. It's as if they've forgotten how to be gracious."

"Too much profit-taking withers the spirit."

"Nay, it's not that. The village is poorer than ever. If there is profit, it's being bled from Fendwarrow before it reaches the common folk. There's an ill feeling there. It's difficult to describe, but it felt as if I was being watched, though I never saw the watcher."

"And the other Gifters, did they come to help you?" asked Tabitha.

"That was a strange thing—they only arrived after three days, when the trail of the Shadowcasters was cold. They've stayed to help in the search, but I doubt they'll find anything."

Tabitha was incredulous. "But you sent the Courier. We saw you."

"Maybe it got lost, or never arrived," Trisha said, her voice trailing off. It appeared she had been so absorbed in her work that she hadn't given the matter much thought. "The Swordmaster sent one of his men to summon the Gifters. Hah! He shook the Swords up something fierce when we got there. I was glad I wasn't standing in their shoes that morning." She smiled at her private memory. "That is one fearsome man, Glavenor."

"He's a gentleman too," Tabitha agreed. "He bought me a drink at the Tooth-and-Tale, even though I had showered him with glass."

"Yes, he told me of that. He spoke quite highly of you." Trisha's cheeks dimpled. "Seems you made an impression, though I'd be surprised if he forget the name and face of anyone he'd met."

"What did he say?" Tabitha asked, moving to the edge of her seat.

"Enough for me to know you made an impression," Trisha said simply, "though little good it will do you, my girl. For all his charm and strength, Glavenor is still the Swordmaster of Eyri, a duty you should never forget."

"Everyone keeps saying that! What difference does it make? You're a Lightgifter, and you married a farmer!"

Her father said nothing, but Tabitha was suddenly ashamed. It wasn't like her to speak before she thought. She squeezed her father's arm, to let him know she hadn't meant any offence.

"Just because a man likes the way you sing doesn't mean he wants your hand," Trisha said sternly. "I don't think Glavenor is the marrying kind," she added.

"Why?" Tabitha asked, less sure of herself.

"He puts his duty before his happiness."

"How can you know that?"

"He ran all the way to Fendwarrow, because he thought it would be faster to keep me and Sword Ayche in the saddle."

Hank nodded, as if he had expected it. "A better man the King couldn't find as his hand of justice."

"It's no surprise he's good," Trisha said. "You know how harsh the challenge is for those who seek the title of Swordmaster. Only one man can hold that blade in Eyri."

"What's wrong with liking him then?" Tabitha asked.

"Oh, I don't blame you, my treasure, he'd set any maiden's heart aflutter, but I think it will always be his sword he holds tighter than the hand of a woman. Let Glavenor be, unless your paths continue to cross. He has the work of ten men in Fendwarrow alone, and I suspect the task won't end there."

Trisha rested her hands on the table. Tabitha noticed again how haggard her mother was. She set aside her dreaming for a moment.

"What else happened, mother? There's more, isn't there?"

"It's not something which telling shall ease, but it's a burden nonetheless, and it must be told, for you both should know why I must go."

"Go?" challenged Hank. "Where? You've only just returned. You're in no condition to travel again."

"I know, my love," Trisha answered, touching Hank's arm. "But I can't stay more than a day or two, at most. Not until I am done with this."

Trisha reached into the folds of her cloak, and produced a white kerchief, folded many times over. She opened it, delicately, cautious.

It was empty. An empty white kerchief.

Tabitha searched her mother's face for any signs of jest.

"What?" Tabitha asked. "There's nothing there."

Trisha shook the kerchief gently. Something skittered onto the table-top, making the rolling sound of a spun coin.

Round, round, round. *Drrr.*

It was quiet. Tabitha strained to see what was obviously there. All she could make out was a clearness, a small circle of colourless substance that bent the light but did not reflect it. She reached out her hand to touch it, but her mother caught her in a firm, almost painful grip.

"What is it?" she asked, surprised by her mother's strength.

"This is what the Darkmaster scoured Fendwarrow for. This was his ring. But I found it, before any of his minions did. A stroke of good fortune for the Light."

Hank's brow was deeply furrowed. "Nothing but trouble will come from this, Trisha."

"Nothing but trouble already has come from this, my love. I plan to end that trouble, before it preys on more than one poor village."

"But why would you want to keep such a thing?"

"To strike back at him! If it has value to the Darkmaster, then it hurts him to have it gone. Have no fear, I plan to be rid of it. I considered throwing it away many times on the road, allowing it to fall into some deep bog, but I couldn't risk it. What if the Shadowcasters find it again, what if some innocent finds it? It has some power I do not understand. I think the Darkmaster drew some of his inspiration from it. No, he will not get it back!"

"Why don't I take a hammer to it?" Hank offered, reaching for the ring. Trisha stopped his hand.

"No, my love, it won't work. I tested it with the largest rock I could lift, and it didn't show a single mark. I have a better idea. I will travel to Southwind, and take a boat past Stormsford to as close to River's End as I can. If the ring were to float in a bottle over the falls, it shall not be found again."

Tabitha's gaze was still locked on the ring. She didn't want to turn away, lest she lose its position and never find it again. The way the light bent through it was fascinating. The longer she looked at it, the more she could see within its clarity. The individual fibres of the table appeared in crisp focus in the middle. The ring's circumference was outlined by compressed reflections. The ring looked as if it was forged from hammered air, it seemed *clearer* than clear. It didn't look like an evil thing; it was quite beautiful, perfect.

She felt herself being drawn forward, as if the circlet was *gathering* a part of her.

"What does it feel like to touch?" she asked her mother.

Trisha gave her a sharp look. "It is as cold as a midwinter's frost. I'll not hold it for long, lest I find a hook hidden within it." Trisha lifted it carefully from the table between finger and thumb. Tabitha was fascinated by it, she wanted to touch it, to feel it, to take it from her mother.

Trisha dropped the clear ring into the kerchief, and folded it away. Tabitha tried to hide her disappointment as she watched the package return to the pocket of her mother's cloak.

· Trisha was consumed by a giant yawn. "It's a wonder that I found it, on the doorstep of Fendwarrow's inn—it pressed up beneath my boot. I'll be glad to be rid of it. I need a while to recover, but then I must make haste to Southwind."

"Not another word," Hank said, and shushed his wife with a kiss. "To bed, and to sleep. You can make plans tomorrow, and I can see to getting a hand for the farm. This time I'll come with you."

Trisha smiled wearily as she was led from the room. Tabitha padded along in her wake, after blowing out the lamps. She tried to imagine what kind of substance it could be, that could withstand the crushing weight of a rock, yet remain unblemished. She wondered what hand could craft such a perfect glass, without flaw or facet to reflect the light. What wanted to know what it felt like to touch. Just once, before it was gone from Eyri forever. Something that beautiful couldn't be so bad.

◆ ———————— ◆

It took until noon on the following day to get her chance. Tabitha slipped out of the kitchen door, and tiptoed past the back of the homestead.

She had waited a long time for her mother to fall properly asleep. She had played all of the lullabies she knew, and had ended with nearly an hour of improvisation on her lyre. It would surely be another day before Trisha attempted to travel again. Her mother had looked tired enough to sleep through a thunderstorm, but ever since Tabitha had arisen, Trisha had been awake.

During her singing, Tabitha had positioned herself on a chair in the corner of the bedroom, beside the cloak at the door. Her curiosity had plagued her. Whenever she thought her mother was deep in slumber, she had tried to reach for that nearby pocket, but every time, Trisha had been roused, tossing in her sleep before settling into the covers once more. It was as if her mother sensed her wilful thoughts and tried to warn Tabitha against what she was going to do. But at last, her mother drifted off, unable to protect what might be stolen from her own room.

Tabitha tried to convince herself that it was just *borrowing*, not stealing. She was just going to have a look. She'd return it straight away. Her hand slid into the cloak. She found the pocket, and the folded kerchief within. She could feel the hard shape of the ring through the fabric. She took it, and fled from the house.

High in the meadow behind the homestead was a single silken tree. A wind-chime dangled from one of the spreading boughs, tinkling in the breeze. The air was always full of sprites here, dancing in and out of the fluttering white leaves. It was one of her favourite places— open to the sky, well clear of the dark forest behind. Anyone who approached from the farm would be seen labouring up the hill toward her. Tabitha set her lyre down beside her, and sat on the grass at the bole of the tree.

Tabitha breathed out slowly. She was safe, she told herself, safe and alone. Mother was still asleep. Father had left for the neighbouring farms long ago, to see about a caretaker for Phantom Acres—a guardian for the farm and for Tabitha. She had already learned that she would not be going on the journey to River's End.

What if the ring really is bad? she wondered.

Just a peek, and I'll put it back.

She laid the kerchief on her lap, and folded it open. She told herself that the trembling in her hands was because of the sudden breeze. The ring glistened in the sunlight, like a circle of clear water supported, unbroken, upon the white fabric.

When she first touched it, pain shot into her fingertip. She jerked her hand away. Her mother was right. The ring was as cold as ice.

And yet it had left a thrill in her blood. It wasn't bad, or evil, or dangerous—it had just given her a sudden sting of cold. She wanted to touch it again; she couldn't keep her hand away from it. The jolt came again, but this time it felt good, energizing, exciting, like the charge in a thunderstorm. She lifted the ring off the kerchief, testing its hard edge between finger and thumb.

The initial chill faded, and was gone.

She dropped it into her palm. It was lighter than a feather, yet it felt solid and strong. Its surface was so smooth it could have been polished with silk. She turned it over and over in her hand, marvelling at the feel. It was perfect, no blemish or scratch marred its surface.

It was growing warm.

A thrill of anticipation wriggled down her spine. She raised the middle finger of her right hand and slipped the ring on. It fit her finger snugly, and yet it seemed to slide around the base of her finger, circling continuously like a restless snake.

The world brightened around her, in an expanding circle, as if a cleansing wind passed away from her and had cleared a haze from the air. The sweep of grass below her took on a different appearance, each individual blade seemed washed and sharp. The walls of the homestead became detailed, whereas before they had been blurred by distance. She could see the wood-grain of the kitchen door clearly. It was the strangest sensation. If she wanted to inspect the door, it seemed crisp, but if she relaxed her interest in it, it seemed to fade again.

The trees, all the way over the rise, all the way across the high ground to the southern peaks, they were all a richer green than she'd ever noticed, each a subtly different shade to the others. The sky was a deeper blue. The clouds were tumbled by the upper winds like fresh foam.

The ring was warm on her finger.

Something else had changed, beside the visual clarity, but it took her a few moments to understand what it was. She smelt the faint traces of the wood-smoke from the homestead, the feathery warmth of the chickens, the freshness of the fields—so many faint things were intensified. She heard the distant bleating of the sheep as if they were beside her.

Sounds, smells, sights; she could focus her attention upon any detail. She felt her awareness become startlingly clear. Even her thoughts, her memories were becoming more distinct.

As the fogginess in her mind cleared, something which had been hidden for many days emerged. She could remember the words of the dream-song! She wanted to sing, before she lost the strange awareness or forgot the moment altogether. Her hands reached for the lyre. She struck the first chord without thinking. She had practised the tune enough—it was the words she had longed to find, and now she knew them, she could feel them, as if they were sculpted from solid sound. The vibration of the lyre ran through her body. Tabitha rejoiced in the resonance.

She lifted her clear voice to the sky, and sang.

Sing high from your heart with courage,
and sing with true faith in your eye.
Sing high with elation, to all of Creation;
before the soft echoes die.
All Life comes as grace from another,
all Life can be taken away,
so share your new wishes out wisely,
there might come an end to your day.
Share all your wishes so wisely,
for Life echoes the music you play.

The words were shaped for the music; they joined in a seamless harmony. Every word resonated in the deep way that she recognised from the ascent-note of the Glee of Genesis—a power that touched the world around her. She imagined that she saw a strange clarity rush away from her, down the slope, past the homestead, through the fields below—it could have been the tears of joy forming in her eyes. The strings of the lyre hummed after each plucked note. She sang with all her heart, and she was lost for a timeless moment to the flow of creation.

The words ended as quickly as they had begun. Only one stanza, yet that was all she knew from the dream. Silence descended like a blanket, wrapping her in warm fulfilment.

She set the lyre in her lap. Her pulse was racing, her mind was alight. The singing left her with a glow, as if the sun had been right inside her heart. She gazed over fences of Phantom Acres, and the fields beyond, and felt a part of all the land. Her song had unusual lyrics, yet they had been the right words, without a doubt. She wondered if they had been sung before, or if she was the first.

A powerful song; one to cherish, and practice, and sing again. If she could impart a fraction of what she had felt in the singing, her audience in the King's Challenge would surely be spell-bound. She wished for a parchment and quill, or tablet and knife; anything to record the lyrics. Yet she knew in the same moment that she would never forget the song.

The dream-song. The Lifesong, a name which rang with the certainty of truth.

A distant figure was travelling up the road toward the farm. Her sight was sharper than ever. She recognised the long stride of her father, though she doubted he could see her from so far away.

She suddenly realised the consequences of being discovered. *The ring! She was wearing it!*

She found its clear surface, and pulled at it. It seemed to clutch ever tighter to her finger.

Off, off! It must come off! It must be replaced before Father returns.

Her finger was too dry, the ring's grip too tight. She ran her tongue along its upper edge.

Wham! ... fizz. The world was gone.

She lay on her back. A tree stretched over her, reaching to the sky beyond, its white leaves fluttering.

She remembered nothing, at first. The grass was cool beneath her. A breeze brushed wisps of hair across her face. As her awareness slowly returned, she realised how blank her mind had been—emptied of thought, vacant, stunned. She remembered to breathe. She was Tabitha Serannon.

For an instant, she had lost it all.

Her mouth was filled with a sharp, numbing taste.

Then it all came rushing back. She jerked upright. Her father strode toward the farm. He was a quarter league away.

She clutched the Ring tight. Her finger had been moistened by her tongue, and when she pulled again, the Ring slid free. A horrible emptiness swept over her. She had ended a special moment, she had lost something precious when she'd taken the ring off.

Father was coming!

She centred it quickly in the kerchief—that clear, glistening, beautiful thing. The world had emptied of all its richness, her life would be so dull without it. Oh, to fold it away was sadder than ever. Yet she knew that it had to be returned before her mother woke and searched the pockets of her cloak.

Tabitha hastened toward the homestead. Her father would reach the home after her, but not by a great margin.

The ring. It was a wonderwork, a thing of beauty, strange and powerful. It didn't deserve to lie in the foam of River's End, cast forever from the realm of Eyri as her mother planned.

Her mother wouldn't let her keep it. It belonged to the Darkmaster, didn't it? It was dangerous, evil.

How could she ever tell her mother what she had felt. The wonder of it. The clarity.

But I'll never touch it with my tongue again, she decided. That clarity had been too intense.

She reached the kitchen door and sneaked into the house. The stairs creaked softly underfoot as she climbed to her mother's bedroom. She stood for a time in the doorway, holding the kerchief. Trisha was still asleep. Tabitha imagined that the ring had grown cold again, colder than ever. She yearned to draw it from the kerchief and feel it warm under her hand, to slip it on and experience the world in that wondrous way.

Heavy footsteps shook the house from the front stair.

"I wish I could keep you," Tabitha whispered. She kissed the folded kerchief. Finally, she slipped it into the pocket of her mother's cloak beside the door.

"Hullo, dear," came Trisha's voice from the bed. "Have I been sleeping long?"

Tabitha froze. Her mother propped herself up against her pillows. Had she seen her?

Trisha blinked with owl-like vacancy. She rubbed her eyes.

Tabitha breathed a quiet sigh of relief. Her mother had seen nothing.

"Sleeping? Not long. Not long at all."

◆ ——————— ◆

When Twardy Zarost heard the song, he halted at once. He was in the marketplace of Flowerton. People jostled him, grumbling at his obstruction, but he gave them no heed. He stood with his palms turned to the sky, revelling in the ancient aria, grinning like a Merryfest melon. He was hearing a higher sound, a song he knew the villagers couldn't hear, for it came from far away to the south, probably even as far away as Meadowmoor County. He mouthed silent words at the noonday sun, and swayed upon the cobbled street, dancing to the enigma. His hat did its best to cling to his head.

The song ended after a few verses.

Only one stanza of the Lifesong. A pity it was not more, but it was enough. It was a start, a great start. The biggest explosion in the universe was in the beginning. He dropped his attention from the sky to the bustle of the market.

It was high time to leave Flowerton. He slipped from the crowd.

He soon reached Horse and the cart, and used the orchards to cover his passage from the town. It would be better that no one remembered which way he had departed.

They rode fast, for the load was light. Only one barrel remained of what he had hauled from Ravenscroft, one he had been keeping for a little tavern in Levin, on the return. It wouldn't matter if he sold it someplace else, he decided.

The air was scented with the first eager spring buds. Three weeks until the month of Bloomtide, when the boughs would be thick with colourful fragrance. For now, the land was mostly green punctuated by the grey-brown trees, and the low white stones of the occasional stacked wall. They joined the traffic on the road to Fig Tree well clear of Flowerton.

The Lifesong had been sung. The fair voice had come from the south, not the east. He knew who it was. The young woman who had sung the Shiver in the tavern contest, the Lightgifter's daughter from First Light. It had to be.

Her sudden power could only mean one of two things—he had not recognised her ability at all, or the Ring had moved, and she had used it. For either path, he had a pressing duty. The Lifesong was a great spell, it would be a beacon for those who coveted power. Others within Eyri might have sensed the singer, just as he had sensed her distant call. They would be drawn to the source like thieves to gold. He would be needed, if only to warn of the danger.

Oh, he had been too late for fair sister Syonya. So long ago in Oldenworld, in their merchant-house in Kaskanzr, before he'd even ventured to the Three Kingdoms, yet the memory burned like molten lead, heavy and hot. Her blood on the red-stone tiles, in the room that overlooked the sea. Oh Syonya! He had been so young; he had believed in the Philosophers of Kaskanzr then, in their high moral principles and their puritanical cause. By the blazes! He had been rising in stature amongst them. But her beautiful song had brought forbidden magic with it, it had been branded as heresy. Her defiance made a mockery of the men who had outlawed her. While Zarost had argued her case in the Moothouse, she had been silenced.

Zarost had not gone quietly into the wilderness. They had paid in blood for their horrendous crime. Zarost had not enjoyed the retribution, but he had cried out his sister's name aloud upon each death. Such vengeance was not a solution, it was merely a stronger flavour of failure—he had learned the bitter taste of it. His father's house had been ruined. Syonya was forever dead. Fair Syonya, oh my sister, oh!

He gritted his teeth.

No, he would find the singer before the others did.

Zarost hoped that the Darkmaster didn't search for his Riddler prematurely—he was only expected in Ravenscroft by the end of the week. It was important that he was not followed on this journey, more important than ever before.

"Come on, Horse," he said, flicking the reins, "we have a long way to go, and a short time to do it in."

Horse improved on her quick trot. The cart wheels spun swiftly over the hard-packed earth.

"Were it not for the Riddler's Oath, we could be there a lot quicker," he added. But he had worked and waited for too long to cast the chance of success aside through a moment's indulgence. The first flower of a new spring had revealed itself. Twardy Zarost was determined to see it endure.

"May time pass as slowly for the others as it does for us," he wished aloud. Horse tossed her head. The day sped by to the rhythmic measure of hoofbeats.

◆ ——————— ◆

Kirjath Arkell kept to the shadows amongst the buildings in Fendwarrow. The village reeked of Lightgifters. Their spells were undoing the fine work which had been layed down over months. Fear was being tainted with new hope, oppression was being washed away with relief, pain dissolved with healing. He even heard somebody laugh as they passed by in the dirty sunlit street.

He spat the stale jurrum out, and cursed.

It was all such a waste of sprites, that empowered essence which could have been turned to the Dark. It was the Swordmaster's fault; without him, there would be no need for caution. The Gifters wouldn't be here, and Kirjath wouldn't need to hide.

One rancorous thought led to another. If the Ring hadn't been lost, none of this wastage would be happening. The Darkmaster had made a mistake; he was losing his edge, growing old and cretinous. The Master expected Kirjath to find the Ring, but it was ridiculous. With all the Lightgifters around, he couldn't isolate any new magic which might alert him of the talisman's discovery.

The village was full of Light essence, full of the touch of Gifters. Their magic was everywhere the same, all sickening and inept. They spread dependancy, offering it in the disguise of strength and health. Do-gooders. Lifting people from despair and making them all the weaker for it. As soon as the Gifters left, the false crutch would be taken from the Fendwarrens, and the people would be defenceless against the return of Darkness.

And the Lightgifters would leave. Many wise villagers already closed their doors against the visitors. Such folk knew who controlled things in Fendwarrow. Most of them were tightly bound into the web of deals and debt. They didn't wish to encounter the Darkmaster's wrath when things returned to normal.

One Lightgifter had departed early, a blonde woman, the one who had arrived with the Swordmaster. She had worked long hours ministering her healing in the house up on End Row. For a moment he had thought that she might have discovered the talisman. Her magic had seemed loud, and strong, as if augmented. But when the other Lightgifters had arrived, he had not been so sure that her sprite-work was unique. Her apparent skill could be due to his unfamiliarity with the Light. He was so used to the motes of Dark essence that anything else was like a trumpet call on a still morning.

He folded another jurrum leaf into his mouth. The first bite was always the best. It sent a shiver of visions down his spine. The future was sweet. He was sure that the Ring was lying unclaimed, somewhere in the village. When the Swordmaster and the others departed, he would retrieve it, and claim his pleasure.

That woman, up on End Row. He remembered kicking down the door, and the triumph of what had come after. The fear had been delicious on her. He wanted to taste it again. She had been healed by the Gifter, just for him to break her. The second time would be even better than the first.

He chewed, and swallowed the juice. He allowed his senses to spread out through the village while his mind lingered on the fantasy. He would have to wait. Many Gifters were in the village, and the Swords scuttled nervously about, driven by the Swordmaster. Maybe tonight, or the next.

A powerful, high-pitched song pierced his receptive ears. He stifled a howl as it jangled his nerves. Even though it sounded as if the woman's voice came from afar, the jurrum in his veins bubbled in response to the strange power. He was grasped by agonising cramps. The few villagers he could see in the street passed by without showing any reaction to the sound. The aria carried on in his ears, jarring him to the bone, bringing him to his knees. He wrapped motes around his body, but the song penetrated the shroud as if it were no more than a shadow.

It was a spell for sure, unlike any he had sensed before. The pain wasn't physical—he couldn't dull the agony by welcoming the pain and turning it into pleasure as the Darkmaster advocated. The spell-song boiled in his blood, plaguing him with horrible sensations, doubts and fears he didn't need. He struck out at the air, then smashed his fist into the ground instead. Blood welled out from between his fingers. The violence defined him again, it gave him strength and certainty. He was Kirjath Arkell. He was terror.

Yet the song carried on and on, driving through him, making him feel so small, and insignificant, and wrong. It rejected his violence, it dissolved it, as if it contained the essence of peace.

He snarled and forced himself upright.

The music had to be stopped.

He turned his face until the sound came equally into both ears. Straight ahead, to the west. He had been right to suspect the blonde Lightgifter. She had ridden early from Fendwarrow because she had taken the talisman. The song had to be a spell of Light, else it wouldn't repell him so strongly. Magic, augmented by the power of the Master's talisman. He winced against the eldritch din. For once, he wished he hadn't been born so sensitive to magic.

The Gifter lived somewhere near the high hamlet of First Light. He had noted the farm during his recent journey there. For the spell to travel so far meant it was extremely powerful. It rivalled the Darkmaster's best. He wondered what he would be capable of with that talisman in his hands.

The music ended abruptly, and with it, the effects of the spell disappeared.

It would take a day to reach her.

Kirjath cleared the outer buildings of Fendwarrow and began the trail along the shore. He maintained a long, ground-eating stride. West, where the pinnacle of Fynn's Tooth stood white against the midday sun, and the Swords were thinly spread. There, just down from the forest and the High Way, he would find his prize.

He smirked.

He might even have the chance to pay a visit to that girl, the darling who had interfered with his child-snatching in First Light. Yes, she would not escape him again. He would find out who she was, where she lived. He spat the jurrum aside, and wiped the spittle off on the back of his sleeve.

First, the Ring. Then the girl. He would decide which of them to return to the Darkmaster.

6. THE DEAD OF NIGHT

"When you can't find your shadow,
then are you in darkness."—*Zarost*

They stood close in the living room. Tabitha's mother was eager to be off, but she was determined to share the Morningsong with Tabitha and Hank. The red of dawn filled the living room. Tabitha watched the white crystal at her mother's throat change to pink. A moment later, the sunlight struck the Lightstone directly, and the orb glistened brightly. They waited in silence for the dawn to reach Levin, lower in the basin of Eyri.

Trisha took a breath, then began to sing the Morningsong. Tabitha knew that her mother heard the distant voice of the Assembly in the Dovecote. It was a wonder which could never be shared—she could only see the sparkle in her mother's eyes and wish that one day she would bear the sensitive crystal orb and hear the faint communion of the Lightgifters herself.

The benediction was familiar, and came easily. They all sang the second verse. Trisha summoned sprites to her hand and guided them to touch her Lightstone.

The essence came from everywhere; between the floorboards, from the rooms nearby, through the front door which stood open to the breeze. Hundreds of faded sprites passed over the Lightstone, dull little sparks. They became bright as they were recharged by the Morningsong. When the song was complete, sprites trailed away from Trisha's hands like jewelled dust glinting in the air.

The new day was blessed. Trisha's orb retained its luminescence; a sphere of Light above her heart. She recalled some of the sprites, and they formed a fuzzy cloud around her shoulders.

"You're not bringing more for the journey?" Hank asked, gently.

"I'll summon them if I need to, my love," Trisha answered. "There is always some essence around."

Hank nodded, then approached Tabitha and held her close.

"Goodbye, treasure. We'll be back by midweek, for sure. You leave early enough today to reach the Tooth safely. Shepper will be here to care for the animals this evening, and he'll be here when you return."

Tabitha felt a sudden chill when her mother kissed her and turned to leave.

"Be careful," she said. Her mother smiled.

The two horses had already been saddled and loaded with travel-packs. Tabitha's parents mounted, and trotted the hired steeds from the farmyard. They were fine animals; they must have cost her father dearly. Tabitha leant heavily against the door-post, unable to shake the feeling that it was all unreal.

She waved as they passed through the lower gate, and they returned her farewell. Her parents had departed for River's End.

There goes the Ring, leaving Eyri.

Why did it feel so sad. Why so untrue?

They shall not reach River's End? Or they shall lose the Ring?

She couldn't be sure, but the deeper she probed her intuition, the more certain she became that something was wrong. Her talent for sensing the truth had made her a Truthsayer in First Light. Yet there was an emptiness in that inner place, when she considered her parents.

She wanted to run after her mother with the warning, but the horses were cantering, and had already reached the limits of Phantom Acres. She would never catch them. Besides, she wasn't entirely certain that there was danger. The hollowness that she felt might herald only the futility of the quest. It might be a reflection of her disappointment, her sense of loss. The Ring had departed with them. There was no chance she would wear it again.

She wished she could reclaim the clarity of thought which the Ring had induced. The day seemed dull, now that the dawn was passed. The sun was smeared across the sky by hastening clouds, and a shadow passed over the farm. She shrugged against the chill, and turned from watching the empty trail.

She busied herself with farm chores. Bread for the evening at the Tooth and Tale. A few candles for the store. She collected the eggs and fed the chickens. After throwing a few bales of fodder to the sheep, there was nothing to do but await the afternoon, when she planned to walk to First Light. Another Friday night, another weekend at the Tooth-and-Tale, a chance to earn her way. She considered departing at once. Time passed too slowly in the silent homestead.

She reached for her lyre, but a small sound made her hesitate. A scrape and thump in the barn, or somewhere nearby, as if something had toppled. Tabitha crossed the floor on tiptoe. She eased the front door open. A gust of wind met her. The yard was empty.

There was scuffling within the barn. A horse snorted and stamped. A solid thump.

"Damn and blast you!"

She recognised her father's voice. A second later he came out of the barn, clutching his elbow.

"Cursed horse is supposed to be lame." Hank worked his upper arm with his fingers.

"Father, why –" Tabitha began.

"Horse shied, and backed into a ditch. Stupid thing. I should never have paid so much for it."

"What did the horse shy for?"

"A shadow amongst the trees, nothing more."

A cold foreboding brushed Tabitha's heart.

"What kind of shadow?"

"A shadow, Tabitha." He held her gaze. "Don't you have wild fancies on it, now."

"Where's Mother?" She couldn't shake the sense of present danger.

"Calm yourself, treasure. She rode to the neighbours to see if we could borrow another horse for the journey. She'll be here soon."

"And the Ring?" Tabitha blurted out.

Her father looked at her strangely, and paused long before answering. "It is safe, with her. Why do you ask?"

"I—I just had a feeling, is all. This morning. That something was going to go wrong."

"Well, now that it has, it is behind us. We can go on with our task. Here comes your mother now."

A horse and rider galloped into view. They raced along the crest of the middle-horizon toward Phantom Acres.

Tabitha spoke her thoughts aloud. "Why is she riding so fast?"

Trisha galloped at break-neck speed. A copse of trees obscured her for a moment, then she emerged again, leaning low against the horse's neck.

A black bird dived from the sky, directly above them. It swooped at the horse's head, and the stallion swerved, stumbled at a fence, and crashed through the poles. Trisha was thrown to the ground. The horse ran on, through scattering sheep. The big bird climbed, and dived again. It looked like a raven.

Tabitha ran on her father's heels. Where her mother had fallen was partly in view. Trisha hadn't moved.

The panic spread to the sheep. They scoured around the limits of their pen. Some found the break in the fence, and they scattered in mindless terror. The raven swooped. Its terrible cry drove the flock before it.

When they came upon her mother, they found Trisha curled up on her side in the long grass. Blood trickled down her temple. Her eyes were closed, and she gave weak, tremulous breaths. Tabitha ran her hands lightly over her body.

"Nothing broken," she said, meeting her father's distressed gaze.

Hank stroked Trisha's hair away from her wound. Despite the blood, the gash was small. Hank scooped his wife up as if she were a lamb.

Tabitha scanned the sky. The black raven was gone. The horse paced in a corner of the field, weaving one way then the other. The sheep were dispersed all about, bleating and milling in knots. Some of the ewes dropped their heads to the turf, the bird and panic already forgotten.

They laid Trisha on a pallet on the living-room floor. The fire licked through fresh logs in the hearth. She helped her father to clean and dress the wound. Still Trisha slept; her breaths were weaker than ever.

"Can I get the spritesalt from the safe-chamber?" Tabitha asked.

Hank just nodded his assent. The safe-chamber was reserved for her parents' valuables and as such she had never opened it. Her father sat beside Trisha, her head in his lap. His face was crumbling inwards.

Tabitha knelt at the base of the hearth. The fire was hot against her face, but the hearth-wall was thick, protected from the heat above. She had seen her father work the turn-stone before. She pushed it inwards, and began to twist it.

"Here, let me help," her father said thickly, his hand suddenly over hers. "Stone will lock if it isn't turned right."

He guided Tabitha's hand, and the turn-stone moved. It kicked outwards against her palm, and Hank drew her hand away. He pulled the stone from the low hearth-wall.

"Mason charged us the earth for this, but she wanted a safe all the same. Ah, Trisha!"

He stood back, his gaze on Trisha.

The vial of Spritesalt was resting close to the mouth of the chamber. Tabitha drew it out carefully. The stopper had only been removed from the vial twice in Tabitha's memory. It was a highly treasured prize of special potency.

She glanced at her mother's still form. There could be no question that the Spritesalt was needed. She poured a generous portion into her hand, then spread the balm gently across Trisha's forehead. The Light faded from the salt as the healing spell was released.

But Trisha remained as pale as milk, and didn't rouse. Tabitha used more spritesalt. It vanished without effect. Wood cracked in the fire. The room was too warm, and still.

"It's that Ring," Hank said, bitterly. "She has borne that tainted talisman too long. We should have been far from here, yet here we are, not even begun. That thing turns fate against us."

A strange defensiveness awoke within Tabitha.

"Hush, Father. A shying horse, a strange bird, how can they be blamed on a little piece of glass? Nothing has that kind of power." But speaking of the accident raised a sudden doubt in her mind. *A black bird, just like the one that warned the Shadowcaster in First Light.*

"Think who the talisman belonged to, and you have your answer," Hank responded.

"But maybe this is another ring, maybe it isn't evil. The Shadowcasters couldn't know that mother has it. It's invisible."

"When did you become the expert on it?"

It was a caustic comment, unnatural for her father. They were both behaving strangely under the strain.

Her father's level gaze bored into her. Her indignation dissolved as her cheeks coloured. Tabitha bit her tongue. It was wiser to be silent.

"Nothing but ill fortune will come from that talisman," Hank asserted.

That's not true! It helped me find the words of the Lifesong.

She couldn't explain to her father how the words had slipped into place when she had worn the Ring, for that would mean admitting she had taken it from her mother's pocket. She hadn't forgotten those words.

Her lyre was where she had left it, leaning against her mother's larger instrument beside the window. The day had turned foul rapidly outside; low clouds poured down from the forests, driven by a fast-approaching storm.

Tabitha hummed a quick scale, running her fingers lightly over the strings. Her father bowed his head over Trisha's sleeping form. The oblique firelight made his brows appear deeply furrowed, his face more than haggard.

From the first note she played, the Lifesong filled her, almost overwhelmed her. She held on to the words of the stanza she knew. The lyrics offered the solid certainty that she felt when she spoke as the Truthsayer; they felt right. She sang louder than she had intended. It was a glorious release. The room was filled with the wonder of music.

She experienced the sounds as if they formed a river and she was trailing her fingers upon its rippled surface. She could sense other themes passing by beneath the simple melody she played, other currents within the liquid flow of the song.

The Lifesong thrummed in the wood of her lyre as if the instrument was alive, quivering. The air cleared around her. Trisha seemed to shimmer in sympathy with Tabitha's notes, as her body responded to the song. Tabitha imaged that the music was rippling through every living fibre, releasing the curse of her mother's condition. She sang, pouring love into her song.

The stanza came to an end. Tabitha's voice tailed off.

Trisha stared up at Tabitha with a look of deep wonder. She was awake! A log collapsed gently in the hearth. Hank breathed a sigh of relief. Finally her mother spoke, in a weak, clear voice.

"That song, that song! You have found the healing verse."

"It was the dream-song, the Lifesong. You remember? I learned the words."

Her mother's awed gaze was difficult to hold.

"You—called me back," Trisha said. She smiled, then winced suddenly, and touched her head. "Oh, oh oh. It's the drunkard's best headache I've earned myself. How did I do this?"

"You don't remember?" asked Hank, pulling her close in a gentle bear's embrace.

"I remember the horse bolting. I fell?"

"On your fair head." He kissed her temple where she had wounded herself.

"That I can heal. Oh, thank you, Tabitha, you brought me back from a very cold place." Trisha shifted gently from Hank's arms. She summoned sprites from where they played in the fire. They were dull, having paled since dawn, yet they would hold enough Light for Trisha's spell. She wove them into a pattern between her hands, layer upon layer of flickering particles, bonded by her thought and the words of the Healall spell. Tabitha knew the words, but without the Lightstone and the mental training of the Dovecote, she had no command over the sprites. Her mother raised the delicate net of Light to her head. For a moment Trisha looked like a queen with a crown of sparks. The essence sank into her hair and disappeared.

Her mother breathed a sigh of relief, and eased into Hank's arms once more. She regarded Tabitha with eyes that were tired but clear of pain.

Little was said for a while. It was good just to be together. When the fire burned low, Tabitha collected more logs. There was no question of her mother travelling that day. Her father went out to gather the sheep, and to stable the headstrong stallion, if it could be found.

They shared a frugal dinner. Nightfall found them together in the living-room again, beside the companionable fire.

"Well, it's good that we're all here, safe at home," said Trisha.

Tabitha felt the room filling with cold, as if the door had swung open and allowed the night to gust into their home. Her truth-sense rebelled at her mother's words. The foreboding was like ice deep in her heart.

"We are not safe at home," she whispered.

"What is it, treasure? What do you sense?"

"Something is coming here tonight. Danger."

A Shadowcaster. Could it be?

She couldn't bear to speak the word, for fear of it ringing true. But in the end, it was worse to hold the statement at bay, and to doubt, than to have the dreadful premonition confirmed.

Her throat was so dry.

"A Shadowcaster."

True. She knew it.

Fear coursed through her like a cold poison; her truth-sense was washed away, she would learn no more.

A Shadowcaster. Lone farms and Lightgifters.

Something clanged outside.

It could have been one of the horses kicking against its stall.

"Mercy! Have I drawn a tail from Fendwarrow?" cried Trisha, rising swiftly on unsteady feet. "Are you sure the danger is here, tonight?"

Tabitha nodded.

"We cannot leave, into this storm," Trisha declared.

"Then we'll fight!" boomed Hank, glaring out the window. "Let a Shadowcaster cross the threshold, and he shall feel my fist!"

The muffled clang sounded came from outside again. This time she was sure it came from the direction of the barn. It might still be the horse, restless.

"You don't understand, my love," Trisha said in a small voice. "You can't fight a Shadowcaster. You don't have a Lightstone, you can't command the essence. Only I can face this foe. Hank, this is a Shadowcaster, not an ordinary man."

Hank spun to face her, his fists clenched tight. "Then tell me how I can help you! I will stand at your side if he threatens your life. If it's true he's coming." He shot Tabitha a glance, but his gaze held no distrust, only a grasping hope that she might recant her pronouncement. He knew Tabitha's ability well enough.

"I don't know how to fight a Shadowcaster," Trisha answered. "I've never faced one before. They always evade us. They are a rumour, hidden in the dark, an unseen predator. But I know they are capable of violent acts."

"A blow to the head took you down today. I vouch the same will cripple a Shadowcaster."

"Maybe. Oh, Hank, be careful if you do!" Trisha summoned sprites again, and allowed them to pool in her cupped hands. The Light cast a strange illumination on her face, and in it Tabitha saw hollowed eyes and a gaping mouth, vivid and frightening. White as bone, cold as stone.

Tabitha's stomach rolled, and she stifled a cry. She couldn't tell if the vision was the truth, or a nightmare fantasy.

She stumbled to the large window, and pressed her forehead to the cold glass. The night was dark, thick with dreadful secrets. The fire crackled sullenly in its hearth, its light framed the window with a dull red glow. Off in the distance, Tabitha heard a nightjar screaming its nocturnal sermon. She tried to calm her breathing.

A face lunged out of the darkness beyond the window. The glass swirled out of focus, the roof and walls and floor spun dull red, but in the centre of the sudden confusion, the attacker's face was as clear as etched stone. His cold, marbled eyes were grey stained with yellow. She knew those eyes, they pierced Tabitha to the bone. Then he struck the glass with his forearms, and the window exploded.

Vicious shards splintered over her body. A thousand tiny teeth bit her, she cried out as the many blades cut her legs. The fear was like a wall, so solid that it drove her backwards, reeling. She felt naked and helpless. The window was empty. The Shadowcaster hadn't jumped into the room as she had first thought. He had vanished.

Blood welled up from cuts in her face and scalp, and soaked into the collar of her woollen jacket. She turned, violated, toward her parents.

Hank's rage burst. "You will not touch my child!" he roared at the night beyond the shattered window. A cold breeze pushed into the room, rippling the curtain. The Shadowcaster was gone. His explosive appearance had torn the night. His disappearance was unanswered.

"No!" Hank roared again. He ran to the window, crushing the shattered glass underfoot. He looked capable of tearing down a tree with his bare hands, so angry was he. He cleared the jagged shards from the bottom of the frame with a sweep of his boot, and leapt out into the dark night. The top of the window remained like a fringe of broken teeth. Hank thudded to the ground below.

Her mother issued a strangled cry after Hank, but he was gone, running away in pursuit. Trisha went to the gaping exit, but then she froze and recoiled. A dark shape suddenly filled the window. The Shadowcaster dropped from the windowsill to the floor, and surged into the room, pushing Trisha backwards with the threat of his presence. His black cloak swirled wide, preventing escape, bringing a wave of terror. Tabitha wanted to scream, but her own fear had clasped its bony hands around her throat. She stood transfixed as the Shadowcaster advanced and her mother retreated across the room in front of her.

He was taller than her mother by at least a foot. The cowl of his cloak had fallen from his head, exposing a bristling cut of steel-grey hair. His eyes were unflinching, determined, even more cold and merciless than she remembered from her encounter in First Light. His face was a work of pasty stone, except for his bright red lips. He grinned, an expression which suggested impending release, rather than mirth. There was no warmth there, only hunger. A pure black orb dangled on a chain at his throat.

Tabitha wished she could sink into the floorboards and disappear. His attention was on her mother not upon her, but she knew from his first glance that he had recognised her. He had promised to return, that terrifying day in First Light.

"Lightgifter, your husband is chasing an illusion, but he will return in a moment. Decide! Meet my demand, and I will not kill him."

Trisha met him with a square stance, her sprites gathered around her like a shield of sunlight. But her voice quavered when she said, "What are your demands?"

"Only one. I will have the Master's Talisman from you. I will have the Ring."

Trisha staggered where she stood.

Blood stung Tabitha's eyes. She drew the back of her hand across her eyes, but her hand was bloodied as well, and it only made her tears worse.

"Ring?" she heard her mother say. "I don't know of any ring. I am a Lightgifter, not a jeweller."

"Gifter, don't toy with me. You are too weak. The lie is already in your eyes. I know you came to Fendwarrow, and left with the talisman. I have sensed the use of it, yesterday and today. The stench of a new magic is all over this place, in this room! You sang that spell-song today, it stung me again. You're using the talisman, I know, but the Ring does not belong to you. It is mine! I have come to collect it for the Darkmaster."

Tabitha's vision cleared enough to see her mother's eyes narrow.

"I will see it destroyed, before your kind spread your Dark blight any further through Eyri."

A faint shout came from outside.

"Then your husband dies," the Shadowcaster stated.

"No!" Trisha cried. "Murder is a High Crime. You will be executed!" It was a desperate powerless threat, and her mother must have known it.

"The King's law doesn't touch me, you stupid crone. I won't be found."

"The Swordmaster will track you!" Trisha was shaking, trapped halfway between defying the Shadowcaster and fleeing the room to forestall Hank. "You can't kill and get away with it!"

"Your faith is charming, but you are wrong," the Shadowcaster stated. His presence alone made Tabitha weak. It was a wonder that her mother could speak at all, having to hold his eye.

"My husband has nothing to do with this," Trisha retorted. "I took the Ring."

Tabitha gasped. Defiance in the face of the coercion. The shadows swirled around the black-robed Shadowcaster, and an aura of fear swept through the room. He gathered more motes around his body; a Dark nemesis to face Trisha's halo of Light.

Hank Serannon pounded past the window, heading for the front stairs.

The Shadowcaster smiled, a disheartening exposure of his discoloured teeth. "Good. Now save your husband, dear woman, and give it to me." The Shadowcaster stretched out his hand. He looked calm, poised, deadly. He had meant everything he had said.

The force of compulsion was thick in the air. Tabitha wanted to cry out and plead for mercy. It was all she could do to be silent, for her mother's sake.

The front door slammed, and a moment later, the heavy curtain of the living room doorway was ripped aside. Hank stormed toward the Shadowcaster, crossing the room in an instant. He nearly flew through the air, arms outstretched to tackle his opponent to the ground.

He knew nothing of the Shadowcaster's terms.

The Shadowcaster was almost negligent in his defence. He jumped aside, his cloak billowing, and slapped an open hand to Hank's neck. A black stain remained where he touched. The Shadowcaster whispered, a sound like dead reeds in a breeze. The stain on Hank's skin became a snakelike coil, a glistening black band.

Hank was on his feet in an instant. His eyes smouldered with fury. He charged the Shadowcaster again, but took only two steps, then faltered. He clutched at his throat, his face darkening, his eyes bulging. The black collar drew tight, a writhing noose of motes. Tabitha stood rooted in horror as her father dropped to his knees in front of the Shadowcaster, and then fell, thrashing on the wooden boards of the floorboards.

Sprites arced from Trisha's hand toward Hank, but the Shadowcaster deflected them and speared Hank's body with another scourge of motes.

"Freeze," said the Shadowcaster, raising one hand with a flourish.

Hank jerked hard, once, and was still.

"What have you done to my husband?" Trisha cried. She threw sprites toward him again, and again they were turned aside, wasted.

"He'll live, if you behave. You have little time." The Shadowcaster turned his palm upward, and whispered again. A wisp of darkness settled there, pooling like oil.

"Yes, Dark essence," the Shadowcaster stated, "so much more power than the Light, as I'm sure you have observed." He pushed

Hank's inert body with his foot. "There is a word I could speak to release him, but nothing will help him if it is spoken too late. Best you hurry with that ring, woman." He gazed nonchalantly at Trisha, as if he had all the time in the world.

Her mother fled the room.

Tabitha was shocked. Surely her mother had the ring in the pocket of her cloak? Why did she run from the room? Why had she left Tabitha alone?

The Shadowcaster stepped closer. "Hullo, pretty. You have saved me time, by being here for me."

"The Swordmaster will find you," she stammered. She understood why her mother had called upon his name. In the face of such despair, she needed something to hope for.

He dismissed her threat with a smirk, spread both hands, and whispered his summoning. The Shadowcaster seemed to grow darker, his cloak reached further around him, a swirling fabric of black satin, or motes of Dark essence. The cruel wind became colder. The chill night seeped into her bones.

Tabitha retreated, until the wall struck her firmly from behind. She was beside the fireplace, but even the fire was affected by the chill, and it smouldered weakly, barely able to glow, let alone offer warmth.

Blood trickled from her cuts. Her pulse was still racing, but like a mouse caught in the open, she was too scared to move lest it caused the predator to pounce, too scared to utter a squeak lest it betray her. She was captured by the terror which pooled like lead in her feet. She pressed herself back against the wooden panelling beside the hearth, and wished her father would move, or that her mother would return to save her.

The Shadowcaster's gaze pinned her to the wall as if it were the point of a blade. A cold, terrible blade. He gestured toward her, throwing some of the blackness that surrounded him in her direction.

Dark essence!

It cut through her waist, denying her all feeling of her body below. Vitality leached from her limbs, painful at first, then less so. A numbing cold overwhelmed her body.

"Despair," she heard the Shadowcaster say.

The blood stopped flowing from her wounds. It didn't matter, really. She was going to die. Even her terror became a numb, distant compulsion. She was too weak to fight, too small and powerless.

Better to give in. The peace of black silence filled her mind, the allure of endless sleep. She began to slip further into the void, and the sound of an icy wind filled her ears. Blowing, howling, whispering. She was surrounded by the darkest night.

"No!" her mother cried.

Tabitha was vaguely aware of a warm presence in front of her. Tabitha's blurred vision began to clear again. There was an intense light before her which blocked her from the Shadowcaster.

She heard a wracking cough from the floor where Hank had lain.

A sudden rush of warmth and light washed through her.

She recognised the words of her mother's Healall spell. The rush of Light restored her, but left her confused and strangely pained.

"You never intended a trade," her mother accused the Shadowcaster. "You intend to take the Ring, and to deny our witness by death!"

There was something waving behind Trisha's back, twisting backwards and forwards in Trisha's hand. Tabitha's vision was still playing tricks with her, and her mother's back became a smeary aura of light for a while, like paints mixed by a child. She blinked. Everything came into focus. She saw the words scrawled on her mother's white kerchief.

Take this. Run.

Hasty letters, written with rough charcoal on the white weave. Her mother's body shielded Tabitha and the kerchief from the Shadowcaster.

She knew what was contained in the folded fabric.

For a second, she couldn't find her any strength to move. Her mother was going to fight the Shadowcaster. She would only want Tabitha to flee if she expected extreme danger. Or failure. Her mother was wreathed in sprites—she must have summoned all she could have during her brief absence.

Oh Mother, is it worth so much to you, to deny him the Ring?

Then Trisha spoke the words that helped her to understand.

"I know your face, you cretin! She described you in detail. My sister is scarred, part of her will never heal. You will pay for your evil, if it is the last thing I do." Sprites left her hands in a twinned blast of Light, aimed at both the Shadowcaster and the still figure on the floor.

Everything was tilting, sliding, slipping, the world was falling inwards to crush Tabitha. There was a terrible note of finality to her mother's threat. She saw her father recover with a sudden jerk. He leapt from the floor, taking the Shadowcaster's legs out from under him. Her moment was now, or not at all.

She took the kerchief from her mother's hand, and ran. The five strides to the door took forever.

A cold blast followed her into the room on the other side. She crashed into the kitchen table, scattering pots and glasses. Then she was through the back door, and stumbling, tripping, running out into the night.

She fled.

The moon seeped through a hole in the stacked clouds overhead, and everything was bathed in its ghostly light for a moment. She passed the solitary silken tree which stood sighing in the wind. The chimes jangled an agitated dirge. The worn path through the high meadow was hard beneath her feet.

Panic fuelled her legs; her terror found release. She tried not to think of her parent's plight, only the simple command. Take this. Run. Trees flicked by.

An image of her father assaulted her. He was swamped in Dark essence and clutching at his throat.

How can they fight him? How long will Mother stand?

Tears streamed from her cheeks as she ran. The wind whistled through the trees, and buffeted her with hard gusts. The path was steep. A heavy raindrop stung her face, then another. She hardly noticed them. Her mind spun with the crazy shards of the scene she had left behind. A cavernous nausea yawned in her belly. She was a traitor, running away. Yet her mother had demanded she run. Her mother was fighting for her life, fighting to give her time.

What good will time be, if Mother fails?

Her thoughts tortured her, leaving an angry poison in her blood that roared like a wild thing above the pounding of her heart.

She reached the forest just as the hail began to fall. The trees shielded her, but it became much darker, for the moon was hidden again. Pine needles softened her footfalls. Her heart ached with every running step.

She reached the junction on the High Way and turned right, towards First Light. She laboured for breath. The road was wide, worn by the decades of travellers.

Tabitha pushed herself to the limit of her stride, not caring if her heart burst from exertion. The pain and fear and chaos of uncertainty churned within, driving her panic to an ever higher pitch.

The earth blurred underfoot. The forest was filled with moist, groping darkness. The roar of water pulsed through the air, and the undergrowth grew thick along the sides of the road. A river came out of the mountains to her left, rushing under a broad, arched bridge and away downhill. Tabitha ran out across the River of Falls, and the hail stung her without remorse. Her footfalls thudded on the slippery planking. The wood was worn and slick. She was high over the rushing water, and moonlight swirled wetly in its currents, gleaming through the spaces in the dark bridge.

The strength drained from her body as if the Shadowcaster had renewed his touch on her. Fatigue and despair gripped her spirit. If she crossed the bridge, she would truly be abandoning her parents. She stumbled over a gap in the planking, veered towards the edge of the bridge. Her shoulder caught the slender rail, and she was repelled. Her breath rasped in her throat. Her head throbbed. She slipped hard to her knees.

Tabitha clung onto the bridge rail. She couldn't go on at this delirious pace.

The Dark essence had already claimed her strength.

Her mother's brief warming touch had loosened the Shadowcaster's grip, but she knew that not all of the motes had been driven from her body. Now that she had stopped, she could feel the cold worming its way deeper inside. There was nothing she could do to repel it.

The pounding in her head threatened to drown out the roar underneath the bridge. She sank back from her knees, pushed her body against the railing. Hail pelted her. The wide river poured between the piled rocks below. It ran a short way downstream before disappearing into a roaring mist of white spray.

She stared blindly in the direction of Phantom Acres. Her tears fell to the river, far below the bridge.

Take this. Run.

How far can I run, Mother, knowing you face the Dark?

The Shadowcaster's threat was not so immediate any more; it was dimmed by the distance and Tabitha could almost imagine that her mother had a chance, after all. She gazed into the dark mystery of the night beyond the falls, trying to sense what was happening on the farm.

◆ ——————— ◆

Kirjath Arkell was relishing his game. The Lightgifter's challenges were quick, but she was no match for his power. She was good at defence and healing, but useless with attack. He had hoped for more of a contest. He had allowed the young one to flee, because he knew he could catch her later. He wanted the talisman first. He could have it now, he could take the Lightgifter down, but it was better to give her time. It was always better for hopelessness to really sink in.

Lightgifters were easily bested. They should have been crushed long ago. The Darkmaster was too cautious.

The blonde woman had a diminishing supply of sprites, yet she kept wasting her essence to heal her husband. Pathetic.

Let the man lie, you stupid crone. He's to die anyway.

Every time the farmer rose, Kirjath dropped him to the floor again, with the briefest of spells. The man was a simpleton. *Can't he see how much Dark essence I command?* Any sensible man would abase himself before such a mighty adversary as Kirjath Arkell. The farmer shouldn't fight a Shadowcaster with his fists. *I should break his mind, freeze him to keep him still.*

But there was a good reason to keep them alive. Both of them.

Kirjath deflected a wash of Light with a simple curtain-shield, confusing the sprites amongst the ripples and folds in his cloak of Dark essence.

He shaped a Morrigán, and whispered a command to the raven, before sending it swooping over the Lightgifter's head. The bird would rub her nerves raw, hiding behind her at the limit of her vision. She would be aware of it, but would never move fast enough to meet the source of her distraction. When he needed it, Kirjath would strike her from that store of Dark. He cast an illusionary body to the left, and moved to the right.

Tonight was more than just a reclaiming of the Master's talisman. It was a test of his own special art, the private lore which the Darkmaster had revealed by trying so hard to conceal it. The lore that went beyond the simple push and pull of Dark and Light, a power far more ancient and wild than the impotent essence.

Kirjath had found the hidden scrolls of the Morgloth lore.

The Gifter was confused by his trickery, and threw her attack at his illusionary body. He took the opportunity to cast a spell of Breaking. At the base of the farmer's spine, before he rose again. He released his motes, and they found their mark.

The scrolls, sealed in the deepest cavern of Ravenscroft, had revealed the pattern of the Gateway, the access to the powers Kirjath had believed only existed in legend. The Darkmaster had feared the knowledge, he had feared to use it himself for what it would summon.

Old fool. He shall not rule me for much longer.

Kirjath Arkell had no qualms about seizing the feared knowledge. He was the master of whatever he summoned. The Gateway had been drawn, and opened on the darkened earth.

His beast was coming.

He could track its footsteps, feel its raw hunger. Its mind was within his mind, contained by his superior intellect. He commanded the Morgloth. It came to do his bidding.

To let the woman fight for life, while he knew that her death was sealed, gave him a heady thrill. But he couldn't draw it out any longer. The Gifter was getting more aggressive in her spells, and was learning to discern the flows within the Dark essence. She disrupted the Morrigán spell, and scattered the motes.

Kirjath cast three illusionary bodies within the Dark, and sent them outwards from where he stood. It would divert the woman's attention for a moment.

He guided the beast to the homestead, and lured it through the window with a single thought.

Food.

The Morgloth's terrible screech was carried on the wind of its arrival. It burst through the few jagged remains of glass when it shot through the window. It spread giant wings wide to land, heavily, on the floor beside Kirjath. It crooned, a strange, wet sound, and looked down at him with a baleful red glare.

The Lightgifter was making the mewling sounds of a strangled kitten.

Kirjath marvelled at the big creature. The legends never did them justice. Morgloth were more deadly than the worst tale he'd heard told, more blood-thirsty than an enraged bear. It was not a beast that could be adequately described in words. Its presence had to be experienced, and none experienced a Morgloth so vividly as its Lord. He knew everything the Morgloth sensed, and was awed for a moment by its ruthless appetite for the souls of the living.

[Lord?] came the Morgloth's alien question. Kirjath still found it unsettling, the way he could understand the beast, though it didn't speak. The Morgloth inhabited his mind, and they communicated in images.

The man, he ordered, regaining his self-control.

The Gifter was backing to the far wall with a horrified, doomed expression. She cast a pitiful spell of Light at the beast. The sprites were absorbed into the Morgloth's skin with no effect.

The Morgloth leapt onto the farmer's back. The farmer was conscious, Kirjath knew, but the Breaking had left him paralysed. The Morgloth struck like a snake, its elongated head a deadly hammer. The farmer's skull cracked, and the demon feasted on his life.

The sensation was one of overwhelming bliss. Kirjath was unprepared for the ecstasy. His beast had never killed before, at least not while he was its Lord. Always the summoning, and the returning, he had practised it many a time. But never the hunt. Now he understood why the beast hungered so. To take a life was sating a hunger he had never fully understood. He raised his unseeing eyes to the roof as the convulsions of pleasure passed through his body.

The farmer's life poured away into the Morgloth. The beast didn't seem to consume any flesh, or at least Kirjath couldn't taste any through the awareness he shared. Only the force of spirit, the living energy, it roared over the falls into the blackness. Then it was gone.

Before Kirjath could return to the present, a body slammed into his, lifted him from the floor.

The Lightgifter. Damn and blast her! He scrabbled for balance, but the woman drove him too fast. His heels struck the hearth, yet still she drove him, her strength extreme, her eyes insane. They fell into the coals, and sparks exploded around them.

Pain.

He tried to cool the flames with Dark, to wrap himself in protective cold. He would defend, this time. She would need the Light she summoned for her own healing. He could smell the burning of flesh, and knew it wasn't only his own. The bite of the coals lessened, yet the pain did not cease. He tried to throw her, but she sat on his chest, deep in the agony of the swirling heat. Flame caught her hair, and she burned bright.

But she didn't use the last sprites she summoned for healing, or warding, or any of her gentle Gifter spells.

"Burst, flame, burst for me!" she cried, her arms spread wide.

The Light essence became fire. The hearth became the centre of the sun. Heat scoured his body, took the air from his lungs. More essence than he had seen all night. More pain than he had ever felt in his life. The Dark was blasted from his command, fire filled him.

Coals were flung outwards, and the ceiling caught fire. The room became a swirling inferno.

She had released the essence that could save her life, to kill him. The Lightgifter had sacrificed herself. She burned like a torch, and he, beneath her.

Take her, he commanded his Morgloth.

The charred stench of his own body was choking him.

The Gifter was wrenched from his chest. Pain raged through him, nerves burnt within his ravaged flesh. Somehow he managed to flick himself from the bed of coals, onto the floor below.

[No life], the Morgloth objected. *[No food.]*

He didn't care for the beast's disappointment. Agony filled his senses, commanded his mind. The Morgloth tossed the woman into the fire again. The Gifter crumpled, burning like a dry stick.

Kirjath rolled away from the scattered coals, but wherever he moved, he burned. He was mad with torment.

Acrid smoke swirled, blinding him, stealing his breath. What Dark essence he could summon, he wrapped tightly around his body, a thin skin of magic against the overwhelming assault. But the Dark essence couldn't give him air to breath, nor could it heal the pain. Panic and desperation soiled his mind, breaking the discipline. He felt his command of the Morgloth waver. His attention was absorbed as its animal presence grew. In a horrible moment, he saw exclusively through its eyes. It stood, watching its Lord, the one who bound it to service, the one who allowed it to exist beyond the underworld.

The walls were sheets of fire, panelling alight, flames gnawing at the beams overhead. Wood whistled and wheezed the dirge of its own immolation. Yet the great Morgloth was untouched by the flames. It peered around the room, looking for life.

A charred form lay before it, in the middle of the floor—a heap of black rags, like filthy laundry tossed into a hasty pile. The heap bulged. The Morgloth took a step backward, and watched. The lump twitched, and a charred piece of meat ventured out from the heap of smoking black rags. The meat became a stump, the stump a fist. The fist opened into four fingers and a thumb, blackened and spider-like. The Morgloth tilted its head, trying to decide.

[Food?]

The hand pressed itself down into the floor, and the heap of rags was drawn along behind it, sliding over the floor. Slowly, slowly, the body moved itself away, across the floor, toward the window. The

Morgloth wanted to eat it, but something gritted against that desire. Something growing, something returning.

[Lord?]

Kirjath crushed the beast's mind within his own, snatched the reins of mental power back from disaster. That had been too close. It must be banished, now. It had almost dominated him, and broken the raising spell of command.

"Go to hell. Through your Gateway, be gone!" he screamed hoarsely. He had to concentrate intensely to drive his order against the rebellious mind. Then the pressure was gone. He was wracked with a spasm of coughs, but he saw the Morgloth leap through the window, and flap away. Gone with the wrenching wind and suffocating smoke, into the night.

A beam tore from the ceiling. He wasn't quick enough to avoid its fall. It caught him on the back, slamming him to the floor. His cowl caught alight, blazing around his head like a halo.

He cast a Freeze spell, using the motes that had protected the rest of his body to extinguish the flames, for they were the only essence near. The agony of roasting returned with immediate intensity.

He tried to summon more motes to his aid, but couldn't pronounce the words he whispered. His coughs would not cease.

Damn the Gifter!

He would survive. He heaved himself from beneath the beam, and made a last gambit for the window, where the smoke billowed out into the night, sucked out ahead of him through the burning frame.

He wished the Gifter was alive, so that he could beat her to death himself. The talisman would be lost in the fire, hidden in layers of ash and debris. Out of all the defences she could have chosen, the Lightgifter had taken the only one which could foil his plans.

He dragged himself up and over the burning windowsill, then fell to the ground outside. He slammed into the earth, and the breath was driven from him. He cursed, in silence.

The house collapsed in on itself.

He rolled away across the wet earth, teeth bared against the torture. A thousand needles drove into him from the sky. No matter how far he rolled, the assault continued. Some kind of storm. Wracking coughs kept his face to the dirt, and his strength ebbed with every breath; he couldn't fill his lungs. He drew inwards like a trodden spider, a small black heap, curled up in the dark beneath the pounding of the storm.

◆ ──────── ◆

Inside her woollen jacket, Tabitha shivered. The hail had lessened, and the trees sheltered her from the worst of the wind, but the River of Falls issued a breeze of its own making, chill and insidious, able to find every gap in her clothing. Her breathing had calmed while she clung to the railing of the bridge, but not her thoughts.

Mother, should I return? Have you defeated him? Did Father strike him down?

And the darker, more terrifying fears; the other outcome which could not be. She searched the dim and starless night for answers, but her truth-sense was muddled. Too much fear, shock, desperation.

"They have won," she whispered to herself. Then, with an ache in her heart, she tried the alternative. "They have lost."

She didn't know. The truth eluded her grasp, and despair gnawed like a rat feeding on the last few rinds of her strength. She tried to stand up, but then discovered how deeply she had been weakened. The cold remains of the Dark spell lingered in her blood. She collapsed again. She couldn't go on like this. There had to be a way, to know, to end the nightmare.

Or to confirm it.

She found herself staring at her lap, where the folded kerchief lay, unopened.

Throw it into the river. The Shadowcaster will never find it.

Her mother had wanted to destroy the Ring, take it beyond the reach of the Darkmaster. Here in the River of Falls was not far enough from his reach.

The Ring had cleared her thoughts before, allowed her to see things she had missed, the hidden words of the Lifesong. Maybe it could help her.

The kerchief opened. With the shivering of her hands, she almost tipped the Ring off her lap, but she caught it as it slipped. It was awkward in her numbed fingers.

It glistened in a pale moment of moonlight. A perfect circle. Strangely beautiful.

"Will you show me anything of Phantom Acres?" she asked the Ring.

Silence. Only the faint patterns and arcane letters danced within the glossy sphere.

She had to know.

She slipped the Ring onto her finger.

It surprised her with its sudden warmth. She took a moment to adjust to the heightened sensations, all the faint night sounds, the sharpness of the railing, the smell of the wet rocks, the dark outline of the trees, visible upon the darker background of the night.

With the Ring came clarity, and with clarity, she knew the truth. Her deep intuition screamed the truth at her. Death howled in her ears. Death tore her breath away. Death ripped the last spark of hope from her breast.

Dead. Her parents were dead. She knew, with the clear certainty of a Truthsayer, amplified a thousand times by the clarity of the Ring. The Shadowcaster had killed them.

He had come for the talisman, he had come for the Ring. He would come for her.

She staggered to her feet, gulping for air. The bridge tilted suddenly in the dark, and she stumbled down the apparent decline, onwards and away.

The truth was like a hound at her heels—no matter how fast she ran, she could not escape its awful bite. The Ring had seemed to be a blessing, but it was truly a curse. It rode on her finger, gripping too tightly to loosen, too perfectly-shaped to remove with her cold fingers, plaguing her with lucidity. Her mind flooded with tragic alternatives, she couldn't avoid considering every possible bloody way in which the fight on the farm could have ended. No matter which way she came to it, the truth was the same.

Her parents were dead.

Pine, spruce, alder, and silken trees flicked by, she noticed each kind and remembered every detail, the shape each branch formed. A fox ran deeper into the woods. An owl hooted far away. All this came to her because of the clarity of the Ring. The night was full of things she didn't wish to see, loaded with sensations she didn't wish to sense. She could see so much, yet she didn't want to see any of it. Overhead, the clouds were heavy with imminent snow.

She ran on, wishing she could escape what she knew.

The road was dark. The wind had begun to howl in the trees. Blue lightning lit the night, then thunder rolled as the clouds cracked. Snow began to swirl down, cold and cheerless in the dark. Snowflakes caught in her hair, brushed the tears on her cheeks.

She wouldn't ever see them again.

It felt like forever until Tabitha tripped and sprawled on her face in the pathway. Her breath rasped in her throat. She considered just lying there, where she had fallen, but a glimmer of strength remained in her body. With strength, she might survive the night. She had to be exhausted first, or she might not die.

She would run and run, until she fell and couldn't get up again. Then it would all end, and she could escape her misery.

She pushed unsteadily against the snow, and found her feet again. Onwards she ran, along the High Way, on its course through the forest. The road should have been difficult to follow in the darkness, yet when she searched for it, she could sense where it was, even though it lay hidden beneath the thickening snow.

Tabitha ran. Her strength waned. She pushed on and on, until her heart pounded frantically in her ears and she was reeling. The snow pulled at her boots with every step she placed inside the wagon-ruts. She ignored her fatigue. She ran over exposed rises, where the cold night wind stole the warmth from her legs, she ran into tunnels of quiet forest where furtive night-creatures watched her.

Faces flickered across her mind. Mother. Father. The Shadowcaster, with his evil grin. The yellowed eyes which had filled her with terror, frozen her limbs. The fear which had swirled from his shoulders like a cape. Grey eyes, black clouds of ice. He had come for the Ring. It belonged to the Darkmaster. It was not hers to keep.

Throw it away. Throw it into the forest.

Maybe he had ways to find it. To cast it away would be a betrayal of her mother's final wish. She kept it on her finger.

If the Darkmaster had ways of finding his talisman, he would have found it when it lay in Fendwarrow. Maybe she had a chance to escape with it. Maybe they'd never know.

She was forced to slow to a jog, then an agonising walk. The trees clustered closer, leaning inwards. The trunks moved from side to side, skittering about the forest floor, circling her, circling. Or was it just the dizzying sensation of movement? Blood pounded in her temples, deafening her to the sounds of the night.

The Shadowcaster's words rang clear, as she remembered.

"I have sensed the use of it, yesterday and today. The stench of a new magic is all over this place, in this room," he had said.

She had sung the Lifesong. For the second time. Its magic had woken her mother. Its magic had drawn the Shadowcaster. It was her use of the Ring that had brought him to Phantom Acres.

She was responsible for what had been drawn onto her parents.

She was the reason for her parents death.

The sky tilted at a drunken angle. She lost her balance, and the ground came up to meet the side of her head with a numbing slap. Everything was turning, swirling, spinning. She lay where she had fallen. She didn't care if she never rose again. She cried until the snow covered her body, until she slipped into a dark unconsciousness, on the High Way of Eyri.

The Dark spell of Despair claimed its victim.

7. DARK DREAMS

"If a dream's in your head and your eyelids are tight,
can there be colour, without any light?"—*Zarost*

Ashley Logán turned in his bed, pulling the sheets awry.

He had been having strange dreams for more than a week, ever since the erratic intrusion of extraneous thoughts had begun to plague him. At first the dreams were just visions of a dark, sultry woman, brief fantasies which dispersed like smoke in the wind when he awoke. The groping of his waking mind had only dissolved the vague image when he tried to recall her face. He wasn't sure whether she had spoken to him or if there had been more. But as the week had passed, the dream recurred, changed, became more intimate. He had begun to develop an appetite for sleep.

Tonight, the dream was richer than ever. The woman returned, her raven-hair falling about her shoulders and spreading upon her black silk gown. Secrets and wildness smouldered in her eyes. The doorway in the low-roofed building, the strange rune on the door, the smell of cheap smoke, cloying musk, and wine, the muffled sounds of rowdy indulgence elsewhere; all familiar elements of the dream. Yet for the first time, the woman did not close the door before him. She beckoned, and his blood pumped thick and wild in his veins. Her glamour pulled at him. He needed little encouragement. At her throat was a stone of the deepest black. He wondered what it could mean.

"At last, you find your way to power," she whispered in his ear. "I am Gabrielle."

Gabrielle. The name lingered on his lips.

"Come, taste your reward."

"No," he heard himself say. A deeper voice, not his own. "I serve the Light."

He twisted and turned, then woke with a start.

It was a shock to find himself in bed. He had been elsewhere. He had felt different. Bigger, taller. Older. The world of the waking took some getting used to.

The night was cool, and quiet. He pushed his coarse hair out of his face, yawned, and looked toward the high windows.

The moon peered back at him, saucer-faced. Got you.

"How many windows do you spy through, Fool Moon?" Ashley muttered, watching the white flares curl around the moon's whole rim. A pretty picture, framed with a dusting of snow at the base of the glass. It was rare to see the Fool in spring, for the moon was usually hidden in cloud at night, until well into Bloomtide. It was an ill omen to be seen by the Fool after midnight, but there he was, goggle-eyed, and there was naught Ashley could do to pretend otherwise. An old legend anyway, the touch of the Fool, like tales of the Seven Wizards, or the Morgloth. Nothing but empty words used by bards and old wives to scare children.

"What do you see tonight?" he whispered again.

The moon hushed into the room; touching the trunks, the six beds, the sleeping apprentices, but saying nothing. The beds lined the near side of the room, simple mattresses stuffed with straw, laid upon wooden lattices. His companions slept loudly.

Ashley sighed. He was too awake to catch the dream again. Gabrielle was gone, for tonight. It would be hours before the dawn. Hours he could better spend stalking another mystery.

Ashley rose stealthily, and padded across the tiles to his trunk. The wood creaked softly when he cracked the lid open. He sneaked a robe over the rim of the chest, and eased the lid back down. He donned the coarse white garment and tied his rope at the waist, using the familiar half-knot that marked him as an apprentice.

One of the apprentices stirred as Ashley passed, but settled down once more. Ashley tiptoed to the doorway, and slipped into the men's corridor.

He was on the ground floor of the tiered Dovecote. Silence was thick throughout the building. Even the south wing, dedicated to the kitchens, scullery, dining hall and common-room was still. The walls of the corridor rose as he progressed towards the Hall of Sky. Murals and runes flickered in the soft sprite-light cast by the widely spaced sconces upon the curved walls. The roof formed an arching tunnel. The floor rose smoothly into the pale brown walls. So much more natural than the modern architecture found in the city of Levin, where sharp boundaries, tilted angles and practical lines were the fashion. The Dovecote had endured many years of change, yet stood as it had been created, and only the smoothness of the stone underfoot hinted at the passage of time.

A solid oak door sealed the end of the men's corridor from the Hall of Sky. Ashley knew that the door was barred from the far side, from within the Hall. Once the Rest had been announced every night, the Rector Shamgar himself closed everyone in, and only with the approach of dawn would he open the door again. This was necessary, the Rector didn't neglect to remind them, to protect the apprentices from the dark powers which swam through the ether at night, evil magic which would lead them astray from their studies.

Evil magic. Ashley chuckled.

More likely to prevent the men from swimming through the ether to the women's quarters, when they should be sleeping.

To protect the apprentices from being lead astray by dark powers, indeed. He grinned. The barred door had frustrated him for as long as he had been an apprentice, not because he had any woman to go to, but because the door was there. It was a challenge to his inquisitive nature. Even his teachers, full Lightgifters, were restricted to the gender-defined quarters. The women slept on the distant side of the Hall. A similar oak door sealed them in their wing. Celibacy at the Dovecote was not only sworn, it was enforced.

Ashley backed up a pace to the Light-sconce. The shallow pool of sprites cast no smoke. The small grains of essence flickered with a slow rhythm of dancing waves. The sconces were employed sparingly about the Dovecote at night, just enough to light the passageways. He drew essence to his hand, using the gentle words and pattern of the Summoning that came so easily to his mind now. The Light formed a small puddle in his palm, warm and familiar.

I'll be flayed if I'm caught.

Outside of training classes, the sprites were strictly reserved for full Lightgifters. Rector Shamgar would be apoplectic if he caught an apprentice summoning his own Light. But then Rector Shamgar was not going to find out. Nobody needed to know. That was why it had to done in the dead of night.

An organic design was inscribed on the wall beside Ashley, a skull submerged in leaves. Vines twined through the eye sockets, and tangled outwards. A fine work of art, a bit morbid for Ashley's taste, but nothing more than a design. He had passed it by many a time without a second glance. The design ended in curled roots near the end of the corridor. Just shy of the oak door, the roots wound through runes both ancient and enigmatic. It had been an innocent assignment from Father Onassis which had transformed those runes forever. All the apprentices in the rune class had taken an inscription from somewhere within the Cote to translate. Ashley had chosen the runes at random, yet when he had deciphered them, he had found more than expected.

A touch of Light begins the way to the—a twisted rune, shaped like two fish with twining tails.

Onassis interpreted the closing rune as 'the heart', rendering the message benign. Ashley found an older meaning in the Dovecote texts. The twisted rune was sometimes used to name a place called the Inner Sanctum, a place of the most valued secrets from the founding days of the Dovecote, when the Sage had lived.

The Inner Sanctum. He kept that discovery to himself, and searched elsewhere in the Dovecote.

The secret of the heart lies beneath the earth, carved on the base of the steps of the East-door.

The abundant wisdom of the heart, a step beyond Death's door, written in one of the oldest books in the Study.

In the middle of the song is the heart, inscribed along the edge of the Scribbillarre in the Hall.

All clues to the Inner Sanctum, the most secret of hidden secrets. Yet if it was a place, hidden, there had to be a door. Either that, or he was chasing a whim.

Ashley ran his free hand over the stonework. There was nothing but the vines and skull scored into the walls. No latch, no handle, no hollow section in the wall, nothing. Just smooth, hard brown stone.

He brought his other hand up, tipping the sprites against the wall. They spread in a puff of radiance, rolling outwards from the point of impact like dust from a stamped foot. Light sparkled down the curved masonry to rest at Ashley's feet. He didn't notice the wasted sprites. He watched the wall, transfixed. A luminous line had appeared, a faint vertical. It wouldn't have been visible in the brightness of day. Where the sprites had found the hairline crack in the stone, they remained, caught in the engraved vines beside the skull.

Ashley beamed. He had known it was here somewhere. He summoned the sprites from the floor, and repeated the throw. The line in the stone grew. As he worked, an outline formed, running up from the floor to form an arch before descending again. A doorway in the stone. In the instant that he completed the radiant outline, the wall in front of him swung silently away, into the gloom beyond the corridor.

A touch of Light begins the way to the Inner Sanctum.

Ashley's breath quickened. He could see nothing in the gloom. He summoned another handful of sprites from the sconce on the far wall. He muttered the familiar words of a Flicker over the sprites, binding them into the same dancing form they had held in the sconce. Holding his hand high, he entered the door.

Strange objects leaned towards him; unmoving, yet crowding him with furry heads or tails. The way wasn't clear, his foot struck something with a loud metal clang. He bit his lip, praying that no one would be alerted by the sound.

A bucket! Damn fool. He recognised the place. It was an alcove off the Hall of Sky, where cleaning equipment was stored. Brooms, brushes, mops and buckets poked their way into the circle of light created by his Flicker. He'd spent many an afternoon with one or other of the implements, working off a transgression. Ashley tiptoed through the tangle of objects, and emerged from the alcove.

It was disappointing to find himself in such a familiar place, though he should have expected it. Where else could the door have gone to, placed where it was? It bypassed the barred oak door, but didn't lead anywhere exciting. He walked quietly across the Hall of Sky. Maybe there was another clue he hadn't yet discovered.

He paused, taking in the grandeur. The Hall looked different at night, but there was certainly no 'swirling evil' as the apprentices had been warned. The Hall was huge, the vaulted ceiling three stories above the floor. The Fool Moon caught him again with its baleful glare, through the high dome of glass that formed the apex of the vaulted Hall.

The crystal wonder of the Source dominated the Hall. The Source towered on its white marble dais, over twice Ashley's height; a perfect, ghostly obelisk. The moonlight filtered through its surface and formed spidery lines that twisted and turned at random, as if currents swirled in the heart of the Source. Reflected moonlight shifted in restless patterns against the curving stairways and across the marble floor. Inscriptions and symbols patterned the floor, stretching the knowledge of the Scribbillarre to the bluestone channel that rimmed the Hall. It was said that the entire lore of the Lightgifters was encoded in that floor, though Ashley knew that some of the more recent developments had not been added—such forbidden spells were omitted from the apprentice syllabus as well. The Rector wouldn't allow the 'defilement of our heritage with perversions', as he saw it.

Ashley wandered onto the Scribillarre, holding his Flicker high. He scanned the runes of the floor. There had to be another clue, a hint to where the true door to the Inner Sanctum could be. Lines, sigils, patterns and words spread out at his feet. Nowhere could he see the twisted rune of the Heart.

A boot scuffed on stone, high above, somewhere in the Dovecote. His stomach clenched.

Ashley ran light-footed for the alcove and the stone door. He hoped desperately that the spiral of the staircase hid him from the boot-scuffer. His pulse raced. He forced himself to slow down as he picked his way through the mops and buckets.

Then he was through. He pulled roughly on the stone door behind him.

The door rushed toward him. *Too hard*, he cursed himself. It was going to make a boom when it slammed. At least it would be closed. He could run, and be out of sight of whoever came.

He flinched, but there was no boom as stone struck stone. The door sealed with a soft suck, and the Light essence that had marked its rim showered to the floor. The stonework was smooth under Ashley's hand, except for the faint score-marks of the complex roots and vines. Ashley scooped up the sprites and ran for his bedroom, dumping the Light essence into a sconce along the way.

Safe, by the skin of my teeth.

He heard the bar on the door at the far end of the corridor being removed behind him. He ducked into his room. Then he was in bed, with the blanket pulled high over his robe, and his heart pounding.

The Moon peeped over the rim of the high windows, almost gone from view. He hoped the Fool would keep his silence about what he'd seen.

Footsteps approached down the corridor. Ashley was sure someone stood at the door for a moment, though he was too afraid to open his eyes. He tried to breathe in long, slow breaths.

All was quiet.

8. THREE MORNINGS

"Every morning is the death of night."—*Zarost*

The sun lorded high in the morning sky. It was screeching, a harsh, piercing shriek like the sound of a pig being slaughtered. No, it was a shrill hiss, like green wood put to the flame. Or a child, hoarse from crying for long hours. The sound bored into Kirjath's headache. The sound was worse than the brilliance of the sun. On and on, relentless, the screech screwed into his tender head.

"Shatter that sun till it falls!" he cursed. Kirjath squinted, and winced. The sun was glaring directly at him. His eyes watered, and he searched for his cowl which usually hung behind his neck. His hands found nothing, apart from the ruined burnt fabric of his tattered robe. Burnt cotton, and pain. A boiling pain, which began in his fingers and ran over his entire body, pooling in awkward places; his hands, his back, his legs. And his head, by the cursed light of the shattered sun, his head! He touched his crown, and drew a sharp breath as his sore fingers touched a lumpy, sticky surface of ruin. There was no hair, only the charred crepuscular scalp, though his fingers yielded little feeling themselves.

"Skraaaaak!" screeched the sun once more.

"Shut up!" answered Kirjath, his mind reeling. He had been burnt badly, burnt like a bloody sacrificial lamb. How had it happened? He turned his hands over before his eyes. The left was an angry red, with fat digits which preferred to stick straight out, blistered and swollen like sausages. His right was worse, the fingers crisp and black, yet there was no pain in them, no feeling at all. That worried him more than pain would have. There should be pain, at least. His right hand reminded him of a spider, a wounded spider with three of its eight spindly legs torn off, leaving only the five useless digits.

"Skraaaaak!"

It was not the sun. Something lower, sitting on a pole. A dark shape … he closed his eyes, then tried again, squinting against the bright day and the blinding white patches of snow.

"Skraaaaak!"

A raven sat on the burnt remains of a fence-post, eyeing him with a mocking tilt to its head. Kirjath uttered a string of curses that would have turned an Amberlake fisherman green.

A messenger bird from Ravenscroft. Ah, by the cursed scut of a hoary goat!

No one rivalled the Darkmaster in the art of creating an ugly Morrigán. The only message he had ever received from the Darkmaster was a summons.

Kirjath swore again. What he needed was rest and healing, not bloody frantic travel, to run back to Ravenscroft like a wayward hound. He was still trying to collect his scattered wits. But the Darkmaster brooked no mercy; when a Shadowcaster was summoned, that Shadowcaster was expected in Ravenscroft. No excuse had ever spared a Caster from the lash of Cabal's wrath. You were summoned. You went. Immediately, unquestioning, subservient. It angered Kirjath more than anything else—he was treated like a servant, when he was Kirjath Arkell. However, if he wanted to work the magic of the Dark essence, he was forced to bow to the Darkmaster. There was no other way.

Soon, that shall change.

Kirjath spat into the ashes near at hand. The Darkmaster knew of his rebellious nature—three junior Shadowcasters had been promoted past him to Vortex, while he strained against the debasing leash of the Shadowcaster rank. He snarled at the raven, wishing he could learn to conceal his contempt better.

He caught himself—his thoughts had been scattering again, as if part of him couldn't face the present, or the recent past. He gritted his teeth as he extended his left arm, then called to the bird.

"Alight, Morrigán, and deliver your word."

The raven looked back at him askance. It dropped off the blackened fence-post, swooping low to the ground as its wings spread. Then it swung up onto his outstretched arm, and exploded into a shower of motes. The message was in the Darkmaster's voice. The words were precisely pronounced, cold and disdainful.

"I take it you are done with the task I set you, in which case you are summoned to Ravenscroft, *Shadowcaster* Kirjath. Immediately." That was all. The remains of the raven-form had disappeared completely. The wind spoke of nothing more. The sun glared off the melting snow.

The task done? What task?

It came back to him slowly, painfully. He had been sent for the talisman. The Master's ring. The horror of the night returned to mind with full force. The agony of the fire. The defiance of the Lightgifter, the disastrous explosion of her flaming suicide. She had never given him what he had sought.

Kirjath glared at the ruins of the farmstead. Surely nothing had survived the fire, nothing was left of the talisman? If it had not melted in the intense heat, it would be somewhere in the ashes. The house was burned to the ground, the husband dead, the Gifter dead. The only loose thread was her daughter, the girl who had run away during the fight.

Something still bothered him about that girl. He strained to remember the events as they had happened, but they were entangled in the agony of the fire, and the ecstasy of using the beast. The Lightgifter had returned after pretending to fetch the Ring for him, then she had attacked him with the barrage of Light essence, and the girl ... the girl had bolted at that moment from the Gifter's back. If the Gifter had passed something to her daughter, he would not have seen the movement. Yes, it could have happened.

He gazed at the broken poles and carbon timbers. Such a young woman, on a stormy night, she could not have gone far. The Darkmaster would have to wait, this time. The Ring was important to both of them. Kirjath's mouth twisted into a wry grin, which he abandoned at once as his damaged lip split and spilled a sour taste into his mouth. The summoning had been quite specific. 'I take it you are done with the task'.

Not done, not just yet, you cretin. I have reason to ignore the summoning, by your own words.

He remembered the way the girl had stared at him, as blood had coursed down her face from the broken glass of his arrival. A pretty face, clear-eyed, smooth-cheeked; she would be easy to find. She would be amusing as well. She would tell him if she had secretted the talisman away. She would scream it to him. After that, he was sure of one thing. The last member of the Gifter's family had to be silenced.

◆ ───────── ◆

A bony hand pulled at Tabitha's shoulder. She was cold, frozen. She wanted to remain in the snow, to be left for dead, but the hand upon her shifted, and she was rolled over like a log. She clenched her eyes shut against the bright daylight. The memories she had wanted to avoid burst into her mind instead.

The Shadowcaster had come. Her father had fallen. Dead, her

parents were dead. She had run away through the forest.

She was being pinned down by a somebody. She kicked frantically at the ground, trying to escape. Someone was speaking to her in a strange voice.

"Fight if you would, but it will do you no good."

The voice was strange, warbling, almost musical.

She dreaded what she might see if she opened her eyes. Was it the Shadowcaster? His cloak so dark, his eyes as grey as slate. No, his voice had been harsher.

She cracked her left eye open. She could see a jutting black-and-white beard above her. A weathered, tanned face, wrinkled like bark. Bright brown eyes, slightly mismatched, the nearest one held more gold upon the iris. Dark bushy hair, topped by an old hat made from some striped pelt.

"I have found you first, so you've avoided the worst," the stranger reassured.

She was confused by his presence, confused and disorientated.

What did he want? Was he with the Shadowcaster? Tabitha tried to roll away, but he held her firmly. "Gently now, gently now! No need to take fright. I am here to help."

There was truth in those words, a truth she could hear. Tabitha slumped back onto the snow. She didn't need to fight him, he had come to save her. What did it matter? He was too late. Her parents were dead. She felt his hands shift—one slipped underneath her shoulders, the other beneath her knees. He scooped her up without straining at all, and set her upon something above ground level.

Tabitha was wrapped in a thick woollen blanket. From somewhere behind her head, a horse snorted. The stranger issued a light whistle, and there was a lurch through the cart beneath her. The cart turned in a slow semicircle, then surged forwards as the horse began to trot. The trees marched sedately across the sky. The cart bounced over some uneven terrain in the High Way, then settled into a steady, vibrating rhythm. Unconsciousness swept over Tabitha once more.

◆ ———————— ◆

The East-door stood wide to the morning sun, and a fresh breeze pulled past Ashley through the Hall of Sky. The voices of the assembled Lightgifters and apprentices soared in song. The women's delicate voices raised the music to the vaulted ceiling. The men's tenor harmony danced between the rays of light. A few deep basses intoned a continuous chant which resonated in the very floor of the Hall. The three parts blended into the compelling spell which was the Dovecote's Morningsong. It was a beautiful song that left both the singer and the essence charged. The air swirled with clouds of sprites; their dull brown transformed to brightness as the Morningsong took effect.

The Source was brilliant. Sunlight radiated from it, splitting and joining, flashing out to the walls and floor, marking some of the upturned faces with bright rays, leaving some dull. Not only would the Source empower the sprites, it created new Light essence, drew it from the air.

Ashley sang by rote. He could feel someone's eyes on him, and he scanned the Assembly surreptitiously. Most of the Lightgifters were absorbed by their singing. The Rector stood on the raised dais, directing the flow of essence through the Hall, weaving the sprites in and out of the empowering light.

The Rector? He couldn't be sure, but Shamgar had turned his head just as Ashley looked his way.

Surely the Rector couldn't know about last night? The Creator spare me!

The Rector's round face protruded from the raised collar of his purple mantle. His cheeks puffed out at odd moments as he wove the flows of Light through the hall. The Rector turned slightly, and raised his slim eyebrow as he caught Ashley's eye with a pale blue gaze of piercing superiority. Ashley flicked his gaze away immediately. He sang louder.

The Morningsong faded at last, leaving the Hall in an expectant hush. Sprites shimmered in the confinement of the bluestone channel which circled the Scribbillarre. The gathered Assembly faced inwards, to the only man who raised himself above floor level, the man on the dais at their centre.

"Good morning, Assembly," the Rector began.

"Good morning, Illumination," the Assembly echoed, as one.

"Light to your orbs."

"And to yours."

"Today," the Rector began. "Today is a day unlike the days before it. A day unique from those that follow. The task you will face today can be done only once, so try to do the best you can." Ashley was accustomed to the Rector's motivational speeches, every morning different, yet endlessly the same. The man showered them with disdain.

"Gifters and half-knots, hear me now." The Rector's gaze fell on Ashley again. He suddenly felt like a specimen pinned to a board. "There are always forces that would pull a Gifter away from his true course. Such forces must be denied. We all feel the lure of Darkness, it hides in all the pleasures and desires of the world. But a Lightgifter must never give in to the temptation."

Mutters and jostles passed through the Assembly, drawing attention away from the Rector to the source of the disturbance. The Rector's voice inherited a sharper edge. "A Lightgifter must never break the rules set by the Dovecote."

A space was clearing between the Lightgifters. Ashley joined the majority of the Assembly by looking away from the Rector, trying to see what would emerge from the diverging crowd.

"A Lightgifter must never ignore the command of those divinely selected."

"Rector, she has a vision!" someone exclaimed, cutting through the Rector's litany. A tall, clean-shaven Lightgifter stepped forward, a newly-ordained Gifter called Rosreece. "We must witness," he insisted.

The space cleared further. Ashley was surprised to see Sister Hosanna isolated in the centre. She was as groomed as ever, but for once she did not appear regal at all. Her eyes were rolled back in their sockets, and she swayed on her feet as if guided by an overpowering presence. She was receiving a vision. Ashley had heard rumours of her unique skill, but had never seen it in action. Vision-casting was as rare and unpredictable as a violet sprite. They would all witness a wonder.

"Come, come, we have seen this woman's fits before," the Rector asserted. "Attend to what I have to say." The Rector compelled them with a rap of his sceptre on the dais.

Ashley was torn between getting into trouble, or missing Hosanna's performance. It was not true that they had all seen it before, he knew many apprentices who would be as keen to witness her as he was.

"Gifters! Half-knots!" Again, a sharp stamp of the sceptre. The Rector blew his red cheeks out, but before he could begin what he wanted to say, Sister Hosanna declared her vision.

"I see a farm, in high fields near First Light."

Hosanna was poised on the tips of her toes, as if she were weightless. Her arms were outstretched like a dancer's. Sprites formed a nimbus around her body, and more Light swirled toward her, drawn from the channel at the rim of the Scribbillarre. The essence enveloped Hosanna like liquid radiance. She sank to her knees, and drew the essence into a pool of Light on the white marble of the Scribbillarre. Within her pool, forms began to appear, guided by her vision. A small homestead took shape.

"A young woman sings with a lyre." A miniature figure sat beneath a translucent tree. Then the figure melted into the pool of sprites, and new figures emerged.

"Soon after, a Gifter fights a terrible foe."

Ashley pushed closer through the gathered onlookers. Hosanna's pool showed two figures facing each other, gesturing and moving, but nothing more was clear in the rippled surface of sprites. The taller figure spread its arms wide, and split into three. The sprites were sullied within those forms, dirtier, darker.

"A Shadowcaster," Hosanna pronounced. "There is something else, in his command. It comes. It –"

She jerked where she knelt, her body rigid. Her voice was a strained whisper. "A Morgloth. A Morgloth comes to Eyri!"

The pool of sprites warped into a winged creature, with a wicked head and slashing claws. "Oh, the hunger. The evil!" Hosanna gave a stifled cry, and bowed her head to her knees. The pool of her vision ruptured, and sprites scattered to the walls.

There was a dazed silence in the Hall of Sky. Someone bent to Hosanna's aid. When she rose on Rosreece's arm, she looked tired and haunted. She covered her face briefly with her hands, then said, "I am sorry, I see no more. But I know that a terrible fate comes upon Eyri. I have seen it. The Morgloth return."

"Are you quite finished, Hosanna?"

She composed herself with a quick breath. "Forgive me, Rector, for my intrusion. The vision took me." The crispness of her customary demeanour returned to her face.

The Rector regarded Hosanna with tight-lipped disapproval, and Ashley heard his voice within, just as he had on the day of the starburst, that strange sense of intimate eaves-dropping.

"One day this woman is going to have the wrong kind of vision, and everything could be ruined," thought the Rector.

But when the Rector spoke out loud, he used very different words. "Your ravings do not become you, Lightgifter Hosanna. Next time you should remember your manners and excuse yourself from the

Hall."

Rosreece stepped to the fore. "Forgive me as well, Rector, but I believe the vision proved its worth. The Morgloth concerns us all."

"Morgloth!" the Rector scoffed, puffing his cheeks out. "I do not credit such wild fantasies."

"The Darkmaster would never have gone that far, to release such beasts into the realm," he thought.

"Rector, she has never been wrong before," Rosreece objected. "How can we forget the flood she foretold, or the kidnapping of the crown Prince? We ignore her prophecy to our detriment, to the detriment of all."

"This trumpeter fancies himself too much," the Rector decided. *"And she must be sent away before she foresees something more damaging."*

"I am well aware of Hosanna's odd talents," the Rector snapped. "Visions are usually misinterpreted."

"Can we not send a quest to First Light?" asked Rosreece.

"And get them all out of my way," the Rector mused.

"Very well," said the Rector. "Some Gifters need to travel to the Meadowmoor to discover the truth of this vision, or to warn those who live there of the Morgloth."

That word sparked a riot of nervous mutter and whispered arguments. Morgloth. It was a mythical creature, too terrifying to be real.

"Silence!" boomed the Rector, slamming his sceptre on the dais so hard that he lost his grip on it. The rod skittered down the steps. His skin acquired a darker shade, and one of his eyelids developed a sudden tick. "I have a full day, and little time to waste, what? Hosanna, do we know if this vision has happened, is happening, or is still to take place?"

"Close to this time," Hosanna answered, her head held high. "Whether it was before, or after, I don't know. I never know that."

"We should alert the Sword!" Rosreece blurted out.

The Rector glared down from the dais. "No, I shall not have anyone crying wolf to the Sword without proof. Gifter Rosreece, you will lead the quest, since you feel so strongly about Hosanna's visions. Hosanna, you will accompany him to First Light. Father Keegan and Sister Grace shall be your Gifters. And as apprentice, I select Ashley Logán. May you curb this Shadowcaster and his mischief in time. Light to your orbs."

"And to yours," the Assembly echoed the reflexive litany.

A few surprised faces turned towards Ashley. Rosreece was one of them. "But Rector, this is not training exercise! The Half-knot has no ability yet. What danger might this second-year apprentice face?"

"There are four of you, Rosreece," stated the Rector. "That is surely enough to protect one Half-knot. I have spoken. You will find use for him, one way or another."

"Rector." Rosreece dipped his head.

A strange leader, considering the group and the task. Father Keegan was fifteen years the senior of Rosreece, and he would have been Ashley's choice of leader amongst the four Gifters. He searched for the brown-bearded Father in the Assembly, and found Keegan, tight-lipped, already striding from the Hall. Sister Grace watched him leave as well, a look of studied patience on her brow. She gave Ashley a faint smile when he caught her eye.

"To your work, people," the Rector announced. "We shall await word from Rosreece's team before discussing this event." He made a pounding movement with his fist, then scowled. His sceptre was not in his hand, it lay upon the floor.

"Laziness is the root of evil," he declared. "Be gone, all of you!"

◆ ——————— ◆

Ashley was so excited and nervous about their quest that he noticed very little of the journey's beginning. They had packed, and moved out quickly. He had little time to consider Hosanna's vision, for he was soon trying to master a horse upon the steep descent through Levin.

The tension between Rosreece and Father Keegan compelled them to speed through the bustle of the city. There was no time for talk. Their horses pounded along, cantering where the streets were wide, prancing in frustration when the traffic of merchants, buyers, ordinary folk and ragamuffins blocked their way. The streets wound ever-downward from the Dovecote.

Some time later they reached the city limits. When the sun climbed to its zenith, they were well into the countryside at the junction town of Fig Tree. The gnarled namesake stood in the centre of the circular junction in the town square, casting its mighty shadow upon the weatherworn signboards affixed to its trunk. Flowerton to the north, nestled deep in the farmlands of Vinmorgen County, where the good wines and fruit came from. Respite away to the east, where most of the traffic on the stoneroad originated, wagons loaded with the metal goods from the forges at Chink. They turned due west, to Stormsford, the Fig Tree said, and in smaller text—Llury, Brimstone and First Light. They rode.

They rode wide of the slow-moving wagons and people on the road, taking to the turf on either side which was easier on the horses' hooves. The town of Stormsford passed with only the briefest halt to water the horses, and an even briefer argument between Keegan and Rosreece about the choice of trails. Keegan preferred the Southwind route, but Rosreece was adamant. The High Way would be quicker, for the horses would remain cooler within the Great Forest. The plains of the lakeside district blurred by like a patchwork quilt, with swathes of verdant green sewn between the many tilled fields and farmhouses. The sun rode with them across the sky, a swirling circle of fire, glaring and hot despite the season.

"We should slow," Father Keegan called out, angrily. It was the first word to break the sweaty silence of hours.

"I'll decide when we have need, Father Keegan," Rosreece replied over his shoulder. He kept his horse a few strides ahead of the others. "I am leading!"

"You'll run the horses into the ground," Keegan shouted at the younger Gifter, "then where will we be? These are not the horses of the King's Sword, for heaven's sake man! These are Dovecote nags."

The horses defied Keegan's pronouncement by continuing to canter, but Ashley knew his mount was tiring. They had been driven too long by the severe pace of the lead-horse. Rosreece reined back a little to argue with Keegan.

"We must race," he said. "We have a Shadowcaster to catch, or worse. Do you doubt Hosanna's vision?" His eyes seemed to glint in the sun.

"I doubt your wisdom, Rosreece," Keegan snarled. He was a big man, broad-shouldered and bear-like, easily stronger than Rosreece and senior to him. But the Rector had defined the pecking order otherwise, and Ashley doubted that Keegan would defy that command.

Rosreece did not slacken his pace. They were carried along by his urgency.

Ashley's bottom ached from the hard ride. He wondered how the others found the strength to endure it. Hosanna seemed to be managing on her roan stallion, but behind him, Sister Grace was gripping the pommel of her saddle for dear life. She would surely need a rest, if only to let her wide eyes close for a while. She rode with a stiff-legged posture that gave her no respite from the choppy stride of her small horse.

Ashley wished he could help her. He resolved to speak up, but when he turned to face Rosreece, the Gifter met him with a fierce glare. Ashley held his tongue.

The way became tougher as they climbed from the oat-fields that surrounded Turnmill. The soil became harder, and the road began to wind in tight zigzags, cutting higher into the hills; pastureland, dotted with sheep, the farmsteads sparsely placed. They had to wait while a heavy-laden cart from Tarbarn nudged its way down a narrow pass. The forest loomed ahead, a wall of planted quickpines which butted against the older oaks of the Great Forest beyond. Rosreece shouted the advance as soon as the way was clear. The horses strained up the steep incline, snorting and lathered with sweat. Then they were on the flat again, and galloping.

It happened as they passed the first of the old trees. Ashley felt his mare shudder, then with a surprised squeal she fell over a tangle of roots and crashed to the ground. Ashley was flung onto the hard-packed earth, behind the pounding hooves of Father Keegan's mount.

He came up spitting dirt. His elbows were bruised, his forehead heavily grazed. His mare stumbled to her feet, and limped off a few steps down the road.

Keegan called a halt immediately. Ashley didn't hear if Rosreece made any comment.

"You all right?"

Ashley nodded.

Father Keegan dismounted with knotted brows, and stooped to inspect the injured mare. "She's been made lame," he said angrily, facing down Rosreece.

"We shall ride on to First Light," Rosreece said, looking down at the elder Lightgifter from the vantage of his saddle. "The boy can walk his horse to Llury, and return to the Dovecote tomorrow."

Ashley ground his teeth at being called a boy, but he felt dazed and not a bit foolish from the fall. Rosreece seemed a lot taller, mounted on his horse.

Father Keegan clenched his fists. "We will walk on to Llury.

Together. I'll not be leaving a Half-knot in the woods alone, considering what we are sent to investigate. Our horses could do with the rest."

"You forget yourself, Father Keegan. I was ordained leader of this quest, by the Rector Shamgar. You may have led quests before, but not this time."

"We will walk," repeated Father Keegan, his fury contained under a slow, even tone. "Ashley, lead your horse for a while. Sister Grace, join us now."

She's probably ready to fall from the saddle, Ashley thought grimly.

"Hosanna –" started Keegan.

"No!" Rosreece cut in, through Keegan's command. "We ride, Hosanna. If these weaklings want to rest, so be it. But they will fail the Light, as surely as they will arrive too late. I will see the Shadowcaster captured, and the disaster averted."

A brief glance was exchanged between Rosreece and Hosanna. She looked to the others, then wrenched her gaze away. Hosanna spurred her stallion into a gallop beside Rosreece, and they plunged into the gloom of the forest.

Father Keegan stared after the retreating pair of Lightgifters. "An unfair twist to the bond of lovers," he said.

"Rosreece and Hosanna are lovers?" Ashley asked incredulously. He saw that Sister Grace shared his disbelief.

Keegan was determined. "Very discreet, I'll grant you, but one has to be within the Dovecote. I don't know what she sees in the man, he is all arrogance, and no heart." He gripped his saddle and vaulted up to it. "Now we can set a proper pace. Come, let us move while there is light to this day."

The three of them set off; Father Keegan scanned the shadows, Grace rode stiffly in her saddle, and Ashley led his lame mare on foot.

He spent much of that afternoon mulling over likely couples within the Dovecote. He began to feel increasingly naive. At one twist in the trail he encountered Sister Grace's eyes on him, and he blushed fervently, more for the thoughts he had been entertaining than for any speculation in her gaze.

Ashley doubted that Rosreece would reach First Light before the tail end of the following morning. The Gifter's extravagant haste glared back at them from every hoof-print they passed on the road to

Llury. Rosreece and Hosanna maintained a long stride. They would be fatigued when they reached their destination, too fatigued to deal with any real threats. And because of the clash of personalities, the quest was already divided in two. They were all the weaker for it.

The Rector couldn't have selected a worse group for the task.

9. FRIENDS AND FIENDS

"When do you know someone through and through?
When you cease to surprise them,
or they cease to surprise you?"——*Zarost*

Tabitha woke, but lay quite still. She smelled fresh linen. Something soft pressed against her cheek. She dared to open her eyes. A bedroom with a thick-beamed ceiling enclosed her. Russet carpets lay beside the bed. The windows were shuttered, admitting only a sliver of light. The sounds of the street outside were muffled. A horse snorted. Two voices were engaged in conversation. The words were indistinct at first, but the voices were rising.

"Then you can tell me the moment she wakes." A man's voice, vibrant and vaguely familiar. "I must see her, for goodness sakes!"

"Not now you won't," answered a stern woman.

"Later better not be too late, In'madam. It better not be too late."

The horse whinnied, then hooves clicked away across a cobbled street.

She sat up gingerly in the strange bed. Rumpled blankets covered her legs. Her forehead itched, and she raised a hand to scratch, but her fingers met with fabric. A bandage was bound around her head.

Bandage?

She frowned. A pale brown tunic of lambs-wool covered her, soft and loose. *I was wearing a dress, a blue dress and woollen jacket, when -*

A sudden forgetfulness came over her, a welcome mist. She concentrated on her surroundings. The room smelled clean, of warmth and wood polish. A small fire burned in a hearth. Her blue dress and woollen jacket hung over the back of a heavy chair. She recognised the room.

The Tooth-and-Tale. I'm in the village.

A gentle knock at the door, then it swung inwards.

Lyndall Quilt entered. Her usually carefree expression was drawn. Tabitha seemed to see everything about her, too clearly, she noticed a hundred little details. Lyndall's blond plait needed to be tidied. She had missed a button a third of the way down her jacket, and there was a faint stain of mead on the toe of her leather boot. And all those freckles on her forearm, had they been there before?

Tabitha closed her eyes to block it all out.

Lyndall drew a breath, and Tabitha heard every whisper of the inhalation. There was no way to escape it. She wanted to be asleep again.

"I was so worried about you, coming in so pale like that," Lyndall said. "I thought you'd caught the death of cold. What happened, Tee?" Lyndall plopped down next to Tabitha, making the bed creak in surprise.

Tabitha's stomach turned. She wanted to forget for a moment longer.

"Not yet," she whispered.

Lyndall hugged her, and said nothing.

"How did I get here?" Tabitha asked, when they parted.

Lyndall looked surprised. "The Riddler brought you to us this morning. You thanked him, don't you remember? Before we popped you into bed. What happened to you, last night? You missed your shift in the bar. We got worried when no word was sent."

"The Riddler. Who's the Riddler?"

"The funny man with the floppy hat. Twardy Zarost. Surely you can't have forgotten him? He's a laugh!"

Now that she thought about it, there had been a face, brown and weathered like smooth bark, a bearded man peering down at her.

Lyndall laid her hands on Tabitha's arm. Her touch was warm, her skin smelled of soap, and there were rough calouses in two places on each of her hands. Too sensitive, she was aware of too many details. The forgetfullness in her mind threatened to clear. A memory rose up, a night that would not be forgotten.

Lyndall looked worried. "Are you feeling all right?"

The cold snow, the running, the dark forest. Phantom Acres.

"What happened, Tee?" Lyndall was so full of concern for her, so caring. Tabitha could feel her defences crumbling.

"He came to the farm, Lyndall, because of my song, because of me, he fought with her, and Dad fell, and I think they both lost, Lyn, I think he k-killed them! Because of me!"

"Oh Tabitha. Oh my dear dear friend!"

Tabitha clung to Lyndall's shoulder as the memory overwhelmed her. Lyndall rocked her, on and on, as Tabitha purged her terror with her tears.

Later, Tabitha gazed numbly over Lyndall's shoulder. The fire had burned low in the hearth. Gone, her parents were gone. In one dark night. She felt hollow and cold, as if she was made of only skin and emptiness.

"We should summon the Sword at once, Tabitha. The murderer should be tracked down."

Tabitha pulled away, and looked at Lyndall on the level. "He was a Shadowcaster."

Her friend looked aghast. "Again, so close to First Light? But how can that be!"

"He came to reclaim something taken from Fendwarrow." Tabitha dropped her gaze to the blankets. She found a detached place in her awareness which helped to dull the pain. "He's still out there."

The images of the night flickered through her mind. Slate-grey eyes, streaked with yellow. Hullo, pretty.

Lyndall stood up rapidly. "I'll come back. I think mother needs to hear of this. She'll know what to do." She crossed the room. "What if he comes here? This, this murderer!" She opened the door, and was gone.

Shadowcaster. The word seemed to fill the room with cold for a moment, driving away the warmth of the fire. Tabitha shivered. An evil man, with the stalking movements of a predator. He had wanted the Ring. Her mother had fought to the death to prevent him, to keep the Ring away from the Darkmaster. And now Tabitha had it.

Take this. Run.

Tabitha slid off the bed, balancing for a moment on her unsteady legs. She hadn't realised how weak she was.

Her woollen jacket was draped over the chair near the fire. She searched the pocket and found the soft, crumpled kerchief. She traced her fingers over the smudged remains of her mother's scrawled missive. There was more writing scrawled inside the kerchief.

Legacy in chamber. Know I love you.

Legacy. The word was too heavy to bear.

Oh, Mother, you knew it, yet still you fought. Is this a thing of such power, that you died to keep it from them?

She held her hand up to the fire. The Ring was invisible in the dim light, yet she could feel its smoothness at the base of the middle finger on her right hand. It was cool and slippery when she touched it with her fingers. She was sure it had been warm only a moment ago. She tried to pull it off, but it would not be dislodged, having tightened its grip with the cooling, no doubt.

The unbearable richness of sensations had faded as well. She was only aware of the lambent warmth of the fire, and the cold aching knowledge of her loss.

◆ ──────── ◆

Some time later, there was a knocking on her door. Tabitha rose slowly from the bed. She remembered opening the windows and shutters at some time, then closing them against the chill of evening. Lyndall had banked the fire for her. The room was warm. Nothing really mattered, everything was distant again. People had come and people had gone, and she was left the same.

There had been Mrs Quilt, full of matronly sympathy. She had given Tabitha a pair of grey woodsman's trousers to wear while her dress was drying. The trousers were small enough to be comfortable. Then there had been old Steed, the greying Captain of the local Sword. He had responded with gruff indignation to the news. He had promised that a commando would be assembled, to depart at dawn. They would search for the criminal. If there was murder, Steed promised to see the King's justice enacted. The Shadowcaster would not walk free.

The Captain's statement had lacked complete conviction, as if he considered her story might be a troubled fantasy. She had no proof other than what she felt. Her parents had been alive when she had fled.

The knocking came again. Tabitha realised she must have sat down, despite her intentions. Her mind was wandering, far away. She rose from the bed again. She reached the door and opened it with a reflexive question.

"Who is it?"

She already had the door wide open. Tabitha froze. A strange man stood in the hallway, a spry figure with olive-brown skin and a jutting beard of black and white. On his head perched a brown-striped hat.

"Supper," the stranger identified himself, proferring two heavily laden plates. He bowed from the waist. His eyes held a twinkle.

Tabitha fumbled for words as her wariness faded. The smile on his lips was geniune.

"You're, you're ... the Riddler?"

"Twardy Zarost. Other folk I've tried to be, but I'm not them, and they aren't me." He raised an eyebrow suggestively, and offered the plates once more. "Shall we eat inside, or will two plates of the Tooth-and-Tale's best fill my belly alone?"

The aroma of cooked food, softened by a gravy, and freshened with steaming vegetables, came through the door. The plates were huge, they looked as if they held a feast. She wasn't sure if she could find her appetite, but she felt a sudden urge to talk to the Riddler. Funny, a moment ago she had wanted to be left alone. She retreated into her room.

The Riddler followed.

He was odd. His clothes were outlandish, or of a style that had long since passed from fashion. The leather boots were standard enough, though the tips curved upwards like cheeky snouts. His purple trousers billowed loosely. The black robe ended uncommonly at his thighs, and was belted at his waist with a fraying sash. Slightly grubby white cuffs protruded from the robe at his wrists.

Tabitha took him to the small oak table beside the fireplace. She was thankful for the easy silence which Twardy Zarost assumed. He devoured a good portion of Mrs Quilt's cooking before meeting her speculative gaze. He spread his leathery hands.

"I am sorry for your loss, young Tabitha. Your friend Lyndall told me about your parents."

Tabitha flinched, and set her unused fork back on the plate. She resisted the rising sorrow, but the pressure was insistent.

Anything, anything but that! That's why I wanted your company, to take my mind elsewhere.

She had to avoid a show of weeping before the newcomer. It seemed important to keep her poise in his presence. She couldn't afford to come apart at the seams.

"How did you find me?" she asked.

"How? By horse, and a cart." Twardy Zarost held her eyes with a steady gaze, his face impassive.

Tabitha's mood darkened. His humour was ill-timed.

"Questions do funny things with answers, questions do." Twardy speared a small potato with his fork, twiddling it through a patch of cheesy sauce before popping it into his mouth.

Tabitha took a deep breath.

Can't the silly man see I want to cry? She didn't want to play his games. But his challenge gave her a spark of anger, and she felt her tears recede a little.

"If you don't mind me saying so, Mister Zarost, you are strange in these parts. What were you doing on this stretch of the High Way?"

"Mister is another's name, my name is Twardy," he said in his rolling, musical way. "I've been here before, but not to be noticed. I seldom come here, because there's nothing to do. If you don't mind me saying so." His laughter tumbled like water through sunlit rocks. "But it sounds as if something happened here last night. I was travelling the High Way towards you, and you came towards me. Our paths crossed, you could say. And now, they're all tangled up."

He was still being evasive, but he was the man who had brought her in from the cold, after all. Her irritation faded as she remembered her manners.

"Thank you," she said. "For saving me."

"Not so. I cannot do that."

"I'm warm. I'm fed. I would have died. You saved me."

"Ah, but what of the fellow who followed us to this village? I cannot protect you from him."

Tabitha's blood ran cold. "W-what fellow?"

"Black cloak and orb are the marks of Shadowcasters, yes? He was one of those, but he's burnt like a roasted potato. Bad at hiding too, for I saw him many times today, though the villagers see him not."

"He's here, in First Light?"

The sickening smile, the eyes of slate. Clouds of midnight cold about his shoulders. Her father fell to the floor. Tabitha could hardly draw a breath. *What happened at the farm, that he was burned?*

"I don't remember him being scarred," she said, grasping for hope. "Maybe it's—another."

"The way he watches your room, I'd say he's a stalker. He doesn't seem the kind to leave empty handed. You are in danger until he gets what he is looking for. You have it with you?"

Tabitha stared at the Riddler.

"The Ring? How do you know about the Ring?"

"Ah, so you know that's what it is. That is good. Be careful of speaking so openly of it, for many would like to own such a thing."

"You know of it?"

"The Ring is a different thing to different people. Do you have the Ring with you then, that he follows you so?" Twardy Zarost leaned towards Tabitha, suddenly intent.

She felt awkward under his altered gaze. Surely he couldn't have noticed the clear band on her finger—it was invisible in the dim light. Her right hand went to her trouser pocket, where she could hide it. She shook her head.

A painful cold lanced through her finger. Things were progressing too fast. The effort of conversing with the Riddler was tiring her, trying to puzzle the meaning in his words. Already he seemed to know too much. She didn't want him guessing that she wore the Ring, and couldn't get it off.

"My mother, before she died, she hid it." Again, the unbearable cold from the Ring. She tried to finish with a neutral comment. She had never been much good at lying. "I know where it is. But why is it so important?"

The Riddler fidgeted in his chair, and spread his hands wide as if to say he had no idea. His brown eyes held a hungry look.

"Where is it?"

"In a chamber in –" Tabitha gasped. The Ring was a blade of ice, threatening to sever her finger. With sudden dread and clarity, she understood something about the talisman.

She could not lie, while she wore the Ring. It made the compulsion of her Truth-sense clear and commanding.

"Somewhere that I know of," she said. A vague warmth penetrated her finger around the Ring. "That's all I'm telling," she ended hastily, folding her arms across her chest. She was not going to be backed into a corner again by the Riddler.

Twardy Zarost laughed. His grin was so wide and geniune it was difficult to imagine he had seemed threatening only moments before.

"You have the makings of a fine Riddler, Tabitha Serannon. It will be good to see what you become in time. I do know that you bear the Ring." His eyes held a joyous glint.

"How do you know?" she whispered. Her hand was still firmly ensconced in her pocket. He couldn't have seen the Ring when her hand had been free.

It was invisible, she told herself.

"The Ring you bear is one of great power. And so, those who know what they speak of, call it the Wizard's Ring. It is my business to be close to it. I have promised to see the Ring taken to the wizard whom it was made for. Never fear, I won't steal it from you, but I must guide you and the Ring to the wizard. That is my task, that is why I am here."

"The Ring must be returned," stated Tabitha, a little disappointed.

"Re-turned, yes." He pronounced the word strangely.

"So the Ring is not something evil?"

"Evil or good, that is always something you choose for yourself."

"Is it dangerous?"

"The path to the wizard is always dangerous. That is the path you shall need to follow. You will lose the Ring if you do not walk that way."

"Can't I give it away? Can't I give it to you?"

Twardy Zarost threw his hands into the air. "Oh no, it's not for the likes of me. But you can give it to the Shadow-man, if you want. No? First, you should know this. If you choose to bear the Ring yourself, your duty will grow every day, until you will never be able to set it down."

There was no need for caution any more. She drew her right hand from her pocket and grasped the clear solidity of the Ring between the fingers of her left hand.

"What if I can't get it off now? Does this mean I'm already bound by the duty?"

"You cannot get it off because you really do not want to," he said, chuckling all the while. His eyes were bright with knowing. "Only later shall it be your duty which prevents you."

Tabitha tried to pull it from her finger once more. As she touched it, she remembered the music, faint and clear. The Lifesong. The Ring was too beautiful to throw away. It had showed her things already. It would not always be hers, but for the moment, it could be, if she wanted.

"How do I find the wizard?"

"The Ring will show you, follow what you see."

"Is the wizard to be found in Eyri?" she asked. It was a silly question, she supposed. There was nowhere to go outside of Eyri. Yet wizards were the things of legends, and she had always thought of them residing in the sky, or far, far away.

"The wizard? Wizards go everywhere. Who can say where a wizard begins, and where a wizard ends? But surely when you know where to look for the wizard, the wizard shall be near, that is true. You see, the wizard needs the Ring, but you must find the wizard."

The story seemed to be bending in curious ways in the Riddler's hands. Her earlier wariness returned. She wasn't going to let him puzzle her so easily.

"Where? Where do I find the wizard?"

"North, south, east, west, wherever you decide. It is the path to the knowledge of the wizard you must follow. I cannot tell where the wizard shall be found."

The Riddler's evasiveness was becoming exasperating.

"What do you suggest, Twardy Zarost?" she asked. "Where should I go?"

"That is the third asking upon the same riddle, and so the final answer." He paused for a moment to steeple his fingers. "What do you inherit from your parents?"

The directness of his question took her hard. She was forced to face the thoughts she most wanted to avoid. Her parents, assumed dead at Phantom Acres.

Inherit. It had been written, in her mother's hand. She pulled the crumpled kerchief from her pocket, and smoothed in on her knee.

Legacy in chamber. Know I love you.

There was only one chamber it could be, beneath the hearth in their homestead. Her mother really had foreseen the end. Her inheritance awaited at Phantom Acres. It should not be abandoned, to be stolen by thieves. Whatever lay there, was precious. She had to get to the farm.

Strangely, the decision to collect her inheritance left her feeling empty and cold again. It seemed too much like setting things aside, getting on with her life. But she could see the clear course winding ahead like an illuminated path through the empty darkness of her thoughts, and she knew it was the path she must follow. The Ring was warm on her finger.

"You have decided?" the Riddler asked.

"I shall return to Phantom Acres."

"And then?"

Tabitha paused.

"I shall go to the Dovecote in Levin. I shall present myself to become a Lightgifter."

Zarost's eyes reflected golden candle-light. "When do we leave?"

Tabitha was taken aback. He seemed ready to depart at once. "I must wait, until the—Shadowcaster—is arrested," she answered.

"You will be taken away, by the Shadow who hunts you," he warned. "The Sword is no match for him." Zarost looked certain of that, and the more she considered it, the more she feared he might be right. Old Captain Steed had probably never dealt with a murderer in all his years of patrolling First Light.

"Best for you to make the first move," said Zarost.

"But how? If *he* is out there," Tabitha said, pointing to the shuttered windows, "he'll attack the moment I leave. How can I go there, how can I go anywhere at all?" The certainty of her purpose began to crumble beneath her, dissolve into that hollow darkness. She shivered.

Twardy Zarost rose from his chair. He stacked their plates and cleared the morsels from the table with a sweep of his hand.

"I can help, but only if you call upon me to help."

He waited, his eyebrows raised expectantly. It took Tabitha a long moment to understand his strange request.

"Can you help me to escape from the Shadowcaster?" she asked.

Zarost bowed, a delighted grin creasing his beard.

"Yes. It is now your path and not mine that we tread. It is time a riddle was laid for our stalker. We shall be riding in the morning before dawn. Be ready for the knock-knocking upon your door."

Tabitha nodded mutely. The Riddler was leaving, and he took something from the room with him. The shadows gathered beyond the range of the fire. She felt herself sinking. The Riddler turned at the door.

"Good night, Miss Serannon. We ride in the morning."

"Good night, Twardy Zarost," she whispered.

Back to Phantom Acres. Where she would find her parents.

The door closed.

Mother, give me strength!

She had to go. She had to retrieve her inheritance before … she shuddered. Would the Shadowcaster really be fooled by the Riddler? How far would she have to run to escape his reach? Surely the Dovecote would protect her? The Shadowcaster wouldn't dare to follow her there.

Questions, questions, but no answers.

She remembered the biting cold of the Dark essence, and the look in the Shadowcaster's eyes. He didn't seem to be the kind who would give up. She forced herself to ignore the conclusion, to blow out the oil lamps, and to pretend that the thickening darkness held no threat.

She almost fooled herself.

She stripped, and slid beneath the bed-covers. The embers glowed a dull red in the hearth. Tabitha lay on her back, and stared at the ceiling. The beams were hidden in vagueness. So many people had come and gone. Now that the night was finally her own, the vaporous memories of the day dispersed, revealing the gnawing void beneath. She had pretended to be involved during the questioning. Now there was silence, and nothing else, only an empty place within her heart.

She did not want to care any more, the caring hurt too much. She wished to be swallowed by the deep black emptiness.

The Riddler couldn't help. He couldn't bring her parents back.

When she closed her eyes, the room ceased to exist. She felt as if she were dissolving, vanishing like the day, crumbling like so much sand piled against the tide. The hollowness washed through her, taking everything, leaving nothing. She didn't care.

The Ring was warm on her finger. At least there was that.

She lay for a long time, neither asleep nor awake, in the space between one thought and the next. The sounds of the night were distant—the muffled voices from the common-room, a faint clatter of pots from the kitchen, even a scuffing of feet outside her window—all belonged to a world far beyond where she was.

The emptiness stretched forever, and all the while she was sinking. A force tugged at her spirit, like a current which pulls a log toward a waterfall. From that river of empty darkness, she fell into an abyss of nothingness.

It felt as if her life was draining from her body. She was so weak, so tired, so peaceful. She didn't try and understand—she didn't care enough to try. All she could do was to watch, and wait, and witness what the Ring was showing her. Falling, falling.

Then she was still.

In that moment, she knew the awful proximity of her own death. There was nothing driving her, nothing keeping her alive. She had long since ceased to draw breath, but she couldn't find the part of her that should be breathing, the part that should care. She had no form, no colour, almost no existence. She was a place of clarity, and no more.

The Ring took her further.

She heard a voice, a delicate small voice, singing a song which was woven under the surface of everything that lived. The lyrics touched her own clear memory.

She sang. The Lifesong vibrated in her core. Her spirit shimmered. A wind snatched at the air, swirling it around her. She sang against the hungry void, against the end, against death. Rapture took purchase in her soul, and somewhere beyond it all, she felt her body returning, as if she were becoming more alive, born from the void to the world again. Life coursed through her veins. She gasped, and drew a searing breath. The stanza of the Lifesong had ended.

Her bedroom returned with a rush. The solid beams of the ceiling loomed overhead in the gloom. The room was quiet, but blood roared in her ears. The soft sheet touched her body. The embers glowed. She was safe.

The Ring burned hot against her skin, but even as she made to release it from her finger, the strange glass cooled, and the need to remove it was gone.

The Lifesong was a gift, the Ring was a powerful tool. She resolved to learn about both. They had cost her too much to surrender them, or to waste them by giving up.

"Thank you, for making me strong," she whispered to the clear circlet. She considered all that had happened to her.

A ring, a riddler, a slayer, a song.

Her life had been turned upside down. Zarost had offered to be her guide. There were forces at play which she didn't understand. But she was certain of one thing.

She twisted the sheets in her fists even as she fell asleep. Her fate was cruel, but she was not willing to be washed under by the tide of Dark. She had found the will to fight. The Shadowcaster had a lot to answer for. And he would not get the Ring from her.

◆ ———————— ◆

Twardy Zarost did not return to his rooms once he had delivered the plates to the kitchen. Instead, he swung the back door gently open, and slipped out into the cold night. He frowned as he searched the nearby darkness. He walked a way down the small street, then pulled back into the deep shadows and all but disappeared. Nothing moved. The moon cast a fey illumination upon the rooftops, picking out pale wood planking and speckled thatch. A cat yowled from across the cobbles. It padded along the street, but didn't even look his way. With tail erect, it turned and marched off down a nearby alley. Nothing else stirred in First Light.

The Riddler shook his head, and moved into the street once more. The guard was missing. He slipped through the village, and came at last upon a large, squat building, set slightly apart from its neighbours. Thick rough-hewn timbers enclosed barred windows. A lamp burned beside the iron-bound door, casting a pool of light on the wide stone forecourt. Set into the centre of the door was the emblem of the Sword—the gilded hollow circle of Eyri divided into four equal parts by the lines of a sword's cross-guard, blade and tang. It symbolised the Sword's fairness with every segment of the population, and the presence of the King's justice in all things. So they said. In truth, the segments were not equal, and one segment escaped justice altogether.

Twardy stepped into the light, and knocked.

"Who is it?" boomed a voice from beyond the door. At his answer, a heavy bolt was slid, and the door opened outwards. A man dressed in uniform motioned for Twardy to enter. The guard was gruff-looking, his cheeks bore stubble, his brows stern or staid. He closed the door with a thud once Zarost had passed.

A commanding veteran looked up from his desk.

"What news, Riddler?"

The greying captain sat with his quill raised expectantly above his journal, his lined face lit by a flickering candle. Oil lamps lit the wall behind him, filling the room with a functional glow.

"I have not seen the man again, Captain Steed," Twardy Zarost answered. "Very good at hiding he seems." He advanced to the desk, and drew up a wooden chair.

"Doubtless," the Captain agreed. "One of my men has confirmed that the Shadowcaster is lurking in First Light. Ayche saw him, though the cretin vanished just as soon as he tried to close. I must say I did not believe you at first, thought you to be jumping at shadows. But I've stationed two Swords at the Tooth-and-Tale now. If he is here, it can mean only one thing—he is after the Serannon girl."

"The girl, and other things, but the girl is the most important. The guards at the Tooth couldn't guard their own bungholes, Captain."

The Captain stiffened, but Zarost continued.

"I found the back door unguarded."

"Curses! I'll have his sword for this. Ayche!" the Captain barked, "find that juggins Victor and return him to the Tooth. He must be 'patrolling' the Grone Street bar. And stay there tonight, as commanding breech-kicker."

The guard who had admitted Zarost nodded sharply and lifted a dull helm from beside the door. He saluted the Captain with a raised fist before striding out into the night. The Captain gave Zarost a wry look.

"Our blades are perhaps a little rusty in these quiet parts."

"Not so quiet any more, my Captain, not so quiet at all."

Steed closed his journal, and rested his hands on the leather cover. "We shall wait until this Shadowcaster shows himself, and take him into custody. Then the peace shall return."

"I am giving respect to yourself and your men, Captain, but you won't catch this fish without a hook. And if he reaches the girl, she has not a chance."

"I see." Captain Steed eyed the Riddler for a while, his lips pursed. "You have something you wish to suggest?"

"There is a way to catch such a fish, even with a blunted hook."

The Captain watched the wax candle burn down.

"Very well. I can't afford to spend every day protecting one girl with all of my men. What are you getting at, Riddler?"

"Lay a net he does not see."

"And how do you propose we do that?"

"Let me tell you what I shall do come morning, and you can decide if you'd like to fish."

Ashley pushed the empty plate aside, and leant back in his chair. The Dormouse in Llury served hearty portions for a silver and six; they were accustomed to feeding loggers and hunters. The ache in his belly was gone. He wished there was a similar cure for the ache in his butt. He would gladly pay another silver. Walking had seemed a welcome respite from riding at the time, until he had discovered how tiring it was to walk at a horse's pace. The scoured road to Llury had seemed to go on forever.

They hadn't seen the other Gifters again after they had ridden ahead.

"What do you think happened to Rosreece and Hosanna, Father Keegan?"

Keegan ignored the question, taking a deep draught from his tankard instead, then closing his eyes.

"Damned cub won't be quiet," thought Keegan. *"Suppose I was full of questions until I was ordained."*

Ashley gritted his teeth. *Cub?* But Keegan hadn't spoken the word, and he couldn't challenge it. Ashley pressed his hands to his temples. He wished he could find some control over the intrusive voices in his mind. Willing them away didn't seem to work when he was tired. It was possible he was just having hallucinations.

Sister Grace was savouring her apple pie and seemed to be too tired to take an interest.

Keegan answered at last. "They might be riding still, but they'll not yet be at Brimstone."

"More likely they've halted and are shameless in the forest. Hosanna, naked in a saddle, feet in the stirrups."

Ashley concealed his burning embarrassment by dropping his face and pretending to scratch at an itching forehead. Stars above! He hadn't expected such a carnal thought to come from an ordained Lightgifter. Sister Grace gave him a quick, puzzled glance when he looked up.

"What happens to Gifters if they're caught—together?" he asked.

Grace looked greatly surprised, but it was Father Keegan's reaction he wanted to see. He wanted to know if he had heard the Father's thoughts correctly.

"Where does that question come from?" Keegan growled.

Out of your mind, thought Ashley, but he bit his tongue. It didn't prove anything, he decided. He still didn't know for sure, and he couldn't risk asking outright.

"Gifters can marry, Ashley," said Grace, "but they go right out of the Dovecote." She gave a short, flat whistle. "The sanctity of the Light must be pure around the Source, and that means chastity, honesty, and dedication."

"Hah!" said Keegan, but when they both turned to him for explanation, he buried his beard in his tankard. *"If the Sister only knew how empty the Cote would be,"* Keegan thought.

Ashley stifled a laugh; Grace was regarding him with a level gaze, as if he'd been the one entertaining fantasies, not Keegan. He wasn't sure that he was entirely blameless, now that her eyes were on him. He seized at the first question he could bring to mind.

"Hosanna's vision," he stammered, "when the Shadowcaster fights the Gifter, and the Morgloth appears. Is that—it's surely a metaphor for something bad? Not a real Morgloth, not a real demon."

Sister Grace's level gaze wavered. "We can't be sure, Ashley. Too little study has been done on vision-casting, and she is the only one with the gift at present. She sees—shapes and patterns, a short glimpse of events."

Father Keegan wiped the foam from his beard with the back of his hand. "There must have been an evil beast in the world to give birth to the legend of the Morgloth, but the tale has grown horns and teeth over the years. I doubt we'll ever see its like."

"But if Hosanna has seen true, then it will come again," Grace asserted. Her fatalism was alarming.

"How would we fight a Morgloth?" Ashley asked.

"There is nothing you could do," said Keegan, looking suddenly bereft. "It would gobble you up, boots and all." Behind his mask of mock sincerity, he thought, *"The cub is so gullible he could be sold a three-legged horse."*

"Keegan!" Sister Grace scolded, "Stop taunting the young man. You know Eyri wouldn't be entirely defenceless against a Morgloth. If the legends are correct, the threat of the Morgloth was met, and cleared."

"That's just a legend," Keegan retorted with a laugh. "You're using one legend to defeat another."

"How were the Morgloth defeated?" Ashley asked.

Grace ignored Keegan's continued laughter. "The Book of Ages says The First Swordmaster of Eyri stood before the horde, and they were petrified by his blade, and he slew them as they stood, until all lay defeated before him, or returned to that hell from whence they came."

"That's so typical of the lay of legends," scoffed Keegan. "Beasts and heroes, gods and wizards, all utterly implausible."

"But why did the Rector send us?" Ashley asked. "If it's so implausible, he wouldn't waste our time and sprites on this quest."

Keegan gave him a pitying smile. "You really do believe this ruse, don't you both? It was just a way for the lovers to skip the stifling strictures of the Dovecote. There's no Morgloth."

"You can't be sure, Keegan," Sister Grace objected.

Keegan shook his head. "We are here because the Rector had to answer such a blatant interruption without losing face. Rosreece stood up to the Rector as well, and marked himself for retribution, but that was obviously their plan from the start."

Something about Father Keegan's logic didn't add up. Hosanna. She wouldn't have falsified her vision just to earn her abscence from the Dovecote. She was always so impeccable, yet Father Keegan blithely assumed that lust had overpowered her reason.

Then again, Ashley hadn't guessed that Hosanna even had a lover. After the way Rosreece had compelled her to join his lead, Ashley's ignorance was plain. Keegan was wiser in the ways of desire.

"And us? What are we doing on the quest?"

"As for Sister Grace, the Rector feels threatened by her talent, for it surpasses his. So the Rector uses his prerogative whenever he can to send her away. And you—doubtless you know what it is you have done to deserve his petty anger."

The Hall. I breached the sanctity of the Hall at night.

"We're on a mission for fools," Keegan concluded, his brow gathering. "Morgloth! When we reach First Light, we'll find only the laughter of the ones we come to warn."

Sister Grace put a gentling hand on Keegan's fist. "Don't rile against our fate, Keegan. We serve the Light, not the one who commands us. I still believe there is more to Hosanna's vision than you credit."

"Thank you, Grace. Ah, I see there's no convincing either of you. If you wish to chase Morgloths at dawn, we'll need to be strong. I've hired a fresh horse for Ashley from the Inn, we shall make good speed." He rose from his chair. "For one, I'd like to test if the beds are as good as the meals here."

As they retired from the dining room, Ashley caught the wisp of a curse from Keegan, though it went unspoken.

"Blast and set fire to it! I must keep an empty bed, yet those ahead of us get away with it. I should accept the offer in Fendwarrow. Ah, but that would be good!"

Ashley promised himself he wouldn't filch another thought. Ever. Some things were not meant to be known. He had no right to learn of Keegan's fantasies.

But that night he dreamt of a sultry seductress named Gabrielle, a woman with a wild hunger in her eyes, her voice husky with promise, her dark hair tumbling over a black silk gown that clung to her body wherever she moved. He didn't want the dream to end.

He couldn't be sure it was entirely his own dream.

10. WINE
"To all wines is added a taste of mischief."—*Zarost*

Dawn broke crisply over the eastern horizon. Sunlight lanced across the basin of Eyri, and struck the high cliffs of Fynn's Tooth on the western rim. Clear ice and snow glared, the skirt of talus became a shattered grey, and the spears of a thousand trees cast long shadows against its flanks. The sun was punctured upon the jagged maw of the Zunskar Mountains; its bright assault spilled into Eyri.

The day always began with the breaking of the night, Kirjath decided. He pulled his smarting eye back from the hole in the wall. The welcome gloom of the stable returned.

The night had passed all too quickly. He had located the girl, yet the presence of the soldiers had frustrated every attempt at entry. On any other night, they would have presented no barrier. But his supply of essence was badly depleted. And he was hurt. He would not admit that he was also very weak.

His burns plagued him. They were so bad he wanted to scream and never cease. The continuous strain grated on his nerves. Hour by hour, he had bled energy from the Dark essence, depleted the supply that he had brought from Fendwarrow. Hour by hour, he had consumed the mana. Motes flickered over his skin like feasting flies, numbing the pain to a dull ache. His left hand had begun to ooze during the night, adding a sickly-sweet smell to the other aromas. He kept the motes concentrated on his head, wearing them as a thick crown, chanting softly to bind them to his body.

There were no new motes in First Light; none had ever been turned this far west. He had tried to summon more Dark from Ravenscroft, but the task surpassed his ability. And for all his knowledge of spell-casting, he could effect no healing; only a Freeze to numb the agony, to contain the damage. It was an abuse to his body he knew he couldn't sustain. He had to find a healer. A poultice or a balm, from a herbalist or mender. Not a Lightgifter. Never a Lightgifter. He spat a chewed lump of jurrum into the straw.

He was on borrowed time. He had ignored the Master's summoning. He needed results if he was to avoid the retribution. The girl and the Ring, before healing. But with the Swords all around, he had to wait for a gap in the defence. He couldn't risk using the beast in his weakened state. The Morgloth's rebellion was only too fresh in his memory. No, the Morgloth was a last resort. It eased his frustration somewhat, knowing that he had the means to kill them all. He could be patient.

He smothered a hacking cough with his robe. The tattered garment reeked of smoke. He pushed his eye up against the knot-hole again. There was some activity outside the inn.

A small man sat in a cart, a striped hat perched on his head. Two uniformed Swords loaded a heavy barrel of wine onto the cart. A wagoneer, then. He looked vaguely familiar. Strange for a full barrel to leave the inn, but Kirjath supposed it had been traded at a profit to someone in desperate need. Especially if it were Dwarrow-wine. Folk soon acquired a taste that would be sated by no other. There would be a small amount of Dark essence in the wine. For a brief moment Kirjath considered summoning the motes to his own hand. He would have to breach the barrel to do that, and expose himself in the process. Best he leave it be.

Two more Swords rode into view, leading extra mounts with them. They halted at the door to the inn, beside the three men already there. One of the footmen knocked on the door of the Tooth-and-Tale, and stood back.

The door opened to reveal a large woman.

One of the Sword greeted her in a loud voice that carried on the wind.

"Morning, Madam Quilt. We have come to collect the Serannon girl. She is to come with us on a search for the Shadowcaster. We have word that he was seen on the north road."

The innkeeper acquired a stony look.

"How dare you suggest Tabitha is to ride? With all she's been through, and a dangerous killer loose, whom you have failed to bring to justice? The girl needs rest, and safety!"

"She is the only one to have seen this Shadowcaster. We need her to identify the man."

"Whoever heard of such a thing! She can identify him when you drag him back here on his ear. She does not leave that room." Kirjath didn't miss where she pointed; the last shuttered window of the inn frontage.

"I can't station men here and do the search," the Sword objected. "She'll be safer with us."

The innkeeper folded her arms across her heavy bosom. "I shall protect her here! Nobody enters my Inn against my will!"

The wagoneer shook his head. "Little good such arrogance did her parents, and little good it will do for you. The Shadowcaster is dangerous. He could be in the Inn and out again, and have the girl in a twist of his shadow. Madam-inn, how are you going to fight him? With a broom?"

The innkeeper's face reddened, but her jaw was set.

"I will not allow it! The girl stays here!" Turning on her heel, she shut the door firmly in the face of the men gathered on the street.

They stared at the Tooth-and-Tale for a while, and muttered between themselves. Finally, the Captain gave a sharp order, and the Sword closed rank. They rode north, the wagoneer with his wine-barrel trailing along behind. Off to search for the wicked Shadowcaster.

Let them search, the tinpots!

Kirjath couldn't believe their stupidity. Maybe they didn't know how badly he wanted the girl. They had identified her position, and left it unguarded in the same fatal moment. He would be done with his task, and be well on the way to Fendwarrow before they had any idea.

He lurked in the stable a while longer. Then he checked the street. First Light was waking, and a few villagers went about their business. No sign of the Sword.

He used the motes to hide him within the shadows beside the stable wall. He slipped around the side of the building, and paused at the corner. A few milkmaids passed by, pails balanced on their heads, tongues wagging. When the street was clear, he slunk quickly across the cobbles to the Tooth-and-Tale.

The back door stood open. A cook was in the kitchen, busy behind clouds of steam. When her back was turned, Kirjath entered. The frying pan which he used to hit her with made a dull, ringing sound. He hoped it would pass for a kitchen sound, as well as the heavy thump as she fell to the floor.

The corridor had many doors leading off it, each to a different room. He wasted no time, he knew the room he wanted—the last room which looked out over the front street. The door was closed, but Kirjath did not knock. He twisted the door-handle, and flung the door wide.

◆ ——————————◆

It was dark, inside. The cart lurched over the last of the broken ground, and settled with a thump onto the road once more. The barrel shook, but never toppled. Fingers drummed rhythmically upon the lid.

"How much further?"

"Wine takes time to mature," said a singsong voice outside.

"The bumps hurt."

The cart slowed, and came to a halt.

"But you must pretend to be wine, then you'll not be hurt by the bumps," the muffled voice declared. A sharp tapping of a hammer jarred the wood above.

"Watch your head!" warned the Riddler.

The wedge came free from the lid, and sunlight burst into Tabitha's world.

"Poof! Why do people ever drink this stuff? It's really awful," she muttered, wriggling out of the barrel. Her legs ached, but it was bearable to stand. She smoothed her tunic, and tucked the coarse woodsman's trousers into her boots.

"Ah, but Dwarrow tastes better after the first goblet, and better still after the second," answered the Riddler, gleaming with good humour. He handed her a heavy overcoat when she took her place beside him at the front of the cart. She hoped Mrs Quilt wouldn't miss the clothes. The Riddler had been adamant that she say nothing to the innkeeper of where she was going.

"The Swords are gone?" Tabitha asked, glancing around at the quiet forest.

"Yes, they turned back long ago. We've backtracked as well."

Tabitha recognised the road. They were on the High Way, to the south of First Light. Zarost clicked to the horse, snapped the reins. The cart lurched forward, and settled into a good pace.

"No telling how blunt the Sword really has become. I want to be gone from Phantom Acres before the sun is high." Zarost pointed to the east, where the sun lay tangled in the boughs of the trees. He urged the grey into a canter. Tabitha held onto the seat with both hands to steady herself.

She didn't know what to dread more, the Shadowcaster escaping from First Light, or their imminent arrival at Phantom Acres.

◆ ——————— ◆

Kirjath stared down the long blade pointed at his throat. A Sword, where there should have been a girl.

Shatter the sun! It was all too easy, too bloody easy! I should have known.

He flung himself towards the open door, away from the Sword. He could outrun the soldier. The man looked to be thirty pounds overweight, and not a little out of shape.

A whistling sound warned him an instant before he was struck, but his reflexes were slower than usual. A staff struck him across the head, and the corridor swirled. The staff whistled and struck again. He raised his arms over his head to ward off the blows. He caught a glimpse of a thick dress, and stout legs standing in a firm stance. Then he saw the whole of his attacker. The innkeeper raised her broom for another blow.

A woman! She dared to strike him! He was being beaten by a woman with a bloody broom!

He regained his composure in one furious moment. He flung most of his Dark essence at her, retaining only the bare minimum to protect his body.

"Freeze!" he commanded.

The Sword rushed at him from the room, blocking his escape to the kitchen. He fled the corridor to the front exit of the Tooth-and-Tale, out into the street.

Three Swords and their Captain waited for him. They were mounted and ranged in a semicircle around the exit. They closed rank as Kirjath slipped on the cobbles.

Trapped! By the balls of Krakus! And I haven't enough essence.

The Swords dismounted and closed with weapons drawn. The blades were dull, but they'd be sharp enough. Kirjath spun. The fourth Sword emerged from the inn, completing the circle. He forced Kirjath back with violent slashes. The air was suddenly filled with the whistling of blades, all around him. Then he felt cold steel touch his neck. A sword rested there, its point coming from behind to end under his chin. Another sword slid across his belly, the point of a third pressed into his back. The fourth blade pressed against his chest directly over his heart.

The Captain urged his horse closer, until the beast towered over Kirjath.

"Shadowcaster, you are under arrest for the suspicion of murder. If you try to escape you shall be executed without question. I presume this Darkness of yours is alike to the Light essence. Release it from your command!"

Kirjath held his head high, and drew a long, slow breath. The Captain stiffened in his saddle. The sword at Kirjath's neck bit, and a warm trickle ran over his chest.

"Do it, now!" ordered the Captain. Kirjath steeled himself, and released the Dark. He howled as the motes scattered towards the shadows. They left raw pain behind. His hands boiled, and his scalp felt as if it was smothered with burning pitch.

"You shall come with us now to the Swordhouse," the Captain said, glaring down at him.

He met the Captain's glare with his own. He remained silent, but he knew his thoughts were written across his face.

You will die a horrible death, Captain. You, and all of your miserable toy soldiers.

Strangely, they did not respond to his threatening glare. Someone hobbled him with a leather cord. The same guard then bound his wrists tightly, raising an eyebrow at the charred and blistered flesh, but pulling the cord roughly nevertheless. Kirjath wanted to scream with the added pain, but he would not give an infidel such pleasure. He glared straight ahead, refusing to look up at the Captain again. A rope was tied into a simple noose, and slipped over his head. The Sword who tied it grinned slackly, then jerked the rope tight. It pinched Kirjath's throat, but he defied them by breathing—a rasping, forced respiration.

"Ayche, stable your horses. Men, let's move!" ordered the Captain. They began their procession through town—the Captain leading on his tall horse, the Swords and Kirjath on foot. Villagers paused, shocked and delighted at the spectacle of a captured criminal.

Kirjath decided which of the guards would die first. The man at the end of the rope pulled him forwards with wild jerks, trying to topple Kirjath to the stones as they walked. Then he would giggle to himself.

"Enough, Victor!" barked the Captain over his shoulder.

They continued at a more steady pace. Now and again the rope still twitched. Kirjath shuffled at the limit of his hobbled stride to avoid the point of the sword at his back. The guards formed a close escort around him, their dull blades still drawn. Kirjath gritted his teeth against the pain, and concentrated on reaching the Swordhouse without tripping on the cobbles.

As he was led across the village square, a terrible realisation settled on his shoulders.

He did not have enough essence to open the Gateway.
He could not call to his beast.
He was in trouble.

11. INHERITANCE

"Trickster, liar, traitor, thief—
one part laughter, three part grief."—*Zarost*

The north wind was bitter, it cut to the bone. Tabitha's teeth chattered. Her hair swirled and stuck to her wet cheeks.

The homestead was a wreckage. She saw everything with the unforgiving clarity that the Ring induced. Broken timbers lay like abandoned spears on a battlefield. Disturbed ash swirled, and collected in the lee of the ruins. The grass was burned to the scorched earth. The trees close by the homestead, all black pillars, with a sharp, stale smell. No warmth remained in the homestead; it was cold, empty, dead.

She trod unsteadily through the debris. There was nothing left of the front staircase except one of the stays. She climbed that into the carbon corpse of what had been her home.

The devastation of the family room was complete—a broad swathe where the floor had been, rude stumps of blackened timber at the walls. The hearth. The sight hit her with all the force of a collapsing mountain. Ash. Timbers. A skeleton on the raised stone. She knew without a doubt.

She snagged her sleeve on a beam as she sank to the floor; the weak support broke and fell away. She hugged her knees close. The faint sound of chimes came on the wind; the sound of shattered dreams, memories turned to ice, then broken, the shards blown with mockery across her heart.

Father made those chimes.

Her gaze dropped to a jumble of burnt timber, into the ash below, where a gruesome relic protruded. A skeletal hand, the spoiled leather of black skin pulled tight over bone. The digits pointed negligently across the floor. She knew who that was too. The clarity of truth was merciless.

She hunched over sharply. Both of them were gone, her parents were dead.

The tears never came. She had expected a flood. She almost wanted the ravaging release, yet she found that the river of her grief was dry, her heart was a desert. She stared at the carbonised floorboards.

She had done her weeping the night before. She found herself in a place beyond emotion, a place stripped more bare of feeling at every passing moment.

The Ring formed a glistening stripe on her finger, clear and bright. Violence and murder had been committed. She had no power to reverse the act. She could not face the Shadowcaster. Yet she felt a purpose growing within. The Dark had inflicted this wrong. The Dark that spread fear through the night, Dark that festered in Fendwarrow, and brought death to her door. Against that foe, she could fight in another way.

She would right this wrong.

"I shall dedicate my life to the Light," she whispered. She was certain. If they wouldn't take her as apprentice at Yearsend, she would find another way to serve. She would resist the Dark with every breath she took. She looked up to see the Riddler watching her.

"I dedicate my life to the Light," she repeated.

He considered her with a grave expression.

"Once is for whim, twice desire, but three times makes a vow entire," he announced. "What shall it be?" He held up a hand, as if to forestall her immediate answer.

The pause for thought only made Tabitha's resolve complete. "As you are my witness, I shall say it a third time. I dedicate my life to the Light."

"Then you have bonded yourself to that course with your word. Nothing can change it."

"Nothing shall," answered Tabitha, meeting his stare as she rose to her feet.

"Yet everything shall try to. Of that be certain."

"I will become a Lightgifter. I will remain a Lightgifter."

The Riddler dipped his head, and stepped toward her.

"Then it is only fitting that you are orbed. Will you accept your Lightstone?" He held up a silver chain. On it dangled the pale crystal orb of a Lightgifter.

Tabitha was stunned into silence. Wonder swept her common sense aside. A Lightstone! For so many years she had desired nothing else but to wear the orb. She reached out her hand to touch it. The stone was cool, white, though slightly smudged from Twardy's hands. Such stones were sacrosanct. Surely only the Rector of the Dovecote could orb her?

"Do you wish to be a Lightgifter?" the Riddler pressed.

"Yes," she said, unsteady. "But –"

She didn't get to voice her confusion. Twardy Zarost moved too fast. He slipped the smooth chain around her neck. The clasp clicked shut.

"How do you come by a Lightstone? Where –"

The terrible truth of the Riddler's trickery dawned on her. She yanked at the chain, trying to break the clasp open.

"How can you give me my mother's orb!" she cried.

He must have lifted it from her body where she lay.

"You claimed it yourself, with your words." He backed away from her anger.

"How could you do this?" she shouted. She fretted at the clasp with her fingers. The chain was tight, the orb hung close to her throat. The clasp would not open.

"I don't want this! I am not accepted by the Dovecote yet." Panic gripped her. Everybody knew you couldn't steal a Lightstone. It had to be blessed by the Dovecote, or the bearer would lose all sanity.

"I shall go mad! It's not right! Take it off!" she cried. The chain cut into her neck, but still she pulled, frantic and wild. Twardy stepped up close then, and grabbed her hands roughly.

"How easily a tale is believed," he said gently. "You shall not go mad, but there is magic in the clasp. Only death can release the orb now."

His voice became firmer, a warning. "Stop, there is nothing you can do. Who better to bear your mother's orb, than you?"

She strained against his grip, but he was immensely strong for a small man. She knew he was right, but it didn't stop the anger. She had trusted him.

"Once the clasp is closed, an orb is borne for life. Did your mother not tell you? You can never set aside the vow to serve the Light."

Twardy released her hands. She swung a fist at him, but he danced out of range.

"Oh, be calming down, girl, it won't kill you. It's a useful piece of rock. You shall have great need of it, if you are to survive on the course you have chosen."

She glared at him a while longer. Yet her thoughts were too clear, the Ring's touch too revealing to hold onto her anger. She was mad at him because he'd tricked her, and he'd only been able to because she had been dumb. The anger was useless. She needed him. There was still a Shadowcaster somewhere out there, and it was a long road to Levin.

She tried to pull the Lightstone into view, but the chain was too tight. The best she could manage was to push half the orb past her chin, where her eyes had to strain to see the smudged crystal. More soot came off the orb as her fingers rubbed its surface, revealing a stone as opaque as pure snow.

"Twardy, I am not sure if I am ready for this."

"Oh, you shall learn, surely you shall learn."

"What will they say, at the Dovecote? How can I come in before my Age, already orbed?"

"They shall accept you, if they have any sense."

What if they don't? she thought, but said nothing. She let the Lightstone drop back on its chain. It nestled snugly against her throat. It had no effect on her, not like the intense clarity of the Ring. Yet she knew it was the gateway to the Lightgifter's magic, she could learn to command the sprites through it. Wearing the Lightstone was comforting, in the way she supposed a sword comforted a soldier. It made her feel less helpless in the shattered, ruptured world that surrounded her. She would learn to command the Light.

She pushed past the Riddler, and stepped gingerly across the unstable flooring to the hearth. The skeleton upon the stones lay in delicate repose amongst the choked ashes.

"Thank you," she whispered.

The empty sockets of the fire-blackened skull seemed to moan with the passing of the wind, chilling her to silence. Nothing could ever erase the sense of duty she felt in that moment, bearing her mother's orb, and standing before her open grave.

Her mother had left her one final task.

The safe-chamber was by her feet. She knelt, and searched for the turn-stone. It was soot-stained but intact, as was most of the hearth. Ironic, she thought. The only place that survived the fire was directly beneath the fireplace. She pressed the turn-stone deep into the wall, felt it compress the mechanism at its far end. She rotated the stone on her fingertips, then pulled her hand away. The turn-stone jumped back at her through its channel, and came to rest slightly proud of the wall. She worked it free, and set it down with a thump. The safe was a secretive darkness before her.

Suddenly the Riddler thrust himself between her and the wall, his head blocking her view. "How does this work?" he asked, his voice partially swallowed by the safe.

"Do you mind?" Tabitha snapped. "This is a private place."

The Riddler peered into the safe for a moment longer, but pulled away before Tabitha could push him aside. "Wonderful!" he exclaimed. "So simple." He seemed inordinately pleased. "Go on, young Gifter, go on! Aren't you going to retrieve your pot of gold?" he asked.

"Hardly that," Tabitha answered curtly. The Riddler was beginning to work on her nerves. She knew she ought to be thankful to him for all he had done, but he was just so—irreverent.

Hardly a pot of gold. She knew they had stored their wealth in the safe, but how much would a farmer and his wife the healer have earned and saved? Yet her mother had thought it precious enough to warrant the message on the kerchief.

She reached into the depths of the safe.

The first item she found was familiar. The vial of rare spritesalt. It glistened in its translucent tube. She set it carefully in the breast pocket of her cloak.

The second time she reached into the safe, her hands found rough stone, then leather. A small bag. It was heavy, and when she pulled it out, and opened the drawstring, coins glinted up at her. The Eyrian wheel not in blackmetal, but in silver, and even gold. She jerked the drawstring shut, suddenly nervous with so much money in her hand.

A fortune. They left me a fortune.

There had been something else in the safe. She leaned in, and retrieved the last item. A leather scroll-case. She traced her fingers over the delicate design. A dove, clutching a lyre in its feet. She worked the lid loose. Dust-coloured parchments protruded from the tube, rolled tightly inside one another. She tugged at the layered scrolls, and they came free in one sheaf. The sheaf was followed by a cloud of sprites, a sudden puff of radiant dust which was wrenched away in the wind. The scrolls fluttered in her hand, restless. A page folded away from the sheaf with a snap, and Tabitha caught it before it could tear. When she folded it back against the others, she saw her mother's unmistakable script inked across the scroll.

The Riddler poked his nose over her shoulder.

"Spells?" he enquired.

"It's a song script, but it's too windy to open it out," Tabitha said, rolling the parchments quickly and returning them to their case. She was certain the scrolls were special, and secret. She would read them when she found some privacy.

She replaced the heavy turn-stone, sealing the safe. It was a useless gesture, she supposed, but she needed to feel that at least one small place in the devastation had been left intact.

Blackened ruins; broken remains of the past.

The wasted homestead was no resting place for her parents. They should be buried.

She left Zarost without explanation, and descended toward the barn. The roof was burnt, yet some of the walls were intact, and the tools lay in their place beside her father's workbench. She collected a pick and a spade. As she left, she noticed two broken ropes tied to a post. The horses must have run from the fire. At least they had lived. Maybe they had returned to the stables they knew, to wherever her father had hired them from.

Digging proved to be hard work. Her sweat gathered on her brow and became icy in the wind. She was absorbed by the simple task for a while.

Zarost joined her in silence. They used the cart to move her parents' mortal remains from the fire site to the hill behind, beneath the spreading silken tree that held such a commanding view. Her special place, her secret place. They would rest there forever.

She was planting a second silken acorn in the freshly packed earth, when steady hoofbeats made her heart leap. She whirled to face the forest. No figure was visible in the gloom of the dense trees, yet the sound was clear, the pace a steady canter. She strained desperately to identify the rider.

What if it's the Shadowcaster, come to claim the Ring?

The Riddler spoke at her side. "That rider comes from the south fork, not the west. It is not who you fear it to be."

Despite the Riddler's assertion, she noticed that he edged closer to his horse and cart.

"We should be off. We have a long, long ride ahead and a hunter at our back."

The rider burst from the trees, blue cloak swirling. A tall Sword, on an impressive roan mount. His helm glinted brightly. Twardy Zarost scuttled up to the driver's seat of his cart.

"Let us be gone!" he urged Tabitha.

"But what of the rider?"

"It's just a Sword, and we must go. He may have other business."

Tabitha accepted Zarost's hand, but paused in the motion of boarding the cart. She recognised the poise of the approaching rider, the dark, strong features, the powerful bearing.

Garyll Glavenor.

She released the Riddler's hand.

"It's the Swordmaster!" she exclaimed. "We must wait for him."

The Riddler sat atop his cart for a moment longer. His beard twitched. Then he slipped off the far side of the seat, and sprang away upon the grass. "I left something in the ruins," he called, over his shoulder. He scurried off downhill.

The Swordmaster took a while to close the distance to her. She had forgotten how clear her sight had become, how far she could see. She stood under the silken tree, wondering what she would say to Glavenor. Her surroundings told a desperate tale.

He arrived in a flurry of hooves and armour, and dropped to the ground. He took in the mounds beneath the tree, the soot and earth on her clothes and the devastation behind her all in one glance. The depth of compassion in his eyes said all he needed to say.

His strong arms encircled her. She knew he stared over her head as he held her close, knew he took in the extent of ruin. She felt his arms swell hard against her. When he pulled away from her at last, his eyes smouldered.

"Your parents." The blunt tone of the question told her that he had already guessed the truth.

Tabitha nodded mutely.

"When?" The word was loaded with gathering fury.

"Two nights ago. The S-shadowcaster, the same one, the one who came to First Light. He came, and my mother fought him. Then –"

Her voice caught in her throat. Garyll bowed his head.

"Afterwards, he followed me. To First Light. Captain Steed set a trap for him there this morning, but I don't know if it worked."

Garyll looked as if he was about to ask something, but he only nodded.

"Did you find Shadowcasters in Fendwarrow?" she asked.

"The evidence of their presence is undeniable," he said, his eyes on the ruins once more. "But they seem to avoid my sight, no matter how close I come." His knuckles cracked in a gathered fist.

"Describe this Shadowcaster for me again, if you can."

Tabitha told him what she could remember—the slate grey eyes, yellowed and cruel. The cowled black robe. The aura of cold fear. His bleached skin, red lips, empty smile. The midnight orb he had borne at his throat.

"Like that one, but dark?" Glavenor asked.

Tabitha's hands flew up to cover the Lightstone, but when she realised how ridiculous it was to try to hide, she dropped her hands again.

This is the Riddler's fault. Garyll must think I'm a grave-robber.

He didn't say anything.

The stone the Shadowcaster had worn was identical in shape and size to the Lightstone. Yet the colour at its heart couldn't be more different.

"Where is the driver that brought you here?" he asked, indicating the horse and cart nearby.

"He—went to find something he'd lost, in there." She waved a hand toward the ruins, not wanting to see the devastation just then. "He's been so kind. He found me—that night—and took me to the Tooth."

"Does he have a name?"

"Twardy Zarost. He calls himself the Riddler."

Garyll looked like he'd just bitten into a lemon. "Little wonder he has made himself scarce."

"You know him?"

"Come with me," he said, taking the reins of his horse, and leading it down the slope. "I have seen him in Fendwarrow, though not of late. He has much to answer for."

"He's done something wrong?"

Tabitha wouldn't put it past the trickster to be on the wrong side of the law. Yet she couldn't help feeling she was betraying her ally.

She slowed Garyll by his wrist. "Promise me something. Please don't do anything to him. I need him, now." Garyll met her eyes briefly.

"All right," he said at length. "For now. There are more severe crimes I must pursue."

When they reached the blackened ruins, Garyll cupped his hands to his mouth. "Come out now, Riddler. I shall not arrest you today. You are lucky to have a friend in Miss Serannon."

"Is that a truce?" came a hidden voice.

"For the moment."

"How long will that moment last?" The rolling nature of the Riddler's speech made it difficult to pinpoint where he was.

"For today," answered Garyll, ranging his attention through the ruins.

An area of stacked debris toppled outwards. Twardy Zarost emerged with a tricky grin.

"Swordmaster Glavenor, what a surprise it is to see you."

"I hope to repeat the surprise soon enough," Garyll said briefly.

Zarost jumped down from the rubble. "I know you are a man of your word, so I shall expect you to surprise me. But then it cannot be a surprise," he ended, with mock disappointment.

"None of your clever words!" warned Glavenor. "You can begin your reparations by telling me the truth. What can you tell me of this Shadowcaster I must pursue?"

"I suggest you ride hard, Swordmaster. The Captain shall need your aid. The man they were to capture this morning is more than he appears to be."

"You mean you think he shall evade capture."

"Oh, Captain Steed is good enough to catch a netted fish, but I think his blade is too blunt to scale it. He underestimates the Caster, who he knows, and who knows him. Especially who knows him."

"You seem to know a lot about this—criminal."

"That is my secret, and I cannot tell," answered Zarost, taking a wary step away from the towering Swordmaster. "You said a truce."

"For today. Now here's your side of that bargain." He glared down at the Riddler. "You take care of Miss Serannon. You break that bargain, and it'll be your neck, not your explanations I come to find."

"Garyll, it's all right," Tabitha said. "I trust him. We are going to Southwind, and on to Levin. But I had to come back here. To know."

"On my word, I shall take care with Miss Serannon," promised Zarost. "You take care with the Shadowcaster," he added.

Garyll's steely regard bored into Zarost. "A Riddler's word is not one I would always trust."

"Yet it is always spoken true," answered Zarost.

"That remains to be proved to me. You look after the girl, Riddlerman," Glavenor said gruffly. Twardy Zarost nodded gravely.

Garyll mounted his horse.

"Goodbye, Miss Serannon. I shall find you once I'm certain that justice has been served on this Shadowcaster." He clenched his reins in a tight fist.

"Thank you, Garyll. Go now. I'll be all right."

Glavenor turned and galloped off toward First Light. The Riddler watched, beside her.

"And so he's drawn to the place where he's needed the most. He understands justice well. Let us hope that his sword can cut through the shadows."

Garyll's figure was soon small, his helm glinting randomly between the trees, his horse galloping like the wind.

The Riddler guided her with a gentle hand towards the cart. They set off without delay, down toward Cellarspring and Russel, and finally Southwind, where the Amberlake glittered under the steely noon.

Tabitha watched the mounds of her parent's graves diminish with the distance. The clarity of the Ring allowed her to remain there for almost a half league. Up upon the high meadow, below the sighing silken tree. Her neck ached from the awkward position.

"Thank you, for my life," she whispered. Even quieter, so that only the rushing wind could hear her words, she breathed, "I shall serve the Light in your name."

The remains of Phantom Acres smeared into the hazy distance at last, and was lost from view. They rode.

12. GATEWAY

"Fairness is the hardest riddle of them all."—*Zarost*

"What was that?" said the Sword, sharply.

Kirjath met the soldier's gaze.

Let him rot in hell.

The soldier muttered something unintelligible in the direction of Kirjath's cell, then continued to sharpen his blade, pulling his whetstone with an even rhythm, filling the Swordhouse with the rasp of steel.

Kirjath slowly released his breath. It was crucial for the guard to remain distracted. He wasn't even sure if his plan would work, but he had to try. Time was running out. He knew that the Captain of the Sword waited upon a scout who had been sent to the Serannon farm. Once the messenger confirmed the charges against him, there would be no delaying justice. The Captain had made that much clear, for Kirjath was a murderer.

He smiled discreetly. There was no going back now. And there was only one way out. He focused on his task again, trying to keep his voice below the rasp of steel.

For a High Crime—that of murder, rape, treason and grand theft—the penalty was death by beheading. If they had any idea of his talents, they would have acted swifter, for he had earned the honour of all four counts.

The guard rose to fetch something from the far side of the room. Kirjath steeled himself for his desperate plan. He blended the pattern of the Summoning of Essence with the Gateway to the Underworld. It was a complex mental exercise, to join the two spells—one the call to Dark motes, the other the opening to call for something far more powerful, far more deadly. The Morgloth. He hoped that if they were cast at the same moment, something would come of it. He had failed to raise any Dark essence in the vicinity of the Swordhouse.

Kirjath chanted the words of the combined invocation as loudly as he dared. The air remained still before him. He repeated the words, straining to pull the Dark through the Gateway pattern with mind-power alone. His headache increased. Nothing happened. He needed Dark essence to carry his spell. Without motes, he was an impotent cripple in a cage. Kirjath stared at the rough timber walls.

The Sword returned to his sharpening.

Cursed whore of a day! How did I allow these bounders to snare me so easily?

Without magic, the Gateway would not form, and the beasts beyond could not be summoned. Kirjath closed his eyes. It was unacceptable. This could not be his end. There had to be a way.

He ran his eyes over the interior of his jail-cell. He had done it a hundred times already, searching for some weakness, some means of escape. But the cell had been designed to thwart such attempts—the small window set high in the wall was heavily barred. The walls were constructed of thick timbers, far too broad to break. The grille which separated his cell from the main room of the Swordhouse was made from iron bars as thick as his wrist. Apart from a cast-iron pail with a lid, and a low bed of packed straw, the cell was empty. Just as it had been the last time he had checked, and the time before that.

His eyes lingered on the straw of the bed, and for a second he considered the commotion he would cause if he could set it alight.

Burn! like the Lightgifter's farmhouse.

He shook his head—he had no means to light a fire, and the thought of it only brought the pain of his naked scars to the fore with a torturous jolt. He bit back a whimper.

Curses and pestilence upon them all!

He noticed an oddity in the straw mattress. Something was stuffed into the fibres, a pale scrap of paper rolled tightly to the size of a finger. It was well hidden, but the longer he looked at it the more noticeable it became. He checked on the soldier outside his cell. The Sword was now intent on polishing his blade with an oiled rag, having satisfied himself with its keen edge. Kirjath rose from the stone and sank onto the straw.

"Find comfort while you can, Shadowcaster," mocked the Sword, "it is surely your last rest." The soldier smirked, then returned to polishing.

Look closely at your reflection in the blade, tinpot. It shall be your last look.

Kirjath shifted his body on the straw. Without the shield of Dark essence, his legs, head and hands formed an unrelenting throb of agonised nerves, but he managed to reach the rolled paper. He bit back a curse as his swollen skin brushed the parchment, his fingers were clumsy and they stung continuously. He hooked the note at last, and rolled over to face the wall. It took a while to unroll the paper's tight folds, his blackened right hand being useless for the task. When the missive was finally flattened, it was a rough script he discovered, a morbid rhyme of a past prisoner.

> *My head's on the axeman's block*
> *dark beneath my neck the rock.*
> *I looked for aid, but all did fail*
> *until I turned to the iron pail.*

A prisoner capable of poetry? It was absurd, he supposed, but people acted strangely in their final hour. He understood the panic and pressure the man must have felt, the kind of desperation that conjured images of dark rock beneath the neck. He lingered over the final line.

Nonsense. What was the iron pail, and how would that have helped the doomed man? The poet must have been delirious, drawing words from his surrounds to complete the rhyme. There was the pail of water in his cell, though. Despite himself, Kirjath crawled over to it, and worked the lid free.

The water was as dark as oil.

Although the pail was almost full, he could move it with ease. The liquid didn't slosh over the rim either, it stayed at the same level. Perfectly still. Weightless. Dark essence.

The message had been for him. He had an ally. The note must have been placed in the cell before he had been brought to the Swordhouse. Someone had known he would come there, and had provided him a way out. Who but a Shadowcaster could fill a pail with motes? Too many elements didn't add up. Yet the questions could wait. Time was wearing thin.

He had a new plan.

He summoned the motes. There would be enough for the Gateway. His body's needs would have to wait.

The main door to the Swordhouse burst open. A tall, severe soldier blocked the daylight. Kirjath recognised the angular face immediately. The Swordmaster of Eyri.

He ignored his rising panic, and spoke the first words of the Gateway, pushing his motes outwards to form their pattern. A second soldier burst through the door, and stood to a weaving attention before the Captain—the scout that had been dispatched earlier. He blurted out his report.

"The Serannons have been murdered, the farm is burned to the ground. Justice on that man!" His finger stabbed the air.

The Swordmaster was already running toward Kirjath's cell. His sharp eyes had spotted the slither of motes, no doubt.

The motes completed a wide circle before Kirjath's feet. Slick filaments of Dark wound across the stone floor, flickering to their place inside the pattern. Then the Gateway was complete.

All he had to do was to say the word.

The door to his cell was unlocked, wrenched aside, and the Swordmaster had drawn his blade all in one precious moment. But he was too late. Kirjath drew his lips back in a snarling, triumphant grin.

The Swordmaster's broad blade whistled towards him, but Kirjath ducked and rolled away.

There was no mercy in the eyes that hunted him. Kirjath hadn't expected any. He was going to need all the speed he could muster. He formed a command in his mind, to be ready for his beast.

Throw the first man aside.

"Step through the Gate, and enter my mind," shouted Kirjath, running to avoid another sword-strike. The stone inside the circle darkened.

"What?"

I speak to my Morgloth, and not to you.

The stone had become a swirling pool, a whirlpool of night, reaching down into endless depths. The spell was complete, the Morlgoth called. Kirjath felt a surging hunger. And the demon was upon them.

The beast launched through the Gateway with its purpose already set. Black talons gripped the Swordmaster, and lifted him. He was thrown hard against the iron bars of the cell wall. His helm skittered over the floor. The Swordmaster crumpled against the bars.

At the others. I must escape.

The Morgloth leapt for the cell door, and dived outward at the nearest Sword. The jailhouse was full of easy prey. The men stood stunned, mouths agape. The first Sword didn't even raise his arms in time to ward against the vicious jaws. He made a squeak before his head was bent back on sharp talons.

Kirjath savoured the familiar mind-link of the channelling—strong, clear, wild images flooded him. The Morgloth felt more powerful than the last time. Kirjath revelled in the death-ecstasy for the briefest moment. The Morgloth tore the Sword's head off at the neck.

The remaining Swords scattered.

The guard who Kirjath had marked for death, the one who had yanked the rope during his passage to the jail, was running for the main door, wailing. Kirjath bent his will to change the Morgloth's path, and the demon launched itself at the fleeing man. The beast cloaked the soldier with its giant wings, and crushed him to the floor. Kirjath could sense the hunger and blood-lust in the beast as if the thoughts were his own, exciting, almost disgusting in their intensity. He shared the fatal bite again. The exhilarating rush. The mist of the soldier's spirit was swallowed into the emptiness of the Morgloth's hunger. Bliss, strength and ecstacy.

Cold steel against his throat brought Kirjath instantly back to reality. He was being cut, deeper and deeper. The Swordmaster had recovered from his fall, somehow he was right there beside him. Glavenor spoke harsh words into Kirjath's ear.

"Halt your beast, or you'll die. This sword goes through your throat." Kirjath sensed the demon launching itself from the far side of the Swordhouse, its attack focused on Kirjath's assailant.

"Halt it!" the Swordmaster shouted, jerking his sword deeper into Kirjath's neck. "You'll die before I do."

Blood was already flowing, and a small jerk on the grip of the sword would be the end. Kirjath threw his desperate mental command at the lurching demon, adding his voice in a hoarse croak.

"Back! Get back!" He waved his hand at the Morgloth, gagging on the pressure on his throat. The beast resisted within his mind, as if part of him wanted to continue the strike, to fall on the dark-haired Swordmaster who stood with blade outstretched, to bite into the neck so proudly exposed.

At the last moment, the beast halted its strike. It slid to a halt an arm's length from Kirjath. Its eyes were red and hell-fired. It strained against his command, but made no attack.

"Banish your beast," the Swordmaster demanded. Again, the punctuation of the blade.

The bastard will kill me the moment it's gone.

"Free passage," Kirjath wheezed, fighting back a cough. "I want free passage."

"You'll die before I let you escape."

"So will you, if you kill me now. My beast lives on."

"I have no fear of death. I do what is right."

"And your compatriots, friends, and innocents?" Kirjath retorted. He noticed that the other Swords lingered near the door, unsure whether to flee, or to trust their Swordmaster's might. "The beast knows no end to its hunger. If I am not commanding it, if I do not banish it, it will feed on every life it finds. You've felt its strength already. You shall not match it, you shall never stop it."

It was a gamble. The Swordmaster had not yet killed him, which meant he did not understand. Without Kirjath's active will, the demon would cease to have access to the mortal world. Kirjath's mind was the real gateway through which the Morgloth lived. A swift turn of the Swordmaster's blade would end both him and the threat of the beast. But the Swordmaster had not yet killed him. He didn't know the truth.

Blood dripped from the Swordmaster's blade to the floor. The Morgloth screeched with frustration, but stayed where it was. If the Swordmaster became any redder with his fury, he would ignite all on his own. "My word, then," the Swordmaster said between clenched teeth. "Banish the beast, and you'll have passage from this Swordhouse, but only from this Swordhouse."

"I should take your word?" scoffed Kirjath, his arrogance swelling. If the Swordmaster was offering a deal, there was possibility for more manipulation.

"My word is my deed," the Swordmaster growled. "Banish your beast now. I shall let you reach the door."

Kirjath sneered. "Do you think I am an idiot? The cowards at the door shall cut me down the moment the beast is gone." He considered the deadlock for a moment. "Call your friends into the cell, let them stand here before my beast. One twinge on your sword, and they will die before I fall. Then you shall die, with the future blood of Eyri upon your hands."

This might just work, Kirjath reflected, trying to piece the moves together into a plan. Give and take, truth and fake, there had to be a way to freedom.

"Only if the cell door is locked, so your beast can't escape," Glavenor countered. "The Swords have sworn their lives to the protection of Eyri, and we are all prepared to fight to the death. But I will not risk the lives of innocent Eyrians to your demon."

Kirjath swallowed against the pressure of the blade. He could feel more blood trickling down his neck and into his cloak. "The

Morgloth will depart, but you chase me then, and I'll call his name before I fall."

Glavenor nodded his assent, and prompted the first move. "Men, to the cell. Trust me in this." The command in his voice was intense. Even so, the Swords came with reluctance. They knew their lives were being traded, and could only hope that the Swordmaster knew what he was doing. Kirjath saw the greying Captain shoot the Swordmaster a warning glance, but even he stepped into the cell and stood beside the men. They formed a nervous huddle against the wall. All of them needed a two handed grip to steady their light blades. Kirjath savoured their expressions for a moment.

Testimony to their stupidity that they believe their Swordmaster.

They were bait, in a delicious trap based solely on a bluff. The Swordmaster could have twisted his blade at any time, and ended it all. He didn't know.

Kirjath focused on the area of his own consciousness that was the Morgloth. He felt a resistance to his command. The demon was displeased to return to the Underworld. The hunger was not sated, it would never be sated. The beast flashed wicked fangs at its master as it crossed the stones with a ponderous gait. It halted just short of the circular void that was the Gateway, shifting and weaving with frustration. It would only be a short lunge from where it stood to the fearful men.

"I want to feel the breeze of freedom on my back, before I surrender my beast," said Kirjath. "At the door, you remove your blade. I shall banish the beast." He began to back slowly toward the cell door, away from the towering form of the Morgloth. Glavenor matched his pace exactly, stepping with fluid grace, as if in a dance. The sword remained steady against Kirjath's throat. The Swordmaster pulled the cell door after them. It clanged shut, and he slid the heavy bolt into place.

"Right, a little space then," ordered Kirjath, eyeing the tall Swordmaster over his shoulder. "Remove your blade, and I'll remove my hungry friend."

The Swordmaster took a step away from Kirjath, lowering his blade to a ready position. They eyed each other like alley cats, poised for action should either relent on their word. Glavenor tracked him as he backed to the main door.

"Move against me, and the Morgloth has a feeding frenzy. I just need a word," Kirjath warned. The Swordmaster nodded in silence, his stance as taught as a drawn bowstring. His free hand rested on the door handle, barring Kirjath's exit.

"Banish it."

"You'll never open the door."

"And if I do, you'll not banish the beast."

So the Swordmaster was not so stupid after all. Kirjath searched for a solution to the recurrent deadlock.

In the instant that his thoughts wandered, the Morgloth strained against its mental leash. Hunger, bloodlust, anger and frustration assaulted Kirjath's mind. He barely regained his dominance in time. The Morgloth screeched and yowled at him, resisting him with every fibre of its being. It had to go.

The main door was wrenched open. It caught the Swordmaster by surprise, and for a moment he was forced to move away from Kirjath as a soldier stumbled into the room, a sheepish grin on his face. He smelled of cheap wine.

"Victor, stand clear!" The Swordmaster's warning was too late. Kirjath had seen his opening. With a snarl, he threw his body weight at the man, striking the soldier viciously against his breastplate. Kirjath's ruined hands hit armour, and pain ripped through his arms, but the drunk fell heavily against the Swordmaster, knocking him away. Kirjath came away with the soldier's dagger in his hand, but he didn't pause to use it.

He leapt instead through the open door, and slammed it closed behind him. He dropped to his knees, and wedged the dagger under the door jamb. The mental command he gave to a certain beast was simple, and clear. Although he knew he should run, he couldn't resist a shout of triumph to the man inside the door.

"That is what you get for opposing Kirjath Arkell. If you follow me, you shall taste worse!"

Then he drew his tattered black robes close, and ran away through the back streets of First Light.

The door shuddered behind him, but held. If he judged the Swordmaster correctly, there would be no pursuit. Not at first. The screams of soldiers filled the air. Kirjath smirked as he bolted past uncertain villagers. The gloom of the forest beckoned in the distance.

Glavenor would save his men, before he thought to give chase. He was too noble a man, too just to be ruthless enough, too honest to sacrifice his men. A burly villager stepped into the street to block his way, but Kirjath simply ducked down an alley, and continued in his flight. The wind of freedom gave speed to his gait. He ignored the pain. No one would catch him now.

The Swordmaster really did not know the first thing about the beast he faced. Already Kirjath could feel the link fading, weakening as he moved out of the Morgloth's range. He would not be able to continue the channelling for much longer, he was already further from his minion than he had ever attempted before. Once beyond the limit of his mental range, the beast would be gone, wrenched back into the Underworld whether it wanted to or not. But for as long as he could, Kirjath Arkell was going to hold onto the Morgloth, keep it this side of the Gateway.

For his beast was feeding.

Garyll Glavenor knew before he heard the scratch of the dagger that they were in trouble. He heard the Shadowcaster's taunt. His shoulder rebounded from the jammed door. He spun, just in time to see the nightmare beast pounce upon Sword Ayche within the locked cell. Ayche's screams were cut short.

Glavenor raced to the iron door, with a sickness and rage building in his throat. Another Sword he recognised beat against the bars, but Garyll didn't blame him for his cowardice. The Morgloth was draining the life from its prey just behind him. The Captain was the only other man still standing in the cell. His sword scythed across the beast's elongated head, issuing a screech of tortured metal. The Morgloth batted the Captain aside.

Glavenor shot the bolt and wrenched the cell door open.

"Form at my shoulder!" he commanded the Sword. The terrified man turned reluctantly as Glavenor blocked the exit, but he seemed to take courage from Garyll's advance on the beast.

The Morgloth had consumed what it wanted from its third prey, and was rounding on the Captain. Steed had regained his feet, but slashed the air dazedly as he backed toward Glavenor. The Morgloth avoided his blows easily.

Glavenor swung his massive blade in a full circle overhead, hoping against hope that Felltang would have enough speed to penetrate the awful skin of the Morgloth. His sword whined as it cut the air. The Morgloth halted its advance, its head tilted in puzzlement.

Glavenor struck, aiming for the glistening neck. But at the last, as

Felltang shrieked its death howl, the legs of the Morgloth buckled, and it dropped beneath the arc of Garyll's blade.

Surprise lasted only a fraction of a heartbeat, for he knew his art. He used the off-balanced energy of the missed strike to swirl himself in a full turn, then brought the blade downwards in an arc that intersected the Morgloth's wing. Felltang found its mark, and bit deep. The wing was sliced almost to the trailing edge, yet there it held his blade with the tough grip of boiled leather.

The Morgloth launched itself at Garyll with all the strength of its pain and rage. Whatever spell had brought it to its knees was gone.

Garyll was seized in a clawed hand and hurled toward the roof. He yanked Felltang free. He braced himself as his helm slammed stars into his vision. Then he was falling toward the beast. He pointed Felltang downwards at the gaping maw of teeth below. The Morgloth may have jumped clear of his descent; he was too dizzy to be sure.

The impact of the floor brought the stars rushing back. He couldn't see where the Morgloth was, and all he could do was to swing Felltang in a desperate circle around his body. The low howl of the fluted blade surrounded him. His vision cleared once more.

The Morgloth was unsteady before him, weaving on soft legs.

Did I hit it on the way down?

He swung Felltang overhead, an instinctive reaction to the opening in his opponent's defence.

Before he could sink his blade into the beast a second time, the Morgloth jumped away. It issued a terrible screech, and jerked backwards over the stones to the dark circle it had emerged from. It didn't look like retreat to Garyll, for the Morgloth threw its talons outwards to the rim of the crater, clutching even with its ruined wing to the stone. An instant later, it was gone, sucked through the strange gateway into the depths of the Underworld.

The dark hole closed up. The dull grey of the original stone returned. Garyll did not attempt to understand what had just taken place. Justice was more important.

"Captain, I must pursue the Shadowcaster," he shouted as he ran. "If you should ever see him again, kill him on sight."

◆ ——————— ◆

Barely an hour after the Swordmaster had departed, two figures approached the Swordhouse. Captain Steed watched them through the narrow front window, his gaze as empty as the goblet in his hands.

A tall, fervent man and a regal blonde woman. They were dressed in the garb of Lightgifters. They looked weary, though the man had a hungry look about him. He wanted something, he needed something, and the imminent demand he bore irritated Captain Steed the way a loose splinter irritates a wound. He had no time for pompous visitors. He had no time for anyone.

He was sinking in his private sea of despair. He had lost three of his men, and because he hadn't acted swiftly enough. The Shadowcaster should have been executed the moment he was brought into custody. Instead, it was his men who had paid the ultimate price. They had been a little blunt, but they had been his Swords, his companions. His friends.

The Lightgifters entered.

"If you're here for the Shadowcaster, you're late. He's already left," Captain Steed muttered. He didn't bother looking them in the eye. They could hang for all he cared.

"The innkeeper at the Tooth-and-Tale tells us you took a Shadowcaster prisoner for murder," the man said. "You've let him go?"

"He has escaped. You can see for yourself what it cost us," Steed said in a toneless voice. He waved his empty goblet to where Victor was preparing the bodies for burial. Ayche was being bound in white linen, beside his two fallen comrades.

Of all the men, I'm left with the drunk, he thought, then regretted the spiteful sentiment immediately. He didn't wish to exchange death for death. He wished them all alive.

"Who are you to ask?" Steed said gruffly, still not looking directly at the intruders. He sloshed another portion of the dark wine into his goblet from a depleted bottle. It had started with two fingers, just to steady his nerves.

"Why don't you pursue him, man? You're letting a murderer get away?"

Captain Steed took a long time to answer. He forced his hands to remain steady on the desk.

"Our best man is already tracking him. It is none of your concern." Steed heard his own voice hardening. "I say again : who are you to ask?"

"My name is Rosreece," the tall Lightgifter answered. "Is the tracker the same best man who let him escape? It sounds as if you need our abilities to apprehend this Shadowcaster."

Steed snorted. This Lightgifter was terribly full of himself. "Your healing essence won't be enough."

"Hah! It sounds like you are in awe—of a mere Shadowcaster!"

"Ros, don't –" the woman began, in a pacifying tone.

"It seems the might of the Sword is not what it was," Rosreece asserted, ignoring the woman's gentling hand as well. "We shall apprehend him, of that you can be sure."

The goblet buckled in the Captain's hand, metal crumpling like paper. Liquid trickled over his white knuckles.

"Have you ever dealt with a Shadowcaster, cockerel? This man has a beast at his command, the likes of which we have never seen. A vicious, deadly demon."

"The Morgloth!" exclaimed the woman. "Oh Ros, it's true! Oh Mercy!"

"That's why we're here!" Rosreece said. "To capture the creature of the Dark, to meet the Shadowcaster's threat. Doesn't seem as if your tinpots do too well at it."

Captain Steed cleared the desk from his seat. He had the arrogant Gifter off the floor with a stranglehold before he could restrain himself. The crumpled goblet skittered across the floor in his wake. With his free hand he forced Rosreece's head to point towards the corner of the room, where the three bound corpses rested. "Open your eyes, Gifter. Look at my men—ravaged, dead. My men! Your ignorance of this Shadowcaster's power will lead you straight to the grave."

Rosreece's eyes bulged, but he struggled to make his voice heard. "I don't expect mere Swords to have an understanding of matters of essence. You have been fooled. There are ways to counter the illusions of the Dark. Put me down."

"A fool, am I?" the Captain hissed. Rosreece's face reddened under the intensified grip. "Leave us now, before I do something permanent about your manners." He threw the Lightgifter back towards the woman. Her shocked gaze had not left the bodies in the corner.

"I'm leaving, I'm leaving," said Rosreece, in a voice that aimed to be threatening but came out more like a petulant whine. "At least one of us cares about upholding the law. I am going to bring this Shadowcaster to justice, seeing as how the mighty Sword has failed once already. Come, Hosanna." He spun on his heel, and made to grab for the woman. But she avoided his hand. She met Captain Steed's eye.

"Was it a Morgloth?" she asked, hushed.

Captain Steed bowed his head. "Yesterday, I would have called you a fool to suggest such a thing. Today I have seen the legend return. There is a Shadowcaster who commands a Morgloth. May you have better luck than us when you cross his path."

13. FISHERMAN'S REVENGE

"The fish that learns to spit out the hook,
always feeds well."—*Zarost*

Riding beside Twardy Zarost in his cart was better than walking, but not much better, Tabitha decided. The hard-sprung wheels felt every bump and crack in the bad road, and the wooden seat passed the message on. She wished there was more than just a blanket underneath her backside.

Twardy Zarost grinned at her and bounced clear out of the seat as they passed over yet another rock. He seemed to be enjoying himself immensely. His racoon-striped hat perched defiantly on his head. They reached a straighter section of road, and Twardy clucked to the grey mare, urging her into a trot. Tabitha grimaced as corrugations juddered her view of the countryside. Her hood slipped from her head, but a sharp glance from Zarost told her to pull the cowl up once more as a group of farming youths with herding dogs approached. They were harmless locals, probably returning from selling livestock at Cellarspring, but the Riddler had made it clear from the first that her face must remain hidden or she would be returned to the wine barrel.

The land fell away steadily as they rode through Meadowmoor County towards the Amberlake. From time to time, the road ran precariously close to the rim of a deep river gorge on their left. The River of Falls thundered down the cleft, filling the air with its moist breath. Alders, pines and silken trees flanked the river like proud sentinels guarding their precious water.

Tabitha just absorbed the detail of the scenery, not wanting to think. Her mind was filled with waterfalls and gentling hills, shimmering trees and the twisting brown course of the road to Amberlake. The road improved once it had descended from the high ground, and by mid-afternoon they passed through the bustling town of Cellarspring and took the turn to Russel. As they traversed the lower farmlands, they passed farmers driving ploughs through the fertile soils of spring. It was the first week of the month of Furrow, a good time for sowing.

Seeing the familiar activity reminded Tabitha of one farm that would not be worked at all. Here, the ploughshares turned around and around, ignorant of how they cut deeper into her grief. And so the wind which blew at their backs found its bite again. Tabitha searched for another distraction.

"What does a Riddler do?" she asked, breaking the long silence.

Twardy Zarost grinned and jutted his beard into the air. "A Riddler's work is a simple thing. I must hide the truth without lying."

"Do you ever speak straight?"

Zarost laughed. "You mean to say am I ever not a Riddler?"

"When do you say exactly what you mean?"

"Always will I tell the truth, always near the Ring, forsooth."

"But you're always confusing me. All your answers have two meanings, or more."

"If some people do not understand the Riddler it is because they are not hearing properly." He waggled a finger at her. "If some people listened more dearly, they may be able to hear things clearly."

He had slipped through her fingers again. Tabitha understood Garyll's wariness of Zarost. To a man like Garyll, who lived by separating right from wrong, the Riddler's riddles would be infuriating.

"What did you do to anger the Swordmaster?"

Zarost leant close to Tabitha, and whispered, "I stole his sword, his great big sword, upon the wharf market in Levin." He drew away from her again, beaming with glee. "He's lucky I didn't steal his boots. Or his underwear." He laughed, immensely pleased.

"How? How do you steal the Swordmaster's sword?" Despite herself, she couldn't shake the image of Garyll Glavenor standing in a busy market, having recently lost his clothes. She hid her grin.

"He was distracted."

"But he discovered you," Tabitha asserted, trying to be stern once more.

"Much, much later. I tried to sell the sword many times. Everybody knew about it. Strange that nobody wanted to buy the sword, when I told them to whom it belonged."

"But why?" It seemed a risky thing to attempt.

"I wanted to show one man that the thing he most treasured could be lost if he did not take care of it."

Tabitha regarded him anew. The Riddler was stranger than she had ever suspected. Risking the ire of the Swordmaster, purely to lay a moral lesson? It sounded unbelievable, yet she wondered if his tale was supposed to hold a lesson for her as well. Her fingers found the Ring, then the Lightstone at her throat, and finally the bag of coins. Acknowledging her treasures only made her feel her loss more keenly. The greatest treasure had already been taken from her life.

"Where am I to go, if I am to take care of my treasure?" she asked.

"The Ring will help you to see the path to knowledge, but you may not always have the courage to do what is right."

"Why do you hide everything in twisted words, why do you try to confuse me with answers that aren't answers. Why can't you just tell me what I should do?"

"I am here to be the Riddler, nothing more."

"Why?"

"I made a promise to the wizard, whose ring you wear. I must guide you to find that wizard."

"But why don't you just take it to the wizard yourself?"

"Bear the Ring? That really would be the end of me." He laughed, though Tabitha didn't catch the joke. "No, far better you wear it, and I be riddling all the roads for you."

"You make no sense at all!" Tabitha said, turning away from his insistent smile. Her frustration had reached breaking point. "Crazy man," she whispered, well below audible level given the noise of the cart and the passing breeze.

"I am not completely without a heart, young Tabitha," he reprimanded her.

Tabitha felt abashed. She had not meant to be mean. The Riddler waved her apologies aside.

"You are mostly right, for everyone misunderstands me. That is how it should be—few are worthy. If I didn't riddle, then I would lead. And so, you would follow me and not seek your own truth. No new talent would be born in Eyri, Chaos would finally overwhelm us all, and we would lose the war."

Tabitha tried to stave off the question, but it was impossible to ignore the glaring inconsistency.

"What war?"

"The war against Chaos, it continues as we speak. I do battle in my own way."

Zarost really was crazy.

"War? We've had peace in Eyri forever!"

"So it would seem, so it would seem. You live under a powerful protection."

"King Mellar and his Sword uphold justice. Who would we fight? The Shadowcasters, maybe. But that's not a war, is it?"

"You should study your legends more closely, Miss Serannon. Just because things appear at the dawn of Time doesn't mean they don't endure. The appearance of peace doesn't mean that Riddlers aren't needed."

"There wasn't a Riddler at the dawn of Time," Tabitha stated flatly.

Zarost chortled. "If there hadn't been a Riddler, there would be no Eyri at all. Not as you know it. No, it would be something else, entirely." He looked up towards Fynn's Tooth. "So would the world. So would the world. All because we have a Riddler."

"What are you doing with me then, if you have a war to wage?" Tabitha asked, shifting in her seat to look directly at Twardy Zarost. He returned her gaze with a twinkle in his eye, his browned face crinkling like parchment.

"Why, riddling, of course."

"But why with me?"

"You are trying to find the wizard, you have the Wizard's Ring. That you succeed is important in the war. Especially now that everything has begun to change." He raised an eyebrow in her direction.

"What is changing?"

"The fabric of the universe, I believe. You forget what is in your heart, and in your hands," the Riddler said slyly. He clicked and twitched the reins, urging the flagging grey mare into a trot again.

Tabitha realised with a start that she held her mother's scroll-tube. She had been tumbling it over and over for minutes, without being conscious of it. She hastily tucked the worked leather case inside her cloak once more. Out of sight, where it belonged.

They slammed over a ditch and bounced high, but Twardy Zarost did not slacken his pace. Ahead, a long straight led downwards between two large hills. The rich green slopes were dotted with sheep and the first of the spring's bright daisies. Beyond the vee of the hills was a glistening body of water, tranquil and jewel-like in the centre of Eyri. Amberlake. When she turned to look back to Fynn's Tooth, it seemed far away. The sun was already falling through the western sky. They had yet to reach the artist's village of Russel, where the houses were built upon stilts amongst the reeds. Soft-press paper and oil-paint came from Russel, and some of the best paintings in all of

Eyri.

Tabitha wondered if they were still extending the stoneroad from Southwind along the shore. It would be dark by the time they reached that lakeside village.

The man who had challenged the theft lay unconscious in the dust of the stable-yard on the outskirts of First Light. Kirjath had wished to kill him, but he had neither the time nor the energy to summon the Morgloth again. He needed to be frugal with the little Dark essence he could summon.

It hadn't taken many motes to still the farmer's thoughts, to render him cataleptic. The man had stared blankly as Kirjath had clubbed him to the ground. The farmer would awake later with the mother of all headaches, and not the best of moods. He would likely be unfriendly towards Shadowcasters. All of this worried Kirjath naught, for he was long gone.

The black charger he had stolen was big and fast, but it fought his command every step of the way. It fought while it ran in terror, for it dared not vary its course from the one that the swooping ravens demanded.

Give this bloody horse an inch, and it will turn against me.

Kirjath held on to the pommel of his saddle with his swollen left hand, grinding his teeth against the agony. The reins were tied short, and they lay untended on the stallion's mane. He didn't need the reins, he just needed to stay mounted—his birds would do the rest. His thighs ached.

Two Morrigán bracketed the stallion, flying in tight formation on either side of its head. Whenever the horse veered left or right from the road, the ravens closed, making to strike for the stallion's eye on the offending side with horrible screeches, wicked beaks wide open. After the first few strikes, they only needed to maintain formation at the limit of the horse's vision. It ran, in a panic-stricken gallop, with ears laid flat against his head, and rolling eyes.

The speed had been necessary to escape the Swordmaster. As Kirjath had pulled ahead, he had been able to draw more Dark to himself, and it had become easier to avoid pursuit, to lay false trails and cast illusions into the woods until he had completely shaken his tail. Then he had sent one of his ravens ahead.

The Morrigán had brought him news of a cart with two passengers, one with a striped hat, the other hidden beneath a cowl. He had driven the horse harder, but he had reached the burned farmhouse too late.

There were footprints in the mud beside the gate, footprints in the ash of the devastation. Two sets of fresh footprints—a pair of soft-soled leather boots, and a small pair with a light tread. The girl, and the wagoneer, he was sure. Who else would have visited the ruins, and built two fresh graves on the hill?

The twin tracks of the cart had been easy to follow, leaving the farm on the Southwind road. It was just a matter of time.

◆ ——————◆

A chuckling stream emerged from the hills to their right, and cut across their path on its way to the larger River of Falls. They descended the winding path to ford it at its narrowest point. However, when they reached the water, Twardy Zarost dismounted from the cart, and urged Tabitha to do the same.

"Help me with the harness."

"I thought we had to hurry!" Tabitha said. She looked over her shoulder. A copse of trees stood rustling on the crest of the bowl. "Why are we stopping?"

"If your bottom is stiff, then think what Horse feels, and you'll know why we stop."

Tabitha winced as she stretched her legs down over the side. She ached in every joint, not just in her behind. The horse was lathered in sweat, and hung its head gratefully down to the water. Twardy loosened the bridle, and together with Tabitha, lifted the harness from the horse's back. He slapped the mare's rump, and she took a few steps out into the cooling stream, snorting thirstily at the water.

"What's her name?" Tabitha asked.

"I call her Horse," said Twardy, with an amused expression. "Because she's a horse."

"That's not a real name! You can't—she must –"

Tabitha frowned, and placed her hands on her hips, the way Mrs Quilt did when she ordered something in the kitchen and expected to see it done.

"Lazy," he suggested, his face cracking into familiar lines.

"No! She must be something more special than that," she said, looking at the lopsided burst of white on the mare's forehead. "What about Starburst, or Flicker. Or Blaze!"

"Be lazy, then," Zarost announced, raising an eyebrow. Tabitha didn't get it, at first.

"You mean Blazey?"

"B*lazey*," he agreed, much amused.

Tabitha held his eye. She knew he would turn every name she suggested upside down or inside out. She gave up trying to outwit the Riddler. The horse would be called Blazey, and she'd know what it meant.

The horse was taking long draughts from the stream. Tabitha kicked off her boots and waded out into the stream. It was cold. She halted uncertainly at the mare's side, and shot Twardy a tentative glance.

"Can I?" she asked, scooping up some of the chilly water with her hands.

He nodded. "Keep the sweat off your clothes, or we'll have to rename you as well."

Tabitha washed the sweat-stains from Blazey's legs. The mare nuzzled her briefly, then returned to sucking at the water.

They rested for a while in the glade. The stream chuckled incessantly. Then all too soon, the Riddler harnessed up again.

"Come on, B*lazey*," he called out.

The horse twitched her ears. The bumpy ride resumed.

◆ ——————— ◆

Long after the visitors had moved from the ford, after the cart had disappeared up the steep bank of the hollow, leaving deep cuts in the loam, the sound of a galloping horse filled the trees. The black horse snorted deeply with each breath, compelled by its fear to bear its dark rider. It emerged from the copse of alders at a desperate gait, and launched itself down the steep slope. Five giant leaps finished the winding descent by a forced short-cut, and the stallion bore its dread passenger into the ford. The charger struck a submerged rock, and it stumbled to its knees. The stream exploded around it with icy water.

The stallion eyed the water longingly, and made to quench its raging thirst. But the rider hissed, and the vicious birds swooped in close. Squealing with panic, the stallion heaved itself upright, and jumped through the shallows. It strained up the far bank, kicking loose stone and soil out as the rider forced another short-cut, and then it was gone, the hoofbeats leaving a shocked silence in the glen.

◆ ——————— ◆

Tabitha breathed a sigh of relief. They had made good time, and the twilight had barely begun to thicken the shadows as they entered Southwind. They had been on stoneroad almost all the way from Russel, and it was smooth and level and easy on the wheels.

Most of the windows of the buildings they passed were lit, and the smells of cooking spilled out into the narrow main street. The low dwellings were made from slender planks, and they crowded into the street in an almost jovial way. Their thatch roofs, capped with sand-bags, extended close to the ground. The street curved from side to side as various buildings blurred on the straight line. A disordered place, yet friendly.

The village inn boasted a double storey. A sign hanging slightly skew on its knotted white rope boasted that Southwind's finest food was at the Kingfisher's Breeze. They passed the inn by, though not without Tabitha giving its open doors a longing glance. She hadn't eaten since the night before at the Tooth-and-Tale. She'd taken no breakfast before she had been bundled into a certain smelly wine barrel. It seemed like an age had passed since the morning.

The villagers whom they passed offered gentle greetings, as peaceful as the lake that lapped against the shore nearby. The Riddler guided the cart along the main street to a large wharf at the water's edge, then turned left along the shore to a lone building which stood half on stilts. The fading pink of dusk lingered on the wooden walls— one storey on the landward side, but a full three where the house projected ponderously over the lake and dropped to a lower level of jetties. Small watercrafts were moored below.

"Mulrano lives here. He might speed you on your journey," said Zarost. He brought the cart to a halt beside a large door set in the side of the house. He jumped down, and walked around Blazey's drooping head. He whistled a clear starling's call at the upper window, then hauled the door open along its grinding track.

"Bring Blazey through, we'd best be out of sight," he said, waving Tabitha on as he scanned the darkened sky. Tabitha looked back into the darkening village, and she felt a twinge of fear as she grabbed the reins, but there was nothing sinister in Southwind that she could identify. Still, it felt as is somebody was watching her. She twitched the reins the way she had seen the Riddler do. Blazey plodded forwards on leaden feet, and they passed into the concealing gloom of the boathouse.

The owner of the boathouse soon appeared. Mulrano had a friendly, weathered face, with bushy black eyebrows and a big grizzled chin.

He welcomed them in, by way of a back-slapping hug for Zarost and a shake of his oar-like hand for Tabitha, but he didn't say a thing. There was something strange about Mulrano.

He ushered them into his softly furnished lounge. He smiled and nodded. He showed Tabitha to the washroom with a gesture and a bow of his head. He prepared a meal for the weary travellers without a word. They ate in silence.

When they sat in their woven cane chairs beside the fire, and Tabitha complimented Mulrano on his fine cooking, he acknowledged her with a nod of his head. Tabitha's questions about the prosperity of Southwind brought yet another smile, but no answer. He listened attentively as Twardy Zarost told their tale, his eyebrows rising in his craggy face as Tabitha's need for hasty passage to Levin was explained.

He seemed to chew for a while, though he had already cleared his plate of food.

"Please, Mister Mulrano, I can pay for my passage. Will you help me?" Tabitha asked.

Mulrano made a strange gesture at Twardy, twiddling the first two fingers of his right hand.

Maybe he can't speak, Tabitha thought. She shot the Riddler a sharp glance. Zarost grinned indulgently.

"Yes, friend Mulrano is as mute as a minnow, or more truly a mule, for he can make a sound, but the words do not come out as he intends, do they Mulrano? So he prefers to say nothing."

"Why didn't you say?" she challenged Zarost, colour rising to her cheeks.

"You needed a puzzle to keep your mind occupied. Mulrano wants to know if you can swim."

She looked incredulously at the Riddler, then at Mulrano, then hastily looked away.

Mercy, he can't speak. How was I supposed to know?

It was obvious, she supposed, but a little warning would have spared the silly questions. It was Zarost's way, she was discovering, to surround himself with as many riddles as possible. She made a hasty attempt to answer Mulrano's question.

"In summer we swim in the river-pool. I know enough not to drown."

"Your canoe will be the fastest," Zarost told Mulrano.

Mulrano shook his head, and frowned at the Riddler. He rolled his hands, and pointed to himself.

"I fear the morning will be too late," said Zarost.

Mulrano shook his head again, with not a little anger in his eye. He gestured at Tabitha with one raised finger, then pointed to the dark night visible through the lakeside windows. His hand made an obvious sign of a capsizing boat. "Foop!" he said.

"But we do not know where the Shadowcaster is!" Zarost argued with Mulrano. "Already in this village he could be, touch wood that's a fallacy. She must go tonight. The canoe is the fastest thing she can handle. She does not know how to sail, do you, Tabitha Truthsayer?"

She averted her gaze. Admitting to a sailor that one couldn't sail seemed like admitting to a farmer that you didn't know which end of a sheep to feed. "N-no." She picked at the hem of her cloak. The furnishings were so soft, the fire glowed so warmly, and the aroma of their meal lingered in the air. "Do you really think the Shadowcaster is still after me?" The threat of the Shadowcaster was something which belonged to the night outside. "Are you sure Captain Steed didn't catch him? Maybe we could just stay the night."

"Shatter the sun!" the Riddler exclaimed, jumping to his feet. "There is your answer!" He pointed to the window. They spun to face the blackened glass.

At first Tabitha saw nothing, but Mulrano stiffened beside her, and then she made out a vague shape on the windowsill in the darkness outside. A glassy black eye peered at her. A sharp beak glistened with reflected light. Then with a grating cry, the raven lifted off the windowsill and disappeared into the night.

"Morrigán!" Twardy spat the word out. "You can be sure his caster is close behind. You must go, girl. Not to Levin, but to Stormhaven, there's no time. You'll be safer on the King's Isle than anywhere in Eyri."

Mulrano placed a firm hand on Zarost's chest and held his gaze. He tapped on his own chest with the free hand. Tabitha wondered what he could mean, but Zarost looked at Mulrano approvingly, then held him close and clapped his back.

Mulrano ran deeper into his house, and he could be heard rummaging about. Zarost turned to Tabitha, and produced something from within the folds of his robes.

"You must keep this close, and not drop it in the water," he said, handing a leather tube to her. The leather was worked with the design of a dove, clutching a lyre.

With a start, Tabitha realised that the song-scroll had gone from her jacket pocket. She had been unaware of its presence for some time, but had not noticed in her fatigue. What with the unfamiliarity of Southwind, and Mulrano's curious reception, she had completely forgotten about her mother's legacy. Zarost was gleefull. She plucked the scroll out of his grasp, and shoved it deep inside her jacket once more.

She turned away to hide her embarassment.

Thief, she muttered under her breath. *The little thief!*

But he had given it back.

How long has he had it for?

He had stolen the sword from Glavenor to teach the Swordmaster the value of precious things. She vowed to keep the song scrolls closer than her own underwear.

Mulrano swept into the room, a leather bag slung over his shoulder. He scooped some fruit into the bag from a bowl, then looped it tight and made for the door, gesturing vigorously that they should follow. He led them down the stairs into the boathouse. Twardy Zarost pattered after Mulrano, still chuckling merrily, and Tabitha followed.

Mulrano selected a small skiff. It sat fairly high in the water, and had only three seats; one fore, one aft and a box against the masthead. The large volume between the seats was filled with murky green fishing nets, which smelled quite strongly. At any other time, it would have been quite unappealing.

It could be filled with dead fish, and it would still look good tonight, she thought. Somewhere within the night beyond the house was the Shadowcaster, and he knew where she was now. She stood nervously on the jetty. Mulrano sniffed the air, and collected a pair of oars from the boathouse wall. He strapped them tightly against the gunwales, then un-cleated a thick rope from the mast. He dropped the boom, and a triangular sail unfurled itself neatly. The stern of the boat swung gently out away from the jetty, but Twardy held on to a securing line and kept the bow close. Tabitha waited for Twardy Zarost to board.

"I shall stay, to delay the pursuit," the Riddler said, ushering Tabitha over the bow and onto her seat. "I cannot involve myself any more. I am afraid I have done too much already." He pushed them off from the jetty. Mulrano gave him a hard look, then nodded, and sat down beside the tiller.

The Riddler waved as they drifted away.

"Goodbye, Twardy Zarost," Tabitha called out, "and thank you."

"We'll be seeing each other again. Remember that things are not always what they seem to be. Wait! I have something for you." He fumbled in his clothes, and produced a small object. He tossed it across the dark water separating them. It was an accurate throw, and Tabitha caught the wooden disc easily.

"Go now!" shouted Zarost, waving them off. "The dark must not find you yet."

Tabitha turned the disc in her hands. It was a circular mirror, bordered and backed with wood. There was something inscribed in the backing, but it was too dark to make it out. She slipped the mirror into her deepest pocket. A strange gift, from a strange man. He had already retreated along the jetty, and was squatting beside a canoe.

"Goodbye, Blazey," she called out. A horse snorted from the depths of the boathouse. The wind caught the sail, and the ropes pulled tight with a snap. The water muttered underneath the bow, and Mulrano guided them out across the great rippled realm of the moonlit Amberlake.

◆ ——————— ◆

When his Morrigán returned to him, he drained it of its vision. The bird's essence dissolved into his hand, yielding what it had seen. Kirjath wasted no time. The girl was clearly visible, eating a meal with the wagoneer and a bluff fellow with black hair. The raven's parting view showed the boathouse, on the outskirts of town. She was close.

The stallion quivered with exhaustion, but he drove his heels deeper.

"Chase the horse, make it run," he commanded his second Morrigán. The raven dived and croaked, the horse stumbled toward the lake, dragging its hooves. Even fear could not drive it much further with his weight on its back. He didn't care; he had no need for it once he had reached the girl. It could collapse and die.

As soon as Kirjath neared the end of the main street in Southwind, he knew something was awry. A skiff was heading out across the lake, moving slowly across the rippled moonlit water. The lone boat could only mean one thing. The girl was still fleeing his pursuit. He kicked the horse beneath him, driving his heel against its bruised ribs. It gave a short squeal, and shuddered into a trot.

It went no faster than that, no matter how he kicked.

Where there's one boat, there must be others.

When he reached the jetties, he noticed a small figure sitting at the end of one, his feet dangling over the edge, with a fishing rod in his hand. The line drooped into the dark waters below the jetty. On his head was perched an unmistakable striped hat.

"Wagonman!" Kirjath shouted, as if the name alone were a sufficient curse. "Where is the girl! I will have the girl!" He leaped from his horse and winced as the pain of his abused legs reminded him of the hard day in the saddle. "Speak, or I will strike the grin from your face as you sit."

The man watched him approach. "Good evening to you sir. I am the Riddler. Who might you be?"

Kirjath strode down the last planks of the jetty, and grabbed hold of the man's shirt-front roughly with his left hand. A blister broke between his fingers, and he ground his teeth.

"Liar! You can't be the Riddler, you aren't the Riddler! He is advisor to the Darkmaster." But there was that recurrent familiarity about the man, about his voice. It couldn't be. Kirjath swallowed against the ugly taste of uncertainty. If this was the Riddler, he would have to be careful, very careful.

He drew himself up. "I am Kirjath Arkell, and I will have the girl who you spirited away from First Light. Don't deny it, I have tracked you both. Is she on that boat?" Kirjath pointed a crooked right hand at the now distant smudge of darkness out on the lake.

The man who called himself the Riddler nodded, suddenly cowering from Kirjath's intent stare. That alone proved he wasn't the Riddler. Cabal's advisor had never been afraid of anyone. He had been an enigma, always heavily cloaked in Ravenscroft, his face hidden. But never scared. This little man was nothing more than a cheeky wagoneer in a silly hat. At first his voice had seemed familiar, but the more Kirjath decided that he was an imposter, the less familiar it sounded.

"She runs from your embrace, though I can't imagine why," the wagoneer said. He even had the cheek to grin at his own witticism.

Kirjath's backhand blow caught the hatter below the chin, and he was knocked on his side. Kirjath poised himself. The false Riddler clutched to his fishing rod, and looked up belligerently at Kirjath. Somehow, his hat clung to his head. But he did not retaliate, and Kirjath exhaled quiet relief. It was not the Riddler. This man was powerless.

He was extremely cheeky, for he spoke again. "I'll not be letting you use any of these boats, if that's what you're thinking. They belong to my friend, and he's not one to lend boats to strangers."

Kirjath's rage pounded in his ears. The tatty imposter was defying him. Lying, provoking, and defying Kirjath Arkell. The last of his Dark essence, that which was tending his wounds, came quickly to his hand. He drove the motes into the wagoneer's ears, choosing a simple pattern that suited his needs.

"Despair," Kirjath whispered, his breath washing against the little man's cheek. The imposter would not be moving until the essence was recalled. His worst fears would lock his mind into a trap where every direction was closer to danger, and the only safety was in remaining completely still, not resisting, not daring to fight back.

It was a basic Dark spell, one that worked only on the weakest of minds, but it was all that Kirjath had power for. There was no more Dark essence around. It looked to be good enough. The doomed hatter was already staring crazily into the night, and he had begun to gibber.

Kirjath struck him with another backhand blow. "I am Kirjath Arkell. Remember to fear my name, and maybe you'll live a while longer." He kicked the man in his ribs, then kicked again, his lips curling back into a wild grin. His spell held the man in a grip of terror. He was definitely not the Riddler.

The sudden shriek of a horse broke the silence. Hoofbeats thudded away along the soft shore, an unsteady gallop which splashed through shallows, then returned to the ground, then into the shallows once more.

The bloody raven was chasing the horse, Kirjath realised. In his fury he had forgotten about the second Morrigán bird. They were simple creatures of magic. Without guidance, it had continued with its original instruction: chase the horse, make it run.

Well, the horse could run. It would likely drown itself when it stopped, the stupid beast. But he had a desperate need for the Dark essence. With a sharply voiced command, and the accompanying mental symbol, he recalled the bird.

A flurry of wings beat the air before his face, then the raven landed on his outstretched arm. His recently abandoned wounds screamed to be numbed with the touch of Dark, but Kirjath had a more pressing task. Before the Morrigán could dissolve, he sent it off across the glimmering waters of the lake. He needed to confirm who travelled in the lone vessel.

But he knew.

With every second, the girl was getting further away, and closer to the distant goal of Levin. She would be easy enough to find in Levin, but that would take time, time he didn't have. A worse possibility would be if she stopped off in Stormhaven. The King's Isle meant Swords, and Swords meant trouble. He had to reach her before she made the isle. But even with her headstart, it would take the best part of the night for her to reach Stormhaven.

He surveyed the boats which lay in the slack water beside the jetties. A big, tall-masted boat sat low in the water. Probably holed somewhere, he thought, glancing into its flooded hull. Then there was a punt, a barge-like boat with three sets of oars, and a canoe. The canoe lay with its single-bladed paddle jutting out of the bow, ready and waiting for him. The wind had been dying all afternoon, it was likely to be dead before the night was through. The canoe would be the fastest, though he would have to paddle one-handed.

Just then a flurry of wings announced the return of his messenger. He received its news. The cooling touch of Dark was almost as welcome as the vision of a young woman, looking forlorn in a small sailing vessel, seated beside a bluff fisherman.

Shatter the sun, but I'll paddle one-footed if I could get that girl in my grasp! He boarded the canoe, and settled himself in the rounded hull. A wide cork stopper was jammed in a rude gap in the base, near the bow. It looked to be a recent repair, the cork was not yet soiled by grease or weathered by the sun. He eyed it warily, but the plug showed no sign of leaking. *If it works for the fisherman, it'll have to do for me.* He pushed himself off the jetty with the end of the paddle, and drifted past the entranced wagoneer. The man was still clutching his fishing rod, and staring hopelessly out over the lake.

"Have a nice night, *Riddler.*" Kirjath sneered. "I'm sure you'll feel better in the morning, when my essence returns to the shade." And with that, he paddled out into the deeper water, biting curses at his awkward grip. The lake glistened smoothly under the failing breeze, and the canoe left a widening trail of ripples in its wake.

◆ ——————— ◆

As soon as the canoe reached a safe distance, Twardy Zarost let the Dark essence drain out of his ear. It dripped onto the planking like oil, and seeped through the gaps to the water below.

By the light of the Creator, that was cold! Nonetheless, it had been necessary, to appear to be helpless and harmless. He could not fight Arkell, he should not be opposing him at all. Arkell was Tabitha's problem, her first rival on her path to the wizard. Zarost knew that a Seeker should not be protected from her rivals if her development was going to be successful, for if she was not the best on her own, then she should not be the one to find the wizard.

He had decided to disobey the rule in Tabitha's case. For pity's sake! She sang the Lifesong!

Yet for a Riddler, there were consequences to every action; he had to try his best to ensure balance in all things. He had maintained the balance in First Light, by assisting both the Seeker and Arkell, in different ways. Here he had gone beyond that, he had chosen sides, and his actions would create an imbalance. He couldn't afford to fight Arkell, that would still be up to Tabitha. All he had done was to delay their meeting. He hoped the Gyre would forgive him for that small indescretion.

He stared out over the water.

Mulrano had impressed him. The bluff fisherman had crossed the Shadowcasters once before, and had suffered for it. Still, he was not cowed; the anger ran too deep. They had made sure of the fact that Mulrano would never speak of what he had seen that night the Crown Prince was abducted, of where he had tracked them to. When the Swords had interrogated him, he had not been able to speak to defend himself, and so he had been branded a traitor, because it had been his boat the Shadowcasters had used during the abduction.

That he was risking the journey to Stormhaven himself to see Tabitha clear of the Shadowcaster's danger, told volumes about his character. He defied his tormentors, and the unjust prejudice of Stormhaven.

Yes, Mulrano was a good man for the Seeker to know.

Zarost pulled his pipe and flint from his pocket, and soon had a glowing bowl to chuff upon. He remained seated on the edge of the jetty, and watched the thin fishing line pay out from his reel as the canoe receded across the lake.

◆ ———————— ◆

Tabitha awoke from the biting stiffness in her neck. Something had changed with their movement, and she blinked owlishly around her, trying to puzzle it out. The sail was furled, the boom was raised and tied tightly against the mast. They hadn't travelled that far, she could still make out the receding shoreline in the distance, though it was far enough away to be an arduous swim. The distance remaining to Stormhaven was surely far greater. The rhythmic creak of oars measured out the time. She could make out the hulking form of Mulrano seated against the mast with his back to her. He had a strong, steady stroke which propelled them through the slick water. Overhead stretched a velvet night sky, studded with stars. The wind which had carried them from Southwind had died.

The moon stood high above the western horizon, a waning three-quarter orb, casting a path of ghost-light across the lake. Her gaze fell on a black shape in the glistening highway. Her breath caught in her throat. Something was paddling toward them, an angry, mistimed paddle which alternated erratically from left to right. But even though the paddler was inefficient, the sleek craft was borne closer to them with every pull.

Mulrano nodded resignedly when she touched his shoulder and pointed to their pursuer, as if he knew already. His pace remained unchanged, and Tabitha was about to urge him faster when she noticed the steam coming off his back. His shirt was slicked with sweat; not a dry patch remained. He was rowing as fast as he could manage, and had evidently been doing so for some time. She flicked her eyes back to the pursuer, gripping the mast tight with her fingers as she saw the unmistakable shape of a canoe, and the black-cloaked figure of the Shadowcaster within.

◆ ——————— ◆

He would have her soon. Kirjath dug the oar in deeply, and pulled through the incessant pain.

Just a few more strokes, and the little screamer will be mine!

He would kill the fisherman too, for his interference.

Suddenly, the canoe struck something in the water, a submerged log or a big fish. The nose of the canoe dipped slightly. He felt cold water rushing around his feet, and he cursed. The hasty repair he had seen earlier must have been dislodged—he bent down to search for the cork plug inside the canoe. Water gushed in through the gaping hole, but nowhere could he find the cork.

Blast and befoul this craft! Damn it, it's sinking!

He stamped his foot down, but the hole was an awkward shape, and the water continued to flow in around his toes. It was a serious breach. He pushed his foot deeper into the hole. The hull gave way as he pushed hard against it, and cold water gushed over his legs.

In a desperate gambit, he threw the fading Dark essence in the water and commanded the motes to Freeze. But its power had waned, the motes all but consumed in numbing his wounds. His Freeze spell yielded only a few cubes of ice, which floated away from his thrashing hands as the canoe sank. He howled in his frustration.

"I will find you, girl!" he shouted over the water. "I'll catch you, and I'll make you pay before you die!"

He knew his shouts would carry the short distance, yet no one within the vessel responded. The fisherman rowed the boat away with strong oar-strokes. The glistening ripples of the bow-wave receded towards Stormhaven.

Twardy Zarost sat on the end of the jetty, his feet dangling above the dark water. He reeled in the last of his fishing line, and watched a piece of cork skip across the water towards him.

"Depending on the hook you make, you can catch some strange fish in the Amberlake," he said over his shoulder to the darkness. He was answered by a deep neigh from within the boathouse.

"Finish up your hay," he added. "I believe it's time to be off, off and away."

Tabitha would be safe for a while now, he hoped. She needed time to become accustomed to the Ring. She wasn't quite ready for his riddles, he could see, she became frustrated, and that meant she wasn't ready for answers. Let her look deeply into the Mirror of Self-Reflection, and consider the truth it offered. That little mirror he had given to her was a paradox in itself, because it came from his time with the Philosophers of Kaskanzr, but he had covetted it despite the bitter memories, he had kept it all these years, because the view within it had been so very valuable. He had seen many things in its honest glass, but none so instructive as the face he had seen that morning, when he had risen in the alpine hamlet of First Light: a Riddler who had grown old with trying, with a bright new hope burning in his eyes.

He would do anything to keep that hope alive.

14. ORDER

"Rumours and tales are powerful spells,
powerful spells indeed."—*Zarost*

The morning sun brushed the great brown heights of Stormhaven with gold. The battlements and the city walls loomed over the harbour. Remnants of mist clung to the ground like a fallen nightgown wrapped about the city's feet. Loose thread of mist crept across the harbour.

Tabitha could make out a few vessels through the gaps—here a boat with giant sails, there a yacht with a proud, slim bow. Two great stone wharves encircled the harbour, offering a narrow passage from the lake, but within the harbour there was ample space. Beside the far wharf was a sleek craft painted in bright gold and blue, with row upon row of oars sculled in parallel lines. Burnished shields marked off regular intervals along the gunwales. In the centre of each shield was the crossed symbol of the Sword.

She had been counting the rowlocks to pass the time when the surprising presence of the Morningsong swept all other thoughts aside. The singing came from within her Lightstone.

The music of the Dovecote Assembly filled her ears. She mouthed the words, but she couldn't bring herself to sing. She was afraid that she would be detected somehow—an unworthy intruder upon the sanctity of the spell. She was not a real Lightgifter.

The voice of the choir was beautiful. No wonder her mother had begun every day with such joy in her smile. It had been explained to Tabitha how the Lightstone transmitted the true Morningsong sung in the Dovecote to all Gifters, but to feel it within, transcended description. It washed her doubts aside. She was part of the family of Lightgifters, a worthy sister working to spread health, hope and happiness through Eyri. The inspiration of the song reached deep into her, igniting a fierce determination to do what was right, to be true to the Light, to be pure, and good, and honest.

But she recognised her own hypocrisy. She had promoted herself to the rank of Lightgifter, without the Rector's blessing.

Not me, it was the Riddler who did it.

Nonetheless, she tucked the Lightstone under her collar. The Morningsong continued, surged to its climax, and faded away.

Mulrano passed her a hunk of bread. She accepted it gratefully, and wolfed it down with the pieces of orange he offered. They floated close to the central quay, but Mulrano had not ventured to dock. He seemed determined to wait for something. Tabitha washed her fingers clean in the water. They were safe now, she thought. The night had seemed to last forever. Every time Tabitha had woken, Mulrano had been there, leaning his back strongly against the oars.

Now he stared at the city with distaste, then went back to munching on his breakfast. Tabitha searched the towering buildings for clues to his discomfort, but she could see none. Stormhaven looked beautiful—it rose from the gentle green isle in brown splendour, stone walls gleaming.

Not stone, stonewood, she remembered.

Her mother had told her about the legend of Stormhaven. It had been born in another time, in the time of the Seven Wizards. The defensive city had been a gift, awarded to the first King of Eyri. Certainly, it had been Eyrian carpenters who had raised the original walls from huge timbers. But it was the Seven Wizards who had cast their powerful spell to transform the wood into stone. Or so said the legend.

Real wizardry, Tabitha marvelled, not the simple magic of the essence. *Will the Gifters ever learn to create stonewood?* she wondered. She knew the answer. Not even the most advanced Lightgifters could escape the limits of the essence. Things could not be transformed by the Light, only healed, warmed, illuminated. The Dark? What she remembered of her encounter with the Shadowcaster was fear, despair and cold. She guessed that it was still based on essence, the touch of subtle energy. She remembered the way the Shadowcaster's motes had swirled about him, like a halo of deadly flies. The Dark surely had no power to transform the world, only to terrify the people in it.

There was nothing that equalled the power evident in stonewood, and no lore advanced enough to unravel its mystery. She knew the Gifters had tried. Her mother had despaired of the task after many, many years. But the evidence of the wizardry was undeniable.

The legend of the Seven was lost in the mists of time, but Stormhaven stood proudly for all eternity. It sparked a yearning within her to discover the Wizard's Lore. Twardy Zarost had said she must try to find the wizard, the owner of the Ring. Maybe she would have the chance to learn something of their ways.

As she considered the Ring, it warmed slightly on her finger, and she became aware of details she had missed with her casual glance.

Stormhaven's walls were streaked with the beautiful woodgrains. They appeared new to the world, even though the barrier had stood through four centuries of Eyrian history. The walls which fronted onto the harbour boasted clean patterns of deep brown, with knots and streaks of darker hues.

The northern curve of the harbour wall formed a causeway, the Kingsbridge, which spanned the Amberlake with massive arches. The far end of the bridge was lost in the mist, but Tabitha knew it ran all the way to the shores of Levin, a distance of nearly a full league. Heavily laden wagons trundled along it. People walked, some rode, all inward bound, to the City Gates—a giant, cavernous entrance in the mighty walls, yawning at the morning sun, bristling with battlements that peered down from above.

A bustle of activity near the end of the quay caught her eye. A portly yellow-robed figure with a balding pate was striding importantly toward their vessel. He was accompanied by two stern guards. Mulrano stiffened in his seat. The portly man waved at the boat as if to shoo away a fly, and shouted long before he had reached their side.

"Be off with you. Have you not learned your place on the far side of Amberlake? You have no business here anymore, be off!"

When he reached the end of the wharf, he peered down into the fishing vessel. "Your daughter is no more welcome than you, get thee gone, fisherman." Mulrano turned away from the little man, with an angry glare. He glanced at Tabitha, and jerked his head back toward the official on the wharf. She was expected to speak for them.

"I am not his daughter, but you have no right to talk to him that way. He saved me from the Shadowcaster. He is a good man."

"He is associated with criminals, and has no place on the King's Isle. Hah, yes bite your tongue, smuggler," he laughed at Mulrano's back. "I am an Official of the King's Court. What is your business at Stormhaven, girl?"

Tabitha's mind whirled. She had little idea of how to deal with a Court Official, if that was who the disagreeable toad was. She had not expected to be challenged, yet it was obvious that Mulrano had. It explained why they floated quayside, but hadn't tied up. Technically, she supposed that meant they hadn't landed at Stormhaven. Mulrano must have known there would be trouble for him in the docks.

She used the first faltering answer that came to mind. "I am Tabitha Serannon, I seek sanctuary. I am pursued by a Shadowcaster."

"Strange passage you chose, at night, with a smuggler. And where is this—Shadowcaster—now?" His words were steeped with mockery.

Tabitha didn't bother to turn and search the harbour. She had put that fear to rest. The Shadowcaster had not followed after the sudden mishap of last night, when his canoe had disappeared beneath the waters.

"We, ahh, Mulrano, evaded him last night. His canoe sank. I haven't seen him since."

"Then you have no need for sanctuary!" announced the Official, triumphantly. "If you're looking for charity, you had better be off to the Dovecote in Levin. This is the King's Isle, and only people on the King's business may land here."

She searched for the Ring on her finger, felt its clarity infuse her mind. She knew what to say. The truth cut through her nervousness.

"No, I claim sanctuary. My parents were murdered by the one who pursues me, and justice has not been done." It sounded so cold, stating it out loud as fact. But it felt right, too.

"Do not lie to me, girl, or you will not step onto the King's Isle. You accuse the Sword of negligence for an unpunished crime, you claim pursuers who aren't there. How am I to believe such wild tales?"

The man cared nothing of her woes. If he was too blind to see the truth of her plight, she would have to make it clearer for him. She stood up against the mast, and brought her eyes to bear on the men above. The path ahead was clear. She knew of the custom she could call upon which he could not refuse.

"I demand an audience with the King by the orb of the Lightgifter," she said slowly, feeling the weight of her words as they were pronounced across the water. She had spoken true words, yet she knew they would be interpreted another way. She demanded audience by the orb, she hadn't said she was a Lightgifter. The truthful duplicity made her feel a vague kinship with the Riddler.

An audience could not be denied. She may have to wait for it, but her audience would be granted. Lightgifters were nobility, and carried the royal favour wherever they went.

"You try too hard with your lies, girl," the Official scoffed. "I had almost believed you. But a Lightgifter, in woodsman's clothes, with a farmer's surname, in a smuggler's boat? Hah!"

The guards remained impassive. They were either well-accustomed to the little man's insidious nature, or they were trained to show nothing of their own opinion. Tabitha wanted to throw the toad into the green depths of the harbour.

Maybe that's why he walks with two guards—I'm not the first to think it. She reached inside the neck of her high-collared tunic, and pulled her mother's orb out on its short chain.

There was silence for a time. One guard shifted in his armour, creaking the leather. The water rose and fell gently on the poles which supported the wharf. The Official peered down at Tabitha, as if she were a rare specimen found floating in his soup. As his eyes focused on the orb and showed him his mistake, his face attempted to slide into an expression of welcome. But it was an unaccustomed expression, and his frown remained, making him look like a child who had just wet his own nappy, and was not yet sure what to do about it.

"Aren't you a little young to be wearing the orb, then?"

"That is the Dovecote's decision, not yours," she said, with swelling courage. A Lightgifter would act imperious, not cowed. This was a delicate game, to answer only with truthful words, yet not reveal her gambit. She was not really a Lightgifter. Not yet.

"What matter do you wish brought before the King, Miss Serannon?"

She had claimed the Lightgifter's privilege. She would have to go through with it.

An audience with the King! Mercy, I'll look a fool.

The Official needed an answer. "I would discuss the dire threat of the Shadowcasters."

"Do you have knowledge of such?"

"First hand knowledge. But I would discuss it with the King, and not to all in the Stormhaven harbour." It was a dangerous demand, but the game of delicate truth was making her nervous. She had to get herself onto the King's Isle. The Official puckered his lips.

"Very well," he said, looking plainly displeased, "I shall have to escort you to chambers." He regarded her for a few seconds. "How much longer must we wait for you?"

With a start, Tabitha realised he meant for her to come ashore. She touched Mulrano on his shoulder and he turned to face her. His earlier fury had faded, but a trace of it remained in his gathered brows.

Mulrano dipped his oars into the water, and moved the boat to the base of a flight of steps which were cut into the stone wall. He passed Tabitha the leather satchel that held the remains of their hastily packed provisions. One of the guards descended, and held out a hand to help Tabitha alight. As soon as her feet were on the slippery stone of the base step, the guard kicked strongly at the boat, and shoved it back into the harbour waters. His face remained impassive as he crowded Tabitha up the stairs. Tabitha was appalled.

"But my friend, Mulrano, what about him?" She tried to see over the guard's shoulder, but he herded her up the last of the steps onto the wharf.

"Stop pushing me! Stop it." She emerged in front of the Official and his second guard. "He's just rowed the whole night. Why can't he come ashore?" she demanded.

The little man sneered. "That traitor is lucky to be alive. If it weren't for the mercy of our King Mellar, he wouldn't be. If I'd had my way, he would be lying at the bottom of the Amberlake, chained to a large rock. He doesn't set foot on the Isle."

She was surprised to see Mulrano already halfway across the harbour, pulling hard on his oars. The leather bag slipped in her hands.

I haven't even thanked him for what he did.

Mulrano was facing her, his bluff features visible as he leant back on each stroke. On a sudden impulse, she brought her hands up to her lips, and blew a kiss out across the water. She wished him strength, in whatever he did. She spread her hands, palms out towards the water. A surge of warmth passed her. Sunlight sparkled and played across the water, a hundred ripples of light tracked toward the little fishing boat, then were gone.

Sunlight or sprites? she wondered, but they were gone, and the harbour water had returned to its placid blue-green hue. It was a foolish fantasy. The Light needed a pattern and spell to guide it. You couldn't just wish strength to someone, the sprites wouldn't move unless you were a Lightgifter. She touched the white orb at her throat self-consciously. The orb would be difficult to explain, if she met any Lightgifters. She tucked it under the high collar of her tunic once more.

Her escort had not seemed to notice anything. She turned away from the last sight of Mulrano, who was hoisting his sail in the harbour mouth. The bag which Mulrano had left her was soft and light, and fitted snugly to her back.

The Official grumbled, and set off. Tabitha was led from the harbour district toward the entrance to Stormhaven proper. They were stopped at a checkpoint before the arching City Gates. Stonewood walls towered to either side, smooth as polished glass. The walls would frustrate the most determined attempt at a scaling assault. Tabitha saw movement on the high battlements, and the glint of steel.

At the Official's behest, one of the escorting soldiers announced them from the back of the crush.

"Make way, Lethin Tarrok with the King's business!"

The crowd parted reluctantly, but the escort soon reached the City Guard. The gatekeeper copied down some brief details. They entered the mighty gatehouse.

Now that the portly Official had her in his grasp, he wouldn't shut up. He talked incessantly while they walked, listening little to what Tabitha had to say, offering only a curt "humph!" or "ach!" before launching on another monologue. After discovering that Tabitha had never been to Stormhaven, he smothered her with his knowledge of protocol. He seemed determined to make her feel as unsophisticated as possible, as if knowing that her request for an audience was ill-considered.

Tabitha began to doubt the wisdom of her course. Stormhaven enveloped her with massive walls. Hundreds of busy, important people, rushed by, their voices joining in a hubbub. The grandeur of the city was overwhelming. The Official droned on.

"Your stay will be brief; once you have attended your audience you must return to your home, or the Dovecote, wherever."

She began to explain that her home was destroyed, but the Official cut her off without so much as a pause of acknowledgement.

"You must know that there are many people who seek an audience with the King, and he has little enough time as it is, without wasting it on whimsical fantasies. You will be lodged in the Boarding until such time as you are summoned, and you are to make little nuisance of yourself. You may be a Lightgifter, but you are still a young woman with a tall tale, in my eyes, so don't you get airs and graces, especially not when we talk of the King of Eyri. I shall put your case to the King, and we shall see if he deigns to an audience. You would do well to remain out of sight until then. The city is not as safe as you think, and there are those who might consider a young woman on her own an easy target."

There was a warning note in the Official's voice. Tabitha looked nervously around. The two soldiers continued to pace alongside, in escort. A jingling sound accompanied every second step. She tried to identify which piece of armour made the sound. With a start she realised it was coming from her pocket—the heavy bulge contained the pouch of coins she had collected from Phantom Acres. She hastily transferred it from her cloak to the leather bag. The coins would be quieter on her back. People became funny around coin, she knew.

Maybe the Official had been trying to be helpful with his warning, but she couldn't ignore the shiver that passed down her spine when she caught his eye on her. The sooner she could be rid of the man, the better.

The Official hurried on, taking a route through the streets that seemed to bypass the main traffic. They climbed, and she began to tire. It had been a long night, and an even longer day before that. The empty feeling of her loss was always there. She ran her eyes over the architecture of Stormhaven, trying to find peace in the distraction of its beauty.

Most of the city appeared more like a sculpture than a building. Tabitha had seen drawings of Stormhaven, and knew the city to be a complex geometric design, a giant, tiered octagon. From street level it was the individual buildings that were most impressive. Everything was big, reaching for the azure sky with crenellated ridges or steeply pitched roofs. Ancient stonewood defined precise arches which spanned the street high above. In places, it seemed that tree-trunks were folded into the architecture as cornerstones, though no trace of branches remained. Some roofs were rippled, as if made from water-worn wood. Yet it was obvious that the ancient design had been overlaid by a pressing modern need for development. The stonewood buildings were set far apart, and between them were crammed ruder structures of wood and stone. The low houses and inns would have been elegant anywhere else, but beside the arching grandeur of the stonewood architecture, the newer buildings seemed crude.

A cobbled brown mosaic passed underfoot, patterned in long swathes of black and gold. From high on the battlements a design might become clear, she supposed, but where Tabitha walked, she felt like an ant traversing a page of holy script, wondering at the curve of each letter.

They were in the heart of the city, and the oblique sunlight began to clip more and more gold capping on the high roofs. Tabitha could not hide her wonder. Garyll Glavenor had downplayed the wealth of Stormhaven.

One piece of roof-capping would make a man rich.

It was not all glory and wonder, though. A powerful odour betrayed the city's image of sophistication. A shallow gutter ran along the side of the road, and a milky brown rivulte flowed in its confines. There was always a dark side to a city.

They emerged to a great open plaza. The grand Palace of Stormhaven loomed on the far side of the forecourt. Wide steps rose beside it, built upon the transition to the highest grounds of the city. It had a domed roof, surrounded by a parapet which rimmed the walls three stories up. Gold outlined every detail finely, as if a cloud of pure sunlight had rained upon the construction. Below the gold trim, massive pillars of pale stonewood leant together to form an A-frame, inside which doors stood wide open. A grand stairway led up to the doors from the deep green lawns. Some trees, darkwood or mellina, stood sentry in perfect symmetry beside approach. Closer to hand, the palace grounds were bordered with a fence of gold-tipped spears, which were linked by black iron crossbeams. Five guards stood at the entrance to the palace grounds, each gleaming in the morning sun.

The insistent voice of the Official penetrated Tabitha's thoughts again.

"For of course you shall have to be presented to the House of Ceremony. Your arrival is premature, and I don't have the time to train a girl in protocol, no matter what you bear. They will summon a guideling from the House to take you to your hostel."

Tabitha hadn't heard of a 'guideling' before. Doubtless another aspect of the Court she would have to learn. The Official led her around the city-side of the forecourt. The nearest buildings had low roofs that capped a single floor each. Carved blocks of white marble were mounted before the open doorways, each heralding a different House. The House of Law. House of Coin. House of Ways. Waters. Scribes, Ceremony, Builders. Tabitha's eyes flicked around the semicircle, marking off the boldly scripted signs in rapid succession. All the Houses had the same tidy look of regular use.

A riot of colourful flowers crammed into a flowerbed outside the House of Waters, and a neatly trimmed vine crept up the wall of the Singers.

The people who ducked through the doorways appeared both hasty and important. They were all dressed in fine clothes. Capes seemed to be in fashion, and from the look of the few women Tabitha spotted, tight-fitting waistcoats over loose dresses. Everyone bustled about with pre-occupied frowns, as if they had a long list of things to do, and were struggling to order it all into the time before noon. No one paid a second glance to Tabitha and her escort.

A vocal man rushed past Tabitha, surprising her out of her reverie. "Unconscionable! Thirteen silver to a gold, yet they won't exchange it! Unconscionable!" Tabitha couldn't see anyone to which the outburst had been addressed. She wasn't even sure she knew what 'unconscionable' meant. It had to be something bad. The man was lost to the traffic.

The Official led her toward the wide door of the House of Ceremony. The soldiers halted, and the Official faced her for the first time since the harbour. Beads of sweat stood out on his forehead despite the cool morning air, and the armpits of his yellow robe had become damp.

"I have a busy day, and you've already made me late. Tell them you are here to await an audience, and that I shall be presenting your case to the King. You should be seen to presently."

With no farewell or further comment he turned and huffed briskly off toward the palace, his soldiers flanking him.

Unconscionable man, Tabitha decided, feeling better for his departure. She swung back to face the House of Ceremony. Her nervousness grew as she considered her situation. She was alone in the strange wonder of Stormhaven. Her leaden feet took her forwards.

Small pennants fluttered stiffly against their bonds beside the door. A whiff of parchment, ink and burning wax passed her on the breeze. The House of Ceremony looked dark inside, when compared to the reflected light of the street, the burning gold of the rooftops, the white of the heavy marble sign.

"Come girl, be about your way, be about your way!" urged a deep voice from behind. A strong hand pushed her in haste, not in anger. She was swept through the door and the man passed her by without a backward glance, scarlet cape swirling in his wake. Tabitha was left in the foyer, gazing about like a startled mouse.

The House of Ceremony appeared gloomy at first, but as her eyes became accustomed to the pale light from the windows, Tabitha noted the drapes which were spaced along the walls. Embroidered heraldic shields woven in rich colours were centred upon the dark fabrics, and tassels of copper and gold dangled from their lower edges. The hallway stretched in an elongated semicircle before her. It contained a few low couches set against the walls, and ended with two counters which thrust out from the walls at obtuse angles. The gap between the counters admitted visitors to a wide corridor which led deeper into the rooms of the House.

A soft, peaceful voice reached her ears.

"Marriage, celebration, birth or death?"

A woman watched her from behind the one counter. A large woman, with a kindly face. Dimples pulled at her cheeks. Her thick forearms rested on the countertop, tucked beneath her bosom.

"You'll be new to Stormhaven, then," the woman said in a slow, soft voice.

"Aaahh, y-yes," stammered Tabitha. "I don't really know where to go," she spread her hands wide, and dropped them to her side once more. The lady of the House smiled generously at her, and Tabitha felt welcomed for the first time since she had stepped onto the King's Isle.

"I'm Maybelle Westerbrook, but you can call me Miss May. I am the Lady of Ceremony, which means I am the historian of Stormhaven too. Now who are you?"

"Tabitha Serannon, Lady Westerbrook, and I have requested an audience with the King, but the Official seemed to think I needed to learn some protocol, he wouldn't believe that I sought sanctuary—" Tabitha stopped short. She wasn't sure if she should divulge all of her dark tale.

"Trisha's child? Trisha Serannon?" Tabitha nodded. Lady Westerbrook looked delighted. "A better Lightgifter one could not find. I see there is more to your tale, but let it wait until you are ready. You know you'll have to wait awhile for your audience?"

"Yes, he—he told me so when we came up from the harbour this morning. He said he'd see to the requesting of audience."

"You have arrived this morning? Which Official received you, only to leave you unheralded in my hallway?"

She couldn't remember his name, though she was sure he had mentioned it at some point in his litany.

"It was a plump little man in a yellow robe, with two guards. They escorted me up here, but he left. He said he had important business." She paused. "He wasn't very nice."

May pursed her lips, and inked some details into a large register.

"Lethin," said May, "Lethin Tarrok. Possibly the most unattractive man on the Isle. If he weren't the King's nephew, he would have found poor fortunes in Stormhaven." She shot Tabitha a sympathetic glance. "Even for a spinster like me, there is better company to be found in the alleys behind the Journeyman's Cider on a midwinter's night. An ill fate that you should have him as your first company. I wonder why he deigned to escort you? He's usually far too busy stirring his spoon in the King's court."

"I don't think he came to meet me. I was delivered by a man whom he considers a smuggler."

"A smuggler? Really, I wouldn't take much heed of anything Tarrok says. Who brought you here?"

"Mulrano of Southwind."

May's eyebrows shot up so high they threatened to leave her face.

"He must have had a mighty powerful reason to offer you passage. He's not too welcome on the King's Isle, not too welcome at all."

"What did he do wrong?" Tabitha asked. "He's such a nice man, even though he can't speak."

"He could speak before his tongue was branded. Better that than death, I suppose."

Tabitha's jaw dropped. They *made him* into a mute?

"But why? What did he do?"

May glanced down the corridor behind her, then beckoned Tabitha closer. "He ran foul with others of his kind," she whispered. "It was his boat that was seen in the harbour on the night Prince Bevn was abducted. Whatever bargain he had struck with the criminals turned sour, for they silenced him. And so it was that when the King arrested him for questioning, he maintained that he knew nothing, and that his boat had been stolen. Tarrok headed up the investigation, and it's no secret that Tarrok wanted the fisherman dead. The King pardoned his life for lack of evidence. That was an act of great mercy, considering it was his own son who was gone."

"When was the Prince—abducted?"

"Two months ago to the day. It has been kept quiet—at least, beyond Stormhaven, that is."

No wonder Mulrano had received such a cold reception at the harbour. He was considered a traitor, and had only been partially pardoned.

A group of people came into the reception hall and approached the counter where May and Tabitha stood. May spread her hands apologetically.

"I would hear more of your tale, Tabitha, but for now I must attend to my duties. A guideling will be here soon, to take you to the Boarding. Tell her of your needs, should you have any. You do have coin to pay for your stay?" she added, with a concerned note in her voice. She sounded motherly though, not wary.

"No—ahh, yes!" Tabitha answered, remembering the coins in her bag. It was strange to have so much wealth.

"Good then, until later," May said. She dismissed Tabitha with a broad gesture, then greeted her next customers. Tabitha drifted across the hall and sank onto a couch. She closed her eyes, and knuckled them gently to ease her tiredness.

It really had gone on too long; the fight, the running, the hiding and riding, the long dark night crossing Amberlake, and the march through the city. Underneath it all, her mourning spirit lurked like dark water under cracked winter ice, waiting for a misplaced step. She felt delicate and thin—trying to behave normally in all the strangeness was a strain.

◆ ——————◆

"Excuse me, Miss Serannon?" a little voice enquired.

She opened her eyes. A girl dressed in a pale tunic and indigo pants stood before her. She was very young, maybe eleven years old. Her black hair was tied back.

"I am Pia. I will take you to your room," she said with rehearsed care. She pressed her hands together at chest height, and bowed.

A guideling. Something about the young girl's wide-eyed concentration told Tabitha that she was new to her profession, but determined to do well at it. She smiled weakly at Pia the Guideling.

"Thank you. I'd like that."

Tabitha waved a farewell to the Lady of Ceremony, but Maybelle Westerbrook was surrounded by a press of new customers, and could only smile briefly in acknowledgement. Pia led her from the House of Ceremony into the bright bustle of the street. They turned away from the forecourt and the grand Palace that dominated the skyline.

Tabitha worried about the audience with the King. There was nothing false about the attack of the Shadowcaster, and her desire to seek justice, but demanding the King of Eyri to consider the matter might have taken things too far. The certainty she had felt when facing down the Court Official now seemed like a reckless fervour. It was the Ring's fault—it made her feel so sure, so clear of her purpose at times, but when the clarity faded she was left with her uncertainty.

Ever since she had first seen the Ring, her life had been changed. It was as if she was being carried upon a river in flood, and the sides of the gorge were becoming higher, giving her less choice in where she was being taken. She followed the guideling through the bustle and clamour of Stormhaven, and tried to avoid gawking at the towering buildings around her. She hoped that she appeared city-wise. She hoped that she had made the right decision, to be there at all.

After traversing a few blocks, Pia led her toward a tall lodge. Inside, they found the matron of the Boarding filling a tally-book with determined vigour. The matron was stout, as wide as she was deep, with skin the colour of fired clay. She looked like she could wallop an ox and leave it bruised for months. The rules of the House rattled off the matron's tongue as soon as it was established that there was a place for Tabitha.

"Soap to be left dry. One bath a day permitted after the evening meal. Bed to be kept tidy, folded neat with the dawn. Chamber pot to be cleaned in the drop, but never at night. Lights out at nine bells."

Tabitha scuttled away with Pia as soon as they were allowed. Her room had a tall window, and a view over the bustling capital of Eyri. Stonewood beauty and gold highlighting, mighty walls and cobbled mosaics. Pia assured her that she would return at the Noontime meal, if it pleased Miss Serannon.

The room seemed empty when the little guideling was gone. A lofty dimension to the emptiness made the sounds of the city seem dull and diluted. Sunlight pooled on the bed. Tabitha couldn't resist its temptation. For a moment, she could escape the rushing current of her life, and be still. She sank onto the blankets and curled up on their warmth.

Something poked her from inside her pocket. She pulled it out; the small, circular mirror, the Riddler's gift. She could read the inscription carved in the wooden backing.

See thyself as thyself see.

She turned it over, and over. It was finely wrought, the mirror flawless, the binding strong. All along the rim lay a carved serpent, its scales delicately crafted, following a perfect circle before the head found the tail and swallowed its end.

A strange gift, from a strange man; Twardy Zarost. She gazed at the image within the serpent. A tired pair of deep brown eyes stared back at her, framed by her slack, dark brown curls. Her reflection became unfocused. She felt the smoothness of her blanket against her cheek.

Sleep took her, despite the fact that it was early morning.

15. SURVIVAL
"If you fall, get up.
This is the secret of life."—*Zarost*

Kirjath's day began badly. He crawled from the chill waters of the Amberlake only moments before dawn. A place where the rushes were thick and farms few. He wasn't sure how far from the village of Southwind he was, but nobody had seen his arrival, or spotted him where he lay. He hugged the ground shamefully as if it were a saviour, then beat it with his bare hands when his exhaustion eased. He howled with fury as he tore at the earth, then howled with pain as his softened wounds exploded under his rage. The girl had evaded him.

A girl!

And now she was in the safety of Stormhaven, where he could not risk his magic. She was safe in the protection of the Sword and the King's Isle.

Failed. To return to Ravenscroft without the Ring.

The lake had almost drowned him. At first his heavy cloak had weighed him down. He remembered tearing it from his neck, then tearing his tunic free, keeping only his trousers and boots. The lake was cold, and had begun to mist over in the dead of night. He had paddled like a dog, snorting bubbles into the water with each laboured breath, his eyes yearning for the distant shore which had seemed to retreat rather than near as the hours passed. The strength had leached out of his limbs, his head had sunk deeper with each stroke. The moon had set. Only his bloody-minded anger had kept him going through the night. He found no Dark essence to aid him. It had been a cruel lesson. He was flawed with weakness as if he was an ordinary man.

Later, when the Morrigán found him on the lake shore, he wanted to tear it apart. A useless gesture, he knew—but he wanted to destroy it nonetheless. He needed it to feel pain, needed something to cry out as he twisted it limb from limb. He needed something to ease his rage.

The Morrigán cawed loudly, mocking him. The bird was a creation of essence, and would merely scatter to the breeze, feeling nothing. It would be from Ravenscroft. He couldn't dare to spurn it. The black raven maintained a circling distance until he accepted its missive by raising his arm.

He knew what it would say before it dispersed, before the motes struck his skin. Motes! He drew them eagerly into his wounds, though their power was already diminished by the spell they had been part of.

The Darkmaster's hissed command lingered in the air. "You will come to Ravenscroft immediately!"

Kirjath cursed the sun, cursed his suppurating wounds, cursed every Lightgifter that had been whelped from their miserable mothers, but he headed away from the lake. He could explain his refusal of the first summoning, but this one was undeniable.

When he found the road, he turned east towards Fendwarrow and beyond, where the pass to Ravenscroft lay concealed. There would be no pursuit of the girl now, no chance for him to turn his failure to success.

Walking was painful. His leather boots had not dried properly, and his toes had begun to chafe. His thighs cramped from the strain of the ride followed by the swim, and his skin suppurated where it had been burned. Kirjath cursed whenever his legs failed him—his stride wobbled across the road like a drunkard. It was unforgivable, that a body should fail so.

Having a purpose helped to keep the jagged edge on his anger, which kept his exhaustion at bay. Anger at the Darkmaster, anger at the girl, anger at the canoe which had failed, anger at the wagoneer, the one who'd claimed to be the Riddler. He had sat so still on the jetty, frozen and overpowered, but Kirjath couldn't get rid of the nagging suspicion that the hatter was somehow responsible for his downfall. He didn't like things he didn't understand—they made him feel cheated, as if everyone was laughing but he didn't catch the joke. He would have to ask the Darkmaster about the Riddler.

Blast that little man!

Kirjath spat a dark lump of jurrum into the grass. At least he still had jurrum. Soggy as the leaves were, they eased his nerves.

As he walked, the day improved, for the closer he came to Fendwarrow, the more motes were in evidence. He summoned Dark essence from wherever he could find it—the shade beneath logs, the dark flecks beneath leaves, from the cracks between broken rocks. The motes covered his skin like feasting flies, easing his burns with their numbing cold. The motes balked at the sunlight, and he had to repeat his invocations to keep them from the shadowed folds of his trousers. Dark essence flickered over his naked chest and back in agitated, frenetic patterns. To have something serving him eased his anger slightly, even though it was just the tiny particles of Darkness.

He hid from those who travelled on the shore road that morning, using his motes to assist where the cover of reeds or scrub was too thin. He skirted the village of Waxworth, and thereafter there was no traffic at all. Little reason for anyone to visit the lepers in their pools at Rotcotford, or to go any further into Bentwood County unless you were aiming for Fendwarrow. After seeing no one for a while, he grew careless, and so some travellers caught up to him on the road beyond Rotcotford, as he was walking through a grove of silken trees.

He heard the hoofbeats too late to weave the Dark motes into an illusion. He drew the motes hastily into his mouth instead, and swallowed. Better that they were concealed. His stomach groaned under its painfully cold contents. He hoped the riders would pass him by quickly—the fewer the folk who knew he was a Shadowcaster, the better. He had no time for a challenge with some bright-eyed Lightgifters, or a patrol of zealous Swords.

"Hsss! Leper!" he heard a man warning his companion. "Ride clear! Ride clear!"

The two riders passed him, giving him a wide berth before cutting back onto the road ahead. They turned to face him there, and halted. A tall, youthful man, and a slender woman with a regal expression. The crystal orbs at their necks left no doubt about their profession.

Lightgifters!

Their white robes were travel-stained, and both tried to deny their tiredness by sitting a little too upright in their saddles. Kirjath noted the stiff line of the man's lips.

Blast and set fire to them! He wasn't in the mood for challenges, or conversation.

"Halt there leper! Come no closer, we will have none of your disease. Halt, I said!" The man rose slightly in his saddle. Kirjath came to a halt, keeping his gaze on the ground before his feet, concealing his obsidian orb beneath his chin.

"We seek a Shadowcaster—have you seen any?" The man sounded as if it disgusted him to have to ask questions of an evidently diseased peasant.

"You do know what a Shadowcaster looks like, don't you, leper?"

Despite his initial resolve to let the riders pass, Kirjath clenched his fists to create fresh pain. Pain always helped to focus his mind. Kirjath eyed the woman from under his eyebrows. He winced against the cold in his guts. He could use her.

"Speak up, beggar, or shall I open your mouth for you?" The man looked not a year past twenty-one, yet he was arrogant enough for one twice his age and rank.

Yes, the woman would be very useful. No need for the bantam cock, and no way to avoid him.

Kirjath held a dangerous pattern in mind, the triple looped prism of Decay. An apt curse for one who had named him a leper. It was good to have adequate resources again.

The tall man glared expectantly down at Kirjath. Kirjath raised his head and opened his mouth wide. He spewed the Dark essence out, filling the air with a swarm of motes which rushed into the pattern of his chosen spell.

"Decay!" he shouted, his arms thrown wide.

The Dark essence struck the tall Lightgifter full in the face. He screamed in his saddle, waving his arms desperately to ward himself. He made a feeble attempt to summon Light to his hands, but already the Dark spell was wreaking its havoc, and only a few sprites came to his panicked command. They would be consumed as he ministered his own healing.

The woman fell backwards from her horse, landing somewhere beyond the animals in the dirt.

Curses! The woman had placed herself in the only protected area. Whether it was skill or fright, Kirjath couldn't gauge. He had enough Dark essence to fight them both, but only if he drew them into the same place and could use one spell.

A rush of sprites pulled through the grass from all directions towards her, summoned from the silken trees, from rocks which glinted in the sunlight, from the bright flowers beside the road. She was good, and fast. But she was a Lightgifter.

"Web!" he shouted, a new pattern in mind. He clapped his hands. His blackened right hand struck the blistered left. He howled with pain, but it was done. The motes spiralled outwards and collected in a swirling, spherical web which cut through the air around him, blocking any attack from the Light. The exhaustion he tried to deny showed in the meagre lattice which failed to cover more than a quarter of a sphere. It would have to be enough to hold the attack.

The woman was still summoning Light essence—her radiant

aura towered over the horses. She was stronger than he had thought. He would need more shielding to check her power. He recalled the motes from the mounted Lightgifter with a sharp gesture, binding their added essence into his shield. The man toppled from his saddle, gasping first, then screaming as his limbs failed to protect him from the fall. The rot had bitten deep into him, and his healing was not complete. There was a loud crack and groan as he hit the ground.

The Morgloth. I need the Morgloth!

The thought came with a powerful desire, a rushing tide of lust for the demon's presence, a yearning for the might he would command through it. Yet he knew it was also becoming an addiction. He tried to use logic to suppress the eagerness. He could win against two Gifters.

But not during the day, not weakened as he was.

Far better if I use the Morgloth and finish them off for sure.

He did not have enough essence to create a gateway inside the shield, not enough to complete his purpose and remain protected.

A blast of sprites cut past his head. The Lightgifters were working in unison, channelling the collected Light essence into a blade which burst through his flickering shield.

By the balls of Krakus!

They were too good. The young man was on his feet again, and he worked in perfect synergy with the woman, meshing his flow with hers to create a unified spell. She must have countered his Dark spell already. It was too late to change anything, Kirjath realised. His hasty plan had to succeed. He closed his eyes, trying to ignore the chaos of energy swirling around him. Heat scorched past his head.

It was going to hurt.

The symbol of the Gateway was clear in his mind. He recalled the motes from their shield, drew them to his hand. He managed the first words of the Gateway before the Light seared through his chest. The rest of the words came out in a harsh shriek. It had to work.

He forged on, guiding the motes to their place in the circle, holding the pattern grimly in mind. A twin spell raced through his legs, bringing him to his knees.

It wasn't Healing these Gifters brought. It was Fire. The Darkmaster had assured them all that such spells had been outlawed in the Dovecote. Obviously not all of the Gifters followed their Rector's command. Every nerve in his body screamed. The Light really was the nemesis of Dark.

"Morgloth, serve your master!" he cried to the darkening circle at his feet. He fell onto his stomach to avoid the next searing flash of sprites.

"Morgloth, I command you!"

A familiar presence swelled in his mind, coming like a charging bull. He offered the target of a certain tall Lightgifter to the mind within his mind. It was time to feed.

A spell of lightning brilliance shot from the Gifters' hands. The air crackled with its heat. But at that moment, the demon emerged from the Gateway and blocked the attack with its bulk. The beast took the assault full on its chest and spread its ragged wings wide. The power of Light would have left Kirjath screaming, yet the beast didn't even flinch. The essence was absorbed into its slick black skin.

The horses wheeled, and fled.

The Morgloth leapt, and descended on the tall Lightgifter. Kirjath stiffened as the anticipation swept through him. He forgot about his pains. He smiled as the woman screamed. She stumbled backwards on the road, and fell to the dirt.

The Morgloth filled him more than ever, it was stronger than ever, and he welcomed its presence. The bite, the suck, the life-force which drained into his body like water falling from a cliff, the empty sensation of an unlimited void, the sweet purity of a moment of satisfied lust, all this washed over Kirjath like an intoxicating drink, filling his mind completely with raw power and ecstacy.

He saw the world through the Morgloth's eyes, he was the Morgloth, and his chin was wet with blood. He tossed the sack-like remains of the Lightgifter aside.

It was only when he saw the woman crawling backwards away from him on the dirt of the road, felt his wings spreading wide for the strike, that he realised what was happening. He had lost his mind.

"Stop!" he shouted at the demon. "I am the master, I am the master!" he raged. It felt as if his mind would burst. The demon had landed on the woman, its black wings arched into the air, its legs straddled her, and part of his mind could smell the sharp scent of fear.

Not my mind, the demon's mind. He clenched his fists. Pain.

"Stop, stop, stop!" he screamed at his beast, clamping his thoughts around the parasitic mind within, forcing it to submit. He was stronger, he was the master.

Submit, damn you! you foul, beautiful beast. I need this woman alive. He grinned as he felt the animal mind crushed inside his. It felt good to overpower the demon. It proved how strong he was, how immense his skill. He was Lord Kirjath Arkell. He wet his cracked lips, and approached the demon. In the mud at its feet was its quivering, terrified prey.

Tears streamed down her cheeks, and she babbled incoherent words like too many invocations jumbled together. She tried to scrabble backwards through the undergrowth, but came up against a large boulder. Kirjath commanded his demon aside, and straddled her himself. The black beast stood close by, flapping its wings in frustration.

Kirjath held her chin in his good hand. Her eyes looked as if they might roll back in her head and be lost forever.

"Heal me, Lightgifter," he commanded.

She stared back at him, uncomprehending, her fear pushing reason and logic far from her mind's reach. He slapped her, once, with the back of his left hand. Pain jabbed at his flesh like a thousand thorns. But he saw the shift in her eyes, the return of some intelligence behind her gaze. She knew what she was dealing with now, a man who was beating her. Her nostrils flared a little in anger. Kirjath smirked.

He slapped her again, then grabbed her chin in his suppurating hand and forced her wide eyes to look at his.

"Heal me, Lightgifter," he repeated, "my hands, my head, my skin—you can heal these?"

Her expression hardened, but then her eyes flicked to the right, to the hungry beast, its skin like dirty oil, its muscles rippling as it shifted from one barbed leg to the other, its taloned hands curling restlessly at its sides. All resistance left her face. Kirjath struck her again.

"Try to fight, and my beast knows to tear you apart. Remember that as you work, and keep a steady hand."

"I need to rise," the woman said, staring blankly at him.

He backhanded her again. "Did they not teach you any manners in the Dovecote? You will address me as *my Lord*, for that is what I am."

She continued to stare blankly.

He raised his hand for another blow.

"Please my Lord, I need to rise."

He struck her anyway.

Once Kirjath had released her, the Lightgifter rose mechanically to her feet. She kept her gaze downcast, though Kirjath knew she still harbored a burning anger. It was going to be a pleasure to drown the flames of that particular fire.

The woman closed her eyes, and Kirjath shifted uneasily as she searched for Light essence. He reached for the Morgloth, and felt the demon stiffen in anticipation.

Any sign, and you rip her head off.

Sprites pooled between her hands. She muttered a few words of invocation, and approached his side with a sullen expression.

It was horrible being touched by the Light—a prickling, uncomfortable feeling like sunlight crawling under his skin. He wanted to scream. He watched in silence as the Light essence filled his wounds. The sprites pooled where the Lightgifter pointed to. She continued to cover his damaged body as if smearing salve, chanting all the while. He pulled his trousers up to expose the raw skin of his calves, and she added sprites behind his knees. Then she began a new incantation, words unfamiliar to Kirjath's ears, words with a lilting sing-song sound to them, though there was little joy from the singer. He gasped as heat swept across his body. It felt like he had stepped from a blizzard to stand before an open furnace.

He grabbed her by the throat. "I'm warning you! No tricks."

"The warmth is part of the healing," she said tonelessly, when he eased his grip.

He reluctantly allowed her to continue. The breaks in his damaged flesh began to seal. The angry red of his burns faded to a shiny pink beneath the sparks of Light. The sprites faded, and fell from his body like dust, their power spent. He could still feel nothing in his right hand, but the skin had lightened from black to grey.

His scalp itched furiously, and when he ran his left hand over it, it was dry and hairless. Scar tissue rumpled the skin, but it was clean. It was bearable.

"I can do no more now," said the woman, turning her back on both him and his beast. Her statement came out in a monotone. "I can only heal, not re-create. Your skin is permanently damaged. It will not fester now. With time, your right hand may recover. It will never have strength." She paused for a moment, then said, "I will not try to attack you again. You and ... that thing, may leave."

Kirjath cackled. The woman certainly had nerve.

"Well, you *may not* leave," said Kirjath, grabbing her arm and spinning her to face him. "I have further need of your services." He leered at her as a lecherous fool would leer at a serving maiden, then laughed again. Not that, not *only* that. He had far greater plans for her. She would serve him in many ways.

"We shall ride together from here." He shot a glance at the Morgloth. The beast was still eyeing the woman with an intense hunger. Kirjath grinned. The mastery, the sheer nerve of his domination of the beast made him feel jubilant.

Retreating down the road a short way, Kirjath came to the corpse of the Lightgifter's partner, the tall man with the once-too-sharp tongue. Blood had pooled at his shoulders, staining the white fabric of his robe with a deep red collar.

Kirjath removed the white cord from the man's waist, then pulled the robe from the body. When he donned the robe himself he found that it fitted him well, leaving only the toes of his boots and the tips of his fingers exposed to the sun. The cowl shaded his head comfortably; soft, wet fabric cooling his itching scalp. He smiled down at the vacant corpse and rolled the slack head with his boot. A fly settled in the man's open mouth.

"Speak up, or I will open your mouth for you," he mimicked in a wheedling tone. Then he kicked the slack jaw shut. The teeth clocked together with a hollow sound, and the jaw hung slackly once more. He smirked towards the woman. He saw she had averted her gaze, but not enough to be unaware. She looked ill, and tears fell from her cheeks.

"Remember your partner here, should you have any clever little ideas. Do you understand, wench?"

There was a pause. "Yes," she replied at last, eyes still downcast.

Kirjath waited, his gaze menacing.

"Yes, my Lord."

The monotone could not fully conceal the loathing.

The Gateway still spun idly in the road. Kirjath scooped a small amount of Dark essence from the Gateway spell, pooling it in his left hand. Holding a new pattern in mind, he spoke the words of Silence, and directed the motes into her face, her mouth, her throat. A look of panic became resignation a second later.

Morgloth improve women's behaviour, Kirjath mused.

Without her voice, she would have no way to command the Light. Just like him, she needed both word and pattern for her spells.

She stared woodenly ahead of her. She was his.

Without warning, the Morgloth launched itself at the woman.

Kirjath cursed. He had lost concentration for a moment; already the beast infused a large part of his mind, like ink soaking into blotting paper. It wanted to feed.

He tried to isolate the demon again in the chaos of his thoughts. The Morgloth pushed the woman to the ground, forced her head back with sharp talons. Kirjath didn't even bother to shout, he gripped the demon's mind with all his mental power and clamped down fiercely, desperately.

Would it turn on me if I lost control?

To be ravaged by the hands of his own creation would be the ultimate failure. He had to keep a grip on himself. He spoke the command clearly, and banished the Morgloth to the Gateway. The pressure in his head became immense and painful. The beast issued a guttural growl. Kirjath felt a shudder within his mind, like a rotten fruit rupturing underfoot.

And still the Morgloth resisted.

Kirjath tightened the net of his psychic hold, and felt the demon scream. With a slash of its tail, the Morgloth leapt for the Gateway. It fell into the void with a screech, and was gone.

Kirjath stared at the earth as it faded from jet black to the brown of the surrounding roadway. The tension slowly eased from his shoulders. There was much to be learned about demons. The Darkmaster might have been wise to hide the Gateway spell and to never use it. The Morgloth seemed to be getting stronger every time.

He surveyed the woman as he returned. She had learned enough about him not to run. That was good, she knew he would kill her, if she gave him reason to. She had a willowy build, not full-bodied enough to really enjoy. And her dark, arching glare would need some training.

"Have you ever felt such perfect fear, Gifter? You've lived in shelter for too long. I am your Lord now, and I shall teach you more of fear. Much, much more." He moved close to her, close enough for her to smell the blood on the stained white robe. "Move," he commanded, and pushed her roughly into the road, towards Fendwarrow.

It was some time before they came across the Lightgifters' horses. The animals were well-trained, and had waited beside the road after running from their fright. They cropped the grass, and nickered when they saw the woman. The steed Kirjath took was skittish when he mounted it, but seemed to be pacified by the fact that its companion bore the woman, and it recognised her presence. They had forgotten the beast, and their fear. He didn't think the woman had.

16. PURSUIT
"The faster the arrow,
the greater the miss."—*Zarost*

The Kingfisher's Breeze was a comfortable inn. The door to the common-room was thrown wide, and it overlooked the main street of Southwind. Ashley sat together with Father Keegan and Sister Grace at a low table, enjoying the afternoon meal set before him. Potatoes fried with sharp spices, ale the colour of sunlight, and fish which steamed through melting butter. To the regular patrons it was good fare, to the travel weary, it was a feast.

Captain Steed sat across the table from the Lightgifters. They had travelled hard since before the dawn, on their separate courses. Ashley had a lot to digest besides the food. Of the two, the food was far more palatable.

A soft leather parchment was spread upon the table. Ashley traced their passage idly over the Captain's map. Yesterday, the village of First Light had yielded the awful news. The scourge of the Shadowcaster and the Morgloth would have been an unbelievable tale, had it not been for the stark honesty of the Captain, and the three coffins he tended. The Lightgifters' mission changed in that instant. They would not return to the Dovecote to discuss their findings. First, they would see justice done.

This morning, the broken remains of the Serannon farm, and the two fresh graves above the homestead, had told them all they needed to know. Hosanna's vision had been true. The blessing that Keegan had offered over the mounds had been spontaneous and heartfelt. They had pushed hard to reach Southwind, while their anger chafed against their slow passage through Meadowmoor. They would catch the man who had killed poor Gifter Trisha Serannon and her husband. Such a wicked murderer should not go free.

Captain Steed had travelled the direct route—through Brimstone, and Westmill. Three coffins lay in his carriage, destined for an honour burial at Stormhaven.

They ate mostly in silence.

The doorway darkened. A large Sword entered the common-room, and approached their table. His armour was streaked with the grime of hard travel. He smelled of sweat and leather. Ashley thought he should know the face.

"May I join your meal, Captain?" the newcomer boomed.

Captain Steed looked not a little surprised. "Master Glavenor! By all means join us, but why are you here, when you left a day before us?"

The big soldier dragged up a stool. "A frustrating tale, for I have run a loop!" He turned to the Lightgifters. "My apologies, all," he said, rising again from his chair. "My urgency has ambushed my manners. I am Garyll Glavenor." He extended a hand to Sister Grace, then to Father Keegan, and finally Ashley.

"Swordmaster Glavenor?" Ashley stammered, suddenly realising why the man had seemed familiar. A legend he, though seldom met by the likes of apprentice Gifters.

"Aye, but make no fuss of it. I have a big sword, but just now I wield it clumsily. The Shadowcaster—" He paused in mid-sentence, turned to the Captain. "They know?"

Captain Steed nodded. "They were sent from the Dovecote upon a premonition, though too late it seems. We do not dine together by chance."

Father Keegan leant forward, looking past Ashley to where Glavenor sat. "We have a common goal," he said. "This Shadowcaster must be found. We may be able to assist you, and you us."

"You have horses?" Glavenor asked. At their nods he continued. "There is no need for you to expose yourself to such danger. This man is vicious."

"There is every need," said Father Keegan. "A fine member of our Dovecote was murdered, her husband was murdered, and her home was destroyed. I intend to see justice served on the man responsible."

"Well spoken, Father. I hope your companions feel as strongly as you do about the quest." Glavenor's gaze ranged slowly over the Lightgifters. Their sincerity must have impressed him, for he nodded, and said, "We will make a good team, then."

"Swordmaster, you said you ran a loop. How so?" asked Sister Grace.

"At first he used his strange art to trick my eyes, and with that he gained a lead. I soon learned to track the Shadowcaster's horse, for its trail was true. But it seems the horse threw him, and ran wild. I found it after a long day in the saddle, far into the highlands. There was a madness in its eye, and it would not come close. It shied from my presence, I think that is why the chase was so lengthy and so misleading. I came here for news, for this murderer must have evaded me on foot."

"He travelled by boat," Captain Steed answered. "He tried for the King's Isle."

"Stormhaven?" Garyll looked vexed. "That is the last place I expected."

"The Serannon girl was taken there. The Shadowcaster followed them."

"Where does this tiding come from?"

"The local Swords," Captain Steed answered. "They say a man fitting the description of the Riddler passed through here yesterday with the girl. They think that a fisherman delivered her to Stormhaven during the night, though they can't be sure, for the man cannot speak, and I'm not sure we can trust him either, being who he is. But he was adamant that the Shadowcaster had followed them, and capsized in the lake. He was quite jolly about it."

Glavenor looked stunned. "Is this Shadowcaster so mad, that he would brave Stormhaven to reach the girl?"

"Maybe the threat of Stormhaven was exactly why he tried so hard to reach her. He is also partial to jurrum, so does not see the world as others see it. We found leaves on him when we arrested him."

"Who was the fisherman, to run such a risk for her?" Garyll asked. "He must be commended."

"A man called Mulrano. You remember him."

"Mulrano the—silenced one?" Garyll was suddenly alert.

"The same," Captain Steed answered.

"Well there's another turn I did not expect. Could the Shadowcaster have drowned?"

Captain Steed shook his head. "The fisherman didn't say that. He doesn't know. My guess is he can swim, and he's slunk off somewhere, tail between his legs. Not even a madman would try to accost her on the King's Isle."

"Fendwarrow," Garyll stated. "All roads of crime lead to Fendwarrow. That is where he must be headed."

Gabrielle! somebody thought. Ashley hadn't even tried to reach out with his mind; the thought had leapt into his head with its eagerness.

"Perfect!" shouted Father Keegan, rising to his feet. "Then to Fendwarrow we ride."

Glavenor raised a restraining hand.

"Father, allow me to replenish my strength. I have not eaten for a day. I shall leave with all haste."

Father Keegan looked surprised at his own outburst, and sat down abruptly. Glavenor beckoned to a serving girl. He ordered a large meal and some supplies for the road.

Ashley pored over the Captain's map again. Fendwarrow was to their east, six or seven leagues along the lake shore, beyond Russel and Waxworth and the leper's hideaway at Rotcotford. He kept his head down, trying to ignore Keegan's eyes, though he could feel the Father's regard.

Gabrielle. The image of the sultry woman lingered in his mind. Ashley had promised himself that he wouldn't snoop. But that thought had been fired at him, rich with dread and delight. From Keegan? What could Keegan know of Ashley's recurrent dream, why should Keegan know Gabrielle at all? Ashley tried to concentrate on the simple lines of the map, and force the other thoughts aside. It did no good to sneak into people's minds.

Fendwarrow seemed to grow darker on the map, wedged tight into the cleft of the Black River, a secretive, forbidden place.

Dread and delight.

His stomach churned.

Father Keegan left the table, and the sensations subsided. Ashley watched the map a while longer. He couldn't decide whether to be more worried about meeting the Shadowcaster at their destination, or the implications of what Keegan expected to find.

17. STORMHAVEN

"Which is stronger, the storm without,
or the storm within?"—*Zarost*

Tabitha was woken by a gentle shake.

"Hmm," she answered, her eyes still closed. It was all right, her mother always shook her gently when she fell asleep at the fire instead of in her bed. She was in the living room, and father had been telling a story.

"Hmm," she commented, tugging her blankets closer to her chin.

"Miss Serannon, Miss Serannon, it's time for the evening meal. Lady Westerbrook said to wake you."

Tabitha smiled groggily through the clouds of cosy dreams.

Where's the brook? Westerbrook?

She sat up. A little girl dressed in blue stood beside her bed. In a room that was not her own, with polished wooden floors, tall drapes, and a wide stone windowsill framing the pale mauve of an evening sky. She had fallen asleep in her clothes. The last wisps of her dreams swirled out of sight, and were replaced by the reality of Stormhaven.

She was alone here. She was safe. Everything else about her life was upside down.

The young chaperone seemed like a little angel.

"Pia, isn't it?"

The guideling nodded, and extended a small hand. Tabitha let the angel lead her down from the Boarding, out into the wide, paved street. Dusk was settling, and faint music could be heard. An armoured Sword passed them sedately, nodding in a friendly manner to the girls.

"Where are we going?" Tabitha asked.

"To eat, Miss Serannon. The evening meal for the Boarding is served at the Bee. It's only five doors down." She waved along the street in the direction they were walking.

"Why not at the boarding house," Tabitha enquired, a little nervous at being out in the strange, grand city at night. "Surely they serve meals there too?"

"They say there used to be a kitchen, but it was closed before I was a guideling. All food in Stormhaven must be prepared by a member of the Guild of Cooks, and the Boarding never has lots of people in it. Besides, it's more fun at the Bee," Pia added gaily.

They soon came upon a squat stone building that was trimmed with dark wood. An oil lamp lit a sign which had become softened at the corners. The gilded mascot of the Bee flew through the letters. Beyond the sign, great stained-glass windows spilled colourful light into the street. Great swathes of dark ivy climbed the walls. As Pia pulled the door open, the music and babble of voices rushed over them.

It seemed to Tabitha that everyone in Stormhaven must have come to the Bee. The common-room was packed. A bard played a lute boisterously upon a small stage. Finely dressed patrons leant casually towards others seated on tall stools. Women in beautiful dresses, with the fashionable short outer bodices, bantered gaily at a long bar. Men carried tankards across the room, women returned with slender wineglasses. Everywhere, people talked. Mouths wagged, and the words blended into a confusing hubbub that swallowed their meaning.

It really did sound as if she was inside a beehive.

Pia disappeared into the crowd, then darted back an instant later, offering Tabitha her hand again. The guideling wove between the bodies like a ferret through grass, finding a course where Tabitha saw none. Coals glowed in a hearth. They passed through an arched, open door into another room. Tabitha relaxed as the sound level dropped to a more mellow buzz.

Benches ran alongside large tables, the air was cooler, and kitchen scents drifted her way—she took a deep breath, and looked around the dining room. Some couples dined at separate tables, a few Swords occupied one nearby. They hunched over their meals, paying no attention to Tabitha and the guideling. Pia led her to the far side of the room, where a large group of adolescents bantered. They all wore the same blue guideling uniform, though in various fashions from rumpled to neat. A shapely girl who looked to be almost Tabitha's age wore a tunic that seemed intentionally too tight.

Pia guided Tabitha to a space near the end of the table, beside the open window.

"All us guidelings sup here. Miss May says it's a wonder we aren't all twice the size, with the meals we eat, but she forgets how much we run around the city for her during the day."

"Where is Miss Westerbrook, Pia? Does she eat with us?" It was unlikely that the Lady of Ceremony would dine with mere guidelings, but she could hope. Maybelle had seemed so gentle and comforting.

Pia pointed to a side door. A large figure was backing through the opening while talking to an equally well-proportioned man in an apron. Tabitha honed in on May's voice before she realised she was drawing on the Ring to do so. The clarity arrived with a rush of warmth in her right hand. She couldn't remember what she had done to trigger the Ring's aid. It seemed to respond to her need.

"I think the pumpkin pudding would be best, Kettle, and they can have the stew before. Oh, and there'll be an extra portion at our table for a few days." Maybelle Westerbrook emerged from what had to be the kitchens, and approached with a broad, motherly smile.

The guidelings calmed their banter as soon they saw her, and they all rose from their places, pressing their hands together to greet their mistress. Tabitha wasn't sure if it was appropriate, but she copied the gesture and bowed.

"Good evening, Tabitha. I hear you sleep very soundly." Maybelle winked, and came around to settle in a chair at the head of the table, close to Tabitha.

Two boys opposite Tabitha argued in loud whispers.

"Guidelings! Hush." Maybelle commanded. The two boys fell instantly silent, but glared at each other under their eyebrows.

"I want you all to say hullo to Tabitha Serannon, who's awaiting an audience with the King. She's new to Stormhaven, so you're to help her if she's lost."

A murmur of unsynchronised greetings rippled through the guidelings, as all eyes turned Tabitha's way. A boy with sandy hair was blushing, and it looked as if he kicked his neighbour beneath the table. He caught Tabitha watching him, and became crimson.

Thankfully, the guidelings soon turned their attention elsewhere. Bread arrived from the kitchens, and was devoured before it touched the table. A chunky, rich stew followed, and suffered the same rapid fate.

Tabitha wanted to hide, but the Lady of Ceremony kept up a lively conversation with her. May asked her about the spring weather in First Light, and if the sheep were ready for shearing, and how one spun wool to get the best thread. She told of the way the city had been extended since the early days, what weddings and ceremonies were taking place, and her frustration at how the Houses of Rule seemed to work against each other in everything they did. Apparently, nothing happened in haste in Stormhaven, for the centuries of rule had allowed the refinement of precise laws and procedures.

Tabitha began to relax in Maybelle's presence. The Lady of Ceremony had a natural gift for light conversation. Even so, a chance question broad-sided Tabitha.

"So how is your mother Trisha keeping?"

The colour leached from the room. The sights and sounds seemed to become a pale distraction, a desperately thin veneer of normality stretched over a deep, aching darkness.

"She isn't. She's—dead."

The nearest guidelings fell silent. May was appalled.

"When did this happen?"

"Three nights ago."

"What are you doing here?"

"S-sanctuary. I was pursued."

"Who would do such a thing?"

The Shadowcaster. Eyes like stained slate. Her father, at his feet.

"Can we talk about this some other time?" Tabitha pleaded softly. The thought of crying in front of the troop of youngsters was too much. Many of them were gawking at her.

May placed a hand over Tabitha's.

"I'm so sorry. Forgive me, I—this is terrible. I'll not pry where there's so much pain. This is why you have requested the King's audience? Good. He must know."

Tabitha bowed her head for a moment.

"You wish to talk of something else?" May asked gently.

Tabitha nodded; anything to draw her back from the yawning chasm of grief. "Tell me about history, if you will, something really old." As Stormhaven's historian, May must have a wealth of information.

"Of the city, or the realm?"

The further from the present day the better. "Has there ever been a war in Eyri?"

"Why do you ask?"

The Riddler had referred to a war, when they'd been riding to Southwind. He had spoken of it presently, as if the chaos might return at any time.

"Someone—uh—mentioned it. I didn't believe it at the time. Was there ever a war?"

"That takes us back a time," May answered, looking distant. "There are few who know the legends that well. Most folk today are too caught up in modern things. There was a war, if the legends hold any truth to them. The war was tied to the formation of Eyri in ancient times, before the coming of the Seven Wizards and the crowning of the First King. That is one period I have not studied well. You want to visit the Stormhaven Library, down on Greentree Street, it has scrolls and books from the early days, templates and drawings, oh wonderful things!"

May leant a little closer to Tabitha. "Truth be told, I would spend all my time there if it weren't for my other obligations. There's so much work these days, and so little time to study history." She looked wistful. "Which reminds me —" she said, rising from her chair to address the table. "Guidelings, it's way past the Set. Your parents await you, and we have a busy day in the morrow. Your dishes to the kitchen, then off with you!" She clapped her hands. "Thank you for a day well done."

May supervised the rapid clearing of their table, and led them all out of the dining room. The common-room was hot, pulsing with the throb of voices, but an air of restraint touched the people as Maybelle Westerbrook glided past, her line of blue goslings in tow.

Maybelle took Tabitha's arm as they stepped out into the street. "Take care not to hold the hurt forever inside. I shall make time if you'd like to finish your tale to me. I have so much to attend tonight, but would you care to join me for Noonday tomorrow? We can discuss the things of which you may not speak here."

Tabitha appreciated May's discretion. Three guidelings were still accompanying them. Tabitha nodded gratefully to May, honoured by the invitation.

"I'll send Pia in the morning. You'll be wanting to visit the Library, I don't doubt. Pia can show you where to go."

Tabitha voiced her thanks. She could spend a morning pretending to be an avid student of the histories. It would probably do her good to learn more of the legends of Eyri, however clouded their origins.

A remote bell sounded in the city, nine mellow chimes.

They parted at the Boarding. Tabitha was glad that May had been so friendly to her, but she was also relieved to be alone. The stairs creaked as she passed silent rooms. The hallways of the Boarding looked different beneath the sparse, flickering touch of lamplight; darker, bigger, full of shadows.

When she had readied herself for bed, Tabitha lit a candle and set it on the windowsill. She noticed that her leather bag lay on the floor, where she had left it. It would be wise to keep a closer guard on it.

The coins would be the first to go. She caught her breath.

If I should lose mother's scrolls now, I wouldn't even know the songs.

She would read them immediately, she decided. Songs she'd never seen, the legacy of a mysterious knowledge, to be read in secret. Her pulse quickened as she reached out for the leather bag and drew it close. She found the tube within. She was about to pull it free of the bag, when someone appeared at the door to her ward. She froze.

"Already the first night and you want to break the rules. Did I not say lights out at nine bells?"

She had forgotten about the matron and her rules. Tabitha snatched her arm back from the bag. The beefy woman crossed the room, glared down at her, then snuffed the candle between finger and thumb.

"Lights out means lights out!" was all she said, before turning on her heel. The sharp scent of smoking candle-wick lingered in her wake.

"Sorry."

"First offence, Miss Serannon. See that you don't commit another in your stay, or you'll have a premature departure." The doorway was filled, then it lightened faintly, and footsteps boomed down the stairs.

Tabitha slipped beneath the blankets. The song-scroll would have to wait.

She stared through a chink in the curtains at the night sky. The song-scroll would have to wait for the next day. The stars appeared as pale smears on the imperfect glass. She watched them for a long time. There seemed to be far too much dark between the smudges of light.

18. RAVENSCROFT

"Does your own reflection look you in the eye?"—*Zarost*

Cabal of Ravenscroft, how Kirjath hated him.

With the hate, came respect. The aged Master was a twisted, tyrannical ruler, but he was no fool. His command of the Dark essence was as complete as could be imagined—he was the first Shadowcaster, and so his lore was always more practised and deadly than anyone's. That knowledge kept Kirjath Arkell on his knees in the throne room, despite his rage at having to debase himself so.

One day, old man, I shall strike you down, and take your throne. I have another power, one you were too afraid to test.

Kirjath ran a darting tongue over his lips, and tasted his crusted wounds. They only served to remind him of his failure, which brought his anger to the fore.

Why not now? Rip his head off.

He stiffened, and forced the bloodlust away. The Morgloth's presence clung to him even though the demon itself was gone. With every channelling, the beast's mind became harder to control. He could overpower the Morgloth, but he could not risk losing that command. Here in the throne room of the Darkmaster, he wasn't sure what would be thrown at him. Better to endure the Darkmaster's wrath, than to challenge him prematurely and risk losing control of his own beast.

He remained kneeling, and waited for Cabal's touch.

The black curtains which adorned the throne room gave Kirjath the usual headache. He knew that the curtains were designed to make subjects nervous and unsettled. They rippled and swirled erratically, making the periphery of Kirjath's vision a torture of warped angles, curling patterns and sudden human forms. The fabric was a delicate weave of Dark essence, refined to a complex pattern no one could equal—a reminder to all of Cabal's mastery.

Kirjath kept his eyes lifted proudly from the floor. He would not bow his head as the Master expected. His gaze did not penetrate far. The single brand suspended overhead cast a pitiful pool of illumination on the glistening obsidian floor. A few paces of lit stone, then the shadows. Kirjath was an easy target, a penitent figure in a circle of guttering light. For the first time he wondered if the white robe he wore was irreverent, in this, the heart of the Shadowcasters' domain.

At least the robe was stained with blood.

The arrival of the Darkmaster was a staged indulgence. Kirjath abhorred the theatrics. They were the same every time. When you entered, the throne was so thick with darkness that nothing could be seen of its occupant. One walked to the lit stage, at the base of the throne, then turned and knelt, so that you faced away, the way you had come in, the way you hoped to leave. It did no good to anticipate the Master, for he was entirely silent in his approach. Sometimes it took hours for the Master to deign an audience, sometimes longer, but once you had been summoned to the room, you never left before the Darkmaster granted leave.

The stone bit into Kirjath's knees, but he ignored the pain. He had endured far, far worse in this place.

Cold, bony fingers touched Kirjath's neck from behind. He jumped, despite himself.

There was something about that hand which always brought a chill sweat to Kirjath's brow. The Darkmaster was not a pleasant man to have under your skin.

He dropped his gaze to the floor.

"Still so proud, Kirjath Arkell." The Master's voice was the sound of dry scales disturbed by a breeze.

Kirjath did not answer. Sometimes it was better to be silent, when you knew your voice would quaver and betray you. Kirjath smarted on his own weakness as he waited. The icy hand withdrew from his neck. The Master remained behind him. The curtains rippled.

"You did not come when first called, Arkell."

Kirjath pronounced his words with a forced, steady command.

"You presumed my task done, Master, which it was not."

Kirjath tensed in anticipation of discipline. It was only now, in the Master's throne room, that he realised how insolent his actions had been. The Master's presence altered behind him, but whether Cabal had stepped closer, or further away, he couldn't tell. Cold crept through Kirjath's legs.

"I see. And why did you linger with your task?"

"The Lightgifter would not release the Ring. She fought."

"So you surely succeeded in your task then. The Lightgifter did not overpower you, did she?" A belittling tone underlined every word.

"No!" snapped Kirjath, resisting the urge to lash out with Dark essence. He had to remember who he was talking to, he couldn't afford anger here. "I overpowered her. She lies in her grave."

"You killed the Lightgifter? Under what authority?" The Master's voice crackled quietly, the way that ice wheezes when placed in water.

"The Lightgifter resisted. She chose to fight. She was too talented in the use of essence. I had to kill her. Her and her husband."

"Are you a complete idiot? I should tear the lining from your brain and feed it to the crows." The threat was not an empty one—Kirjath knew of at least two Shadowcasters who had ended their service in just that manner. The Master was suddenly close, his lips against Kirjath's ear.

"Give me a reason to stay my hand."

Surely the Master couldn't be serious? The Light was the enemy. What did the death of one Gifter matter? *I don't have to take this humiliation. I am Kirjath Arkell. I kill with ease.*

"I used the Morgloth to do it." He smirked at the empty stone before him. *Chew on that! Push me too far, and I'll use it on you.* The bloodlust surged through his veins, bringing strength and a wild abandon.

The curtains ceased their movement. The throne room became as still as a mausoleum. The Darkmaster was somewhere behind him, waiting. Kirjath turned, a gesture forbidden in the throne room.

The Master was at the limit of the illumined circle, his cowl thrown back. His pale, lined face displayed no trace of the shock or awe Kirjath had expected. Dark eyes bored into Kirjath. His confidence began to crumble, a pitiful castle of sand before the winter gale.

"You have need to study your history better, Kirjath Arkell. Such beasts are dangerous beyond your comprehension."

"I command them! And I had to! Without the Morgloth—I would have been executed in that cell in First Light. Anything is justified to avoid such a fate."

Why does the Master shake his head?

"It is worse than I imagined, then. You faced down the Sword with your Morgloth?"

"None other than the Swordmaster," Kirjath said, pride swelling briefly in his heart. "My beast left three of them dead."

"Then it has begun," said Cabal, his stare cold and unreadable. His hands curled into fists, then he hid them within the sleeves of his robes. "The Swordmaster will not leave that particular trail. And your trail leads here, to Ravenscroft. Idiot! You'd best be gone through Fendwarrow before the day is out. Intercept him there, and lead him away. We can't afford to have Ravenscroft discovered, not now." The Master paced into the gloom.

Footsteps followed a loop in the darkness, then suddenly the Master was there again, in the pool of light. Kirjath noted the essence which had collected in an outstretched hand.

He tensed, bracing himself for the inevitable punishment.

But what formed in the Master's hand was not a spell of torture. With a brief command, the Master created a raven from the motes.

"Bring me news of the Swordmaster of Eyri. Where he is, and who accompanies him. Go!" He released the Morrigán, and it swooped to the door, leaving the throne room with a mocking cry.

"I give it a task, it is done. Why does that not happen with you?"

A cloud of motes swept towards him.

Kirjath felt a desperate shame. Inadequacy flooded him. It was a spell, he knew, but the knowledge made the compulsion no less compelling. He abased himself on the stone.

"Forgive me, Master. My task was more complex than the Morrigán's."

"You do have the Ring, though?"

Straight to the heart of matters.

The tone of the Master's voice warned Kirjath of worse to come, but there was no way to deny him the knowledge. Kirjath cursed.

"No, Master, but I know where it is. I am sure it is borne by the girl, the daughter of the Lightgifter. If I could be free from the need for this audience, I would complete my task."

Kirjath's sentence ended at a far higher pitch than he had intended. He heard a sound from the direction of the Darkmaster he would rather not have heard. Knuckles cracked as fury gripped Cabal by his bones.

When he spoke, the wheezing voice was so close to Kirjath he could feel the tremor of the Master's rage against his cheek. He didn't dare move.

"Think how the Swords will search for you now. Your actions have destroyed your chance at succeeding in the task. Your mission was not one of murder. Your mission was to retrieve the Ring! I must have the Ring!"

I must distract him, mollify him, or I won't survive this.

"Why, Master?" Kirjath asked, in his most grovelling tone. "Help me to understand, that I might serve you better. You are so powerful already, why do you need a trinket like the Ring?"

"My plan is almost complete, the triumph is counted in days, not in years. But the Ring is too dangerous to be at large! I must have it before I strike! You have failed me in the most critical task." He pointed a crooked finger at Kirjath, and a fine thread of motes speared Kirjath through his stomach. Kirjath couldn't resist the scream which broke from his mouth—there was a needle pressed into his spine, in a place so sensitive and fundamental he was driven near to madness.

The Master's voice came through a haze of pain. "I am poised to strike. But what if the Ring is used against me? What if someone learns of its power before it is reclaimed?" The question was no more than a whisper. A second needle lanced into his groin, making the first seem benign by comparison.

Kirjath's throat worked hard to keep the bile from rising into his mouth. He was not afraid, he told himself.

"But what does the Ring do, Master?" he squeaked.

"The fundamentals of essence, I learned from that Ring. When I wore it, I could see beyond the Lightgifters, to the possibility of the Dark, and beyond. I learned the most powerful spells; the Turning, the Devotion, the Web, before I reached the Ring's limit, before it fell from my finger in Levin."

"But did you not lose your ring in Fendwarrow, Master?" Kirjath asked, desperately hoping that the Darkmaster hadn't noticed how his torturing had eased when he pondered the mysteries of the Ring.

"I could not wear it, you fool! It fell from my hand over a decade ago, and would not be replaced. I kept it bound on a chain, lest it be lost, and found. That chain broke in Fendwarrow. I cannot risk another adept finding it, and growing to power. I will command this realm, in its entirety!"

Kirjath felt at once relieved and excited. The Ring had just become an immensely appealing treasure. He knew where it was. The bearer was hardly an adept, she was just running scared.

"A girl carries it." He snorted his disdain.

The pain of the twin probes returned with merciless pressure.

"You careless idiot! She has already evaded you. Do you think it pure luck that she escapes? She is learning from the Ring! The longer you take, the less likely your success."

A sobering thought, even without the persuasion of torture. Yet

Kirjath wasn't entirely sure it was the Ring's fault the girl had escaped, from both First Light and Southwind.

"She had a companion, a man who claimed to be the Riddler, though I know it is impossible. He was guiding her."

The Master's spells broke, the motes scattered to the shadows.

"My absent advisor works against me? The Riddler?" The Master's rustling voice hardened to a crunching, gravelly sound.

"No, no, you misunderstand," Kirjath reassured hastily. "This was a little man, a beggarly-looking fellow, with no skill in the Dark and a ridiculous hat. He couldn't have been the true Riddler, the great oracle of Ravenscroft."

"Did you ever see the true Riddler, Arkell? See his face?"

"Ah—no. His cowl was always—but he was bigger. Not a Shadowcaster?" he ended lamely. He had always taken the Riddler for a powerful Caster, second only to the Darkmaster. He had never dared cross the Master's advisor.

"Few have ever seen his face, here in Ravenscroft. It was one of the privileges he asked for, and I granted it for the wisdom he imparted. He wore the robe of the Shadowcasters, but no orb. He was an advisor. His power was a masterful illusion."

"You say he was an advisor, not is?"

"I have not seen him since he departed on a wagon run, before my Ring was lost in Fendwarrow. Damn him! He has tracked the Ring like a bloodhound on the scent."

"You're saying that the little hatter could have been the real Riddler?"

"When the Riddler does the wagon run, he wears a striped hat and outlandish clothes. And he is very, very good at evading the Morrigán when he wants to. You miserable slack-wit! He has defected!"

The Master was quick to summon the essence, and weave a fresh messenger raven.

"Speak your description to the bird, Arkell. Tell it what the Riddler looks like in the light of day."

Kirjath recalled what he could—the brown skin, the bushy beard, the racoon-striped top hat.

"Find that man!" Cabal ordered. The Morrigán departed with double the haste of the first. "You, as well, Shadowcaster, that is your task. The Riddler must be found, and brought back to me, he knows too much of my purpose. Damn him! How did I not see his danger?"

"He was too close to you, perhaps?" Kirjath commented, then bit his tongue. The Master did not welcome criticism. Cabal seemed to ignore the slight.

"And the Ring, Master?"

"Of course the Ring, you sluggard! They'll likely be close together, the Ring and the Riddler. That may be what he was after, all along. Go now, you whining whelp, go!"

Kirjath rose on unsteady feet. His legs ached cruelly. The part the Master had tortured was excruciating. But Cabal had commanded, and he had to obey. The compulsion originated within his Darkstone. There was nothing he could do to resist the Darkmaster's hold on his Stone.

"Master, may I employ the aid of the Morgloth in my task?"

"I don't care how you achieve their deaths," the Darkmaster answered in a crisp whisper. "But you broke into a most private vault in Ravenscroft to gain the demon-lore, so chew on this while you execute your task. It may offer a good reminder of the value of things left unbroken."

A curling ball of motes shot from the Master's hand, too fast to avoid. Kirjath heard the tooth crack in his jaw before he felt the pain. Splinters of dentine gouged into his tongue. He ground down on the ruined tooth, just to spite the violation, to make it his own will that caused the agony. The taste of blood was sharp.

He said nothing more.

Yet so much changed as his feet bore him across the hard surface of the throne room, through the gloom beyond the torch, to the arched exit, and the cold passage beyond. With each step he took away from the coercive influence of the Darkmaster, his own anger returned. He could think for himself again, and only for himself. A clear purpose filled Kirjath Arkell, clearer than any he had ever known before.

Cabal was wrong to punish him for daring the demon-lore. The Master had pushed him too far.

Kirjath vowed that his days of being a servant to the Darkmaster were over. The Riddler and the girl would die, but for his own reasons. He would return with the Ring, and the Morgloth, more powerful than the tyrant could ever be.

Kirjath had discovered a compulsion stronger than fear.

Hatred.

He spat a mouthful of blood against the wall. The Darkmaster would taste an infinitely larger amount of that before he died. Kirjath would take great care that his enemy died slowly.

19. ECHOES OF ETHEA

"Secrets love to be told."—*Zarost*

Tabitha gazed at the parchments which lay on the giant oak table. Three sheets of crackling paper, each covered with her mother's upright script. She spread the pages flat with the outside of her arms, but the corners still curled defiantly inwards. The library was quiet, as still as a cave, apart from the librarian who scuttled past infrequently. Most of the scholars who were present were bent over their own work, hidden at tables amongst the tall shelves of bound scrolls, books, manuscripts, and tomes of law. The alcove which Tabitha had chosen was dimly lit. A fat candle squatted on an iron saucer. Its red skin collected wax in warts and blisters as time breathed slowly over it.

The first page was a disorganised collection of writing. It looked as if Trisha had built up a poem over many months or separate entries. The ink was faded in some places, and arrows redirected text across the page. Dominating the page was a musical score, exactly scribed, needing no alteration. The melody marched through the chaos of words, binding them together. After the final rest, a comment had been added.

Echoes of a distant voice—Yearsend 402.

Tabitha recognised the date. She had been born at the end of that month, on Midsummer's Eve. She wondered if it was coincidental.

The lyrics were difficult to follow from start to finish, but after a while she had sorted the order.

The string of the lyre plucked in tune
can shed off its notes with a shiver.
A voice that is pure can unleash the allure
of the Singer, the Saviour, Lifegiver!
All lives might be woven together,
all bitter cruel warring might cease,
when the song in your heart is sung in full,
when that resonance finds release.
When the Song of Life is sung in full,
and the Universe feels its peace.

Lifesong. The title she had used for her own song, the one she had learned in the daydream, the song she had sung to bring her mother back.

The melody was different, but the score had as many pauses and silences as her own version. Rests, where a normal song would have had notes. She didn't have a lyre, but she could follow the music in her head. She didn't dare to break the silence of the library by singing out loud, but she risked a quiet humming of the tune. It was a light, delicate, and strangely timed piece, enchanting in a familiar way. The same powerful word tied the two songs together.

She traced her fingers over the jumbled lyrics, wondering if she had got the sequence right. It seemed to rhyme, the way she had sung it.

Mother wrote this? Did she ever sing it?

She imagined her mother sitting in the living room, playing gaily on her twin-stringed lyre, her golden hair catching the sun. The image dissolved with a piercing sting of truth. Her mother would never play music again.

The second page bore no music at all. It was filled with patterns, three complex diagrams made from pale and delicate threads.

Light. Spell-patterns of the Light!

She knew such diagrams were forbidden. Only the Dovecote held spell-scrolls. The Gifter's knowledge was strictly protected, yet here stood spell-patterns, she was sure, written in her mother's own hand.

Tabitha scanned the labels.

Flameburst. Spriteblind. Truthfury.

The names conjured up images of a Gifter in battle, the Light used as a weapon, with a deadly intent. Tabitha was stunned. Violence was not the Lightgifter's way, not according to what she had been told about Lightgifters.

Maybe these spells are not taught in the Dovecote.

A burn-scarred Shadowcaster. Phantom Acres in ashes. The fire might not have been set by the Shadowcaster. It might have been her mother's last act of defence.

Tabitha followed the intricate designs. Within the curling patterns, delicately scribed under the threads, stood the words of each spell.

It took her some time to decipher the writing, and even longer to memorise the spells. The patterns were so complex she resorted to covering each of them up, to study them in parts. The candle burned lower.

It was ironic that the first spells of Light she was learning were patterns of violence. She wondered how one practiced such spells. However, it made her feel good, to have begun her learning as a Lightgifter. She would surely be trained in many spells in the Dovecote. She wasn't so sure they would ever teach her the Flameburst, Spriteblind or Truthfury. It would be her secret, kept with mother's spirit.

At last, she was ready to turn the page. The last scroll was another musical score. She recognised the unique timing at once. She eagerly mouthed the words as she followed the special music.

Sing low from your heart with grieving,
and sing back the faults you have cast,
Undo the hurt in the words never meant;
for hate can return from the past.
All Death is an end to a circle,
all circles must close to be tight,
better the truth than the lies of before,
when wrong was held to be right.
Better the truth than the falseness before,
when you hold the Creation in sight.

Something was different about this Lifesong stanza, it felt like a dirge, not a dance. Her mouth was dry. She noticed a remark penned in the border.

Played during Summerset 410. Wasting death amongst the animals despite Light healing. Worst winter in memory. Hank and Tabitha sick. Is this linked?

Tabitha searched for a memory of the bad winter. She would have been seven years old in that year. She drew on the Ring, and clarity infused her. Tabitha's memories became a matrix of detail, neatly ordered, layer upon layer, every year unique, every sight and sound present in her thoughts. The immensity of what the Ring allowed her to see was overwhelming, but her need drove her onwards. She held onto her purpose—to find the time when she had endured the effects of the second stanza.

A memory burst across her vision. A bed, her mother's healing, an emptiness that never filled, her own frail arms pulling at the blankets, an incessant cough. She had all but forgotten it. Once recalled, the memory was vivid, so vivid she began to cough and tremble in her heart. The snow had blocked the windows until well past Wintersbreach. It had seemed that the essence had been drained from the world around her, and that everything was hollow, without substance. It was the first time she had ever feared that she might die. Thankfully her mother had only sung the stanza once, and had neither practiced nor perfected it.

She let out a long, slow breath. The vision faded.

A footnote was scrawled at an angle beneath the last verse.

Long have I prayed for a song to heal the hurt I have caused. I fear to sing either of these verses again. Beware. There is a power here I do not understand.

Tabitha stared at the second stanza and its anecdotes. The candle wax spilled over the rim of its saucer, and pooled slowly on the desk, flowing into a knotted depression. The flame guttered, and died, leaving a trail of smoke rising through the returning gloom. The words became indiscernible.

Beware.

There was much Tabitha didn't understand of her mother's writing. Little wonder her mother had never spoken of the songs, never shared the knowledge with her. It was secret. The horror of the last song had spoiled the joy of the first, that was plain. For the first time, Tabitha considered that maybe her mother had not bequeathed the scrolls at all. Maybe they were private, and should have joined the ashes of Phantom Acres, the secret kept intact to the grave. Maybe she should not have learned the violent spells, or read the verses of the Lifesong at all.

She slipped the scrolls into their sheath. The leather tube was a heavy burden in her bag as she made for the exit, but she knew it was the kind of knowledge never intended to be left in a library.

Tabitha's noon engagement with Lady Westerbrook was at the Leaf of Merrick. She found May at a private table in the arboretum which overlooked the grounds. Spring played through soft leaves beneath the sun. Beyond the verdant gardens, the buildings of Stormhaven dropped away to the distant City Walls. Even the glinting allure of Amberlake was bright in the clear air.

The food was served on fine earthenware. Salads, oils, herb-bread and cheese soon settled her belly, and a mild drink of honey jasmine soothed the last of Tabitha's nervousness away. The Lady of Ceremony was as respectful and open-hearted as always. After a few pleasant minutes of light conversation, she could not avoid May's probing sympathy.

"Finally, I get the time to hear about your journey," said May, smiling. "Are you happy to talk of it, or shall it wait for another day?"

Tabitha set her bread aside. It would do no good to avoid the truth. She nodded to May.

"Your mother died," May began gently, "and yet you sought sanctuary here. Your father? Dead as well?"

Tabitha dipped her head again.

"Mercy me! And this morning, a certain Captain Steed of the Sword was seen arriving, with a heavy burden—three fallen comrades from First Light. I have been asked to prepare a Ceremony of Memorial. He wouldn't speak more of it. Is there a link in this tragedy?"

The Shadowcaster. The face at the window. Father falling. The burnt remains of Phantom Acres. Blackened skeletons in the ash.

The suppressed memories flooded her mind. Tabitha wished that she had more control over the Ring's intensity.

"Oh dear, oh dear!" said May, placing a comforting hand on Tabitha's arm. "I didn't mean to upset you so."

"No, it's all right!" Tabitha said, too sharply. "I want to talk, I need to tell you. I just wish –" Tears stung her eyes. "I just wish it didn't hurt so." She paused to steady her voice. "I feel so alone without anyone knowing."

"I understand, I know," May comforted. "You tell me when you feel it's right."

When did it all begin to go wrong?

"He came at night," Tabitha began, "and he struck father to the floor with his Dark essence. He was a Shadowcaster, one of the Dark Essentials. He wanted –" Tabitha paused, feeling suddenly uncertain.

The Ring. She bit her cheek, and closed her eyes for a second.

You have to trust somebody.

"He wanted my mother's Ring," she continued. "Mother wouldn't give it to him, and she gave it to me, made me run, out into the night, and leave them there. When I returned, after two days—they were both dead, lying in the ashes of the fire."

Tears stung her eyes.

May's gentle touch steadied Tabitha. Nonetheless, telling the whole story hurt like a fire-brand pushed through her heart. She told

May everything—of the Riddler, and her escape from First Light, the ride to Southwind, the night of terror on the lake, Mulrano the hero, their reception at Stormhaven. There was only one secret she wasn't prepared to share. She kept the Lightstone hidden beneath her tunic.

When Tabitha had finished, May rose and came to hold Tabitha tight. Tabitha took strength from the embrace.

May returned to her chair, shaking her head. "It seems we are living in terrifying times, and you are right at the centre of events. The past few days are likely to shake the whole of Eyri to its roots, and I don't think it will stop shaking for some time."

"Do you think they'll catch the Shadowcaster, May? The Swords, will they stop him?"

"Yes, my dear, they will have to, but it sounds as if he is terribly dangerous. To leave three of the Swords dead, as well as your parents! This is more violent a man than any rumours we have collected from Fendwarrow of Shadowcasters. He shall be brought to the King's justice," she ended, with a level stare.

"Executed?"

"I don't doubt it."

Seeing the certainty in May's eyes made Tabitha feel a little better, but her sadness remained. Killing the Shadowcaster wasn't ever going to bring her parents back.

"You spoke of a ring your mother treasured. Was that all that the Shadowcaster sought? His actions sound extreme for a thief."

Not really a thief, Tabitha thought. The Ring hadn't really belonged to her mother, either.

"It's not an ordinary kind of ring," said Tabitha. She held up her right hand to the light. The Ring glistened like wet glass, a band of moving clarity. "Promise you'll keep this a secret?" she asked.

"But there's nothing there," said May, at length. She shot Tabitha a concerned glance.

"Here, feel it," Tabitha insisted, reaching out and taking hold of May's hand. She guided May's fingers to the Ring.

May gasped. "I still can't see it!" she exclaimed, "but I can feel it. It's so cold." May squinted. "Yet completely invisible."

Strange, it's warm to me. Can't she see it at all?

"This is incredible!" said May. "I've never heard of such a thing." She touched the Ring again, then withdrew her hand as if stung.

"It's bitterly cold. Why do you wear such a thing?"

For the clarity of thought, the sight of a hawk, the hearing of a hound. Because with it, I understand more. Because it is a beautiful thing. Because I cannot remove it.

Every reason was too private to reveal.

"It's mine," she said. She knew it sounded lame.

"Yet the Shadowcaster knew about this ring, even though it can't be seen. He came to your mother to collect it."

Tabitha caught a warning glint in May's eye.

"Did it belong to anyone before your mother?"

She has reasoned out the Shadowcaster's pursuit. How do I answer truthfully without making Mother seem to be a thief?

"The Riddler said it has passed through many hands, but that it belongs to a wizard."

"A wizard! The only wizards I've heard of live in the myths of the Forming, and who knows how fanciful the pens which wrote that history were? There are no wizards in Eyri, Tabitha."

"But the Riddler said it was my quest to find the wizard."

"This Riddler, he wouldn't be a small, brown-skinned man with a bristling beard and a striped pelt hat."

"Yes!" exclaimed Tabitha. She realised that she had only alluded to him in her tale, but never described him. "You know him?"

"That trickster preyed on the Swordmaster when he was in Levin."

"You know about that?" Tabitha said, incredulous.

"Not many know, but I am a historian, Tabitha. Collecting knowledge of events is my skill. Now if this is the same man who rescued you from the Shadowcaster, my advice would be to be thankful, but don't believe a word he says."

"Twardy Zarost speaks in riddles, but I think there is always truth in what he says. He seems very wise."

"Wise at appearing wise, no doubt. Tricksters always are, and they're always after something."

"But Zarost hasn't taken anything from me."

"Are you sure? Have you counted your coin recently?"

"I've never—there's so much—I never thought to check."

She reached for her bag beneath the table, then thought better and looked up at May sharply.

"That's not like Twardy, he wouldn't have stolen anything from me. He wouldn't even take the Ring, when he saw it and I offered it to him."

"He can see the Ring as well as you? Then it is a strange thing I don't understand. How can one person see it, and not another?"

"Twardy Zarost is clever that way. He saw the Shadowcaster too, when the Swords wouldn't believe him in First Light."

"Just—be careful around him," said May. "And be careful with that ring. Your pursuer must covet it greatly, to have risked so much to follow you."

Tabitha suddenly considered another alarming possibility. The lone Shadowcaster might not be the only one to be sent after her. The more secret she kept the Ring, the less of a target she would be.

"Please. Don't tell anyone about it."

May regarded her coolly. "You will speak of it to the King, when you have audience with him? He must know the whole story, to understand your pursuit."

It was something Tabitha hadn't considered, baring herself to the King. It was unavoidable, she supposed. He was the King of Eyri, and she had requested an audience.

"Yes, I'll tell him," she promised.

"Good, then let us finish our meal, and speak no more of it. I'll hold what we have said in confidence."

They shared an elegant dessert that was laden with the taste of sharp orange, sweet apple, and soft cream. The breeze rustled through the arches of the arboretum. Small, chirruping birds descended on their table the moment they left, to scour the plates for crumbs.

May settled their account, then hugged Tabitha in parting.

"Ask the librarian to show you the ancient histories, like the Legend of the Forming," she said. "It will answer a lot of your questions about wars, kings and wizards."

"Thank you, May, for everything. You've been so kind to me."

May smiled. "Never fear to call on me, when you have need. Messages travel swiftly with my guidelings."

Tabitha was soon mounting the stairs to the Library for the second time that day. The doorman nodded in recognition as she passed.

"Closing time is four bells, missy."

His gruff words followed her down the vaulted admission corridor. She was sure to be done in two hours. There was only so much one could take in, and to Tabitha it seemed that the whole of the last week had been saturated with detail. In truth, a few minutes of poring over the ancient histories would probably be enough to put her to sleep.

But when she finally sat before the thick tome of The Forming, and opened its heavy leather cover, she found that she was drawn into another world. The book told of battles and sieges, of wild magic, the formation of Stormhaven, and the inauguration of the first King of Eyri. Vivid illustrations mirrored each page of text, showing the action and tragedy, heroism and valour, terrifying beasts, armoured men, and the ravages of war. It was history, but a history so colourful and rapid that Tabitha scarcely noticed her second candle of the day failing in its saucer. The hours passed by in the blink of an eye, a blink filled with learning.

War was a strange thing for Tabitha. She had lived all her life in peace, her ancestors had lived in peace. Before the Shadowcaster's evil deed, she would have found it difficult to imagine real battles and bloodshed. Yet such strife seemed to be the norm in the ancient times, according to the legend.

There was no clear enemy, but the invasions into Eyri never ceased. They battled fierce dusty men with shaven heads, the northern Lûk, whose pointed staffs and great woven shields made them difficult targets, and whose devious thrownets were said to grip like iron cables. The Lûk claimed the Eyrian land belonged to them, that it was a holy place, the source of the Ever-running Waters, and should not be set foot upon. The Eyrians claimed that they were there to stay, and so they fought.

A vicious clan of axe-wielding miners who had travelled through the Zunskar, apparently seeking to extend their lode of gold, claimed ancestral ownership of all the mountains around Eyri. The Eyrians said they could stay if they wanted to mine and trade in iron, but that they would never own the mountains. This led to a battle in the Broken Lands which lasted for three bitter winter months before the miners surrendered.

The westland was infiltrated by cloaked archers, and the stronghold of Llury was besieged by a band who announced their kind as Hunters from Eastmark; leather-armoured, swift-footed, difficult to track or even face, for they shot from afar, from the trees, from the dark. They offered no truce or treaty—they came for women, they had few of their own. Nowhere within the surrounding Great Forest was safe, even after the Eyrian men learned to ambush the Hunters by dressing as women with blades concealed in their clothes, and to steal the horned-tipped bows from those Hunters they killed. It cost many lives to regain command of the pallisaded Llurian village.

Eyrians had been divided in their warring, for it appeared that there was no unified Sword or even a King of Eyri. The inhabitants of the realm were herders, trappers, fishermen and traders, yet all were called upon to be warriors. Few crops were grown, and nothing was said of crafts except for the iron-forgery at Respite, the site of many harrowing battles. Only the strongest or the luckiest survived. The people were gradually forced inwards from the rim of Eyri, to the great defensive settlement of Levin.

And then the worst threat of all fell upon them—the beasts of black hunger, the nightmare of the winged Morgloth. A single beast was said to claim one hundred lives. There seemed to be no defence against its scourge. One artwork depicted five Morgloth circling the town, with terrified people scattering beneath.

It was there in Levin that the Gyre of the Seven Wizards appeared. It wasn't clear in the writing where they came from, or why they came. They drove the Morgloth back. They were always depicted as a group, standing close to form a circle. A great meeting of the peoples was called soon after the Gyre's arrival.

The Gyre set a trial. They laid a sword upon the ground within their circle, a sword unlike any ever seen before, of fine craftsmanship and apparent lightness. The aged wizard who demonstrated it to the crowds wielded it with ease despite its size. It was forged, they said, to be wielded against the Morgloth. The beasts had been driven off, but they would return.

Any man or woman who could breach the Gyre's circle was said to be worthy to receive the gift. A day of furious attempts ensued, but every hopeful was repelled, no matter how hale or hardy they seemed. The people became frenzied, for the sword was obviously valuable. Everyone wanted to own it. But the circle of the Gyre had a warding, some hidden device of sorcery that shielded the wizards. Even the rocks that were thrown in frustration rebounded at the throwers. The people must have felt cheated fools, until at last, one warrior breached the circle.

Stevenson became the instant hero of the people, even more so when his tale was told, for he had approached the circle wanting the blade not for himself, but for the defence of the people of Eyri—he was truly prepared to face the Morgloth. Thus did the blade Felltang pass into Stevenson's hands. Stevenson was later named the first Swordmaster of Eyri, for his selfless use of the sword against all foes.

That must be the blade at Garyll's side, Tabitha marvelled. *Felltang.* At least a part of the myth was true, if all the rest sounded wild and fantastic.

There came upon the Eyrians a time of desperate war, for the Lûk came renewed from the north. But the Gyre did not abandon the people to die. They caused the bedrock to rise up from the Amberlake, linking the land at Levin to the distant wooded isle in the lake's centre by a narrow causeway. The Gyre made a strange offer—for those who would swear fealty to the crown of Eyri, the Gyre would assist to build a mighty defence on the isle, and there the people would be safe. But there was confusion, for Eyri did not yet have a King. In answer, the wizards produced the Kingsrim, a golden coronet of fine crafting. They explained that it would be sufficient to kneel before the crown alone. The monarch would be chosen in good time.

Now the Eyrians were fierce survivors, and were suspicious of things they did not understand. How could they swear allegiance to a King who had yet to be crowned? The offer seemed too open to trickery and abuse. But as they argued, the assault intensified. A new force of leather-faced men descended on horseback from the southern highlands, bearing fletched spears and wickedly barbed throwing discs, adding to the threat of the Lûk. The invaders were devastating, but they were crippled by their own diversity. They fought as much with each other as with the Eyrians. Over all this the Morgloth swooped, taking lives wherever they wished, paying no heed to the changing sides of battle. It was from this bloody chaos that Stormhaven was born.

One by one, the Eyrians swore fealty to the Unnamed King, and retreated over the Kingsbridge to the isle, for their burden of battle was grievous, and they could see the inevitable end of their kin.

Soon, the city of Stormhaven began to take shape, and from the first moment it offered the Eyrians a reprieve from their war. The Kingsbridge was narrow, and easily defended. They had feared that their wooden walls would prove too weak, until the Gyre had revealed the wonder of stonewood. There was fish aplenty in the Amberlake, orchards and forests on the isle, and even herds of mountain goats on the higher slopes. There was much speculation about the Gyre in those days, about how they caused the fruit trees to bear fruit enough to feed all, how their magic caused waves to wash attackers from the Kingsbridge, how they sank any boats that tried the crossing from the distant shores, yet all these accounts smacked of heresay and speculation. There was even an ill-tempered rumour that the Gyre had instigated all the attacks in the first place, to bind the Eyrians to them with a single cause.

The invaders continued to throw themselves against the growing defences on the Kingsbridge, and Stevenson was often called upon to rally the men to his aid, to meet the assault with wits and steel. All the while, Stormhaven grew under the guiding vision of the Gyre, the City Walls were raised, the mighty Gatehouse constructed, the ramparts and tiered inner defences took shape. It was a time of back-breaking work, but it was a time of hope as well. For the Eyrians could see that their strength was growing, not waning. A pride unified them as Stormhaven rose higher and mightier against the sky.

At last, the Gyre announced that Stormhaven was properly founded, and the time had come for its ruler to be chosen. The King was to be named. The Kingsrim was raised to an expectant crowd, and set upon a chair. The Gyre formed their circle wide around it, and issued their final test.

"The man who shall reach the crown is the one who can accept the full responsibility with a truthful intent. Wait!" they cried, halting the crowd's advance on their circle. "Hear first what the responsibility is. The crown shall form the centre of Eyri, and the centre it must remain for the realm to be. Its outline is the horizon, the limit of Eyri is the limit of the realm, and there we shall place a shield that none may penetrate, so long as the crown remains in the centre, in Stormhaven. But know this—the Shield of Eyri shall bind invaders out, but it shall bind you in. This is the responsibility of the one who would claim the crown—to never leave Stormhaven, and to accept the border of Eyri as the limit of the world, for himself and for all future generations of his people."

"What if the people do not wish to be bound thus?" came the angry cry from the crowds.

"It is not for the people to defy these terms," the Gyre's spokesman answered. "You who inhabit this isle have already given your word, and by it you are bound, for it was given in the presence of seven wizards. You serve your King, in everything."

Most of the crowd were sobered by this, but some of the more hot-headed pushed to the fore, intent on assault. It was Felltang that they met, the blade of Stevenson. The solidarity of their Swordmaster pacified them, offered them leadership in their confusion.

The crowd's chant became one for Stevenson, urging him to try for the crown.

"King! King! King! King!" The call resounded from Stormhaven's high walls.

"How shall I use this sword in the defence of Eyri if I am to remain in the Isle?" answered Stevenson. "We must reclaim the land to the four horizons. Nay, if the King is to remain as the centre-stone of our new order, I shall serve him best as his Swordmaster. Those men who wish to join me, will be in my fighting squad, the Sword of Eyri."

The matter of the King of Eyri still remained unanswered, and so the trials began. The Gyre's filter of magic was stronger than ever, the people threw themselves against the barrier to no avail. The day drew on towards sunset, and still the Kingsrim gleamed from its chair in the centre of the Gyre, untouched. That no one was worthy seemed a spiteful trick.

It was a young boy, no more than thirteen years, who finally entered the circle of the seven wizards. A hushed silence grew upon the crowd; part disbelief, part wonder. The most greying member of the Gyre announced the King of Eyri.

"This boy has succeeded where you have failed, because his heart does not desire other things. His intent is pure on this—to rule fairly, to sacrifice his freedom to rule, to honour the Shield and protection of Eyri forever."

Inspired more by his courage than by a trust of his judgement, the people of Eyri applauded their new King. They had no choice, their word bound them. The Unnamed King had been named. Richard Mellar.

The family line is unbroken, Tabitha marvelled. There was still a King Mellar on the throne, the legacy had lasted that long. The seven wizards, the first young King, the Swordmaster Stevenson and even the scribe who had recounted the coronation would all be long dead, for the mythical Forming had taken place over four hundred years in the past. Apart from the fanciful illustrations of the fearsome Hunters, fiercer Lûk, and winged Morgloth, another aspect of the legend raised a question which couldn't be answered. Why would a group of seven wizards work to create a kingdom, then leave it and never return? The parts of the history of Eyri didn't add up to a whole.

"Last call," came a gruff voice, interrupting her thoughts.

The doorman poked his head into Tabitha's alcove.

"Missy, you cannot spend the night here, no missy no. Four bells is gone and you don't come by."

"Sorry, I didn't hear anything. How late am I?"

"Early for sunset, missy, but not by much."

Tabitha closed the book of the Forming carefully, and followed the doorman through the long aisles of the Library. She wondered if wizards really existed anywhere beyond ancient legends.

20. MIDNIGHT'S PASS

"Be careful of the little men,
for they will have the biggest dogs."—*Zarost*

The Crowbar was a dark and sprawling inn. It hid in the mists of Fendwarrow's evening like a highwayman, lurking in concealment until traffic passed close by on the main street. Kirjath savoured the rich aroma of pitch that seeped inwards from the log walls. It was dark and smoky inside, pulsing with urgent secrets, with lust and Dwarrow-wine.

The man who owned the Crowbar guaranteed discretion. Mukwallis was no fool in the ways of the world. The wine at the Crowbar was always rich, dark and utterly intoxicating. The entertainment always drove the patrons wild—to further drink or into the arms of the main commerce done in the Crowbar.

Mukwallis had been discreet about the Lightgifter whom Kirjath had deposited on his way to Ravenscroft. It was not the first time that the cellars of the Crowbar had hidden something other than jurrum and Dwarrow-wine. The woman had evidently been washed, and fed, which was more than Kirjath would have bothered with. When the Gifter had been brought to his private room, Kirjath had waved the innkeeper's offers of extra services aside, and closed the door abruptly.

He had been keenly anticipating the moment when he could vent his fury. All the way down the long return from Ravenscroft, Kirjath had chewed on his broken tooth and tasted the bile of being a Shadowcaster. He would return to defy Cabal. No one treated Kirjath Arkell like a slave, not even the Darkmaster.

The walls of Kirjath's room were thick, sound would not travel far. His door could be bolted from the inside. Oh, how he loved the Crowbar.

He kicked the blonde again. Her head plunged into the steel basin on the carpet. She was unwilling, but naked all the same. Kirjath knew he could have stripped her himself, but that wouldn't have had a sufficient taste of victory, no thrill of domination. She had to be the one to undress, but she had refused. It had been good to get reacquainted with her.

She had soon remembered the Gateway, when he had completed the design on the carpet with spilled red wine. She had understood very quickly then, and her clothes had fallen to the floor.

He traced the circle idly with his foot. A touch of Dark essence, and the Gateway would be ready. The Morgloth were just on the other side. Sadly, there was no real need to say the word. The Lightgifter was obeying his every whim now. She was already proving to be boring.

But he did renew the spell of Silence which held her voice, just in case. She had found her lungs the last time he had used her.

"Dye yours as well," he ordered the woman, scooping her white robe from the floor with his foot. She drew the robe into the basin of red wine. Kirjath watched the way the skin of her back stretched over darkening bruises as she kneaded the robe in the basin.

◆ ———————— ◆

Ashley didn't like Fendwarrow. The air had an acrid scent to it. It was colder and murkier than anywhere they had travelled through. A clammy mist made the night seem oppressive. He could almost feel the presence of evil oozing through the town, the eyes that watched, hidden in the shadows. Even the horses seemed affected by the weighted silence, and their heads drooped tiredly as they plodded along the cobbled main street.

They came upon the infamous Crowbar. The years of debauchery seemed to have soaked into the very architecture, for even the walls couldn't stand straight.

"Our horses must rest, and feed," said Father Keegan. "We'll take private rooms. I don't expect I'll see either of you in the common-room tonight, but I must try to fish for news of the Shadowcaster." He eyed first Ashley, then Grace.

Glavenor turned in his saddle as they drew near to the Crowbar's sprawling frontage.

"I'll see what the Swords have to say. Don't wait for me—get yourselves a meal."

"There is a Swordhouse in Fendwarrow?" Ashley asked, surprised that the law and such lawlessness could live in the same town.

"Yes, Ashley, a house filled with Swords who become rapidly blunted. You surely met Victor in First Light. He came from here. Can't hold his drink, or keep his hand from the bottle. I had to replace the Captain here not two weeks ago. The Swords in this town have to be cycled yearly, lest too much darkness soaks into their bones. No one forgets their year in Fendwarrow." Garyll swung his horse away from them, and clattered off across the wet cobbles.

Father Keegan shouldered his pack. "See to the horses, Ashley, and then come through the front and join us in our rooms. I will see to it that our meal is delivered upstairs. I'll not have our meal interrupted by the coarse locals."

Really, how bad can it be? Ashley thought, as he dismounted and collected the three bridles. He led the horses around the back of the inn, where the stables lurked. The stalls boasted more drunken angles than the architecture of the main building.

A groom met him and guided their horses into their empty stalls. The stables were almost full. They passed a restless-looking grey with wild eyes, and a tired roan stallion. Something brushed over Ashley's memory like a willow-frond touching a stream, but it was gone.

The Crowbar, finally I get to visit the Crowbar!

The prospect thrilled him the way forbidden things are wont to do. He was a Lightgifter, and knew he was expected to avoid the Crowbar's trade. Which was why it was so alluring.

It won't hurt just to look.

Music pulsed faintly through the steamed windows at the rear of the inn, and Ashley's hand trembled with excitement as he reached the door and turned the handle.

Air laden with heat, sweat, smoke and ale passed over him like the gust from a summer storm. The bard's song threaded urgently through the scents. Lamps filled the haze with a ruddy light, voices clamoured and roared from half-lit faces, dark cloaks swept by. The floor felt uneven underfoot. It was covered with wood shavings.

The door swung shut behind him, and Ashley found himself facing a group of rough-looking men. They were circled about a table where two burly Swords arm-wrestled. Two men in black cloaks leant against the bar and eyed Ashley. The one tilted his head toward the other, said something unintelligible, and they both roared with laughter. They continued to watch him as he walked unsteadily through the crowd.

The men in the common-room blended into the dark shadows when compared to the women present. Ashley felt his throat go dry as he took in their dress. The fashion seemed to be deep open cloaks with raised collars, and then underclothes, nothing in between. Ashley gulped as he realised the woman before him was returning his gaze. She wore a low-cut bodice which barely covered her to her thighs.

Her smooth legs were naked to the tops of her high leather boots. He felt his face burning as he caught her eye again. She watched him with an impish, cunning grin. He felt like a chicken being eyed by a fox. His pulse thundered in his ears.

It was a delicious sensation. He kept his gaze on the floor, and wove his way further through the common-room, closer to the bard and the distant exit.

He pushed through a knot of people, and found himself close to the small stage where a woman danced. He recognised her instantly, and felt his knees go weak. The noise of the crowd swirled around him. He was in the centre of a whirlpool of lusty, drunken heat.

It was Gabrielle. The dark woman of his dreams. Her face was unmistakable, the waves of raven-hair, the secretive smile, the black silk bodice covering her voluptuous breasts. And at her throat, set on a silver chain, a black crystal orb. She must be a Shadowcaster. His feet rooted in fear, Ashley stared at Gabrielle.

How could I have seen her in my thoughts, when I've never seen her before? How could I know her, without ever having been here?

Gabrielle moved in time to the bard's lilting music, her feet shifting fluidly to the melody of his pipe, her body pulsing in sensuous curves. Her hands wove empty patterns in the air, and from time to time she threw her head back and slid her hands through her hair, or over her body. She caressed herself in ways every man present wanted to, and yet there was a restraint to the crowd, a sense that no one would touch her without her word. For she was dangerous. The forbidden nature of her body increased her glamour, and Ashley became aware of just how many men were grouped around him. She didn't seem to notice him in particular; she danced to the crowd. He was just another moth drawn to the flame.

My dream girl?

"What's the matter, Lightgifter? Missing your Sisters back home?" teased a loud man behind Ashley. A hand shook him roughly, but he didn't dare turn. He knew that tone of voice—it always led to trouble.

"They fall young, these days," someone added.

"Gifters always come sniffing at the door of the Crow, wanting more than their starched white virgins," taunted the first speaker. It was one of the black-cloaked men whom he had seen at the bar.

"This one's sniffing all right, oh yes he's sniffing!" bellowed the second fellow, a heavy-set man with a cauliflower nose.

"You joining us for a drink, young man?" cajoled the black-cloak.

"Uh, er, I've got to go," Ashley stammered, trying to back his way out of the crowd. The men were all too big, burly, unfamiliar. Closing.

An iron grip stopped his retreat. He was shoved into the centre of the circle.

"Drink," a rough voice ordered from behind him. From the corner of his eye Ashley identified the second black-cloak.

Another Shadowcaster, it must be. How many here are Shadowcasters?

A tankard of something thick and dark was forced into his hand. The brute with the cauliflower nose clashed a similar tankard against it. Ashley struggled to maintain his grip, and some of the fluid slopped over his wrist.

"Oooh, can't hold his drink," taunted someone within the crowd. Ashley tried to take in the whole group of men. The danger could come from anywhere in this crowd. He felt very conspicuous in his white robe.

"Welcome to Fendwarrow, lad," roared the flat-nosed brute, and the others tittered. "Let's see if those wobbly knees are made of steel or soap." He lifted a tankard to his lips, and with his spare hand guided Ashley to do the same. Ashley's nose burned with the alcoholic vapours. The group of men pressed close, spoiling for sport, or a fight, Ashley couldn't decide which.

I'll take the drink if they'll leave me be.

Ashley tilted the tankard and swallowed the first draught of the cold, thick liquid. It seared his throat instantly, and he made to drop the tankard, but the brute continued to tilt it as he upended his own. Ashley took another gulp, then another, swallowing air at the same time in his haste to avoid drowning in the rush of liquor. The last of the drink spilled past his nose. The guiding grip was removed to the accompaniment of a gap-toothed smile.

Ashley spluttered as the full force of the drink hit him. His eyes watered cruelly, and it felt as if something had removed his lungs from his chest. No air seemed to be getting down his throat.

"Nectar of the Gods, lad! Now you know what proper Dwarrow-wine tastes like, but not what it feels like. Genn'lmen!" Ashley was shoved across the group by strong hands. "The Crow Twister!"

He was shoved back the way he had come, then turned, then pushed, spun, pushed, twisted, pushed again. Every time he felt as if he would fall, but strong hands grasped him roughly, and he was tossed across the circle again. The world whirled with red lamplight, dark faces, rustling cloaks, and pulsing sound. The pushes became more and more rapid, and he presumed the circle had narrowed, but he had no way of seeing. Everything whirled about his eyes.

"All right, boys, you've had your fun with him," a deep voice cut in. Ashley fell to his hands and knees—the pushing stopped, but the world continued to spin. A pair of polished leather boots came into a vague focus before him.

"Let him be."

Ashley looked up to see a fuzzed image of one of the muscled Swords who had been arm-wrestling near the door. The man rested his right hand casually on his sword hilt. The Fendwarrens seemed to respect the Sword, for they parted slightly and allowed Ashley to stagger to his feet. Even so, Ashley caught a few muttered curses directed at the Sword. Ashley burned with shame when he realised that the dancer Gabrielle must have witnessed the entire charade. He broke from the circle, and headed for the door.

"I think the Lightgifter pissed himself," someone shouted close behind him. He felt his robe being yanked up, and something splashed against his legs. Roars of laughter and cheers chased his back as a tankard clattered to the floor. He ran for the door and out into the foyer.

A toad-like man sat behind a reception desk. When he saw Ashley burst into the room, he chuckled into the many folds of his chin. He was cloaked in a oily green garment which reminded Ashley of pond-weed.

"Three-oh-four-'n-five," was all he said, pointing up to the stairs at his back. He went back to polishing a gold plate on the desk.

When Ashley fled up the stairs, the after-effect of the Dwarrow-wine gripped him. A banshee had been released inside his head—his blood pounded, his thoughts roared, and his breath burned like fire in his chest. He missed his footing many times, but didn't care. Every step put him further from the rude laughter and heady scents of the common-room. And Gabrielle.

◆ ———————— ◆

When Garyll finally joined them in room three-oh-four, they had all but finished their evening meal. Keegan had insisted on a separate room, but Grace had offered to share hers with Ashley. There were two beds in each room, so the offer was surely innocent enough, but knowing what he knew, Ashley couldn't help but wonder about the Sister's quick smile. Sharing a room would conserve their funds, he supposed. He was suddenly conscious of his dishevelled appearance, and the cloud of Dwarrow-fumes about him. He wished desperately that Grace's eyes would linger on something else but him for a while. But he had accepted the offer, to a quickening pulse.

You're seeing things that aren't there, he berated himself. *She's a Sister, you're a Half-knot, she can't possibly be interested in you.*

The food had been well-prepared, a little spicy for Ashley's palate, but anything was welcome after their gruelling day in the saddle. Ashley's head still swam with the memory of the common-room, and he didn't trust his tongue with long words. They had spoken little during the meal.

Garyll brought news which forced discussion.

"There's no sign of the Shadowcaster Arkell, but your Lightgifter friends are staying here at the Crow," Garyll said as he eased himself into a chair beside the door.

"Rosreece and Hosanna?" Father Keegan asked.

"The innkeeper wouldn't give me any details at first, said it wasn't proper. But one of the Swords says he saw them enter Fendwarrow yesterday on the Southwind road. A blonde woman and a tall man who kept his hood drawn, in white robes. Sound like your friends? They stabled at the Crow. I had to remind Mukwallis of my blade before he would give the room number. He said they've ordered five bottles of Dwarrow, and don't want to be disturbed."

"The horses!" Ashley blurted out. "That's what I saw. Their horses are stabled here."

"Well why didn't you speak up sooner, boy?" Keegan bristled. "Too busy carousing with the locals?"

Ashley couldn't defend himself from the quip.

"The room number?" Keegan asked Garyll.

"One-ten, down the passage on the first floor. It's your affair, I'll not interrupt their evening. Who knows why they've stayed here two days?"

"Ashley," Father Keegan commanded, "go down and call them to meet us."

Ashley just wanted to hide in a corner, but he couldn't exactly refuse the senior Lightgifter.

"What if they are," Ashley faltered, "um, busy?"

Sister Grace gave him a surprised look.

"Oh, shatter them!" Father Keegan snapped. "We are here to bring a murderer to justice, not to throw a party. If they are acting indecently they deserve interruption. Tell them to meet us here in three-oh-four."

Ashley found his way down the stairs, and through the foyer. He cast a wary eye toward the revelry in the common-room. Thankfully, no one noticed him. The front-desk was abandoned. He crept down the corridor, counting the numbered doors as the sounds grew fainter again.

One-eight. One-nine.

He raised his hand to knock on the thick timber door at the end of the corridor, drawing a breath in nervousness.

Two days? What were they up to?

His knuckles rapped the door lightly. The sturdy wood absorbed the sound, and he was just about to strike the door with more commitment, when a short cry made him pause. It was muffled through the woodwork. He wasn't sure if it was pain or pleasure, but the cry unsettled him.

It is not my place to get involved. Lover's quarrel, lover's problem. She's old enough to look after herself.

Ashley didn't have enough to go on, and he knew that his blood ran thick with Dwarrow. But he brought his hand down hard on the door with the second knock, and kept on rapping for a time.

He shifted uneasily. Something squished under his tread, and he kicked it clear of his boot. Jurrum-leaves. Used ones.

This place is a cesspool of debauchery.

It didn't stop at the jurrum. On the floor beside the leaves, was a collection of something that looked like flaked skin. Revulsion skittered up his spine. He wanted to leave the Crowbar, and never come back.

"Who is it?" came the muffled voice of a woman through the dark oak panelling.

"Ashley Logán. Is that you, Hosanna?"

There was a pause. "Yes."

"Can I come in?"

"No." Another pause. "What do you want?"

"We need to meet. Father Keegan sent me. We're in three-oh-four, with the Swordmaster. Can you both come when you –" Ashley faltered again, and blushed furiously as he realised what he had been about to say. "When you can," he ended lamely.

There was a long silence from the other side of the door. Not quite a silence, Ashley realised. Angry whispers teased the limit of his hearing. He probed with his mind, hoping that his erratic ability would serve him.

Nothing.

"Give us a while," Hosanna said in an odd voice. "Now go away. We don't wish to be disturbed."

Ashley felt like a little boy caught spying. He gritted his teeth, and backed away from the door. The next time Father Keegan could call them himself.

Suddenly an angry thought snaked through the ether, shockingly intense : *Lightgifters be damned! How many shall I have to rid myself of?*

Ashley recoiled. He felt shamed for trying to snoop in Rosreece's mind; he had intercepted a thought he shouldn't have known.

Ashley expected Rosreece to wrench the door open and blast him with a wave of indignation. But the door remained firmly closed. Maybe the Gifter was drunk, to be so angry at the disturbance. It was not Ashley's affair.

He retreated from the corridor as fast as he could. An uneasiness followed him like the echo of that first small cry he had heard.

When he reached the foyer, he veered left, away from the common-room and the stairs. He didn't want to face Keegan's judgements, and he needed to find somewhere to relieve the Dwarrow-wine. He passed a few rooms, a bustling steaming kitchen, then a scullery. The smell of wasted food washed over him as he pushed through a door to a courtyard.

Smells about right, he thought wryly. He spotted his goal. A low building squatted against the far wall of the courtyard. A walkway sheltered by a sagging roof hugged the wall and led toward the outhouse. Two lamps glowed along the walkway, the others had burned themselves out, or were too blackened for their flames to be visible.

When he returned from the outhouse, he entered the Crowbar behind a couple wearing hooded crimson robes. The vegetable waste of the kitchens masked their smell at first, but as they staggered through the corridor ahead of him, Ashley caught the reek of alcohol. They disappeared into the common-room when Ashley took the stairs from the foyer.

Ashley shook his head, he couldn't believe that they needed to drink any more.

♦ ———————— ♦

Hosanna and Rosreece had still not arrived. Ashley sat quietly beside Sister Grace. Father Keegan paced the floor. Garyll sharpened his sword, but ceased when Grace gritted her teeth at the torturous sound. Sister Grace wove a Healall spell, and Ashley felt his riding-pains fade. As he sobered, he became aware of a singular unease; a worry like a mosquito on the back of his neck, pricking him with its intuitive proboscis. Something was wrong. He just couldn't fit the missing piece into the puzzle.

The horse had rolled wild eyes at him, Rosreese's horse. It had been frightened by something, yet apparently it had been stabled for a full day. The horse should not still be nervous. And Hosanna and Rosreece had been riding hard, their trail should have been cold, yet here they were, barely hours ahead.

Ashley chewed his lip.

Five bottles of Dwarrow-wine?

He had tasted a few mouthfuls in the common-room, and it was not fair to call it wine. Distilled poison would be closer to the mark. One bottle would down two men; after five bottles the Gifters would surely never wake again. The extravagance didn't make sense.

Celebrating their success? Or drowning their failure?

Rosreece had not spoken, Hosanna had sounded tense and angry; failure then. But if they had failed to capture the Shadowcaster, then why was there freshly chewed jurrum in the corridor outside their room?

Captain Steed had mentioned the Shadowcaster's habit. They had seen jurrum at Phantom Acres. Jurrum on the road to Fendwarrow.

In a dreadful moment of deduction, he knew.

The vicious thought from beyond the door of one-ten had not been Rosreece's at all. With a cry he leapt to his feet.

"The murderer is with Hosanna!"

"What makes you say that, boy?" Father Keegan demanded.

Ashley felt suddenly trapped. He couldn't tell them of his mind-skill, they would ridicule him. "Jurrum," he said, "beside the door of one-ten. Wet, chewed jurrum."

"So how does that tell you it's the Shadowcaster we seek?" Keegan retorted. "Many of them here chew jurrum. The Crowbar's renowned for it."

"I saw flakes of skin as well. The Captain said the Shadowcaster was burn-scarred. He must have scratched his scabs outside the door. And i heard—a strange voice there."

Garyll was on his feet. "Your eyes and ears are sharp, Ashley Logán. You should have spoken of it sooner."

"I only put it all together now."

Keegan glowered at him. "Your mind was clouded by all that carousing, no doubt."

"He's thinking clearly now!" said Glavenor, making for the door. "This explains Mukwallis's manner, if he were hiding the Shadowcaster." The Swordmaster rushed from the room.

They crowded through the door, and pounded down the stairs after him. Ashley prayed that he hadn't made too many assumptions. If it really was the Shadowcaster who was with Hosanna, then where was Rosreece?

Glavenor was already pounding on the door of one-ten with the hilt of his drawn sword when they caught up to him. They halted a few paces clear.

There was no answer. Glavenor tried the handle, but it was locked. The door stood firm and mute against them. The Swordmaster made ready to shoulder the door in.

"Oi, Oi Oi!" came a shrill voice from the front-room. "What on earth is going on here? You people cannot disturb my patrons at this hour!" The squat form of the innkeeper swept down the corridor, green pond-weed cloak trailing.

"Mukwallis, open this door!" commanded Glavenor.

The innkeeper pushed past the Swordmaster to stand in the way of the door. "If they will not open, that is their wish. These are my guests!"

Garyll had his sword to the innkeeper's throat in a blinding flash of steel. "If I have to break open every door in this house tonight, Mukwallis, do you think the King will be pleased with what I find? We shall have access to this room, or you will find your inn stripped apart. Tonight."

"I run a reputable business, I have nothing to hide," Mukwallis objected.

"Like the murderer concealed in this room? If you want to be an accomplice, you will join him in the gibbet."

"A murderer? Nonsense!" Beads of sweat had formed on

Mukwallis's brow. "The guests in there are Lightgifters, here for private reasons. They don't wish to be disturbed," Mukwallis complained, but he backed away from Garyll's blade, and fumbled at his belt for a great key-ring.

Garyll beat the door again. "Open up, I say!"

Father Keegan summoned the Light, what little there was to be found. Grace had used her supply to heal them, Ashley had none. Sprites were rare in Fendwarrow, it seemed.

The key turned, and the door swung inwards, moaning against its worn hinges. The space beyond the doorway was dark, and still. They followed Garyll's blade into the room.

A fire in the hearth. A basin. A rumpled bed and a guttering lamp. Nothing else; no sign of Hosanna.

Garyll hissed a warning. "Be alert! This is the design of the Shadowcaster. He used it to summon his beast in First Light. Stay behind me, stay in the light!" he commanded.

Ashley's heart leapt into his throat. His eyes scanned the gloom frantically. He saw the stained circle in the carpet that Glavenor had referred to.

There were too many shadows. Too many places where a beast might lurk, poised to strike. Too many corners where a Shadowcaster could wrap himself in Dark essence, and be hidden.

They stood in silence, not daring to breathe lest they muffled a movement. Then Keegan muttered a spell, and the sprites in his hand flickered into flame. He held his hand high, throwing light to the four walls.

Nothing.

The bed! Ashley thought, in the same instant that Glavenor leapt for it. He ran his sword swiftly behind the draping blankets and scooped them clear, retreating in a fluid step to survey the floor. Nothing but shadows.

There was a steel basin beside the hearth, filled with a dark fluid. Dwarrow-wine, by the look of the breached bottles in the corner.

Why a basin of wine?

Close beside the fire stood two high-backed chairs, which seemed to be stained in dark crimson blotches, as was the carpet beneath them. The same colour as the circle design, stains of dark, deep red.

"Hang me!" Ashley exclaimed. "They left half an hour ago, they passed right by me in crimson robes." Ashley pointed to the basin of wine. "Dwarrow-wine makes a good dye."

The Shadowcaster had escaped; he was surely long gone on Rosreece's anxious horse. Ashley crossed the room to the window, and pushed the shutter wide.

"Look out!" shouted Glavenor, but his warning came too late. There was a confusion of beating wings, a sudden wind and a scratching cry. Then the bird was gone, leaving Ashley with the metallic taste of shock in his mouth, and a heart beating like the hooves of a galloping horse. Ashley steadied himself on the windowframe, and stared out across the walled yard. A few stars pierced the dark night above a cluster of beggarly, barren trees.

"Morrigán!" Father Keegan cursed, at his back. "This Shadowcaster uses every trick in the book. He doubtless left it here to warn him of our pursuit. Did you see which way it flew?"

Ashley pointed to the right, where the raven had disappeared over the roofs of Fendwarrow. "A Morrigán, Father? What is that?"

"The same as our Courier, a messenger bird, only made with Dark essence."

How does the Father know so much about it?

"I'll meet you at the Swordhouse," Garyll shouted, running from the room. "It is on the Levin road, and the Sword on watch can say if our quarry passed. Make haste! We cannot let the Shadowcaster escape with Hosanna."

◆ ─────────── ◆

Kirjath rode down to the boats. He yanked on the reins to the horse behind him.

Blasted Lightgifters!

When the youth had pounded on his door, he had been using the woman, breaking her spirit like glass underfoot. The pleasure had been wild and delirious. The woman had been his, her body battered, her resilience broken at last. He had filled her mouth with Dwarrow, he had soaked her with it until she was drunk and yielding, yet she knew what acts she performed. And the youth had pounded the door.

Lightgifters. How he hated their kind.

Mukwallis would pay dearly for guiding them to his door.

He rode like a guilty fugitive. The anger it awoke almost made him turn, ride back into the village.

I'll slay them all! Let them feel my Morgloth tearing their necks open, feeding on their lives.

But he didn't dare to turn; he knew he had drunk too much of the

Dwarrow-wine himself. He had needed something to drown his rage at the Darkmaster. The Dwarrow had worked its wonders, but it had taken a heavy toll. His mind was not completely his own. He couldn't risk a channelling. And he wasn't sobering up, for the fumes from his red robe were heady and overpowering.

He kept the horses headed for the boats. The Morrigán returned, cawing loudly, bringing the news that the Lightgifters had finally breached his room.

The woman fell from the saddle, then, drunk out of her mind. She didn't seem to care at all when she struck the ground. Kirjath considered leaving her where she lay.

She was his possession. Her broken spirit was his creation. He enjoyed the feeling that gave him. He wanted to see the look on her face when she sobered in the morning, and fully understood her descent into hopelessness.

It was only when he lifted her to his own saddle that he realised what she was trying to do. She was resisting him in the only way she could. Trying to slow him down, so that their pursuers would succeed. Her will was not yet broken.

He struck her hard on the temple. A bone cracked when she hit the ground. He retrieved her. She was better behaved.

He loaded her over the front of his saddle, a slack lump like a sack of flour. He considered the spare horse for a moment. It wavered slightly in his vision. Then his lips peeled back in a grin.

It was perfect.

Lead them to the heart of Darkness. That will keep the Master busy!

A lesser man would have been afraid to consider it. But he, Kirjath Arkell, was not a lesser man. With a bark of laughter, he summoned the Dark essence to his hand.

Casting the illusion of two riders took some concentration, but he created a passable decoy and covered it in a black shroud of motes. He slapped the horse's rump, and it set off for the centre of Fendwarrow at a canter.

It'll run faster than that.

Kirjath drew more motes from the night, and cast himself a Morrigán. "Chase the horse, lead it home, to the Master, to Ravenscroft," he whispered into the bird's ear. He threw the raven after the retreating horse. Its harsh, splintered croaks soon had the horse galloping in panic.

The horse would pass the Swordhouse, and then lead them all up the secret trail that they would never find alone. The Darkmaster would have a lot to contend with, at the break of day.

Kirjath smiled, and mounted his horse behind the slack load.

At the boatyard, he found a small skiff, its sails furled around the mast. There was a steady breeze from the west—he would have no need to paddle, this time. The memory of his previous trip to Stormhaven fuelled his anger again, and he spat a lump of jurrum into the sand.

No more failures.

He would find the girl, and the Ring, and return with power. The Master would regret ever having spurned a man called Kirjath Arkell.

He dumped his woman in the bow, and pushed the stolen boat out onto the rippled surface of Amberlake. The rigging dropped, and the sail snapped tight.

◆ ——————— ◆

"We'll catch them soon," the Swordmaster shouted over the pounding of hooves. "I've ridden this trail before, it ends against the cliffs ahead. They'll have to return."

Ashley rode close beside the Lightgifters and the two Swords from Fendwarrow. They followed Glavenor.

Dark rock rose on either side of them, rising higher as they pressed deeper into the ravine. The Black River slid by close at hand, slick and sinuous.

The lone horse up ahead was holding an extremely good pace; even though it was burdened by the two cloaked riders, it was gradually pulling away from their pursuit. The Shadowcaster was pushing the horse to its death.

Instead of turning at the head of the valley, Ashley saw their quarry ride out into the river, where the water foamed downstream of a booming waterfall.

"The river is too swift there! They'll both be drowned!" Glavenor shouted as he spurred his horse to gallop. Yet if they were to drown, Ashley knew that the Swordmaster would be too late to save Hosanna.

The pale horse did not swim. It picked its way across the river, as if treading in the shallows. The bird, which had been attending the Shadowcaster all the way, swooped suddenly. The horse jumped from its course, and thrashed to regain its footing in the rushing current. Yet the two riders remained in their seat as if they had been glued to the saddle. Then the horse plunged into the falling sheet of water, and the riders were gone. The Morrigán overshot them and climbed out. It gave a harsh triumphant cry, then passed away into the night above the falls.

Glavenor waded into the Black River. The water flowed swiftly, yet it only came up to his waist, even though he was far from the bank.

"There's a path beneath this water!" he shouted, wading back toward them. "We shall have to lead the horses. Follow me!" He grabbed the reins to his steed, and strode into the river once more. The horse stamped and shied at the dark water, but Glavenor soon had it following him upon the hidden trail.

The company advanced, leading their reluctant mounts.

The water was like ice. Ashley's robe became heavy and tugged at his legs. He was glad Glavenor led the way, for he couldn't see anything beneath the opaque surface of the river. How they reached the base of the waterfall without mishap, he didn't know.

The falls thundered down. Glavenor tried to lead his horse through the curtain of water, but it dug its hooves in and would not follow. He emerged through the water again, determined despite his soaking.

"There's a cavern in there, the trail continues. Father Keegan, do you have enough essence to provide a light?"

"As I used in the Crowbar," Keegan replied.

"Good. It'll be easier once one of these beasts is through." He mounted his horse quickly. "Already, the Shadowcaster gets away!" He kicked the horse's flanks and shouted commandingly. The horse leapt. The water cascaded over them as they parted the falls. Then they were gone.

Ashley felt his knees go weak. He muttered a curse, and heard it echoed amongst the others. Even the Swords appeared daunted by where their path led.

But Glavenor's bravery was strangely infectious. Father Keegan dragged his horse toward the falls despite its rearing and snorting. They fought amongst the churning waters, then suddenly they were through. The flare of the Flicker spell coloured the water beyond the falls a ghostly brown.

Keegan's light. At least they had that.

Maybe it was because the horses were tired, maybe because the temperament of the Dovecote nags was less headstrong than the soldier's steeds, maybe it was luck alone; Ashley and Grace came through the falls unhurt, their horses followed them with trusting steps. But the two remaining Swords did not fare so well.

When the first soldier broke through the water behind Ashley, the distorted image of his horse reared on the far side of the fall. The reins were torn from the soldier's hands as he was pulled back through the liquid curtain. There was a squealing commotion outside.

When the Sword returned, he wore a sober expression.

"Swordmaster, the horses are both in the river, they swim downstream. What should we do?"

"You won't keep the pace without them. Damn! We have no time to wait, and you'll need the Lightgifters to help you through this darkness. Retrieve your horses when they find the bank, and return to Fendwarrow. If we have not returned by tomorrow evening, send a rider to Stormhaven, and come through here with a full squadron. There must be something more than a trail beyond here, for the Shadowcaster to press so strongly for it, and for it to be so well hidden."

They left the Swords behind. Father Keegan led the pursuit. His Flicker spell lit a narrow tunnel which angled sharply upward through the rock. The horses were spooked by the weird passage of booming echoes, but the tunnel was straight and smooth, and no jagged rocks or sudden twists hindered them. They soon emerged to the cold, crisp night again.

The trail was easier to follow from there on, a hard-packed, winding ascent. Even on the occasions when heavy mists crossed their way, they made good speed.

They saw the horse they pursued three more times that night, but every time it had pulled further ahead, despite its heavy load. Glavenor would not relent, and the Gifters followed as best they could. The Swordmaster seemed aware of the risk he was exposing them to, for he kept the group tight and never pushed far ahead, though the desire to catch the Shadowcaster surely burned fiercely within him.

The night pressed close around them, and it felt to Ashley as if a hundred hidden eyes were watching him. Sister Grace rode near on his right side. Her robes brushed against his leg. After a while she reached out her hand. Ashley couldn't read her eyes in the dark, but he felt the companionship in the squeeze she gave him.

He covered her hand with his. Her skin was cold. Ashley knew she was scared—he was scared himself. For a while, he felt warmer inside. But when Grace's hand slipped away, the gnawing fear did return; darker, colder and more silent than ever.

The watching presence grew as they wound their way higher into the mountains.

They came upon a wide bridge which spanned an awesome chasm. The river was constrained to a tight, deep gorge, and its frustrated thunder echoed from far below. The bridge surface seemed unsteady under the horses' hooves. Ashley was about to say how glad he was to have put it behind him, when he began to sense the queerness of the place they had reached by crossing it.

The half-light of approaching dawn showed a landscape of black rock. What little vegetation there was, clung fiercely to the steep slopes of shattered slate. The skyline was pierced with white peaks. Ashley couldn't stop shivering at the incessant cold. His robe was still wet from their passage through the waterfall. He had endured an ordeal of shivering since that time.

They rounded a bend, and the company reined in sharply. The road fell away, and a valley opened up before them. It held a strange gloom, as if the air was thickened with smoke, yet there was no smell of burning. A giant spire of black rock thrust upwards in the distance. Against its sheer cliffs, hundreds of birds soared, tiny dark specks against the pale sky. Tilled fields formed a grey-green patchwork upon the valley floor. A dirty mist filled the far end of the vale, and only the sharp spines of the higher ground was visible there.

Ashley was stunned. A land completely hidden, totally unknown to them, yet within Eyri. He wondered how many people inhabited this secret realm. He searched the vale for buildings, but it was impossible to see clearly against the dark slopes. If there were any habitations, they were built of the same black rock that littered most of the vale.

"Jurrum!" cursed Glavenor. "It had to come from somewhere."

The Swordmaster had dismounted, and was bending low to a bush on the roadside. It was a broad-leafed plant, squat and hardy-looking. Many of them dotted the landscape, clustering near to the shelter of boulders. It looked as if the hedgerows at the edge of the nearest crops were jurrum as well. Possibly all the hedgerows.

Grace stiffened at his side, and pointed to the giant spire. "There, at the base, there's a Keep."

Ashley strained to find the shape in the jumble of ridges and rocks.

He gasped. He had been looking on too small a scale. The Keep was massive, its walls towered high above its entrance. It seemed to slant outward from the mountain as well, as if leaning threateningly toward them.

"Where are the people?" he wondered aloud.

Keegan's mount shied. The Father settled the horse down, and turned to face Ashley.

"Just because we have forgone our sleep, doesn't mean they would have done the same."

Ashley wasn't reassured—he had heard rumours that Shadowcasters slept during the day. Then again, maybe there weren't any Shadowcasters here, maybe it was just a vale of secretive farmers.

Glavenor spun suddenly on his feet, his hand to the hilt of his sword. They all followed his eyes. Nothing but a few black boulders.

Ashley eased a sigh, but the dull foreboding did not fade. Dread gnawed in his belly.

We should get out of here.

It was too late. The horses shied all at once. Things shifted in the undergrowth. The boulders which had slumbered on the ground shimmered and began to move. Not boulders anymore, but figures, cloaked in black robes, their movement silent. Their faces remained hidden within their dark cowls, but their menace was tangible in the way they circled the Gifters and Glavenor.

The sharp grind of steel told Ashley that Glavenor's blade had been fully drawn. Yet he had nothing to arm himself with. In this place, there was no Light essence at all.

If Ashley had ever doubted the existence of the Shadowcasters before, he knew that he would never have the luxury again.

A force of nearly fifty men and women surrounded them. A haze of dark particles flickered from Shadowcaster to Shadowcaster, linking them in an aura of motes. Ashley recognised the movement of essence. It was the same magical flux the Lightgifters employed, only the sprites he was seeing were as black as night.

What does one do with Dark essence?

The thought chilled him to the bone.

Five Shadowcasters formed a group in the road and advanced. A figure cloaked in a shifting cloud of gloom led them. It was impossible to discern exactly where the leader stood, because of his use of the motes. Nonetheless, Ashley felt the immense weight of the figure's scrutiny.

"Why do you trespass in my kingdom?" the leader demanded, his voice an angry scraping wheeze. The challenger spread his hands. Darkness seemed to rise from the rocks. Ashley felt the sting of something as it took the warmth from his flesh, the sickening bind of a strange spell. He felt as if he had been pushed from a high place. He knew that there was an impact to come.

A wave of nausea washed over him. He felt so small before the mighty man who faced them. The fact that he couldn't see the man's face made the fear even worse.

The Swordmaster's voice held no trace of the terror Ashley felt. "We do not trespass! This is the land of Eyri. You know you are the subject of King Mellar, and I am the King's Swordmaster." Glavenor held his blade at the ready. It glinted pale blue.

"I know who you are, Garyll Glavenor. Sheath your sword," the leader commanded in his harsh, scratching voice. The Dark essence rushed over the company like a spindrift. Ashley was glad he was seated in the saddle, for the crushing despair and weakness he felt would have buckled his knees, had he been standing.

Glavenor's face was cut from stone.

"Are you the leader of these people?" he demanded.

There was a long silence measured only by the nervous breathing of the Gifter's horses.

"I am Cabal, Darkmaster of Ravenscroft. This is my land, and my people. I ask only once more. Why do you trespass in my kingdom?" The edge of menace in the voice was sharp enough to draw blood.

Father Keegan stepped close to Glavenor. They held a brief, whispered conversation. Then Keegan addressed the one who called himself the Darkmaster.

"We chased a man, a murderer, to—this place. He has killed many. We seek only justice."

"Whose trail of blood do you follow?"

"He calls himself Kirjath Arkell," said Glavenor. The name was pronounced with fierce contempt. "I presume he is one of yours." Glavenor was tensed, as if for attack. Keegan rested a pacifying hand on the Swordmaster's arm. They exchanged a brief glance.

"Father Keegan, you are most wise," rasped the Darkmaster. "Yes, I know who you are, all of you. It is only at my mercy that any of you shall leave this place. You would do well to remember that, Glavenor."

The Darkmaster seemed to know too much about them. Ashley

tried to shrink down further into his saddle.

A command was relayed through the Shadowcasters. A horse was led to the fore, a grey, bearing two riders who were hidden beneath a thick, black cloak.

"Are these the riders you seek?" the Darkmaster asked. He extended his hand and issued a sharp command. The bulky cloak flipped open, then dispersed as if the wind had blown it to pieces. There was nothing inside the cloak. A cloud of black particles flew to the Darkmaster's hand.

Dark essence.

"What you have chased was an illusion, but it served the traitor's purpose, in bringing you here. Now I must decide what to do with you."

They huddled in the road. Keegan made to speak, but the Darkmaster had already raised a swift hand. Motes flickered through the air, forming a net around them which seemed to contain a thick silence.

Nothing moved, the air was cold, and still. They waited.

Glavenor seemed to be counting their adversaries. High above, the rose-fingered dawn began to streak the sky, but on the ground, the gloom seemed to linger with the Shadowcasters.

Ashley hoped that the Darkmaster would forgive them for tresspassing.

What am I thinking? This is Eyri.

But he couldn't deny the feeling of desperation and inadequacy. Even Glavenor seemed to feel something, for he sheathed his sword at last. The Darkmaster gestured the motes aside, and the sounds of the vale returned.

"So you can count, Glavenor."

"Our grievance is with the murderer Arkell," Garyll answered. "He must have evaded us in Fendwarrow. We shall ride peacefully from here and bother you no more this day."

"Your words do not hide your intent very well, Glavenor," the Darkmaster responded. "It is clear you wish to return another day, to settle the issue of my rule. No matter, I expected no less of you. And in that, you shall serve my purposes well. It is time I bade my neighbour a warning, and who better to announce it than the Swordmaster of Eyri? None shall doubt your word. Tell Mellar that we wish to trade, that much can be gained from working together, and nothing from resistance. And tell him to send a more—diplomatic—emissary next time."

A hollow laughter issued forth from the cloaked Darkmaster, a sound like shattering flint. For an instant, Ashley thought he saw the figure reduced to a shorter man, with a lined, thin face. It made the Darkmaster's menace no less, only more concentrated.

"You may go, but you shall not ride peacefully. You must be gone from Ravenscroft by the breaking of dawn. You have little time to make the bridge, but we shall help you ride." The Darkmaster raised his arms to the lightening sky.

Ravens descended in droves. They dived from the high cliffs, flocked from the fields, and some were even formed in Shadowcasters hands as Ashley watched. Morrigán.

Glavenor leapt to his saddle. A bird dived and Grace's horse squealed, reared, and fled, with the Sister clinging desperately to its neck. The rest of the horses could not be held back. They charged in panic, away from the driving birds of Ravenscroft.

If Ashley had been a horse, he would have run faster, for a wave of cold fear chased them. Motes pressed the awful spells of the Darkmaster into their backs. They galloped along the wide black road, with the Morrigán sniping at their horses like dark arrows.

The fearsome bridge that spanned the chasm was more terrible in the pre-dawn light than it had been in the dark. The drop was huge on either side. Sheer, broken cliffs fell hundreds of feet. The bridge looked smooth, too narrow to be safe without rails, yet that was all there was—a span of the blackest stone, arching through the air.

But the fear driving the horses was greater, the flurry of black wind and broken cries compelled the beasts to bear their riders over the slick surface at great speed. Ashley closed his eyes, and prayed that the horse did not.

After the crossing, the horses would not slacken their pace. The Morrigán continued to harass them, though not as intensely, and gradually Ashley began to fear their attacks less. They never seemed to strike the riders or the horses. Their task was simply to frighten, to chase.

Peaks passed by, and the sky lightened ever more. The road held no danger, save that it sloped downward. They raced through a narrow defile with the birds screeching and cawing at their heels. They burst into a gentler landscape, where the hills opened outward, and the air was clear. As if responding to a sudden command, the Morrigán pulled up and away, wheeling in a black gaggle behind the company, before heading deeper into the mountains. Their cacophony faded; they had returned to their roost.

The horses took a while to calm, but their pace slackened to a canter, then to a trot, and finally they allowed themselves to be reined in.

The view was spectacular. They were halted on a hillside that had stern peaks on its right, and the Black River ravine on their left. The trail wound downward, towards Fendwarrow. The ravine was thick with mist, and over the lower ground ahead it crept, extending far across Eyri, covering the Amberlake with a soft white blanket. Far across the realm, the unmistakable shape of Fynn's Tooth was fired by the brilliance of the morning sun. Dawn had broken, and the immediate danger had passed.

They let the horses graze briefly.

The voice of the Dovecote Assembly came to Ashley through his orb, but he did not have the heart to join them in the Morningsong. There was no Light essence in this abandoned place. Having witnessed the Shadowcasters, he wondered if the Gifters would ever have the power to resist their spells. He could still taste the bitter poison of despair which had scourged his soul.

Without Light essence, they had been defenceless in Ravenscroft. The same could happen elsewhere. Ashley suspected that the Darkmaster wouldn't be content to remain in his hidden vale forever.

It was the Swordmaster who put a voice to the thought.

"Ravenscroft is a worse threat than the murderer who led us there. An entire army could be hidden within that Keep, and we would not know it."

"Yet they have never sought to invade Eyri," said Keegan, in a pacifying tone.

"No Father, you are wrong. The troubles in Fendwarrow stem from that dark vale up there. They began their invasion of Eyri long ago, only so subtly that we were never alerted."

"The Darkmaster could have killed us!" Keegan objected. "And yet he sent us off with a message for the King. Maybe his intent is not as menacing as you think."

"Or he is immensely confident of his position, to act so boldly," Glavenor countered.

"What of Hosanna, and Rosreece?" asked Sister Grace. "We cannot abandon the duty of finding them."

Glavenor turned to face Ashley and Grace. "We followed a decoy here, so Arkell must have left Fendwarrow by another route. He might still have Hosanna with him, but I fear your Rosreece was eliminated, even before we came to Fendwarrow."

"Why would he keep Hosanna?" Ashley blurted out, then bit his tongue. Keegan gave him a sharp glance.

"Maybe he just needed a healer," suggested Grace, but her eyes held a deeper sorrow. It didn't need to be said. A man who murdered with abandon probably wasn't the best company a woman could hope for.

"We shall pick up his trail in Fendwarrow. I think a chat with Mukwallis is long overdue."

"And what of Ravenscroft?" Keegan asked.

"That is a matter for our King," answered Glavenor. "Come, let us begin the trail, or it shall never end."

The pace was slow, for the horses were tired, and the mists soon swirled around them. A damp mood claimed the morning. They all had much to consider.

When they came to the tunnel above the falls, the horses would not enter. They had reached their limit—too many terrifying incidents, too long a road. None of the horses would step into the darkness, even Garyll's steed shied and stumbled away.

They let them graze on the rich grass above the falls. Ashley searched for another passage, but there was no way down the loose, broken cliff or out of the steep-sided gorge. Glavenor tried to coax his horse through the tunnel with a branch he managed to set alight, but the wood smoked and spluttered and only worsened the horses' unease.

"I shall send my men to retrieve the animals," Glavenor announced. "They can set proper torches in the walls of the tunnel. I intend to place a strong guard here, to ensure no traffic passes through these falls."

They agreed to picket the horses and to march the last league. The falls were as icy as ever, but the daylight diminished the threat. They staggered through the sloping tunnel behind Garyll's smoking torch.

It was late afternoon by the time they tramped into the village of Fendwarrow, weary as plough-horses. Glavenor agreed that they rest overnight while he hunted for clues. He left them at the Crowbar. The inn had a strangely deserted feel to it. The kitchens served poor fare, but none of the Gifters had the energy to complain.

It wasn't long before Ashley had fallen into an exhausted sleep on top of his bed. Even as he dreamt, he was aware of the night falling. He knew that somewhere, in a vale filled with Dark essence, the Shadowcasters were rising.

His sleep was troubled.

21. KING OF EYRI

"Thread by thread, the spiders weave,
but ever less their web can leave."—*Zarost*

Kirjath began the day in high spirits. He hid the boat in the Scrags, the hidden coves of shattered rocks which formed the abandoned south shore of the King's Isle. The woman he tied to the mast, like the pitiful sack of flesh and bones she had become. As the wine wore off, she had become morose and tearful. Kirjath supposed he could give her some jurrum to ease the Dwarrow-bane, but there was a more pleasing alternative.

He wove a Dark spell of Despair, and guided the motes to infest her mind. She would be too hopeless to recover that day. She would want to kill herself, she would feel she had deserved it all, and would not attempt to escape, if he judged her right. She would await his return, that he might punish her. He smiled to her, and set off through the tumbled rocks.

He had evaded the other Lightgifters, and sent them as a present to the Darkmaster. They would be dead in Ravenscroft by now, or fleeing for their lives, if the Master had been merciful.

Mercy from the Darkmaster?

They were dead. The Master would still be furious, ranting and raving, plotting ways to discipline his traitorous servant.

Servant no more!

A flickering doubt tainted his courage. The Darkmaster was a formidable enemy, maybe he had gone too far. His hands found jurrum in his pouch. The juice filled his mouth as he chewed a leaf, and his confidence returned with a thrilling surge. He would find the girl, claim the Ring, and begin to gather his power. With the aid of the Morgloth, no one would stand in his way.

The morning mist was not clearing off the lake, and the sun hid above the vaporous soup. The mist was greasy and dank at water level, infused with the scent of Stormhaven's effluent. That meant he was close to the sewers. There wasn't much shore between the Seep and the Kingsbridge. Then he would reach the City Gates.

There was a movement in the mist ahead. Sudden voices. Swords. Kirjath waded quietly into the chill water of the lake. The Swords would be too suspicious of him, so far from the Kingsbridge. The memory of his capture at First Light was fresh; as infuriating as a weevil in the brain. The tinpots had been too clever for him. He had been caught in the simplest of traps.

Never again.

Kirjath halted silently. He wrapped his body in the gloom of Dark essence, diffusing his shape into a bulky charcoal cloud, a cloud with faintly yellow eyes.

"Hey, what's that out in the lake?" A young guard's voice. Eager to impress his superiors, no doubt.

I'll impress him.

A fantasy with black wings, dread talons, and a deadly bite came to mind. But Kirjath kept as still as stone, and allowed the Dark essence to spread outwards instead, blurring his figure, widening, shifting, confusing the man on the shore.

"Jumping at shadows, Bradley?" an older voice asked.

Kirjath could just make out their forms in the mist as they peered his way. He focused the Dark into three prongs above his head.

"Just an old tree, kipper," the senior guard admonished. "The mist does strange things to the eye. Come, we have a way to patrol yet." The Swords walked on, leaving the water lapping against Kirjath's legs.

He waited until they were far gone, then he waded parallel to the shore for a way. The jurrum was growing sour.

He scratched his scalp, pulling scurf from the rippled skin.

Blast and shatter the Lightgifter!

She may have eased the pain, but she had left him with scars aplenty. His head felt like a burnt potato. He spat the stale jurrum into the water. He had a task today; to gain entry into Stormhaven, and to find the girl.

The City Gate was the only way in—Stormhaven's sheer walls of stonewood were impenetrable. But the guards at the Gate were a mere formality—they would be easily fooled.

He could hide himself beneath the cowl of his robe while he stated his business. A merchant seeking advice from the House of Law, that would get him in. It wouldn't take long to find where the girl was. If she used the Ring at all, she would be an even easier target.

◆ ——————— ◆

Tabitha gazed down at the street from her bedroom window. Most of Stormhaven was wrapped in a woolly blanket of mist, and even in the higher parts of the city, pale threads of moisture curled around the roofs. The Morningsong had come and gone in her Lightstone; familiar words but an unfamiliar joy of communion with the Assembly.

Stormhaven was busy in the mornings. Already the streets were filling as the busy folk of the King's Isle emerged like ants from a nest. Through the merchants, bureaucrats and nobles, marched a strict procession of Swords on patrol.

A voice at her side brought Tabitha back to her immediate surroundings.

"Good morning, Miss Tabitha."

Pia was as neatly dressed as ever. The little guideling was beaming.

"Hullo Pia."

"Miss Westerbrook said you're to meet her as soon as you're ready at the House of Ceremony. I'm to help you dress." She offered a pile of folded blue linen.

"Dress? Why? What is to happen this morning?"

"You're to see the King." Pia could not mask the awe in her expression. "Miss Westerbrook said she will request a special audience." She proudly opened the fabric she held, and layed a deep blue dress on the bed. Tabitha gasped.

The King.

It was a most beautiful garment, as blue as the evening sky, loose-sleeved and finely-weaved.

The King?

A golden sash was folded about the waistline, and embroidered swallows crossed the fabric in pale tones.

The King!

When she donned the silky gown, she found that it was an elegant fit. Pia helped eagerly throughout her hurried preparations, doing naught to calm Tabitha's nerves, twittering of the palace halls, the audience chambers and the protocols she had been taught to keep during an audience with the King.

Tabitha tugged nervously on the Lightstone at her throat, exposed above the low neckline of her fine dress. There would be no hiding the white orb. She squared her shoulders.

Maybelle said I must be honest with the King. Let it begin with the Lightstone.

◆ ———————— ◆

Lady Westerbrook was waiting in the cool foyer of the House of Ceremony. She was elegantly dressed, and a blue-metal circlet held her hair back from her face. She smiled and commended Tabitha on how well the dress suited her. Then her gaze fell on the exposed orb at Tabitha's throat.

"Oh," was all she said at first, but her eyebrows flew high to perch near the circlet. "When did you … is that your mother's?"

The question was too direct to avoid with clever words. Tabitha nodded.

"You were not orbed by the Dovecote." It was a statement.

"The Riddler sealed the clasp," said Tabitha. "But I am sworn to the Light."

"This Riddler has a lot to answer for." May watched Tabitha for a while, with a calculating gaze. "Are there any other secrets to your tale?"

"None," said Tabitha, hastily.

The Ring was a sudden biting circle of ice on her finger. She had vowed to tell the truth.

The Lifesong.

It seemed too private a matter to admit. She hardly understood what the song meant. But her singing had drawn the Shadowcaster in the first place. It was an important fact in the course of her tale. She had to be truthful if she wanted to retain Maybelle's friendship.

"Except, I am a singer. I sang a song that the Shadowcaster heard from afar. I am not sure how he was drawn to it."

May seemed satisfied. "You are an extraordinary young woman, Tabitha Serannon. I was right to call a special audience. These are things that the King should know of, if he is to understand this present threat to the realm. He is wise, our Mellar, but he needs information in the first place. Be sure to tell him everything, Tabitha."

"May, how does a special audience differ from an audience?"

"An audience may take a week to be heard, a special audience is my privilege as Lady of Ceremony. He does not know I bring you or your tale with me, but that is my prerogative."

"Won't the King be—angry?" Tabitha enquired, feeling suddenly foolish in her royal gown.

"Angry? Not our Mellar. Come! It is right for women to keep men waiting, but not for too long, lest they realise they are waiting."

Maybelle winked, and led Tabitha from the House of Ceremony. Pia skipped along beside them. The bustle of Stormhaven passed by in a swirl of coloured cloaks and the trample of boots. Soon the crowds thinned, and they came to the spear-tipped fence that bordered the palace. Five Swords gleamed in the gateway, blocking their passage as effectively as a drawn blade.

"Maybelle Westerbrook of the House of Ceremony, my guideling Pia, and my guest Tabitha Serannon of the Meadowmoor County, for special audience with the King," announced May.

One of the Swords moved to the open hatch of the gatehouse, and nodded to a scribe who began to scribble furiously in a ledger.

"Aye, we know of your audience, Missus Westerbrook," said the scribe. "Miss Serannon," he said, nodding. He indicated Pia with the end of his quill. "The little one may go only to the door of the audience chambers so long as she returns with the escort without any misbehaviour. I'll not be held responsible for a guideling underfoot in the Palace."

Pia beamed at the scribe. He turned and issued a crisp command to the Swords. They stepped smoothly aside, standing to perfect attention. The sunlight glinting on their polished helms and sword-hilts was the only thing which shifted as Tabitha passed by. She wondered how many times they had practised the motion, how many times they would do it again.

They followed their singular escort into the palace grounds. They traversed a short avenue of silken trees, and mounted a grand stairway. They passed between massive stone pillars, and through the engraved doors set therein. The cool interior was vaulted and quiet.

The palace was wondrous. The corridors were floored with immaculate, dark stonewood, polished to a glistening sheen. The scent of crushed leaves and wax lingered in the air. Organic patterns wove throughout, created by the use of varying hues, delighting the eye with whorls and random grains. The walls were a richer tone than the floor, panelled more with red than brown.

It must have been touched by the wizards, to be of stonewood, Tabitha marvelled.

Statues of water-fowl posed in alcoves and lost corners, making to spear a fish with their stone beaks or to beat the air with their outstretched wings. Giant carvings of Eyrian men battling winged beasts and vicious-weaponed foes poised on pedestals. They were so realistic that Tabitha could imagine they had paused their striving only as the procession neared, and would resume their fights once they were hidden again.

Despite the art, the palace had a rigid feel to it, as if everything had its place, and that moving anything would be frowned upon. Even the tapestries were stretched on identical frames, set at regular spaces along the corridors. The art was colourful and alive, but contained within strict borders.

Tabitha smoothed her dress, and her hand fluttered to the Lightstone at her throat. The grandeur of the palace made her feel inadequate and ill-prepared. Even Pia seemed to be affected, for she had not uttered a word since they had entered the palace. Yet the Lady of Ceremony strode with confidence beside them.

Tabitha took strength from the fact that it was really May's audience, and she was a guest. But she knew she would have to recount her tale directly to the King once they were received.

A short man appeared from a side corridor, wrapped in a yellow robe and an aura of self-importance. Tabitha recognised the Official with a sinking heart. His objections were voiced before he had come within ten paces of them.

"What is a guideling doing inside the Palace? Miss Westerbrook, there is no need for her kind here. Take her back to the gates, Sword Tarennin." Pia and the Sword peeled off from the group before Maybelle could countermand it, as if they knew from experience that their presence would only bring further insult and bad consequence.

May's voice held an edge of warning. "Lethin Tarrok, you may be an Official of the Court, but your manners appal me. Who gave you the right to dismiss my companions so?"

"Lady of Ceremony, you of all people should know the Palace is no place for children, and that I command these halls. You should be ashamed that you brought her, not indignant."

"Oh, hush, you mean little man. We come to a special audience with the King, so stand aside."

"I must ask why she accompanies you. Surely you are not bringing her case to the King?"

His eyes slid over Tabitha, then returned to May.

"Whom I bring to my audience is none of your concern," May answered. "I might ask you why the audience Tabitha requested has not yet been scheduled. Her case is of vital importance."

"I would not trouble my King with tales brought by a liar."

The blood pounded in Tabitha's ears, but she could not speak. May was outraged.

"Lethin Tarrok, you forget yourself! You will apologise for that slander."

"Not at all. By the word of the House of Lightgifters, Tabitha Serannon is a name not listed in those orbed by the Dovecote. She gained her entrance to Stormhaven under many false pretences, one of them being that stone." He pointed an accusing finger at Tabitha's throat. He looked entirely too pleased with himself.

May drew herself up. "This young woman fled her parents' murderer to reach Stormhaven. No wonder she wasn't thinking clearly when confronted by one such as you in the harbour. Lightgifter or not, she is an Eyrian, and by Fynn's Tooth she will be treated as one. Now stand aside, we have an audience to attend."

"Not at all," said Tarrok. "If you insist on completing your audience, it is my *duty* to escort you, and announce you to the King. Follow me," he ended, turning away before May could respond. The look that the Lady of Ceremony directed at his back could have burned stone. May took Tabitha's arm without a word. They followed Tarrok, at their own pace.

If I had not revealed the Lightstone this morning, would May have stood up for me?

Tabitha was suddenly very glad she had trusted her friend.

She mulled over the value of honesty as they were led further through the palace. Tarrok ducked into a narrow archway ahead of them, then turned to face them with an impatient, withering expression. Maybelle slowed.

"The throne room –" Maybelle began, pointing along the main hallway they had been walking.

"Not the throne room," Tarrok corrected. "The King is in his private chambers. This way."

They followed the Official down the side corridor. The roof was somewhat lower, the walls were plain. They came to a door inlaid with gold fretwork. Tarrok knocked loudly, then heaved the door open. It swung back on silent hinges.

"The Lady of Ceremony, and her companion," Tarrok announced, as he preceded them into the room. "I must warn you, your Highness, that –"

Tabitha grimaced at the words to come, but May cut off the Official's sentence with a sharp voice.

"You must warn of nothing, Tarrok! And you forget your manners." They were suddenly inside the room, standing before King Mellar. Tabitha's head spun as the King regarded her with wise eyes. She heard May's announcement as if from afar.

"My guest is Tabitha Serannon. Good morning, your Highness."

Tabitha stood frozen in awe for an instant before realising that May had dipped in a curtsy. She hastily copied May's example.

The King of Eyri.

"Morning, Highness," she breathed.

"Ladies," King Mellar acknowledged them both. He faced them from behind a thick desk; a bear-like man with piercing green eyes but kindly features. His head bore copper hair, upon which was set the golden crown Tabitha knew as the Kingsrim. A large portrait of a young Prince hung behind King Mellar's desk, a second painting showed Mellar's son playing with a toy boat on the Amberlake shore. There was a miniature picture-frame balanced on the King's desk which faced away from Tabitha, but she could guess whose face it displayed.

"Welcome to my private study. Your guest surprises me, Lady Westerbrook, but she is welcome. Thank you Tarrok, that will be all." The King's voice was warm, and deep.

"But your Highness, this girl is not—"

"I said, that will be all," King Mellar said firmly, forestalling the other. "You can advise me after, but I'd like to offer my guests an untainted audience."

"She —"

"Out!" boomed Mellar. The command in that voice stunned Tabitha. Tarrok backed away, and the door closed with a hush behind him.

"Sorry about that. Take a seat, please."

Despite her pounding nervousness, Tabitha found herself settling in a chair close to the King's desk.

"I'm sure you're wondering why here and not the throne room, Lady of Ceremony. I had hoped to speak of things which the prying ears and buzzing tongues of the Officials might not hear." A meaningful glance was exchanged between the King and Maybelle, a look which did not go unnoticed by Tabitha.

Maybelle smiled. "I was wondering more why you keep a man like Tarrok in your service."

Tabitha's eyes grew wide. Never in a hundred years would she have considered to challenge the King so. Even Maybelle seemed to realise the implicit defiance.

"Sorry, your Highness, I forget myself in my temper. He is your

Official."

King Mellar made a placating gesture.

"And my nephew, Maybelle. Have no worry. I know you speak plainly and I value such audience. Aye, he may seem rude, when there are so many others with fine manners. Sometimes the seat of rule becomes the centre of a spider's web, binding me to my throne. How that web is spun, and with which threads, is my burden. I cannot deny my older sister's son, when there is hope that he may be coached in some useful profession here. But enough of the court! I come to my study to escape the tangled web of bureaucrats and servants for a moment."

"Yet a weak thread might bring a web down," Tabitha said.

She covered her mouth with her hand—she hadn't intended to speak her thoughts aloud. She wished she didn't have the compelling urges of a Truthsayer. The Ring had only made her talent more pronounced, by bringing clarity to her intuition.

King Mellar held Tabitha with his level gaze. She felt as if he noticed every fine detail—each crease in her blue dress, the rapid rise and fall of her chest, the snow-white Lightgifters orb.

"You speak very freely, young lady. I would value it if you continued to do so. There are few who have the courage."

Tabitha was about to splutter out an apology when she realised the King had accepted her outburst. May saved her from further embarrassment.

"That is one of the reasons I brought her, Mellar. The other is the tale she bears, a tragic, but most extraordinary tale."

"Of course, you are the Serannons' daughter! Forgive my slowness of wit. The Captain from First Light mentioned the farm at Phantom Acres, and the outrage committed there. My deepest sympathies, Tabitha, you are a strong woman to have endured it so well. A credit to the Lightgifters indeed."

"Thank you, your Highness," Tabitha mumbled.

How do I tell him now that it's a borrowed Lightstone?

Her heart ached to tell the truth.

"Why was I not told of your arrival in Stormhaven?" he asked.

"It was Tarrok who received her," May answered for her, crisply. "He doesn't understand her importance."

"Ah, then," said the King, but did not finish the sentence at once. "I take your meaning of broken threads in the web."

"It was not entirely his fault," replied Tabitha. "He wouldn't let me into Stormhaven, so I showed him this orb and claimed the privilege of a royal audience. But he found out about the orb. It isn't mine, this is my mother's Lightstone. I'm not yet a Lightgifter."

The King regarded her sagaciously, then smiled.

"I see you have a compulsion for honesty, Miss Serannon. Why don't you tell me of how it came to be that you bear your mother's orb ahead of time. I presume that is part of the tale Maybelle would have you tell?" At May's nod, he returned an expectant gaze to Tabitha.

She began her tale, beginning with the first night in Phantom Acres. King Mellar's attention never left her during the telling, and he made encouraging comments from time to time. It had become easier to talk of the events, though it still pained her deeply to relive the memories. She told the King everything, of the song she had sung, of the Ring she now owned, of the Riddler, the ashes of her home and the race from the Shadowcaster. When the river of her tale had finally run its course, and washed her up on the shore of Stormhaven, Tabitha's voice trailed off. King Mellar rose from his desk and came around to stand beside Tabitha's chair.

"Don't get up," he commanded, laying a gentle hand on her head as she made to rise. "You have been very brave, and you must be commended for enduring, and telling the tale so honestly."

"I think she has more than a right to be commended, Mellar. She has a right to demand justice on this Shadowcaster, though I know she is too shy to ask it."

"The wheels have already been set in motion for that, Maybelle," he remarked, seeming to take no offence at the Lady's direct approach. "It was not to talk about the weather that Captain Steed of First Light came to me yesterday. His tidings were dark, for three of his men were killed by the same man. Justice shall be swift, of that be certain. The Swordmaster tracks this criminal as we speak. I shall not relent until he is found, and executed."

Tabitha looked up to her King. Their eyes met for a time. When the King withdrew his hand, he took an immense weight from her shoulders. Justice would be done.

The King turned to May. "Something else the Captain spoke of makes me deeply worried. What I tell you now does not leave these four walls. I will not have the panic spread, but I believe you have a right to know this, Tabitha, for a fuller understanding of the events. The Swords were downed not by the Shadowcaster, but by his beast, a beast whose only name could be a Morgloth."

"But that's impossible!" exclaimed May. "The Morgloth are beasts of the legends, the time of the Forming. They are a fantasy! No, Mellar, tell me this isn't true."

"I trust this Captain, and his report was clear. This Shadowcaster has found a way to raise a demon. The beast tore through trained soldiers like a wolf through hens. Only the Swordmaster appeared to have any effect against it."

"But surely it is not raised from some Underworld, Mellar! It must be a big bear, or some illusion of his magic."

"The Captain was quite specific, Maybelle. The beast was summoned from a circle in the floor of his cell, where before there had been nothing. A beast standing taller than a man, with black wings, and a lust for blood. A beast with a head like a long melon, skin as black as ink. A Morgloth."

A stunned silence filled the room. King Mellar sank into his chair. He held Tabitha's eye.

"Now that you understand what a threat he is to the realm, you know how fierce my intent to capture this man is. I shall not abide such a fiend in Eyri. Rest assured he shall find justice soon."

If anyone else had suggested Morgloth to Tabitha, she would have laughed at the notion. But this was the King of Eyri, and the weight of his words brooked no questioning.

Oh, Mother, what did you face?

"Justice does nothing to bring joy to the heart," the King announced, "and of that you are sorely in need, Tabitha. I would like to give you a gift, something to cherish and lift your spirits, if only for a while."

"I don't need a gift, your Highness. I'm glad for the sanctuary of Stormhaven."

King Mellar shook his head. "The sanctuary I provide is for everyone. No, I want to award you something personal. You mentioned that you are a singer. Do you play an instrument?"

"A lyre," Tabitha replied, then felt forlorn. "It was burned with mother's, in the fire."

"A lyre then," said the King, determination in his eye. "When you will, visit the Den of Notes in the merchant's quarter. Tell Yzell that it is the King's wish to award you with a lyre. You will do that?"

Tabitha nodded. "Thank you."

The King reached into a drawer, and produced a stick of sealing wax and a scrap of paper. He held the stick over a candle. Purple wax dripped onto the paper. He waited a moment, then pressed his ring into it.

"It is a small thing," he said, handing her the royal seal, "though I hope it brings a song to your heart. Show this to Yzell, he'll understand. Now what do you plan to do from here?"

The question caught her by surprise. She had never dwelt much upon what she would do after the audience. She had come to Stormhaven to hide. But she could not hide forever.

"I shall present myself to the Dovecote for my apprenticeship. As soon as possible."

King Mellar smiled. "You waste no time, a trait which many in this city could learn." He pulled on a cord behind his desk, and the faint chime of a bell could be heard.

"I would advise, though, that you wait until we have apprehended the Shadowcaster. You will be safe in Stormhaven, but Levin is not so disciplined."

The servant took a few minutes to arrive. When the door finally swung open, it revealed a breathless Lethin Tarrok, damp yellow robe and all.

"Yes, Your Majesty?" Tarrok looked bothered, as if the summons had interrupted matters of greater importance.

"When Miss Serannon requests it, she shall have an escort of Swords to accompany her to the Dovecote in Levin."

Lethin Tarrok nodded slowly. Too slowly, Tabitha thought, as if he was reluctant to do anything.

"Certainly, your Majesty. The men shall be made ready when she asks." He leered towards Tabitha. "Can you ride?" He seemed pleased at himself for some reason, but the King glowered at Tarrok.

"A carriage, Tarrok!"

"Ah," the little man said, "she has become someone of importance. How do women do that, overnight? As you wish, my King."

Mellar's green eyes bored into Tarrok until the Official dropped his gaze to the floor.

"Tarrok, I did not employ you to be my Fool. I shall tell you if I wish to hear your wit."

"Majesty," Tarrok said, in an almost humble tone.

"Now are there any important audiences awaiting my attention?"

"Lord Luross, your Highness, seeks to discuss an upgrade of the High Way. Lady Ahlen of Levin, wanting charity for her hungry waifs. A few minor nobles with minor grievances."

"Good. You can tell them that I shall attend them in the throne room presently. That will be all."

Tarrok bowed, and backed out of the King's private study. Tabitha was certain she saw the man smirk before the door closed with an audible thump.

"Well, the wheels of the kingdom grind on. I must see to the steering. Thank you for coming forth with your tale, Tabitha."

She was being dismissed, she realised. Tabitha stood, and curtsied before King Mellar.

"Thank you, Highness. I shall serve you in all that I do."

The smile that spread through the King's beard was genuine, but he waved a finger at her. "A powerful oath, but might I change it? Serve Eyri in all that you do. Then we shall strive for the same thing."

"I shall serve Eyri."

May rose beside her, and curtsied her leave from the King, but Mellar forestalled her exit.

"A moment in private, Maybelle, if I may."

Maybelle shot Tabitha a merry glance, and made a gentle shooing gesture with the hand behind her back.

Oh.

Tabitha scurried for the door, curtsied again, and pulled it to after her.

Maybelle and the King?

It was possible that they might be talking of policy, and nothing else. Yet the more she considered it, the more perfect the match seemed. Everyone knew that the King had never remarried after he had lost his Queen, so many years ago. He didn't deserve to be lonely.

◆ ———————— ◆

She exited the grand arched palace doors to spectacular light. Everything was white, brilliant sparkling white. The mist had advanced during her audience to lap against the lower steps of the palace. The grounds and the forecourt were smothered in vapours. It was as if a tide had risen, and the city of Stormhaven had been flooded. The buildings of the Upper District poked their stern forms through the vaporous sea, looking like overturned boats with golden keels. The sentry post bobbed closer at hand, with five Swords who stood in the shallows, their legs lost to view. It was beautiful, but eerie too. The mist absorbed the sounds of the city. It was surreal, and it felt as if she was about to step into a dream world.

The guards nodded to her as she approached the palace gates, and they stood aside to let her pass. The mists pulled overhead as she crossed the Forecourt. By the time she had reached the Boarding, the sun was a diffused incandescence. It was too wonderful a day to be indoors, she decided. She turned from the stair.

She found her way down toward the merchant's quarter with an eager stride. The mists became cooler and thicker. Horses clicked towards Tabitha on the cobbles, then the riders emerged from the shroud, only to vanish again as soon as they had passed. Somewhere, a hammer pounded upon iron. As Tabitha focused on the sounds, her Ring brought a wealth of details to mind, piercing the mist for her.

Traders heckled with one another over a bolt of cloth. A tailor complimented a customer loudly. A gaggle of women guffawed. Three youths burst out of a side street, fighting and running at the same time. Through everything, the pungent smells of the city—horses, stone, clothes, people and the less savoury scent of the canals.

Tabitha realised she had halted in the street, overwhelmed by the sensations. She tried to ignore the clarity of the Ring, and focused on finding the musician's shop. The lower district of Stormhaven was a well-ordered network of streets and old buildings. A few enquiries guided her to a door beneath the carved signboard of the Den of Notes.

Chimes tinkled above her as she crossed the threshold. It was gloomy within the shop, but warm. It smelled of wood-shavings, and oil, and parchment. Musical scores were piled on a well-worn desk, and weighted with a bell. A small fire burned low in a hearth. Nobody attended the front room.

Just then a piercing blast come from within the building. There was a clatter of metal, then a vehement curse.

"Ah, beat the piper black and blue! My head, my blessed head. Will you never learn, Yzell? Strings in the mornings, pipes after noon!"

The sounds of stumbling continued for a while, then the heavy thump of a body seeking refuge in a chair. The rasp of a metallic file began. The hidden voice began to chant, an off-key baritone.

"Cursed wine, cursed wine, my head is victim—of the vine."

Tabitha's curiosity drew her around the desk, toward the narrow back door that stood ajar.

"Hullo?" she tried. The filing continued, then was replaced by the thump of a mallet.

"Hullo?" Louder this time.

"Eh? Come in!" came the delayed response.

The room she entered was a jumble of carved wood and half-finished instruments. A pale man with a shock of grey hair gave her a gaunt, apologetic smile. He was deep in the refuge of his chair.

"Hullo Gifter. What can I do for you?" Then to his lap he said, "Trumpets, they make the damnedest noise if they aren't tuned."

"Who were you talking to?" asked Tabitha. There seemed to be no one else in the workshop, though with the clutter she couldn't be certain.

He waggled the brass trumpet vaguely. "The sins of a late-night worker."

"You're Yzell?"

He nodded. "Though I should have retired long ago." Suddenly his ringed eyes brightened. "You're a Gifter. Would you heal me, it's a real pounder this morning." He tapped lightly on his own temple.

"I—can't. I'm still in training."

"Ah, too bad then. Suppose it's my own fault anyway, I should've left the revelry to the younger folk. You know my prices are higher when I've a headache?" he ended, but when Tabitha refused to respond to his mild coercion, the hopeful look faded from his face.

"What instrument?" he asked.

"Ah, a lyre. The King's gift."

At this, he shook off the appearance of sufferance. "You have a seal?"

Tabitha handed the blank slip of paper over.

"He must trust you well, to leave the gift and craftsman undefined. And trust me to destroy the chit." He looked at the paper for a moment, then tore it in two. "The power of a trusting King. A lyre, you said?"

"That's what the King wanted. I—I don't need anything special," Tabitha stammered, suddenly awkward about what she was expecting of the instrument maker. "A wooden seven-string is what I played, before."

"And how would my King feel, knowing I had given you a cheap product to display his thanks? No!" he said, tossing the trumpet he had been holding over his shoulder. "You shall get the King's lyre he sent you to collect." The trumpet disturbed a pile of cymbals, which tumbled with vigour to the floor. "And I shall charge him accordingly," he said over the noise, a conspiratorial glint to his eye. "That's how these things work, young Gifter."

"I am Tabitha. Tabitha Serannon." She extended her hand to the seated musician.

Yzell's grip was firm and dry. He used the handshake to pull himself suddenly from the chair. Tabitha staggered, but retained her balance.

"How will you be playing this lyre? Badly, or well?" he asked. He was taller than Tabitha had expected. He smelled of wood-chips.

"Well enough to keep a tavern filled for a few hours," she said. She did not want to seem vain, but he had to know she could play.

"A tavern singer?" Yzell exclaimed, his eyes bright, "and there I was taking you for a humming Gifter." He left her abruptly and picked his way through the obstacles in his workshop. "What songs do you play the best?"

Tabitha searched through her repertoire; the crowds enjoyed the tankard-thumpers, but she loved the harmonic pieces best. "Treachery's Dawn. The Ballad of the Forest. The Glee of Genesis."

He paused to look at her from the far side of a bench. "You can—complete that, the Glee?"

Tabitha nodded. Yzell's face lit up. He rummaged through his creative debris, muttering imprecations to himself.

"Ever played a strangle-oak?" he asked, an instrument in hand.

It was Tabitha's turn to feel overwhelming surprise. Strangle-oak was rare indeed, a wood so hard it was said to bend chisel-blades. An instrument made of strangle-oak would be light, and strong. And very, very expensive. She had never heard of a lyre being made from such valuable wood.

"Let us see if it likes your hand, Miss Serannon." Yzell passed the lyre to her over his chair. "If it proves to be good, why, then I won't need to make a lyre at all, for you can have this one. It's new," he added, "but it doesn't fit my big hands. I should have thought of that before I made it, I suppose. Just one of those works that takes you, you know? I acquired the wood, and had to craft the instrument. Damndest thing."

"It's—beautiful!" Tabitha whispered. The wood felt alive under her fingers, so smooth it could have been made of silk, so light it almost floated in the air. The dark brown wood was tightly grained. Yzell had worked a gold symbol into the wood near the base, a flowing, delicate rune.

"Ah, that's something I saw written on a musical score once. Strange music, no harmony I could find, but the symbol stayed with me. It just seemed to fit. Come on!" he encouraged. "Play it, feel if it holds a tune for you."

"What shall I play?" Tabitha asked, nervous of having to perform in front of Stormhaven's master instrument-maker.

"Sing the Glee, it's been long since I've heard it played well."

He's forgotten his headache, Tabitha thought.

"Are you sure?"

"Certain." He raised his arms, as if to introduce her to the crowds.

From the moment she plucked the first string, Tabitha knew that the lyre she held was special. A resonant, perfect note trembled through the wood. She couldn't hope to match the music of the lyre, but she could try.

She raised her melody as her voice warmed. It felt good to sing again. An age had passed since she had last performed for anyone. She immersed herself in the ballad of Creation.

Yzell burrowed beside the door for a moment, and returned with a rascal's grin. He set a glass wine bottle on the bare floor. Tabitha raised her eyebrows, but did not falter. The Glee of Genesis was compelling, pulling her along in the current, toward the waterfall she knew was coming, where notes and song would climax. She took a step away from the bottle.

The song coursed through the air with an eldritch power. The notes seemed cleaner than she had ever sung them before—she had a refined sense of when she struck the perfect resonance, and she used the feeling to guide her song. The lyre offered faultless notes. She wondered if the strange clarity in the music had something to do with the Ring. The walls of Yzell's workshop seemed to dissolve before the music, as if she was generating waves of pure sound.

It feels like I am singing to all of Eyri.

She reached the ascent, the final note of the Genesis, the Shiver.

The glass wine bottle shattered to a hundred pieces. The song faded. The instrument-maker lay on the floor.

Yzell clutched his head in his hands. "Blast-ed, blast-ed, mother-of-all-Dwarrow-banes!"

"I'm so sorry," Tabitha said, kneeling beside the musician. "I didn't mean to—oh dear!" She layed a hand on his shoulder.

"Nonsense!" Yzell exclaimed, his fierce expression at odds with his crossed eyes. "That was brilliant. Brilliant! Ah, my head feels worse than the bottle. Oh, oh, oh." He staggered to his feet, and hung onto the chair like an old man.

"How do you -?" he began, then grimaced.

"The glass breaks every time if you sing the note pure," Tabitha filled in.

"Not that," Yzell muttered, straightening from the chair. "The way you sing, it gets under the skin, under everything, like it was setting the world to moving with your tune. Never heard nothing like it."

Tabitha didn't have an answer for him. She had felt it too, the strange intensity to the music. She had begun to think it was her own imagination.

Yzell regarded her with an almost steady gaze. "I swear that if you sang that note any better, you would be walking in the footsteps of the Goddess, singing like mythical Ethea."

Tabitha couldn't hold his eye; the praise was too great. She watched the floorboards instead.

"The strangle-oak. It's yours," she heard him say.

"But I –"

"I would be honoured to know that one with your talent played my instrument."

The honour he bestowed upon her with those words was even more valuable than the lyre itself. She threw her arms around the eccentric musician, and kissed him on the cheek. He stepped away quickly.

"Got to finish this dratted trumpet," he said, but he was smiling broadly as he stalked away.

"Thank you, for the lyre," said Tabitha, "I shall always treasure it."

"You ever change your mind about the Lightgifting, you come here and tell me," he said over his shoulder. "There's work aplenty for one with your voice. Now be off, I've much to do!" He buried himself in a pile of timber and tools.

Tabitha backed slowly to the door. "Good day, Yzell!" she called out above the sounds of his rummaging. "And thank you."

"Leave the front door closed," came his reply.

She took that to mean that his headache was worse than he cared to admit. His prices would be very high that afternoon.

She couldn't avoid disturbing the chimes on the way out, but she took care to close the door to the Den of Notes quietly.

The mist was still thick in the street, the cobbles damp underfoot. She tucked the lyre under her arm.

The City Gates must be nearby. From there, I can work my way inwards through Stormhaven.

It was turning out to be a wonderful day.

◆ ——————— ◆

Kirjath paced the Kingsbridge. It had been infuriating to find the heavy guard at the City Gates, more Swords than he had expected. They stopped every visitor to Stormhaven. They had opened a carriage before his eyes, looking under the seats and through the barrels and goods, despite the carriage-owner's objections. They were even lifting cloak-hoods, revealing squawking sparse-haired crones and indignant nobles to the daylight. No one was spared from scrutiny.

Stormhaven was on guard against something. News of his beast must have come down from First Light. They were scared.

The presence of the thorough guard forced him to reconsider his hasty plan. Maybe he could use the Dark essence to hide his approach, with Silence and Shadow, but he doubted he could pass through the guard without detection, they would notice something moving through their ranks. An attack on the Sword would only raise the alarm, and make stealth in the city an impossibility. He needed time to find the girl in Stormhaven. He couldn't have tinpots chasing him through the streets.

Maybe the girl isn't in the city.

Then the song hit him. He almost stumbled to his knees, but managed to retain his balance and not draw attention to himself. Somebody was singing, and it pierced his ears like a hot skewer. Nausea rushed through him. It was worse than the first time he had heard her sing.

Music like no other. It pounded though his head, making itches run across his scalp. He felt as if he would burst with revulsion.

He cast his doubts aside, and strode back toward the City Gates.

He knew. The bearer of the Ring was in Stormhaven. The same vile magic he had witnessed from Fendwarrow, the same awful voice he'd tracked to the Lightgifter's farm. The people nearby did not seem to hear her.

The song rose in pitch and power. Kirjath tore two jurrum leaves to shreds, and ground them between his teeth. The pain hardly eased.

She must be close to the Gates, to affect me so strongly.

A mere girl!

His plan was simple. Wrap himself in Darkness. Rush the guard, slip through in the confusion. The mists would do the rest. He wouldn't need long to follow the clear trail of magic to its source. Once he had the girl, he could raise the Morgloth, and cut a path clear to the Gates again. The more he chewed on the jurrum, the more sense the plan made.

The Ring shall be mine!

The City Gates loomed out of the mists, with a lengthy queue of people, coaches and animals. The Dark essence he had kept in abeyance surged to his hands. He wove it to a dense web of Shadow, cloaking himself and the road on either side of him in gloom. Animals shied as he passed, and people called out in surprise, but he didn't care. They knew nothing of his intent, these Eyrians. Few would understand the sudden darkness that swept past them. He watched the Swords, with their silly little blades and thin steel helms.

Freeze them, Decay them, let them taste Despair. I have enough essence to take them all!

He strode forward.

But he didn't make it to the Gates. The current of sound that he had been wading against became a raging torrent, then a flood, then a single, high note which ripped through his mind like a ragged blade.

He fell to the road. His essence scattered into the mists.

Pain ruled his world.

When the agony eased, and he became aware of his surroundings again, he realised the danger. The Swords were not more than fifty paces ahead of him, on the limit of the mists.

"Are you all right, mister?" a youth shouted out. A crowd was gathering. The Swords would be coming soon, he knew. His thoughts were in turmoil, tortured by the echoes of that terrible high note. He doubted that he would have enough focus to wield the scattered essence.

Kirjath gathered his red robes, and fled. He broke left from the road, and ran for the Seep, retreating along the course of his morning's advance. Each step carried a separate curse.

There was no sound of pursuit, but he ran hard nonetheless. He only slowed when he was well past the lone temple on the eastern corner of the Isle and into the reeds and marshes of the wastelands beyond. His way to the Scrags was fuelled by the bitter taste of fury. She had done something to him with her song. He felt ill.

Though his captive moaned and screamed under his hands when he returned to the boat, she didn't help to purge his anger. The blond Lightgifter had an unripe smell about her. She had soon screamed herself hoarse within her gag. Soon after that, she was slack and listless in the keel.

Hunger gnawed at his belly.

All he could find in the inlet to eat were the fat brown mudfish. He coaxed them to the surface by tossing insects onto the water to drown. Then he used a Breaking spell to paralyse them. Working with the Dark helped to restore his confidence, but the anger remained. The fish were impossible to scale properly with his single functioning hand. When he bit into them, they tasted of grease and weed.

The only thing which was good about the day was the mist, which did not retreat from the inlet where he hid. He wracked his brain for a way to get to the girl. He was running out of time.

The longer she was left with the Ring, the more power she gained.

He sent a Morrigán flying over Stormhaven, searching for his prey, but he knew he would have a long wait. There were many places to search, and many people on the King's Isle.

22. SHADOWS AND SCENTS

"Beware the failed man,
for he has nothing to lose."—*Zarost*

The morning began as it had the day before—a greasy mist clung to the lake. The Morrigán brought good news. The girl had been found. She slept in a room on the third floor of a lodge, close to the central court of the city. The bird hadn't been able to breach the window to gain a closer look, but from the vision it brought, Kirjath had been sure enough. There lay his quarry, there lay the girl, the ring bearer, thief. His thoughts quickened into action. The night had been long, and its quiet had yielded a way to enter the city. The boat was tied up nearby, tilting on the slack water.

"Kneel," he commanded. The woman pushed herself up onto all fours. She had learned to obey his voice.

"Water," she asked, in a broken whisper.

"Come here bitch, put your head in my lap."

He denied her the water. A drink could be her reward for good behaviour, should she hold still. She crawled to him over the crumbled rocks and pebbles. The way she moved displayed much of her pain. She wouldn't hold out much longer, without food or healing.

No matter. She was only needed to perform one last trick.

She dropped her head against his thighs. He took her matted hair in his bad hand, clumped as much as he could in his curling fingers, and pulled her head back. Her eyes went wide when she saw the blade he held in his left.

Kirjath savoured that expression for a long moment, but when he brought the knife down, it was her hair he cut, right at the base against her scalp. He hacked and hacked, throwing handfulls of blonde hair aside. It took a long time, and his wounds began to weep. He didn't cut her too much, considering.

When she was shaved, he ordered her naked. The red robe he threw into the ashes of the night's fire. It smoked, and blackened, but did not catch flame. He kicked it around and walked it into the dead coals, until most of the red had become a dirty black. He tossed it back to the woman, but she didn't seem to care enough to dress. That was a change from the early days.

He stood close behind her, and barked in her ear, "Be proud, wastrel. Today, you are a Shadowcaster. Now dress, and walk with me!"

Their pace along the shore of the lake was made slow by the woman's hobbling gait. She went faster after he allowed her a drink. Kirjath even gave her some jurrum to ease her pain, though he had to force the leaf between her teeth, and make her chew it.

He led her into the water as they passed the stinking Seep, to avoid contact with the patrols. They remained hidden with a minimal use of Dark essence. Kirjath called a halt just short of the Kingsbridge, in the shallows, concealed in mist.

A thrill passed through him, a potent mix of lust and fear.

He spun the spell of the Gateway on the shallow water. The Gifter stiffened, her reddened eyes widened in her ash-streaked face. Her head was a mess of chopped bristles, raw skin, and clotted blood. She would do well today. He pulled her cowl over her head.

"Do you want to be rid of me? Do you want to earn your escape?" he asked.

She was transfixed by the circle of the Gateway, yet pulled her gaze away and looked up into Kirjath's face. There was a mix of horror and hope in those eyes. Good. She still wished to live.

He whispered her part in the plan to her, and she listened to every word. Then she started off at a walk for the Gates of Stormhaven.

She would perform, today. She wanted her freedom badly enough.

He created a Morrigán to follow her, to bring word of what transpired. It croaked away into the mist.

He waited beside the circling Dark essence that led to the Morgloth. It wasn't yet the time to call the beast, but his pulse raced at the thought of what was to come. A terrifying plan, but necessary. There was no other way.

The Morrigán returned, at length. It grasped his outstretched arm with claws that stung for only a moment. The spell dissolved, and the vision was released.

A black-robed tattered figure approached the City Gates. The queuing people drew away as it passed. Three brave Swords came charging down from the Gates, blades drawn. The figure shouted, "I know of Prince Bevn!" The men were well-trained, for when they felled the figure, they used the hilts of their swords. The Shadowcaster was carried away into Stormhaven, doubtless to the Swordhouse for interrogation. It had all gone perfectly, according to his plan. They would not be expecting another Arkell in the city. That was all the advantage he could hope for.

He gazed at the dark circle.

"Morgloth, from your hell be born, your master summons you."

He clenched his stomach in anticipation. It had to be done.

The demon rose from the Gateway, its wings beat the cool mist air. It was always the same Morgloth which responded to his call, the one which now bore the scar of service on its right wing. Its animal mind was a swelling, urgent pressure which thrust up through Kirjath's thoughts, aggravating his lingering doubts. He curbed the Morgloth's power by dominating the demon. He shared his immediate plan with the beast and felt the Morgloth consider and understand.

It was too late to turn back.

The demon flew away, then it turned, swooping low. Kirjath spread his arms. He stood straight and tall in the water, facing the lake, into the approaching nightmare of black, ancient evil. The Morgloth extended its legs, as if to strike Kirjath with the barbed heels. There was a hard impact.

The Morgloth's legs closed and linked at his back. Kirjath grasped the demon vigorously. He was lifted, wrenched from the water like a fish by an eagle. The Morgloth strained above him, beating the thick air with heavy strokes. Kirjath's feet dragged over earth, and he commanded the Morgloth to veer over the water once more. If the beast failed to lift him clear, he could not afford to be dropped so close to the Gates of Stormhaven. The Morgloth obeyed, and seemed to ease its flight as their speed increased. Kirjath circled them off the shore, allowing the beast to build height with each spiralling turn. A surge of triumph rushed through his veins. Despite the torn wing, his Morgloth was succeeding.

Don't look down, he reminded himself, but the very words of the prohibition tugged his eyes downwards. He clutched on to the black legs with renewed ferocity. There was nothing below, a sickening, swirling mass of whitish grey, just the same as to the sides, and above. Water streamed from his boots and blew away in the wind. He hoped the demon knew which way was up. He commanded the Morgloth to greater heights. The mist had to end somewhere.

They burst through to the bright morning above. Sunlight glared off a carpet of shattered white. Every beam of light seemed to be reflected directly at Kirjath, piercing his head with the brilliant pain of a thousand needles. In the distance, golden spires and dark walls thrust up through the mist. The Morgloth, affected directly by his master's pain, if not his own, faltered in the air, and they fell through the canopy to the gloom below.

Kirjath screamed within his mind. They spun, but the demon was strong, and recovered after a few stalled beats.

They resumed level flight. Kirjath ground his teeth. He could not afford to lose control, not now; not ever. He had no illusions about what the demon would do if he was to lose his mental stranglehold of its animal psyche. There was a long, deadly fall to the ground below, and the demon would relish every second of its tormentor's end. It obeyed only because it had to. He collected his thoughts, pressing down on the beast's sphere of mental influence which had already enlarged itself within its host.

To the city, he commanded. The golden spires had given him all the bearings he needed. The demon winged silently through the moisture.

◆ ——————— ◆

Tabitha had to lengthen her stride to keep up with Maybelle Westerbrook. The Lady of Ceremony was in buoyant spirits. May had surprised Tabitha by coming to the Boarding and inviting her on a brisk morning walk to begin the day. They walked through the Upper District estates, where all the noble homesteads of Stormhaven were arrayed amongst orchards, tall trees and rolling lawns. Compared to the compactness of the Lower District, the noble houses practically lounged in their luxurious estates. They saw very few people, though Tabitha knew that elsewhere, merchant's doors were being swung open already.

Tabitha had wanted to bring her lyre on the walk, not because she intended to play it, but because she couldn't bear to leave it behind. Truth be told, she had slept with it under her pillow, one hand on the strings. She'd fallen in love with Yzell's instrument, the King's present, for all that it was, and for all that it represented. But she had not wanted to seem too sentimental while accompanying the Lady of Ceremony, so in the end she had left it under her bed.

"It's a most beautiful thing, May," she explained.

"Strangle-oak is rare indeed," May commented. "There's a history to those trees. Do you know it?"

"I heard they grow in their own glades, because they strangle the roots of everything close. I've heard it said that they live so long because they're protected by spirits."

"I doubt it's the spirits' doing," May said, chuckling. "The wood is seldom felled because it is so hard, and so many tools are broken along the way, from cutting to crafting. The strangle-oaks are left alone, and they grow old, very old. There are enough of them around Llury, in the Great Forest. But legend tells that in the earlier years of Eyri, convicted felons were hung upon the strangle-oak. Tree of Justice, it was called, though that name has been forgotten. It was said that if the man were innocent, the bough he was suspended from would break and he would fall to the ground. That custom passed away long ago, yet the memory of the fruit which those strangle-oaks once bore seems to have lingered in the tavern tales."

Tree of Justice.

"Did boughs ever break?"

May shrugged. "I doubt it, for a weak strangle-oak is a thing rarer than silence in Stormhaven. Every part of the tree is as strong as iron. It must have cost old Yzell dearly for the wood, and taken weeks to craft a lyre from it. I suppose he does receive the King's gold for that work now, but he must like you, to have offered such a prized piece."

"It's so perfectly formed, May, I feel honoured just holding it."

"He's an exceptional craftsman, Yzell. That's why Mellar—ah— the King chooses him above all others."

Tabitha yearned to return to her room and to play the lyre again.

Strangle-oak. It must have been greatly feared by wrong-doers.

◆ —————◆

The pressure of the beast was beginning to fray his nerves. Never before had Kirjath held the demon at bay for so long, summoned but not allowed to feed. It had borne him safely over the wall, and was well hidden in a yard close to the boarding house, but it was not content to stay there. The Morgloth pushed fiercely against its mental prison, testing, waiting, for the moment of weakness, when it could break through its Master's domination. Kirjath sweated with the strain of concentration; it was stuffy behind the bedroom curtains. Holding the beast was hard enough. Holding it at a distance was arduous.

Let the beast work up an appetite.

He was not ready. Using the Morgloth now would prove nothing, merely draw unwanted attention to his actions. He had to capture the girl. Once he had the Ring in his hands, the Morgloth would buy him freedom from the King's Isle. He would reward it with a feeding frenzy.

The girl's absence from her rooms was beginning to worry him. He wanted this business over with.

Shatter and blast the spires of Stormhaven! Shall I have to settle this matter in the streets?

He was about to create a Morrigán when he heard footsteps on the stairs. He drew a hushed breath. The footsteps drew nearer, creaking the floorboards one by one. Perfect, she was alone. He whispered to the motes at hand, readied them for casting another spell. The footsteps entered the room, then came really close, not an arm's reach from the curtains. Something was dragged from beneath the bed. Kirjath felt the tightening of his stomach and groin as he anticipated the strike. Then he tossed the fabric aside with his left hand, and threw the motes with his right.

"Silence!" he commanded. The spell struck the person before him with convincing force. But it was not the girl.

A tubby man in a yellow robe stood at the foot of the bed, bulging eyes in a damp face. He had been rummaging in a leather bag, but dropped it to the floor. His slack-jawed terror became more obvious as Kirjath stepped close. The colour faded from the man's skin.

"Where is the girl?" Kirjath snarled. The man jumped, and began to back away, as he mouthed at the air. Of course. He couldn't utter a word. Kirjath cast the more complex spell of Domination, that the man would neither run nor act against his will, then recalled the motes from the spell of Silence.

"Now speak, damn you! Where is the girl?"

"She—she went walking with her friend," the man stuttered. "She'll be back s-s-soon."

"What are you doing here?" Kirjath demanded.

"I—I was going to leave her a note. She is to leave in a carriage for Levin."

Kirjath knew that look. He sent more motes his way, intensifying the Domination. It took immense concentration not to lose his hold on the Morgloth with the distraction of the matter at hand.

"Do not lie to me. It will bring your death."

"She keeps gold in her bag. I came to steal it," the man squeaked.

"Good. What is your name?"

"Tarrok. Lethin Tarrok, my lord. I'm on your side, I work for the

Darkmaster too."

Kirjath pulled a knife from his belt. Sometimes a blade was the easiest way to assure silence.

"Stay, Lethin Tarrok," he commanded. Held in the grasp of Domination, the man could not break and run. If the man's eyes protruded any further, they would surely pop from their sockets and dangle on their threads.

"But you—you were captured by the Swords this morning!" Tarrok gasped.

Pride swelled in Kirjath's chest. They had been fooled. He could afford a moment to savour that knowledge.

"That was not I," answered Kirjath. He put the point of the blade behind the man's neck, at the base of his skull. The less blood now, the better. The neck was wet with sweat.

"You wear no Darkstone. What work is it you do for the Darkmaster?"

"Please do not kill me! I am a spy, a ferret, an informer for the Darkmaster! Cabal of Ravenscroft! He needs me, he'll miss me if I am gone!"

"I care little about the Darkmaster's displeasure," Kirjath said.

"I can help you!" Tarrok pleaded. "I can help you. You want the girl, Tabitha Serannon? I can deliver her to you, beyond the city walls."

Kirjath didn't push the blade in, but held the point firm.

"No, little man, that will not save you. You already said she was coming back here. I shall only need to wait."

"But what if she doesn't? What if they discover that it isn't you in the Swordhouse? I can deliver her to you, so you need not search."

The man wouldn't lie, not with the strength of the spell that compelled his fear. Still, a man about to die would take desperate risks to win his life.

"There is more to your offer," Kirjath breathed over Tarrok again. "Or you would not be so brave. Speak."

"The Swords think they captured you this morning so the girl has no reason to stay here which is why I was arranging an escort to Levin and I can ensure she is on it very soon with the worst Swords assigned to her and you hidden within the coach," he said hurriedly, completing it all in one breath.

The whites of his eyes revealed that his association with the Darkmaster was real enough. The faint yellow streaks were clear proof that past payments for services rendered had not been in gold, but with the leaves of a certain addictive plant. Kirjath felt a certain kinship.

"You will keep your head, but by the Tooth, if I do not see results within the hour, you'll taste your own blood," Kirjath warned. "I shall pay you ten jurrum to keep your mouth shut while you work."

Kirjath withdrew the knife. Tarrok sagged. There were large damp patches on the yellow robe. Tarrok turned to face Kirjath. His hand shook. His lip twitched.

"Fifteen."

Kirjath smiled, an awkward expression, then threw back his head and laughed. The cheeky bastard was trying to haggle. Kirjath could still kill him.

"Ah, Tarrok, your nerve is wasted in Stormhaven. Here, twelve leaves, and your silence shall be absolute."

Lethin Tarrok pocketed the jurrum as deftly as a conjurer, and one leaf found his mouth.

"I shall prepare the King's Stables, Lord Arkell. Remain hidden here, I shall come as soon as the way is clear. I know a way to the stables that is completely concealed."

◆ ———————— ◆

The cobbles gleamed underfoot as the sun pierced the mists. All the way back from leaving Maybelle Westerbrook at the House of Ceremony, the streets had been clearing, opening to the bright blue sky. Tabitha took the stairs to the Boarding, and entered the gloomy interior beyond.

There were wet footprints on the steps leading to her room.

Someone new in the Boarding?

The visitor was likely to get a scolding from the Matron, tramping water all over the wooden floor like that. She placed her foot inside one of the prints. The tread was big—it had dampened the floorboards outside the limits of her boot. She followed the footprints, keeping her steps in the wet marks. A premonition brushed her mind as lightly as a skittering spider. She paused on the landing.

Where have I felt that presence before?

A faint odour of wine drifted on the breeze from her room. Something didn't feel right, not right at all. She tried to sense what was ahead using the Ring. Wine. Coldness. Quiet.

"Tabitha! Tabitha!" It was Maybelle, calling her from the lower hallway. She turned away from her room. It felt as if a dark presence waited at her back.

"Yes, May!" she shouted down. The Lady of Ceremony had begun to climb the stairs, but Tabitha halted her progress by running down to join her.

"I had to come back and tell you, Tabitha. They've captured the Shadowcaster, the one who was after you! Isn't it wonderful?"

"When? Who captured him?" Tabitha's heart was tripping over itself. She missed May's response to her question—her attention was behind her, at the head of the stairs, and beyond. Nothing but shadows.

You're imagining things. This is Stormhaven, nothing can assail you here.

"Sorry, when?" she repeated.

"Come," May said, linking her arm with Tabitha. "Let me take you to the House, there's something I want to give you, before you go."

Tabitha allowed herself to be drawn out to the street. "Go? Go where?"

"The Dovecote. Didn't you want to go to the Dovecote? Tarrok has arranged an escort. Haven't you been listening to anything I've been saying, Tabitha? The Shadowcaster is caught, he will be killed today. They told me just after we parted from our walk this morning."

Tabitha supposed she should be excited at the news, or relieved, or at least surprised. She felt nothing, nothing at all.

"Tarrok surprised me so with his sensitivity," said May. "He said the execution would most likely be public, in the Forecourt, and you probably wouldn't want to attend such a display. And he said the King has been quite enthusiastic of late to see that things are done quickly. A carriage has been arranged to depart in an hour. He asked me to tell you to prepare yourself for the journey."

The sky was blue and empty overhead. Something had shifted, on the limits of her sight. Something about this day was strange.

"Oh, bother, I forgot," said May, halting. "The dress has been taken to be cleaned. I shall have to bring it to you at the Stables, when your carriage leaves. I'll see you there!"

Lady Westerbrook strode off, leaving Tabitha not far from the Boarding, wondering why she was feeling so puzzled by it all.

You should rejoice. The murderer of your parents has been captured.

The Ring was cold on her finger.

Something was amiss.

♦ —————————♦

"The Ring and the Seeker, I find you at last."

The voice at her back made her jump. She spun. A black beard, shot with grey. A racoon-striped hat. And a grin that stretched from ear to ear across the Riddler's leathery face.

"Twardy Zarost!" she exclaimed. She sighed with relief. She had been ready to run. "What are you doing here?"

"Many paths are converging; I thought I may be needed."

"Oh Twardy, will you come with me to my room? I need to know what lingers there."

The Riddler caught her arm firmly. "You should not be poking into shadows yet," he said. "I know a place that's green and bright, and there we must go, to be out of sight."

Hidden in the Riddler's merry voice was a note of urgency. Tabitha did not resist his guiding hand, but glanced back at the Boarding at the last moment. A figure in a yellow robe slipped into the doorway, but no one came out.

Twardy Zarost led her up the street.

His brown eyes were bright. "How does the King care for you?"

"Ah, well. Fine," Tabitha answered. "He gave me a gift."

"A very good lyre, I hear. You should keep it close."

Tabitha shot him a puzzled glance. He bobbed his head towards her.

"Your voice can fly, across land, water and sky."

Cryptic, as always. She watched him closely. "How do you know about the lyre?"

Zarost waggled a finger at her. "Do not chase minnows, when there are bears in the pool, and little water left."

"Minnows? You mean there are more important things I should be asking?"

Zarost smiled. "If I tell you what to ask, there'll be no riddle in the truth, or truth in the riddle."

Tabitha tried another angle. "Why do you think I am in danger?"

"Some covet what you have, and seek to take it from you."

My room. The wet footprints. Somebody came to my room.

She stopped, a hollow in her belly. She had left her lyre beside the bed. "Twardy, I have to go back."

The Riddler frowned. "So soon you forget what brought you to the

King's Isle. You are not ready to face the hunter."

"The hunter—the Shadowcaster? Here?"

"Don't presume you are safe, at any time. Come, come," he said, guiding her up the street once more. "It is too late to change what happens elsewhere, but every step of your own chooses a path amongst many ahead. Think of some better questions, before your feet lead you on a doomed road."

He led her off the street, through an old gate to a garden. Great trees bowed overhead. The scent of growing leaves was fresh. Tabitha recognised the grounds of the Leaf of Merrick.

"Why does life seem to be rushing in a torrent, whenever you are near? Would you be helping me if I did not have the Ring? What do you gain by helping me?"

Zarost raised his hands as if to ward off further questions. "Much better, much better indeed! Now I can try to answer them all at once, or you can try to ask it singly."

Tabitha considered her words. "Why are you here?"

He arched an eyebrow, and it almost hid under the brim of his hat. "Many, many answers sprout from that seed. There is no time to explore them all."

Tabitha would not be riddled aside. "Tell me one of them."

Zarost pouted his lips. "A Riddler's task is to hide the truth from all but those most worthy."

"Yes, but why are you *here*?"

"Because you wear the Ring, and I must see that you have the best chance to complete your quest, though I must not lead you in the task."

Tabitha grimaced. As abstruse as ever. When the Riddler didn't wish to give anything away, he could be infuriating. But she wouldn't let the question go. Even her Ring was warm, leading her on, guiding her to the truth.

"Why are you here today?"

"Because you are in danger of ending yourself."

There was a moment of perfect silence.

"How can you know that?"

"The path of inevitability." He twiddled his fingers one over the other as if in explanation. "Your feet take you forwards to a confrontation for which you are not ready. I offer you an escape, but I cannot compel you to take it, no."

"How do I know I can trust you?" she asked.

"Have you ever come to harm in my company?"

She dipped her hand into her collar, and lifted her Lightstone clear. "You've tricked me before."

"The minimum of tools, you needed the minimum of tools, that is all. You shall need more than that stone aiding you, to survive the beast. You need learning, and that takes time."

The beast. Tabitha was filled with sudden alarm.

"You're talking about the Morgloth, aren't you? The King said the Morgloth was used in First Light. Can the Shadowcaster really command them?"

"It is a crazy man who thinks he commands a Morgloth."

"Yet such a man has come to Stormhaven?"

"I had thought you would be safe here, but it is not so. Thus you must leave, and hide, until you have learned to harness your power, until you understand what it is you face."

"My power? I haven't even begun the Lightgifter's training. I wear an orb, but have no spells. I wear a Ring, but don't understand its ways."

"And you sing. Never forget that you sing."

"My voice is hardly powerful," Tabitha objected.

He shook his head slowly. "You really have no idea of what it is you do. I had thought the spell you cast yesterday was a very wise thing, only now, it seems to be a very luck thing."

"Spell?"

"You sang a most enchanting song."

"Oh, that," she said, recalling the performance in Yzell's workshop. "That was just the Glee of Genesis. It's a tavern-song. How did you hear that?"

"That is no tavern-song, and I heard it sung in a way that would be wasted in a tavern."

She refined her question to pin the Riddler down. "Where were you that you could hear it?"

"Crossing the river at Stormsford."

Tabitha searched his eyes for the signs of insincerity. The Riddler couldn't have heard her from Stormsford—it was over five leagues away from the King's Isle. He held an honest, steady gaze.

He's a good liar, then.

But the Shadowcaster had been drawn to Phantom Acres by her singing. *How far away was he, when he heard my voice? Are they alike, the Riddler and the Shadowcaster?*

She dared not voice that question.

"Is my singing the reason for my danger today?" she asked.

"I don't doubt it. He knows you are here. That is why you must be elsewhere."

"But I am leaving," said Tabitha. "There is a guarded carriage arranged, I'm going to the Dovecote. Within the hour."

Zarost stood a long time, considering, before answering.

"That may be a good escape, but it would be best you are in a place that no one knows."

"Must I run and hide all the time? I want to present myself at the Dovecote, I want to become a real Lightgifter. I tire of pretending."

"You want that strongly enough to risk meeting the Shadowcaster?"

"Yes," she answered hastily, without conviction.

Do I?

Tabitha tried to understand the mixed feelings that the question awakened. She found the familiar smoothness of the clear ring between her fingers, and turned it absently, hoping for some of its clarity to infuse her thoughts. Images of her possible futures flitted across her mind—those where she failed to attend the Gifter's training, and those where she stood triumphant, a masterful weaver of the Light, serving the people of Eyri every day with her healing touch. Tabitha, daughter of Trisha Serannon, Lightgifter and defier of the Shadow.

"Yes." The word held the tone of truth. "I want to go to the Dovecote."

"Very well, so you choose your path," said the Riddler, with teasing solemnity. "But you should know that the path the Ring shows is the one to the wizard, not the path to goodness and virtue."

Tabitha thrust her hands into her pockets. She hadn't realised her display had been that obvious.

"There is another thing I must tell about the Ring," said Zarost. "It has a way of bringing hardship upon you."

"But I thought you said that it was neither bad nor good?" Tabitha objected.

"It has no power of its own. It offers only an altered view, a clearer view, for you to reach deeper into the mystery of life. What you learn depends on where you choose to seek."

"But why should that bring me hardship?"

"The deeper you dig, the more gold is found, and so the more thieves gather around."

"What if I just threw the Ring away, like my mother wanted?" Tabitha muttered. She drew her hand up before her face, and played the Ring through the light. They both knew she didn't mean to throw such a wonderwork away.

"It never becomes easier to bear the Ring. Always, more difficult."

"What if I just keep it and do nothing, tell nobody."

"You cannot avoid its use if you bear it. And so, you show yourself to those who listen."

"How am I ever to find the wizard, and be rid of it then?" Tabitha despaired. Zarost made it seem like she was doomed to face an ever-increasing host of evils.

"I have given the tool to you. What more do you need?"

Zarost held a finger to his lips, then tapped his head. He meant for her to solve the puzzle on her own.

I have a tool? He gave me a little mirror, that is all.

She searched for the small wooden disc. It was still there, in her cloak pocket. She drew it out. It looked the same as ever. On the one side, her image. On the other, the solitary inscription—*See thyself as thyself see.* Even the clarity of the Ring didn't pierce the puzzle.

"Twardy, I –" she began, but he motioned sharply with his hand, suddenly concerned.

"There are some hungry men nearby," he whispered. "They are searching for somebody."

He pulled Tabitha aside, against a thick hedge. Tabitha hid the mirror in her pocket. She heard it too—the stealthy tread of many feet, coursing through the garden. Some of the paths were overgrown, shrouded by tall plants. Tabitha caught a glimpse of a familiar face crossing a gap.

"It's all right," she said, "it's Lethin Tarrok. He's the one who's arranged the carriage for me." She saw a uniformed Sword as well.

The Riddler bolted. He cleared the trees and pelted across the open grass. His hat bobbed wildly, but retained its perch atop his head.

Tabitha stood in a daze.

A sharp voice sounded beside her.

"Swords! The main buildings!" shouted Tarrok. He came close. Tabitha recoiled. Some kinds of sweat you couldn't mask, no matter how much lavender you applied.

"Miss Serannon, what are you doing here?" he said, in a scolding tone, then continued before she could answer. "One of the Swords mentioned they had seen you being lured in here with a strange man. What were you thinking, while we wait for you? It is most unseemly to keep a royal carriage waiting!"

It has been an hour already?

"I—sorry, I didn't think it was so late."

"You didn't think at all. The man you were lounging with is a villain."

"But that's Twardy Zarost! He's not a criminal, he's the Riddler." Maybe if she argued with Tarrok, she could buy Zarost some time.

"The Riddler, eh? And that title makes it acceptable to steal past the City Gates without entry permission?"

Tabitha looked at him blankly.

Three struggling figures crossed the grass. The Riddler returned, held between two burly Swords. Tabitha recognised the soldiers from her arrival in Stormhaven, when they had formed the escort. Tarrok's personal favourites.

"Well, well, well, what do we have here?" trumpeted Tarrok. "By the hat, you can only be the Riddler. I have been warned about you!"

"He's done nothing wrong!"

"Riddler, I arrest you under suspicion of treason. I have been informed that you have been in league with the Darkmaster."

"But that's impossible!" Tabitha objected. "He's not involved with the Shadowcasters. He helped me escape from one."

"Ask him yourself, and you shall see. He claims to never lie, from what I have been told. So, Riddler, what shall you be—a liar, or admitted threat to the crown?"

"Tell him, Twardy Zarost! Tell him you were never involved with the Dark. You came here to warn me."

Zarost held her eye, and spoke with deliberate care. "In riddles speak I, but never can lie."

"What's wrong with you? Tell them, Twardy, or they'll jail you."

Zarost's eyes spoke volumes, but his lips were silent.

Tarrok leered at the Riddler. "Do you deny that you were the advisor to the Darkmaster?"

Tabitha gaped first at Tarrok, then at Zarost when he said nothing. Nothing at all.

"By your silence, you admit your guilt!" Tarrok decreed.

It felt as if a trapdoor had fallen away from Tabitha's feet. She watched the Riddler's face—defiant, his lips held taut, his gaze unrepentant. She could see it in his eyes, she could feel it with her special sense, she could touch it with the knowing of the Ring—it was true.

The Riddler had come from the heart of the Shadowcasters.

He must have tricked her from the first.

"Take him away!" commanded Tarrok. "To the old King's dungeon. I shall be questioning him later."

The Swords hauled Zarost away by his arms. He was facing Tabitha. His heels dragged on the ground.

He tricked me, yet he cannot lie.

"Were you trying to help me today?" she shouted after Zarost.

"I tried, but perhaps I shouldn't have! Now I cannot return, unless you summon me." The Sword to his right jerked on his arm, and snarled a garbled warning at the Riddler.

"If you face death, remember to shake and shiver!" he shouted. The Sword to his left struck him. He was silent after that.

"How rats squeak when they're caught. Come along, Miss Serannon," Lethin Tarrok said, taking her arm in his sweaty paw. "You're lucky we were in time to catch that rodent, before he led you astray. Men like the Riddler get in the way of important business. We mustn't let you be delayed any further from your departure."

Tabitha followed him from the garden and down the street. She was still in shock. She had thought she understood the Riddler, despite his odd behaviour. He had been a rescuer, a teacher. In a way, a friend. Yet now, she felt betrayed.

Her truthsense had never failed her. He came from the Shadowcasters. What if the Riddler had been trying to take her away in the first place, what if the wizard he was urging her to seek was the leader of the Dark? Maybe he was too afraid to handle the Ring, so he had tried to use her as the bearer.

Facts were missing, the explanation didn't work. He had saved her from the Shadowcaster.

But what if that had just been rivalry amongst bounty-hunters?

The conflicting theories swirled through her mind like an angry confluence of rivers, and she came no closer to a solution.

Tarrok allowed a brief diversion to collect her bag and lyre from the Boarding, and to settle her account with the Matron, but he would not leave her side. He led her swiftly through the streets of Stormhaven.

One course was clear before her. She would journey to the Dovecote in the royal carriage, and present herself to the Lightgifters.

23. KINGSBRIDGE

"History is made in that place
where many paths converge."—*Zarost*

They let the horses drink. Ashley's new mare blew heavily at the water. She was a sturdy beast, broad-chested and muscled. There was a world of difference between a Sword-horse and a Dovecote nag. The Swordmaster had seen to it that they all rode fresh mounts that morning, for their old ones were still being retrieved from above the waterfall in Fendwarrow. Glavenor had been adamant—if they were to ride, they would all ride fast horses. Ashley had heard no objections from the Swords of Fendwarrow. The Swordmaster was formidably persuasive when he was angry.

A single purpose had unified them at dawn—to ride to Stormhaven, to bring the heavy burden of news before the King. The Gifters could attest to the matter of Dark essence, the Swordmaster would confirm the treasonous words. They would all tell of the vale they had seen, lest one of them be suspected of madness.

They had agreed to continue the search for Hosanna and the Shadowcaster once they had brought the news before the King. A boat had gone missing from the Fendwarrow jetties. The Shadowcaster had escaped across the Amberlake, possibly to the King's Isle itself.

They had made good time on the road to Levin. From Kironkiln onwards, the dirt was hard-packed and smooth-worn from the passing of the regular clay-wagons, from Wendelnip on it became a stoneroad with a galloping track on the water side, without which they would have been slowed to a crawl by the added traffic of linen-and-garment merchants from Rhyme and Burke Manor.

Levin towered above them to the north-east, tiers and tiers of pale walls and red-grey roofs, a termite's mound of human endeavour. The Lightgifter's Dovecote was visible near the crown of the hill, cinnamon shades worked into the soft sphere of stone. Keegan had sent a second Courier to the Rector from Fendwarrow at dawn, announcing their findings. But it remained unanswered, like the first sent from Southwind.

Maybe the Rector thinks us mad, with the tales Keegan told. Morgloth and murder, ravens and the Vale of the Dark.

The Dovecote seemed so close, yet Ashley knew their first duty was to the King. There would be time for talk with the Rector when they returned.

Duty pressed on their shoulders, and they set off again. Ashley gritted his teeth against the aches. Too many days in the saddle had rubbed the inside of his legs to raw spots, rammed joints to bruising, and strained muscles to incessant stiffness. The Sword-horse's powerful gait seemed designed to shake him apart.

They turned left onto the Kingsbridge. The road led into the distance along the obsidian causeway, like a giant serpent stretched upon the lake. The nearer part was clear, but a great portion of the span was swallowed by the lingering mist. A league or more away, the highest domes and battlements of Stormhaven poked through the shroud.

The sentry post was manned by Swords who watched them with a jaundiced eye. A change came over them as the Swordmaster approached. The sentries suddenly trimmed their stances.

"Good morning, Swordmaster," a junior Sword greeted, saluting with a fist raised to his chest.

Glavenor returned the salute. "We have crossed swords in the training halls, have we not? What is your name?"

"Jonan, sir. I trained with you last year."

"Well, Sword Jonan, I have a task for you and your companions. If you should see a man with a red cloak and burned skin, halt him at this post with all your force. His name is Kirjath Arkell, and we are tracking him for murder. And if any person comes here with a dark stone at their throat, or wearing a black cloak and having burn-scarred skin, treat them as traitors to the crown, and have them arrested."

"Dark stones sir? Shadowcasters? Yes, sir!" the junior replied. The other Swords stiffened as Garyll drew level with them.

Garyll motioned to the Lightgifters to ride, and they passed onto the Kingsbridge with him. He brought his horse alongside Ashley's. "I doubt that'll do much, but it may close a hole we can't afford to leave unstitched. The Shadowcaster is a fool if he tries the Kingsbridge, but it may be his last option."

It was only when they burst into the sunlit courtyard of the Stables, that Lethin Tarrok at last slowed his pace. Tabitha felt instantly guilty at having kept everyone waiting. Six mounted Swords waited in the yard in rigid parallel. A black carriage gleamed, the driver ready atop, with two sleek stallions connected to the traces. The horses stamped on the cobbled yard with their iron-shod hooves.

Maybelle Westerbrook was there as well. Tabitha turned to greet her.

"On board, Miss Serannon!" said Tarrok. "They have all waited long enough in the sun for you."

"Must you be in such an incessant hurry!" Maybelle's voice cut like a knife through the charged air. "Ever since the King mentioned that Tabitha has a more efficient manner than you do, you've been a most insufferable agitator. Don't let him rush you, Tabitha."

Tabitha took the opportunity to approach May, and embrace her.

"Goodbye May. Thank you for all you have done for me here."

May pulled away. "No, no, this is not goodbye. I shall be coming with you."

"What!" exclaimed Tarrok.

"I have decided," announced May, turning on the smaller man, "that Tabitha needs a better sort of company than you'll provide on the way to Levin."

"But I shall not be going!" he explained. "She has them as escort." He waved a dismissive hand at the Swords.

"Well, that's all the better then, for we shall travel with more pleasant company."

"But you'll miss the execution of the Shadowcaster. It's scheduled for sunset!"

"We all want justice for that man, but I have no need to watch his death."

Tarrok looked as if he had trodden on a bee. "But you have duties to attend in the city, Lady Ceremony!" he objected.

"And you think it your place to remind me!" said May, suddenly towering with anger. "You forget your place, court servant. I wish to travel to Levin, and shall be accompanying Miss Serannon in this carriage."

Lethin Tarrok made a strangled sound. "But you can't!" he squawked. "The carriage is collecting supplies, it shall be full on the return."

"Then it shall have to take a lighter load," May answered.

"But I am not certain of the wheels!" he said, his hands fluttering in the air. "I'm not sure they shall bear your weight."

May gave him a hard look. Tarrok reddened.

"Come on, Tabitha. It is time to leave."

Lethin Tarrok stared at them as they boarded, then leaned in and spoke loudly. "I am sure now that the Lady of Ceremony is travelling in this carriage that the journey will be a safe one."

Tarrok closed the door as firmly as he could without slamming it.

"What was that about?" asked Tabitha.

May spread her hands. "A rotten little man who wishes he were more."

The driver cracked his whip overhead.

Tabitha had never been inside such a plush carriage before. It was a beautifully crafted cab—the black wood was polished to a shine, the cushions were wide enough to seat three on both the front and rear benches. The seats were fronted with panelling which suggested a storage space for travelling gear. The deep blue upholstery of the walls was studded with gold. Small, oval side windows offered a fleeting view of Stormhaven. Even the floor was carpeted. The only thing which marred the royal appeal was the faint odour of wine and smoke, which seemed to linger in the fabric of the seats.

Tabitha sat close beside Maybelle Westerbrook. May gave Tabitha's hand a gentle squeeze, then she reached into a bag at her side, and produced a folded blue garment.

"A gift, for when you tire of the Gifter's white or those travel-clothes you are wearing now," she explained.

Tabitha held it up. It was the dress she had worn to the King's audience. She had returned it after the day, and had thought she would never see it again. It was the most elegant garment she had ever worn.

She hugged May. No words were needed.

May looked upon her kindly. "I knew your mother when she was young. I am sure you will become a fine Gifter, just like Trisha. You have her purity."

"Thank you, May."

Tabitha wished she had brought a gift for Lady Westerbrook. All she had with her were the contents of her bag, and her lyre. She would find something in Levin, she decided, and have it sent to Stormhaven.

The scrolls, I should show her the song-scrolls.

It would not be a gift, but an act of sharing that would display her trust. May would know the privacy of the writings were of special value. She drew the leather tube from her bag, and pulled the scrolls free.

"These are the songs and spells my mother kept, the only thing to survive the fire. I thought you might like to see them."

May took the scrolls as if they were delicate.

"You have played this music?" she asked, after glancing at the first sheet.

"I haven't dared to," Tabitha answered. "There's a warning on the last page which made me hold my tongue. I think Mother must have played them, at least once. I've sung something—similar."

Tabitha glanced out of the window as May pored over the scrolls. They were passing through the giant gates of Stormhaven, and a saluting sentry blurred past the carriage, followed by a queue of visitors to the city. Tabitha blinked against the brightness outside. A strong wind was chasing the last remnants of the morning mist, leaving sparkling chop on the water and a clear blue sky.

"Forgive me for sounding ignorant," May apologised, "but these patterns mean nothing to me. What are they for?"

Tabitha looked over to where May held the second page upon her lap.

"Those are patterns for a Lightgifter's spells," answered Tabitha. "It's part of the way we command the essence—part is the word, part is the pattern you have to hold in thought. They're not supposed to be drawn out like that—I think these are secret spells I'll not be showing in the Dovecote. They are very aggressive for a Gifter."

The front bench creaked, once.

"Trisha, aggressive? She must have changed in the years between us."

"Did you hear that?"

Tabitha watched the closed front bench. Something had sounded odd, out of place. They passed over a rut in the road, and the door jumped on its hinges, then squeaks and rattles passed throughout the cab.

She sighed. Just a bump in the road.

"Those are very complicated patterns to remember," Tabitha commented, "maybe she was scared she would lose the knowledge, because she never practised the spells. You're right, I can't imagine my mother using the Spriteblind spell on anyone."

May turned to the last page, and studied in silence.

The carriage rocked in a steady rhythm to the beat of the horses hooves. But Tabitha's nerves were on edge, and wouldn't settle.

Outside, there was nothing but the rim of the Kingsbridge, and the waters of the Amberlake, flecked by the rising wind. Inside, nothing but the two of them in the carriage.

"Why are they risking a public execution for the Shadowcaster, when he's got the power to raise a Morgloth?"

May looked up sharply.

"I suppose the Sword have got their reasons. I know they wanted to make an example of him, to discourage anyone else from repeating his crimes. They must have a terrible death planned. It is a good thing we are away from Stormhaven today."

"What if he escapes again?"

"The Swords won't make the same mistake again, now they know his danger." May searched Tabitha's face, then she reached out a comforting hand. "We've got Swords all around us, and soon you'll be surrounded by Lightgifters. Relax. He has been caught. It is over."

Tabitha breathed out heavily.

"I know, it's just—the biting cold on my finger, sending shivers up my spine. This Ring," she said, holding up the talisman she knew Maybelle couldn't see. "It deepens my sense of when things are right, and when they are wrong." She brought her hand to her mouth. "Something is horribly wrong."

There was another loud creak in the front bench. Tabitha's heart skittered within her chest.

Inside the carriage.

The carriage ran smoothly over the unbroken road surface.

"May—" Tabitha began.

She didn't finish her sentence. The lid of the front bench flew open. A cruel face with yellowed eyes and a feverish grin emerged.

◆ ——————— ◆

Kirjath acted with speed. He had perhaps a slim second before one of them would scream, but that was time enough. The twinned spells of Silence flickered away from his hands, and claimed his victims. He crippled their voices as they were drawing breath. He grinned at the girl, and shocked her with more Dark essence, a painful Freeze just for the pleasure of seeing her writhe. The fat lady rose in her seat, and raised her arm threateningly. He smirked, and planted one foot against her chest. He kicked her back into place, giving her a taste of the Freeze as well. Her head cracked against the back of the carriage, and her legs went slack, but her eyes remained open and vaguely focused. He altered the Freeze, concentrating the motes in only one part of her body. As the blood cooled in her heart, it would beat slower and slower.

He scowled at the fat lady's hopeless expression, and wondered if she could have any use at all. Lady of Ceremony—she would fetch a good ransom. But that alone did not make her indispensable, and it was too complicated an affair to arrange.

The flashing water of the Amberlake confirmed his guess; they were clear of the Isle, and a good way along the Kingsbridge.

The girl reached for the door-handle, but he caught her hand with his left. He twisted her wrist, until she made a good pretence at screaming, her mouth wide. The Silence held, and she made no sound. He continued to twist. She scrabbled onto the floor, turning to save her arm, until she sat at his feet, facing the fat lady, her arm twisted up past her chin.

A little further, and it will break.

"Something is horribly wrong," he mimicked, breathing into her ear. He surprised himself with his own laugh—a cackling, sickly sound like a hoarse turkey.

Be cursed! Too much jurrum.

Too much strain as well, keeping the Morgloth at bay. It had been hours now. And the distance grew ever more.

"Move, and your arm breaks," he warned. "And you, fat lady. Try anything, and your friend here will have a useless arm of shattered bone."

He eased the lid of his bench down, and sat, the girl still held in the armlock.

As if it matters. She won't live for long.

The view was quite pleasant, really, if a little bright. Travelling in a royal coach was something he could definitely get used to. He reached over with his free hand and clawed the curtains closed. The wind and the noise of the horses would take care of the rest. This was his moment, and nothing was going to distract him from savouring the victory. There had been so little to savour of late, and a great debt of misfortune to be repaid.

"The Lightgifter's legacy!" Kirjath mocked as he took notice of the spell-scrolls he had heard them discussing. He lifted them from the fat lady's lap. He pretended to peruse them.

"Aggressive, for a Lightgifter. Tell me, how do you cast a spell if you can't speak, or if you're dead?"

He put his ear against the girl's soft cheek, pretending to listen.

"Yes, quite right. You say nothing. Nothing! Because it's impossible, isn't it?"

The fat lady was going pale in the face. She had the look of desperate appeal, like the runt of a litter about to be drowned. Beads of sweat were collecting on her upper lip. Fear had a delicious effect on women.

He eased some of the Dark out of her body. It wouldn't do any good to kill them now, and cheat the Morgloth of its promised meal. He threw the scrolls to the floor.

"No one should know the tricks your mother used," he told the girl, "and no one should have the Ring she stole, no one but me. Where is it?" He could feel it was not on the fingers of the twisted hand. He wove a thick spell of Despair and sent it into her ear.

Let her feel the full agony of her end. Let her be crippled by hopelessness.

He waited a moment for the Despair to take effect. He didn't want her trying for the carriage door again.

When he felt her proud shoulders slump, and saw her head drop, he knew the Dark spell had lodged deep within her. He shifted his body over hers, and released the twisted hand to find the other, where she surely wore the Ring. She writhed beneath him. There was a whistling sound, and he caught a glimpse of wood, an instrument held in her left hand, swinging up toward his jaw.

He jumped, but the surprise blow clipped him nonetheless. The wood was as hard as iron. His head rang with a full chord. He grabbed her arm and wrestled the weapon from her hand. He searched her fingers for the Ring.

He found it on her middle finger; a hard, cold band, smooth as ice. He wedged her arm between his legs, then pulled hard on the Ring. His fingers slipped without dislodging it.

He tried again, then again. It was like trying to grasp a greased pip. "Why won't it come off!" he shouted. He gripped her wrist tight, lifted her hand to his face.

If it won't be pulled off, I'll bite it off.

He stuffed her middle finger into his mouth, and closed his teeth on the base. He felt the Ring against his tongue, and tasted its numbing, metallic tang.

Wham! ... fizz.

The world vanished.

He lost everything. The Morgloth. The spell patterns he had engaged. Even his feeling of victory was erased. For an instant, there was nothing but clarity, like an empty limitless pool.

◆ ——————— ◆

He was sitting on a bench in a carriage. A girl faced him. She had a bright hand, sprites of the wretched Light collected there. She was holding a paper in the other, speaking words which he didn't understand.

A Lightgifter. The girl.

The Ring! It came rushing back to him with a thunderclap. He launched himself at her just as the sprites were bonded, just as her spell was completed. He hadn't expected her to have any command of the essence—she didn't appear to have a Lightgifter's orb, but maybe she wore it under the high collar of her tunic.

The flames which burst against his body were made of Light.

The heat consumed him. Every inch of his skin screamed, the memory of fire was all too fresh. He fell upon the girl and grasped her throat. He squeezed her throat hard. If he could damage her vocal cords, it would save him essence. The fat lady cried out. He renewed the Silence spell on her.

The fire was rampant.

He summoned more motes and wove a quick Web to protect himself from the worst of the heat. He didn't have the time or the essence to quench the flames—the girl's Flameburst spell was everywhere. Fire ate at the curtains, consumed the wood panelling, burned on the floor. Smoke coiled against the ceiling in an acrid cloud.

Let them burn!

He had been in command a moment ago! It was now desperate chaos. He kept the girl in a strangle-hold, he could take her with him, but he needed assistance to escape.

He had to find the Morgloth. With the strange jolt that the Ring had given him, he had lost contact with the beast. The Morgloth had been with him so long that he had become accustomed to the headache, the place in his thoughts where the other mind raged against its containment. Now that it was gone, he felt a worse pain, somewhat like the agony of finally dropping a fire-iron that should not have been picked up—the absence of the branding-rod allowed the burned flesh to scream. He searched in that ravaged place in his thoughts, and found a glimmer of the Morgloth's spirit.

The demon's mind returned to his, wild with impatience. The Morgloth was in the place where Kirjath had left him, hidden in the yard in Stormhaven.

His command of the demon was frayed by the distance between them.

Fly, you evil, fly! I need you here!

He felt a surge of familiar fury. The Morgloth would screech as it took to the air, an enraged bellow of animal hunger, but it would leave the alley and Stormhaven behind on its powerful wings. Kirjath watched through his sharpening mind's eye as the City Gates passed below, complete with the upturned, gaping faces of the populace and sentries. The beast issued a chilling cry.

Behold my beast, my power, my mastery!

The Morgloth followed its master's summons along the Kingsbridge. The demon was furious, rebellious, frustrated.

Soon, my servant, soon you will gorge yourself. Fly fast!

Kirjath directed the beast down to the sloping rock beside the Kingsbridge, where the approach of the black wings would be concealed by the glistening obsidian.

The carriage was filled with dense, acrid smoke. His eyes smarted.

He grasped the girl's wrist, twisted it again, found the Ring in a fierce grip. With the crippled hand, he reached inside his cloak, where he kept his knife. He hooked the weapon out with some difficulty.

He placed the blade against her flesh, just above the Ring. The girl croaked like a Morrigán when he plunged the knife down on her finger. Her vocal cords were too damaged to issue a scream. But the handle slipped in his weak right hand, and he knew he hadn't severed the bone.

The coach came to an abrupt halt, and he was thrown to the front seat. The wood was burning. The bloody finger pulled from his grasp, and with it, the Ring.

The fat lady fell onto the floor.

The girl kicked against the door, and it flew open. He grabbed for her, and caught hold of her clothing. She began to strike him with the hard instrument again, then she was pulled from his grasp by someone beyond the door.

When he heard the rasp of swords being drawn, he knew that he needed his beast more than ever.

A man jutted his head through the smoke.

Kirjath felt the rush of wind over his dark wings.

The man stepped up on the running board. His sword lanced for Kirjath's throat.

He swept over the edge of the Kingsbridge, and swooped for his target.

The Sword's second thrust missed again, because his balance was upset.

The Morgloth wrenched the man from the carriage door. The Sword uttered a brief scream as he was lifted into the air by his neck. Horses squealed out on the Kingsbridge.

The taste of blood. A rush of life-force so heady, it took him down, despite the pain that kneeling caused him. He saw the Kingsbridge through the eyes of the Morgloth.

Three chargers bucked their riders to the ground.

The carriage lurched off, the horses squealing and galloping.

The driver shouted as he fell past the door.

Kirjath was vaguely aware that the temperature was rising. He drew the Dark essence tight, but the flames bit through his protection. And yet, it didn't seem to matter. He had a hunger, and sating it was more important. The lust controlled his mind.

A blade flashed against his black talons, glanced off without effect. He grasped the second soldier by the head. The bite was swift. The pleasure raged through his body, pleasure and pain, pain and hunger again. His blood pounded in his temples, his breath short and shallow. He opened his eyes to check the progress of the fire, but the view of the Morgloth remained. He was swooping down from the sky, aiming for the back of a fleeing rider.

He panicked against the vision, but the Morgloth's view remained. The beast was vital, its power filled him with lust and wild strength. He arched as he struck the fleeing horseman. He felt the death-bite directly, as if inflicted with his own teeth, the fresh blood in his own mouth.

He shuddered.

Three down, three to go.

Pain seared through his ecstasy. The flames were killing him. He couldn't breathe. He had to get out.

The urgency of his panic brought some of his awareness back to him. The carriage was an inferno. The fat lady was gone. She must have jumped from the carriage.

He dived through the door, spread his arms to swoop away, and discovered that he was not a Morgloth. His face slapped against the hard-packed surface of the Kingsbridge. He rolled and tumbled, and finally came to a stop in a heap. As he stood, he stumbled, and that weakness saved his life.

Hooves thundered past him, and a blade howled over his head, missing him by a hair. A nasty screeching blade, one he remembered. A tall armoured man reined his steed in hard, and turned to renew the charge. The Swordmaster.

He turned, and ran.

The way was blocked by three Lightgifters. He avoided their first assault of essence, a scattered spell as bright as lightning. He summoned Dark essence, but it was a pitiful supply, and not enough to retaliate with. He had only enough to strengthen a defensive Web.

The Swordmaster bore down on him. He feinted to the left, then jumped right. The charge went wide—a wind struck him, nothing more. The Swordmaster dropped from the saddle. Kirjath fled, but the footsteps at his back closed fast. He knew the Web would not be enough to turn the blade that came for him.

The Morgloth broadsided him with such a force that it snapped ribs. His breath was driven from his lungs, his vision burst into a thousand stars. He was well clear of the Kingsbridge when he regained some sense of what had happened.

The Morgloth had acted on its own. He was clutched in its talons, they were flying, clear of the Swordmaster, clear of his pursuit. It had saved him. But it had acted on its own, and that meant he had lost command. The Morgloth's thoughts burst through his mind, brutal, invading, striving to conquer all of him.

He fought against the domination. They could not leave the Kingsbridge, not yet. He did not have the Ring.

Return. Return! he tried to commanded the Morgloth. *I must have the girl.*

He felt, rather than heard the answer.

[Too many men. You would die.]

He argued in images, clawing a little authority back from the beast.

The girl is further back on the bridge. There. You kill her, I need only her hand. Then we escape.

The Morgloth turned, and Kirjath delighted as its course became a diving descent. He was the master again. On the Kingsbridge below stood the girl with the lyre, face upturned, alone. The Morgloth would do his bidding.

There was just one thing that didn't make sense. Why had the beast saved him?

The Morgloth answered without being asked. With horror, Kirjath realised that their thoughts were pooled. There was no division between them. His control was an illusion.

[You are my Gateway. If you die, I cannot feed.]

♦ —————————— ♦

The winged creature turned, and aimed towards Tabitha. The Shadowcaster was still caught in its legs. She could only guess the Morgloth had gone mad and turned on its master. Now it came for her. She watched with detached fatalism. The horror of the beast's appearance had terrified her so much she had passed beyond fear into a stunned fugue.

She had almost fainted from pure fright when the soldier who had helped her from the carriage had been attacked by the Morgloth. His head had been ripped off in front of her. The beast had drunk his life away. She had crawled away from the horror, gagging on her bile and the agony of her crushed throat. The nightmarish legend was real—it had come to the Shadowcaster's aid, and it killed with greater zeal than the wildest rumours she had ever heard told. She had known then that it was only a matter of time, before the beast would chase down all the other prey, and come for her. With the augmented clarity of the Ring, she saw every detail of the Swords' deaths. Now she looked into the face of her own.

Its black wings rippled in the wind of its dive. It dropped the Shadowcaster as it levelled out on the far side of the Kingsbridge. It would take her unhindered. Tabitha didn't know what to do, she was rooted to the spot by the inevitability of her own impending death.

She knew Glavenor and the three Gifters were charging down the Kingsbridge, she had seen them arrive, but she knew they would not reach her in time.

And what would they do, against this dreadful beast?

Its jaws were wide. Teeth stained red. Hunger in its eyes.

Time slowed, and the last few moments before impact seemed to stretch out forever.

She did the only thing she could. She let out a desperate scream, of the highest pitch. It lasted a scant moment, for the damage to her throat turned the rest of the scream into a grating screech.

The Morgloth tossed its head, and faltered in the air. Its wings tilted, it tumbled, and swept toward her suddenly out of control. It slammed into her, knocking her flat, but it spun clear, and ended a few paces beyond her on the road. Its cruel, hell-fired eyes locked onto Tabitha the moment it regained its feet. Evil oozed from the Morgloth's slick black skin. She could sense its hunger, its emptiness which yearned for her spirit.

But she was sure that her scream had made it falter. The Morgloth had winded her, but she drew a wrenching breath, hoping against hope that she could fill her lungs in time.

If you face death, remember to shake and shiver.

The Riddler's strange warning suddenly held meaning. She reached higher with her voice, and screamed again. But her injury split the sound into a scattered pitch. The Morgloth tossed its head. It made to cover its ears with its wide wings, then shook itself as soon as Tabitha's shriek ended. It didn't only look hungry then, it looked angry as well. Muscles rippled beneath its skin as it tensed for attack.

A surge of Light rushed over her, cast from the Lightgifters. Pain shot through the points where the Dark had frozen her flesh, but the pain subsided where the fire had scalded her, and her throat was infused with sprites. The result was a sensation of shifting, being transformed. Then it passed, and she felt healed. The Lightgifters couldn't know how much she had needed it. They were galloping toward her, with Glavenor running in the lead, closing on the Morgloth. The beast suddenly turned, and sank, ready to leap on the Swordmaster's advance.

May I sing like the Goddess Ethea.

She plucked the lyre once. She knew before she sang that her note would be true. The Ring gave her clarity. It was more than a glass that would shatter with this singing of the ascent of the Glee of Genesis. The Shiver pierced the air.

◆ ———————— ◆

The girl sang the highest note, and Kirjath truly understood. His mind exploded. His every nerve was scraped raw, every sense was assaulted by jagged glass. The sound penetrated all of his thoughts, it surged through the space he shared with the Morgloth in an instant. The fundament of his being was attacked, assaulted, blown away. They were paralysed, he and his demon both, and Kirjath watched with horror as the fluted blade of the Swordmaster sliced down through the air. The sword screeched with that horrible note as well—it was identical in pitch, only harsher than the girl's voice. There was something about the note that drove fear through his soul, agony through his mind, and paralysis through his body. It was the Morgloth's nemesis, the answer to the beast of endless hunger, the antithesis to the creature of evil.

He was still inside the demon's mind when the Swordmaster's death-blow struck. He was trapped in a psyche which resonated with a torturous note.

Felltang scythed through black flesh. The demon fell to the ground, and its life poured upon the stone. With a final surge in the singer's voice, the Darkstone on Kirjath's neck shattered.

Kirjath Arkell knew absolute pain.

It was not a conscious decision that urged him to action. His mind was a wasteland of shattered images, his thoughts as broken as slate pounded by a thousand hammers. He ran to escape his own thoughts. He was mad.

Splinters of light drove their way through the jelly of his brain. Screams, laughter and an endless wind chased each other, and he felt as if he was running on bare feet through twisting labyrinths of blades. Lightning crashed behind his eyes, then blood, then darkness, then lightning again, as if he was witnessing the beginning or end of creation.

He leapt from the edge of the Kingsbridge. For a brief moment of sanity, he knew it was impossible to clear the sloping rock before reaching the water. Then he forgot about the leap, for he believed himself to be a bird. Then a stone, then a man once more. Madness scattered him in all directions.

He believed the impact to be from a giant horse's hoof. He bounced from the rock, broke the surface, and sank through the sun-shafted waters of the Amberlake.

He was a rock.

He was a fish.

24. LOVE AND LIES
"At the heart of a riddle
lies truth, truth lies."—*Zarost*

The ringing sound continued in her ears. Tabitha realised she had been sitting on the shoulder of the road for some time since her legs had given way from relief. The youngest of the three Lightgifters was speaking to her, but his words made no sense at all. The Swordmaster was still patrolling the rocks below, his unsheathed sword glinting. The rocks were steep where the Kingsbridge met the water. Garyll Glavenor picked his way along the uneven terrain like an egret searching for a tick.

Tabitha was sure that the Shadowcaster wouldn't surface. He had been under too long to survive, and the wet patch where his head had struck the rocks was clearly visible.

She was still stunned that she had harnessed the Light essence. She hadn't really expected sprites to come to her desperate summoning, but she had tried nonetheless. She knew how to gather the Light— she had witnessed her mother's spells all of her life. But she had never suspected that the sprites would come to her own hand, so soon and in such great numbers. Suddenly, her hand had been filled with Light essence. The scrolls had shown her how to use it. Yet even that violence had not been enough. She had been driven to use her voice.

She had felt the effect of the Shiver directly, the way the note had reached out, touched everything around her, linking her to the Morgloth. She had been so focused on the beast, at the end, that she had not concentrated on the Shadowcaster at all. Yet it was as if they were inseparable parts of a union. When her note and the Swordmaster's blade had converged on the Morgloth's head, she had heard a small shattering sound from the Shadowcaster. She knew that her note had affected him deeply. He had fled, and leapt from the road.

And then the Morgloth's severed head had tumbled towards her. She had recoiled from the horror of its black blood spilling over the road. Carnage littered the Kingsbridge. Three men lay dead on the road, their necks torn open from behind. The flaming skeleton of the carriage threw smoke to the wind. She had stumbled away, in the Shadowcaster's footsteps, to the point where he had jumped. There her legs had given way, and her lyre had tumbled to the ground beside her.

The surface of the lake held only the white wound of his plunge—the Shadowcaster must have sunk like a stone. The water was deep, and nothing had risen to the surface except a few pink bubbles.

The waves washed all traces of the event away.

It was over.

"It is hard to wish that soul a peaceful afterlife," someone said beside her. Tabitha turned away from the lake at last. The young Lightgifter was standing close, his blue eyes on the lake. He had an honest face. He turned towards Tabitha.

"You have a powerful voice," he said.

"I had *no* voice, until you cast the Healall," Tabitha answered, her thoughts finding the here-and-now at last. "Thank you."

He nodded. "I knew it was needed." His eyes slid away briefly, as if to hide something private, but then he shrugged and smiled. "Your voice—I was afraid my Lightstone was going to shatter as well," he said. "Though that would have been preferable to facing the Morgloth."

Tabitha tossed her head towards where the beast lay on the road behind her. She couldn't bear to turn. "Is that the first time you've seen—it?" she asked.

He nodded a few times.

"Me too," Tabitha whispered, leaving the rest of her thoughts unspoken. She hugged her knees close.

"I was terrified when it turned on us," the young Gifter said. "I'm glad it was Glavenor and not me who had to wield that sword. I would have dropped it and run."

Just to hear that she was not alone in her terror made her feel better. The legend had come to life, a nightmare incarnated. She knew it would be weeks before she ceased to see the creature's wings spread wide, its gaping maw closing on her. Within her mind the Morgloth dived upon her, over and over, despite the fact that the Swordmaster had slain it.

The young Gifter extended a hand. "I am Ashley Logán. You must be Tabitha Serannon."

Tabitha was caught by surprise. She reached up to take his hand. It was dry and warm.

"How do you know?" she asked. "I've never met you, have I?"

"We've been following the trail of the Shadowcaster. If we'd known he would pursue you so hard, we would have come directly to Stormhaven, and not wasted time in Fendwarrow. We were at your farm," he ended. "I am so sorry."

Tabitha nodded to let him know it was all right.

The other two Lightgifters came up behind Ashley then—a dignified elderly lady, and a stern bearded man, both wearing smudged white robes.

They've been riding with Garyll. That must be hard travelling.

"Tabitha, this is Sister Grace, and Father Keegan," Ashley said.

"Hullo." Tabitha didn't trust her legs to stand reliably yet. She was ash-streaked and dishevelled; she hoped they didn't care. She bowed her head respectfully.

"Your friend the Lady asked after you," Sister Grace said.

"May! Is she all right?" Tabitha asked, stung by a pang of guilt. She hadn't even gone to search for May. Instead, she had stumbled to the edge of the road, and had succumbed to shock.

"She was burned," said Father Keegan, gruffly. "She broke an arm when she fell from the coach. We healed her as best we could, but she'll need much rest. We cast a Sleep on her, to better aid the healing."

"She's on the cart," said Grace, pointing. A flat-bed was negotiating its way around the Morgloth, and it bore a bundled form behind the driver. Another cart followed, commandeered by one of the Swords, laden with the bodies of the fallen.

"Come! It's time we pressed on for Stormhaven," Ashley said gently. He offered his hand to Tabitha once again. She rose to her feet. But she didn't want to leave without at least thanking Garyll for his sudden aid. He was still down on the rocks.

"I was going to the Dovecote," she commented.

"We'll be going there just as soon as we've met with the King," Grace reassured her. "Why don't you come with us?"

"Thank you," Tabitha replied. "I just need to—I just need a moment." She picked her lyre up from the road, and brushed it off. Her eyes were not on the instrument.

Glavenor turned from the water's edge, and scaled the Kingsbridge. It seemed he had finally accepted that the Shadowcaster was gone. There was a fire behind his eyes when he crested the rise, but Tabitha was sure his expression softened as he approached her.

"Miss Serannon," he said, bowing low. "We are all in your debt, I believe."

She was swallowed by his powerful gaze. "I should thank you, for saving us." She shuddered. "You killed the Morgloth."

"And you held its feet when it counted most. I have never heard a voice before that could set my sword to shaking."

"It's a special note," Tabitha said lamely. She couldn't explain how the Ring had given her the ear to find its perfected form, how she'd felt her voice reaching through the universe in that moment.

A smile spread across his severe features. "Aye, I have felt its bite before. It's a special singer who sings it. I'm glad that we came when we did, and not later."

"Thank you for coming," Tabitha said, truly grateful.

Garyll dipped his head.

A mounted patrol galloped toward them from the city, forestalling a question Tabitha wished to ask. It would be good to hear from Garyll's lips that the Shadowcaster was dead.

"Swordmaster!" the lead rider greeted, saluting as he drew rein. "We saw the beast, but didn't know where it would strike until we saw the smoke." The rest of the patrol of ten reined in. The horses were lathered with sweat. The men stared at the bier of Swords.

Glavenor returned the salute of the leader.

"Never mind! It is done. Your men can be put to good use. I need a patrol set up along the length of the Kingsbridge on this side, on the water's edge."

"What should we search for?"

"The Shadowcaster named Kirjath Arkell. If his body should float to the surface, I want it brought to me."

"That is not possible, sir."

"Why not?" There was a tight note of warning in Garyll's voice.

"Sir, I just left them interrogating the Shadowcaster Arkell in the Swordhouse in Stormhaven. We captured him this morning at the City Gates. You needn't search for him here."

"No!" Garyll asserted. "I have just battled him here! I know that man, I have held him on my blade before. Arkell fell from the bridge not a half-hour ago, right here!"

"And when I left Stormhaven not a half-hour ago, he was still in the interrogation room, as he has been all morning," asserted the rider.

Tabitha could see that the rider was nervous of defying the Swordmaster, but he held to his story and did not waver.

A questioning look settled on Garyll's brow.

"What does your Arkell look like, and what has he said?"

"Black robes, a badly-shaven scarred head. He has a web of black magic which doesn't seem to leave his body. He doesn't say anything, save to repeat his name, and that he knows the whereabouts of Prince Bevn. That answer alone is the only reason we keep him alive. He seems a bit weak-minded, sir."

"Weak-minded?"

"He cries a lot, sir."

"Can there be two of them?" Glavenor asked aloud. "This is something I must see! Your horse, Sword."

"Sir?" The man dismounted unsteadily. Glavenor was atop the steed and turning it about an instant later.

"I'll see you all in Stormhaven!" he shouted over his shoulder. "We have business with the King, later."

Then he was off, in a thunder of hooves.

They followed, at the pace of two wagons, one with a heavy load.

It was then that Tabitha discovered another bitter cost to the victory on the Kingsbridge. Within the burned husk of the carriage was a handful of silver and gold coin, too hot to handle without the help of the Swords' gloved hands. They collected the scraps of her life into an upturned helm. There was nothing to find, except the coins.

Her mother's song-scrolls had been burned to ashes. Despite her chagrin, she sensed a kind of completion. Everything that had begun at Phantom Acres had been ended.

Her parents had been avenged.

◆ ———————— ◆

King Mellar's study was crowded.

The King himself was seated behind his desk. Besides Tabitha and the three Lightgifters, there were three others in the private audience. A Sword who Tabitha recognised as Captain Steed from First Light sat upon a stool. Lethin Tarrok lingered in the background, not yet dismissed. Garyll Glavenor paced the floor.

"The woman was a decoy, your Highness," Garyll stated. "As soon as we employed the Gifters here to break the illusion, we could see she was not what she had seemed to be. She wears the orb of the Lightgifters."

"Did you recognise her?" the King asked of Father Keegan.

"Not at first, but it didn't take long to figure it out. Hosanna is one of our own, she rode ahead and was abducted by the Shadowcaster

Arkell three days ago, we believe. She must have endured a horror in his presence."

"I had not expected to care about our captive." King Mellar said soberly. "His—her head was going to fall at sunset. Very lucky for Hosanna you returned, Glavenor. How is she? Can she be questioned about the Shadowcaster?"

Garyll shook his head. "She is distraught. She shivers, she does not speak, and she makes no eye contact. The Shadowcaster has left too much ravage in his wake."

"You ended that scourge today," the King reminded him.

Garyll shook his head, and his jaw clenched tight before he spoke.

"We were there, right there in Fendwarrow! He had this woman in the same inn we used, and he evaded us. Ever since First Light I have chased him with one purpose—to drive my blade into his rotten heart. The way he took his life today denied me even that. And the way he set up his attack makes us look like fools. With respect, your Highness. I take it upon my shoulders that the Sword were so slack. Somewhere, their training has gone awry."

"I do not blame the Sword for their weakness against the Morgloth, Glavenor. From what I've heard it is a terrible beast to face."

"It was the man who was more dangerous than the Morgloth. He threw the woman at the gates because he wanted the sentries to lower their guard, which must have taken place. Miss Serannon says Arkell must have been inside the carriage before it left the Swordhouse this morning. How does a felon find his way into the city, and into that exact carriage, undetected, without a severe lack of vigilance by the Sword? Unless he had help from a traitor."

They considered his assertion in silence. It seemed to grow hotter in the room.

"I found another servant of the Dark in the city," blurted Tarrok suddenly from behind them, "I had him arrested."

Tabitha turned in her chair to look at Lethin. He held his head erect, and his expression was indignant, but there was a fine sheen of sweat on his brow, so fine Tabitha doubted anyone else had noticed. Then again, she had seen him sweating every time they had met, so maybe it was his usual state.

"This man had evaded the sentries, for I found no record of him in the register at the City Gates. He is an admitted accomplice to the Shadowcasters, and his presence has been noted at scenes of recent trouble. He must have shown Arkell a secret route into Stormhaven. They must have plotted this attack on poor Tabitha together."

The insincerity in Tarrok's eyes brushed her like his faint scent of garlic. Tabitha felt her sense for truth being twisted past its limits. The man was lying, but what part of his statement was untrue, she couldn't tell.

"Who was this man?" Garyll asked, his attention hawk-like.

"His name is Twardy Zarost, though he claims the title of the Riddler," answered Tarrok, somewhat smugly. "I believe you've run into him before."

Garyll cursed, then shot a concerned glance at Tabitha.

She struggled to find her own position on the Riddler. He had seemed to be a friend, at first. He claimed to never lie, yet if his words in the gardens were true, he had branded himself as an accomplice to the Dark.

"Is this not the same man you spoke of?" the King asked Tabitha.

"Yes. But he helped me escape from the Shadowcaster in First Light. He can't be working for the Dark." She turned again to Tarrok. "He set up the trap that caught Arkell."

"A trap which was not too hard for the Shadowcaster to escape from, I hear," Tarrok retorted archly.

Garyll stiffened. "I'll not trust the man, but I don't think that is fair," he cut in. "He escaped that trap because I did not act swiftly enough."

"What if you had not arrived when you did, Swordmaster? Would Arkell not have got away with ease?"

Garyll did not answer that, but Tabitha knew the question made him wonder, and that was all the answer Tarrok needed to drive his point home.

"Was he really aiding you, Miss Serannon, or was he just trying to get you away from those who could protect you?"

"But he took me to Southwind, it was his idea to send me here with Mulrano!"

"And *that* fisherman is a known traitor. It's a wonder you survived that night."

Tabitha felt the cold teeth of doubt gnawing at her belly. She had survived that night on the lake because the Shadowcaster's canoe had sunk. Were it not for that, she would have been caught. A disturbing possibility slithered through her thoughts. Zarost could have been trying to get her out of the way. It could have been by accident alone that she had evaded the Shadowcaster on the lake.

"Hadn't he already found you today, wasn't he trying to accost you when I intervened?" Tarrok asked. His eyes had a fervid cast to them.

He had the ability to make her feel pawed over with his sweaty hands, even though he stood beyond arm's reach. She wished his words didn't make so much sense, for then she could spurn his attention.

"No!" she said. "It wasn't like that."

"And what was he doing, if not accosting you?"

"He came to warn me, and urged me to leave –" her voice trailed off, another terrible doubt forming in her mind. "He said I should leave Stormhaven. I told him about the carriage, and he suggested it might be a good idea." A hollow nausea rose as she realised how she might have been manipulated. It had been a great enough shock to witness Zarost admitting to his involvement with the Dark when Tarrok had confronted him in the gardens. But to think he had been actively working to trap her was something far worse. She couldn't find her tongue.

All his assistance, was it just to gain my trust?

"I think I shall have a chat with this Riddler when we are done," said Garyll, sharply. "Where is he?"

"The old dungeons, Swordmaster," Tarrok answered proudly.

"I shall learn of his exact involvement with the Dark. If he refuses to speak, he shall spend a long time down there."

"Would it not be better if he were dead?" asked Tarrok.

"What use to us would he be then?" demanded Glavenor. "No, Tarrok, you overstep your mark as advisor. Justice is my domain. You are commended for apprehending him." The Swordmaster gave Tarrok a curt nod.

"You are all to be commended!" cut in King Mellar. "You all played a part in today's victory. But that is not why you have been assembled." Mellar turned toward the three Lightgifters. "The Swordmaster has reported the grave tidings from beyond Fendwarrow. I don't doubt his word for one moment, but he suggested I hear your accounts as well. Tell me what you found of the Shadowcaster's realm."

Tabitha sat bolt upright. Another realm? A kingdom of Shadowcasters?

Sister Grace began. "Their leader called it Ravenscroft. I saw a force of fifty, all black-robed, all wielding the Dark strain of the essence. The Darkmaster claims to rule a separate kingdom, as if he is not within the borders of Eyri, or subject to your rule, Highness."

Father Keegan grunted in agreement, but didn't have anything to add.

"It looked like it's been established for years," offered the young Gifter Ashley. "There were tilled fields, a hard-packed road, and a mighty-looking entrance to a keep. I didn't look at the valley too long, for the Shadowcasters surrounded us. I was afraid, Highness. I could almost believe they have the talent to weave fear with their essence. It was a terrifying vale to be in."

Sister Grace looked to Ashley before addressing the King. "It was night, and I was tired, but I believe I felt the same. A spell of despair."

"That's a part which my Swordmaster omitted from his report," the King said with a dry smile. "Though I have heard this reported from Fendwarrow as well. They must have powerful spells of concealment as well, for their comings and goings to have passed unnoticed for so long."

Tabitha knew her eyes were too wide, but she couldn't contain her alarm.

A kingdom of Shadowcasters?

"You mean there's a whole colony of them?" Tabitha asked nervously, not wanting to intrude, but unable to contain her incredulity. "Where are they hidden?"

"Ravenscroft is far above Fendwarrow, in the mountains," answered Garyll. "The trail passes through a waterfall close to Fendwarrow, a trick that deceived me completely until now. I'm an idiot! It must have been the drain for all stolen goods, and a supply of many things. No wonder that I could never find the source of the rot in Fendwarrow, the root of its evil. Now we know—there is a community at the end of that trail, and a sizeable force of Shadowcasters. Who knows how many more there are in that vale, under the rule of the man who calls himself the Darkmaster?"

King Mellar scratched his head, then removed his crown and set it on the desk. "What is his intention, Garyll?"

"What puzzles me, your Highness, is that they could have stopped us earlier on the trail; I'm certain we were noticed. With their numbers, they had the upper hand, yet they allowed us to push in all the way to their hidden valley. It was as if the Darkmaster wished us to see it, wished to announce his presence. He declared a desire to trade, though he must know how ridiculous that sounds, when he defies to acknowledge you as his King in the same breath."

"So he incites us to react, then," the King declared. "What would your immediate response to his provocation be?"

"To send a strong force of Swords into that valley, and clear it out. It is a mire of evil, I agree with young Ashley here when he says you can feel it when you near that place. No good can come from these Shadowcasters and their Dark ways. Those who conceal their activities must be up to something suspicious. We must not hesitate to crush the Shadowcasters."

Tabitha held her breath for the King's response. This was war talk. The King steepled his fingers.

"If they are all the same, Swordmaster, then I agree with you. The murderer Arkell was clearly a criminal, and his death was justified many times over. There is surely more evil in Ravenscroft, but I don't think it would be wise to march in and lay waste to them, until we understand fully what they are capable of."

"What do you suggest, your Highness? By the Darkmaster's admission, they all commit treason against you." Garyll looked ready to swing his blade through a stone wall.

"We must know if they have more of these Morgloth at their command."

The King's words chilled her to the bone.

"I saw many ravens," said Ashley, "a spell like our messenger birds. Maybe the Morgloth is the same."

Father Keegan disagreed. "No, the Morgloth is a creature, not a construct of essence. If it were made of Dark, then our Light would begin to disrupt the pattern, yet our magic has no effect on it, our essence is absorbed by its skin like rain into parched earth. It may be summoned by a spell of essence, but it is a deadly beast itself."

"What if they have fifty, or a hundred of those beasts?" said the King. "It would be immeasurably worse than poking a hornets' nest."

The sky would be full of Morgloth, a flying wave of death.

The King continued. "I can't bring that upon Eyri. We must devise a defence against the Morgloth, if we are to be wise. That is why I seek your counsel. You have all survived this beast."

"If another comes, I can slay it," asserted Garyll with conviction.

"That one beast, how many Swords did it kill before you took its head?"

Glavenor paused, his expression darkened. "Six."

"In the Swordhouse," Captain Steed interjected in his gravelly voice, "you had more effect than the others, Glavenor. There's something about you, or your blade, that made the beast shy from your blows."

"I don't think I have any special advantage," Garyll said, "only my training with the sword. It was Miss Serannon here who had an effect on the beast. She brought it to its knees before I had swung my blade."

All eyes fell on Tabitha.

"I just screamed, when it swooped on me," she said, knowing that was not the whole story, but not knowing how to explain how the Ring had cleared her senses to find the power that lay waiting in the perfected Shiver.

"Yet when I healed you, you sang higher," said Ashley. "There was something that ran through all the air around you then. I could feel the power even from where I stood."

They need the truth in this.

"There's a song, called the Glee of Genesis," she answered. "I took the high note from that, the Shiver. It's the note I use to shatter glass in the taverns. I gave it my all, and sang it as pure as I could. It seemed to work. The Shiver seems to confuse the Morgloth, or cause it pain, I can't tell which."

"This—Shiver—is it a spell, or something every singer can do?" King Mellar asked.

"I suppose it has a kind of magic to it, but not like the Lightgifter's art. It's a note, a special one, it's fills the air with a vibration. Something about it upsets the Morgloth. That's why Garyll, I mean, Swordmaster Glavenor can harm it. He has the power of the Shiver."

Garyll looked at her sharply. "I do not."

"But you do! Your blade makes the same note."

A sudden realisation dawned on Garyll's face. He moved aside, drew his sword from its scabbard and described a slow arc around his body. There was not enough space to complete a circle though, despite the Gifters and Captain Steed shying from the blade. They rose, and shuffled to stand beside King Mellar's desk, allowing the Swordmaster the room to swing his weapon.

The sword ripped through the air. Garyll swung it in a circle above his head, his grip shifting to contain the force. Tabitha and the others flinched every time the blade swung in their direction. As the angle on his blade changed, so a shriek filled the King's study, the howl of a banshee, but unsteady, surging from faint to loud. A piercing tone rang from the blade for an instant.

"There. That's the note!" Tabitha exclaimed.

Garyll slowed the blade, and its blurred edge became sharp, then still before him. He looked excited. It was a strange manner for the Swordmaster of Eyri, but Tabitha had never seen him looking as handsome as he did in that moment.

"Of course!" he declared. "There's a form which I was trained in, a form called Dancing with the Demon, which uses the overhead strikes. I'd always thought the moves to be wasteful, big swirling circles and long exposed spins. But it was all to make the blade sing! Dancing with the Demon. Painfully clear now. The old masters must have known. Thank you, Tabitha."

He gave her a warm, heart-stopping smile.

He had called her by her first name.

"These holes, in the centre of the blade, I'd always thought them strange. But it's the holes that create the sound, they train the wind to that piercing note."

"So," said King Mellar, "we have a weapon."

"One weapon is hardly enough against a troop of Morgloth," Father Keegan noted.

But Tabitha had an idea, and as she considered it, the Ring warmed on her finger. It might just work. She followed the idea to its completion, visualised every Sword with the device, every Sword with a chance against the Morgloth. They had to try.

"What if you drill the other blades out in the same way?"

Garyll shook his head. "No, Tabitha, that would weaken them terribly. I don't know how the smith forged this blade, but it is unique. A normal steel blade would split down the centre if it had these holes."

Tabitha would not be diverted though. She could sense that the idea she held was vital. "What if Yzell made an instrument to reproduce the blade's note?" she asked.

There was a moment of silence. Lethin Tarrok was the first to break it. He looked more unhappy than ever. "What, shall we have all the soldiers setting their swords aside, and playing their lyres into battle?" he scoffed.

The King cuffed him over the back of the head. "Miss Serannon is wiser than you think. Not lyres, no, it would have to be something small and light."

"A whistle, with the note of the Shiver," said Tabitha.

The King clapped his hands together. "Brilliant! Yes, this we must try. I shall set Yzell to the task at once. Tarrok!"

"Certainly, your highness," answered Lethin, somewhat sullenly, "I shall find him down in the bowels of the city." He rounded the desk and passed close by Tabitha, offering her a pale leer before making for the door.

She was glad to hear the door close behind him. A tension seemed to leave the room.

"You know that my Bevn is still missing," the King said quietly, mainly to Glavenor. "I fear –"

Garyll nodded. "You fear he may be held by those in Ravenscroft."

"If you discover they hold my son, the war begins in that moment."

"Your Highness." The Swordmaster met the King's eyes for a long moment. Mellar's face was creased with concern.

"Glavenor, my son must not be hurt."

"So we must prepare for the worst," said Glavenor. "I shall train the men on what they can expect, from what little I have learned."

"I think your men shall be expected, no matter how soon they go," Mellar warned. "It's up to you to make sure we can turn the surprise, so prepare your men well. But this challenge must be answered, I cannot let such a threat to Eyri lie, now that it is exposed."

"Are they such a threat, your Highness?" asked Father Keegan. "Is trade not an option? I am sure they are mostly an ordinary folk, and would have as little desire to die in a battle as I do. Surely you could negotiate?"

"We do not negotiate with those who commit treason," said Garyll in a clipped voice.

"I understand your compassion, Father Keegan," said King Mellar. "Your gentle training in the Light commends itself well to peace and healing. But there are times when one must act with a concern for the realm and not the individual. I shall not be the King who let Eyri be overrun by Morgloth, murderers and moral decay. No, these Shadowcasters have too much to answer for in Fendwarrow alone."

Keegan nodded, but said nothing.

"They shall be given the opportunity to surrender," King Mellar added. "There is something you could do to ensure mercy is present, however ruthless the battle becomes. Take word to your Rector, tell him that I seek the Lightgifter's support for our Sword. Your skills may well be needed in earnest."

It looked to Tabitha as if the King was pressed deeper into his chair by the burden of rule. Yet even as she thought that, he set his shoulders, and rose, a sign that the audience was done.

"Thank you, everyone, for your counsel, and your deeds today. I take strength from your victory."

They bowed in turn, and made their exits. As Tabitha passed the threshold, she heard the King address one of the Lightgifters behind her.

"Sister Grace, how is May, the Lady of Ceremony?"

"She will heal well, your Highness. She is strong."

"Thank the Creator for that. I shall come to see her when she wakes."

The cool passages of the Palace slid by underfoot. The Swordmaster walked in step with her. His presence was large, and mighty. Tabitha didn't know what to say; she wanted to say too much, yet nothing at all.

"You answered a question I have pondered for years," said Garyll. "The reason behind the shape of my blade was lost in the long succession of wielders before me. I never guessed that the blade was forged specifically for the Morgloth. I suppose it's difficult to imagine such a beast until you see one. A week ago, I would have believed it a fantasy."

"Is that sword really Felltang, the one from the legend?" she said, indicating the weapon sheathed at his belt.

"So they say," answered Garyll, his broad hand touching the hilt. "It has been handed down from Swordmaster to Swordmaster through the ages, since the time before the Kings."

"Do you really think it was gifted by wizards, as the legend tells it?"

The humour in Garyll's face was mixed with sobriety.

"The Gyre of Wizards? That is almost more difficult to believe than the Morgloth. But if the second is true, then maybe the first is as well. Felltang is a unique blade, and no Eyrian smith has been able to equal it in his forge. This blade is lighter, and holds a sharper edge, than any metal we have. And Felltang is not the only legacy of unnatural things from the ancient times."

He swept his hand through the air, indicating the walls of the palace—dark-grained, polished masonry.

"Stonewood," finished Tabitha.

"So, yes, maybe something of the legend is true. Hard to know the truth about the wizards, but I believe you identified the purpose of Felltang. This blade was made to deal with the threat of Morgloth."

"And the Swordmaster has always been the one to wield it?" Tabitha asked.

"Since it was awarded to Stevenson," Garyll confirmed.

"I was glad Felltang was in your hand today," said Tabitha, with a sincere smile. Garyll held her with a deep, steady gaze while they paced on. His face was tanned, and a short stubble roughened the clean lines of his jaw.

"I did nothing but execute a beast you had already crippled. You deserve more credit than I."

Glavenor was as good at deflecting compliments as he was at parrying sword-strokes. Tabitha was determined to find her target.

"I had no way to kill the Morgloth," she countered. "It recovered as soon as my breath ran out. I needed you, and you saved my life."

He nodded, but took her arm gently and drew her aside. They were somewhere outside the palace already, and it was bright. Tabitha's whole attention was captured by the man before her. She was aware of the Gifters passing behind her on the path, but in a vague, hazy way that made their voices sound as echoes from afar. The closeness of the Swordmaster seemed to overwhelm the clarity of the Ring she bore, and even though it was warm on her finger, the rest of the world was awash with a buzzing light. One part of her world was clear, clearer than the crystal Ring.

Garyll was holding her close, looking directly into her eyes.

"On the Kingsbridge, I tasted fear for the first time," he said quietly, to her alone.

"The Morgloth is a terrifying beast," she agreed, hesitantly. It was strange to consider Glavenor capable of fear. He was the Swordmaster, an invincible pillar of strength and certainty.

Garyll shook his head. "The Morgloth was an adversary. I do not feel fear for adversaries. There is only a battle, and the best possible outcome."

It was the answer she had expected—cold logic, nerves of steel.

"What did you fear?" she asked, her voice no more than a whisper under the weight of his intense regard.

"I feared that you might die. I have never felt such a fear before."

Caring and concern were mirrored in his expression, and something deeper that made her breath catch in her chest. Something like a surge of Light essence ran along the back of her legs, up her torso, through to her fingertips.

She stepped towards him and rose on tiptoes. Her heart thundered in her ears as she realised what she was about to do. He looked surprised. She pushed her face closer to his, her nose so close to his skin she could smell the soap of a brief, recent wash and the sunbaked travelling he had endured beneath it. His clothes smelled of leather, horses, steel and his worked body.

She kissed his cheek. His stubble was harder than she had expected, but strangely exciting.

Get back, girl, you'll be making a fool of yourself in a moment.

She withdrew from the surprised Swordmaster. He must have seen the surprise on her face as well, for he laughed then, a deep, gentle laugh as one shares between friends, full of mirth and intimacy.

"And I had wondered if I should ever dare to do the same," he said, taking her arm and leading her onwards again. "You are truly a wonder, Tabitha Serannon."

She hoped he didn't notice how she leaned on his arm for support for a brief few strides. There were too many emotions chasing through her mind to risk answering the Swordmaster's compliment.

◆ ──────── ◆

The young Lightgifter Ashley waited for them beyond the Palace guards. He looked mildly embarrassed at having to intercept them, especially when she and Glavenor parted hands to stand before him.

How much did he see?

But the mischievous cast to his eye told her. He had seen everything.

I don't care. I don't have to hide anything about the way I feel. Except perhaps the weak knees.

"Ah, sorry to intrude," Ashley began.

"Not at all, Ashley," Glavenor reassured, his voice even.

"Miss Serannon, we'll meet you at the stables in the morning, if you'd like to accompany us to the Dovecote."

It was like a pin prick in the soap bubble of her daydreams. She knew she concealed her disappointment badly, but didn't scruple to remedy it. Garyll was watching her, his expression unreadable. He seemed suddenly distant, a man unknown again.

What was I thinking? He's the Swordmaster, and I should be on my way to the Dovecote. It's what I always wanted, to be a Lightgifter, isn't it?

"Thank you, Ashley, I'd like the company. How early shall we be leaving?"

"At dawn, just after the Morningsong."

"Tomorrow morning, then," said Tabitha, smiling.

"Goodbye, Swordmaster," said Ashley, extending a hand to Garyll. "It was an honour to travel with you."

"Thank you, Ashley, and likewise," answered Garyll, shaking hands briefly, "but keep your farewells for the morn, when I can better thank the others for their efforts as well. And I doubt it's goodbye—I may be needing your aid sooner than you think."

"In the morning," said Ashley by way of farewell, and he trotted away from them across the cobbles of the Forecourt.

"Always thus," said Garyll, reflectively. "I must attend to preparing the troops for Ravenscroft, and then shall be on the campaign. You must surely go to your studies. I am certain you shall be one of the finest Lightgifters Eyri has ever been blessed with."

His compliment softened the wall which had begun to grow between them.

A snatch of song came to Tabitha. "We have but moments in the moonlight, moments to share alone."

"What?" asked Garyll, looking enchanted and uncertain at the same time. Tabitha had never imagined the King's Justice could be feeling any of the crazy emotions she was feeling.

"It's a song, the dreamchaser's lullaby," she answered, turning towards Garyll and trying to absorb as much of him as she could, before the inevitable parting.

"Forgive me for asking you on such a day as this, but we are too soon parted. Would you like to dine with me this evening?"

Tabitha knew that her smile was extreme, and that maybe she was being too plain and obvious in her delight, but she wanted nothing to contain the feeling. She felt like a flower beneath the sun of Garyll's attention, or was he the flower and she the sun? For he grinned at her in much the same way; guilty of happiness. He was truly handsome when he smiled.

◆ ────── ◆

The hours passed so swiftly that Tabitha didn't have the luxury of feeling nervous. She scarcely had the time to find a room in the Boarding, bath, visit May at the Healers, and find something to wear, before Glavenor was due. Garyll had been adamant that the tavern they would dine at was an informal place, suited to traveller's clothes and relaxed manners, but whether it was out of a soldier's natural prudence, or in sympathy for Tabitha's appearance, she wasn't sure.

She had visited the cutter's shop in the merchant's quarter anyway, and purchased a shirt to replace the soot-stained woollen tunic she wore.

It was a fine, indigo garment with a thin lining of fleece that peeped out of the collar and cuffs. The grey woodsman's pants would have to do with just a brushing—they were clean enough, or dark enough not to be noticed. As she waited for Glavenor to arrive at the Boarding, she twined a few small flowers into her hair.

Garyll had changed his uniform for a coarse red tunic, but his broad sword remained belted at his hip. He was clean-shaven, and his dark hair was drawn close against his head into its customary short tail. He seemed taller at night—he towered over her as they walked the streets of Stormhaven, filling the evening with order, piercing the shadows with a vigilance that was second nature to him.

The first tavern they passed, the familiar Bee, was so full that the patrons had spilled out into the street, and some of the music and sounds of revelry had flowed out through the open door. Garyll led her past the crowds, keeping them on the opposite side of the street. More than one of the patrons looked nervously to the night sky before pushing back into the crush.

Tabitha's hand rested only gently on Garyll's arm, yet she could feel the muscles ripple beneath his skin; he was ready and alert, despite his calm exterior. She wondered if it was deliberate that she was on his left side, so that he kept his sword-arm free.

The Traveller was a tavern tucked up against the looming north wall of Stormhaven, right at the point where the Upper District dropped to the Lower. It overlooked the roofs of the merchant's quarter from its vantage. A crowd plugged the doorway of the Traveller as well, but Garyll drew her aside before they reached it. They entered via a small door in the adjacent alley.

It seemed that they were expected, for a jolly tavern-keeper welcomed them beyond the door, and ushered them through the warm kitchens to a simply furnished but cosy dining room. A fire played in one corner. A wicker screen formed one wall, separating the room from the hubbub and music beyond, though much of it filtered through. Wooden tables, thick reed mats and cushions were ranged about the floor. Almost all of the low tables were occupied. The patrons ranged from middle-aged to old, from well-weathered to genteel.

Many patrons noticed their entrance, and it seemed to become quieter in the room for a moment. A greying man tipped his hand to his brow in a suggestion of a salute. Garyll raised his hand discreetly and nodded his acknowledgement. The patrons returned to their meals and conversations.

Garyll unbelted his sword, and set it beside the table, before folding his large frame down onto a cushion. The host returned with a basket of steaming bread, and a wide-lipped bottle of light Honeydew wine. Garyll broke the bread and offered it to Tabitha. It burst with goodness; soft on the tongue, moist in the centre, with a crust that crunched.

"Quite silly that we have to hide from our own fame," he commented, between bites.

"How so?" asked Tabitha. She hadn't given much thought to their entrance, she had presumed it was Garyll's usual route into the Traveller.

"There's no tavern in this city we could use tonight that would offer us privacy through the front door. I'm thankful for the Traveller's design."

"You mean you didn't want to be seen by those in the common room?" she asked, indicating the room behind the screen. She could only see into the larger room in a vague way, but she could see enough to know it was packed with people, many in animated discussion. Much ale was being consumed.

"Trust me, you don't want to go out there," said Garyll. "We wouldn't get a moment to ourselves if they knew we were here."

"Why?"

"Listen," he instructed, tilting her glass as he poured to prevent the Honeydew from gurgling. "Life is becoming legend."

Tabitha ranged out. She knew the Ring was probably working to augment her senses, yet the volume of noise still surprised her. She tried to isolate just one or two voices in the cacophony of revellers.

"- seen the corpse hoisted in the breeze above the City Gates? It's a Morgloth, no doubt -" offered someone with a deep, hoarse voice.

"Dead as a doorknob. 's the Swordmaster what killed it," slurred someone else.

"-'scuse me."

"Aye, here's to his shiny spike!" proposed a youthful card. There was laughter, and cheering. "Glavenor!" was the toast. "His shiny spike," said a few of the more inebriated voices.

"I heard it was the girl. She sang to the beast, and put it to sleep."

"For sure," said a mocking baritone. "And she sneezed, and blew the Shadowcaster from the bridge."

"More a woman than a girl," someone corrected.

"—'scuse me."

"Old Steve says she's been working in the tavern in First Light."

"Working, or working?" There was a suggestive inflection to the end of his question.

"You be thinking of her like that, and she'll scream at you, 'n break something!"

"—was a scream what stopped the beast, is what I heard."

"Nay, she's a singer, all right. Seen her with a lyre in town."

"—'scuse me, you're standing on my foot."

"She's a Gifter, you fools! I saw her with the Swordmaster, so you best be careful with your tongue, if you want to keep it."

The conversation turned quickly from the speculation about Tabitha.

"—Morgloth," someone whispered. Suddenly everyone had a loud theory.

"—rips through Swords like they was children with sticks –"

"—hungers for blood –"

"—stands ten feet high –"

"—Shadowcasters keep them as pets, feed them from birth –"

"—spawn of Krakus himself –"

"—feast on the life of men –"

"How many more gloth are there?" asked a wiseacre.

"—Morgloth," someone whispered again.

Tabitha discovered that she could see through the wicker screen if she leant close to it. Ale was vanishing into gullets like water into drain-pipes. Empty tankards lined the bar faster than the serving man could count the coins for their refilling. Tabitha suspected it was the barman who muttered 'Morgloth' under his breath, for he had smiled broadly every time she heard it said, as the crowds downed their drinks and ordered anew. Tabitha wondered how many of the crowd would awake the next morning beside their tankards. The tavern-keeper was exploiting the hysteria for every coin it was worth.

"Here's to a woman worth saving from peril," said Garyll, his deep voice bringing her back to the dining room. He watched her intently, and tilted his glass toward her.

The room was suddenly warm against her face. She took her own glass, and clinked the rim against Garyll's.

"To a man who is leading me into it," she teased, smiling broadly.

The Traveller, for all its informality, had a kitchen that excelled itself. Bowls of soup were soon placed beside the bread on the table—a thick, spiced butternut flavour lingered on her tongue like the delicate traces of cream on the sides of their bowls. They talked of this and that, small things of Eyri, things she did not remember afterwards, only that the conversation had been easy, for the most part, yet silent at times, when she thought that Garyll held back from asking something, as if mindful of the mood. She didn't probe, the evening was too wonderful. She used the silences to alternately watch his face, or his strong, tanned hands. His eyes were altogether too deep and dangerous.

The carafe of Honeydew retained little of its contents. By the time they had reached the end of a sticky, meaty platter of ribs, her cheeks were aching from smiling too much. The shared indulgence in the lusty feast with Glavenor made him more Garyll and less the Swordmaster. Tabitha found herself smiling at him again.

I hope we're going to become friends.

"I've been thinking about what you said," Garyll told her, "about the note my blade makes, and about other legacies of the ancient time."

There was some basting sauce on his upper lip, at the corner of his mouth, where his cheek dented when he spoke. She wanted to kiss it off.

"Felltang was awarded to the first Swordmaster in a time of war. He used Felltang well, and led the Swords to slay all the Morgloth and to drive every threat from the borders of Eyri."

She daren't kiss him where he sat, with all the patrons in the dining room watching.

"Yet it seems strange to me that nothing has come upon Eyri since that time. There have been no battles against invaders since the formative years. Nothing has come into Eyri to threaten the Kings' rule."

She reached over the table, and with her finger, made to wipe his lip. He pulled back reflexively, but then held still and watched her with amusement. The electric rush of contact tingled through Tabitha's finger. She cleaned with a touch, then withdrew her hand.

"Doesn't that seem strange to you? A realm the size of Eyri, and no invaders have ever chanced to come here, from—Outside. Not even a traveller or two? In over four hundred years?"

She licked her finger absently, then blushed when she realised what she had just done.

"Strange? Er, ah, yes?"

"So I checked the records of House of Ways as well. There has never been a journeyman who has left Eyri, to return with news of the lands beyond. No routes through the mountains or the Great Forest. It seems Eyri is impenetrable, from inside or out. I've never thought about it before, I've never needed to think about it. But if this is true, then why the wars in the formative years? How did our ancestors ever come to this place?"

Tabitha was in danger of appearing slow-witted. She carefully set her wine glass on the table, resolving to drink no more.

Where did all the Honeydew go?

She found a point to challenge Garyll on.

"What about Fynn? Didn't he explore the Zunskar, and the South Highlands?"

"And found nothing. He said of the Zunskar 'the mountains became ever more severe, and the snow more blinding, until it seemed the earth itself turned me back to the gentle arms of Eyri'. He became thirst-blighted and delirious in the Highlands, and doubled back on his own trail without realising it. And we both know what happened to him in the end."

She had sung the song often enough—Fynn Fell Down. He had climbed the Tooth above First Light to see beyond Eyri, and came down with the avalanche as a snowball.

"So no one ever heard his final tale," Garyll finished.

"You're saying nobody can escape Eyri?" Tabitha asked.

"I don't know what I'm saying," answered Garyll, swilling his wine speculatively. "But after twice meeting a Morgloth, and the purposeful note of Felltang, I'm reluctant to discard anything of the legends."

"You believe in the Seven Wizards, then?" she teased. She was enjoying Garyll's speculative mood, so at odds with his usual precise manner. It was exciting to find another man under the armour of the Swordmaster.

"What else did those who created stonewood do?" he mused. "What changed when the crown was placed on the first King's head, that the invasions ended?"

Tabitha took up the fanciful thread. "What if the Seven Wizards cast a spell, to keep everyone out?" she suggested.

He laughed, realising his own folly. "It is a bit daft. They would have died long ago, and how could anyone have the power to keep out an invasion along an entire border?"

Something in his words sparked a memory. She had read something in the Stormhaven library, in the legends of the Forming.

"That's what they did in the beginning!" she exclaimed. "The test to earn Felltang was a circle of the Seven, a circle which no one could breach. The test for the Kingsrim was the same."

Garyll was observing her with a wary expression, as if he was uncertain whether she was serious, tipsy, or having him on.

She grabbed hold of his hands to show her sincerity. His hands were warm, and strong.

"What if they extended that barrier to the edges of Eyri, so that no outsiders could ever penetrate the borders?"

The entire border of Eyri? Who could possibly have that much power?

It was an interesting theory, but it was otherwise flawed. There were outsiders in Eyri.

"What about the Shadowcasters?" she said, deflated. "What about Ravenscroft? They're all invaders, aren't they?"

Garyll considered her for a moment, then shook his head. "Ravenscroft is within Eyri, or at least the borders defined by the Kingsrim. It is within the horizon you see from Stormhaven. I believe their vale is peopled by Eyrians, folk somewhat akin to Lightgifters gone bad. They are not true Outsiders, the invaders of the legends. The Shadowcasters may well be the ones who disappeared from the eastern villages over the years. There have been rumours about creatures from the Broken Lands, taking children at night. The fuel for that rumour may well have been the Darkmaster, abducting new apprentices to his cause."

"Including Prince Bevn?"

Tabitha regretted the observation the moment she gave it voice. Garyll's expression hardened, his hand formed a fist; the martial poise of the Swordmaster returned.

"That is a fearsome thought," he said. "And probably true. I should hasten my campaign to clear the decay from Eyri."

"If I can help you in any way –" Tabitha began, her voice trailing off as she considered the unlikelihood of the statement. This was the Swordmaster she was talking to.

Garyll shook his head. "You have suffered enough at the hands of the Shadowcaster. You are too precious. It shall be my mission to ensure you are kept safe, far from any involvement with the Dark, far from the perils of any future battles."

"Not too far from you, I hope," she said, hoping to draw him back with her smile to the intimate world they had shared until a moment ago.

"You don't want to be near me," he rebutted, his eyes distant. "Not with what I face. Not until we have claimed victory."

He had been right to keep conversation light, before. Thoughts of the impending confrontation had raised Garyll's armour faster than a poke in the ribs with a sharp stick. He did reach out a hand and brush her face gently, but then he rose from the table. He belted his sword to his side. Their special time at the Traveller was over.

When Garyll approached the tavern-keeper to settle the account for their meal, the host waved his coin aside. "Not tonight, Swordmaster, not tonight. You may have been seeking to hide from the crowds, but your deeds deserve credit nonetheless. It is the least I can do, to lay a meal for the hero of Stormhaven and his lovely companion."

Garyll considered the host for a moment, then shook his hand, and paid compliment to his fine cooking. When Garyll ushered Tabitha into the street, a glimmer of a smile played across his lips.

"Now I have to invite you again some time, to have properly taken you out to dinner."

She took his arm.

The walk through the streets to the Boarding was cold, which allowed Tabitha to nestle closer to Garyll. Even though he set a slow pace, it was over too soon; a brief passage between the dark buildings, beneath the channel of crisp stars. She tried to hold onto him for a moment longer, but she knew that they must part.

They halted at the base of the stairs. She looked up into Garyll's face, but he watched the eaves of the Boarding high above. His body stiffened.

She placed her hands about his neck, and rose on tiptoe.

A scuffling sound high above made her pause. Garyll did not drop his gaze to her, though she knew he must feel how her body was positioned, close against his. She glanced up.

A dark object the size of a roof-tile fell. It came whistling down at them from the eaves.

"Watch out!" shouted Garyll. He pushed the palm of his hand against her chest. She was thrown backwards, away from the Swordmaster, her feet scrabbling for purchase on the cobbles. She tripped, and sat down heavily. She expected the roof-tile to shatter on the street between them, but the piece of falling masonry spread its wings, and swooped low overhead. A hoarse croak mocked them. The raven flapped away, down the street, and was lost between the dark buildings.

Garyll was at her side instantly, lifting her from the ground in his arms, holding her close as if she weighed nothing at all. His face was close.

"Oh, I am sorry Tabitha, I am such a fool. I thought it was going to crack your head. Raven! That was no ordinary bird."

She just looked up at him, dazed, shocked by the force of Garyll's blow, by the suddenness of the attack from above, by the overwhelming conflict of emotions she felt. A moment ago she had been meaning to kiss him. The opportunity had been stolen, by a Dark messenger. She didn't know whether it was fear, relief, sadness or anger she felt. Her heart pounded, and she was glad Garyll carried her still. A shiver passed through her body, a delayed excitement at having been so suddenly separated then brought close again.

She felt his lips on hers.

She thought she saw a reflection of her own surprise in his eyes. Before he could end the kiss, she caught his head in her hands, and kissed him back. His hair was thick and smooth.

When he finally pulled away, and set her upon her feet, the night was different. The darkness was not so dark, the warmth of her own body pushed the cold away.

"Goodnight, Tabitha," he said, his broad smile gradually fading. "I think I shall make a patrol of Stormhaven, to see if I can disturb any more things that do not belong in the city. You get safely indoors now. I shall see you off at dawn."

"Thank you, Garyll," she said, but didn't move. "I had a wonderful time with you."

He bowed low, then turned and paced away.

"Goodnight," she called after him. He waved, a smile creeping over his shoulder. She blew a kiss to his back, watching his determined stride carry him through a street now commanded by the Swordmaster of Eyri.

She took the stairs to her room two at a time.

◆ ─────────── ◆

The Darkmaster smacked his sceptre into the floor. He wished for the power to split the rock beneath, that all of Ravenscroft might shudder and tremble at his strike. His plan had failed.

No! His plan had not yet succeeded!

Kirjath Arkell was missing, and might even be dead.

Cabal had sent Morrigán after Morrigán out to search for the errant Shadowcaster, but Arkell was nowhere to be found. During the Midnight Mass Cabal could feel the loss of his servant directly. There was a place of deeper silence, a missing link in the network of Darkstones. The Midnight Mass swelled and echoed within Ravenscroft's chambers, but one Shadowcaster was absent. One voice did not chant its unswerving loyalty to the Master. One presence was gone.

It had been enough of a shock to see the corpse of the Morgloth being hoisted to the battlements of Stormhaven. That was the first vision that his Morrigán had returned to him. Arkell had been doomed the moment he began to play with the Underworld. Yet with access to such devastating beasts, Kirjath Arkell should have had no problems retrieving the Ring.

Cabal had fuelled Kirjath's anger well enough before sending him on his quest from Ravenscroft the last time. With the suggestions planted in his mind, the Shadowcaster should not have been able to stop until he had reclaimed the Ring. And then, Cabal would have reeled him in like a fish on the line. But someone had killed the Morgloth, and Arkell was lost. He had to assume the worst.

Which left a horrible consequence in its bloody wake. The Ring was not yet reclaimed, and he could not risk the confrontation he had been planning. The Swords would have to be delayed until he had the talisman secured.

His latest Morrigán had still not returned.

He ended the Midnight Mass prematurely, cutting his devotees off with a terse mental command.

"Enough!" he shouted, stomping his sceptre into the floor once again. "Silence!" It was a command as well as the spell he sent rippling through the Keep. Dark essence bonded to his pattern, and Ravenscroft became as still as a graveyard.

The mental union of devotees fragmented in confusion.

Let them wonder. Let them fear my wrath tonight!

He had never cut short his favourite pleasure before. He usually delighted in the multiple domination of the Midnight Mass.

He sat quite still.

It was a Morrigán that finally broke the silence, returning to its Master with a croaking cry and a circling flutter of wings.

"Alight, messenger, and deliver your vision."

The bird released the sights it had been sent to find, and so became motes of Dark once again. Cabal saw the girl, her face upturned in surprise, at the base of some stairs. So she lived still. That fact only underlined Kirjath's miserable failure. Cabal caught a glimpse of a figure beside the girl, the unmistakable defiant pose of a fighter, tall, black-haired. The Swordmaster Glavenor.

Cabal's sceptre smacked the floor a third time. A fragment of stone chipped at the base and skittered away in the darkness.

I cannot afford them to be together.

They surely would be drawn apart very soon. The King would have to answer the challenge of Ravenscroft with an invasive army. If Cabal judged him correctly, Glavenor would lead the army himself. The girl, he was sure, would be left behind.

All that was needed was a little time.

The soldiers would have to be stalled, until the threat of the girl had been eliminated. He needed to be sure that the Ring would not be used against him in some accidental discovery of magic.

He massaged the knuckle of his middle finger on the left hand, where he had worn the Ring those many years ago. It ached still, that bite of cold which had heralded the end of its tolerance for him.

His own discoveries with the Ring had come upon him with rapid bursts of enlightenment. The Decay spell he had learned in one night.

The next night he had watched its deadly effect on a dissident trader.

Yes, the girl had to be silenced before she could learn anything of the sort. The Ring was a stepping stone to knowledge of devastating power.

Such possibilities, yet it had long since ceased to be a boon to him.

Even when he bore the Ring on his neck-chain, using it to gain insight into new spells was like trying to draw blood from a stone.

What if she has already learned something new. What if she defended herself from Arkell by using magic?

The Morgloth was dead. His Shadowcaster was gone.

What has she learned to do?

But then an oily smile spread across his face as a new possibility dawned on the Darkmaster.

She didn't have to represent a danger. She could be a tool.

He realised he had erred in sending Kirjath to claim the Ring. It wasn't the Ring he needed to claim; it was the girl.

25. ENTER THE DOVE
"Learning makes us younger;
it's the forgetting that causes age."—*Zarost*

The Morningsong began Tabitha's day. The voices of the distant assembly in the Dovecote surrounded her in sleep, but the volume of sound soon diminished as she woke. She was fuzzy-headed, but excited. The Lightstone brought the last verse of the song to her, a delicate blend of Lightgifter's voices made small.

To wake thus was fitting—it was a special day. She was finally going to Levin, to begin her apprenticeship to the Light. She fumbled her things together—the lyre, her coins tied on a thong, the little mirror Zarost had given her; all that remained of her possessions. She supposed that she could purchase more clothes with the ample money she had, but there seemed little point in that, on her way to the Dovecote. She would wear the Gifter's whites when they welcomed her into the fold.

She donned the clothes she had worn the evening before, and stuffed her old tunic into the pocket of her heavy cloak. There wasn't time to breakfast. Ashley Logán had said they departed just after dawn. She was already late.

She ran, her lyre in hand, a joyous thrill spurring her on. Someone else beside the Gifters would be there, to see them all off.

◆ ──────── ◆

They were all waiting for her when she reached the stables. The three Lightgifters sat in an open carriage, with two Swords up front. Garyll Glavenor was chatting to one of the escorts, but he turned on her arrival. His broad smile was all she needed to make her day perfect.

Last night was not just a whim.

He gave Tabitha a private little nod, but greeted her formally. "Good morning, Miss Serannon." He even bowed at the waist.

"Morning to you too, Swordmaster Glavenor," she returned, dipping in a bow as well. The stiff behaviour made her want to giggle, it seemed out of place, but she supposed in the presence of his men, and the Gifters, he couldn't exactly sweep her up in his arms, and kiss her full on the lips, as he had on the steps of the Boarding. There was an awkward moment as she considered what would be a proper gesture of parting. He solved that problem for her, by stepping close and offering her his hand. He led her up the carriage steps, and kissed her hand in the manner of a gentleman.

"You'll make a fine Lightgifter. I shall seek you out when I return."

He didn't have to announce where he went. She knew he meant the dark vale of Ravenscroft.

"Good luck," she said. She squeezed his hand.

It was as brief a parting as that. Garyll stepped down and away from them, and bade farewell to the others in the carriage. The driver flicked the reins, and the carriage swept out of the stable. The tall, pensive figure of the Swordmaster was lost to view. Tabitha was swept on by the swift current of the day.

What little conversation began in the rear of the carriage, died away as they passed through the great City Gates. The Morgloth had indeed been hoisted to swing from the battlements, a sign to all of judgement passed in the King's name. Tabitha shivered at the sight of the demon, its slack wings hanging far past its truncated body. It seemed to Tabitha as much a token of victory as a warning of evil, for if one Morgloth could be brought to be, so could another.

She supposed the King was wise to alert the populace to Eyri's present danger—if Ravenscroft held close to the numbers of Shadowcasters reported by Garyll and the Gifters, then great hardship was coming. Everyone should be on their guard.

It only strengthened her resolve to become a Lightgifter. At least with command of the sprites, she could use her mother's orb to assist the healing of the land, or to fight for goodness, should it come to that.

She hoped Garyll could contain the threat of Ravenscroft within its own valley, and that nothing escaped. No Eyrians deserved to face a creature like the Morgloth.

The events of the previous day haunted them all in different ways. Silence ensued until they were well past the place of the battle, until they were closing on the tiered city of Levin. Slowly, the enthusiasm she had felt on waking returned. She was going to the Dovecote, to become a Lightgifter. Her excitement rose with every winding street they ascended.

◆ ———————— ◆

They were taken directly to the Rector's chambers on arrival. Tabitha was awe-struck—the hall they passed through was large enough to accommodate a fully grown silken tree. The crystal obelisk, the Source, was much bigger than she had expected from her mother's tales. It was a glorious sculpture of flashing, sparkling sunlight.

They ascended two flights of stairs, and were ushered into the richly-furnished rooms of the Rector Shamgar. Luxurious couches and furs were arranged within the pale walls, but the layout seemed obscure, for there was nowhere for the visitors to seat themselves when addressing the seated Rector. They were left standing like schoolchildren brought before a teacher upon a misdemeanour.

The three Gifters greeted him as 'Illumination', and Tabitha followed suit, bowing briefly from the waist as she had seen the others do. The Rector said nothing. He was half-turned in his broad chair to look out over Levin. Three great oval windows showed the western panorama, from the forests to the lowlands to where boats sailed the Amberlake along the dividing line of the Kingsbridge. The Rector swivelled his chair to regard them critically.

The leader of the Lightgifters was heavy, Tabitha decided, for it was too much of an effort for him to rise from his chair to welcome them. He puffed his cheeks out while he ran his pale blue eyes over the newcomers.

"Morgloth on the Kingsbridge, and you in the thick of it, I hear, what?" He eased the sash that tightened his purple robe around his belly. "Well, report to me, Keegan. What have you been doing to spread peace and healing?"

Keegan bunched his shoulders, but answered in a steady, bored tone. "We followed the trail of Shadowcaster Arkell from First Light. He captured Hosanna—she was ahead of us with Rosreece. I fear Rosreece was murdered by Arkell, for we have not seen him again, and Hosanna bursts into tears at the mention of Rosreece's name."

"She cries at anything you ask her," noted Sister Grace, her voice full of compassion.

Keegan nodded, and continued with the report. "Arkell evaded us in Fendwarrow, but sent a decoy to the Darkmaster's hidden lair, which we managed to follow. A full settlement of Shadowcasters, a whole vale with its own Keep, tilled fields, and a hidden access. They call it Ravenscroft, a foul, bitterly cold place. Who knows how long they have harboured their power there?"

"How much time did you spend in Fendwarrow?" the Rector asked

Keegan.

"Not more than a few hours, Rector. Ravenscroft is beyond it —"

"I worry for the people of that village," the Rector cut in. "Too much darkness and suffering, for too long, what?"

Keegan stood stiffly before his superior. "But it's the doorway to the Dark, they gather in Raven —"

"Yes, yes, the vale of the Darkmaster. As I understand it from your strange messages, a remote place high in the mountains. My concern is for things closer to home."

"We should take a force of Gifters to Ravenscroft, and help the Swordmaster in his campaign," objected Keegan. "He plans to conquer the Shadowcasters, for they claim no allegiance to the crown. He has requested our assistance, and I believe the Dovecote owes him that."

The Rector blew his cheeks out, his expression darkening at Keegan's insistent defiance.

"Maybe you mistake yourself for a Sword, Father Keegan. Ours is the way of healing, not of war. If the Shadowcasters choose to hide in a place called Ravenscroft, then they are causing no harm. The Swordmaster can go on his hunt with his own strong men, I'll not be risking good Gifters for the sake of picking a fight. But harm indeed is often seen in Fendwarrow, not so? Sickly babies, women the victims of trouble, the waterborne madness. Tell me, when you passed through there, did you see any signs of Light?"

"No, Rector," Keegan answered slowly, his shoulders still bunched. "From there, and all the way in to the mountains, not a sprite or silken tree."

"And yet here in Levin, there is a surplus of sprites, not just in the Cote, but in the streets, down at the water's edge, up in the trees. Think of Stormsford, or Llury, or even Respite. Everywhere in Eyri, we have taken the Light to the people. But in Fendwarrow, there is none."

"That is because it has been used up, in healing," said Grace, plainly.

"In a place where there is no light, that is where darkness grows, what?" the Rector stated.

"Do you wish something to be done about it?" asked Keegan.

"Take Light essence to that place, to Fendwarrow. I shall issue you with a large supply of sprites. A mission of mercy, if you will, to the poor folk of Fendwarrow, what? See what good you can do there,

Father Keegan. I am sure your time will be better spent in that than in chasing shadows. I have spoken to you."

Keegan remained silent.

"Sister Grace, explain to me how it is that your group went to Stormhaven on the Kingsbridge but did not report to me before doing so? You rode past Levin."

"We had to report our findings to the King," replied Grace.

"Just as well, or we wouldn't have come upon the Shadowcaster in time," Keegan added.

"Silence! Did you not hear me say I have spoken to you? The King rules Eyri, but it is I who rule you, even if you wish it otherwise," he said loudly, turning his glare upon Grace. "And it is to me that you should report first. I shall decide whether to report it to the King. How can we work in unity if your priorities lie elsewhere?"

"I would have thought helping a fellow Gifter out of trouble would always be to the benefit of the Dovecote," said Grace.

"What do you mean?"

"Well, Tabitha here, she's a Lightgifter, is she not? We helped her defeat the Shadowcaster, and his Morgloth."

The Rector turned his attention to Tabitha for the first time. She almost wished he had not noticed her, for his gaze was an uncomfortable thing to endure. She felt pinned to the spot, scrutinised, and found wanting.

"You are Trisha Serannon's daughter?"

Tabitha nodded, earnestly.

The Rector snorted, and continued to hold her with his gaze while he addressed Sister Grace. "She may hope to be a Lightgifter, but I have neither tested this one, nor found her worthy yet."

"But she bears the Lightstone. I thought –"

"What?" bellowed the Rector suddenly.

"She bears –"

"I heard you! Show me," he demanded of Tabitha, his expression dangerous.

A wave of guilt washed over her, driven by the Rector's disapproving stare, and further strengthened by the shocked expressions of the three Gifters. Tabitha pulled the Lightstone over the collar of her shirt, where she had kept it concealed for the day.

"What!" the Rector shouted, jumping to his feet. "I never orbed you, girl! How dare you bear the Lightstone?" The Rector advanced on her. Though he was not much taller than Tabitha, he had the ability to look down upon her as if from a great height.

"It was my mother's," she whispered, too afraid to back away. The Rector grabbed hold of the orb, and yanked hard, as if to free it. The chain held, and bit into the back of her neck. The Rector's eyes widened in surprise. He reached behind her head.

"How did you seal this clasp?"

"The Riddler, after the fire, he put it on my neck. It wasn't my idea," she pleaded.

"Impossible!" the Rector exclaimed, pulling on her chain again. At least he had the care not to pull so hard that time, but it still chafed against her skin. He dropped the chain,

"One of the oldest rules of the Dovecote, and you break it before you even arrive. You see these two hands?" he said, shaking his hands in the air before her face. "Do you see these hands?" Tabitha nodded, wondering desperately how she could escape. It was all going horribly wrong. She hadn't expected to begin her apprenticeship provoking the wrath of the Rector, but it was too late to avoid.

"These are the only two hands that may orb a Gifter!" he roared, behind a fine spray of spittle. "Only the Rector learns the spell of the Vow, only the Rector selects the apprentices to take that Vow and join the service of the Light. Who is this Riddler to force an apprentice on me, who are you to so wantonly break the rules?" His voice tapered off to a clipped demand, but his eyes retained the dangerous cast.

Tabitha cringed in her own skin. She became painfully aware of how the others who stood before the Rector were robed in white, while she wore motley traveller's clothes. She was an interloper in the house of Lightgifters. They watched her expectantly, a little warily, as if puzzled by her duplicity. But Ashley Logán's expression hardened to a firm resolve.

"How was she supposed to know the rules of the Dovecote, if she was not yet here?"

"I did not ask for your opinion, half-knot!" the Rector snapped. "You hold your tongue, or you shall get another week's window-cleaning on top of the one you have just earned."

Ashley didn't speak again, but he shot Tabitha a quick commiserating glance. She took encouragement from the fact that he had stood up for her. She didn't feel so alone.

The Rector looked her up and down. His expression was still indignant, but his eyes had become sly.

"How old are you?"

Tabitha hesitated, knowing she was cornered again. She was not yet of age to be a Lightgifter.

Truthsayer, you cannot lie. He could find out anyway, from the records of births and deaths in Stormhaven.

"I shall be eighteen at Yearsend. I was born on Midsummer's Eve."

"Another rule you break then, pretending to be a Gifter, but not yet of age! You surely knew this from your mother."

Tabitha didn't need to answer—everyone in Eyri knew the Gifter's apprenticeship began at eighteen. She decided, instead, to appeal to the Rector's heart. Surely one who taught healing and compassion would have some sympathy for a recently orphaned girl.

She swallowed. "My mother taught me well, and I know what shall be expected of me as a Lightgifter. When my parents were murdered by the Shadowcaster I dedicated my life to serve the Light." She lifted the Lightstone on its short chain. "I will do anything to make amends for this, anything at all, but as I must continue to bear it, please let me bear it with your blessing." She met the Rector's gaze with her genuine appeal, then bowed her head. The Rector's eyes were as cold as an empty winter's sky.

She heard Sister Grace speak, though she dared not look up. "Rector, she could serve in the stables, or the kitchens, until the turn of the year. I believe her heart is true, she wants to be a Lightgifter."

"Many people want to be Lightgifters, Sister Grace, but few have what is needed to join the Dovecote."

Tabitha picked her eyes up from the fur rug. "I hear the Morningsong every dawn. I can call to the sprites, though I have little training in what spells to cast. With Ravenscroft exposed, won't you need all the Lightgifters you can get? I want to learn, I want to help, I don't want to do the wrong thing."

The Rector considered her for an uncomfortable moment of silence, then walked to his chair and sat, turning to gaze out the windows at Eyri.

"Very well! You shall work off your guilt," he said, still facing away. "If you wish to prove how you have reformed, how you can be dedicated to the rules of the Dovecote, then you shall have no dealings with the magic, until Yearsend, when I shall test you. You shall wear grey, like all the other servants, and you shall cover that Lightstone which you have no right to wear. You shall stay in the women's wing. One complaint about your conditions, or the work that is set before you, and you shall be dismissed. You have already stretched my tolerance to its limits. See that you behave from now on."

Tabitha didn't know what to say. Although she would not even be an apprentice, she had a chance to be, when she was of age. That wasn't too far in the future. She would stay in the Dovecote. He had not turned her away.

"Thank you, Rector Shamgar."

The Rector didn't acknowledge her thanks, he had already dismissed her as being nothing more than a servant until Yearsend, it seemed. He was turned to face Sister Grace.

"Why has Hosanna not returned with you?"

"They require her for questioning, Rector, regarding her time with the Shadowcaster. But she doesn't speak. I gave her my best healing, but she is –" Sister Grace closed her eyes. "She is damaged, in here," she said, tapping her temple with a finger. "All the healing spells work on the body. There's nothing I know for the mind."

"Well, if she was in such a bad way, why did you leave her?" retorted the Rector.

Ashley rolled his eyes at Tabitha.

Grace answered the Rector with calm patience. "Sister Vanessa is the Healer in Stormhaven, she was caring for her, as well as I could."

"I think my own skills are more likely to yield success with such a patient," declared the Rector. "You should return to Stormhaven, and bring Hosanna back to the Dovecote for healing. I would like to hear from her what happened to the unfortunate Rosreece, and what she knows of the Shadowcaster's magic. Tell the Sword we shall allow her to be questioned once she is healed."

"Rector, I don't think –"

"You question my ability to heal her?" the Rector challenged, leaning suddenly forwards in his chair towards the Sister.

Grace remained nonplussed, and Tabitha admired her calm. "I don't think she will travel all that well. She had a fit of screams and tears when we tried to move her from the cell in the Swordhouse."

"Well, that is something for your expert hand to solve then," he replied, easing back into the depths of his seat. "Bring her back as soon as you are able, and I shall attempt the greater task of reclaiming her mind."

Sister Grace nodded. The Rector smiled, but only briefly.

"Half-knot! Take servant Serannon down to the stores, get her fitted in a grey, and a neckerchief, don't you forget, and present her to Wyniss. Then get to cleaning your windows." The Rector dismissed them both. Keegan and Grace stayed in his chambers. Tabitha bowed as she left, and again at the door when Ashley did so. They scurried into the warm corridor.

Ashley sighed deeply when he had closed the door behind him, but indicated with a finger to his lips that Tabitha should say nothing. They walked softly to the stairs, and descended. The central volume of the Dovecote's hall dropped away beside the staircase. There was a purity to the light and air that made Tabitha feel like singing, after the tension in the Rector's chambers. She wondered if they would let her join the Morningsong the next day.

"Do servants get –"

"Shhht!" Ashley said, a quick warning glance.

Only when they had reached the middle floor did Ashley explain.

"We are not supposed to speak on the Rector's floor, unless we are speaking to him."

"That whole top floor is the Rector's?"

Ashley nodded, leading Tabitha on toward the grand curving stairs that led down to the ground floor.

"Is he always like that?"

Ashley nodded again, but gave her a wicked grin. "You'll learn very quickly here to avoid drawing attention to yourself."

"How do they stand it?"

"Who?"

"Keegan and Grace, he treats them like children, yet they take it with humility."

Ashley looked puzzled. "He is the Rector."

"But they are Lightgifters!"

"You have not yet taken the Vow. You will understand when you take the Vow, at Yearsend. It is a fundamental as old as the Dovecote— to be a Lightgifter, you must accept the Rector as the Illumination, the sole channel to the Source, the final link in the chain of Gifters to the Light. The Rector is the one to allocate our essence to us. That gives him the power to withdraw the right of any Gifter to essence, which renders them powerless. Keegan and Grace are just protecting their own interests in there. Try to imagine what it would be like to be a Lightgifter, without Light to gift."

"So we must obey him, all the time?" It seemed an impossible task

342

for Tabitha. She had already had a taste of how demanding the Rector could be.

There was a twinkle in Ashley's eye. "I didn't say we always obey him. Just make sure you aren't caught not obeying him. Life would be miserable if we followed Shamgar's rules to the letter. Yet while you are in the Dovecote, it is best to appear to be doing just that."

♦ ———————— ♦

Washing. There was a heavy wooden bucket to carry to the well, a heavier bucket to return. A cauldron squatted on the kitchen hearth, swallowing more water than Tabitha thought possible. While it heated, she collected the aftermath from the dining hall—cups, bowls, platters, boards, and spoons—and brought them to the scullery bath, an armload at a time.

She tried to make light work of it, pretending it was just another night in the Tooth-and-Tale, but there were so many people at one sitting that she knew it would take hours to finish the cleaning alone. There were close to one hundred Gifters and apprentices in the Dovecote, all told. And besides the Gifters there was the staff of ten—cooks, cleaners, grooms, the store-master and Mistress Wyniss the Matron. It all amounted to a lot of serving, a lot of collecting, and a lot of washing.

Tabitha scalded her hand on the cauldron, trying to scoop too much boiling water into her bucket. The coarse scrubbing cloth she was given had a manner of sending bristles under the fingernails. The cook had favoured oil in the food, and the residues soon fouled the water, so that she had to replace it with another bucket from the cauldron. The soap was an ineffectual cake which liked to break apart and stick to surfaces rather than clean them.

Sweeping. The thick-bristled broom that she was issued with did a bad job of coaxing the dust from the twisting corridors of the Dovecote, but a hard look from Mistress Wyniss had cut off any thoughts of complaint. Tabitha watched half-knots file out onto the Sandfield for the instruction that she wished she could attend. She soon learned that sweeping there was best left until after the class had tracked their dirt into the lower corridors. Even though the apprentices seemed diligent in wiping their feet on the mats, they left a trail of grit in their wake, a trail Tabitha was expected to have spirited away by sunset. She began to sweep again.

Cooking. The onions stung her eyes to tears, but the pile would not get any smaller by crying at it. She stripped them by feel alone, diced them, and added the pieces to the cook's stew. There were two other assistants in the kitchen, but there was so much to prepare that they all worked at a frantic pace. The others were more efficient in their scurrying. Orders were shouted through the steam and scents of the kitchen, vegetables were collected and dispensed, herbs were retrieved from the gardens, pots were hung over the fire, and others taken from it. All around was the heat, and the overly-rich aroma of cooking meat being turned over the open flame. Once braised, the meat would join the mountain of stew in the cauldron.

Tabitha cut her finger when an onion slipped beneath the knife, and she earned a frown from the cook. She caused delay by seeking out a bandage, but she knew her presence itself was a boon for the kitchen. The sting of the onions returned the moment she set her knife to the pile once more.

Washing. Water for the cauldron. Collecting plates and platters. Fighting the tattered cloth that pricked her fingers.

When a strident singing voice called out through the Dovecote, she had just finished her pile of cutlery and set it in the fire-box to dry. The cook ceased tying herbs to an overhead string, and called to Tabitha.

"Come on, luvvy, that's the Evencall. We must be out!"

They had just enough time to reach their room in the women's wing before the great oak door boomed shut at the end of the corridor, sealing them from the Hall of Sky.

There was little talk shared between the servants that night—like the others, she washed, found her allocated bed, and fell upon it.

Her last thought before she fell into an exhausted sleep was how far away the Lightgifters had seemed all day—she hadn't seen Ashley at all, and despite the other Gifters being close in body, they disregarded her with a gaze which passed right through her, as if she weren't there. She had had no opportunity to talk to anyone other than the servants. It was as if being a servant made one unworthy of attention. She supposed it was better than being shouted at.

◆ ——————— ◆

The Morningsong was touching, powerful, joyous and sad in the same moment. It brought to Tabitha memories of family, singing together in the crisp morns of Phantom Acres, a time that would never return. It evoked feelings of sharing, the unity of the family of the

Light. Each and every Lightgifter, no matter where the sun had found them, would be joined in song with the choir of the Dovecote. The sheer volume of sound overwhelmed Tabitha, even though she stood at its fringe. The voices swelled through the Dovecote.

Mistress Wyniss had been very firm in her answer—no ghosts took part in the Morningsong, ever. Tabitha had found that the only way she was allowed close to the Hall of Sky was to continue fetching water for the baths, a task which brought her past the singers with every bucket.

On the second pass, she couldn't resist setting the work aside, and creeping up to the arched hall doors. She longed to be standing amongst the ranks of Lightgifters, in the Assembly.

Sprites swirled through the air, over the Gifters' heads. The Gifters who she could see were turned away from her, facing inward to where she knew the obelisk of the Source would be. She spun her warm Ring absently around her finger. The Morningsong pulled at her with its familiar joy. Even though her Lightstone was carefully tied inside the black neckerchief she had been given, she could feel it vibrating in sympathy with the song.

Yet as she stood listening and felt the spell deep in her bones, she became aware of a discord in the sound. There was a silence in the pattern where there should be a voice. There was a missing thread of song without which it could not be complete. It was not unlike the moment when she had discovered the words to the Lifesong, on the hillock behind Phantom Acres. She could no more deny the sudden knowledge than she could stop herself from singing.

She added her voice to the theme which surrounded her. Her song was like a bird's, following no structured melody, yet piercing the gaps with pure music. Her song had a strange lilting rhythm.

The sprites spun incandescent through the Hall, joining into streams, suddenly thick with Light.

She became so absorbed in the perfection of the song, in the sensation of rightness that rang through her body, that she forgot her caution. She leaned further in to the Hall, her eyes feasting in the brilliance of the Source. It was a delicate fury of Light that weaved through the Gifters.

The Rector Shamgar caught her with his pale blue gaze.

He was standing beside the Source, his arms raised as if guiding the sprites, his lips set in rigid parallel.

Tabitha jumped back into the corridor, her heart pounding. The

Morningsong continued its unbroken melody, but her voice had caught in her throat. She hurried away. She hefted the bucket to her side, and made for the well.

Second day, and already I've broken one of the Rector's rules.

Her inspired mood was chased by the spectre at her back. She had little chance of surviving the ten weeks until Yearsend without breaking the rules again. The Rector could dismiss her at any time.

Despite that knowledge, she shouldered the burden of her duties for the day with determination. Deep in her heart, a seed had found purchase. Singing with the Lightgifters had been like opening a door to a bright new day. She tried to hold onto that feeling as the day wore on, as the hauling of water became sweeping, the sweeping cleaning, then cooking, washing, making soap, mucking out stables, cooking again, washing, beating dust out of mats, and the tired scurry to bed as the Evencall was called.

On the fourth day, she found someone to talk to, at last. She was sweeping the women's corridor out through the Hall of Sky, when a clatter and a thump from above drew her attention to the windows overhead.

She gasped. A figure moved past one of the many glass panes, high above in the vaulted ceiling of the Hall. The glass was irregularly transparent, but when the figure dropped to his knees and pressed his face to the glass, she recognised the youthful features of Ashley Logán. He waved, and Tabitha returned the greeting from three stories below. But then she noted that his hand held a rag, and he was cleaning the glass. She couldn't be sure he had waved at all.

Later, she tracked him to the well, where he drew water for his cleaning work. He was dressed in a grey robe, just like Tabitha. He should have been in white, like the other Lightgifters.

"Hullo stranger," she greeted him. There was more of a sting in her voice than she had intended.

"Hi Tabitha," Ashley replied mildly. "I'm sorry if I haven't been around to talk to, I suppose it's become so much a bad habit of mine that I don't even think about it. We're—forbidden to talk to ghosts. At the moment, I'm trying to keep my neck out of trouble, with the Rector the way he is."

"Oh."

"But I'm a ghost for a few hours today, so I suppose we can talk."

"You're a ghost?"

"The greys," he explained, lifting his robe at the shoulder. "All the apprentices have a grey, we all get to be ghosts from time to time. But I'm expected to perform all the duties of a half-knot as well, so my days are rather full at the moment."

Ashley wound the well-handle. The mechanism creaked as rope twisted tight around the spindle, bringing his laden bucket to the surface.

"Ashley, why doesn't the Dovecote have more servants? Surely there's enough money in the coffers, with all the healing work the Gifters do? Why doesn't the Rector employ another ten?"

"Are you tiring of it?" he asked.

Tabitha nodded. It wasn't so much the work she was doing, which was simple enough, if burdensome. It was the work she wasn't doing because of it—touching the Light essence, learning the ways of the sprites, the spells and patterns that had been her mother's art, all forbidden by the Rector. She had yearned for it so long, and to be so close to it, yet denied it, was a grinding frustration. The nine-and-a-half weeks that stretched before her to Yearsend seemed to stretch forever.

Ashley swung his bucket to the rim of the well, and unhooked it from the rope. His expression was sympathetic.

"It's supposed to teach us humility, this sort of work."

"How much time do you spend learning humility, and how much learning magic?"

"Hah!" Ashley laughed. He looked around the yard quickly. "The Rector is keen on humility. Even when I'm not a ghost, I have to run errands to Levin town, collect faded essence, copy scrolls. Then there's the Meditation, which is three hours. I have one, maybe two hours a day when I'm trained in the Light. It takes a long time to perfect anything, and even longer to learn new spells, especially with the meagre amounts of essence we are allowed to use. Sometimes I despair of ever being allowed to become a full Gifter. It is said that in the old days, it took but a year to reach full Gifter status. I'm coming up on the end of my third year now, and still haven't mastered all that I need to."

"Is that because there's more to learn, or because you are given less time to learn it?"

Ashley shouldered his bucket, and Tabitha walked with him from the well. He considered her question for a moment. "I've heard that the more extreme spells have been outlawed by the Rector, so we don't learn those any more. Only the spells of healing, light, and warding are taught, but the level of perfection required of us seems to rise every year. I know my spells work as they are, yet the Rector always finds fault. He is the Rector, so I suppose he knows what he is doing."

"How is it that you have meagre amounts of essence to work with? We're in the Dovecote!"

"The Rector—is very strict with the sprites. Like yesterday morning, even with the bloom of Light we had during the Morningsong, we got no more than usual for practice. The extra was sent with Father Onassis to assist Keegan in Fendwarrow."

They approached the sloping wall of the main Dovecote building. A rope dangled from somewhere beyond the high curve of the roof.

"You had more sprites than normal?" Tabitha asked.

"A whole wave of Light," Ashley answered, a smile on his lips. "We still can't figure out why it happened. It was as if the sprites unified in a great pattern for a moment, and when that fell apart, the Hall was filled with Light. The Rector couldn't explain it. He became quite angry, and accused one of the older Gifters of using the forbidden spells."

"Something like the Spriteblind spell?"

Ashley stopped so abruptly that water sloshed from the bucket, wetting both of them.

"Damn! Sorry, sorry," he apologised, setting the bucket down with both hands. "What do you know about the Spriteblind spell?"

She didn't know why she had spoken of it, only that she had wondered about the forbidden spells of old, and the song-scrolls her mother had left. When she was silent, Ashley bent to tie the rope to the bucket, but he continued to watch her as he did so. Tabitha had the unnerving feeling of fingers brushing over her mind.

"I don't know much," she said. "It was mentioned once, by my mother."

And I haven't forgotten that pattern or the words.

Ashley was watching her intently, his eyes wide.

"You know the Spriteblind spell," he pressed.

How does he know?

She couldn't deny the outright truth. Besides, she wanted Ashley to be her friend. It wouldn't do to begin a friendship on lies.

"I know something of it," she hedged.

"Teach me. Please. I'd give anything to learn that old spell. It's one of the forbidden ones."

He wants me to teach him? I'm the one who needs to learn spells, and they won't teach me until Yearsend.

A possibility bloomed in Tabitha's mind like a spring flower.

"A trade," she said, smiling broadly. "I'll show you the patterns of the Spriteblind, if you teach me the first spells you learned."

The excitement slipped from Ashley's face.

"Oh, I can't, Tabitha! I would have to defy the Rector's order, and I'd also have to steal Light essence for you to experiment with. I'd be in such trouble if I was caught. I'd be expelled!"

"I know Truthfury and Flameburst as well."

"The burning carriage. That was you?" His jaw hung with slack incredulity, then he caught himself. "We all thought it was the Shadowcaster, that he started a fire to drive you out of it. You cast the Flameburst?"

Tabitha gave him a little nod. The intensity of his gaze was unnerving. She couldn't tell if he was angry, or excited.

"Hah!" He exclaimed, and clapped his hands. "Hah! I knew it. I knew it! Damn them, they make it seem so complicated, and shroud it all in mystery. Yet a raw novice can master the old spells." He looked around suddenly, as if worried that someone might have heard his outburts.

"I wouldn't say that I'd mastered anything," Tabitha warned. "The fire went all over the show, not where I had intended."

"But you cast it, nonetheless!" he exclaimed. "How much training did you have from your mother?"

"I saw the pattern once before I used it on the Kingsbridge. Mother never taught me, it wasn't allowed."

"Hah! I knew it! Simple as the Flicker spell. Or otherwise you've got an enormous talent for being a Lightgifter. Spriteblind, Truthfury, and Flameburst," he repeated slowly, grinning, "for the spells of Courier, Healall, and Shield."

He's offering to trade!

Three basic spells for the three she knew. It seemed an unbalanced trade, until she considered the risk Ashley would be taking to train her. She wasn't sure she could remember all three patterns perfectly, anyway.

"When?" she asked.

"I can't risk it until this week has run its course, I have too little time. If I were caught while I was supposed to be on ghost duty I'd have double punishment, without a doubt. But on Saturday, I'll come and find you."

The flaw in her plan became glaringly apparent.

"Oh dear! I don't have a moment free from dawn till the Evencall, Ashley."

"But after the Evencall?"

Tabitha shot him a puzzled glance. She knew that once the Evencall was sung, the corridor to their bedrooms was barred by an oak door; the men's corridor likewise. There was no way to meet after the Evencall.

"Do you sleep in the women's wing, in one of the servants rooms?" Ashley asked.

"Yes, but –"

"Then I'll find you. Make sure you stay awake on Saturday night. I'll come when I'm sure the others in your wing are asleep."

He shot her a broad, dazzling smile. "Now get back to work, ghost, or you'll still be sweeping come dinnertime, and I will be wanting food, not dust, to fill my belly."

He laughed, grabbed the rope, and began to scale the sheer wall. Tabitha swung her broom at him in mock rebuke, but he had already scaled the rope beyond her range. She noticed that the rope had knots tied into it at regular spaces. When he reached the domed level of the roof, he stood, and dragged the bucket up after himself.

She hoped she was never set the chore of cleaning the windows to the Hall of Sky. It looked terrifying.

About as terrifying as the consequences of being caught in the spell-trade, she mused.

She hefted her broom in her hand. She was determined to wade through the slow week of chores without losing hope. Saturday held a solid promise. She really was going to become a Lightgifter.

◆ ———————◆

Tabitha lay in bed, listening to the gentle breathing of her roommates, trying to stop the room from swirling in and out of focus.

The chores which had been stacked upon her throughout the week had left her feeling exhausted long before the Evencall was called each night, and although she had fallen into her bed with the intent to sleep, her misgivings about the meeting with Ashley had kept her awake, so that she never slept enough, and each morning was more of a struggle against the clutching blankets.

Now that the meeting was upon her, her nervousness had given way to fatalism. If she was caught, so be it, she could not go on at the Dovecote without learning something of the Light, and who was the Rector to punish her for wanting to be a Lightgifter anyway? Ashley did it for his own reasons, it was his problem if he was caught, that guilt wouldn't be hers.

She knew also that these were irritable thoughts born of her tiredness, but that didn't stop them plaguing her mind.

Maybe he won't come at all, then I can sleep.

But her curiosity wouldn't allow her to sleep either. Saturday night stretched on, the moon rose, the room spun lazily in her vision, and Tabitha truly began to believe that the young half-knot wouldn't come.

A single sprite stung her nose with a small puff of Light and warmth. She felt the faded essence slide down her face like a grain of sand. A flickering illumination and an area of thicker shadows beyond the door told her that someone waited in the corridor.

Ashley. He didn't forget.

She slipped from the bed, her heart suddenly racing. She wore a tunic and leggings already, having donned them before pretending to retire. The servants did not alter the rhythm of their sleeping susuruss.

Ashley held a delicate swarm of Light in his hand, bound in a Flicker spell. The flame threw strange patterns on his face. He placed a finger on his lips, and led Tabitha down the corridor, away from the Hall of Sky.

The last doorway before the baths was the entrance to the laundry room, where Ashley ducked inside. The residual heat from the bath-furnace next door warmed the room through one cracked and distended wall. Hanging robes on a line appeared eerie in the wavering light, like a company of disembodied Gifters witnessing their furtive arrival.

Stacks of laundry were piled on the floor and the high table. Two disused garment-stands stood in a corner, looking like harshly-pruned fir trees. Ashley pulled the door closed with infinite care. He dropped some towels on the floor and shifted them to seal the bottom of the doorjamb, before approaching Tabitha.

"We've got to be as quiet as mice," he whispered to her. "I don't want any of the women to wake, or to see the work of light under the door."

Tabitha nodded to show that she understood.

"Can you summon the essence?" Ashley asked. He offered his palm to her, where the sprites played in the binding of the Flicker spell.

She reached for the Light, and called out softly in the words of the summoning. The pattern was a simple double-loop, the only one she had known before her mother's song-scrolls. She had summoned before, on the Kingsbridge. Yet this time, it didn't work. She tried again. The sprites remained in Ashley's left hand, an unbroken Flicker spell.

She looked at Ashley with pleading eyes. "Why doesn't it work?" she asked, a little louder than she had intended.

"Shhhh." He tapped his right hand against his Gifter's orb, where it glistened against his throat. "You must focus your will in the Lightstone."

She had grown into the habit of keeping hers hidden, since the Rector's command. The more she thought about the orb, the more it cast a soft glow through her neckerchief.

When she tried again, the sprites came to her hand with ease. They danced over her upturned palm, waiting for a spell command.

"The Healall. What's the pattern?" she asked.

In an instant, Ashley had the sprites in his hand. Tabitha bristled.

My sprites.

She summoned them again, repeating the pattern and command. The sprites began to leave Ashley's hand, then curved up and back to his palm, where they remained.

"The clearer your pattern, the tighter your focus, the more success you will have wresting control from me. But wait!" he cautioned, hiding his Light-laden hand behind his back. "Let me show you the pattern. We can test your will another time."

Of course, he needs the sprites to demonstrate with.

Tabitha subdued her gritty jealousy.

Mercy, I'm more tired than I'd care to admit.

Ashley brought his hands together, then drew them slowly apart again. The Light was stretched to form a surface between them. As Ashley's mind guided the sprites, so they resolved into a recognisable pattern, like an enlarged honeycomb.

"But that's so simple!" she exclaimed, suddenly ecstatic. "It's the same six-sided thing. It's like a badly made sheep pen."

"Shhhh. There's a twist in it, see?" He focused on the sprites for a while, and the pattern changed to hold only one hexagon, enlarged. There were two twists in the pattern, opposite each other.

"Let me try." Tabitha tried to summon the sprites from his hand, but he kept them firmly in his command.

Ashley gave her a warning look. "A good healer makes a very fine network, so fine you don't see the individual patterns, it just looks like a haze of Light. The more times you can repeat the pattern in your spell, the more powerful the healing."

Tabitha wasn't interested in his explanation, she wanted the Light back. The Ring warmed on her finger, and the laundry room filled with detail and sensations.

What had been empty darkness began to swirl with faint currents, as if the air retained the disturbances of people long gone. Heavy scents of soap, fabric, the wood of the table, warmed mortar, even the faint odours of the hanging robes came to her. Tabitha's enhanced awareness brought an overwhelming flood to her senses.

Ashley Logán had become sharply defined, she could see every detail of his face, every nuance of his patient expression. In his hand, the Light essence appeared brighter and more delicate than ever before. Tabitha could identify individual sprites, the tiny spinning particles, little containers of energy, harbouring a fleck of Light within. Fine tendrils of Ashley's will wrapped around the essence, holding it in his command. It was a simple thing to part the threads of his command with her own, and then to summon the Light through the gap created.

It's just a matter of seeing what you're doing, she marvelled.

The Light formed a sphere around her right hand.

"What shall I heal?"

Ashley looked surprised, then frustrated.

"Why don't you heal your own tiredness?" he grumbled.

She was going to snap an answer at him, but she knew he was right. Her mood was as unstable as ever; she had gone from being angry to joyous to angry again in a few moments.

"I can cast the Healall on myself?"

Ashley nodded.

"How do the sprites know what to heal?"

"Any lack or discomfort within is really just a lack of Light. The sprites will fill that deficit. The more you can hold the target in mind, the more concentrated the healing is, but once they're in the pattern of the Healall, the sprites will heal that area on their own. Don't worry too much, you're going to make mistakes in your first spell, just try it, see what happens."

Mistakes? I'll show him a first spell he won't forget.

Tabitha recalled the pattern which Ashley had demonstrated. The Healall spell grew between her hands, a lace of Light, growing ever finer as she repeated the hexagonal fundamental at its edges. She sensed the delicate shapes and was able to refine them long after they had become too small to see with the naked eye, as her demand drew more awareness from the Ring.

Yet the increased sensitivity had a side effect—awareness of the very small brought awareness of the very big as well. Her senses were wide open, and she was aware of things beyond the limits of the room. A woman turned, restless in her bed. The Hall of Sky was quiet, the Source a flickering giant of pure moonlight. Men snored, the kitchens smelled of flour, oil and thyme. The Dovecote was a smooth dome capped by clean windows. There were roaches in the drainpipes, ants marching through the foundations.

She had reached her limit. The Healall pattern rippled, like a pool of reflected sunlight, then seperated all at once, guided by her dispersing attention.

Zing!

There was a brief flash, and the smallest sting of warmth, but nothing more. Streaks of light flew past her head like hurried fireflies, and disappeared into the ceiling. Almost all of the Light had missed her, and Tabitha felt no less tired than before. But the sudden abandonment of the sprites left a room as black as pitch.

"Bugger," Ashley said in the darkness. "I think you've used up all the Light essence."

"Is that normal?"

"No," he whispered. "No, the essence fades, one spell-casting is never enough to drain all the Light from it and make clear essence. You must have sent the sprites all through the Dovecote, everywhere but here."

"So my spell was a flop?"

Ashley chuckled. "I think you may have made the air better to breathe."

He's being nice.

"How much of a flop?"

Ashley's gentle laughter bubbled through his words. "I have never seen such a disastrous spell. The weave was tight, but even my worst mishaps have not had such a wide focus. You were supposed to heal yourself. How big do you think you are?"

Tabitha was glad it was dark. He couldn't see her red face. They sat for a while in the dark without speaking.

I had the same problem with the Flameburst spell. I wanted to attack the Shadowcaster, but set fire to the whole carriage.

"I've just blown your chance to learn the Flameburst tonight, haven't I?"

Ashley didn't answer.

"Can't you get some more from the sconces?"

"I daren't take any more tonight, in case the Rector notices the lack in the morning. I've already siphoned from both corridor Flicker-spells."

The silence was thicker than the darkness between them.

"Ashley?"

"mm."

"You're not mad with me, are you?"

The chuckle she heard set her fears to rest. "I was just wondering what's going to happen when I teach you the Courier spell. We are going to have feathers all over the sky. No, don't worry about the sprites."

Tabitha heard him rise, and tiptoe toward the door. He cracked it open, and a faint of illumination came in from the corridor beyond.

"Come, there is nothing more to be done tonight," he whispered.

Tabitha followed him until they reached her room.

"How did you get here?" she asked.

"My secret," he answered. "Now go to bed. We'll meet as soon as I get the chance, so sleep while you can."

"Thank you, Ashley. It's your turn next time."

"I know." His grin was a faint altering of shadows. "That's why I'll be back."

He padded softly away toward the Hall of Sky. Tabitha strained to follow him with her eyes, but he was outlined against the Hall's paleness for only a moment, as he slipped through the distant door. A very soft thump and the sound of a bar being shifted into place announced his movements, then the silence was complete. Tabitha tried to guess how he achieved the meeting.

If he'd been in the Hall of Sky, he could have opened the door to the women's corridor and left it ajar. But how did he get into the Hall in the first place? Either he had found a way to unlock the bar from within the confines of the men's corridor, or he had a route that bypassed it entirely.

When her bed took her weight, it pulled her down into the blankets with merciless hunger. She snuggled into her pillow and accepted the fierce embrace of sleep. She was going to be a Lightgifter, despite what the Rector tried to put in her way.

◆ ──────── ◆

The kitchen was filled with clamour and steam all morning. There was only one sitting to be prepared for Sundays, and that was the Noonday meal. It was to be a minor feast, and the cook kept Tabitha running to and fro, fetching supplies from the stores, washing, peeling, drawing water, and finally kneading a mountain of dough under attendant clouds of flour. There was a levity to the conversation in the kitchen, the servants bantered with one another, even with the newcomer. Tabitha found herself enjoying the work for once.

"A whole procession of them, polished down to the buckles on their boots," said one of the kitchen hands, a solid girl with plaited hair who Tabitha knew only as Val.

Tabitha's interest was piqued, but she continued to pound the dough. She knew the cook beside her would be quick to scold; the good mood didn't reduce the amount of work that needed to be completed before noon.

"When did the Swords go by, Val?" the cook asked.

"The little hours o'morning. I was coming up from the waterfront."

"You mean coming up from your latest man," the cook interjected. The wry humour in her tone surprised Tabitha. She had always taken the cook to be as austere as a wrinkled lemon.

Val giggled. "No rules on Saturday nights for me," she said.

The cook grunted. "It's true, you missed a quiet night in the Dovecote. But the best sleep I've had in years."

"Where did the Swords go?" Tabitha asked, risking a question in light of the gay mood.

"Going to clean out Fendwarrow at last, I'll wager," replied Val. "Off on the Dwarrow road, ninety, one hundred horses."

Tabitha had to ask. "Was the Swordmaster with them?"

"The Swordmaster, he rode at the head of the squadron, and on his gauntlets were the words stitched 'beware, sinners, beware!', and he wore a purple flower in his hair." Val shot a mocking glance at

Tabitha, from across the bread-making table. "I don't know, luvvy. I was half a league away. Just saw the procession ride. Wish I could bag myself a Sword, one day," she ended dreamily. "Any one would do. They make a good wage, the King's men."

If the Swords had ridden out, Tabitha knew that Garyll would be with them. Their preparations for battle must be complete, the march on Ravenscroft had begun. She envisioned Garyll fighting in a pit filled with Morgloth, manic Shadowcasters all around, throwing spells of despair and darkness at the beleaguered Swordmaster and his men.

A sharp prod in the ribs accompanied the cook's scolding voice. "The bread's not going to bake of its own accord!"

Tabitha shook herself and set to work. The mountain of dough had to be separated into twenty hills. The fire beneath the ovens needed stoking. And when that was done, there was butter to churn from milk, oranges to squeeze, loaves to tend, and salt to break.

Yet nothing could distract her mind's eye from following a procession of Swords along the imaginary shore of Amberlake, to Fendwarrow and beyond. She was scolded three times before Noontime. It began to feel like a normal day in the kitchens again.

◆ ————— ◆

Sweeping the men's corridor, she had discovered, was best done when the half-knots were training outside, for the teachers would accompany them, and only a scribe or similar Gifter would wander by from time to time. She could get most of the dust out of the corridor and through the Hall's east door before the trample of many feet would render the task impossible.

The door which sealed the end of the corridor at night was the same as the one on the women's side of the Hall—thick, ironbound oak, crafted to seal tightly against the doorjamb. A heavy bar with a pin was used to hold the door in place. There was no way she could conceive of getting through such a door from within the corridor once it was closed. No blade would be able to lift the bar, the pin would prevent that. Yet Ashley Logán had found a way. The search for an answer to the puzzle helped to pass the time.

She checked all the rooms for secret passageways as she swept them, but each cubicle yielded the same simple structure—beds, chests, high windows, four solid walls, and a doorway each. There was nothing unusual about the bathrooms either. She began to wonder if

Ashley had hidden in the Hall of Sky all night just to be able to make their illicit meeting. It was a possibility, but the risk was enormous. She knew it was the Rector himself who came down into the Hall to open the doors in the morning, and he would surely be aware of someone in the Hall when he closed for the Evencall. There wasn't really anywhere to hide. There had to be a way around the door.

It was when Tabitha decided to search along the walls for any irregularities that the Ring began to augment her vision. She was straining to see something in the worked stone when she noticed footprints. All along the men's corridor were ghostly trails of footprints, a trampled confusion of many feet. She swept her broom over the nearest marks, but they remained, a faint glistening disturbance on the pale stone floor.

The Ring was warm, and she knew that she was using its power, so she guessed it was something peculiar about the Ring, an extension of its clarity. The footprints hadn't been visible to her when she had been sweeping, yet now that she ranged out with her senses, they came into vision. She walked a way down the corridor, then looked to where her own feet had passed. Overlaid on the fading patterns beneath, were brighter prints matching her own.

The many prints below had to be traces of traffic, of the Gifters and half-knots who had emerged from their beds that morning, or walked to their rooms during the day. The Ring was allowing her to see the delicate imprints of their presence.

There was one set of footprints that deviated from the common traffic routes. Someone had stood close to the wall near the oak door, beside a design of engraved ivy leaves. Once she was standing in that place, her sharpened gaze found the faintest of cracks running through the wall, a hairline imperfection that scribed the outline of a door.

She was suddenly certain that the footprints belonged to Ashley Logán. She had found his secret access.

◆ —————— ◆

Mistress Wyniss gave Tabitha Wednesday afternoon off, and for the first time since her arrival in the Cote she wanted to play her lyre. The lift in her heart, to be awarded free time after the seemingly endless grind of labour, was enough to sing about.

Then Ashley found her, and showed her the sprites saved from his training session. All thoughts of singing fell by the wayside. Ashley seemed nervous to talk to her in the open. He led her to his private place, high in the wall of the Dovecote. The climb was scary, but the alcove, when they reached it, proved to be secure.

There was no rim to the recess, but it formed what could have been a balcony for the window set deeper in the stone, and as such was tall and wide enough for the two of them to sit a comfortable distance apart. Iron bars sealed the window, and the room beyond was small and mostly gloomy bare stone. They were high enough to be on the third floor of the Cote, but if the Rector had ever used the room behind the bars, Tabitha reckoned it hadn't been during the last five years. The chamber smelled faintly of cobwebs and disuse.

The view was worth the climb. A silken tree hid the grounds below behind rustling white leaves. The green western horizon from Fynn's Tooth to the Great Forest was visible through the uppermost boughs. Bright towers of cloud filled the sky. To the right, the roofs of Levin dropped away steeply, to reveal the snaking foam of the Storms River in the distance, as it wended its way through coloured spring fields. It was such a clear day, she could even see the haze of River's End, where the mighty falls threw moisture to the air at the northern rim of Eyri.

The thrill of vertigo gnawed at her stomach, heightening her awareness of the splendour—it was a perfect day to set her first dove to flight. But she just couldn't seem to master the Courier spell.

"But it tickles!" she squealed, the essence falling from her hands.

"Shh," urged Ashley. "We're hidden from sight up here, but not from sound." The sprites collected around his hand when he summoned them.

"You have to keep the flow going through the pattern," Ashley pointed out.

"It's got to flow?"

"Yes, it's like a river contained by the pattern. Look." He wove the sprites into an egg-shaped basket of Light threads, and spoke the words to activate the Courier. The sprites swelled to the shape of a neat little dove, which fluttered its wings a few times before settling on his hand.

"Find Tabitha Serannon," he whispered into its ear. "Tell her it's Ashley's turn with the Flameburst now."

Ashley's dove hopped over the stone to Tabitha.

"Alight, messenger, and deliver your word," she said, offering her hand as a perch. The Courier flew up to her palm, and exploded into sprites once more. The Light essence was slightly dulled, but there was still ample to work with.

"It's Ashley's turn with the Flameburst now," echoed the soft message of the Courier. He grinned at her. "Show me the pattern again, I must have missed something the first time."

The technique of shaping the essence into a spell fundamental had become easier with practice. The Lightstone at her neck seemed to have something to do with it, for when she copied Ashley's mannerism of lifting the sprites to the stone, the pattern she intended formed faster. The clearer she could recall the pattern in her mind, the clearer it formed in her hands. It was focusing the spell on a target that was the complicated part for Tabitha. She dared not risk another episode of wide focus with a spell, particularly this spell. So she just brought the sprites into the pattern of the Flameburst, and held them there for Ashley to study.

"Bejiggered if it isn't the most intricate pattern I've ever tried to copy," he said, staring at the convoluted threads of Light in Tabitha's hand. "How do you remember it all?"

She hadn't really thought about it much. She had seen the spell in her mother's scroll. She had used it once. She remembered it.

When Ashley attempted to cast the Flameburst spell, it resulted in a widening circle of sparks, which flared briefly and went out. The sprites fell to the stone between them, a duller shade of Light.

"Bugger."

"No worse than my Courier," whispered Tabitha.

Ashley tried three more times. Tabitha felt the heat of the last one against her face, but the flames were still no bigger than fireflies.

"How did you ever learn this spell so quickly?" Ashley asked.

"I—"

She couldn't tell Ashley about the Ring. It was a secret too strange.

"I've got a good memory," she offered.

She wished Twardy Zarost were around to ask. Although his answers were as crooked as a stick, he was the only one who knew something about the Ring. It seemed to be playing an ever greater part in her life.

Suddenly, she realised her error with the Courier spell. She had been confusing Ashley's pattern and her memories of the one her mother had used. The older memories were imperfect, made up of her childhood recollections of vague patterns in the sprites, seen when she had not worn the Lightstone or the Ring. She discarded those, and was left with the clear pattern Ashley had offered.

The little dove formed perfectly in her hand, a delicate creature of Light.

"I did it!" she exclaimed. She lofted her hands, ready to throw the dove into the freedom of air.

"Wait! It has to have a target!"

She brought her hand back just in time. She whispered into the Courier's ear. It flew a brief circle, decided on Ashley, and dissolved when he accepted it.

"If you hadn't done that," he explained, "the poor thing would have flown all around Eyri, looking for nobody. We'd have lost those sprites until they faded completely to clear essence."

A distant voice echoed from within the volume of the Dovecote, a plaintive, repetitive call. Ashley scuttled to his feet. "That's the crier for the end of break, I've got to go back to class." He stood at the rim of the alcove, in preparation for climbing down. "You're welcome to stay up here and practice on your Couriers. Just send them to yourself, and they'll do a short hop before dissolving."

"When shall we meet again?" she asked.

"Try to find me when you get time off in the day." He lowered himself over the edge, and found the first foothold to balance upon.

"Why not at night?"

"I'm worried about sounds carrying in the quiet. I tried to come to you once, since last time, but the door to the women's corridor had a new wedge closing it, one that would have made a noise releasing. I think the Rector suspects something. Do you realise the kind of trouble we'll get into if we're caught?"

"Why don't you just use the door in the ivy-pattern?" she asked.

Ashley looked thunderstruck.

"How did you find out about that?"

"I've got a sharp eye," she said, slowly.

Ashley smiled, broad and deep. "You are proving to be quite an exceptional ghost. I fear we shall all look like novices when you become a Gifter."

"How does the door open?"

He pulled himself up to the alcove again. "So you found it without knowing how to open it, without using the sprites?"

She nodded. He looked impressed.

"It opens with the Light. If you throw the sprites at that section in the wall, they cling to the outline of the door. But there's nothing there to see with the naked eye."

"There's one on the women's side as well."

"Then we *can* meet!" he exclaimed. He considered something for a moment. His eyes were a sparkling blue.

"Can you keep a secret?"

Tabitha nodded.

"There's a place I've been trying to find, another doorway. I have seen clues to it all over the Dovecote, but can't find the access. It is called the Inner Sanctum, and no one speaks of it, I don't think anyone else knows about it, but I know it must be there. It might be marked with this sign." He summoned the sprites from where they lay on the alcove floor, and created a pattern in his hands with them.

A curving, double rune, like two fish with overlapping tails. Tabitha recognised it at once. The symbol was carved on her lyre.

"It's called the Heart," he explained. "But I believe it also stands for the Inner Sanctum, where the secrets of the Sage are rumoured to be kept. Somewhere in the Dovecote there might be a door leading to the Heart, used in the old times. Maybe you can find it."

"I'll try," she said uncertainly. If nobody knew about the Inner Sanctum, then there would be no recent footprints leading to it. It would be difficult for her to find.

"Don't tell anyone about it," he added. Then, as if he had suddenly remembered the crier's call long past, he scuttled downwards.

"Take the essence to the channel in the Hall of Sky when you're finished," he called up to her. "That's where all the other pale sprites are left. Try not to drain all the Light out of it, or it won't listen to your summoning. They get recharged with the Morningsong."

He reached the ground, waved discreetly, and jogged off to find the class of half-knots which had surely begun already.

A hidden place called the Heart, marked by the double-rune. That Yzell had carved the same rune into her lyre was intriguing. She picked the lyre up, and ran her fingers over the engraving. It was evidently an old rune, long forgotten. *How old?* she wondered.

She practised the Courier spell, drawing the essence into the fundamental pattern, refining it, then setting the bird to flight. Despite Ashley's caution, she failed to exercise sufficient restraint. One moment she was molding the glowing essence into a Courier, the next it dissolved in her hands, clear, empty essence, all the Light spent.

It pooled beside her on the stone floor of the alcove, a patch of clarity not unlike the Ring—she could touch it, but it was as transparent as water. She could not collect it in her hands, for it spread beneath her touch, then reformed into the puddle as soon as her fingers withdrew.

Clear essence. The end of a sprite's life.

A breeze rustled through the silken tree. Strange, she thought, that no sprites danced in its leaves, as they did in the rest of Eyri. Here at the Dovecote, all the sprites were used in the training, or taken away by the Gifters on missions of healing. She hoped the Rector wouldn't miss another handful of sprites, for there was no way to take the clear essence with her.

She gave up trying to collect the puddle of clear essence from the stone floor of the alcove, and began the daunting climb down the outside of the building. Going down was worse than coming up. Ashley had made it look a lot easier than it was.

♦ ———————— ♦

Late that afternoon, Tabitha visited the Hall of Sky. In part it was to marvel at the grand architecture, and to witness the crystalline beauty of the Source. But in truth she hoped to find the access to the Inner Sanctum, and surprise Ashley with her skill. The prize of the hidden door would repay in some way the risk Ashley had taken on her behalf to bring the sprites and train her in secret.

Tabitha decided that the Sanctum had to lie close to the Hall of Sky, for it was the centre of the Lightgifters' monastery. The Hall was vast in circumference. Beginning at the east-door, it took almost an hour to search along the pale stone walls, where the reflections from the Source formed delicate traceries of light. She had to move every time someone passed nearby, lest they considered her interest in the walls to be curious.

Only in two places was there anything remarkable in the smooth masonry. Where Ashley's secret door opened from the men's corridor, and at the similar access leading from the women's corridor, the stone revealed a fine incision. Tabitha could only notice the doors when she drew on the power of the Ring to aid her sight.

Having exhausted the walls for clues, Tabitha stepped over the channel where pale sprites already awaited their replenishment, and strode onto the white marble of the Hall's centre-circle.

The Scribbillarre, Ashley called it.

Complex engravings surrounded the dais upon which the Source stood. Words, runes, random lines and intricate patterns had been cut into the floor with precise artistry. It was a difficult place to sweep, that much she knew from the days gone by.

The moment she began to pace the Scribbillarre, she knew her task was impossible. She had no experience in the old runes of Eyri, and not enough experience of Lightgifting to identify any spells in the patterns, should they be there. The infrequent words offered no clues to the Heart or Inner Sanctum.

She used the augmentation of the Ring to search for abnormalities in the floor. An overwhelming number of ghostly footprints appeared. They tracked all over the Hall of Sky in heavy concentration, like the prints of sheep in the mud around a feeding trough.

She tried to ignore the traces of traffic, to see beneath the confusion. Nowhere amongst the small glyphs and sigils was there a sign of the double-rune she sought. The late afternoon sun warmed her cheek softly. She stood quite still beside the Source, mesmerised by the intricate play of light and shadow on the floor. She allowed her eye be drawn where it wanted.

Time flowed like a river, and the people using the Hall flickered by.

If anyone thought she was simple-minded, they didn't interrupt her reverie to tell her so.

The sun sank to the western horizon. The brilliance of the Source began to fade.

At last she realised what it was she was staring at. The pattern of the Heart-rune stood before her on the floor in shadow. It was a giant pattern, spanning the entire Hall in its breadth. The way it overlapped the edges of other designs and the seams of floor made it difficult to identify. She doubted she would have seen anything had it not been for the Ring. The way in which the fluctuating light of the Source had been visible to her eyes had revealed the only area in which the scattered illumination did not fall over time.

The twisted rune of the Heart, across the entire Hall. And in its centre, in the place where the two tails overlapped, was a square scribed in the floor, marked at each corner by a six-pointed star. There were many stars scattered across the Scribbillarre, but Tabitha knew she would not forget those particular four and how they were placed. For when she scrutinised that part of the marble apron, she identified four perfect lines, linking the four stars, lines as barely visible as the outlines of the other portals she knew of.

There was a door in the floor of the Hall of Sky.

♦ ——————♦

At the evening meal, she ensured that she served Ashley's end of the table first. She found a short moment to lean close to him.

"I've found the door."

He choked on his stew.

"Meet me tonight in the Hall," he whispered, between coughs.

The sparkle in his eyes was all the thanks she needed.

♦ ——————♦

Moonlight, a soft glow against the corridor beneath her bare feet. Her indrawn breath sounded loud in the Dovecote's silence. Her heartbeat was sure to wake everyone from even the deepest slumber. Yet no one rose to stop her as she tiptoed to the oak door, and no one noted how she stole sprites from the sconce. She worked the Light into the outline of the secret door.

Tabitha cringed when the door opened with a sucking implosion. It was terribly loud; she was certain the Rector was descending the stairs from his high rooms already, woken by the breach of the Hall of Sky. She sighed out one ragged breath, then another.

Silence.

At last she summoned the nerve to step through the door. The frame glistened with the sprites she had placed, so that it was a frame of Light she stepped through. The stone door was cool to the touch, and swung effortlessly away.

A figure, standing suddenly close in the gloom, made her heart stop altogether.

"It's me," whispered a familiar voice. He pulled a cloud of light from the deep sleeves of his robe.

Ashley.

Relief flooded through her legs.

"Bring your sprites with you," he whispered. "You can open the door from this side as well, but we shouldn't leave them open, in case —"

His voice tailed off, but Tabitha had no desire to finish the sentence. They both knew that the consequences of being caught in the Hall of Sky would be dire. She summoned her sprites from the frame, and pushed the stone door gently to. It sealed with a thud both as soft and clear as distant thunder.

When they crossed onto the Scribbillarre, Tabitha felt as if she were treading across a pool of silvered water, and that her feet might break through the surface at any moment should they be placed too heavily. The Hall was larger than ever, stiller than ever, colder than ever. It seemed that all the stars of the night sky were reflected in the Scribbillarre. The designs that had been so memorable in the daylight were altered under the moon, the patterns which had bracketed them seemed larger and more indistinct. She began to wonder if the Sanctum was only meant to be found during the day, while sunlight cast the subtle marking pattern upon the floor.

Ashley shifted nervously while she searched, but he said nothing. She was grateful for that; they stood exposed on the white Scribbillarre, like mice upon whom the fearsome owl might descend at any time. They shared many a nervous glance to the Rector's room beyond the highest level of stairs.

Finally Tabitha identified the square cut of the trapdoor with its four marker-stars. She knelt, and sprinkled the first of the sprites to the four corners with a shaking hand. Ashley completed the rest of the outline.

The stone ground gently as the section sank away. A puff of warmer air escaped with a hiss and blew dust against their faces. Tabitha fought a sneeze, willing herself to make no sound. The square stone trapdoor rested no more than a finger's breadth below the surface. Ashley reached out a tentative hand, and pushed against the inner slab. It sank further, then returned to near the surface when he released it. He tested it with a leg, and the stone sank far beneath the floor. He gingerly transferred more of his weight onto the stone, and so descended until his head was below Tabitha's knees where she knelt. He came to a rest there.

Ashley cast a Flicker spell. The dancing light revealed a stairway, leading down into thick darkness. Tabitha hugged her chest. Now that the way was open to the Heart, she didn't know if she wanted to step down into the yawning maw.

It was decided upon a sneeze. She had fought the effect of the dust resolutely, but at last her nose betrayed her. She erupted with a muffled blast.

She looked up in horror, expecting to see the Rector's round face peering over the high railing of the third floor.

Ashley whispered sharply to her, and she scrambled into the hole. Ashley took some of her weight, and guided her feet down to the stone. As soon as they stepped clear of the entry slab, it rose up, borne on a rocker arm as thick as a tree trunk.

"The sprites!" warned Tabitha. Ashley summoned them just in time—they slipped past the slab as it swung into place. The entrance to the Heart sealed with a dull thud above them.

"The door! How do we open it again?" Tabitha asked in a panicked whisper.

"It doesn't matter. At least we're hidden." Ashley raised his Flicker spell high. Set underneath the rocker arm was a large ring. Ashley mimed the action of pulling it downward. "We'll need sprites to break the seal, same as above," he guessed aloud.

Tabitha sneezed.

They hurried to be away from the entrance. The stairs were steep, but dry with dust, and their footing was certain. There was a hand-rail, cut from the stone wall. The passage had none of the polished look of the Dovecote architecture—rather, it was rough, the walls uneven, as if constructed in haste, or secret. The illumination of the sprites did not penetrate more than a few steps down the stairway. Thick shadows lurked below them.

They descended.

The passage split in two upon a narrow wedge of stone. To the left, the stairs continued downwards, wide and evenly spaced. To the right, the passage was constricted, and the indistinct stairs seemed to be broken and treacherous, leading only to a blank wall.

Tabitha's senses were sharpened by her instinctive fear of darkness. She strained to see in the flickering half-light. The passage to the right had an unfinished look to it, a feeling of abandonment, or destruction. The Ring brought her a sense of foreboding from that place, an emanation of something unsettling.

A shiver crept up her spine.

What if this inner sanctum is a tomb or a trap? What are we doing down here?

The more she ranged outward with the Ring, the more unsettled she became. There was something in the right passage. A movement, though her ears told her of silence, and her eyes showed her that the jagged stones beneath the jumping shadows were still.

There was nothing there, and yet it moved.

"Let's go left," suggested Ashley. "It doesn't look as if that leads anywhere."

She wanted to avoid the strange aura of the right passage as well, but it had begun to intrigue her. The Ring warmed as she stared into the dark cleft. There was nothing to see, but there was something to sense.

Ashley descended into the left fork, bearing the Flicker spell away. The mystery within the right fork lured her. A movement, like a current in the air, curling to form a pattern of nothing but motion. The clarity of her senses brought the shape of it from the darkness.

The Heart rune. It marked the passage they should take.

"Ashley, wait!" she cried.

But her call came too late to save him from the trap.

A rock thumped to the floor, somewhere deeper in the passage. A ball of sprites came shooting from the darkness like a sparkling comet. Ashley backed up a step in surprise, but did not ward himself from the Light in time. It struck his face, and formed a glowing network over his head. Then the spell matured, and the flash of its climax was blinding in the gloom, even where Tabitha stood.

Ashley wailed and fell to his back. His Flicker spell scattered, the sprites thrown like sand upon the stairs. Darkness swelled from the depths of the unknown cavern, hiding everything but the faint glow of essence.

"Ashley!" Tabitha cried. She wanted to run to him, but could manage no more than a crouched hobble, for fear of losing her steps in the gloom.

Ashley moaned, his hands to his face.

"The Creator have mercy!" he cried. "I've been blinded. I've been blinded! Tabitha!"

"I'm right here," she whispered, reaching him and putting a hand on his shoulder. He found her hand, and gripped it with both of his.

"I can't see! I can't see!"

His eyes were wide open, unfocused, ranging around to find Tabitha's face. His pupils shone with an inner glow. His hold on her arm was desperately strong. She couldn't think of anything else to do but to sit there with him.

"Should I try a Healall?" she asked at length.

"No! No more Light!" His pleading expression was made all the more awful by the radiance behind his eyes. Tabitha moved herself closer, set his head on her lap, and smoothed his hair away from his face. She tried to ignore her childish fears of beasts crouching in the gloom. She didn't know the pattern for the Flicker spell. With Ashley crippled, there was no way to defy the darkness.

"Was that a Spriteblind spell?" she asked.

"I suppose so," he said at length. His grip eased slightly. "Then it's temporary." He shook his head from side to side, and moaned at the result.

"Is it painful?"

"Yes?" he answered, his voice thick with uncertainty. "No." Some of the tension left his body. "No," he repeated, "but it's terrible, Tabitha, like staring at the sun. My whole head is filled—with Light, and nothing else."

"Can you recast the Flicker spell?" she asked hesitantly.

"Why? Oh." He summoned the sprites, and the flame of essence formed above his palm. It was as Tabitha had hoped—the Lightgifter's skill did not rely on sight, only on the words and guiding mental pattern. At least one of them could see now.

The stairway was clear. She didn't hesitate to help Ashley to his feet, and guide him upwards, away from the passage he had chosen in error. When they came to the fork in the passage again, Tabitha halted. The Heart-rune was still there, as a disturbance in the air, deep in the cleft. It appealed to her curiosity. A secretive charm.

"I'm going to look in the other passage. Will you wait here?"

"No, Tabitha!" Ashley gripped her arm tighter. "What if there's a trap in there?"

"There won't be," she said, knowing the truth of it. "You went down the wrong passage."

"How did you know that? I heard you warn me, but too late."

"I can see—a guiding mark in this one."

"I saw nothing there."

"I have sharp eyes."

"And I—see even less than I did before," he ended bitterly.

She gave his hand a squeeze. "Will you wait here for me?"

"No." Ashley squared his shoulders, and stared her down. His blindness caused him to look slightly amiss of where she stood. "If you're going in there, I'm coming with you. You need my light."

It was slow going. The steps were badly hewn, some were missing altogether. The walls slanted increasingly inwards, forcing them to walk hunched over, using their hands to push away from the rough boulders. Ashley's blindness, compounded by the fact that he had to keep one hand free to hoist the Flicker spell aloft, made it difficult to lead him. But they came upon a sharp turn in the passage, where the rock underfoot levelled, and they could walk easier. They passed through a narrow entrance, and were suddenly in a small, rounded chamber.

Tabitha gasped.

"Tabitha, what is it?" Ashley whispered.

"A man," she answered, "the figure of a man, in Light."

Facing them across the chamber was a robed Lightgifter, an old man with long, sparkling beard and a thick mane of white hair. The figure didn't move, but the sprites did, swarming through the outline to create the shifting illusion, a shell around empty space. The spell was reminiscent of a Courier dove, yet this was a masterful version— the figure showed fine detail, down to the individual cords in the rope at the man's waist, the wrinkles of care in his brow, and the wise cast of his eyes.

"What does he look like?" Ashley whispered.

Tabitha vocalised what she could see.

"The Sage, you're describing the Sage!"

"You mean the founder of the Lightgifters?" Tabitha said, awed.

There was the faintest trace of warmth from the figure. Although the sprites were plentiful, they were pale, and offered little illumination.

"Damn! I wish I could see this, to be sure. It is rumoured the Sage's messenger birds were eagles, so great was his skill in the Light. If it is anyone, it is him you see."

"Could a spell last that long?" The Sage had been dead for over two hundred years.

"The Sage was powerful. It would make sense, it ties in with the references to the Heart I've studied—all in the first days of the Dovecote, in his time. Our skill has diminished greatly since then. No one has ever equalled the Sage's mastery of the essence."

The Sage's apparition stared fixedly at the intruders.

The wise founder of the Lightgifters had created a spell which allowed his form to be hidden for centuries. The secretive chamber was a strange place for a monument.

She felt unworthy of being there. She had no right to breach the inner sanctum.

Tabitha averted her gaze from the figure, and glanced around the rest of the chamber. It was smooth-walled, womb-like and empty. There was no exit from the chamber save the opening they had entered through. The only thing they could possibly find in the Heart was the glowing figure, the spell that the Sage had left behind.

Maybe the entire figure is a messenger.

The more she thought of it, the more sense it made. A messenger, left to convey a most valuable secret to the future. Knowing its purpose didn't make her any more worthy of receiving the Sage's message, though. She felt watched, as if someone was probing her thoughts.

Strangely, Ashley seemed to have been mulling over the same possibility as Tabitha.

"Alight, messenger, and deliver your word," he said aloud, and extended his hand. The words sounded hollow and disrespectful in the presence of the Sage. The figure didn't move.

"Who could be more worthy of receiving the Sage's message than those in service of the Light?" Ashley asked, as if by way of explanation.

How does he know I was feeling unworthy?

She stepped away from Ashley, suddenly nervous of being close to his uncanny prescience. She approached the figure of the Sage, and scrutinised the fine weave of the sprites. They formed a near-perfect surface, smooth and continuous, from where the robe touched the floor, to the crown of his head, from fingertip to fingertip. Except in one place. There was a delicate twist to the sprites that were set in the centre of the Sage's Lightstone. She reached out, and touched the Heart-rune there. The Sage collapsed over her hand. Sprites scattered and tumbled in a cascade of sparks. The perfect form of the spell was broken. The many pieces of the spectre shattered on the stone beneath her feet.

She almost cried out in surprise. She hadn't meant to destroy such a wonderwork. She hadn't wanted to ravage the ancient treasure of the Dovecote's Heart. Curiosity had drawn her forwards, and she had gone far further than she ever should have dared. If the spell had been a messenger, then she lacked the skill to receive it, for there was only silence.

Or was it near-silence, with the tiniest disturbance nibbling on the edge of the quiet?

My breathing? Ashley's?

It was a little sound, like the gurgle of water in a gutter, or the patter of a beetle's feet across a leaf. But when she focused on it and used the power of the Ring to clarify what she heard, the faintest whispering voice came to her ears. There was a message after all.

"—for only you who wears the Ring could hear my word, or find this place. I know the ways of the Ring so well, and I miss its power every day, but that is why I must warn you, Seeker, and hope –"

"Tabitha –"

"Shh!"

"—it must be refused, as early as it can be. I left it too long, I learned too much from its second sight, so much turned to goodness I never thought—"

"What is it?" Ashley interrupted again.

"Shh! I'm listening."

"But there's nothing –"

"Shh! Be quiet. Please!"

"—that I had to cut my own finger from my hand, for the bond of the Ring was too strong. I refused where the path led, I still refuse it, for to find the wizard, you must walk the darkest path. To turn on all that I have created, and declare it only half of my whole, would make a mockery of the Dovecote and all the principles of goodness. I have banished the Riddler and his furry familiar from us, for it is him that leads me to this darkness as much as the Ring he has helped me to understand. I knew the sign of the Heart would draw you here as it drew me to many truths and temptations. Beware of the Heart-rune's lure, for it marks the path of the Seeker and may not lead to goodness."

The Sage's delicate whisper ended. Tabitha dared not breathe, in case there was more to the message. Her caution was wise.

"I can only hope you heed me in time, Seeker. Take it from your hand, and destroy it in a better way than I employed. If you are here, then the depths of Amberlake were not deep enough."

The silence that followed was complete.

The weight of the words she had witnessed descended upon Tabitha Serannon with the force of a mountain. There was too much to accept at once, but one thing was clear : the message had been intended only for one who bore the Ring. The rock beside her bare feet was speckled with the failing glimmer of sprites. She watched them for a long time.

"Tabitha?"

"Yes."

"Are you finished hearing voices?"

"Yes."

She turned to Ashley, where he stood with the pale remnants of flame above his palm. It was not going to be long before that spell gave out as well.

"What did the messenger say? It was a messenger, wasn't it?"

"We have to go, Ashley. Your Flicker is going out."

"Is it? Everything is still so bright."

"There is some essence on the floor, maybe you can summon that."

He did so. When incorporated into his Flicker spell, the sprites made the chamber slightly less dim. She guided him from the chamber by his arm.

"You didn't answer my question," he pointed out.

"No, I didn't."

Their return seemed infinitely quicker than their arrival had been. Tabitha didn't relent when they reached the main stairs, but pulled Ashley onward until they were at the head of the staircase, below the exit to the Hall of Sky. The darkness crept ever closer as Ashley's flame faded.

"Release your essence, I've got to open the seal," she instructed.

"Are you going to tell me what the Sage said?"

"Ashley! Now is not the time to be churlish with me. I need the sprites."

"I'm being churlish? I took the risk of this quest as well, you know. Look at me! I've been blinded, who knows when it shall fade? I have borne a greater cost than you. I deserve to be told the secret we came to discover."

"I can't." She searched his face for some sign of sympathy, but saw only bitterness. "The secret was only for me."

"Are you so special, because you have sharper eyes, and ears?"

He couldn't have come much closer to the truth.

"Something like that," she said miserably. She couldn't begin to explain the Ring to Ashley while the dark consumed his last few sprites. She knew the Sage had not intended the words for anyone but her—the Seeker, the holder of the Wizard's Ring. The trap Ashley had triggered proved that beyond doubt.

"I will tell you what I can," she promised. "When I can."

"That is small comfort." He did break his command of the Flicker spell though. He offered the sprites to Tabitha.

It was awkward to reach the slab from beneath, for part of it was blocked by the rocker arm. When she had the four sides of the outline completed, there was nothing left of the sprites in Ashley's hand. Tabitha hung on the ring overhead and the seal gave way with a quiet suck.

The paleness of the moonlit Hall was a welcome sight over the rim of the square stone. Tabitha worked her hands onto the top of the marble slab. It took all of her weight to depress it to the ground. She guided Ashley closer.

"Give me a leg-up," she whispered. He cupped his hands and braced himself without a word. He was still angry, she could tell.

Once she had shimmied up to the floor level above, she reached down and guided Ashley's hands to the rim. He pulled himself awkwardly up. The stone under his feet seemed to offer some assistance, and when he rolled clear of the hole, the marble slab thudded up to the surface. When the sprites sealed the edges they were lost beneath the floor of the Scribbillarre. The way to the Heart was closed, the fit was seamless.

The Dovecote was asleep. It was the deepest hour of the night, and even the moon was resting on the western horizon, beyond the tall lower windows of the Hall.

"You've got the sprites?" Ashley asked.

"No," Tabitha answered, in a small voice. She realised that she should have summoned them before they had escaped past the trapdoor. They had no essence to activate the secret doors to reach their respective bedrooms. They could not leave the Hall of Sky without leaving an unbolted door behind. The Rector would know that someone had been out.

Ashley was the first to recover.

"The oak doors can be opened from this side. Open the men's side, and I can find my way to my room. You can take some sprites from the sconce. Then close the door from this side again, and go through the side-door to your rooms."

It was a good plan. Tabitha was grateful for Ashley's quick thinking, and felt all the more miserable about his mistrust of her. They ghosted to the door in silence. Ashley held a hand out all the way, as if he did not rely on Tabitha's lead.

The bar set across the men's door was secured by a pin, which came out quietly enough. But the bar itself was heavy, and it was awkward to stabilise and lift clear. The hinges creaked.

Nothing moved.

Tabitha led Ashley part of the way to his room, collected a handful of essence from the wall sconce, and returned to the Hall.

The Dovecote was still wonderfully peaceful, but Tabitha's pulse was not. Her feet were heavy with the dread of discovery. She endured the creaking of the door with a grimace, but then it was closed, and the bar in place, quieter than she could have hoped. It was the metal pin that let her down. In her haste, she did not grip it firmly enough, and it clattered to the floor. She scooped it up, thrust it into the securing hole, and fled across the Hall.

The sprites she spread on the secret door were already drained and pale, having been taken from a sconce which had offered illumination to the men's corridor all through the night. She should have anticipated the weakness of the Light, and taken more, but hindsight wouldn't open the door. The sprites made an attempt to break the seal, but in doing so merely drained themselves of their energy, and fell to the floor as clear essence.

Tabitha was driven by the fear at her heels.

If she opened the women's door and took all the sprites from the sconces in that corridor, she could return and close the door properly, then unseal the side-door. It was her only hope for remaining undiscovered.

She worked the wedge out from above the bar in the big oak door, tapping it from side to side. She was lifting the heavy bar to free the door when she heard the soft rustle of clothing behind her. She froze.

Footsteps approached, halted.

She dared not turn. She knew she would scream if she did. She eased the bar slowly down to where it had been, and held onto it tightly. There was nothing else to do.

"So it is you, Miss Serannon, who has found a way to jimmy my locks." The Rector's voice was made all the more terrifying by its falsely pleasant tone. Blood pounded in her ears.

"I give you a chance to show yourself worthy of one day becoming a Lightgifter, and how is my mercy repaid? By sin?"

The heat of Shamgar's anger pressed against her back.

"What do you have to say?"

"I am sorry, Rector." It was a hopeless plea, but it was all that came to her confused and panicked mind.

How much did he see? How much does he know?

"You are sorry? You violate the oldest of the Dovecote codes, the vow of chastity, and you are sorry? Which failed man has been your prey tonight, I wonder?"

Chastity? What is he on about?

"I slept with no man tonight, Illumination."

"Your time for playing the fool with me is over. I heard the door to the men's corridor being closed. I know you were there tonight. And when all the tall tales have been told and retold, the truth of it comes down to one thing. Rutting."

Tabitha felt her face colour, but she didn't turn, or answer back. Now was not a good time to defy the Rector. She wished she were made of essence, so she could just shake to pieces, and be swallowed by the floor.

"Please forgive me, Illumination."

"Forgiveness is born of service, and good behaviour," he retorted, "both of which you have offered in short supply. Turn around."

She let go of the oaken bar, the only support left in her world. She turned on leaden feet, and faced the consequence of her actions.

Rector Shamgar was remarkably calm. He even favoured her with a spectral smile. But his eyes were strangely clouded, as if deep, hungry fires burned in his soul.

"Come with me," he said.

He turned on his heel, and strode to the broad staircase. Tabitha had no option but to follow him. She couldn't risk his anger. She had defied his command already. They climbed the stairs up to the third floor.

"Wait here."

She was placed outside a heavy door, close to the Rector's rooms. The Rector returned with a key, which he turned in the lock beside her. The door protested when he shouldered it open, then swung back on aching hinges. What the room contained, could not be seen in the darkness.

"I have not had to use this room of solitary confinement for eleven years," said the Rector, looking down his nose at her. "Know that you are the first to need such discipline in over a decade of the Dovecote. You tarnish the record by your presence. Reflect on that while you atone. If you try to call out to anyone, it is me who shall come, and it is not sympathy you shall find. Only in deprivation will you appreciate what it was you were offered in the Dovecote. Only in atonement will you find the chance for grace. Then we may begin with your service, and the behaviour needed for you to find my mercy."

The Rector pushed her away, through the door and into the dark. Disturbed dust assaulted her nostrils.

She couldn't think of one word in her defence. The truth of her actions would be seen as more sinful than the lie Rector Shamgar believed.

"In time, I shall come to ask you again of the men you have lain with. See to it that you have an answer for that question, if you wish to ever leave this room."

The door was slammed very hard. The key turned in the lock. The darkness was complete.

26. GOOD TIDINGS

"If you gift a light to someone,
where does the darkness go?"——*Zarost*

The Darkmaster had already retired for the day when the flutter of wings interrupted him. He hadn't been asleep, but he didn't wish to be disturbed in his private chambers. Dawn was about to break outside, and he was irritated by the failure of his Shadowcasters to slip through the line of Swords. The invaders could be held off indefinitely at the bridge, that was not the problem. They would never gain access to the vale of Ravenscroft while he did not wish them to. But while they were massed at the edge of his domain, his own Shadowcasters could not get out, which meant a critical task could not be achieved. He pushed himself up from his pillows.

His new apprentice stood at the foot of the bed, his pale face glowing with earnest dedication. He held a tattered white dove with many feathers missing on his hand. The apprentice was trying to hide his giggling.

"The Morrigán have been playing again," the boy said.

Cabal grunted. There had been a time when he would have laughed, but it was not amusing when the messengers that were now intended for him, became as bedraggled as this Courier, or sometimes lost completely. He couldn't break the Morrigán of their habit.

"Take your miserable backside out of my room!" Cabal ordered.

The apprentice bobbed his head, deposited the dove on the blankets, and ran for the door, giggling. He still believed it was all a game. Cabal waited until the door was closed, and all was quiet, before turning to the small white dove.

"Alight, messenger, deliver your word."

The sprites stung. He endured the discomfort. There could be only one Lightgifter who would be bold enough to send a message direct to the Darkmaster. The voice released by the Courier was smooth and supercilious.

"I have deigned to oblige you. The girl has been isolated from the others, in a way none will question. She can be held indefinitely, but every day shall cost you the price of the contract again, in advance."

Cabal closed his eyes, and reigned in his anger at the double-cross.

The Lightgifter liked to believe in his superiority and independence, which is why he could never be relied upon, and why his price was always the highest. It had been out of urgency that Cabal had considered the Lightgifter at last. But the task had been done.

Held indefinitely.

It had a nice sound. The girl was out of the way. The gates to Ravenscroft could be opened, and his plan could be set into motion. But to have the girl a prisoner in the Dovecote was not enough, and it would turn out to be more costly than necessary.

He rose abruptly, and paced through the darkness of his room. Smooth gravel crunched underfoot, easing his mind with the sound of breaking bones.

The solution tied in so well with his plans that he laughed out loud when it presented itself.

He had almost forgotten about the one who hid. The report of the broken man had come to him the previous night. Cabal hadn't been able to think of a use for the wastrel, but he would be desperate to regain favour, desperate enough to obey his Master's word completely. He was beyond the line of Swords. Now that the girl was held, a simple task could be set for the shattered minion, a task a child could complete.

In the headboard of Cabal's bed was a collection of black crystals, resting in holes where they could better absorb the presence of the Darkmaster. He picked a slim Darkstone from the spread, one of the oldest, one to which his connection was as certain as an iron leash. He threaded a chain through the ring at its apex, and cast a spell over the chain's clasp. Primed with the Master's word, it would seal when closed around someone's neck. The Darkstone would confer just a taste of what the Dark had to offer, yet a taste was all anyone needed. He would have another Shadowcaster.

Cabal summoned motes to his hand, and wove a Morrigán. When it had left with the Darkstone, he dressed, and strode from his rooms. He roused the Shadowcasters from their beds with a far-reaching jolt of cold. They would know to come to the Cavern.

There was a real battle to prepare for, at last.

27. THE DARKEST NIGHT

"The greater the bridge,
the higher the toll to cross it."—*Zarost*

Garyll stared into his gruel. All that could be said for it, was that it was hot. Three days, this the fourth, and still the icy wind tore through their camp.

It was not his manner to dwell upon failure, but that was all he had achieved since reaching the chasm. There was little to look forward to in this day, except another tragedy of fruitless endeavour on the Wall. The wind, always the wind, whistling into his ears, telling him he couldn't do it, he should stay where he was, he was too weak, he was tired and cold and sore. It was an incessant, maddening whisper, and to escape its effect he had to deny every statement he heard.

It was worse in the moments of sleep, when the voices took hold of his dreams and created a torture of mockery and confusion. He woke not knowing if those he trusted should be, not knowing if the hungers he had dreamt of weren't really his, and wondering if the woman he held dear would ever be safe from harm. For in his dreams she had been pursued by a hundred Shadowcasters, and he had led them all to Tabitha Serannon. He had foregone sleep since that first night, and the grit behind his eyes was the evidence of his fatigue.

He shook himself, realising that he had been caught by the wind's despair yet again. Today they *would* succeed in breaching the Wall. He forced himself to spoon some gruel past his lips. He *was* strong and steadfast. In a moment he *would* leave the warmth of the tent, and rouse the men to execute his latest plan. The Wall *would* be shattered, and the rock beneath scaled. He *would not* be swayed by the Darkmaster's will.

He remembered how the wind had begun when he had led his troop past the falls above Fendwarrow. The righteous determination of the soldiers endured during the ride, up until that point. After that, for every step they took, the confidence seemed to slip from their faces as the cold wind gusted tears from their eyes. The ravens flocked to plague them with their desolate cries. The Swords could feel their enemy watching them through the many eyes of the dark birds. But of the Shadowcasters themselves, they saw nothing.

Thick clouds plagued them in the higher reaches of the mountain pass, a soup of grey vapours that drove a chill damp into their clothes, and rimed their armour with ice at night.

He had believed himself well-prepared for the battle to take Ravenscroft. Two full troops, of fifty-five Swords apiece, formed his army. Every man bore a Shriek, the whistle that might offer defence against the Morgloth. The men were hand-picked by the Swordmaster for the task—hardened men, experienced men, the kind who kept their blades sharp. He had expected trouble from the Shadowcasters, he had expected fierce resistance at the bridge, or a pitched battle in the vale of Ravenscroft itself. He had not expected the Shadowcasters to break their own bridge down.

What was left on the far side of the chasm was an insurmountable cliff of ice. It was a giant's tongue which protruded from the mountain where the landing of the bridge had been. It fell in a glistening sheet as broad as the river to the base of the ravine, where it ended short in ragged, dripping teeth. The men had named it the Wall.

Getting to the Wall was hard enough, for without the bridge, they first had to descend the sheer cliff where the road from Fendwarrow ended. The rocks were slick with cold moisture. Ropes had been used to build a ladder down the treacherous slope, down to the deep base of the gorge. The river was a raging torrent, sucking at the boulders and spitting at those who walked upon them. The Swords had built a hasty bridge, basic, but strong. Then they had reached the base of the Wall, and their endeavours had become fruitless, and the failures had begun.

Climbers had been sent to gain the summit and then cast ropes down. They never reached the top. They were the first to die, their hands suddenly finding no purchase on the melting ice, though they had been certain their daggers and spurs were going to be enough. They had landed amongst the men with a breaking sound that left little doubt, and a terrible echo in Garyll's mind. Failure.

Garyll had sent scouts back on the trail, to see if they could find another access into Ravenscroft. Half of those men brought back reports of shifting snow, unstable ice, rock-falls and cliffs, terrain that offered no passage even for the desperate. Of the other five, no word returned. Failure.

Garyll tried to begin a high bridge of his own, but the chasm was too wide to throw a grappling hook across. They managed to catapult a rock with a leash of fine cord to the far side, but it would support no weight. Another failure.

They began construction of the ladder on the second day, but it was slow going. Trees were found, and felled—the best to be found were red pines, heavy with sap, and over ten men tall. The horses were used to haul them to the chasm, but the day was brief, and the horses had had to be camped a fair way back to Fendwarrow at the only adequate grazing. By nightfall on the second day, the great ladder was an open A-frame only two trees tall, half the height they needed to achieve. As the light faded, it seemed an ever more pitiful attempt against the looming Wall.

The voices in the wind on the third morning mocked the Swordmaster's meagre accomplishment without respite. When the Swords rallied to work, they found that the ladder of trees had been consumed. The Wall had swollen over the wooden structure. The ladder was trapped deep within the slick tongue of ice. Garyll would not give up hope. He drove the men to pick at the ice, to break it from the structure from the bottom upwards.

It was dangerous work, for the ice broke free in seracs that fell upon the men below. Those who worked upon the Wall had to be sent back to the camp regularly to warm their fingers and toes, lest they lose them to the frostbite. New Swords were assigned, despite the obvious lack of progress; by midday they hadn't reached far into the overhanging teeth of ice. By nightfall, they hadn't even reached the top of the old ladder, let alone built it higher.

Failure, whispered the voices. *Failure, failure, failure.*

Three days, this the fourth, and still the wind tore through their camp. His thoughts were being led in circles. Garyll set his unfinished gruel aside, and burst from the tent into the light of dawn.

Today they *would* breach the Wall.

The wind had lost its bite. The voices hadn't ceased, they never ceased, but the leaching effect of the cold was gone. It was like the first day of spring, a change in the seasons, as if the grasp of winter had finally eased in this high pass. Even the driven clouds had receded to the higher peaks. Garyll felt a moment of hope.

He quickened his pace towards the chasm. It was a short way from the camp to the end of the road, and as he walked, the way became more exposed, ever more a trail scribed thinly over hard, sloping ground. Above, the morning was different from any of the others. The sun shone, defining the peaks with crisp light. The sky was blue. His spirits began to lift. When he rounded the final bend and approached the head of the ropes, he looked to the far side of the chasm, and a thrill coursed through his body.

Today they *would* breach the Wall.

He had expected the ice to have consumed their work again. He had steeled himself for another day of chipping away at the Wall, in the hope of placing at least one more tree on the head of the ladder. Yet what faced him was a gift from the gods.

The ice had sheared where the apex of the ladder thrust upwards through Wall. A massive portion of the face had split off, leaving a jumble of seracs that littered the rocks at the base, and caused the low rope bridge to lie at an awkward angle. But what remained of the Wall was mostly as it had appeared to them on the beginning of the second day. A few hours with the axes, and the ladder would be clear from its entrapment. They could build upon the ladder today, raise it swiftly. Above the Wall, the access to Ravenscroft beckoned.

Garyll spun on his heel. They would need five more trees, and all the speed he could muster from the men. For while they worked at the Wall, they were vulnerable to attack from above. He hoped the Shadowcasters continued to play their watching game, but he vowed to be ready if they showed themselves.

It took the Swords until late afternoon to complete the ladder, but at last the final trunk was hoisted upwards, to be lashed on the uppermost point of the frame. It projected no more than a man's length above the crest of the Wall. The tip swayed as the binders struggled to secure it.

There were many ravens watching Garyll from the higher rocks, and many more circling in the sky, soaring along the looming cliffs in the late afternoon breeze. If their calls had not been so hoarse, they might have appeared to be graceful creatures. But their cries were twisted, like the screams of masochists. Their presence set his nerves on edge.

When the binders raised their thumbs, Garyll didn't hesitate to sound the charge. The Swords swarmed upwards, spurred by the fear of being too late to help their comrades above should they meet resistance. The hundred men scaled the ladder like a swarm of ants. Nothing came upon them. Apart from the Swords, the landing was deserted, and the road led onwards, open and still.

The wind whispered, the river thundered far below. The sun was dying in the western sky, and the peaks were splashed with red.

Some of the ravens flew away toward the east. Garyll set the march.

They had come unto the vale of Ravenscroft, and their presence was announced, of that he was certain.

The vale was gloomy, cold, and empty. Nothing moved in the jurrum bushes and scattered boulders, except the slowly lengthening shadows. The air was dark.

They marched.

A murmur passed through the troops behind Garyll as they closed on the Keep of Ravenscroft. The Keep was an ugly, dominating mass crested with a thorny rim of haphazard spires. It crouched against the feet of the towering mountain. There was nobody to be seen on the battlements, or in the yawning maw which formed the entrance. The ravens were gone. The leaching cold had returned. Yet the sensation of being watched was overwhelming.

Black earth, black rock, black chips of stone beneath his feet. It was unnatural. The entire vale, all the way up to the spire beside the Keep, was the same dark substrate. Garyll kicked a loose pebble. It seemed to ooze into the ground when it came to rest, though he couldn't be sure in the failing light.

"Halt!" he called out. In his own ears, his voice sounded small. His command met silence. The Swords, to a man, had already ceased to advance. Few men would meet his eye when he turned to face their disordered formation. The Swords shuffled into tighter lines, shoulders tensed against the weight of oppression that had swamped them all.

What am I doing? It will soon be night, and the Shadowcasters will be in the height of their power.

Garyll shifted his stance as if readying himself to leave, then gritted his teeth when he recognised the source of the fear—the doubting voice whispering in his ears.

He would not be manipulated by the Darkmaster's trickery. He had a hundred men with him, and if the Darkmaster expected him to leave, then it was the perfect time to press his attack.

"Light the torches!"

The brands were soaked, and sparked with the strike of sword on flint. Garyll selected the ten soldiers best suited to form a rearguard. They were easy to identify. Their faces shone whitest in the torchlight.

He clenched the hilt of his sword, and turned to face the Keep.

Ravenscroft. The hide of the Shadowcasters, the root of all evil in the realm. The Darkmaster had defied the right of the King to rule.

They would surrender and swear fealty, or they would meet with the King's justice.

A multitude of doubts assaulted him from the darkness ahead, carried on the whispering wind. Garyll knew of only one good response to fear. Face it down, make it surrender. He had been wound too tight by the Darkmaster's games. He was propelled at his enemy like a bolt from a crossbow.

"For Eyri!" Garyll shouted as he drew Felltang high.

"For Eyri!" the Swords echoed. Their voices didn't carry far.

They proceeded at a march, three abreast and thirty deep once the rearguard had hidden off the trail. The men loosened their swords, and tightened their helms. Garyll marched at the head, flanked by flaming brands. He kept just ahead of the torches, so that his eyes were sharp. The road bore them into the mouth of the Keep. Ravenscroft's bowels were icy and dark.

It took his eyes a while to adjust to the gloom. Twilight had been bright by comparison. There was an unfamiliar scent in the air, a stale smell, like that of an animal's lair after a period of hibernation. The corridor they marched into was a high tunnel. He commanded a brief halt.

Silence.

Garyll led them deeper, wading against the darkness that seemed to thicken with every step. Wave upon wave of despair washed and broke against him. He could feel the fear running through the men, but he forged onward, refusing to acknowledge the Shadowcasters' power. The impetus of the denial drove him deeper. The air flickered under the torchlight, as if polluted with a current of motes. They were walking into a spell.

They have too much of an advantage in here.

At last he realised that his own fatigue and frustration had been used against him. The Darkmaster had anticipated his mood, and had drawn him in by using the resistant thread of his warrior's courage. Subtle spells pulled his thoughts every which way.

They would have to fight their way out of this one.

"Watch out!" shouted a voice far behind him. There was a grinding of metal, a crash of men being thrown against one another, then a deafening boom of something heavy striking the ground. The screams of one man filled the darkness.

Garyll rushed back along the column of men. A Sword had fallen and was skewered to the ground by a portcullis. The corridor was sealed.

Garyll cursed his own stupidity.

"Grab the bars, lift it off him!" Garyll commanded.

It proved to be useless. The portcullis was too heavy by far, it did not move an inch, even with all the hands they could muster. The portcullis couldn't be that heavy. It was locked.

"Be alert, men!" he warned.

The trapped soldier's screams tapered off, and he began to shiver. Garyll covered the man's hands with his own, and gripped until his knuckles were white.

I chose this man.

"Bloody stupid way to die," the Sword whispered suddenly. He looked up at Garyll's face a moment longer, then he clutched the bars. His legs kicked once, hard.

"You will pay for this, Ravenscroft!" Garyll shouted to the darkness. Only the echo of his voice mocked him from the shadows.

"Swordmaster, what would you have us do?" The question came from a soldier on the far side of the portcullis.

"How many men are you there?"

Mutters passed away into the distance, then rolled closer again.

"Thirty, sir."

And ten outside, the rear-guard. We are split in half.

"Retreat to the rear-guard, and form a defensive unit at the mouth of the Keep. Run! There may be a second portcullis!" Garyll shouted.

Hurried feet stamped away.

Garyll led the remainder of his force onwards. Better to move, than to be a sitting target. The roof lifted itself beyond the reach of the torch-light. The walls fell away on either side. Openings in what seemed to be a vast circular chamber hinted at further passages.

Reception hall. Where are the hosts?

All hell broke loose.

The air was a flurry of wings. It seemed that a hundred ravens assaulted them at once, causing the Swords to cover their faces. The torch-bearers lost their brands. Running water sounded nearby, a sudden rush as if a dam had broken.

Blades were drawn around him. The ring of steel sent blood thundering through his veins, but there were only ravens to strike out at. They were easily destroyed upon a blade, shattering to black dust, though Garyll heard an indrawn breath when a bird penetrated someone's defences.

They retrieved the brands, but one lay unattended for too long. It guttered, and went out with a sudden hiss.

Something was approaching, in the cover of darkness. A gurgling, rushing sound. The Swords bunched together in the centre of the chamber, in the low point of the floor's depression. One man jumped away from an attack of ravens in front of him, and knocked Garyll off-balance. Garyll caught himself by dropping to one knee. There was an unexpected splash.

Water!

The chamber had been dry moments before. He stood. Wet feet, in suddenly soaked boots.

The touch of the Dark is the purest cold.

If they were in the water when the Dark essence was commanded, they would be caught like flies in honey.

"Run! Get out of the water!"

He chose an archway at random and shoved his two torch-bearers roughly towards it, running with them, but when the spell struck his men, almost half of them were wading against the rising current in the depression. From above, in the darkness, a united command was sounded.

"Freeze."

At least twenty Swords were caught in the trap. They stood ankle-deep in a pool of ice. Some hacked at their feet. Water continued to rush into the chamber, washing over the ice, preparing the pool for a repeat.

Garyll launched himself back into the chamber. His feet slipped, and he hit the ice hard, sliding through the gathering water on the surface. Together his men hacked at the ice, and pulled a few feet free.

"Get out, get out, there's no time!" he shouted.

"Freeze." It was impossible to pinpoint where the Shadowcasters were. They seemed to speak from all directions, a hollow, distant sound.

Another five men were trapped in the ice.

It was hopeless. The water poured in. One Sword, who had fallen on his hands and knees the first time, was now trapped in ice up to his shoulders. The water touched his chin. The man fought desperately.

A simple plan formed in Garyll's mind. Find a Shadowcaster, any Shadowcaster, and demand the reversal of the spell under threat of death. There were three corridors leading from the chamber, and a fourth through which the water poured. The Shadowcasters could be hiding down any one of them.

"Split up!" he shouted to the few men who were free. "Find any Shadowcaster, force them to cancel this spell. Kill any who resist you. Go!" He dived down his chosen corridor, pulling a torch-bearer with him again. A few Swords followed.

Garyll ran with Felltang drawn and extended in front of him. If there was anything waiting for him in the dark, better that it met his blade first. He outpaced the torch, and shouted for light. The narrow corridor snaked downwards. Garyll ducked under a sudden overhang. Moments later, the torch-bearer yelped behind him. The torch issued a hiss as it was quenched. Then all was dark.

"Swords! You there?"

Silence. A brush of cold.

Garyll halted. He could sense bodies approaching from both sides. By their silence and stealth in the dark, they declared their identity. He closed his eyes and readied himself.

What has become of my men?

His ears itched. A word was chanted from close by.

"Despair."

He spun and slashed the air with his sword, but whoever had been there danced out of range. The Shadowcaster had landed his blow. The spell clung to him like the weakness that clings to a drunkard in the morning; no matter how much he wished it gone, the spell remained, leaching strength from deep within his bones. It was the spell he had heard in the whispering wind, but a thousand times stronger. He refused to be swayed by its suggestion.

Felltang was heavy. He saw how the ice chamber had been a filter, slowing their charge, dividing them. Just as the portcullis had been. The Swords were separated, and the Shadowcasters could come in close enough to work their magic. The Swords were doomed.

"Despair."

His slash was delayed this time. What hope did he have of finding his target in the dark? They were too strong, he was too weak, he was tired of fighting them, too cold to care, too deep within the heart of Darkness to ever escape.

He recognised the trickery just in time. He reversed his grip on Felltang, and raised the hilt of his sword to his forehead.

Let me serve Eyri, and be strong.

"Despair."

He waited. He sensed the group of Shadowcasters; they spread out around him, one approached from behind. A damp body odour brushed him. A rustle of clothing told him the man had raised his arms, as if attempting to lift something over Garyll's head, or to apply a particularly intense spell.

Without altering his grip, Garyll swung his sword hard, driving the point backwards past his chest. The hold of the Dark essence on his body broke, and Felltang sank almost to the hilt into what had been behind him.

He leapt forward. He was a whirlwind of fury. Felltang howled, scything through bone and flesh alike. He heard three bodies fall to the floor, and a fourth man was limping away, crying like a wild animal.

He heard the movement behind him too late. Something smote his helm, hard. The darkness was complete.

When he regained consciousness, he was already screaming. Pain ruled his left arm, raw agony tore through the core nerves of his fingers. Something was being driven into the end of his forefinger, a nail, or a needle. Garyll wrenched his hand away, but his wrist was held in iron. His muscles strained, his back arched against the restraints. He was bound on all four limbs, and there was a fine chain around his neck. A hammer sounded at the same moment that the pain bloomed in his finger. The nail was driven deeper, against the bone. This time he did tear something in his arm, but the pain of ligaments separating in his elbow was nothing.

His screams were not the only ones he could hear.

Enter the Inferno, he told himself. *Enter the Inferno.*

The skill came to him instantly, despite the years since he'd needed it. To go beyond the pain, he visualised the Inferno, a place where the heat was so immense his clothes became a flash of coals, a fire so cruel that every part of his body was burning, every nerve screamed in multiplied agony. He used his pain to drive his attention deeper into the Inferno, accepting more pain, loading his being with the complete agony he had learned in training. You could only escape the pains of battle, by going beyond them.

He was the mind within the Inferno, burned clean of his body. Any pain belonged to the flames, no pain could supersede the ultimate torture he knew in that place. In the Inferno, he became the mind of the Swordmaster alone.

When the hammer struck again, he fed the pain to the fire. He was beyond his body. He couldn't stop the scream, he didn't need to—his mind was protected by the Inferno. He had accepted all the pain as his own; the hammer was a lesser pain than what he knew in the fire.

How hard-won that skill had been to learn.

His eyes smarted, his vision showing him bleary confusing images. He realised that his head was tied so far back that he was seeing upside down. Torches flared red against black walls which rose into darkness. The hammer sounded again, and the room disappeared for a moment.

A giant cavern, the torches ranged in a circle. Dark figures, robed and cowled. A soft tap of the hammer, worse than before. He fed it to the Inferno.

Other figures were tied to altars in the same manner that he was. Wrists and feet iron-bound, heads drawn back off the end of the raised stones.

He couldn't see his own torturer, but he could feel the man shift his attention to another finger. It had to be a man, the grip was too rough for a woman's. A fresh nail slammed into him, finding bone on the first blow.

When his vision cleared again, Garyll saw a tall figure approaching with rapid stride; cowled like the rest, yet different. The man's presence reached out ahead of him, making him both familiar and fearsome. He knew the man's power in an intimate way he couldn't define.

A crawling sensation surged through Garyll's body, beginning from high on his chest. Despite the separation of his attention in the Inferno, the crawling invaded his mind when it was done with his body. It was a searching, terrible touch, more alarming to Garyll for where it had reached than for what it did. The shield of the Inferno had never failed him before. Yet this man had gone beyond it with ease—he was inside him, too close to block, an adversary who stood behind him instead of in front.

He is the shadow and I am his caster.

The words were not his own, yet they sounded in his mind, and urged him to repeat the litany. He was going mad. Garyll reeled and lost concentration. The pain of his shattered fingers roared through him.

Enter the Inferno.

That was his own thought, he was sure. But there was another inside him. He coughed, and felt a small pressure against his throat, a cold weight.

I am the shadow and he is my master.

Black robes touched Garyll's face.

"You were told to rouse him, no more!"

The voice was familiar from his first visit, that of Cabal of Ravenscroft. The Darkmaster.

A strangled sound came from where Garyll's torturer had been.

"This is the Swordmaster, you fool!" the Darkmaster said. "Do you know nothing of his training? He will not give in to pain. You have already escaped the torture, haven't you, my dear Glavenor?" The robes slid by, and a pale face came close.

Cold eyes regarded him in a way that was both predatory and familial. Garyll saw too much in those steady orbs; they were too deep with understanding, with hunger, with power and possibility.

"No, not to pain. But he will give in." The Master rose.

"I thought only to prepare him for you, Master. Is he not more receptive this way? It has worked on many of the others." The nails in Garyll's left hand were flicked once.

"Leave him! This one is more use to me whole than broken."

"Yes, Master." The torturer sounded disappointed, but his footsteps passed away to the left, and the nails were not struck again. A new scream told Garyll that the torturer had found someone else to work upon.

My men, where have I led my men?

"Pain is not his greatest fear," said the Darkmaster, close by. "No, I have something special for the Swordmaster."

The hand that pushed Garyll's hair from his brow was as smooth as the skin of a snake.

"Gabrielle!" the Darkmaster called out. A woman approached. As she neared, she blocked the light from the nearest torch with her body. All Garyll could see was her outline.

"See that Glavenor finds his way in the dark. He hungers for it already, though he doesn't know it, and it is hidden deep. He is strong, he is righteous, you shall work both from him, or you shall lose your rights as Vortex." Garyll saw the woman stiffen, but she said nothing.

"I need him at dawn, ready to take the Devotion. You may use whatever essence you have need of."

Gabrielle bowed low to the Darkmaster, as if he had bestowed a great honour upon her.

To use essence must be a reward, Garyll realised. But he had heard the words as clearly as she—the Vortex would lose her rights if she failed in her task. He began to feel that the worst of his torture had yet to begin.

She began with the spell of Despair, so concentrated and cold that he could not draw a breath for a long time thereafter. Without Felltang in his hand, without foes to face, it was difficult to find the battle rage that had shielded him before. The woman carried on and on. He knew that he lost something of his resistance with every iteration of her spell, and he knew that she knew it too.

She talked to him, a soft, smothering attention like oil laid thick upon water. He drowned in her words, and where they led him. She offered him a way out of his misery, though he knew it was a false trail. He vowed to ignore her.

She laid one hand against his throat, pressing the cold object there deeper into him. That cold place beneath her hand never warmed. The crawling sensation returned, and her voice became a commanding force, binding his mind to the borders she set. He could do nothing but follow in the flow of her current, and break through the walls of his own principles as she chose to lead him beyond. Her will coursed through his veins, and sought out things he had repressed and forgone long ago.

He would not speak at first, later he dared not, for what he might admit. Just by Gabrielle's suggestions, and where her mind led his, the worst parts of his being were brought to the surface, where they collected, swelled and erupted across his mind, staining the walls with their poison.

His own weaknesses responded to what she described; the exhilaration of beating a man in a fight, the solace of numbing drunkenness after having to execute a convicted criminal, the ambition to prove himself stronger than all other men, his lust for hard sex, harder than any woman he had known could give, hungers like these that had never been sated and, he tried to promise himself, never would be.

He sucked his cheek inwards and bit down on it, hoping the reminder of pain would clear his thoughts. It only made the visions worse, filling them with the taint of his own blood, and a lust for more.

Time stretched onwards in interminable darkness. She taught him how pain could be pleasure. She taught him how the men who could forego their principles could live fulfilled. She showed him that he was no better than those he had judged, how they had followed the same hungers he knew, his own hunger, allowed to rise.

It was many, many hours until he drifted from her towards exhaustion. Yet Gabrielle was not done, and she moved the torturer's nails absently. He dived for the purity of the Inferno in his mind, yet she used even that against him, casting a spell of weakness to drive him toward sleep again. He ran from her in his mind, yet she was always with him.

She was too close to him, her hand on his throat created too strong a link, as if she could use that place to see into his soul. He had long ago guessed it was the stone of the Shadowcasters, chained on his neck. It bound him into their network of Dark like a bond of blood. It laid his thoughts open to the one who touched him. It made him believe he was in an infinite space, a dark place, where a voice, his voice, repeated a mantra.

I am the shadow and he is my master.
He is the shadow and I am his caster.

Sometimes he denied it, in the way that he had denied the whispers in the wind. Sometimes he forgot to ignore it. Sometimes he had to grind the words apart in his teeth, before his lips could betray him.

From time to time a man nearby was unshackled, and taken away. The screams, which had filled the chamber with a cacophony, became fewer and fewer, until all he could hear was his own laboured breathing, Gabrielle's voice, and somewhere at the limits of awareness, a soft weeping which had lasted for hours. He forgave that man, whoever it was.

He found one island in the sea of despair, a place he retreated to at last. Tabitha Serannon. If there was one pure sanctuary in all the world, it was the innocent feelings he had for Tabitha, and the beauty she represented in his soldier's life. He let everything go, knowing he would not need any of his weaknesses, if he could remain on the island, in the protection of hope. He had been shown he was not good, he could not believe in himself. But he could believe in Tabitha being good. He repeated her name, and held onto the hope she represented. There was one thing good in the world.

Tabitha.

"What was that, my dear?" Gabrielle's voice was soft, smooth, as venomous as ever.

Garyll shut his mouth. He hadn't meant to whisper aloud. He took Tabitha into the Inferno with him, and went to the core of his being, where the Vortex Gabrielle couldn't reach. At last, he fell from consciousness, in a plunge that avoided sleep and found the emptiness beyond.

◆ ──────── ◆

The snap of his chains brought him around. He had been moved to a new place, upon the battlements, beneath a freezing grey dawn. He was weak, so terribly weak, as if all of his will had been reamed out of his body, all of his resistance taken with the last of his body-heat. He had never known such a cold, it was the cold of the dead, though his heart beat slowly within him.

He knew he was alive, because his damaged fingers throbbed with every heartbeat, and because the air scraped down his throat as he drew breath. Someone stood beside him. Garyll didn't need to look to know who it was. The man's presence filled him with dread. He knew the fear was fuelled by the motes which flickered between them in a lazy spell, but he had lost the strength to deny the fear. He had only enough strength to notice how his courage was being ground like soft flesh between two immense, dark boulders.

His wrists were shackled behind him, his ankles likewise, and both were connected on a chain to a ring set in the stone. The chains were short, forcing him to remain where he was, on his knees. Even so, he could see over the rim of the spiked battlements. Some forty Swords were collected in disarray on the plain below. They seemed to be waiting for something. With a start Garyll recognised them as the group who had been ordered to retreat, after the portcullis had separated their force. The men on the field below were probably waiting for him to return. They knew nothing of the terrible things that had occurred within the Keep. They had not yet been caught.

There was a fine chain around Garyll's neck, and a weight beneath his chin. The crawling sensation hadn't left his body, the cold only made the touch of Dark more intense and his nerves more sensitive to it.

"It only hurts because you resist," explained a slithering voice.

The Darkmaster stepped out in front of Garyll, regarding him coolly. He produced a sword and laid it on the stone. The sword glistened, its blade as keen as a razor. Garyll eyed Felltang with longing. It was a wasted thought, he knew. He was chained with iron, the blade would be of no use. He doubted he could swing it even if he were unfettered, he was so weak.

"Behold the symbol of your station in life; a weapon, made only for killing other men. What have you brought to the world, what have you created? You have only killed, in your time."

Garyll heard the truth, and it drew his spirit ever deeper.

"How many more deaths shall you be responsible for?"

Garyll stared at the stone between his knees. The Darkmaster gripped his hair, and tilted his head back again.

"Look out there, at the poor soldiers you led to Ravenscroft, so easily fooled by a word from one of their turned comrades. They believe the Keep conquered, and wait for you to lift the portcullis." The Darkmaster bent close, holding Garyll with the intense hunger that shone behind his eyes.

"Are you ready to save their lives?"

Coldness bit into him.

"Accept me as your Master. They shall be spared."

I am the shadow and he is my master.

He is the shadow and I am his caster.

Garyll ground his teeth.

The Master regarded him for a moment, then chuckled. There was no humour in the laugh, only disdain. "Oh, you will fall, have no fantasies about that. The mightiest always fall, and they fall the hardest."

"A demonstration, if you will," the Darkmaster added, indicating the plain below. "Remember, I offer you the power to spare them."

Cabal lifted a dark orb from his own neck, a large crystal, the size of a child's fist. He set his lips against it, then released it and spoke two words.

"Darkswords, advance."

Garyll heard the command echoed within the stone on his own neck. It came with a wave of coercion. He tried to stand despite his fetters, so strong was the urgent need to respond. The Swords who were already gathered on the plain appeared attentive, some raised their hands in greeting. Then Garyll saw what they had—a tight formation of men marching out from the Keep. Men wearing the burnished mail of the King's armoury. His men. His Swords, though Cabal had called them something else; Darkswords. It was worse than he had imagined. Close to fifty men. He knew what they bore on chains around their necks.

"Fight the Dark! Resist! Stop!" he shouted over the battlement. But his voice was hoarse from a night of screaming, and the cold. Cabal wove a spell of motes, and threw the delicate lace over his head.

"Silence."

Garyll guessed his words would not reach far, but he shouted nonetheless. The Darkmaster smiled, a sad, indulgent gesture.

"It is too late to turn them back. They are already mine."

The Darkmaster spoke to the plains below, where the two groups of soldiers would soon meet. "Your fine, loyal rear-guard are true to the King. But those they face have a new master. Shall we see who is stronger?"

The Swords who marched from the Ravenscroft hunched as if bearing a heavy weight. Despite their stance, they looked poised for action. The others had no idea of who approached.

Not Swords, against fellow Swords!

Garyll flashed a sickened glance at Cabal. The Darkmaster raised his orb. Garyll was crushed as the words of doom sounded in his ears.

"Darkswords, attack!"

The Swords were taken completely by surprise. They recognised their comrades, and extended empty hands to welcome them back. They were met with deadly steel, as the Darkswords fell upon them. Garyll screamed for their retreat, strained at his bonds, but to no avail. The Darkmaster stood silently beside him, watching with disinterest.

The ambushed Swords were quick to recover. They returned the attack in fury. The men were all trained fighters and their blows were vicious. The fervour of the possessed was met with the anger of the righteous. The plain filled with the clash and cries and blood of battle.

Garyll could not bear to watch, but neither could he tear his eyes away.

"Terrible, isn't it?" hissed the Darkmaster. "Brother against brother. Whoever wins the battle wins with revulsion at his own actions. Such men are the easiest to turn to the Dark. So you see, I win, no matter who is left standing. But you have a choice—for those who join me now, there will be no bloodshed, no torment. You can call the surrender. You can lead your men and give them life."

The forces were unmatched on the plain below, though it was hard to tell. He saw one Sword swing a desperate blow against another. A blade slashed open someone's face. The anguish of battle, and the cries of the wounded rose on the wind to sting Garyll's eyes to tears. The melee churned in a confusion of the possessed and the pure.

Some Darkswords did not fight with full commitment, some of them pulled their blows. Those that did so, suffered dearly. The others abandoned themselves to the battle. It was the only way to survive, for either side. Only one man turned from the battle, throwing down his sword as he ran for the river. But then he staggered to his knees, and clutched at his head with both hands. Soon after, he returned to the foray.

Garyll guessed the Darkmaster's sudden concentration had a lot to do with it.

By sheer numbers, the Darkswords were beating their opponents down. Another Sword fell to the earth, his head severed from his body.

"A noble decision, Glavenor," the Darkmaster mocked. "Murder them all, for you cannot risk your own precious principles. Many would prefer to serve me, than to end their lives on the point of a sword for nothing. Those who die with the Darkstone at their throat, need not die now either. But as I said, it is your noble decision, not mine, that causes all these men to die. You are responsible for those who shall come to avenge them as well."

The words stopped his heart. Garyll saw the same scene occurring countless times on this damned plain. A squadron would be sent to investigate the disappearance, and another one after that, until the realm was rid of all its Swords. There was no honour in their deaths, and no hope of winning, it was just a waste of life. He was a tyrant, to cast doom on his men because of his own plight. There had to be another way.

"Stop!" cried Garyll. "Halt the Swords! Halt their battle!"

No one heard him above the clamour, except for the Darkmaster.

"Circle them, but do not attack!" the Darkmaster ordered. Garyll felt the words echo in his Darkstone, and knew it carried to those on the plain as well.

The greater part of the battle disengaged, and spread out around the smaller group of Swords within. They were hopelessly outnumbered. Only ten men had survived the onslaught, and even they were badly wounded. Close to forty Darkswords stood guard, heads low, blades raised. One man retched, but nobody broke from the circle.

"You have something to say."

Garyll looked at the cold stone. "What do you want?" he asked. His voice was strange in his ears, distant, as if spoken by another.

"Speak the words of the Devotion, accept the Darkstone. A small sacrifice, for the life of so many."

He knew the words. He had been hearing them all through the night. He had to find a way to circumvent the possession. Maybe he could work around the Darkstone, cut it from his neck when he had the chance. But he could not risk falling under the Darkmaster's domination, even at the cost of another wasted life in his name. He would find a way to fight.

The Darkmaster reached under Garyll's chin, and held the stone. Garyll groaned as the tide of Dark assaulted him.

I am the shadow and he is my master.

He is the shadow and I am his caster.

The worst was not the invading touch of another man inside him, or the sense of invitation to the Dark ways, or the drowning blackness of his own hungers that ached to be released.

The worst was what came after.

"Forward, Darkswords!"

Out on the plain, the cluster of doomed Swords met the attack with their blades.

"You said the men would be spared!" Garyll cried.

"You didn't say the words."

The Swords were surrounded. They pressed themselves into a formation, back to back. There were four blades against each of their one.

"Learn the cost of opposing me, and never think to do it again. I shall ask for your devotion only once more. Be sure to give me what I want, next time."

The Swords were slaughtered. Garyll counted every body. Some memories fade with the passage of time. Garyll knew at that moment that the sound his men made as they struck the ground would never leave him. He screamed at them to stop, screamed as the bloodlust of the Dark surged to fill him, screamed for the laughter to stop in his mind as he ripped at the fetters which bound him. But the last of the ten resisters fell on the plain, and it became silent on the battlefield.

All the Swords that were left, belonged to the Darkmaster. All but one. Cabal dismissed Garyll's burning glare with his parting comment.

"You will come to see my way of things."

"If you wished those men killed, why didn't you use the Morgloth?" Garyll cried after the Master's retreating back. "Why do you waste the lives of those who serve you as well?"

Cabal paused, and showed Garyll an amused smile. "You must learn that only those who serve me well earn the privilege of living. Those Darkswords who have died, they have proven to be weaker fighters, have they not?" Cabal surveyed the plain one last time, and chuckled. "As to the Morgloth, I wish to live to enjoy my rule of Eyri. Only a crazy man walks the road to the Underworld. Only a doomed man. I am neither."

28. ATONEMENT

"Why do birds sing?"—*Zarost*

Tabitha stared at the ceiling. There was little else to do. Stare at the ceiling, stare at the walls, and think.

She presumed a meal would come after sunset, as it had the previous evening. She didn't mind that it was likely to be bread and water again. She was atoning.

She lay on her back on the floor. It was best to lie still, for dust coated every surface of the bare cell, and the slightest movement filled the air with dry, choking clouds. The barred, glassless window allowed some light in. A faint breeze rippled the spider-webs of many years.

Ironically, she was actually glad for the time in isolation. Not glad that she had been caught by the Rector, but glad he had chosen to place her in the high room. He had been lenient on her, he could have dismissed her from the Dovecote when he'd found her in the Hall of Sky that night. Instead, he had offered her the chance to repent. His forgiveness was extraordinary. Tabitha thought she was beginning to understand why Shamgar was the Rector of the Lightgifters, and how unworthy she was of bearing her mother's Lightstone.

With hindsight, it was difficult to accept her wilful behaviour. She knew that she had felt a pull the moment Ashley had formed the rune of the Heart in his hand, when he had told her about the inner sanctum. She had followed that urge without questioning the rightness of her actions. The Ring had led her from one clue to another. She should have been stronger, denied the urge, used her judgement to restrain her curiosity. She had broken not only the sacred rules of the Dovecote, but the sanctity of an ancient chamber, undisturbed for centuries. Only the most high Lightgifters should have been there.

She was not even a half-knot. She was not worthy.

Despite the correctness of her reasoning, she always came up against the same conundrum. The Sage's message had been for her.

'Seeker' he had called her. The message would not have been audible without the Ring, the tests would not have been passed, the signs would not have been seen, without the intense clarity that the Ring brought. Yet the Sage had told her to be rid of it, without hesitation.

She held her hand up to the pearly light from the window. The Ring magnified the pores of her skin beneath a smooth band of clarity. The flesh close to that knuckle was already purpling. Yesterday had been a painful failure and a sobering lesson; the Ring would not come off with any amount of pulling. It was too late. The only way it was going to come off, was in the manner that the Sage had achieved it, by cutting off his own finger. That was too terrible to believe, and it seemed as extreme as cutting off her head because she could not remove the Lightstone from her neck. If she could live with the Lightstone, why not keep the Ring?

When she tested her truth-sense, she found she didn't really want to take the Ring off. That, she was sure, was the problem. That was why the Sage had feared it so much. It had become a part of her, something she did not want to do without. Had she not learned the verses of the Lifesong during her association with it? Had she not sung like she had never sung before, because of the Ring? There was so much more to the world, when she wore the Ring, so much clarity, detail, and wonder.

It had saved her life, on the Kingsbridge. Were it not for the Ring, she would not have found the perfect note of the Shiver, she would not have stopped the Morgloth and shattered the Shadowcaster.

There were two sides to the truth. Were it not for the Ring, she would not have drawn the hunter upon her in the first place. She would not have had to flee from First Light. Her parents would not have died, Phantom Acres would not have burned, and she would have lived in another life.

Too many maybes, and none of them caused by the Ring itself. She could not turn back time. Life had followed one path, and not the other.

Since she had donned the Ring, her life had changed, but she had tried it on because she had wanted to, she wore it because she wanted to. It was not a thing of evil. It did not rule her life, it was just a tool. A tool, the Sage had warned, that led towards a path of darkness.

The Ring had gone there anyway, it had found the darkness that the Sage had feared. Her mother found the Ring in Fendwarrow, after the Darkmaster had lost it. The Darkmaster had worn it, and Twardy Zarost had been his advisor.

The two thoughts crashed into one another, in a burst of enlightenment. Zarost had advised the Darkmaster, but the Master had finally lost his Ring, and it had passed to Tabitha. Then Zarost had found her, and helped her to escape. And before the Darkmaster, the Sage had owned the Ring. He had spoken of a Riddler as well. Three holders of the Ring, three Seekers of the wizard, with the same advisor, the Riddler?

No, that was taking an idea too far. The Sage had lived over two hundred years in the past, so it could not have been Twardy Zarost who had been advisor in that time. But it was true to say that the Ring always attracted a Riddler, and that the Ring had passed through the Light and the Dark before it had reached her.

And it would probably pass on to another after her, she realised. Well it should, for Zarost had told her that it belonged to the wizard. A wizard whom the Sage and the Darkmaster had not been able to find, in all their years of bearing the Ring.

What chance do I have of solving the riddle?

Zarost had said it would fall from her finger when she ceased to seek out the wizard. If that were true, then she needn't cut her finger from her hand after all. Her own lack of progress in solving the riddle of the wizard was going to do the job for her. She was going to lose the Ring anyway, she realised with a mixture of relief and dismay.

How long will it be, before it goes cold on my hand, and slips away?

If anything, the Ring had seemed to get tighter of late, but that meant nothing, for she was surely no closer to finding the wizard than she had been when she'd fled from Phantom Acres.

Maybe I should learn all I can from the Ring while I can.

She could develop the clarity of sight and sense and thought that it offered, develop the talent for singing which had quickened within her. Draw everything she could from the Ring before it was lost to the next bearer in the succession. It would be a sad day when the Ring left her.

The Ring was warm, and tight. Why had she found it, if it were not meant to be borne by her?

It made no sense. And the roaming questions born of her isolation found no answers, for there was no one to ask.

She wished she could talk to Twardy Zarost. It had been so long since she'd grappled with his riddles. She needed his knowledge of the Ring. She was floundering in her own ignorance.

How could she decide what to do about the Ring, with only warnings and guesses? She still could not believe that the Ring was evil; it expanded her awareness, it made her feel alive. She needed to know. She needed Twardy Zarost.

The memory of her parting with the Riddler came to her. He had spoken to her as Lethin Tarrok's guards had dragged him away. Words she had not considered too deeply at the time, shocked as she was by his admission of being the Darkmaster's advisor.

The Ring grew warmer, and the pool of her memories cleared for her. The sights and sounds of the day in Stormhaven filled her mind. Twardy Zarost, hazel eyes beneath his crazy hat, watching her as he was dragged from the garden. His voice, a melody of cheer despite his situation.

"I tried, but perhaps I shouldn't have! Now I cannot return, unless you summon me."

She came back to the present with growing excitement. He waited on her word. In his strange way, Twardy Zarost had told her she needed to send word to him, before he could come. He might be following one of his arcane rules.

Tabitha jumped to her feet. Dust billowed around her, but she made it to the window before it could envelop her. She thrust her head as far as she could against the bars, into the fresh air, but there her sudden excitement left her.

How could she call on Twardy Zarost, when she didn't know where he was? She had left him destined for the dungeons in Stormhaven, but that was just a guess. The notion of singing the note of the Shiver came to her, but she discarded it. Zarost had claimed to be sensitive to her singing, but the note alone wouldn't tell him she needed his presence. Besides, the Rector had prohibited her from calling out. Such a high note would be heard throughout the Dovecote, and the Rector would not be pleased at all. She wished to keep her hope of becoming a Lightgifter alive.

A Courier! she realised. She could send a dove to find Zarost, and tell him of her need. She had learned the spell from Ashley. But there again, she met disappointment; she had no Light essence to use. She stared through the bars at the grey day beyond. The view was a familiar one.

The top of a big silken tree blocked the grounds below. The western horizon of Eyri beckoned. She recognised the alcove beyond the bars. She had been up there with Ashley, it was his secret place. When they had been up there, she had looked into the gloom and cobwebs from the other side of the bars, and wondered what kind of a room it was.

Now she knew only too well.

The clear essence was still there, left aside when she had drained it of all Light. It formed a small, glistening puddle on the stone of the alcove. A possibility formed in her mind.

The Morningsong. Maybe I can fill the essence with Light again?

She was sure she could perform the spell, but to do it she would need direct sunlight. The sun was hiding behind a slate-grey sky. She doubted any sprites had been energised that morning. Disappointment again.

The search for a solution to calling Zarost was becoming a seesaw ride between hope and helplessness. The Ring burned, spurring her onwards, filling her mind with questions.

If it responds to one song, what about another?

She hadn't sung the Lifesong for a while. The first stanza she had learned, the one of creation, was the only one she dared to experiment with. She cleared her throat and took a deep breath.

She sang the opening line, and the puddle of clear essence rippled. She sang louder, and the essence seemed to shimmer with greater agitation.

The beauty of the Lifesong swelled inside her, demanding perfection, demanding that she sing with all her heart. The notes rang true, resonating through her body, clearing her present cares from her mind. The Ring was a band of heat, driving her to sing the perfect melody. On the fringes of her awareness, a hundred voices sang with her, a faint choral accompaniment. Possibilities crowded the back of her mind, half-formed thoughts of things she might know, if she could sing beyond the first words. She felt touched by a spirit greater than her own. She felt timeless, limitless, powerful beyond measure.

She reached the end of the stanza, yet the clear essence did not calm as her voice died away. Rainbow colours swirled across the surface, and it moved as if agitated by an inner vibration. Yet even as she watched, the vibrations slowed, and the essence began to lose the faint colours she had caused. The sense of wonder abandoned Tabitha—without the music flowing through her, she was just a young woman, a servant in the Dovecote, not yet a Gifter.

What did I expect, for the essence to turn into a butterfly and fly away to find Zarost?

The clear essence swirled together, turned into a butterfly, and flew away. It had delicate, translucent wings that held all the beautiful fading colours of a rainbow wash, from violet at the tips, through purple and blue and green and yellow, right through to pale red upon its slim abdomen. Tabitha gaped after it. It flitted over the silken tree, caught the breeze above it, and was gone.

It was a real butterfly.

The clear essence had disappeared. There was nothing where the puddle had been, nothing at all.

"Come back!" she called out, knowing at the same time how silly the command was. A butterfly would take no notice of her words. But if it was a construct of magic like a Courier it wouldn't be free to ignore her, it would come back to the one who commanded the Light essence. She had to be sure.

The window remained empty. Joy welled up from deep inside. She laughed.

She had sung a living thing from the clear essence. Her singing had primed the spell, her thoughts had shaped it. The Lifesong had a power beyond anything she had imagined, beyond anything she had heard of.

She hoped the Rector wouldn't notice one butterfly's worth of essence missing from the Dovecote, because it wasn't coming back.

29. VEILED ANSWERS
"Never ask for a fortune you cannot afford."—*Zarost*

Madam Astro'z scratched beneath her breasts. The bags were full and heavy again. So many coins glittering on the table before she'd packed them in, too many for a stall in the Levin wharf market to have on hand. It was time to transfer some wealth to a Safekeeper.

She parted the tent flap. The warm morning sun caught the cinnamon patterns on her layered dress. The veil was pulled high on her face, so that only her eyes could be seen. Two youths ran by, playing a game of tag through the traffic of people and horses and carts. A scruffy dog scampered after them, barking happily. A knot of men in heavy work-clothes surrounded a noble-cloaked and balding gent. From the raised voices it was certain something was amiss with the money due for the previous day's labour. Madam Astro'z didn't want to get involved. It was a rule amongst the wharf traders; your business was your own. She signalled to Poorboy Jannus, a sardonic youth who was sitting on a barrel nearby, and he nodded his acknowledgment. Her tent would be watched while she attended to her urgent business. She walked briskly away from the bustling market, into the close-walled street which led upwards through the stained lower district of Levin.

She would have to be on the lookout for thieves—the innocuous ones who stood in the doorways and waited on street corners, always alone, the men who seemed too casual and were too quick to smile. Most traders used the services of the Swords when taking their wealth to a Safekeeper, but Madam Astro'z couldn't afford contact with the Swords, because she wasn't really Madam Astro'z.

Twardy Zarost needed to remain disguised. He'd done the best he could with his surname.

They had taken him to the dungeons, and he didn't want to return there. He cast his mind back to that day, when they had seized him from the gardens of the Leaf of Merrick, and taken him down, and left him. He remembered the sound.

Bloink. Blink. Bloink.

There was always dripping water in dungeons, and darkness in abundance.

The darkness was so thick he couldn't see the hat on his own head, though he had felt its weight. It smelled of moss, and other, older things. As soon as the soldiers left him, Zarost scratched at the walls, trying to find a loose block, a loose bar, anything. The Stormhaven dungeons were well made.

He couldn't ignore the growing fear that Tabitha was in danger. The King had arranged a carriage for her, to leave Stormhaven, and the Shadowcaster was somewhere within the city. She should be going to safety, and yet ...

The Official had seemed too pleased with himself when he had led Tabitha away.

No, he had to escape. But the cell was locked, and sealed.

He would have to use magic, but he knew he shouldn't, because magic lingered. The Seeker would be sensitive to the traces of spells past, especially to the powerful spells of a Gyre member. He should not use his magic anywhere within Eyri, at least until she had found the wizard, for the unique atmosphere within the Shield might become tainted; it would spawn nothing extraordinary if he filled it with the magic of Twardy Zarost. The Seeker had to develop her own lore. He had taken an Oath to the Gyre, to be a Riddler and not a Wizard, while he was in Eyri.

Yet she was in danger, he knew it.

He gripped the bars and shook them. According to the Gyre's Directive, he shouldn't even be trying to save her, for doing so would violate the principle of Free Will. The Seeker's choices were her own; if she chose a path to danger, then she was ready to walk it. It had been easy with the others, to leave them alone when their trials came upon them. But Tabitha Serannon! She was an extraordinary Seeker, the first one to discover something truly new. He paced the floor in the dark. He wanted to make sure she succeeded. He wanted to shield her from adversity, and bend Fate to spare her from danger.

But that was wrong, and he knew it.

Fate should be allowed to progress according to the Seeker's vision, or else the Seeker would not find the wizard she was supposed to find. His job, as always, was to be the riddler, the oracle, the source of knowledge she could draw upon. Never the preacher, the instructor. That was the worst kind of teacher, for she would learn his choices, follow his ways, and her own talent would be suppressed, turned to mimic his. He had to wait until she sought more knowledge, until she called upon him.

What if that call never came? No, he had to escape, if only to be near her.

A door creaked open somewhere beyond the bars, and a pool of light wobbled its way down the stairs. Zarost squinted against the flickering of the brand. A familiar figure held it aloft, a sweaty Official in a yellow robe. The man waved an insistent moth angrily aside, slipped one step, then cursed.

Zarost lay down quickly, while he was still shrouded within the darkness. He put his face on the cold stone near the back of his cell. He guessed the Official was here to gloat. If he played dead, maybe the man would be stupid enough to unlock the door, to prod him with a foot.

Zarost couldn't see his visitor, but he could hear his movements as he approached. The torch was set into a brazier on the far wall, its dancing light came intermittently through the long shadows of the bars. A faint odour of garlic and lavender drifted towards Zarost.

"Hullo, swine!"

A stone clipped Zarost's head, but lightly—the official's arm was weak. Zarost waited. He was determined not to give Lethin Tarrok the pleasure of tormenting a caged man.

The next stone missed, and the one after that.

"Bah! You'll get your punishment! You'll be seeing the Master again, once this is all over. He doesn't like it when his advisors run away."

So, Tarrok did have connections to Ravenscroft. Zarost knew that the heckler was not a Shadowcaster, he had no aura of magic about him. He was just a spy.

A well-delivered stone bit him between his shoulder blades.

"Vermin! You count the weeks on your grubby little claws," Tarrok crowed. "You won't get far before the crown will pass to the Dark. And you won't be able to betray the plan to the King, now. I will be well rewarded for capturing you in time."

Zarost kept his breath slow and even.

"You've sided with the wrong ruler, cur! Mellar will be on his knees before the Master, pleading for mercy. The King shall fall, and we shall see how Eyri's ruler deals with traitors."

Zarost stared at the wall. The governance of the realm was not his concern. The use of magic was.

Get yourself involved in the running of kingdoms, and you'll end up an old man in no time at all.

He supposed that he *was* an old man, a very old man, but he had got there at his leisure over a few centuries. His captor had no idea who he tormented. But then neither did the Darkmaster really understand, and Zarost had been beside him for over twenty years.

A piece of bread thumped to the floor, and a steel cup clanked down beside it.

"You'll find I'm always considerate to my prisoners. This is for you, you'll get a fresh serving every day." Tarrok snickered. "Oh dear, there's a rat in the corner! Don't move! I'd hate for your food to be stolen before you can eat it." A stone whizzed through the air and struck Zarost's leg. He heard a scuffling in the dark. The next stone struck the wall.

"Rack and blast you!" Tarrok threw his entire handful of pebbles in frustration, and they clattered around Zarost, some rebounding from the bars. "You shouldn't be chasing lying little tarts, not at your age," he taunted. "There's always a younger man, who will want her more, and be prepared to pay for it. Hee! The thing about royal coaches is, you never know what goes into those storage boxes, or what goes on behind those curtains."

Zarost stiffened. The coach! The Shadowcaster was within it! He should have known that the Official would have helped Arkell, for a little bribe, or perhaps just a threat. She really was in danger. Zarost wanted to jump up and strike the man, but the bars would prevent him.

Maybe he would still get the chance, if he lay still enough.

"I know you're listening, I know you're there!" said Tarrok. "Your food might improve if you choose to talk. I want to know how they grow jurrum, and what the secret is of the Dwarrow-wine. I could make a fortune growing that in my father's lands in Vinmorgen County. No? You little roach! I'm sure your attitude will change, as you grow thinner." He cackled like a crone, and his voice altered as he turned away. The light from the brand wobbled as it was moved. Damn! The man wasn't so stupid after all. He wasn't going to enter the cell; he was preparing to leave. Zarost risked a glance. Tarrok still had his back partly turned while he tried to free the brand from brazier. A single key was looped upon his waistband, worn plainly in sight. Probably shown off deliberately, a reminder to Zarost of who had command of the cell. Zarost memorised its pattern before easing his face away.

"I'm thinking of flooding this floor of the dungeon, to help clear the rats!" Tarrok jeered as he walked away. "So if you wake up and you're drowning, you'll know why."

Tarrok continued laughing at his own joke all the way to the stairs. He dawdled up the flight, then he was gone.

"And if you don't wake up at all, you'll know why," Zarost muttered under his breath.

In the pale afterglow of the retreating light, he made his way to the thin steel cup. As he'd thought, the liquid in it was not water, it was a pale yellow fluid, and pungent. He threw it out hard.

There would be time to deal with Lethin Tarrok. But for now, he had more important matters to attend to. Like getting to Tabitha Serannon, before it was too late.

There was a scuffling along the far wall. A darker shadow with a tail, heading for the bread. The rat was welcome to it—the food was likely to be of similar vintage to the water.

The vague flickering of the torch was gone, and it was quiet. Zarost paused, considering what he was about to do. It was a huge risk to break the Oath, even in the small way he would need to escape. Twardy Zarost scowled at the darkness. It was never easy, being the Riddler. There was no other way.

He concentrated on the handle of the steel mug and gathered the clear essence inside it. Within the metal, hidden in the tiny particles of matter, was the essence that governed the matter's shape and strength. He claimed that essence, and moved it on the second axis of magic towards Energy, striving to be as discreet as possible with his spell.

The steel grew pliable in his hands. He pulled the handle free, then rolled the strip between his fingers. When it was long enough, he twisted the end into the right shape, and pinched the jagged tip flat. He guided the essence within the steel back towards the Matter end of the second axis. The steel hardened.

They had called it Magemetal in Oldenworld. Such a popular spell, the Metalmelt, a simple loop around the zero point of the second axis. They had all cast it, in those early days, before the alternatives upon the third axis had been discovered. It was the *quietest* spell he could employ.

The lock groaned as he turned his key in it, then the bolt slapped open. He locked it again behind him, and pocketed the key. They would know he'd escaped, but they would never know how. Nobody should know of his talents. Let them wonder.

He trailed his hand along the slimy wall as he made for the stairs. A light, oh for a light! An even simpler spell, one of the first axis.

"Double-damn the Oath!" he exclaimed. He couldn't break the prohibition again, not when he had the alternative of guiding himself by dragging his fingers through a century of cold slime.

Cast a light, and next you'll be turning copper coins into gold, and playing with the minds of young ladies. And you will be the only wizard to emerge from Eyri when Time runs to an end.

He gained the basement level, and came upon a linen store for the prisoners in a silent hallway. He donned one of the oldest, most stained burlap sheets, winding it over his clothes and around his head as well, in the manner of a leper. It would help him pass through Stormhaven swiftly, without being hindered. The Swords would be only too happy to send him on his way back to Rotcotford in Bentwood, where his kind belonged. An old tubular bell hung on a frayed hessian rope beside the door. Zarost took that as well, stuffing his hat into the body of the bell to prevent the rusted clapper from clanging until he was outside.

At the exit, there was only one jailor, asleep. Little wonder, Zarost mused, for he only had one prisoner. He was probably used to guarding nothing at all. His keys were close enough to hook with a broomhandle.

And so he left the dungeons, and the palace at Stormhaven, and left the city as fast as his affected hobbling gait would allow. There had been great commotion around the Gates, Swords running hither and thither, and a galloping company rushed by, heading for Levin. He had slipped through.

Then he had heard the high scream, and seen with his hawk-eyes, far away, that horrible beast of the Underworld crouched before the Seeker, and the flaming carriage behind. He had run, careless of his disguise, building a deadly spell between his hands.

A true voice had sung, a glinting blade had swung, and there was nothing to be done at all.

For the girl had held the Morgloth, and Glavenor had slain it dead.

She hadn't needed his spell, she had been ready.

He danced like a dervish upon the Kingsbridge, whirling till his burlap flapped loose, whirling till the horizon became a smooth line separating the blue dome above from the golden waters beneath. He let the essence dissolve on the breeze, so unneeded, so good to release unused. She had passed her first great trial. She had used what she had learned to defeat a great rival. She had demonstrated her claim on the Ring.

By the time the Swordmaster thundered by, bound for Stormhaven, he was a leper once more, sack-clothed and obeisant, his staggering tread announced by the dull clanks from the marker at his neck. He kept his gaze down as the Seeker and her companions passed by. There would be better times to greet young Tabitha, but in the secrecy of his hood he couldn't suppress a smile.

Stormhaven had become too risky for him, and he guessed the Seeker would move on to the Dovecote soon enough. So he chose to disappear within Levin, to be near enough should the Seeker need him, but where he could remain hidden from others who might seek him out. An easy feat to become anonymous in Levin—the city was like a fat old lady, sat upon the lake shore, so large that most citizens were obscured within the many folds of her skirts. Too much trade passed through the great city for any one person to be noticed, too much traffic rumbling in and out, day and night; too much life. Stormhaven might be the head of Eyri, with the Houses of Rule and the King's Court, but Levin was its beating heart.

Thus was Madam Astro'z born; a veiled woman of undetermined age, olive-skinned, attractive to some, if only for the hidden promise of her large bosom and the mischief in her wise watchful eyes. Her name, as unusual as the Madame herself, was pronounced 'Astroze'. If those who spoke to her had chanced to see beneath the veil, they might have noticed that Madam Astro'z became stubbled in the afternoons. But by then the wharemen who came to the wharf market were too tired to haggle with an insistent woman, and the other customers were hurrying for the taverns. When they came to Madam Astro'z again, on the way home from the shoreside watering holes, she did a brisk business in soothsaying, with her star charts and glyph cards. This work she found most delightful, for her customers lost one fortune to gain another, one they would have received regardless of her augury. But she was talented, they all agreed, foretelling things which came to pass within the week. She knew things that cut like a knife.

Madam Astro'z—how much she saw through the slitted veil, how much she saw beyond it.

He had guessed correctly about Tabitha, for after a few days he heard gossip in the wharf market that the singer was on Light Hill, studying to be a Gifter. She would need some time to absorb all that had happened. She would need some time to think, before the questions would begin again.

She would need some time to reflect, and look inward.

And so Twardy Zarost immersed himself in the glinting details of Eyrian commerce.

The best trade was in fine jewelry, for he knew how to distinguish the resmelted finery made in Ayen Manor from the inferior originals made in Chink—although the miner's daughters had tried their best to produce the Ayen Manor style and delicacy, the Rockroute County still had no silversmiths the equal of Shilivar Ayen's house in Vinmorgen.

The rivalry had a history to it. Every generation of miner's daughters tried to improve on their shortcomings. What a shame the fault was in their forge, not in their artistry. Too great a metalworks at Chink, fired by the quickpines brought from the Westfold plantations, fired until the very stones in the street outside the forgery were hot. It was suited for the stronger work in iron and steel; their farming implements and cookware and even weaponry were good, their curled gemstrings not so. Shilivar Ayen could take their best efforts as raw materials for his own compact forge, and produce the same items with less metal and more finesse. His descendants had inherited his clever hands—but for the hairline touches left by the finishing tools Zarost couldn't tell which member of the Ayen family had worked on jewelry.

Ayen Manor's filigreed glassware was also becoming sought after since they had mastered the art of trapping fine veins of gold between two layers of glass. The coloured pottery alternatives from Kironkiln didn't stand a chance amongst those Levinners who appreciated style.

Flowerton had produced a triple-stemmed candle which seemed durable and colourful. Zarost preferred the spring-scented carved birds from Waxworth in Meadowmoor. You could smell the vitality of the Eyrian downs in them, and he kept one burning in his tent upon the wharf almost every day. They made a nice set—an Ayen Manor necklace, a slender-necked glass, and swan candle—especially for those men whom Madam Astro'z had foreseen meeting impressionable women in the near future.

He chose the products that sold, and sold fast. A pity he could not trade in Dwarrow-wine or spirits, but that would put him up against the Licencing Council and the shoreside tavern heavies. As it was he was operating as a grey trader, having paid only the stalls on either side of him for his place.

He sourced farflung items quickly using the Lightgifters' Couriers.

The ministering Gifters came through the shoreside district every afternoon, collecting donations for the 'upkeep of the Dovecote' in exchange for a 'token of gratitude'—a polite cover for the most active message-service in Eyri. Donate a silver, and a written message could be carried with others in a Courier's flight. Donate six, and you might receive a 'token of gratitude' in the form of an entire Courier bird, to speak to and carry your private message to any Gifter in the realm, who in their turn would receive a 'donation' for interpreting the missive. Money passed hands faster than doves could fly. If the Gifters became too busy, the 'donation of minimal significance' merely rose until the crowds had thinned. Zarost thought it was a useful system, but it was also a terrible corruption of the original vision which had inspired the founder of the Lightgifters to begin their Order.

Charity was supposed to flow from the rich to the poor, not the other way around.

He bought and sold as little magic as possible. For anything within greater Levin, he used runners from the poor district, who were cheaper and had a greater need for the money than the Dovecote.

In the second week, intriguing items began to flow into Madame Astroz's market stall. A clock from Respite which needed no winding. Zarost supposed the device must need replacement eventually, but it seemed to find all the power it needed to move the little arms from a clever bellows which measured the changing weight of the sky. He had never seen anything of its kind, and he almost broke the copper-wire finishing whilst trying to take it apart. The construction was unnaturally accurate for an artisan from the Rockroute County. Perhaps the workshop in Respite had lured away an Ayen Manor apprentice with an offer of a Journeyman's pay.

The clock fetched a high price as soon as it arrived.

The first Levin Councillor who came to collect taxes, Madam Astro'z sent away, because the bristle-nosed fidget was not who he claimed to be. The second Councillor, jowled and jolly, was indeed an important man, and he wanted ten golds in taxes for the trading licence and another five for Madame Astroz's indiscretion (or a 'little something for the mistress, something memorable, something discreet'). And so a beautiful painting from Southwind was lost, a depiction of two swans necking upon the Amberlake amidst drifting thistledown beneath a brooding sky. Zarost decided it was for the best—buyers of paintings were fickle folk, prone to indecision. The artwork might have simply gathered dust.

Then there was a soft-spoken Sword who was searching for a troublemaker called the Riddler. No, Madam Astro'z was obviously not the troublemaker, because she was a woman. No, he understood that the Madame might not see everything from within her tent, but maybe she knew something of a bearded man with a striped hat. Where was that accent from, Madame, from Fendwarrow? Or Coppershaft? She was new on the wharf, wasn't she, not from around Vinmorgen? Where had she come from, and when had she crossed Counties? Were there perhaps trade records or ancestral documents to verify the Madame's history?

Madam Astro'z had produced a quire of the rare Russel Soft-press, pale paper that was fine and strong, and utterly blank. The Sword had laughed at Madame Astroz's temerity, but had taken the paper in exchange for not mentioning to his superiors the lack of documentation. The Sword had suspected that something was amiss with Madam Astro'z, but he hadn't suspected the truth of the riddle.

And so Madam Astro'z continued to trade, while all around her tent the commodities moved, through that great working filter that was the Levin trade yard. Building timbers from Llury, twelve foot high and straight as an arrow. Those pungent sticky barrels from Tarbarn which always reminded Zarost of the pallisaded villages in the Oldenworld Hunterslands, or the mountain lodges of Koraman Kingdom. Heavy flour sacks from Westmill. Jocular sailors from Wright in Westfold brought tanned leather and soap and glue. Dusty wagoneers offloaded finespun wool from Meadowmoor County, tapestries from First Light, livestock from Cellarspring. And as much was outbound from the Vinmorgen farms: eggs, salted meat, fruit, cheese and wine. Linen from Burke Manor, garments from the productive switch-looms of Rhyme. Buyers poked at bundles even before they were off the pulleys and wharemen cursed lethargic stevedores.

To be a trader on the Levin wharf was to hold the pulse of Eyri in your hand, and to feel its health in your ledger. And so it was that the coins were heavy in Madame Astroz's breasts that morning as she climbed the street through Levin on the way to the Safekeeper.

Zarost came to Copper Fountain, a small greensward around which the elegant arched buildings of the various Safekeepers and Lenders were arrayed. One of the few open grounds in Levin, it offered him the first unobstructed view of the sky since he'd left the market. He noticed the strange cloud, and stopped dead.

A curled and many-tailed shroud crossed the sun. It was too strange a pattern for an ordinary cloud, forked and cross-ribbed in the style of the glyphic texts of Kaskanzr, in Oldenworld, like the cards of foretelling that Madam Astro'z used. A few Kaskanzan words had been blended to form a message. Refuge stood in the pattern, or Egg. The symbol for Abandonment was there as well, but it was somewhat dissolved, as if the lowest twist of cloud was unintentional, so he couldn't be certain. But over them all was laid a pattern which made his heart stand still. Doom.

It was too particular a design to have been achieved by random motion alone, and yet no one within Eyri would recognise that writing, no one but him. Such a message could have come from one source alone. The Gyre of Wizards, out in Oldenworld, beyond the Shield.

He had to meet with the Wizards.

The glyphic cloud drifted on the high winds, burning its awful decree upon the innocent blue sky of Eyri.

Doom? For over five hundred years the Gyre had faced Ametheus, and they had endured many horrors, but while they stood together, there was always hope. What could they face now that was so terrible they had lost faith? And why had they chosen the symbol for Abandonment? Did they mean he should prepare to leave his refuge, leave Eyri, abandon it altogether? That was too terrible to consider.

The ominous cloud lingered in his thoughts that day, long after it had drifted beyond the horizon. He concluded his business with the Safekeeper, and hurried back to the wharf market. He would have to clear his wares. Madam Astro'z lifted her tent-skirts, and announced a sale.

Then, sometime around noon, when he was in the thick of the bargain-merry crush, he heard a voice of wonder; a song, carried on the breeze, coming from beyond the crowd, beyond even the lower districts of Levin. No, that voice belonged to the Seeker—it came from within the Dovecote. No one but Zarost took any notice, for they didn't recognise the powerful burst in the ether, the unmistakable trace of magic, the resonance that shivered through everything with a rush of life.

Tabitha Serannon had sung. She was exploring the Lifesong lore once more. She was ready to be riddled.

He was so overjoyed that he gave a soft-coloured silk away to the customer who had been haggling with him upon a price of four-silvers-and-seven. He barely noticed the rest of the wares leaving his stall at cut-throat prices. He hummed a melody to himself all through the afternoon.

Only as the colours of the marketplace cooled to shadow, did the tune die on his lips. He could not forget the way the lowest tail of the Gyre's glyph-cloud had curled to complete the symbol of Doom. He knew that he would have to answer the summons from the Gyre first—it was too urgent, too alarming to ignore. He couldn't believe they had really meant to include the symbol of Abandonment.

It could not be the end, not now, with the Seeker so close to power.

He went to bed a troubled woman.

30. SHATTERED DREAMS

"Sanity is a narrow trail,
perched upon a knife-edged cliff."—*Zarost*

The Amberlake slapped against the rocks of the Kingsbridge. Through a narrow slit, the pale starlight flashed off the chop outside. The crevice was deep, and the sharp rocks were slanted at an awkward angle.

Kirjath Arkell wondered what night it was. There was a mess in his mind where his memory should be. He was –

It came again, and he clutched the rock. The jerking, shivering, splintering pain. It took him some time to realise that the attack had passed, and that he could release his grip.

He wondered what night it was.

The Swords had come and gone. There had been nothing for them to see in the gloom of the crevice but dark, and Dark. Most men couldn't tell the difference. That was days ago.

Wasn't it?

His vision spiralled into a hundred stars, which jiggled and spun, then collected into one terribly bright red burst. The spasm which ripped through his body wiped his mind clean.

He was a spider under threat. He knew he must hide. He had not eaten, there was a roaring hunger in his belly, and the cold neverending. But there was water, oh there was lots of water. And he was alive.

Unlike the beast, he remembered suddenly. He shivered. The image of the battle on the Kingsbridge flickered to life in his mind's eye, then was torn apart by the shrieking sword. He had been inside the Morgloth, he had been linked to it. Then the blade had struck, and the scream had shattered his stone. There was only an instant he remembered after that—coming to consciousness, finding himself sinking, too deep in cold water to ever reach the surface in time. He had cast the Freeze spell on himself, even though he knew that it would just delay the inevitable—he would wake up later, at the bottom of the lake, and drown. It was a most extreme measure, to Freeze one's own heart, a trick they had played with in the early days of his apprenticeship, even though it had been forbidden. Then, they had used only small amounts of essence, which caused a deep unconsciousness for a few hours. In the lake, he had used all the power of summoning he could. It was the end, and he had saturated himself with Dark essence. Even as he had cast the spell, he had known it would be the last one he would ever cast. The breakdown of his mind had begun, as his shattered Darkstone raped his sanity.

But he had not drowned. When he'd come to, desperately cold, he'd found himself lying at the water's edge, on the foot of the Kingsbridge again. He'd floated to the surface, but slowly, for the current had drawn him a long way towards Levin. He had no idea of whether it was the night of the same day, or the next. He had no way of finding out. But he'd seen the Sword approaching, and had hid himself in the crevice. He'd passed out then, for a long time, he supposed. He had never known such desperate weakness.

He forgot what he had been thinking of. An image of a great black Keep filled his mind, a place he half remembered, then it was gone. He cursed. Then he cried, for a time, knowing he was probably going to die, despite it all. He hated the tears more than anything. He was too weak to move.

His mind was like a barrel of broken glass. Every heartbeat turned the barrel, and the shards tumbled over each other, shattering his view of the lake and the moon, painting a new vision in place of the old.

He was a demon lord. He was a Shadowcaster. He was a young boy again, watching his father's execution at the hand of the King's justice. He was a Morrigán, waiting on the rocks at the mouth of the crevice. He was a Morgloth, biting a soldier's neck from behind. He cackled at a joke told to him by a fellow along the bar, then cursed when he realised that no one had spoken. There was no bar. He was in a narrow cave.

The kaleidoscope of thoughts was underlined by the excruciating pain of his shattered Darkstone. He spent a while clawing at his throat and the chain. Then he remembered it was useless. Only in death would it release its clasp and pass to another. It was a damaged relic now; all that remained of his orb was a jagged obsidian tooth. The girl had shattered it with her scream. She had shattered his mind.

A flurry of wings reminded him of the dark bird at the mouth of the crevice. It slipped and flapped itself awkwardly towards him, trying to avoid sliding from the rock in the constricted space. Something was tied to its foot—a stone dragged and skipped along behind the bird. The raven paused just beyond his arm's reach, cocking its head to one side, then the other. It issued a hoarse call.

He looked blankly at the bird, forgetting what it was. Then he remembered receiving one before, in this crevice, and sending his own in reply to announce that he had survived. He had sent such a bird to the Darkmaster.

The Morrigán croaked, and Kirjath covered his ears. The raven would not relent, its harsh call slipped past his crooked fingers and burrowed into his brain. It brought the bloom of red light and another seizure with it.

When he stopped quivering, he was a Shadowcaster. There was a Morrigán before him, faded and weak. It must have been cast at least a full day ago, maybe two. Yet he had not accepted it. He felt the first twinge of fear at his condition.

"Alight, messenger, and deliver your word."

The raven pulled its fetter into his hand. Kirjath felt the familiar touch of a smooth Darkstone. He recognised the chain, the open clasp. It was an unbroken orb, a new orb, black as the dead of night. He was to be made whole again. The Master cared. He belonged. Tears stung his eyes. He was a Shadowcaster. It was something he could hold onto.

The raven dissolved, and the words of the message filled the crevice.

"Deliver this orb to my new Shadowcaster and clasp it on her neck. She is held in the Dovecote. There is a small chapel at the end of the northern wing. You will be found there, and the girl brought to you. Clasp the Darkstone, and no more. I do not wish for her to be killed. Tabitha Serannon will bring both the Ring and her skill to me, in time."

The blood pounded in Kirjath's ears. His rage found a focus, the needlepoint which had driven into him at every turn, causing his failure and ridicule. Tabitha Serannon. He knew the name only too well.

"This is your last chance to gain favour in my eyes," the Darkmaster ended.

The waves lapped against the rock, and the reflected stars shimmered and dipped. The crevice was quiet.

The Master had no idea how tenuous Kirjath's grasp on sanity was. It had been a lucid moment when he sent the last Morrigán winging to Ravenscroft. He was having a similar moment now.

How long before I'm twitching and yelping like a crazed cur?

When the barrel of glass splinters turned in his mind, he would be lost to madness. Yet he could be nothing but a servant to the Dark. His orb prevented him from escape, even in its damaged form—he knew that when the Master turned his coercion on him, he would be unable to resist the pull toward Ravenscroft. His defiance was a thing of the past. The Master had spoken. Kirjath had to see to the orbing of a new Shadowcaster.

He could not fight. There was not enough wholeness remaining in his mind to command the Dark with much focus, let alone to hold onto the vice-grip of the demon-spell.

He wept. Then he shouted in rage, not caring who might hear a voice amongst the rocks where there should have been silence.

Then he forgot why he was shouting. He looked at the orb in his hand with puzzlement, lifted it and tried to fasten the clasp at the back of his neck. The magic would not seal.

He couldn't remember what he had been trying to do. He dangled the orb on its chain against the pale starlight, and grimaced as it regularly blocked the narrow opening in his sight, swinging back and forth.

Dark. Light. Dark. Light. He used to have a swing under a big oak tree, and his father had pushed him high out over the water. Father had been strung on a rope in the village square, the King had said he was that bad.

Dark. Light.

The Morgloth had borne him over the castle wall.

Dark.

The pain was better if you bit down hard on your fingers.

Light.

He arched his back, and kicked out against the rock. He lay still for a while. Later, he sighed. You couldn't sleep, when the pain kept you awake. He remembered now. The only way to sleep was to be unconscious. He bashed his head against the roof of his asylum.

Something warm trickled down his cheek. He cupped a dark stone against his lips. He slid into the wedge of the crevice, and was gone again.

31. A TRICK OF THE LIGHT

"Every time you take a breath,
you breath out your own name."—*Zarost*

Twardy Zarost's sleep was interrupted by a gentle fluttering. It must be a moth that had sneaked through the outer layers of the tent. He brushed it aside. It settled again, a few moments later, with the faintest of familiar echoes, a soft voice raised in song.

His heart skipped a beat. It was no moth; it had the pulse of power and a sense of newness to it that was impossible. He cracked an eye open. The light of dawn bloomed in the canopy above. Before his face, a coloured butterfly flitted in the air, swooped upon him, harried him. Its translucent wings held a wash of colour as if it had flown through a rainbow and caught traces of those pastel shades upon itself. It was a creature unlike any he had seen before. Ring upon ring of shimmering circles surrounded it, as if it had been recently touched by magic and was still shedding the traces of it. Yet the butterfly itself was no spell. It was as real as the folded linen beneath his body, as real as he was.

With a flash of recognition, he understood. This was what the Lifesong had created the day before. This was the result of Tabitha's spell, this was her butterfly! That was why the memory of her song clung to it so tight.

It might be no coincidence then that it had found him. She must have guided its course, even though it was a real creature. That was more astounding than the butterfly itself—it had followed the emanations of the specific man she'd visualised, in the manner of a Courier bird. It would have looked for his aura, not his face, and so might have encountered his trail anywhere between Copper Fountain and the wharf, maybe even looping out upon the Kingsbridge before homing in on him.

Life! She had created life! She had tapped into the true power of the Lifesong. She might not know what she was doing, but she was already raising herself to unprecedented levels of perfection, in a kind of magic which had not been wielded with any competence for hundreds of years. She was developing so fast, yet she was unprepared for what she would draw upon herself with her brand of magic. Soon, she would be testing another second stanza, then seeking out a third and fourth. It was an undefined lore, unbounded, it might achieve anything. She might devise spells that would even break through the Shield and expose Eyri to the Chaos beyond. Zarost sat up straight in his bed. In many ways, Tabitha Serannon was still a girl, ignorant of what she touched, unready to face the fate she tempted. He was worried about her. By Ethea's breath! She hadn't even balanced the first axis of magic—she only knew of the Light.

The echoes of the Lifesong resonated in the butterfly. It came to rest on his shoulder, its wings opening and closing like a little book. He threw his blanket aside, and began to make ready for his departure. He would speak to her today, before he hastened to the Gyre meeting. She deserved a warning, or at least a nudge in the right direction.

He dressed as Madam Astro'z, but he had a suspicion this might be the last day she would be seen in Levin.

◆ ——————◆

The Hall of Sky captured the sunlight, the Source scattered it. Sprites flickered through the air with manic disorder, overcharged with the Light. The essence mirrored the excitement within the gathered Assembly. Ashley Logán was amazed. They had applauded the Rector's news, and now they babbled about it, all at once.

The Sword had conquered the Shadowcasters in the secret vale of Ravenscroft. These were the words of the herald who had spoken to the Rector. The strength of the Dark had been broken, and the Swords held the Keep. They required the urgent assistance of the Lightgifters, for the battle had been terrible. Many Swords required healing. The Rector wanted as much essence as could be commanded to be taken to the vale at once, to purge Ravenscroft of its evil taint. The Sword of Eyri had severed the head of the poisonous serpent. Ashley felt light-headed and carefree.

Rector Shamgar stamped his sceptre on the dais. It took him some time to attain a whispered silence, but he was unusually good-natured about the delay.

"Any volunteers to bear the greatness of the Light to help the Swords?"

The Hall filled with clamour again, and the Rector was lost to Ashley's view behind a forest of raised hands. It would be a joyous task—to heal those Swords in need, and to purify the wastrels whom they no doubt held captive. Nothing so exciting had occurred in the history of the Dovecote.

A rushed morning of packing followed. They tacked up the few Dovecote horses, connected them to carts, and loaded those with supplies. The Rector announced that he would remain behind, to care for the Dovecote and the handful of Gifters and half-knots who weren't able to take the march. Everyone in good health was urged to go.

Ashley joined Father Keegan when they departed.

"Have you seen Tabitha?" he asked.

Keegan shook his head. "Maybe she's not coming, Ashley. She's still a ghost, isn't she?"

Ashley nodded. Still a ghost, and her place was with the servants, in the Dovecote. But that wasn't what he had meant.

"Have you seen her recently, in the last two days?"

Keegan shook his head again. "Not since I returned. Why?"

"Nothing. I just wondered where she was."

"I hope that girl doesn't lose spirit under all the work the Rector is loading her with," Keegan said. "She will make a fine Gifter, when she is raised."

"Do you think she will be? Raised, that is."

"I can't see any reason why she shouldn't be," Keegan answered, throwing a mildly puzzled look Ashley's way.

"But she is not ready yet," Ashley noted.

"In the Rector's opinion."

The way he said it left Ashley no doubt. If the decision had been Keegan's to make, Tabitha would be an apprentice already. It set his mind at ease—he hadn't made a mistake in teaching her, albeit in secret. Since her behaviour inside the inner sanctum, he had questioned his judgement in trading spells. It was all right if she were becoming a Lightgifter, but if she was not to be raised, then he was sharing secrets that should not be shared, not with one outside the order.

The way Tabitha had snubbed him in the inner sanctum still hurt. He had expected her to share the discovery, and yet she had withheld the knowledge she had gained in the chamber of the Sage, as if he was somehow unworthy of it. Maybe that was it—she had been avoiding him these past few days, because she did not want to tell him her secret.

It was unfair. He had received only pain for his efforts. It had taken days for the effect of the Spriteblind trap to clear from his vision. That first day after their foray had been the worst. He had been able to see little more than hazy shapes amidst the burning dots of light, and he had kept on walking into things. It had been all he could do to hide his condition from the others.

He set his thoughts of Tabitha aside. She could look after herself, and when he returned, there would be no more secret lessons.

The pace of the Lightgifters was slow despite their eagerness, because of the carts. It took half an hour to descend through the city of Levin, whereupon they reached the level stoneroad leading to Wendelnip, Kironkiln, and Fendwarrow. Liquid sunshine pooled beside them wherever they went. The Light sped forwards in tendrils to form new pools as the Gifters maintained their command over their sprites. Most of the Light had been drained from the Dovecote for the mission, under the Rector's insistence. The Source would produce more, given enough time. It was imperative that Ravenscroft be cleared of all traces of Dark.

◆ ———————— ◆

There had been a commotion within the Dovecote for a few hours; now it was gone. Tabitha held onto the bars at her window. The cell behind was full of boredom, dust and loneliness. The chamber-pot had begun to smell. No matter how she tried, she could not find the peace of atonement she was supposed to be seeking.

It was a bright spring day outside, with a brilliant sun in a royal blue sky. She took a deep breath of the clear air, but it only made her longing for freedom more acute. She sang a soft ballad to the leaves of the silken tree, hoping to find solace in the song. There was no essence to play with, clear or otherwise. The quiet that returned when she ended the ballad was oppressive.

She was almost of a mind to sing again, when the door burst open. The Rector.

Her heart sank. She kept her gaze downcast. She knew she was supposed to be atoning, which probably didn't mean singing, in the Rector's opinion.

He called her to him, and she shuffled across the cell toward the door. When she stood before him, and dared to glance upward, she saw his smile.

"A fine day, what?" His cheeks puffed outward.

"Yes, Rector," she stammered.

"Well, shall we begin with your studies?"

"Studies?" Tabitha was dumbfounded.

He smiled a broader smile, revealing slightly crooked teeth.

"I'd like to test you, to see if you have the aptitude. No point in us having you wasting your time, when there's so much work for a Lightgifter to do. That is, of course, if you still wish to become a Lightgifter?"

"I do," she replied, breathlessly.

"And are you ready to make reparation for your deeds, or do you need more atoning?" He looked her up and down.

"I'm ready. I'm sorry for what I did, Rector."

"Right, well come along then."

He set a brisk pace through the Dovecote, down the stairs to the Hall of Sky, then through the northern doors. When they had crossed the Sandfield and passed into the grounds beyond, he dropped back to walk beside her. The grass sprung pleasantly underfoot. It was wonderful to be outside. She dared a question on the strength of his present good mood.

"Rector, where has everybody gone?"

"Were you not—of course, you wouldn't know. Ravenscroft has been conquered, girl. I sent as many Gifters as I could spare, and all our essence, to the Swords. There is much healing to be done."

If the Sword had been victorious, then Garyll Glavenor had to be all right as well. She wanted to believe the good news, but her stomach had turned cold. Something was strange about the words, something didn't ring true. Why would the Rector lie to her? She knew she should challenge him, but a sharp glance from the Rector warned her not to. His good cheer was only skin deep. She kept quiet. She wanted to earn his approval. She didn't want to spend any more time locked away in the dust. She wanted to be a Lightgifter.

They left the mass of the Dovecote behind and closed on a small stone chapel. Tabitha had never seen the inside of the chapel. She had heard that only the Rector and a few of the most senior Gifters were allowed to cross its hallowed floor. The Rector opened the door, and ushered her inside.

The chapel was cool, and had a pervading smell of damp about it. Two squat antechambers stood side by side. The Rector guided her towards them with a hand low on her back. When they came close, the Rector slowed her by pulling on the fabric of her dress from behind. There were beads of sweat on his upper lip, and a hungry cast to his eye.

A horrible fear began to take shape. His hand was still on the small of her back, his body near. They were alone. His hand slid down an inch. Tabitha closed her eyes, and gathered a scream. But the Rector withdrew his hand then, and patted her on the shoulder, before stepping away.

"Where you stand now has the best acoustics for the Morningsong. Try it. Sing just the first note."

Relief washed over her. She had been mistaken.

What had I been thinking? Fool girl, he's the Rector.

She hastily drew a breath, and began the oldest of the Lightgifters' songs.

The note fell flat amongst the shadows and beams. There was nothing remarkable about the acoustics of the chapel. The many facets and angles of the inside walls made her voice sound dull. She looked questioningly toward the Rector.

"No, no, you must sing in a higher octave, what? It only happens on the higher notes."

She sang the note again, an octave above the first. The Rector tensed, close to her once more. His expression was unreadable, but he nodded.

"Higher."

She was becoming puzzled, but threw her head back and sang the note in the highest octave anyway.

The Rector grabbed the back of her head, and with his free hand jammed something into her mouth. It stank of stale toes and shoe-leather. She gagged on it, and struggled to escape his sudden grasp, but he tied a piece of cord behind her head, painfully tight. Tabitha fought desperately against him, but she could not break free. He bound her hands behind her back, as well.

No, no, no, no please not this, not like this, not here, oh no. No. No!

Tears stung her eyes. The Rector held her from behind, one large arm lifting her breasts, the other hand twisted her chin toward him.

"You are lucky it is only gold I care for," the Rector whispered, his breath hot on her ear. "You would make a tasty morsel. Maybe when my friend is done with you, I shall change my mind, before I banish you from the Dovecote."

The door to the antechamber opened, and she was shoved through.

There was a sharp damp odour, of soggy fabric and of something vaguely rotten. The door banged closed behind her, and the bolt was shot.

The Rector was not with her, she realised. Her lungs heaved against the restraint of the gag. A narrow lancet window did little to pierce the gloom of the chamber. Something moved in the corner, the dark shape of a man. Her legs turned to jelly. The figure crossed a thin ray of sunlight. She screamed into her gag.

The Shadowcaster stretched to his full height before her, his grin a sliver of white beneath yellowed eyes. His skin had a pasty pallor to it.

Her feet scrabbled for purchase, her back thumped into the door. She tried the latch, but it held firm, she couldn't move it with her wrists bound.

Kirjath Arkell advanced, and pinned her to the door. He stank. She turned her face away from him, but his cold, soft hand gripped her jaw and forced her attention forwards. She couldn't bear to look directly upon those bloodshot eyes, so she dropped her gaze. On his collar dangled a shattered piece of dark crystal.

The Shadowcaster didn't speak. He held her pinned against the door for what seemed like an age. She was too terrified to move.

Tabitha risked a glance to his face at last, and beheld eyes bereft of reason, a mad glare that changed its focus with every heartbeat. When nothing had happened for a while longer, she found a moment of courage, and tried to break free. She wrenched with all her might, making to dive clear of the door.

The Shadowcaster caught her. His eyes had cleared, and she was slammed back against the door.

"Surprised to see me?"

Tabitha couldn't respond.

"I've brought you a present, from the Master."

She flinched when he drew his fist close to her face. He opened it, and she flinched again. A dark crystal orb, fashioned like the Lightstone, but as black as night.

"Be grateful!" he shouted. "An unblemished Darkstone! Look at it! Perfect." He closed his fist around it, and hit her. She fell to the floor. He heaved her to her feet again. She tasted blood filtering through her teeth.

"Bitch!" he shouted. Then his eyes became unfocused. He winced, and jerked against her.

"Put it around her neck. Put it around her neck," he whispered.

When she grasped his intention, she went wild. She thrashed under his grip, kicked out at his shins. It was as if he didn't notice, or didn't care. He used his body weight to pin her against the door, and looped a chain around her neck with single-minded purpose.

The snap of the clasp sounded behind her. Tabitha was paralysed with sudden cold and dread.

The Shadowcaster released her, and stroked the Darkstone at her throat. Then he spat upon the Lightstone nestled beside it. He jerked away, like a puppet on a string twitched by another's hand. Then he sat down suddenly.

He began to shout at the walls.

Then he stared, slack-jawed.

He seemed quite mad.

Tabitha was only vaguely aware of the Shadowcaster's actions. A black whirlpool roared in her head, sucking her into a maw she could not escape. Her vision faded to darkness, a silence wrapped itself around her, and cold entered her heart. She knew that her legs had buckled, yet her body was a distant thing, beyond her command. There was a pattern twined through the darkness close by, a disturbance she could feel rather than see, a pattern she was being guided to appreciate. A spell that was both unfamiliar and ominous. She tried to shy away from it, but her body would not respond, and part of her knew it was useless to try. She was not in a place she could run away from. The darkness and the pattern were in her mind. She could only try to turn her attention elsewhere, away from the pattern.

Then she felt him. A presence, within the darkness, someone who watched her without revealing himself, but he was there nonetheless. He was hidden behind her, though turning did nothing to reveal him. A voice filled the silence, rising through layer upon layer of her own fear and dread.

I am the shadow and he is my master.

He is the shadow and I am his caster.

She moaned through her gag, and fled the touch of the Darkmaster in her mind. Her feet thrashed on the floor, but she didn't try to stand. It was within her mind that she had to flee. Any thoughts of the voice or the darkness led her closer to that awful presence. She reached for her memories, and ran through them as if they were autumn leaves, their faded colours vivid against the blackness which chased her heels.

A moment when she had watched her mother baking bread in their home at Phantom Acres. Sleeping under the tree, her father waking her to help with the sheep. The Shadowcaster crashing through the big window, shards of glass raining down on her. The burned ruin of the homestead. Her parents corpses, as dry as the charcoal they lay in.

The Dark tore through her memories, and there was nothing for her to cling to for refuge. The pattern and the voice returned, the presence of the Darkmaster swelled to embrace her, smothering her with fear, cold, and the urgent compulsion to accept Him as her Master.

Lightgifter. I am a Lightgifter!

Laughter echoed in the suddenly paling darkness.

I wait for you. Power waits for you.

Her vision swam with darkness. "No!" she cried. "No!"

She became aware of her surroundings again. She was sprawled on the floor, her breath came in short gasps through the dirty fabric that filled her mouth. The gloomy antechamber appeared bright, compared to the darkness which she had endured. The Shadowcaster was moving in a corner. The door was unguarded. She scrabbled to her feet, with one thought in mind.

A jet of Dark essence burst forth from the shadows. Motes wrapped her legs in fine tendrils which quickly thickened and pinned her to the wall. When the Shadowcaster spoke and the spell matured, her legs were claimed by the terrible cold she remembered from a night she wished she didn't.

She couldn't move, but Kirjath Arkell could.

He came across the chamber with a hungry, feral cast to his eyes. He wet his lips. He laughed, then fell upon her. He ripped her dress open. It tore to the waist, exposing her undershirt. He tore that as well. Cold air touched her breasts. She screamed, but the gag smothered her cry, and a slimy hand clamped her throat tight. He touched the Darkstone, and strange thoughts she didn't want to think assaulted her.

Abandon yourself to the wildness. Taste the blood of your wounds, fuel your anger. Savour the violence, learn to return it. You could beat this rapist, beat him to a bloody pulp. So much power awaits.

What was worse than the thoughts themselves, was the realisation that they came to her not in the Darkmaster's voice, but in her own. The Darkstone was infecting her with its warped perspective.

Kirjath ran his tongue up her neck. "Enjoy it, like all the other dark-whores." Tabitha wanted to vomit.

You could command the Dark, if you would just accept it.

Her leg pulled free of the spell-binding, and she kicked the

Shadowcaster. He cursed and immobilised her feet with more Dark essence. He pushed his body between her legs, his eyes alight with hunger.

"Whore." It was a statement, not an insult.

"Quiet," hissed a voice from the chapel side of the door. "Company."

The Shadowcaster paused in his ravishing, one hand on her breast. His smell was cloying, his nearness terrifying. It was difficult to keep even a small part of her attention on what was occuring in the chapel.

"Who admitted you here, woman?" The Rector's muffled voice was indignant.

"Been told you have need for a cleaner, so to show you how well I clean came I." The cleaner, whoever she was, had a sing-song voice, deep for a woman's.

"Out! We have no need for cleaners. Out I say!"

"Dust and cobwebs, dirty walls, I'd like to –"

"Take your broom and get out!" There was a scuffle, a solid thump of wood, another thump, then quiet.

Tabitha returned her terrified attention to the Shadowcaster. His hands had paused in their dreadful caress. His eyes were unfocused again, searching the chamber as if following the flight of a fly.

The door was flung open. A figure in a cinnamon dress appeared. She brandished a broom as she strode into the chamber. Her face was hidden behind a veil, but some of her tangled black hair protruded from her misplaced headpiece.

The Shadowcaster didn't seem to notice the newcomer, even when her broom cracked against his skull. Kirjath Arkell slumped to the floor.

Tabitha didn't recognise the cleaner. A pale butterfly flitted about her head, and settled atop the headpiece.

"Never did like these little places," the woman said. "Always mischief in these kind of rooms, men up to no good when they should be praying."

The woman eyed her critically, taking in Tabitha's torn clothing and her shocked gaze. The cleaner removed Tabitha's gag, then her eyes fell on at Tabitha's throat. Tabitha covered the Darkstone in shame, but the cleaner shushed her and held her close. Her bound wrists were untied.

"You're safe from them now, child."

The tears came in a flood.

Tabitha clung to the woman. She cried until she could no more. Relief left her weak, and she hung on a while longer, until she had gathered will enough to be sure that she could stand on her own.

The woman was very strong, and seemed to be able to support Tabitha's weight indefinitely. Yet Tabitha knew she could not afford to faint into the cleaner's arms, for the Dark was still cutting into her ankles. The binding spell that Arkell had cast held firm, and could not be untied like the ropes. Not by a cleaner, at any rate.

Tabitha drew away from the woman, and noticed that she had removed her own veil. She appraised the lean, weathered features of her face, the ill-fitting dress, and the surprisingly large breasts. The face looked different without its beard. A wide, riotous black and white beard, if she remembered correctly.

"Zarost! Twardy Zarost!"

The Riddler looked forlorn. "I said you'd make a fine riddler, said I. How did you know?"

"Your breasts are lopsided."

Zarost looked sheepishly at his costume. He adjusted the right breast to be level with the left, and fiddled with their support binding.

"How do women do anything with these weights on their chests?" he said, looking vexed.

Twardy Zarost! If she had ever doubted his allegiance before, he had proved it now. He was no servant of the Darkmaster. He had saved her from the worst moment of her life, and struck down the Shadowcaster in the process. Tabitha felt her spirit lighten. The Riddler was a lifeline, pulling her from the sea of despair. Twardy Zarost, with a touch of colouring worked into the skin around his eyes, and the huge false breasts.

"They aren't usually ... um ... so big," Tabitha replied.

"Ah, I see. But for me, they are perfect." He brightened. "Men see this chest," he said, swelling his bust proudly, "and they don't look too closely at anything else. The rude Rector who lies in the chapel will remember nothing but that he was attacked by a pair of breasts with a broom. He may have trouble explaining that to anyone who cares."

The pain in her legs reminded her that her rescue was not yet complete.

"Twardy, can you do anything to the motes that bind me?"

His expression sobered. "I don't have the orb for either Dark or

Light."

She hastily repaired her clothing. She secured her skirt with the cord which had bound her wrists. Knotting the loose fabric at her waist offered her a makeshift, low-cut blouse.

A scuffled sound gave the Shadowcaster away as he moved on the floor. Zarost whirled, and raised his broom above his head.

A sudden hope rushed through Tabitha. "Twardy, wait!" she cried, but the staff had already fallen, and the Shadowcaster lay still.

"Always takes two strikes with a broom. Always. Never worked out why."

"Damn. I was hoping you could force him to release this spell." She jerked her leg against the restraint of Dark.

"Force a Shadowcaster? And how could I have done that?"

"You could have tortured him, until he gave in. Shadowcasters understand pain well."

"Torture?" he asked, with a raised eyebrow. "You really have changed since I last saw you."

Zarost was right.

What was I thinking?

Zarost looked uncomfortable. "No, I can do nothing more. You called, and I came, and these men stood in my way. But now, now you must decide which path you take to escape the fate that you brought upon yourself." He smiled broadly.

I should have known he would become cryptic.

She picked on the one thing she had understood.

"When did I call you?" She had wished it, but had never found the means, as far as she could remember. Yet here he was, riddles and all.

"You mean this was an accident?" he asked, his eyebrows leaping away from startled eyes. He raised a hand to his headpiece, and brought it back down with the fingers extended. On his hand, a leaf balanced, then parted to form two coloured leaves, joined at their centre. Rainbow markings upon translucent wings.

"You got it!" she exclaimed. "I thought—I thought it was a real butterfly. I thought it couldn't be directed."

"Real it is, as real as you or I, though it is as fresh as the morning dew, and it has lived for only a day. Yet every moment of its life seems to hold one purpose, the same it must have been given at the moment of its birth. To find the man you wished to call. Well, here I am." He bowed theatrically, and his breasts rode up under his chin. They remained too high when he straightened. Tabitha was too excited at what rested on his finger to comment.

"How did you ever know what I wanted, little thing?"

"You mean you did not command it to do so?" asked Zarost.

"I had no idea. It was an afterthought, when I was frustrated that the Lifesong had not created what I had hoped."

"Ah –" he said at length.

"Ah, what?" she asked, after he did not appear to be continuing.

"Ah, you are the kind that stumbles upon things, without needing to understand too much of how they work. That is a most dangerous kind, but could be just the kind that is needed."

"The kind of what?"

The Riddler seemed to catch himself musing. His expression became the enigmatic mask she was used to—the cheerful, infuriating grin of Twardy Zarost.

"All in good time. First, you have a riddle to solve that is not of my making. Come, we must leave this place." He extended his hand for Tabitha to take.

It was just beyond reach. Her feet were bound just as firmly as ever, and the cold cut into her ankles like knives pressed against the bone.

"What am I supposed to do? You can see I am trapped by the bonding spell." Tabitha knew she was being abrupt, but she had neither the patience nor the strength to endure another one of Zarost's riddles. He remained silent. She began to believe that he really wasn't going to assist. After pretending to rescue her, he was just going to stand by.

Maybe he really can't do anything about the motes.

She had an idea, and summoned the Light essence, calling and extending her will as far as she could, but the Dovecote's sprites had been taken that morning and only two sprites spun into her hand. She cast them at her bonds, and they neutralised two motes, fizzing against the Dark before they fell to the floor as clear essence. Her shackles were as strong as ever.

"It's useless, Twardy. There's no more Light."

They waited in silence for a while, Tabitha looking miserable, and Zarost expectant, then agitated. Eventually the little man could bear it no longer.

"Ask a question of your Riddler, and maybe you'll find an answer."

"How can I release the Dark spell?" she tried, keeping the wording as direct as possible. She knew the Riddler's manner well—he had the ability to slip around the truth like an eel evading capture.

"I have none, but you have two."

She felt her face redden. "What has the fact I'm a woman got to do with it?"

He burst into laughter. "Not these!" he said, pushing his false breasts down inside his dress. He rocked on his feet with the strength of his guffaws. At last he drew enough breath to speak. "Not these." He wiped tears from his eyes with one hand. "Oh, young Tabitha Serannon, I have missed your company."

"How can I release the Dark spell?" she tried again. It was a thing she had learned about the Riddler—if you asked the same question, you gained a different answer, to a maximum of three. Sometimes it was the only way to unravel his riddles. Zarost's shoulders stopped shaking, but his eyes still sparkled with mischief.

"To find the answer, you must walk the darkest path."

The statement was uncannily familiar. The Sage had warned her of a similar thing. Tabitha felt a shiver creep up her spine. Thoughts of the Ring brought with them thoughts of severing her finger at the knuckle. She used her last question almost immediately, not wanting to consider the second answer too deeply.

"How can I release the Dark spell?"

"You bear both orbs."

It was as direct as a sword thrust, and it stopped her heart just as effectively. Her fingers found the icy orb of the Darkstone, where it rested against its counterpart. "This is the Shadowcaster's tool. This was forced upon me!" she declared in horror.

"As was the first orb, and yet you do not shy to use that."

The motes. The Dark? I must command the Dark?

Tabitha was horrified. She could feel the chill of the Darkstone at her throat, she knew well enough it was there. But if she tried to command the Dark, in that moment she would be a Shadowcaster! The whispering voice that she had been trying to ignore returned.

I am the shadow and he is my master.

He is the shadow and I am his caster.

She bore the Darkstone. She had been orbed into the magic of the Dark. She could not believe what Zarost expected of her. As if reading her thoughts, he pointed to the Darkstone.

"You bear a powerful weapon, one they think to use against you.

Master it, and you have a weapon of your own."

"Can't you take it off? Is there anyone who can remove it?" She knew the answer before she had finished the question. Zarost had explained the magic to her once before.

He shook his head, but then decided to expand on his answer. "Only the wizard, but not until you find her."

"The wizard is a woman?"

"I think so."

"How do I find the wizard, Zarost?"

He waggled a finger at her. "That question you have already asked, and gained the three answers."

"But I am not going to find the wizard while I am shackled to this floor. Help me, Twardy. I'm a Lightgifter! I fight the Dark, I can't accept the Darkstone, I can't use the motes!"

Zarost was bouncing on his feet, as if standing on hot coals. He looked like he wanted to be anywhere but where he was, doing anything but giving her clues.

"Help you? You don't understand what you ask!" he cried, suddenly animated. "You can do it on your own, you must be able to do it on your own!" He gestured wildly with his hands, and the butterfly sought refuge in his hair once more. "You use the Light, yet haven't been sworn to the Dovecote by the Rector, yes? So why not the Dark? Why not? Don't make me break my oath for such a small challenge as this."

"I don't want to use the Dark. Ever," she said.

"To fight the Dark is to give it power. Learn to master it, learn to use it before it uses you. I have said too much, I cannot say more."

Tabitha knew that she was pushing the Riddler too far. Any moment now he would leave her again, and then she would be in worse trouble than he had spared her from. The Shadowcaster would awake, some time, and so would the Rector outside. What would happen after that did not bear considering.

She chewed over what the Riddler had said, and as she did, her thoughts darkened.

Use it before it uses you. You are not sworn to the Dovecote, yet use the Light. Why not the Dark? You bear both orbs.

It was hard to set aside the revulsion that she felt for the Darkstone, but when she did, the black whirlpool leapt up within her mind, eager to seduce her with its strength, pulling her into the darkness and cold within. The Master's voice was loud in her ears, but she ignored the insistent mantra.

She reached out her hand, and there her will to summon the motes faltered. She knew the pattern and words to summon the Light, but the Dark was another strain of magic altogether.

He urges me to use the Dark, yet knows I have none of the lore. How am I supposed to learn it?

For a while she stood there and filtered through all Zarost had said for a second time. She tried to use the Ring to bring clarity to her thoughts. At first, drawing on the Ring just made her more aware of the pain in her ankles. She could isolate the individual sting of each mote where it bit into her skin, and the rustling voice of the Darkmaster became a roar in her ears. But despite how cold she felt, the Ring was warm, reassuring, pulling her forward on the path she had chosen.

The answer came with blinding suddenness. The Riddler had been the advisor to the Darkmaster for decades. He had to know. And with the Riddler, it seemed, it was just a matter of asking the right questions.

"What is the pattern used to summon the motes?"

Twardy Zarost smiled. "Have you ever seen the barrel they call the Dwarrow-wine?"

Tabitha nodded. Dwarrow had become the most popular request in the Tooth-and-Tale before she'd left it. "What of it?"

"The mark is never ever hid, the sigil's branded on the lid."

She knew it well. It was how they could tell if a barrel was true Dwarrow, or a cheap imitation that would leave the patrons sober and angry. The Dwarrow-sigil had never been properly imitated, for it was always cold to the touch, whereas the forgeries soon warmed, no matter how the forgers tried. Now she understood why. The sigil was the summoning pattern of the Dark.

The Lightgifters were forbidden to draw spell patterns on anything permanent, lest their guarded knowledge was exposed, and yet the Shadowcasters were so bold as to advertise their spells on wine barrels. The Dark had been under everyone's noses, and no Eyrian had really suspected it. People had already begun to associate the summoning pattern of the Dark with unforgettable nights of revelry.

She held the pattern in mind, and whispered similar words to that of the Lightgifter's summoning. She hoped the motes were like the sprites, in that it was the pattern and will behind the command that was more important than the words themselves.

"Darkness, come to me."

The motes were hers to command. The Dark essence pulled away from her ankles, leaving her skin tingling as her body-warmth returned. The motes collected in a roiling mass around her left hand, as if they were flies and her fingers were soiled with what flies love most. It was a sickly mix of pleasure and revulsion that lifted her stomach.

She was free to go.

I can summon the Dark!

Unaccustomed strength flooded into her veins. With the strength came a fierce hatred and consuming anger, at what the Shadowcaster had done, at what he had tried to do, at what he had done long before. She wanted to hurl the motes at the Shadowcaster crumpled on the floor. But first, she needed more from the Riddler. She could command the Dark, a cruel weapon.

"Tell me the pattern of the worst Dark spell, the one which hurts the most."

She wanted to see Arkell's unconscious body twitch, and to know that he would never awake. She wanted him to die. There was surely such a spell in the Dark lore, something so violent only the Darkmaster's old advisor would know it.

Twardy Zarost grabbed her hand, and pulled her from the antechamber at that moment. She strained at his grip, but he was too strong for her, even with the lust for revenge coursing through her veins. He dragged her past the slumped form of the Rector. Another man she wished to kill.

"Zarost, you must tell me the spell. I demand it of my Riddler."

His eyes were chips of stone, but she knew that she had found a leverage, for he ceased dragging her towards the chapel door. His grip did not loosen on her wrist, though.

"I will tell you when you have let the Dark go, if you still wish to know."

She glared at him, trying to identify the taint of a lie in his words. Her sense for truth never failed her when she could look into someone's eyes, but as always with the Riddler, she could find no untruth. His golden-flecked brown eyes were steady. She had to believe him. So she tried to release her command of the motes, and found a strange reluctance in her heart.

"Let them go," Zarost urged, his voice gentle but firm. "Release the pattern."

The summoning pattern dominated her mind, given form by her desire, hardened by her anger, waiting to be changed, turned into a spell. There was strength in the motes, power waiting to be unleashed, calling to her to claim her rightful command of all she could dominate, to use her new skills to get what she wanted. And the voice, one she had forgotten, but which had not forgotten her.

I am the shadow and he is my master.

He is the shadow and I am his caster.

She recoiled, realising her present danger just in time. The presence of the Darkmaster had seeped into her mind, filled the corners she was not aware of. Any longer and she would be on her knees, begging to become an accepted Shadowcaster, begging to give her power away to the man who waited for her in Ravenscroft.

She cleared her mind, and the motes fell to the floor with a soft susurrus. With the departure of the Dark, the lusts and anger left her too.

When Twardy Zarost released her hand, she knew she would not press her last question any more. Somehow, he had understood what she was going through.

She was not a killer. She reached for the door, and they ran from the chapel.

When they burst out into the sunlight and grass, she allowed the Riddler to guide her. He led her away from the Dovecote, toward the streets of Levin.

"Wait!" she called, suddenly realising what she was leaving behind. The chance of an apprenticeship to the Light was gone, it had never been. But her lyre was in her room in the women's wing, along with her boots, her money and the clothes she had worn from Stormhaven. The rest could be replaced, but the lyre was too valuable to discard.

When she explained her need to Zarost, he offered less resistance than she had expected. "You choose your own path. I shall wait for you a moment."

She went to retrieve her things, all the while fearing that the Rector had recovered and would come around a corner while she ran. The Dovecote corridors were empty, and the building echoed with her hurried footfalls. When she reached her room and lifted the lid of her chest, she was greeted by an altogether different horror.

Her possessions were packed as neatly as ever, but there was a bare space where she had hidden her money. She took everything from the chest, yet still there was no sign of the coin-strings. She searched through the other chests in the room. She looked behind and under the beds. Her money was gone.

All that remained was one gold coin and some change which she had kept in a pocket inside her woodsman's trousers. Her inheritance had been stolen, by someone in the Dovecote. She added that fact to the list of crimes against the Rector Shamgar's name. It hurt something wicked to realise she had lost her parent's wealth. She forced those thoughts from her mind. She would tell Garyll, when he returned from Ravenscroft. There was nothing she could do now.

She collected her things, and ran.

She found the Riddler hiding behind a tree near to where she had left him. Soon they were rushing downhill between tall buildings. Some Levinners paused in their activity to watch the strange couple. Twardy had raised his veil again. Tabitha wondered how many of the men would only remember something with a broom and a very large pair of breasts passing by. Some of the men followed them with a wistful, longing look.

When they slowed to a walk to attract less attention, Twardy still drew the odd wolf-whistle. It seemed the Riddler's costume was a better disguise than she would have guessed. She wondered if Zarost's wisdom was due to his experience as a man, or his experience of men.

He led them to a stable.

A familiar cart lay unhitched beside the wall, and in a stall stood a sturdy grey horse, dozing in her nosebag.

"Blazey!"

The horse nickered, and Tabitha stepped into the stall to rub her hand over her thick coat, and down her muzzle. Blazey nosed her good-naturedly.

"Take her and ride like the wind," Twardy said, removing the nosebag. He tacked her up and connected her to the traces. "Stormhaven is the only place that is safe for you, Seeker. The Darkmaster is too strong for you to be close to yet. You have much to study, and very little time. The library holds much more than the books on its shelves. Use all that you have to find the wizard. Maybe you'll learn the next step on your path soon enough."

"Aren't you coming?"

"I answered your call, and will return, but there is something urgent I must attend to—elsewhere."

He reached under his shirt, and liberated a melon. He extended the second one to Tabitha.

"Uh ... no thanks."

"Fruit so fresh from the wharf market? Take it for the horse, she loves the melonskin."

Tabitha hefted the melon into the back of the cart.

"I shall see you in Stormhaven, before the inner war is done." His comment was flippant, as if the event was of no more significance than a passing shower. Yet to Tabitha, it was as if the earth had lurched beneath the cart.

"War? I thought it was over."

Twardy raised one eyebrow. "Events here are a clue to others distant. I saw the Swords go south, but never north did come. Think of the things you have seen, and what they mean. But do it while you ride. Go!"

He slapped the horse's rump. Blazey rolled her eyes, then lurched away at a trot. Tabitha teetered in the driver's seat, and hurriedly grabbed the reins. When she chanced to look back, Zarost was hidden in the gloom of the stables.

The cart shuddered over the cobbles, and Tabitha was consumed by the task of trying to guide Blazey safely down through the city streets at speed. It was only when she reached the smooth surface of the Kingsbridge that she could really consider what Zarost had said.

Think of the things you have seen, and what they mean.

The Rector had handed her to the Shadowcaster, so he had an allegiance with the Dark. Implications spilled across her mind, scattering alarm everywhere. The Rector had sent the Lightgifters to Ravenscroft, on a mission of healing. If the Rector was an ally of the Darkmaster, he would only send the full force of the Lightgifters to Ravenscroft if ... they were walking into a trap. The Swords must have been anything but victorious. And the Shadowcasters were confident enough to lure the entire Dovecote to their lair.

I have to warn them!

There would surely be light essence in Stormhaven, enough to cast a spell with. She let Blazey stretch her stride.

♦ ————— ♦

Zarost hoisted a fire-coloured patchwork blanket from the small pile of belongings that he had liberated from the cart. After some rough stitching with twine, it became a serviceable bard's cloak, fastened at his throat. Bards were known for their colourful garments and more colourful tales. He only had a frayed grey robe to wear beneath it, but that would have to do. He took a pair of working trousers that he found in the nearby cupboard and replaced them with the dress and silk headpiece, and the melon. Then he broke the head from the broom and tossed it aside.

"Every bard has a worthy staff, a worthy staff has he," he sang as he ground the splinters from the end against the floor. "None so good as a staff that has proved its worth already," he added, to himself. It had been a long time since he had plied the trade of a bard. It might be quite refreshing, for a change.

After settling a small debt with a certain discreet stable-manager, and pressing another coin into his hand for his continued discretion, he left from the back entrance. He kept the grey hood of the robe pulled up over his head. He hoped that he would remain a mystery to all who saw him—just a spry colourful figure passing through the streets of Levin, planting his short staff at every second step and whistling into the shadow of his hood. Those who led any chase from the Dovecote or the wharf market would be disappointed, for the sure trail of the large-breasted Madam Astro'z ended in a pile of steaming horse manure. Sometimes it paid to sow the seeds of confusion thicker than thistles.

He could not afford to be tailed, by men or by Morrigán.

He hoped Tabitha Serannon would stay out of harm's way until he returned. The Darkstone would challenge her greatly. It had not been his plan, but it would serve his purposes. She needed balance in her training, and none better than Cabal of Ravenscroft to offer that. That was the theory, but in practice it was always difficult to let the Seeker follow their own path to the wizard, because it inevitably led to their demise. Every time.

Even though he knew that Tabitha was different, he feared now that she might meet the same end as the others. Though it went against everything the Gyre had planned, he was resolved to intervene. It was the first thing he would present to the meeting of the Gyre. She was too valuable to sacrifice to the sovereign principle of free will. It worked for most apprentices, but the Wizards had never expected one such as Tabitha to develop in Eyri. She was beyond what they had planned for. He would petition the Gyre to change the rules.

A delicate, rainbowed butterfly gambolled around his head, and chose a bright yellow patch of his cloak to rest upon.

He quickened his pace toward River's End.

32. ECLIPSE

*"The righteous pay little heed
to what they walk upon."—Zarost*

The Lightgifters were a sorry lot, Ashley decided. After only a day
on the trail, their march had reduced to a snail's pace. So much for a
life of sacrifice; in their years of service to the Light, the Gifters had
become lazy, and soft. Too much opulence, too little experience of
suffering.

Groans of sore bodies plagued the procession like the blisters on
the feet of those who groaned. One Sister was even complaining of
a headache from too much fresh air. Self-administered healing had
run rife through the group in Kironkiln that morning, until Father
Keegan had forbidden further use of their precious store of Light. In
the absence of the Rector's guidance, Keegan had assumed authority
over the group, and no one had objected—he was an experienced
Gifter, and had developed a fierce temper of late. He strode ahead
with purpose, but the train of Gifters in his wake had all the dignity
of a school outing, complete with the children who always limped
pitifully at the back, demanding attention.

They had flitted through Fendwarrow without stopping for
breakfast. The village had seemed strangely quiet. Now they were
high in the mountains, and the trail was steep, winding in switchbacks
over rumpled ridges littered with scree. Despite the warmth generated
from the exercise, the wind drove a cutting cold through the threads
of Ashley's robe. He couldn't be sure it was only the wind.

Doubts plagued his mind. The Gifters were weak. The last time he
had been to Ravenscroft, it had been anything but a place for petulant
companions. He could remember the dread which had smothered
him in the vale of Dark. Had it not been for the resilience of Garyll
Glavenor, he doubted that they would have escaped. It was a wonder
that the Swords had now conquered the Shadowcasters in such a
short space of time. A foe as great as the Darkmaster would not have
offered an easy victory.

A white dove winged to the path. It bobbed its head as it watched
him approach. The Courier had been following them all morning.
Ashley had seen the bird the previous afternoon, before they had

decided to overnight in Kironkiln. It seemed to be intent on him rather than any other Lightgifter. He had tried to lure it closer before sunset, but to no avail.

It was surely the result of a spell constructed by a novice. His own first attempts at Couriers had been worse—his birds had plummeted from the sky, and exploded upon the roofs in Levin's upper district. At least this bird had the correct proportions.

The dove cocked its head nervously, and began to walk as fast as its little legs would take it up the trail, away from the approaching Lightgifters.

The Courier's perfect proportions were causing its downfall. It was a classic mistake of novice Gifters. If you formed a Courier with too much realism, it would try to deliver its message, but every time it neared a large group of people it would behave like a real dove.

The dove lifted from the trail in a frantic beating of wings, and climbed into the stronger winds aloft. Gone, again.

Maybe it would settle at sunset in Ravenscroft, if he could find a place where he could be alone. Maybe it would come down for seed. You never could tell with aberrant spells, what behaviour they would display.

♦ —————————♦

Afternoon had worn thin into a grey sky when they came to the chasm. Their grumbles and groans of discomfort had followed the Lightgifters like a mantra, but when they emerged on the landing, overlooking the frightful drop-off, even the complainers fell silent. They huddled together, pulled their robes closer, raised their hoods against the sudden assault of cold. No one was ready to cross the bridge. Ashley could not still his beating heart.

The wind moaned through the black canyon, tearing a shroud of snow from the higher peaks before tumbling through the torture of knife-edged spines that was the birthplace of the Black River. From his vantage the river appeared white in its haste, but Ashley knew that by the time it reached Fendwarrow, the waters would ooze through the reeds and stain them dark. He drew the Light which was assigned to him close to his hand. The chasm held a foreboding, lurking presence, as if there was a voice trapped in the wind. It had to be a trick of the canyon and the river far below.

The awful stone bridge spanned the gorge like a challenge to their failing courage. When he had last crossed it, they had been fleeing with fear and Morrigán at their backs. It was far worse to cross it voluntarily, when every vertiginous aspect was visible in the stark light of day. The slick, black stone curved down to the nadir in the centre of the span. Ashley knew that bridges should be curved the other way for strength. It was narrow, high, exposed. He wished they could turn back.

His eye caught a tumble of stripped trees, deep in the gorge beneath the bridge, a pile of limbs lying like a giant spider crushed by the seracs of ice that had fallen upon it. It was as if someone had tried to construct another bridge or a ladder, and failed.

Little wonder that they didn't trust this bridge. Could it have been the work of the Swords?

A horn sounded on the far side of the chasm. A neat procession of figures assembled on the distant landing. Muttered words of relief passed through the knot of Gifters as they recognised the armoured uniforms of Swords. Fifteen, all told. Two blue royal banners were raised, displaying the gold cross of the Sword within the circle of Eyri. The banners were placed on either side of the landing where they snapped on their lances marking the access to the conquered vale of Ravenscroft.

"Come across, Lightgifters!" The Sword's voice was faint above the din of the river which filled the chasm. He waved a hand.

Ashley drew a ragged breath, and squared his shoulders. There was no leeway for faltering feet or skidding hooves. It would be a fearsome crossing. Apparently the Swords were going to wait for them on the far side.

"It can hold you all! Come across," urged the Sword's small voice.

Ashley was amongst the first to walk onto the black span. He shuffled close behind Father Keegan, taking great care to stay in the centre of the exposed walkway. He had not yet taken twenty steps when a great cry went up behind him. Ashley turned as quickly as he dared to.

Two horses reared against their lead-reins, kicking out at the men who tried to tame them. A third horse broke its traces, and galloped away down the trail, back into the canyon.

"The horses won't cross that bridge!" shouted one of the grooms to Father Keegan. "They fear it worse than a snake."

Keegan recalled the Lightgifters, and they assembled around the pack animals. Solid rock had never felt so good underfoot.

"Can you foresee them crossing this span, given time?" Father Keegan asked.

The groom shook his head without hesitation. "Father, we'll not get them across that even if we spend a week with whips. They're spooked something fierce."

The two horses continued to rear, whinnying and snorting through flared nostrils, straining to follow their compatriot who had long since disappeared. They were in danger of losing all the animals.

Father Keegan took only a few moments to come to a decision. "Turn the horses! We'll walk them a way down the trail, and offload the essentials we need. I'll need volunteers to remain with them, to take the horses further down to the first safe grazing."

Hands were raised before Keegan's last words had been drawn away in the whispering wind.

When they started the crossing for the second time, the wind had increased to a howl. It whipped Ashley's hair into his eyes and upset his balance with buffeting blasts. He staggered forwards, hunched to be closer to the surface of the bridge should he be pushed off-balance. The supplies he bore on his back were heavy and awkward in their canvas bag. He dared not look over the sheer edge of the bridge.

He focused instead on placing one foot in front of the other, and following the few Gifters who crossed ahead of him. Some of them were almost reduced to crawling. Somehow, they made it across the awful span. At last they were safely congregated beside the Swords.

The Swords made an unfriendly welcoming committee. They did not speak, they did not smile, and they kept their eyes downcast. They all bore the scars of a grievous battle. Some wounds were bandaged, most were left open, but none bled despite their neglect. The cold seemed to have sealed the wounds.

A broad-shouldered Sword with deep-set eyes stood forward.

"I am Captain Brent, leader of the Swords here. Who speaks for you?" he said tiredly.

Ashley was surprised. If Brent was the leader, where was Swordmaster Glavenor? Father Keegan might have been thinking the same thing, for he considered Captain Brent with a grave expression.

"I am Father Keegan. How did you know of our arrival?"

"Scouts," was all Captain Brent offered by way of explanation. "Keegan. Yes, we were told you'd come. You're later than we expected." He motioned for them to follow the obvious trail.

Keegan led them into the increasing silence of the vale of Ravenscroft.

Ashley couldn't shake the queasy feeling. His dread mounted as they were led further along the trail. They passed gnarled low trees and twisted columns of stone that he had not noticed during the first visit. He manoeuvred himself closer to one of the escorting Swords.

"Where are the Shadowcasters?"

"Safely under the control of the victor," the Sword replied tersely. The look he shot at Ashley convinced him that further chatter was unwelcome. The man looked haggard and angry.

Ashley noticed that a few of their escorters were positioned at the tail end of the Lightgifters' procession. He thought it strange, but then so was the vale they were in.

Everything they passed was tainted a different shade of black. Black oaks arched over the trail, searching the sky with their wizened limbs. The grass grew in dark clutches, slightly greener than midnight. Coal black, peat black, soot black. It felt as if the landscape was feeding on the warmth of their bodies as they passed across it, leaching their will with its hunger for heat. Ashley could see some of the Gifters sneaking the power from their essence to warm themselves, though they had been strictly forbidden to do so by Father Keegan.

The Swords led them around tilled fields of jurrum. They passed over a high plain that was empty of any sign of life. Then they neared the giant Keep of Ravenscroft.

Even though Ashley had the advantage of experience, he felt no less dread than his companions. The Keep *lurked,* there was no better word for it. The sensation of walking toward the mouth of a vast watching beast was unshakeable, despite the company of the Sword and Captain Brent's reassurances that Ravenscroft was conquered.

They halted on the cleared ground at the Keep's entrance. Captain Brent addressed them when everyone had assembled.

"Thank you for answering our appeal. Your Light will do wonders here. But first, we have prepared a meal, so you may gather your strength before the heavy task. Come inside." The Captain even made the effort to smile.

Ashley was surprised that they weren't being taken to the men who needed healing, but Father Keegan didn't challenge Brent's announcement. They were the Swords, after all, the trusted King's men. Their honesty not in question. Their very presence was reassuring.

They trooped after Captain Brent into the arching entrance of Ravenscroft. The lofted corridor filled with the tramp of many feet.

Flaming brands had been set in the walls along the way, revealing a well-worn, sloping passage. The black rock glistened in the torchlight. They came to a turn, and descended into a wide, round chamber with a concave floor. Here many torches were set in high braziers. The chill had been taken from the air.

A grand table had been set, with benches long enough to hold everyone. The table was loaded with fruit, meats, breads, and delicacies. Barrels of wine cluttered the walls. Some of them had been rolled and taps struck into them.

Nothing could have been more welcoming. Ashley realised that he had misjudged the sober expressions of the Swords—they were merely tired, not unhappy to receive the Lightgifters.

"The spoils of war!" Captain Brent announced. "Please, eat your fill, everyone. We shall join you for the meal. We all need to be strong, for what will come."

The feasting began with concentrated fervour. Ashley soon found himself on his third portion of meat, and deep into a second mug of the warming wine. It was similar to what he remembered of the Dwarrow-wine, though not as cripplingly potent. Still, he wondered if the warmth it offered was real warmth, or just a numbing of the nerves which felt the cold. He set his mug aside. Very few of his companions followed his example.

The revelry gathered momentum as the last of the day expired outside the Keep. There was an atmosphere of congratulation within the chamber. They had all endured hardship, and deserved the comforts they were awarded. The barrels which had been breached were drunk dry and new ones were struck.

Light essence slipped from many of the Gifters' auras, and pooled softly in the centre of the chamber. There was no danger in letting go, for the sprites could be collected easily, and would come to no harm resting in the pool together.

Ashley tried his drink again, hoping it would quell his increasing unease. But the wine didn't help. Something was not right.

"Where are the Shadowcasters?" he asked of a Sword who stood nearby.

"We locked 'em in their own dungeons. It's a foul, cold place down there. You'll get to see 'em soon enough, I'm sure." The man winked, but his eyes seemed cold.

It's the wine, Ashley told himself. *Jumping at shadows again.*

He turned his attention back to the feast, but his appetite had abandoned him. Ashley rose and pushed through the carousers to the exit. He summoned a handful of sprites to be used in a Flicker spell, should he need it.

"Where are you going?" The Sword had a strange manner, it was almost a confrontation, not a question.

"River for ablutions," Ashley muttered, pushing past the sentry.

The Sword nodded, letting him go.

This place is driving me mad, Ashley thought. *I'd swear that Sword just reached for his blade when I approached.* The strange pressure of the Keep was making even the Swords jumpy, despite their victory.

He trotted down the passage to the main entrance chamber. Again he encountered Swords blocking the way, and they were even more reluctant to let him pass than the first sentry. They couldn't offer a good reason to detain him, though, and they seemed uncertain of what to do. His persistence gained him the right to a quick trip to the river.

He passed out of sight of the sentries. The cold wind bit into his flesh, numbed only by the wine in his veins. The black shadows of building rain-clouds claimed the purpling sky. It was a bad time to be having second thoughts about staying in the Keep.

Better to be inside in the warmth of wine and song.

A flash of movement drew his attention to a white bird weaving madly through the sky. Two dark, swooping forms chased it with harsh croaking cries. Morrigán. Ashley hadn't seen any during the approach to Ravenscroft, but hadn't expected to—if the Shadowcasters were conquered, they should not be using their magic. Overhead, the two ravens dived and sniped at the smaller Courier. Their presence proved that there was still at least one Shadowcaster who was free, for every Morrigán would have a master. The Dark was not conquered, at least not in full.

Cold hands reached into his belly.

The little dove shot overhead, pushing hard against the wind to outpace the pursuit. The errant messenger was still following him, despite the harassment and the cold, unpleasant vale. Ashley had vowed to receive the message, but he had failed every time. In a desperate bid, he shouted his command to the air.

"Alight, messenger, and deliver your word!"

The dove swerved, and bore down on him at top speed. He knew the Courier would pull its flight up short to land on his outstretched hand, so he was slow to react when it didn't. The impact flattened him. The sprites stung, as no sprites had before. A most novice spell indeed, but powerful. There was only one person he knew who could create such an intense spell with so little aptitude. Her voice was scattered, but it was unmistakably Tabitha Serannon he heard.

"Rector Shamgar is working with the Shadowcasters. You must stop the Lightgifters, they are walking into a trap."

The sprites lay scattered amongst the rocks. Ashley didn't move. He lay in the gully where he had fallen, his head spinning.

It is too late. We have already entered the trap. If a trap it is.

The Swords were the teeth who would keep them from escaping the jaws of Ravenscroft Keep.

But why would the Swords be in league with the Dark?

If Captain Brent and his men were in league with the Dark, why offer the meals and drink, why not attack as soon as the Gifters had entered the Keep?

Why do they wait?

The cold which seeped into him from the ground provided an answer. When night fell, the Shadowcasters would be in the height of the power. The Lightgifters would have fallen beside their tankards, snoring the lethargy of their feast away. It would not be a battle. It would be an annihilation. And they with all the Light essence of the Dovecote.

He had to get word through to Father Keegan. If the Father had warning, maybe all would not be lost. He realised too that if he went back to warn the Gifters, he might never escape himself.

"Kid said ... river ... minutes ago." Snatches of voice were threaded on the wind. Ashley backed into a hollow.

A closer voice startled Ashley to silence.

"Well, we'd better find him. Our Master will not be pleased to lose even one Gifter to chance."

Ashley tried to sink deeper into the gully. He could hear footsteps crunching in the gravel.

"He'll come to the fire. There's a bad storm brewing."

Ashley couldn't make out the reply, but the footsteps ground away from him. Despite his pounding heart, he risked peeping over the edge of his cover. He had to know.

A steel helmet glistened faintly as the man marched away into the deep shadows.

It was a Sword who had spoken, not a Shadowcaster.

The first few drops of rain, flung by the storm winds, spattered the ground. It was almost nightfall. Thunder boomed from deep within the Zunskar Mountains, heralding that worse was hastening on its way toward the vale. Ashley staggered to his feet, and leant against the foul weather. His head spun. He suspected it was the legacy of the wine; there had been other things besides matured grapes in the blend.

His legs were unsteady. He turned from the Keep and headed deeper into the vale. He was going to need shelter soon.

He strained his eyes against the failing light and gathering rain, but the walls of black rock beyond the Keep were smooth and unbroken. He trudged on, feeling cowardly and afraid. He should be saving the Gifters from the trap not hiding from peril. Rain stung his back through his robe. He used his last few sprites to warm his body, but the warmth leached away almost at once. His vision blurred. His heart beat like an unsteady drum in his ears.

He had almost resolved to return, regardless of the trap, when he spied the cave. It was cold inside, but dry and spared from the wind which howled past the mouth.

A crack of lightning split the sky. In its flash, he saw that the cave extended deeper than he'd thought. A smooth, worn passage led into the dark. The instant of brilliance was gone. His brain fizzed. The thunderclap that followed was hard and deafening, and it echoed from peak to peak through the vale outside. His ears continued to ring in the dark. The significance of the worn stone eluded his fading logic, and he sighed as he slumped to the floor in the dark.

The wicked wine claimed its victim.

He dreamt a vivid scene which began in a large dining chamber. Torches guttered above the slumped forms of the Lightgifters, who littered the benches and the floor equally. Swords stood by, guarding those who remained conscious. Ashley guessed there had been some intoxicant in the food as well as the drink, for so many Gifters to be downed. A grim Father Keegan gazed fixedly at an empty tankard. His brow was deeply creased. He slammed the tankard on the table, leaving the handle bent askew.

Ashley dreamed he saw a woman appear in one of the shadowed exits. She watched Keegan with a sultry smile. Ashley recognised her instantly. Gabrielle, the dancer in Fendwarrow, the woman who lingered in his dreams. Her low dress was of sheer, black silk. It clung to the alluring curves of her body, leaving only her pale neck and deep cleavage exposed to the dim flames. Her cloak was clasped at her throat by an orb of pure black.

Ashley tried to cry out a warning to Keegan in his dream, but he could create no sound against the deafening silence. He watched in horror as Father Keegan strode through the untended pool of sprites. Keegan drew enough essence to create a small Flicker spell in his hand. He slipped unnoticed from the chamber and followed the faint swish of departing silk.

Darkness finds a weakness, and there it will swell.

The thought was a whispered voice, and he couldn't be sure it was his own. Ashley wanted to make the dream follow Keegan, and his mind seemed to latch on to the Father's presence. It had been a while since he had snooped. It was just a dream, he told himself. It couldn't hurt to follow.

He saw through Keegan's eyes. Lust for Gabrielle ached through every fibre of his body, and he knew that he must have the woman he followed. He had never felt such a roaring need before. Duty to the Lightgifters was a pale and distant thing, when placed beside the urgent demand of consummation. To touch the pale curves which remained just beyond reach, to gain possession of the seductress whom he had refused for so long was all that mattered. Many nights in Fendwarrow had been wasted in denial of her offers, nights wasted in service to the Light. For too long had that aching desire been spurned.

It all rested on a choice.

Tonight, she was his reward.

Her promise was full of conviction. She would satisfy his passion if he could just catch her. His life had been one long road of longing, leading him to this moment he deserved. How many months had he refused her, though he'd wanted her so badly? How many nights had she visited his dreams, until he could think of nothing else but returning to Fendwarrow, returning to her room, taking what she had offered.

She was the drop of dew on the rose petal waiting to be kissed. She was dark, and perfect. Keegan broke into a run, down and down on the winding stair, as his mind was teased and touched by deepening desire. And always, she managed to stay just out of reach, laughing with a throaty breathlessness, so close he could smell her scent.

Gabrielle's presence drew him on, her overwhelming power that held him firm, pulling him closer, ever closer. Her laughter called to him, he thought of her body moving inside the shifting fabric of her dress, a dress that was slowing, turning. His fingers brushed the curve of a breast, sending a wild craving through his arms. A gentle hand on his chest sent fire to his loins. Full lips whispered in his ear.

"You will not believe the pleasure I can give you when you are filled with your Light essence. That small Flicker spell you have is not enough. Go back, summon all you can bear, and bring it to me. No one shall be able to distract you from your task. Hurry. Your reward awaits."

His lips were whetted by a warm, delicate tongue, and his lower lip was sucked outwards. Desire exploded through his veins. Then she was gone, and he was left quivering with unreleased tension. He turned, as he knew he must, and strode with Keegan's large stride. The passage was clear before Keegan, yet Ashley struck a rock.

The dream link was severed, his vision of the passage dissolved with sudden pain. Ashley was brought rudely back to his senses. He was standing, with an aching leg, in complete darkness. It took him some time to recall where he was.

When I slept, it was in the mouth of cave. Or was it a passage? How far have I walked into the labyrinth beyond?

He spun around in panic. It was pitch black.

What was real, and what the dream?

He found a wall, and trailed his hand on it to guide his steps in the dark. A faint light outlined the mouth of a passage some distance from him. The source of light bobbed along, as if being borne by someone walking with a torch. Ashley backed away until his legs struck a boulder. The light approached swiftly.

Ashley slid around to the shadowed side of the boulder, and crouched in waiting. He didn't know who to expect, but in the bowels of Ravenscroft, he didn't want to be discovered by anyone.

He drew a quick breath when the figure entered his passage. The halo of light revealed a familiar face. Father Keegan's white robe billowed out behind his legs. The small Flicker spell waved and guttered in his hand, pulled by the wind of his passage. Sprites were lost from the tattered column of flame, and they were blown onto his chest and over his broad shoulders, streaking up his robe with illusionary fire which curled and vanished into the darkness behind his head.

The stuttering light played across the Father's face, catching his jutting beard and thick frowning eyebrows with radiance, and leaving the hollows of his cheeks dark. He rushed through the cavern like a charging bear.

Ashley was about to rise from his seclusion and announce himself, when he caught a glimpse of Keegan's eyes—a wild, faraway gaze, like that of a hound about to howl at the moon. Fear gripped Ashley's limbs. He couldn't be sure what the Father would do. He couldn't be sure the Father wouldn't hand him over to the Shadowcasters. If any of the dream was true, Keegan was seduced by Gabrielle. There was no other reason for Keegan to be down in the dark catacombs of Ravenscroft.

Father Keegan strode past close enough to whisper to. Ashley remained motionless against the boulder. Keegan showed no sign of having noticed anything—he paced away. Ashley crept out from his hiding place and tried to follow Keegan, but the passage turned, and the weak glow of the Flicker spell passed up a flight of stairs, then faded. The darkness was complete again.

Ashley was sure that something terrible was about to happen. He sent his mind reaching out for Keegan again, hoping to find something to distract him from his doomed course. Instead, he fell into a whirlpool of lust wound so tight it took his breath away. The link with Father Keegan was even more vivid than before. He tried to pull his thoughts away, but lost control to the same power that governed the mind he was touching. A dark vortex wrapped around his thoughts like an intimate hand. There was no way Keegan could escape. He had accepted the promise. He was under the spell of Gabrielle's seduction.

Keegan was clear of the stairs, and was waiting in the shadows at the edge of the dining chamber. Lightgifters slumbered all around. Keegan summoned the sprites from the chamber, building a mass of swirling Light around his body. One of the Lightgifters raised a questioning head from the table, but was smote from behind by a Sword. The Gifter fell back to the table and did not rise. The Sword returned to stony vigilance, disinterested in Keegan's actions, or under instructions not to interfere. No one else made any move. They were all asleep.

It was more a moan than a cry of pain. Ashley's knees buckled when he heard it. He wasn't sure if the sound was part of Keegan's enchantment, or if he had heard it with his own ears, for his mind was a confluence of wild currents, conflicting aspects warring for control. He tried to pull away. His stomach clenched tight. The woman's low moan called to the memories of his most erotic dreams. He was pulled by the vision of a dark, sultry beauty, a black gown wrapped over her shoulders, breasts which thrust upwards from a bodice of pure black silk. Gabrielle. The dream was real.

He ached to answer the urgency in her voice, the reward it offered. Her naked body, her parted lips, her hunger enveloping him. Another low moan came to him through the dark, urging him forwards. There was no illumination save the faintest glow of his Lightstone, but he knew the lay of the chamber from Keegan's passing, and he backtracked along that course.

Gabrielle's husky voice filled his mind, the memory of her wild moan echoed through the corridor of his dream. Part of him knew that Keegan was further away. Part of him knew it was Keegan's mind he was seeing the visions through, yet he pressed on. His lust thundered through his veins. Gabrielle. She was every man's fantasy.

The vortex of desire drew him deeper. He didn't care about Father Keegan or the Lightgifters. He didn't care about the pressing dark. All he could see in his mind was Gabrielle. He found a way through the blackness, stumbling in the places where his trailing hand missed the wall.

Water trickled down the walls, filling the space with a strange dripping melody. The smell of moss and damp rock filled his nostrils. The air was fresh. The glow of a hidden fire spilled out over the rock floor through the outline of a narrow oval archway. Firelight flickered on the walls beyond the archway, calling to him, hinting at the warmth he would find if he ventured within. Ashley moved toward it. His knees shook. He was sucked onwards by the vortex spell of seduction.

Ashley felt suddenly exposed when he stepped into the lit archway. The source of the fey power was here, a power too great to deny, too great to master. He knew he would be lost in it, should he take one more step. In a frantic moment of lucidity, he cast an eye around the room.

A large fire was burning in a hearth on the far side of the room. The warmth wrapped around Ashley even where he stood on the threshold. A ruddy glow streaked the walls. They bore unfinished patterns like abandoned clay in a potter's wheel. Ridges caught the red flickering light and created dark shadows, filling the walls with dizzy geometry.

From a lowered roof, drapes of a translucent black satin enclosed a bed. The black drapes spilled across the floor, rippling gently over hidden irregularities.

He drew in a sharp breath as he saw a figure move on the bed, her outline cast onto the delicate screen of the curtains. The unmistakable shape of a woman, all cascading hair and voluptuous curves. Desire set every one of his nerves afire. The figure turned toward the sound of his sudden inhalation.

"Is that you, my love?" Gabrielle's voice made his blood fizz. It was a voice more husky, more warm and more fulfilling than he had dreamed. It was a sound of molten chocolate, of mulled wine and honey, of yearning and desire blended with cream, a passionate kiss against his ear. The voice sent a shiver down Ashley's spine, a shiver which turned at his toes and returned to his head. He gagged, unable to reply. Reason had been swept away into the vortex of enchantment once more. Gabrielle turned towards the fire, presenting her back to Ashley. She hadn't revealed herself, but her power pulled Ashley ceaselessly forward.

"Bring your Light."

His unsteady legs carried him toward the bed.

I have no essence! The truth of that failure brought him to his senses with a jolt. *This is madness.*

From the dark cavern through the archway at his back, came a deep, gruff voice chanting words he knew only too well. The Lightgifter's spell for illumination, the Flicker. Keegan had returned with the price of his weakness, a prize Ashley could not match.

Ashley was trapped. He backed away from the approaching sound, passed behind the bed where he was hidden by the sheer black curtains, and slipped into the shadows beside the wall. He prayed Gabrielle would leave the bed. He would hide, and escape at the first moment. As he backed across the slippery floor, the fabric of darkness swirled around his ankles. The cold touch told him all he needed to know. It was not silk. It was Dark essence.

He sank to the floor anyway. The heat of the fire passed overhead. He became partly submerged in the Dark essence, his body all but invisible in the leaping shadows. He watched with a terrified mixture of horror and excitement.

Father Keegan strode through the archway. His gaze was fervid. Keegan was surrounded by an aura of sprites which flared up to the spiralled roof, pulsing thickly, a Flicker spell the likes of which

Ashley had never witnessed before. Keegan's command would not hold for long—already beads of sweat glistened on his forehead from the concentration—but he was robed in almost all of the sprites the Gifters had brought from the Dovecote.

The room was filled with light. Ashley panicked—he had lost his cover. But Keegan's gaze did not waver from the bed.

"Bring your Light, my love," repeated Gabrielle.

Ashley tried to retreat farther into his diminished patch of shadows, but the rock was already firmly against his back. He fought down a powerful impulse to squeak.

"What took you so long? I have been slowly freezing in here," Gabrielle reprimanded, her voice maintaining a seductive note despite its sting. All of Keegan's possessed attention was focused on Gabrielle. He strode forward, and parted the curtains.

"You should be used to that, Shadowcaster."

"You know less than you pretend of the Dark, then. Come to me, offer your power, I will show you the pleasure that can be yours, at last. You have led the Gifters well, now come." Gabrielle's attraction suffused the room, plucking at his body as if he was a harp, leaving him resonating with lust. Ashley knew that the enchantment was not directed at him, but he was still partly linked to Keegan's mind, and he could feel the sensations that passed through the Father. He knew he shouldn't be snooping, but he couldn't help himself. He promised himself he would only sense what was happening. He didn't need to see with Keegan's eyes.

Father Keegan drew a ragged breath. The shadowed outline revealed every curve as Gabrielle pulled a garment over her head. Keegan discarded his robe. A black undergarment fell to the floor. Keegan entered the bed, slipping behind the secretive curtain. Flames of Light burst through the canopy, spreading to the spiralled roof, until the sprites curled and flicked as far outwards as the walls. It looked like a giant flower held in a vase of darkness. The light outlined the two figures in the bed with startling clarity.

Ashley tried to contain his own reactions enough to stay hidden, but it took all the willpower he had. The referred passion continued to erupt, threatening to arch his back or clench his stomach involuntarily. A hunger for the Dark wriggled into his core, like a weevil. It was repulsive.

It was delicious. The pleasure! He dipped further into the pool of Keegan's mind, and felt all the passions, experienced all that Keegan did. It was intoxicating, a wild ride into the forbidden. Irresistible excitement coursed through him. He was beginning to realise that he had the same weakness as Father Keegan. He suspected every man did.

Gabrielle had conquered her prey. Her enchantment began to change, from mental to physical. Ashley felt the vortex within Keegan's mind slow and fade, as it was overwhelmed by the surging passion. He was free to release his telepathic link with Keegan.

It was his chance to escape. He knew he should try to run while the lovers were intent only on satisfying their desire. But the strange lust coursed through his blood, his own desire held him captive.

He didn't want to run. The call of passion was urgent, undeniable. Pleasure clawed at his will, begging abandon.

The room became a swirling mass of confusion. The carpet of black satin rose from the floor, and the Flicker shattered into thousands of tiny sprites. The Light and Dark mixed in a sea of swirling particles. Wild currents spun through the room. A mote struck Ashley's cheek, causing a sharp, cold pain. A sprite burned like a hot spark. Again and again he was struck, and he pulled the cowl of his robe up to protect his head. Raw elemental magic, summoned but not commanded in a spell. So much power contained in so small a space.

The tempo of the lovemaking increased. Gabrielle threw her head backwards and mouthed silent words to the air. Father Keegan was locked in her arms. They formed the eye of the whirlpool. Chips of rock flew from the walls.

Gabrielle's words were clear and sharp, like the warning crack of ice before the avalanches of the high mountains.

"Now, command your Light into the pattern of the Turning. You know the one I mean."

Keegan's voice was thick with the agony of his crumbling resistance. "The twisted circle?"

"Only you can do it. I need you, Keegan. Do it, for me."

"Creator have mercy on me," the Father whispered. He was bonded to Gabrielle. Ashley supposed it was like the crazed compliance of a condemned man stretched on the rack—once you were tied, helpless, you would do whatever the torturer asked—except that here, Keegan was being tortured with pleasure, and it was his own lust that condemned him.

"Command it! I need you!" whispered Gabrielle.

Ashley didn't need the telepathic link to know what caused

Keegan's back to arch. Keegan shouted words Ashley had never heard before, certainly never in the Dovecote. Nonsensical half-finished commands. The sprites encircled the bed guided by the pattern Keegan held in mind.

As the sprites shimmered along in the current of essence, Ashley realised that the twisted circle had only one surface to it. Unlike a true ring, with an inside and an outside, a half-twist in the pattern meant that the two sides were linked into one. The pattern seemed simple, but it was impossible to concentrate on for too long. It must have two sides, but it had only one, no matter how he looked at it. It was fascinating. He almost forgot where he was.

Then Gabrielle's voice joined Keegan's, and the half-formed commands became full words. "Hold the pattern, round and round, in the hidden turn, to the stronger will be bound."

Both Lightgifter and Shadowcaster were concentrating on the spell, that was clear from their sudden stillness. The only movement was the flowing Light essence, bound in its pattern. Then Dark bloomed amongst the sprites, replacing the sparkling essence like a blood-stain soaking through fabric. As the current swept on, the blemish spread, turning the sprites to motes, the Light to Dark.

Ashley was stunned. Before his eyes, the essence was transformed. When all the Light had been turned, Keegan cried out and slumped to the bed. The slick Dark essence continued to flow in the pattern of the twisted circle, bound by Gabrielle's will. The room became so dark Ashley could only see vague shapes in the gloom and the river of glistening motes where it blocked the ruddy glow of the hearth. He knew he should go, but feared moving more than anything now. The room was full of Dark essence, and the Shadowcaster commanded it all.

"Now the essence is more useful to both of us," Gabrielle purred, as she spread her hands. "Your reward, my lover! Now you become one with us, and reach the climax." She gathered the motes, then cast them to the walls. A wave of Dark returned, drawing all of the motes in the room toward Gabrielle.

"We shall gather the rest of the Gifters, turn them together. Then the Source, so we might at last create Darkness ourselves. Then we shall have the power to move on Stormhaven. The King shall fall, and our Master shall have all of Eyri. And we shall be granted great favours for our service."

Keegan grunted and groaned, driven by Gabrielle's sudden

movements on top of him. Motes swarmed around her, tightening in her hands, which she suddenly brought to Keegan's Lightstone. She threw her head back, eyes to the roof, and began to chant, moving upon Keegan all the while.

Ashley didn't hesitate this time. He used the gap to run for the door.

Keegan cried out.

"I am the shadow and he is my master. He is the shadow and I am his caster!"

There was a hiss, of fire plunged into water, and a cry, full of violence and ecstasy. The room became a maelstrom of Dark essence, thrown by two Shadowcasters in wild abandon.

Ashley didn't look back. Ice burned the back of his legs. He was propelled through the archway and out into the passage beyond. The darkness was lifted only a few shades by the faint illumination of his Lightstone.

At least mine is still intact.

Cold air drifted through the passage. Ashley took the turns which led against the breeze, hoping it would return him to the entrance he had used. He moved as fast as he dared. Having been released from Keegan's mind and the fierce grip of the seductress, he felt empty and weak. The passages seemed to have no end, twisting, turning, branching out. He heard voices and shied from their source. He ran from sudden footsteps as silently as he could, shielding his Lightstone in his hand. He lost track of the time, and began to shiver from the cold.

The labyrinth seemed to go on forever. But at last the breeze was more insistent. And there, at the end of a narrow straight, was an archway beyond which rain sluiced upon open ground. He didn't hesitate, but scuttled into the night beyond. Escape was the only option worth considering.

It was a raging storm outside. He was soaked the instant he stepped from the tunnel. Yet nobody would see him leaving the vale in the storm. He pulled the hood of his robe tight against his head. He had escaped the Keep, but somehow it didn't feel as if he had escaped from Ravenscroft.

◆ ─────── ◆

It took him the remaining hours of the night to find his way to the bridge, or at least to the place where the road had crossed the chasm. He lost his way often in the driving rain, and found himself in the arms of skeletal trees, or skidding downhill over wet stone. He became desperately cold. His teeth chattered by themselves.

One thought kept him fighting, kept him moving against the mounting fatigue. If the Shadowcasters could turn the Source to release only Dark as Gabrielle had declared, they would have absolute power. The Light would be extinguished from Eyri. He held onto the thought of saving the Source, though he had no idea of how to achieve it. Only that it must be done.

He had been prepared for the terror of crawling across the black surface of the bridge, slick with rain, buffeted by the dreadful gusts of the storm. He had not been prepared for what lay there when he reached it.

The bridge was gone. The chasm yawned hungrily from below, swallowing sheets of cold rain into its turgid flood.

He searched for a sign of the old bridge—a broken stone, a jagged edge, anything—but there was nothing. The road ended abruptly, the line was clean as if cut with a knife. Either he was in the wrong place, or the entire bridge had vanished. A bridge of black rock, rimed with ice. He stared into the rushing torrent far below, and thought about the power of the Dark essence, and what it could be used for.

It was impossible. He was certain that the Shadowcasters could not cause rock to disappear. If they wielded such powerful magic, they would have ruled Eyri long ago.

And yet, there was no bridge.

His mind refused to work. A mist of exhaustion blurred the edges of his vision. He bit his knuckles to fight the advance of fatigue.

Think.

There was a deep channel of water that passed him on the landing. The rain caused it to overflow, but most of it streamed to the edge and feathered in the wind to spray.

Why do they channel water to flow to waste in the chasm?

He strained to see if there was a similar channel on the far side of the chasm, on the landing there. The thick clouds overhead and the driving rain yielded nothing of the dawn but a faded gloom. There was little detail in what he saw, but he thought he spied a frayed stream falling from the cliffs. Beside it, a red-robed figure, arms raised.

The ragged probes of Dark essence which pushed out from the figure's hands left no doubt as to what kind of traveller he was. Ashley jumped for cover behind a boulder.

The Shadowcaster worked erratically at his spell. It seemed to be a very complicated action, which required much dancing around, shouts and howls, sudden moments of inactivity, and short bursts of commanding the essence. Gradually, a transformation took place. The Dark essence was strung across the chasm, a thin line of motes which Ashley knew could bear no weight. The Shadowcaster shouted, but most of the words were torn away in the wind. He appeared to sit in the rain for a while, staring into the chasm, or at Ashley.

He couldn't have spied him from afar!

The Shadowcaster commanded his essence with a harsh cry.

Ice formed on the line that had been cast, right up to where Ashley hid. Black ice, assuming the colour of the essence within it. The spill from the channel collected in the ice runner. Water poured into the curved guide, and was carried out across the span. The Shadowcaster cried out again, and this time the wind did not tear the words apart.

"Freeze."

The runner of black ice was a foot wide, then two. Rain collected in the construction, and the Shadowcaster used it to build his narrow bridge, warped and incomplete, but a bridge nonetheless. The Dark essence created the pattern upon which the ice grew.

The Shadowcaster disappeared into the darkness against the distant cliffs. Ashley resigned himself to a wait. The bridge was not nearly wide enough for a safe crossing, yet once it could bear the Shadowcaster one way, it could bear him to freedom. He hoped that the Shadowcaster would not destroy the bridge the moment he'd crossed.

The figure burst from the gloom, and dived headlong from the distant landing, his stomach to the bridge. He fired across the chasm like an arrow borne upon the ice. The bridge narrowed almost to nothing in the centre. The Shadowcaster avoided falling by twisting as he slid. Moments later, he had slid all the way the near landing, and was over the lip of it, rising from his knees within the ice and water.

The Shadowcaster gave a cry like a jubilant crow. He turned his back to Ashley, stared into the chasm, then clapped his hands. Ashley recognised the red-stained robe and face of a man he had thought dead. Twice dead, counting the bridge he had just crossed. He pressed himself deeper into his place of concealment. He couldn't breathe.

Kirjath Arkell shouted curses at the storm. He bobbed on his feet for a while. He recalled his motes, taking them from the bridge he had made. Darkness collected about his shoulders. What was left of the bridge was no more than a glistening structure of ice.

The Shadowcaster groaned suddenly and twitched as if in spasm. When he regained his composure, he shouted to the wind, then turned on his heel, and strode off towards Ravenscroft, never even glancing toward where Ashley hid.

Arkell is alive. Arkell is mad.

Ashley had to wait some time before his heartbeat resumed a steady pace. He couldn't help thinking of Morgloth, with that Shadowcaster close by.

Ashley stared at the bridge. He had thought it inadequate before the motes had been withdrawn. Without its binding of Dark, it looked even more fragile and impossibly narrow. And yet, it was the only way to escape from Ravenscroft.

A ray of sunlight burst through a gap in the clouds as dawn defied the foul gloom for a moment. The bridge sparkled to brilliance. Light flashed from every surface, making it suddenly beautiful. It also caused the first sound to come from the bridge.

CRACK.

"Creator give me strength," Ashley whispered. He backed up as far as he could, trying to shut out the voice that screamed inside his head. If a Shadowcaster could do it, so could he.

But Arkell was mad.

He hurled himself over the edge.

Time slowed. The ice was as clear as glass, and he could see through it into the throat of the chasm, past its sharpened teeth to the foam and rocks far below. It was a view he wished he couldn't see.

A white crack ran along underneath him for a while, then shot off to beat him up the sloping distant half of the bridge. He made small noises in his throat. He skidded across a puddle. The water clung to him, slowing his body on the ice. He passed the mid-point with the full strength of terror gripping his heart. The bridge was narrower than his body. He closed his eyes, not wanting to see how it would end.

I should have waited for another Caster to make a stronger bridge. This is a stupid way to die.

He knew he was not going to make it, even before he had slid to a halt. There was too much sloping bridge ahead of him. He had not built up enough speed to carry him all the way. He heard the sharp crack of ice, felt the shudder pass underneath his body, and knew the bridge had collapsed. He threw his hands forward, though he knew it was in vain.

His hands found stone. His grip held. He kicked his legs and flopped like a fish onto a level surface. He opened his eyes, and saw the landing. The remains of the bridge cracked and fell away from where his feet had been. It tumbled, end over end, graceful and glittering, until it smashed to fragments on the rocks.

The bridge to Ravenscroft was no more.

The relief was overwhelming. He almost fainted, but he caught himself at the last moment, his head nearly on the cold ground. It would do no good to let fatigue claim him. He was the only Lightgifter who had escaped the vale of Ravenscroft, the only one who knew the truth. He must carry that truth away, no matter how heavy the burden. But for a moment his exhaustion reared like an insurmountable wall.

Footsteps, or a sudden gust of wind, he had no more than a heartbeat to turn toward the sound before the rock smote his head. Thunder boomed. He lost every sense of the world. The darkness that came upon him was deeper and more silent than the most abandoned passage of Ravenscroft's Keep.

33. THE GYRE

"A committee is a dangerous thing.
A committee of wizards is insanity."—*Zarost*

Twardy Zarost crouched in the seclusion of the thicket. He watched the path. He was running a risk as it was, leaving the Seeker in her critical state amidst the turmoil. It would make matters far worse if anyone saw him leave Eyri. There would be questions he couldn't answer even with the most twisted of riddles.

A robin fluttered onto the path, and hopped closer. It reminded him to scan the sky through the boughs. Apart from driving clouds, it was clear. No doves, no ravens. No further messages from the Gyre, but the one glyph-cloud had sufficed.

Zarost stepped onto the path once again. The easy trail through the farms had given way to a narrow track, where the flowers grew wild and sometimes covered the path completely. Zarost preferred it. Here, the vitality of spring burst through everywhere, in untamed splendour. Even so, the butterfly preferred his coloured cloak to the flowers all around. It flitted and danced in the air, but never strayed far.

He came to a gentle pass, and began to climb, using his makeshift staff to steady himself on the brittle rock underfoot. The trail became a track, then vanished altogether. It was little wonder that no one ventured into the northern lands beyond Flowerton. River's End was infamous for the Rimswraith, the vaporous entity who tricked men to believing they could fly only to let them fall to their death.

Zarost chuckled. It was charming the tales country folk would hold onto. He had worked hard to spread that tale and ensure it became firmly entrenched in the folklore. He liked to have complete privacy at the end of the trail. He tapped his pipe out on the staff.

"Wicked, wicked Rimswraith," he whispered.

He reached the lookout that was River's End at noon. The rock jutted out from the crest of the cliffs beside the thunderous falls. Here the Storms River escaped from Eyri, tumbling more than three thousand feet to its death within the turbulent haze far below. The air was wet with the vapours left swirling above the liquid thunder. The cliffs were impressive, cut sheer and smooth, offering no possible route down their treacherous sides. River's End really was the end of the realm. There was no way beyond it for anyone wishing to live and tell the tale.

Twardy Zarost intended to do both.

He lit himself another bowl of weed, and chuffed contentedly at his pipe. It was always good to have a smoke before the journey, it calmed the nerves. The prudes in the Gyre always had something to say about smoking, the damage it did to the body and mind. When you were going to use the same body for a very, very long time, you had to be careful what habits you acquired. That was the Gyre's opinion.

Zarost blew a smoke ring and watched it climb into the bright sky. The sun had crept past its zenith; he was already late for the meeting. All the more reason for a smoke. He watched the mist curl and twist at the head of the falls—the vapours formed a tree, then it was an eagle, then a beast with arms outstretched. The Rimswraith was on peak form today. He would have to let it trick him, the wicked thing.

He watched the Shield. It shimmered with power, out in the air beyond the Rimswraith. It was a division invisible to most eyes, a manipulation of space that reflected all of Eyri's magic inwards and kept what was outside, out. It was a powerful repellant on either side. He could feel its pressure even from where he sat—a grinding, crushing weight, oppressive enough to turn even inquisitive explorers back towards home. So it would always be, so long as the Kingsrim remained to bind the spell, so long as Eyri contained the seed of the Gyre's hope. The Wizard's Ring might finally have found purchase, in the protected soil.

In over four hundred years, no one had learned to balance the first axis of magic. The various Seekers had developed a fair amount of *lumen* lore, using either Light or Dark, depending on their nature, but the mages were always separated upon the first axis, their spells conflicting, their intentions opposed. The Seekers had always abandoned the Ring when it showed them the path to the other side, or the Ring had grown cold and become impossible to hold when those Seekers had demonstrated no ability to achieve the crossing. Yet it was the path to becoming whole, it was the path to finding the Wizard.

Now, at last, there was Tabitha. She had much to learn, true, but she had great potential. He just hoped she didn't burn out with the intensity of her progress, or become possessed by her treacherous foe.

He would ask the Gyre for a concession, he decided. There had to be some way of smoothing the way for Tabitha Serannon without compromising the requirement of self-discovery.

He rose, tucking his pipe into the folds of his robe. It was time to meet the Gyre. He had to be beyond the Shield when he attempted the spell of Transference. He couldn't risk echoes of that spell lingering inside Eyri, where they could be copied by the Seeker. Her development, as always, had to remain strictly untainted, a function only of what she could discover within Eyri, and within herself.

She wasn't ready for the Chaos outside. Not yet.

Zarost took a deep breath. He could almost hold the staff steady in his hand. He waved the butterfly away—it would have to remain in Eyri—he didn't want to waste attention on it during the journey. It would not cross the Shield by itself.

The breeze tugged at his hair.

He jumped. He fell.

Fabric whipped and snapped in the rush of air. Zarost arched his back and splayed his arms. His legs stabilised him, and he angled away from the cliffs. It gave one a much longer ride if you avoided the cliffs.

An adrenalin-charged grin stretched across his face. Yes, if one didn't angle away, the cliffs came up rather faster than expected. If one put a limb out at the wrong angle, everything would spin out of control too. The cliff-face flickered by. He carefully extended the hand that held the staff, and it pulled his body in a lazy spin to that side. The sun slid past, then the cliffs, the waterfall, then blue sky again.

The movement was exhilarating. He extended his other arm, which reversed the turn. His grin widened. Even here, in a wild fall through the sky, there was balance and pattern.

The Shield came and went, an excruciating resistance that pulled at his body and his mind, intensifying, demanding return. His speed and intent carried him through, into the clear air beyond.

The ground was coming up. Still, there should be time for his favourite. Head down, and the speed built up until the world was a roar in his ears, rushing up to meet him, bending the horizon outward.

The ground was coming up. He was sure he could squeeze in just one more. He'd always wanted to know what would happen if you put your feet down and raised your arms over your head. It would be like walking on air.

The whip of fabric was instantaneous. If his grey robe hadn't been fastened at the waist with stout cord, he would have lost it entirely. That might have been better. As it was, the robe flapped around his head, tangling in the fire-coloured cloak which thrashed there already. He couldn't see a thing. He scrabbled at the air, guiding himself hopelessly into a blurring, whizzing tumble of legs, arms and curses. He lost his pipe, and his pouch of weed.

Damn and set fire to it!

The ground was coming up.

Zarost set his alarm aside, and focused on his spell. He hoped that he'd have time to complete the words. He became aware of his body. He sent his consciousness outwards, into the air around him, and accepted that too. He was a part of the air, it flowed through him, thus the air was a part of him. The air that was the Riddler touched the cliffs, the waterfall, the ground below, and so that was part of him as well. Wider, further, faster, outward. The edges of the lands below, across the oceans, over the world.

Ground coming up! a little voice of alarm warned.

The edge of the sky. The moon. The planets. The stars. Past galaxies and galaxies, outwards past the darkest strangeness of growing universes his awareness streaked, a sphere of Being, reaching in all directions. He reached the boundary of endless existence, which wasn't really a boundary at all.

Infinity.

He accepted it as part of himself, and disappeared. For no one could be spread across infinity, and still exist in one place. It was the paradox that drove the Transference. One Being spread across infinity was more than just thinly spread. It was nothing at all.

He knew there would be an implosion when air filled the space that his body had occupied, but nobody would hear it. The roar of the falls would thunder on, where the ambered waters of Eyri were thrown upon the silvered pool hidden below the mists at the base of River's End. The clash between the traces of Order within Eyri's water and the Chaos essence it met in the tainted land would cause the water to boil and writhe and roar as if the water had been thrown on a fire.

Zarost was gone.

It was a queer experience, as always. No one could remain for long in the infinity without losing their mind. It was too much to cope with. Having no form, yet having awareness. He was everywhere, without being anywhere.

The Transference was only completed when he chose one particular point in his infinite attention and concentrated upon it. He had a single destination in mind; the council chambers within the Gyre Sanctuary. He focused on the lone building in the desert, a construction of gold-veined stonewood and dark-coppered magemetal, its scalloped roofs scaled in shimmering green and shielded beneath a complicated web of clear essence, in a place far beyond Eyri—deep in the southern lands of Oldenworld, a region which had no appeal to the Sorcerer, and was beyond his reach.

Zarost chose an entrance point in the chambers that would be visible to everyone. He chuckled. It was always hot in the desert, too hot. What he had in mind would help to keep him cool through the meeting. Besides, it would be a fine prank if he could make the dour Wizards jump.

The speed of appearance from a Transference was determined by the speed of disappearance, in much the same way a ripple returned from the walls of a concentric pool. The faster the ripple travelled outward, the faster it returned, to converge in the wizard at his destination. Zarost knew that most of the Gyre members would have needed ten or even fifteen minutes to stretch their awareness to the boundary, and thus would have arrived in the Sanctuary as a hazy disturbance which thickened over the minutes, giving all who were present time to anticipate the arrival. It was safe, and considered good manners, to appear gently and slowly. But you appeared as you disappeared.

Zarost fell through the air, his robe flapping about his ears. His appearance in the chamber was instantaneous, and he plunged toward the pool that he'd known would be there, the pool which held the liquid augury, placed in the centre of the circle of wizards. He broke the surface with a mighty splash, big enough to wet them all. Then he was under the cold water, and fighting to control his laughter, so that he wouldn't swallow a mouthful or the entire pool.

When he bobbed to the surface, he was met with stony silence. The Wizards were still in their places around the pool. Six of them were soaked, the seventh one sat with her feet drawn up under her body, clear of the floor. The Mystery had been warned by her intuition. Not so, the others.

Zarost shook with laughter. Only the Mystery smiled. He tried not to cry for the other members of the Gyre.

By the giblets of a foul fowl, they are a mirthless bunch!

Nonetheless, they were the Gyre, and powerful wizards all. He should behave! That thought only made his laughter worse. The six soggy wizards rose from their bench as one, their faces stern.

He paddled hastily to the edge of the pool. A good Riddler he may be, but he would be hard-pressed to survive their combined wrath. He knew the strengths of each member intimately; the calm perceptive Mystery, the intense and shock-haired Mentalist, the bitter forceful Cosmologer, the gentle-faced but deep-reaching Spiritist, the sober strict Lorewarden, the dangerous Warlock and the shrewd Senior. Each had power enough to crisp his hide, in their own way.

Together they were almost as mighty as the Sorcerer Ametheus.

He straightened to meet the tirade. Their hostile glares pinned him in his place.

"How dare you!" screeched the Cosmologer, finding her tongue at last. "This is the Gyre's Sanctuary! We are wizards here!" Stating the obvious in high-pitched tones was her contribution to most affairs, Zarost reflected.

"By the cursed Pillar, Riddler, you should be struck from the Gyre for that!" exclaimed the Mentalist. His streaked hair was a fright, as usual.

"The image! You cod, you've made us lose the image!" exclaimed the sweet-voiced Spiritist. She looked worried, which was strange. She had sworn at him, which was even stranger. Zarost began to consider that his prank might have been ill-placed.

"Work on it, bring it back for us!" commanded the greying Senior, the one who led the debates in the Gyre, so chosen because of his experience and composure. "We can't afford to lose its position!" He looked flustered, Zarost realised. Something was wrong, the atmosphere was too tense. He looked from one face to the next—they were rat-eyed, lean-cheeked, tired. Drawn lips and pale faces. They were under a strain he'd never seen before.

The largest of the men present balled his fists. "What if someone had been in the space you Transferred to, Riddler? Such speed is reckless!" The Greater Warlock, a loud man who always took himself too seriously.

Zarost decided not to answer him. The Warlock wanted to fight. What was the matter with all of them?

The young Mentalist was the first of those who had been angered to recover his humour. "Ah, Riddler, we're a little tightly strung. It was a good joke, at a bad time. A very bad time." He backed away towards his seat. "Maybe later you can tell us how you entered so quickly."

Zarost smiled, but the Cosmologer waved an angry finger at him. "There was nothing funny about it!" she exclaimed. "Get aside, Wizards, get back to your places! We must recover what this silverspawn has destroyed!"

"Oh, calm down, Cosmologer," said a cool voice from the bench. "He's the Riddler, not a scion of the Sorcerer. He's part of our Gyre, and we need his strange ways in our octad whether you wish so or not," said the Mystery. She was the one who had laughed at his entrance. "Welcome, though not well come, Riddler. You have been absent for so long I think many of us have forgotten how to be joyous." Despite her short, unruly hair, she wore an aura of dark elegance. Zarost acknowledged her support with a nod. Her green eyes were twinkling still.

The Cosmologer snorted. "Little to be joyous about."

The Senior raised his hand, waited for the awkward silence to settle, then eased onto the circular bench. He rested his level gaze on Twardy Zarost. "I trust that will be all, Riddler. Please join us." The Senior's voice crackled with tension, and when that happened Zarost knew that the Senior was in a dangerous mood indeed.

Zarost nodded. He must have interrupted something terribly important.

He squelched over to an empty place in the circle, and sat. Water ran from the many folds of his robe onto the curved brown stonewood bench. Nobody seemed to care—their attention was on the pool, where the little peaks of Zarost's disturbance played havoc with the Mystery's attempt to project her vision.

The Lorewarden swept the water smooth with a gesture. He had been a powerful Mattermage, before taking up the third axis. He was a serious fellow, so often silent for entire meetings. The Cosmologer linked a flow of clear essence with the Mentalist, and together they assisted the Mystery with her task. The Mystery reached down until her hand had almost touched the smoothened water, and the deep indigo colour of the pool changed to a swirling white-flecked brown as she gathered the threads of her Seeing spell.

Clouds over the desert sands. They sped northwards, for some time. Finally the great saw-toothed mass of the Zunskar Mountains passed by, the realm of Eyri hidden in its western hook. North, they flew, past the wide grey wastelands that bordered Eyri, to the edge of the Evernon Forest beyond that, where the Six-Sided Land of

Lûk began. Twardy Zarost leant closer as they passed the inhabited district of Rek. Little figures moved upon a network of paths that led outwards from the carpet of trees. Life went on, in Oldenworld. The Mystery gestured, and they flowed over more forest, into the interior of the Six-Sided Land, to a place where the great curve of woodlands gave way to the eastern plains.

As they stepped down towards the land, individual trees thrust up at them, and the pale green carpet of grass spread out. A small bird shot by. They began to track east above a trampled path. A field of slender erect blue-flowered flax bowed in the breeze. An open irrigation pipe threaded its way through the flowers, but no water flowed in it, for the well-point was abandoned. Some baskets piled with spider-silk lay strewn beside the path, as if the porters had fled. They had also dropped their sharp-tipped spears.

The hackles on Zarost's neck rose; the danger was close. Spidersilk was valuable to the Lûk—to steal the thread was dangerous, for the spiders of Evernon had grown large and cunning along the gloomy banks of the tainted White River. For the feisty Lûk to abandon their spidersilk meant something worse than ironpigs or an attack of Hunter challengers.

Another bird shot by, flying as if borne on a gale. Zarost recognised the lay of the land. The high grassed mounds of the digging casts with their spiral pathways. The twined spice trees and herb-bushes that the fire-resistant Lûk palates held so dear. This was somewhere near Jho-down, a settlement linked to the western channel of the down of Koom, where the centre of Lûk culture lay. The most important trade from the west passed through Jho. They wove the most beautiful garments here, soft and fine and durable, better even than the wizard-altered silks produced in the heyday of old Moral Kingdom.

The Mystery guided the vision slowly across the long grassed fields, away from the forest, until they passed the first woven trapdoors of the down. The doors were difficult to discern, braided as they were from the grasses that grew around them.

"It was north of here, Mystery, just a little way," urged the Senior.

"I know," she replied, the frustration audible in her voice. "My vision is wandering. The very presence of what we seek throws me away."

The image in the pool began to shudder, skipping left and right of the direction they were following. They passed low over another trapdoor and veered suddenly through an orchard of purple fruit-trees. A whole flock of doves whipped by, heading north, but flying strangely, as if they fought their own wings. The Gyre followed the flock, then crested a shallow rise and swerved up and away. Jho-down's main settlement lay beneath them, a gentle basin covered with red-leaved heartcreeper and golden soapberry bush. It would seem at first glance to be nothing more than a simple landscape, but Zarost knew that hundreds upon hundreds of trapdoors were hidden in the vale, trapdoors which led to a thriving underground community. And there, almost halfway through the settlement, spanning the entire breadth of Jho's basin, as much beneath the surface as above it, spun a hollow maw, a faceless vortex of churning earth and air and rock and water, a horrid wrangle which left behind a body of crushed remains, a tail of sheddings that didn't end, stretching away to the north towards the Winterblade Mountains. The tumbling doves were sucked across the basin and into the vortex as the monster breathed them in. They were gone.

"Now you see the Oldenworld's bane," the Mystery sighed.

Zarost was on his feet. "The worm! The Lûk, oh the Lûk, oh no!" he cried, staring down into the scouring maelstrom that ate through the Jho-down. That hideous thing had no eyes, only a swirling throat into which the debris flew and was crushed upon itself. The rock and air around the edges of its mouth were wrinkled like the skin of ancient lips. Its hunger seemed to pull at the centre of everything Zarost could see, bending even the pool as if it drew the water which contained the vision towards it as well. Bending the pool from such a distance was just as impossible as what Zarost was seeing it achieve in Jho. He took a nervous step away from the edge of the pool.

"We named it the Wranglewrithe," explained the Lorewarden in a dull voice. "For two months we have tracked its course south from Kah. It punctured the Winterblades like a hot poker through snow. We have no means to stop it."

"This is the new sorcery of Ametheus. It goes beyond our knowledge, present or past," admitted the Senior.

"Two months from Kah to Jho? It moves slowly then," Zarost observed.

"Slow, and then fast, and then slow again," said the Senior. "It wanders like a whirlwind, yet its track heads always south."

"It grows by itself," added the Warlock. "And as it stretches against the weight of its contents it gathers speed at the head. It runs faster now than it did in the lowlands."

It had come through the great bulwark of the mountains! Zarost bit on his knuckles as he watched the erratic action in the swirling maw—sometimes the earth flew apart, sometimes the air seemed to turn solid and drop to the ground below as a blue shedding. Then the scattered earth would come together again, so fast and hard the Writhe created a great hollow in that place. Then water exploded to a cloud, and was sucked almost at once through the pinhole around which everything rotated, to form fine particles of white, barely visible in the chaos and gloom of its innards. The Writhe spun and spun, drawing Zarost forward, tugging at his balance, keeping his attention amongst that ruin of Jho. Some patches of the spillage within the tail were stained red. Zarost suspected it wasn't due to the dyes the Lûk stored for flax and reeds. He saw a man running away from the collapsing edge nearest the Writhe, a typical Lûk cable-weaver, strong and grey-skinned, bow-legged, with the elongated face of his kin; the jutting chin and nose, a handsome face, with dark marriage-whorls worked upon his hard skin. His scarlet headscarf was tight in the tip and full in the knots. The weaver made the motions of running away, but he was being hauled towards the edge instead, he was being forced towards the Writhe. Zarost's heart caught in his throat.

"If Jho was always on its path, why did this Writhe find them in their down?" Zarost demanded of the Senior. "Why weren't these people warned!"

"Do you think we haven't tried!" shouted the Cosmologer. "We have been warning people from Spek to See'gi, from Kurum to Rostkaan, while *you* have been dallying in the shelter of Eyri."

Zarost turned to the Spiritist, hoping for an explanation with less acid in it.

"They are mistrustful of us, Riddler, you know how the Lûk are about anyone not Lûk," she said. "They do not believe what they can not see, and if they are close enough to see, they are too close."

"When they are too close, they are always drawn towards it, into the head," finished the Warlock, smacking his fist into his palm. "From a league away, sometimes much more. It varies, it changes. It isn't constant."

In the image, a Lûk maiden clung to an upright of lashed reeds, as the underground corridor she was in and earth surrounding it, were torn apart. The woven interior of the corridor held together well, and it jutted out from the receding raw cliff, but the end nearest the Writhe was soon stripped to the fibres. A sheave of papers battered the maiden as they hurried by, a cane chair followed. She clung on, against the current of debris, her scarlet headscarf flapping wildly, until even that was whipped away. Her hair flowed free, a full luxuriant length of copper plaits. She must have come from a wealthy family, to be allowed to keep such valuable hair on her head. It wouldn't matter any more. None of what the Lûk had done in Jho would matter. Zarost watched the woven veins of the Lûk settlement disintegrate before his eyes. The segment of corridor which had held the maiden broke away and tumbled towards the worm. Zarost's stomach turned. The Writhe was feeding on everything.

"What kind of creature is this? Where within the Annals of all Existence has he summoned such a thing from?"

"It is not alive, you fool," sniped the Cosmologer. "It can not be threatened or lured or tortured out of its way. It does not care. It is a current, manufactured of ruined space, and in it is spawned a gravity which has become stronger than I can turn. If it is left to grow, I fear it will set the orbit of the Earth awry. It might eat into the soil until it has fed upon the planet's core, until its heart is compact enough to draw even the stars towards us. The Writhe reaches for the Ending, it reaches for devastation."

"Oh why does Ametheus do this?" cried the Mystery. "What use is a world that is ended?"

"We only have the same guesses as always, gentle one," answered the Senior. "That this has been his goal all along, that he seeks to rupture Time itself, and that it has taken him these long centuries to gather his awful genius. I fear he has advanced to an eighth-level spell. At last, he may have found a means to reach the End, unless we can devise a way to counter it. The closer he can move towards the Ending, the tighter he will force the bend in Time to be, because he will bypass all those eras that should still be. That corruption of Time would release Chaos of such magnitude that he would have the power to create whatever he desired, to make and unmake on dimensions beyond our own. He seeks power, Mystery. He wants to rule Life itself."

There were children clutching to their walls, and old folk, and healthy youths too. Zarost grew hot inside. They shouldn't be there, the Gyre had failed them, the Wizards were too cowardly to take responsibility for the Lûk and stand beside them against the Writhe. It had to be stopped. He couldn't stand by and watch the deaths of so many innocents. He would go there and use an extended Transference spell to gather as many of them as he could, take them to Koom or Sess or even the deserts beside the Gyre Sanctuary. Anywhere would be better than Jho-down. He spread his arms and reached for Infinity.

"No!" shouted the Mentalist, jumping up to restrain Zarost. "No! You'll kill yourself!"

Zarost broke out of the Mentalist's hold, but the Mentalist was quick and determined, and he was able to keep a hand on Zarost no matter how much he blocked and weaved. To be touched was to be grounded. He would have to take them both if he Transferred.

"We can't be near to it!" shouted the Mentalist. "It is even worse for us than for those Lûk you would save. You will not be strong enough to fight it!"

"How do you know?" Zarost challenged. "How do you know we can't fight it from the ground?"

"We can't. We almost lost the Warlock."

Zarost glanced at the Warlock to confirm the claim. The Warlock nodded gravely.

"What happened?" Zarost demanded.

"I went there, Riddler, I felt as you did about the inhabitants of Kah, to the north. This Writhe is strange, for time is somehow screwed into its mouth as well ... you will think a moment has passed as you cast your spell, but a day will go by in the world outside, and the Writhe can overtake you in that time."

"I'll prepare my spell before I Transfer. I'll be there and gone in a breath!"

"No, Riddler, it can not work. There is more to the Writhe which you do not understand. You know we are larger than the rest, as wizards we extend further into the world around us. The Writhe— well, you can see what it has already done to the magic of the pool."

Zarost looked. The pool was bending more than ever, an awfully concave meniscus.

"It is such strong Chaos, it grips with a bond like a iron cable to anything which has a hint of Order to it. We think that is why it runs through the network of the Lûk downs so steadily. They have lost much to Ametheus over the years, but they have the most structured realm of any of the peoples of Oldenworld now. They have a kind of Order, though it is not essence-magic. The Writhe feeds on it."

Five baskets of spidersilk tumbled across the grass and were whisked across the gulf to feed the worm. Zarost recognised them as the baskets which had lain unattended beside the field of flax. He wondered if the porters were still running, or if they had been eaten.

He met the Mentalist's sharp blue gaze, and dipped his head. He didn't need restraining any more, they had made their point. He might be the Riddler, but this thing was beyond his ken. He was the one who was a step behind, not the Gyre.

"Show me where it has been," he said quietly. "I want to learn what it is, I must see what you've seen."

They took him on a journey then, northwards along the tail. The Writhe had run an erratic course, exploding from the ground in places, sinking, rising elsewhere again. It had formed an immense corridor of ruin before Jho, blasting through many of the smaller downs on the way to Kah and pulling the landscape into awful columns of devastation there which looked like coloured spires of splintered bone, before the trail left the Six-Sided Land and dove through the solid bedrock of the Winterblade mountains.

It emerged again on the far side, amongst the dry foothills far below the snow line, the same scattering of altered, hardened substances upon a punctured and scalloped land. None of the wild folk who inhabited the foothills were visible, even though the sun was baking full upon the rocks. Zarost wondered how many of them had been taken by the Writhe. He shouldn't care—the Scalard were transformed beyond recognition, they had lost their humanity long ago. They were vicious and cruel beings who understood only domination. They wouldn't even co-operate with each other to improve their living conditions. And yet Zarost felt a poignant sense of loss when he was told that they might have been consumed in the same uncaring aperture that had eaten through the lands of the Lûk, for the Scalard were a race whom the Wizards had failed completely—in a way they represented the worst of what had been done to Oldenworld—they lived, and yet they enjoyed no consciousness, no purpose to their actions, no memory of what they had lost. Zarost knew what they had lost, and it made him sad.

They had been altered first, in the old kingdom of Moral. They weren't so much a race as a congregation of victims with a common affliction. All had been cursed with cold blood, and their kind had moved south in those early years of terror until they came to the protected cleft of the Tarnished Hills, where the sun shone hot and clouds seldom drew in. Over the centuries of harsh survival, they had learned to ease the tightness of their toughening skin with the greenstone of the old mines, which left traces of its pigment within their scales. Once they had been lords and ladies of gracious Moral; now they lived in squalor, fighting with covetted weapons no one knew how to forge any more, feeding on live animals or each other's children, dragging branches to their enclosed huts at night to burn and lie beside. As if that degeneration were not enough, they lost half of their number to a second spell, when Ametheus experimented again with changes in nature, and the fire-blooded creatures spawned in their midst crawled away to find the cold solace of the Winterblades. Oh the Scalard had suffered much, for when they sought to leave their Tarnished Hills and travel further south to follow the winter sun, neither the Lûk nor the Hunter folk would grant them passage through the narrow gap at Slipper. They were silverspawn, too clearly of Ametheus, and those that didn't flee were killed at the borders of the heartlands.

Zarost was angry at their deaths, because in a way they were the Sorcerer's own people, they were in his Lowlands, and should have been spared from his inventions. Yet Ametheus cared not, he never had. It didn't matter to him that his creation had run through his own people first, that it had scoured and mangled and scarred the Lowlands before reaching the heartlands.

The course of the Writhe's devastation exitted the Scalard's valley at the old town of Greenstone, where the products of jade and rivergold used to be distributed to the extended markets of the Three Kingdoms. The Writhe had missed the heart of the town, for beyond the river of crushed tallus, the unblemished great square still stood amongst the gorse-bushes, with its tall obelisks and green magestone mosaic, its towering spring-fed fountain and gilded pool, marking the town which hadn't been a town for centuries.

Northwards, the Writhe sank into the earth, and only emerged again near Meliness, where it had ruptured the old road, twisting the northloop of the causeway right over the southloop. The regular staffs of rusted metal beside the road looked like the lopped stumps of a deceased vineyard. They had glistened and shone once, the pride of Moral kingdom, but those streetlights had been vandalised before the Writhe had come, their glass shattered, their sprites consumed. Few streetlights remained anywhere in Oldenworld, and those that were still intact were dark—no one had dared to renew a spritebulb since Kinsfall, for fear of being struck down by the Sorcerer's reactive wildfire net that threaded itself through the sky. Ametheus had been effective at silencing anyone with talent. Only the Gyre dared to practise magic, and only because they cast their spells together, and so could meet his power on equal terms.

That was, they told Zarost, before the Writhe had come.

It was created so far away from their position on the third axis of magic that even if they pooled their talents, they were not able to mirror its magnitude. The orientation of the spell was still close on the third axis, but the level to which it had been taken, the reach from the zero-point, was formidable. As individual wizards, they could not hope to reach beyond the first level. As the Gyre, their power combined, but even so they had been limited by their number to seventh-level spells without Zarost present in their circle, and then only within those rare moments of perfect cooperation. That was the disadvantage of depending on Knowledge for wisdom—none of them could reach beyond the sum of their single-minded total. But the Writhe was at least an eighth-level weave—they couldn't even discern the fundamental pattern that Ametheus had used to drive his worm into existence. They were certain it still used essence, but it heralded the kind of advance only the sorcerer could achieve, by reaching beyond Knowledge, by reaching for his source. Ametheus had tapped into the next level of power.

They needed the Riddler in their circle, they needed eight minds and lores together to reach an eighth-level magnitude of power and so pierce the complexity of the Writhe. Only then would they have a hope of opposing their antithesis and bringing balance to the third axis.

An idle tongue of wildfire licked across the rubbled track in Meliness, and the earth rippled slightly at the touch of Chaos, but nothing came of it, for the Writhe had already claimed the life within that soil. On the edge of the tail of sheddings, the Castle of Meliness still stood, inhabited by bloodbirds and mean-faced trolls since the last Atheling family in Moral had fallen, almost a century past. The northern wall had been stripped from the building by the passing Writhe, as had the outer and inner bastions on that side. The trolls might have been drawn from their lair, to become a few pebbles in the tail of sheddings, for nothing moved within the Castle any more.

Oldenworld was falling further into ruin. Zarost had not believed that Ametheus could do much more to the Lowlands—there was so little remaining of the old beauty of the Three Kingdoms—but here even the ugliness which had replaced it was being torn apart. He urged the Mystery to move the image further, into old Orenland.

There were low wet clouds boiling everywhere west of Thren Fernigan. The Gyre travelled down low, over the wild cotton groves, into the hot valleys choked with vapours and rampant growth. The monsters that hunted and hid amongst the tangled vegetation shouted and howled and barked, a yammering noise that grew ever more as they moved west, where creatures that Zarost had no name for filled the open places, feasting upon fruit, or upon each other, dark unfortunate things which had survived the Sorcerer's latest whims.

Zarost concentrated on the effect of the Writhe alone, to limit his developing sickness of spirit.

The diameter of destruction had been noticeably smaller near Thren Fernigan, the span of two fallen trees, and it diminished to a width barely big enough to swallow the eroded kilns of the old glassworks at Ross Relawere. The last of the beaches were gone, smothered by the advance of the Growing Lands which had flowed in from the sea like a fetid tide and never flowed away from the shore again. Ametheus had grown all manner of things in the warm brine, things which had died and grown hard and allowed other things to live upon the structure of their remains.

The Gyre could not follow the trail of the Writhe much further into the swamps and fens of the western Lowlands, where fat slugs rolled upon one another in the mud and nervous waterfowl dodged through a haze of deadly insects, searching for the rare ones that were palatable. They had come too close to the Sorcerer's presence for comfort, it would be too easy for Ametheus to trace them back to the secret location of the Gyre Sanctuary. They all knew that the origin of the Writhe was in Turmodin; its track continued, due west. The worm would have emerged from the Pillar in Turmodin as thin as a hair; a mere fibre of disorder. An eighth-level spell indeed, Zarost thought, so subtle at its source it would have had no effect at all, and yet it had grown to a maelstrom of destruction, under its own momentum. Such an escalating spell was the worst kind to counter, for it intensified the longer it was left unchecked.

The Mystery reversed their course.

When they followed the course of the Writhe quickly east, then south, back past the Winterblades to the Land of Lûk, a terrible suspicion grew in Zarost's belly, for if the curve of the Writhe was extended beyond Jho-down, it would find Rek, then through the grey wastes, and then the Shield of Eyri. He pressed his palms to his eyes, wanting to block out the visions of inevitability, but knowing he could not.

"Yes, we know where it is heading, Riddler. You must abandon Eyri."

He hardly heard the Senior's words.

"The Shield was finished off by seven of us, when you were left within," the Senior continued. "It holds only a seventh-level weave—we never considered how far Ametheus might go. If this is an eighth-level spell, then the Writhe might burst through the Shield."

"But if you haven't discerned the pattern of the spell then you aren't certain it is an eighth. It might be of the seventh or even the sixth level," he countered weakly.

"Do you want to gamble your life on what you expect Ametheus did? You can't predict Chaos, Riddler."

Flowerton, it would hit Flowerton first, after consuming the falls at River's End. The Amberlake would be sucked dry from the northern end of the Storms River, and the village of Flowerton would be emptied just as Jho-down had been. For some reason he thought of a homely tavern that he had been planning to visit on his return, the Wayfayrer's Inn—it always had a warm hearth, it always held good tales. The folk in Flowerton were totally unaware of what was approaching.

Flowerton, Levin, Stormhaven. That precious sanctuary for all that was good in Oldenworld would be lost. Eyri would be gone. It was too dear to his heart to set aside in a moment.

"The flowers came out late this year, the sheep have better wool. They've learned to make a stainless steel, and a clock that needs no pull." His words always rhymed when he wanted to hide his feelings.

"You have to get out, Riddler," repeated the Senior. "We can not save it."

"The palace dungeon's empty, though it ought to hold someone. The roofs of the Isle glisten still, when they catch the morning sun."

"You must leave! It is over," stated the Cosmologer.

The Lifesong would be silenced. Young Tabitha Serannon would lose her chance to find her power, she would lose her chance at life.

No. He would not abandon the Seeker—he was her Riddler. She must find the wizard.

The Senior watched him from the far side of the pool. "Help us, Riddler. Join us to meet this Writhe."

The Gyre waited. The seven needed one more. He was needed

outside of Eyri.

He was needed within.

"Leave your petty attachments behind," the Cosmologer accused. "It is your duty to join us!"

"Gently, Cosmologer," the Spiritist cautioned. "There is a something the Riddler has not spoken of, and he fights it within his soul."

Zarost watched the water from his dripping sleeve throw ripples in the puddle at his feet. All the while, he could sense the tension in the chamber rising.

Tabitha, Tabitha, Tabitha. If only she had come through earlier; if only there was time.

"We have the brewings of a war, in Eyri," he said wistfully.

"A war, in Eyri?" replied the Warlock. "Then order has been corrupted already, it has failed its purpose. We can set it aside."

"And there is a new Seeker," he added.

The word touched all seven at once, just as the ripples in his puddle had found the edge of the circle in the same moment. Seeker. The vision of the Writhe disappeared from the pool, but no one objected.

"Is he to be another stepping stone, this new Seeker, or does he really have a chance?" the Senior asked.

"She," the Riddler corrected. "She is moving on the path, but her steps lead her towards a danger I do not like."

"There is always danger on the path!" the Cosmologer snapped. "Why should there not be hardships for a Seeker? Have you forgotten the way of your apprenticeship?"

"What danger is she in?" asked the Senior, cutting across the Cosmologer's slight.

"The previous Seeker developed great coercion," answered Zarost. "There is a danger that she shall be turned from the path and be manipulated to become the Darkmaster's minion."

The Mentalist appeared puzzled. "Surely then she shall lose the Ring? If she fails to follow the true path, she shall fail to attract it."

"We can't afford that," Zarost asserted. "Not with this one."

"Why is she any different? Aren't they always under threat?" asked the Cosmologer, clearly irritated.

"You don't get strong salmon without thinning out the minnows," added the Warlock.

"*Thinning the minnows!* Have a heart, Warlock! Have a heart."

It was easy to forget how ruthless the members of the council could be. Power was the only thing which really mattered, in the Greater Warlock's eyes. True of all wizards, though most hid it well.

"I want to intervene," said Zarost. "I want to clear the path before her, before it is too late."

Three wizards spoke at once. "No!" objected the Cosmologer as the Mentalist declared, "Definitely not!" and the Warlock boomed, "Out of the question!"

The Mystery was gazing out the window. She, of all the Gyre, listened with a different ear. She could probably hear that he wasn't calm, beneath the calm words. Her attention would return soon, he had no doubt.

Even the Senior appeared unsettled. "The magic must evolve in its own fashion, Riddler. If intervention is truly needed, you would be supporting the weaker strain. It can't be allowed."

The Cosmologer looked down her nose at Zarost. "That you should even question it! What has caused such poor judgement?"

"I pity you who see this judgement poor! The Seeker calls upon the Lifesong," he announced.

The silence was complete, except for the slow drips from Zarost's clothes.

The Cosmologer was tight-lipped, her indignation battling against uncertainty.

"How sure can you be?" the Lorewarden asked, at length.

"As sure as one can be after hearing her first stanza echo off the sky. It ran through everything in Eyri, even though the sound was faint due to her inexperience."

"Others heard it?" the Lorewarden asked.

"I had to work hard to ensure she survived what she had brought upon herself with that first singing."

"So you have already interfered with the course of events!" the Cosmologer crowed, desperate to find some fault with him to make herself seem better.

"No, Cosmologer, he did the right thing, so long as his efforts were balanced," said the Lorewarden. "Using the Lifesong! That is something beyond imagining. You have not used magic to interfere, have you, Riddler?"

"I have ground my teeth on the oath, but I have heeded it."

"Always speaking truth in crooked ways, but never crooked truth," said the Spiritist, smiling gently, her grey hair framing her sprightly face. Zarost hoped she was the only one who truly understood his riddled answer. Heeding something was different to obeying it. Just a little.

"Good Riddler," she continued, "many singers have heard echoes of the Lifesong. How can you be sure that the Seeker isn't just a good listener? What has she achieved that shows she has gone beyond the words and is able to use the power?"

"She used the high note, the Shiver, to hold a Morgloth."

"Full of concealed news today, aren't you?" she scolded, but Zarost could see the Spiritist was impressed.

"How long had this girl been under your tutelage, when she used that Shiver?" the Senior asked.

"Ten days."

The Warlock was incredulous. "In ten days this girl has learned enough to hold a Morgloth? What have you been teaching her, man?"

"She has always been a singer. Since she took up the Ring, she has begun to see what lies beneath the surface of the world. I have only been answering that which she asked, in the riddled way. She explores her own power."

The Warlock whistled softly. "She reaches beyond knowledge then, just as Ametheus does." His eyes grew hard. "How do we know she will not unleash Chaos upon us all?"

"No, Warlock, not Chaos! Not with the Lifesong!" objected the Spiritist.

"How do you know? Who knows more than a chapter about that lore?" He swung his gaze around the circle, but no one could provide an immediate challenge. "If she mastered a lore so different to ours," he continued, "she could take her power in any direction she wished. Either end of the third axis would respond to her call. How would we contain her, if she worked a different lore?"

"From what I remember, the Lifesong is a vibration, a resonance, and it is not dependant on any of the three axes of magic for its power," said the Cosmologer. "She might not need essence at all. But that is of no use to us! We need a Wizard in our circle, not a Bard."

"Magic, without essence?" asked the Mentalist incredulously. "Is that true, Lorewarden?"

The Lorewarden rubbed his chin. "Ahm—possibly. The Lifesong is so ancient, and so badly scribed. We knew little more than the melodies, even in the time before the Sorcerer, and most of the books which mentioned the actual practice of the lore were lost in Kinsfall.

We've all read the piece in Creation And Control which the Warlock referred to, which describes it as the 'lilting echo of the Goddess, carrying more than the words of each verse, spilling forth like a wind from the chosen voice as if through a window, unseen, undeniable, its sovereign force linking everything in the dominion of life'. What it carries, and how it achieves this is not known, but I can say that the First Masters of the College spoke of it with great awe, forgive me if I include you wrongly there, Senior."

"Fair words, Lorewarden, quite fair—I was one of those awed Masters. A true singer of the Lifesong! It is rare to wield even a hint of such an ability. It is not like most other lores, you could practise it all your life and grow no better at it. Admittedly there is little available to study. I set the songs aside when it became clear that I was not chosen for it. There is power there, but only for those to whom the power comes."

"Yet if it can change the world without the use of essence, it poses a threat to our effectiveness," the Mentalist said. "How could we hope to keep Order in our spells, if something contrary worked beneath our patterns, something which could change those patterns itself?"

"I agree!" said the Cosmologer. "Maybe it is better this Seeker does not emerge from Eyri. We have enough Chaos to contend with as it is."

Zarost rose from his seat. In all his years of working with the Gyre, he'd never felt as different from them as he did now. They were *arguing* about the value of the Lifesong! He would get what he wanted from these belligerent wizards, or he'd eat his estranged hat.

"She will not wield Chaos, you idiots! Three days ago, she created life with her first stanza. New life! She has tapped into that higher world, she has sung with the voice of Ethea."

The Lorewarden was suddenly animated. "Then she walks in the footsteps of the Goddess! I agree with the Riddler, this lore is so rare, this Seeker is too precious to risk to the challenges of the conventional path—she must be protected, until she has mastered her art."

Zarost raised the palm of his hand. He wanted to catch them before the current mood of wonder had faded, before they bickered and bargained about specifics. "I appeal for the Gyre's vote! Let me promote the Seeker now, and take her from the crucible. She can come here, to learn her way."

They were still excited, but only the Senior, Spiritist and Lorewarden supported him. The Mentalist, Warlock and Cosmologer did not, and they voiced their objections simultaneously. Three votes to three, and his own vote wouldn't count, for he had brought the appeal. Zarost turned to the Mystery, who held the casting vote. She was still faced towards the window, but she returned slowly from her muse. She would decide the Gyre's course. Zarost knew that she had been listening, all along. The private sparkle had left her eyes. Sometimes, Zarost wished she wasn't so wise.

She stood, which caused the many layers of her green gossamer dress to dance upon her body. "Listen to yourselves. Only because of the Writhe are you considering this. Can you not see that the presence of Chaos is inducing disorder in your own thoughts? Riddler, you have tried to manoeuvre us from the path of clear reasoning with your dramatic delivery of news, which tells me that you know what you ask would not be granted were we to consider it fully. To make things easier for an apprentice is never the way to find the wizard. Especially with one more talented than most—she should have opportunity to prove herself against all challengers, not have the world tamed for her. And yet, we need the ninth member of the Gyre, we need you to succeed—Ametheus is in a growing phase now, he's reached this eighth-level horror of the Wranglewrithe, which we shall be hard-pressed to cure. What if he reaches a ninth-level manipulation, I am thinking? He could shake the eight of us off the opposing pole of the third axis, Order would be naked and the Sorcerer's misrule would be unchecked. If the Gyre becomes nine, we might hold him, we might turn him before he grows! We have this one chance, and we must not waver so close to the victory. We may have succeeded, she may well be the one we have hoped for for so long, but she has not yet found the wizard, and that is always the key. If you take her out now, she will be too influenced by the great Chaos prevalent in Oldenworld. She must learn her way within the purified environment of Eyri. So I must vote against your appeal—we cannot intervene: if she is destined to find the wizard, she shall overcome the challenges she faces in Eyri, and grow stronger by doing so. The greater the crucible, the greater the wizard she shall find in its centre.

"Oh Riddler, don't despair, if you believe in her potential, then you must accept the risk of returning to Eyri, to guide the Seeker to find the wizard, while doing nothing to clear the path ahead. And we must accept the risk of battling the Writhe with only our seven until you have succeeded or failed for sure. What is certain is that you do not have much time. The Writhe shall reach the Shield in less than a week. You must be gone from Eyri by the sixth day, Riddler. We shall do what we can to slow the Writhe, but we have little hope of turning it, without you. "

◆ ──────── ◆

When the meeting adjourned, Twardy Zarost climbed the stairs to the High Quad. It was an open square of pale stonewood, half-recessed into the curve of shimmering green roof-scales, half-exposed on its northern sides where a low encircling wall guarded the edge of the drop and the panoramic view of the desert. Empty dunes swept away like a great tan-coloured sea on that side, too vast and arid to cross on foot. Even the transient Armad peoples who roamed the desert from the west coast to Azique didn't come this far south. Only via Transference could one reach the Sanctuary. Only via Transference could one leave it.

Zarost inhaled the hot desert air.

He was disappointed by the outcome of the meeting, but he supposed he shouldn't be surprised. He was the only one who truly understood Eyri. Maybe he was becoming too attached to the place, maybe he cared too much for the life within it. He knew he cared about Tabitha Serannon. The other members of the Gyre were jaded by years of exposure to Chaos, in the vicious world beyond the Shield. In Eyri, life was good, precious and pure. The Gyre had forgotten such a life, and maybe he had forgotten the true burden of living exposed. Then again, they had the use of their magic every day; he lived a life of restraint. Differences were bound to evolve between them, but whichever way the circle of the Gyre turned, he would not abandon it, for it turned around the pool of their strengths.

His fire-coloured cloak hung slack and heavy from his shoulders, but he could already feel the moisture being baked from it despite the lack of any wind. It would soon be unpleasant to be at the Sanctuary, but there was one task he wished to complete before departing, a task which could only be achieved here, beyond the Shield, in a place where he could employ his magic to the full.

The Restitution. It had been twenty years since his last use of the wizards' sovereign remedy. Under the watchful eye of the false Seeker, he hadn't dared to use it, for his transformation might have brought Cabal of Ravenscroft closer to solving the riddle of finding the wizard. Even though the Darkmaster had ceased to develop as a mage and had shackled the Ring to his neck just to keep it, he would have been entitled to promotion if he had found the wizard. And so Zarost had never dared to cast such an obvious riddle at his feet. Every day, Zarost had been weathered under the ceaseless caress of time, just the same as everybody else.

But now! Now the Seeker was Tabitha Serannon. His Restitution might be just what was required to speed her along the path. It was a riddle she would surely solve, and in so doing, she might solve the riddle of the Ring. If she could see what was at the end of the path, she would be there herself. Zarost was determined. If the Gyre required her to become a wizard before she could be released from Eyri, then a wizard she would be, or he would feed himself to the Wranglewrithe.

He sat down on the low wall at the edge of the Quad and closed his eyes. The spell of Restitution required complete concentration, and he was out of practice, he knew. It wouldn't do to get it wrong.

He reached backwards in Time, past the centuries of his riddling in Eyri, past the formation of the Gyre and the years of rising Chaos which had caused it to form, earlier still, to the time when he had first found a misplaced clear ring himself, and nervously put it on his hand. He had been young, on that day in the College in Kings Meet, too young, according to their rules, and yet for any profession other than wizardry he would have been considered a man.

He had been lithe and strong. He held that moment in thought, remembering every fine detail of that body, feeling the way it had felt, knowing the youth and confidence. He had been a handsome acolyte, and bald, in the fashion of the time. He remembered the cool feeling of his shaven head, and the smell of the oils he had used to nourish it. He had worn a beautiful cloak, one of those streak-patterned silk weaves imported from the Empire of Azique.

He anticipated the transformation with a deep breath, then discarded the tired pattern which held him together on the roof-quad of the Gyre Sanctuary. He reached his arms wide, and accepted the perfect memory of the younger man he had been, in another place, another time.

Truly remember your youth, and young you shall be.

He felt the tightening, then the searing heat of Restitution as his body changed. The spell did not create anything new, or make anything disappear, it merely encouraged what was already there to rearrange itself, to become re-ordered, to reject the slow disintegration and chaos of age. It was a spell on the third axis, a spell of pure Order.

Shivers, it felt good!

He was outrageously hungry—his new form needed filling in. He would have to make haste to Eyri, lest he starved to death. He opened his eyes, eyes sharp with youth. He was looking forward to presenting this riddle to the Seeker. He had some good twists in mind. It was a joy being young again.

As he rose to prepare for the return to Eyri, a hand touched him hesitantly on the shoulder. The shock-haired Mentalist stood back as Zarost turned. A surprised look crossed his face.

"Riddler? It is you! Ai, sorry, I didn't mean to interrupt your Rest."

"It is done."

"Ehff. You, ah, your change is very impressive. You go back so far!"

It was unlike the Mentalist to compliment a spell, for he considered himself superior in most regards. Zarost hadn't forgotten that the Mentalist had voted against him. But the young savant wanted something now. Zarost could guess what it was.

"It is hot for games with words, Mentalist. How can I help you?"

Zarost kept his expression impassive. Let the Mentalist believe he was safe. It was never too hot for a riddle.

"Your Transference," said the Mentalist, looking awkward. "I want to know how you achieve such speed. It would be useful to me."

"Who is left at the Sanctuary?" Zarost asked.

"Just the two of us, and –"

"– the Cosmologer," a high-pitched voice took over, "who is leaving. I don't care what it is you want. There may yet be time to warn the Hunters of Bradach Hide, in case the Writhe veers west. " She passed by briskly. Even so, she was unable to conceal the dilation of her pupils from Zarost's sharp eye.

And you always thought you were the next in ability after the Mystery in retaining your youth. He chuckled to himself. She wasn't nearly as good as he was at Resting.

The Cosmologer sat stiffly with her back to the two men, and stared off across the desert in meditation. Zarost indicated they should watch in silence—the example would be useful to prepare the Mentalist. It took ten minutes of fading until she finally disappeared with the softest of whispers like a guttering flame. Zarost shook his head. She was so pre-occupied with time, she didn't notice how much of it she wasted herself. There was a much better way to cast the Transference spell. He turned to face the Mentalist.

The Mentalist looked like a boy about to be given a treat. His blue eyes were bright; the gold flecks in each iris, the marks of his years, shimmered with the wizard's desire for knowledge. "Show me. Please."

"If you want to learn my method, you will take a binding vow— you must use my trick to leave the Sanctuary now."

The Mentalist eyed him warily, and not without reason. One did not accept a binding oath from a wizard lightly, but the lure of the reward was too great. "I accept the oath. I shall use your method to leave the Sanctuary, or I shall not be able to leave at all."

Zarost wove the conditional seal out of clear essence, which when the Mentalist had accepted, bound itself to his aura like a plaited noose. It would not fail until the conditions of the oath were fulfilled. The Mentalist mistook Zarost's grin for comradeship and slapped the Riddler on the back. Zarost began with his brief instruction at once to prevent his rising laughter from escaping. Oh, the Mentalist would wish he hadn't sided against the Riddler.

"The Cosmologer fades so very slowly, because her heart is like stone," Zarost explained.

"Like stone? You mean still? But you have to meditate!" the Mentalist argued. "If you are not still, you will hold onto something of your self, and you'll never reach infinity."

"There are other ways of urging the mind to let go."

"You mean you use—stimulants?" the Mentalist asked, looking shocked. His supercilious attitude was going to be his downfall. Literally.

"The heart is the pulse of your thought. Make the heart run, and your departure will be short."

"But how do you raise the heartbeat so much? You appeared in an instant. Not a minute, or a half, but a snap of the fingers! Such an accelerated heartbeat could kill a man."

"But of course. And there ends your instruction, for that's all there is to it."

Zarost winked. The Mentalist looked blank.

Zarost picked up his short staff, ran to the edge of the roof, and leapt.

The last words that Zarost heard before he disappeared were those spoken by the Mentalist, who peered, palefaced, over the edge of the high roof of the Gyre Sanctuary.

"Oh, no. You're insane! You devious, rotten, unscrupulous –"

The wind of the fall drowned out the Mentalist's curses. The thrill of the risky dive drove Zarost's heart to racing. That was the secret. He disappeared in an instant.

♦ ——————♦

Twardy Zarost leaned back in his chair. It creaked under his weight, but he was not yet content. His new muscles needed a lot of filling. It had been a long, hard run from River's End to the Wayfarer's Inn in Flowerton.

"A trotter's ribs, to fill my own," he told the serving girl, and pressed another silver into her palm.

Her hands were slender, yet strong. The girl's dark eyes widened.

"Are you sure, sir? You've already had four servings." Her voice was warm. She leant close to clear his plate from the table. Zarost almost succeeded in looking away in time. He was sure that her dress had not exposed quite so much of her fine cleavage the last time she had come to the table.

"I've never seen a man with such an appetite."

Zarost had forgotten how subtle the whole game was. It was a pleasure being in a young man's body again.

Even more so, to be in a young woman's.

He was thinking differently too, he realised. He had to be careful not to lose his way here, this was a stop for nourishment, nothing more. "When fine food is served, a man must rejoice and relish it for as long as he may."

"So long as you wish to eat, I shall serve you," she said. That look in her eye, again.

"Would you like to join me while I sup? I would enjoy your company, oh so very much."

The girl blushed and leant close to whisper. Zarost could smell the scent of flowers in her hair. "It is not something which my father would allow. But he has forgotten I am past eighteen, and he would sleep very soundly after midnight, if you'll pay for an extra glass of Dwarrow." The way she said it left little doubt that she had tested her father before.

Zarost smiled. "What is your name?" he asked.

"Samantha."

"Thank you then, Samantha. I regret I am too hasty tonight, prefer to return when I have a greater appetite for such a rich dessert. For now, I'd be appeased if you would bring another rack, and a mead."

She looked disappointed. "What's your name, traveller? In case you pass by again and I can hold you to your promise."

He drank, to hide his hesitation. It wouldn't do to go under the name of Twardy Zarost, or even the Riddler, if he wanted it to be a fair riddle.

"Tsoraz. Tsoraz the bard, pleased to make your acquaintance. Looking forward to deepening it some time."

She smiled, beautiful in the candlelight. Her dress swayed as she retreated through the swing doors of the kitchen. Zarost reminded himself that he was old enough to be her great-grandfather many times over, but he couldn't stop seeing the world through the eyes of his youth. He wondered if he'd been a bit too hasty in using the full Restitution. He'd been a reckless young man, back then. It wouldn't do, for the Riddler to be reckless.

Truth be told, he *wanted* to be reckless. There were ways to ensure he didn't plant a seed.

And they all involve the use of magic, you fool. You have no time to be chasing skirts.

He turned his gaze from the swing doors, now at rest.

Six days, the Gyre had said. Already, too much time had slipped through his fingers. But he had needed the meal, he still needed more. Just one plate, he promised, and then he would make haste to Stormhaven, to the Seeker.

34. BLACK RIVER

"Those who try to juggle wisdom, power and greed,
drop one of the balls, every time."—*Zarost*

Ashley Logán awoke to the bubble of soup. He was inside a large tent. Horses champed outside. A rotund Lightgifter pushed through the tent-flap, bringing with him a gust of blustery cold, and wan afternoon sunlight. The flap fell back as the newcomer joined the other three Gifters who sat on crates beside a brazier. Their cowls were raised. A pot was balanced over the coals, and one of the Gifters tended it with a wooden spoon. Beside him was a dish containing a small number of sprites.

Ashley sat bolt upright. His head pounded an instant later.

"Where am I? What day is it?"

"Ah, feeling better then, son?" The rotund Gifter enquired, twisting on his seat. Brother Onassis. The one who tended the soup gave him a brief glance, revealing the wizened features of Brother Finnian. The other two kept their heads turned away, but he guessed they completed the four left behind at the bridge, those who had all been eager to tend the horses rather than enter the vale.

"What day is it?" Ashley repeated, fingering his head tenderly. There was a lump on his crown, and his skull ached at the slightest pressure.

What happened to me?

"You've been asleep for quite some time. Frozen stiff when I found you. Lucky thing I was up at the bridge, or that rock that fell on you would have been the end."

"How long have I slept?" Ashley couldn't keep the rising panic out of his voice.

"You've dreamt the day away since I found you. Never fear, you're safe," Onassis added, seeing Ashley's face pale. "We're awaiting word from Father Keegan and the Gifters in the vale, but we've food enough to last a week."

A full day. The Dark might be poised to move from Ravenscroft.

"The Gifters won't be coming back. They were captured."

"The Gifters were—captured," Onassis said, his voice trailing off. "Ah."

"All the Swords in the vale serve the Dark too," Ashley said.

The Gifters shifted uncomfortably on their crates.

"I see," said Onassis. He turned away from Ashley, and whispered something to the Gifters at the brazier. They laughed briefly. A mug was passed across to Brother Finnian. He dipped a ladle into his pot, and filled the mug.

"Here, come and take some soup, you'll feel better," old Brother Finnian said, offering the mug to Ashley.

"No!" Ashley strode toward them, but stopped short of the proffered mug. "No, you don't understand. The Dark was not crushed. It was a trap, the Lightgifters walked into a trap!"

"No need to shout, lad, we're not deaf yet." The mug waved about in an unsteady hand, and he took it, to avoid Finnian spilling good soup. He was hungry, but what he had to say was more important.

"Why won't you believe me?" He confronted Brother Onassis. "I saw it with my own eyes. The Dark is coming."

Onassis sighed. "You've been hit harder than I thought, lad. Drink up, then you can tell us the story." He wore the glazed look of a resigned comforter.

Ashley began with the tale of their entrance to the Castle, and the feast which had awaited them. He spoke to the four Gifters, but he could feel his words were not getting through to any one of them, they merely seemed to be waiting for him to finish. Two of them didn't even look up.

They think I'm mad.

Onassis urged him to drink his soup.

Ashley despaired of his explanation. The urgency of it was making his head pound.

"I saw Father Keegan lying with a Shadowcaster seductress. I saw him give up our collected Light essence to the Dark."

Onassis cuffed him across the ear.

"You have said too much. You rave, half-knot! Drink your soup, and be still now."

"But it's true!" shouted Ashley, not caring that he defied Father Onassis openly. They had to see, they had to believe. His head rang.

The two Gifters who had kept their cowls up and their gazes downcast looked up suddenly. He didn't recognised them. Both were large men. The significance of their strangeness did not impact on his mind at once.

Onassis was angry. "Father Keegan? With a woman of the Dark?

That is too wild. To say nothing of Light essence being given to the Dark. What were the Shadowcasters to do with it, for goodness sake?"

"The Dark is created from the Light in a spell of turning."

"Oh for the love of the Light! Your imagination runs away with you."

Onassis turned to the two strange Gifters. "The cold has bitten his mind. His sanity should return, later. For now, silence would be best."

"Rector Shamgar is an agent of the Dark," Ashley declared.

"Outrageous!" Onassis said, whirling. The two large men in Gifters robes separated, approaching Ashley from either side. Onassis held his attention by stepping up close. "How dare you insult the leader of the Dovecote with such slander!"

"Tabitha Serannon sent me a Courier," Ashley said.

"Serannon? The new girl, not even an apprentice? You take her word for truth, and the Rector's for false?" Ashley backed away from Father Onassis. Old Finnian still sat at the brazier, but the other two men were somewhere behind him. He couldn't turn to look and still watch Onassis.

"We must return to the Dovecote!" Ashley exclaimed. "We must save the Source. They plan to take it, turn it to their power."

"Turn the Source to the Dark? You really have learned a lot in one night. Far too much."

An arm grabbed Ashley from behind. His mug broke on the ground, a stain of red-brown soup on trampled grass. He fought the grip, but the strange Gifter possessed an immense strength. He was turned, despite his thrashing legs, to face the other white-robed figure who had circled around him. Between that man's hands, a dark cloud had formed, composed of spinning motes.

In one dreadful moment, he understood why he didn't recognise the two men in white robes. They weren't Lightgifters at all.

Seeing his shocked expression, the man who wove the motes gave Ashley a predatory smile.

"It is not the robe that makes a man, but this," he said, dipping his hand behind his collar. What dangled on the end of the chain he retrieved was a stone of the purest black. "You shall have one, soon enough."

Ashley pulled hard against his restrainer to look at Onassis. He still wore a Lightstone, as did old Finnian, but Ashley doubted the orbs meant much to them. They had defected to the Dark.

"Yes, Shadowcasters, dear half-knot. You'd be wise not to resist them. The last two who tried that, lie at the bottom of the Black River. Without their robes, of course." He signalled to the Shadowcasters. "Time this one was silenced, until the Darkmaster calls upon us."

Ashley realised that the falling rock on the bridge had been no accident. He was being stopped from escaping Ravenscroft. The nightmare was not over.

There was only one spell violent enough to give him a chance, and hardly any Light essence for the task. The meagre supply which Finnian kept in the dish beside him took a fraction of an instant to summon—it was that small. He hoped he had the pattern right when he spoke the words of the Flameburst. He had managed to practice it only a few times since Tabitha had shown him the complex weave. He chose a target that would generate the greatest response from the smallest assault.

His restrainer roared in pain, and released Ashley instantly. He guessed his spell had worked. Then the motes from the other Shadowcaster were humming through the air. They thumped into his chest. Ashley gasped against the sudden cold and panic. He ran past the man who had acted as his restrainer, a man who now beat at his flaming crotch with both hands. Ashley dodged the bulk of Onassis; the Father was too overweight to react quickly, and too surprised to do more than flail his arms.

Old Finnian blocked the exit. He had risen beside the brazier, and held a mug deep in the pot. With a jerk he loosed a scoop of boiling fluid toward Ashley, but the aim was high. Ashley ducked, and upset the brazier and the pot when he stumbled. Someone screamed close behind him, and Finnian fell back from the tumbled coals. Ashley burst through the slack canvas of the door, and didn't stop. The horses grazed close by, picketed on long halters.

He took the first horse he came upon, a dun-coloured gelding that shied from his approach. There was no time to saddle him up—he tore the picket from the ground, and leapt upon the horse's back. The gelding weaved and tossed its head in anger, almost unseating him, but when the Shadowcaster emerged from the tent, the gelding needed no encouragement. It fled from the motes which flickered through the air after them, and squealed when the spell missed its mark and found the horse instead. The gelding kept its footing though, too large a beast to be taken by whatever attempt the Shadowcaster had aimed at the rider. Ashley didn't look back. All he could do was to hold on.

It was a long time before Ashley found the chance to check for pursuit. The slope become more gradual over a league, as the trail followed the course of the Black River from the mountains into lower hills. Mist collected in the folds of the ravine to his left. All the while the horse galloped, whether the trail was narrow or wide. The gelding had a flowing stride, but without a saddle and reins, he had little control over what it did, besides holding onto its mane and the halter rope for dear life. The trail bent close to the Black River, and they had almost entered a bank of mist when the gelding's gait slowed. Ashley was bounced vigorously with the new stride, and his thighs could grip no longer. He managed to hold on long enough to reach a large bush, and he used its spiny mass to break his fall. The horse galloped away from the trail up a grassed slope and into the curling fringe of the river mist.

Ashley called out to it, but the gelding was gone.

There was no sign of Shadowcasters. He knew that one of the Shadowcasters would be loath to ride a horse at that moment. Maybe the other had been caught by Finnian's scalding soup, and couldn't see to ride. Onassis was too fat to be riding in pursuit, and Finnian too frail. He felt a small surge of triumph at his escape, but almost at once he noticed dark spots above the Ravenscroft trail. The pursuers grew larger as they flew down the ravine. Black ravens. Morrigán.

Ashley began to run. Shrill cries pierced the sky far behind him. Ashley reached the cover of mist and kept running, even though the trail became treacherous underfoot.

The Morrigán came closer and closer. Each call was louder than the last, until it sounded as if they croaked inside his head.

He stumbled onwards. He kept expecting a bird to burst through the grey moisture and find him, but the mists seemed to frustrate them in their hunt. The Morrigán cawed close overhead, but after what seemed like an interminable torture, their hoarse mocking sounded further away, in widening circles that lifted ever higher.

Ashley ran.

The ravens came again three times that night, always in greater numbers, but the mist held, and every time they were thwarted by it.

35. MOSAIC

"The forbidden lies deep within us all."—*Zarost*

Tabitha sat alone in her bedroom at the Boarding. The bustle of Stormhaven passed below the window, yet the sounds did not penetrate far into Tabitha's retreat. The curtains were drawn against the sickening brightness of the sun; only a sliver of light ran across the floorboards, in which a pool of sprites turned idly, awaiting her command. Tabitha's attention was neither upon the sprites, nor on the discarded lyre on her bed. She sat on the floor. Her grey robe was rumpled.

A fresh tear trickled over her cheek. She ought to have drained the reservoir of tears by now, yet there were always more, and they did nothing to quench her shame. It wasn't fair, it hadn't been her fault, but the Shadowcaster had left his mark on her, touched her in a way she could never forget. The stain was too intimate.

She closed her eyes tight. She was tainted. Water with a drop of poison was poisoned water. The tainted part could not be separated from her whole. She was the result of a Shadowcaster's ravaging, and was ashamed to be seen, ashamed to talk to anyone, for was it not her fault that she had been caught by the Rector in the first place, and expelled from the Dovecote into the hands of the Shadowcaster? It was her fault, because she had not defended herself with the Shiver. She had allowed herself to be taken by Arkell. Her shoulders shook.

She couldn't bear it. There was always the chance of infecting others with the same evil which coursed through her veins, the poison which spread with every beat of her once-pure heart. She had to hide from the world.

It would have been better if Arkell had raped her, and left her un-orbed. She would have born that shame better, despite the nausea that image brought with it.

Her hand found the cold stone at her throat. The Darkstone. It was everything she hated, yet her hands always returned to its smooth face. Her anger and shame flared as soon as she realised she had done it again. She slapped herself, hard. It would renew the bruise there, but she didn't care. No one would see her, because she would see no one.

She sat on her hands. She knew that those hands would escape again. What made it worse was that the urge came from within herself, as if there were two personalities in one body, straining against one another for the use of her will. Part of her savoured the pain of the slap. The anger was her own, though she had never felt it as such a raw emotion. Before.

The Darkstone was cold in her fingers.

Always, within it, there was the whispering voice of the Darkmaster. His presence crept around, searching for the unguarded places in her mind, relentless, on and on and on. He was a coercive enemy, like an eel moving through the dark waters of her mind, trying to ensnare her. She was barely able to resist him. She was surprised that she could refuse the words of devotion that he wished her to utter. Maybe it had something to do with the distance, or his attention. She doubted she could hold out if he was closer.

What she couldn't bear was her own darkness, rising within her. She knew it was her own, and not the Darkmaster's. It heightened her shame.

The Sage had warned her.

The Ring shall take you on the darkest path.

That could not be denied. The pool of Dark essence beside the peaceful sprites was proof enough. She hated the motes, hated herself for their presence. She had summoned the Dark to her room. It glistened, enticing her eye. She knew none of the spells, yet she could not bring herself to banish the motes, not yet. It was terrible. There was power in the Dark, power with which to tear down those who had been so cruel. The Darkmaster would pay for what he had done. Kirjath Arkell would pay. She needed the power, but she had no mastery over the evil motes. She wanted nothing to do with the tainted magic.

Tabitha summoned the Light essence to her hand, and watched the sprites dance in the air. Just holding them close helped her to remember who she was, who she wanted to be.

I am a Lightgifter.

She dropped the sprites into the pool of motes. There was a brief squeal, like that of an iron pot placed too quickly into cold water. For a moment there was an angry writhing of Light and Dark contained in the one pool, then it was gone, and all that remained was clear essence.

She hid the Darkstone under the scarf that already hid her

Lightstone. She retied the knot.

How many times have I retied this knot?

The cycle was endless. Three days, and each the same. The more resolutely she denied the Darkstone, the sooner it seemed to emerge from the scarf which hid it. At least she had discovered the way to destroy the foul motes that she summoned in her moments of weakness. She prayed she wouldn't waste too much Light in doing so.

There had to be some way to escape the touch of Dark. Tabitha scooped her lyre from the bed. She stood facing the bright slit in her curtains for a long time. Her fingers wouldn't strike a note. She wasn't worthy of creating anything beautiful, and she didn't know of any songs which reflected her mood.

The intruder surprised her. He was so stealthy that she only noticed him when he voiced his greeting beside her.

"Miss Westerbrook said you were doing poorly, Tabitha Truthsayer. I am here to bring some cheer."

She jumped, and spun to face the intruder. A youthful, athletic man, brown-skinned, his bald head smooth and un-weathered. He wore a fire-coloured cloak over a simple grey robe, and he carried a slender staff. He was a complete stranger.

"Go away," she snapped. She was full of anger; anger at being intruded upon, anger at wishing he would stay, anger at being angry. He looked crestfallen.

"I mean, thank you, I have no need to be cheered up," she added, remembering her manners. "The door was locked for a reason. I'd like to be alone."

"Now that is quite wrong, I must say, you really would like me to stay."

Tabitha glared at the stranger. She wasn't sure what to do with all the anger she felt at his presumption. Dark anger. She held her tongue, trying first to find clarity within her warring emotions.

"I see you have a lyre," he said. "Would you let me play a song? Just a simple one?"

"Do you promise to go away when it is done?"

The stranger considered this for a moment.

"Certainly. When the song is ended, or when you smile."

There was an uncanny familiarity about the man, something about the way he stood, or his speech, but she knew she had never seen his face before. He had a vigorous presence, and it lent her strength. He was a distraction from the agony of being alone. He deserved at least a moment of her time for that.

He better not sing like a bullfrog.

She handed him the lyre, and he set his staff aside to take it. The stranger plucked a few experimental notes.

"A fine instrument this, fine beyond words." He struck a simple tune, and launched forth into song, with a good voice. The lyrics, however, were familiar and appalling.

> *Oh, past the bridge came a wide-bowed boat,*
> *where does the river end?*
> *a wide-bowed boat with a cow on board,*
> *where does the river end?*
> *a wide-bowed boat with a cow, and a cat,*
> *where does the river end?*
> *a wide-bowed boat with a cow,*
> *and a cat and a red speckled hen,*
> *where does the river end?*

The stranger sang on. It was a common tavern song, and one which involved adding items to the list until memory could not hold them all. Even a fully inebriated man could make the song last for too long; the stranger was as sober as a fox. The song was never, ever going to end.

He had agreed to leave.

When the song is ended, or when you smile.

She grimaced; it was the best she could do, in her current mood. The stranger was a rascal. He continued to play with a dead-pan face, as if there was nothing devious about his choice of tune at all.

She realised what made him seem familiar—it was his eyes, the golden-brown gaze full of laughter. He reminded her of Twardy Zarost. There was a resemblance to his features as well, but he was young, his skin smooth, where Zarost was old and weathered like tree-bark. Zarost had a forest of hair; the stranger had not one hair upon his head. Zarost was a wiry little man, the stranger was of similar height, but well-muscled. He was even quite good-looking.

She wondered what had happened to the Riddler. He had promised that he would return. She could do with some answers. Then again, she wasn't sure she wanted him around. He had urged her to use the Dark.

The stranger's humour was infectious. His lyrics became more inventive and ridiculously funny by the minute. It wasn't so bad to smile. He stopped playing then, and returned her smile with a scurrilous grin.

"Do you have a name, stranger?" she enquired.

"Tsoraz, humbly at your service." He bowed his bald pate low before her.

"Tsoraz. Where do you hail from?"

"Flowerton, most recently. I live where I find my audience."

"You'll find little audience on the Isle. Only the King's bards may perform in the taverns."

"It was other prospects which brought me to Stormhaven, not singing."

"What is your business here? If I may ask," Tabitha added hastily. She had not meant to be so assertive. She had not been so aggressive. Before.

"I am talking to her."

Tabitha stiffened, suddenly self-conscious and wary.

"What interest does a bard have in this young woman?"

Tsoraz raised a caustic eyebrow. There was laughter in his voice when the bard spoke. "In your case, my interest is more of a duty. But don't hear that wrongly, you are a beautiful young woman."

Tabitha blushed, despite herself. He had no right to flatter her. He shouldn't even be in her room. She chose her question carefully. The bard's answers left nothing answered at all. She got the distinct feeling that even though she was asking the questions, it was he who was directing the conversation.

"What do you want from me?"

"That will become clear to you in time. You can trust me, my intentions are wholly honourable," he said with as much credibility as a blackguard.

"You look so much like a friend of mine. Do you know the Riddler Zarost?"

Tsoraz nodded his head repeatedly, a smile growing on his lips.

"So by truth am I bound. He said you were one to know the truth sooner than any other. He was the one who sent me to you."

"You know Zarost? You're related to him, aren't you?"

"You could say that I am his son."

"Son?" Tabitha was amazed. "He never spoke of any family."

"That's because he was a riddler, and my identity is a secret. He hasn't seen me for many years."

"Was a riddler. What has happened to Zarost?"

"Was? Is. Oo-er." Tsoraz shot her a vexed glance. "He did warn me you'd be twisting my words around in an instant, have me thinking backwards and tripping over my own stupid feet. I meant when he spoke to you of his family, it was as a riddler that he spoke."

"He didn't speak to me of his family."

"Y-es. That is what I meant. You mustn't tell anyone of my link to Twardy, it is an important secret to keep. Twardy made some enemies in Eyri, over time, and I would hate to fall into their hands."

Considering the Riddler, she could understand the request.

"So where have you been all this time that you haven't seen your own father?"

He danced from one foot to the other, a mannerism that was familiar. Tsoraz had acquired all the agitated energy of his father.

"Barding around, taverns and inns, some places too dark to enjoy. We disagree with each other, Twardy and I, and so we seldom see each other."

"And your mother?"

"She—ah—died. A long time ago."

Tabitha could feel the truth of the story being strained at the seams.

"When did you see Twardy?"

"Never did, to be true. He sent a message to me. When he does that I know it's important. He said he had to go away, and that I must come to Stormhaven, and look for a girl called Tabitha Serannon." He spread his hands wide, as if to say 'and here I am.'

Tabitha didn't believe a word. His eyes were shifty. And yet there was truth beneath it all.

"I see there is a lot of your father in you," she said.

"Miss Serannon?"

"You tell the truth in a roundabout way, but you cannot tell a lie well at all."

Tsoraz eyed her for a long time. Tabitha began to feel uneasy under that stare, and thought to retract her hasty words. He was a stranger, regardless of his parentage, and she had been rude to him.

Mercy! I practically called him a liar!

"I see I have tried to answer too much," Tsoraz said at last. "I don't have to answer every question, but if I speak, I speak the truth."

"That is Twardy Zarost's code. You have a lot of your father in you."

"You could say that he taught me everything I know."

Tabitha looked at him askance. Tsoraz unsettled her, despite his friendliness. She wanted to test him. If he was who he claimed to be, maybe he would share some of the Riddler's ability, and be able to see things most folks didn't.

"Would you know anything of this?" she asked, raising her hand.

"The Wizard's Ring? So you are still searching for the wizard, are you?"

He had identified the Ring; she had to believe him. Questions suddenly filled her mind.

"How am I to recognise the wizard? Why does the Ring grow warm and cold on its own? Why is it invisible to some people, but not to me? What does it do to me? Will the wizard be able to take it from me?"

Tsoraz held up his hands to forestall her.

"When Zarost left he laid his duty upon my shoulders until his return. I must follow the path of the Ring and advise the bearer. I would greatly love for you to learn all you need to find the wizard. I would be proud to present that success to Zarost, but I won't riddle with his vigour, and I do not have his age. One thing he did teach me well, for times such as these. Reflection is a great tool."

He raised an eyebrow, just as his father would have.

"And so?" asked Tabitha. The words were vaguely familiar, but she didn't see the present significance.

"How are you going to recognise the wizard, when you see him?" It was her own question, turned upon her. But he had missed something.

"Twardy said the wizard was most likely a woman."

Tsoraz grimaced. "Yes—he would have. Either way, it doesn't change what he told me of the Ring, or the value of reflection. How are you going to recognise the wizard?"

"I've never really thought about it. I suppose she would look different to—others. I've heard that wizards have an aura of magic, though that's probably fantasy, for how can you see magic, not the sprites and motes, but real magic, the kind wizards use? If I could see that magic, perhaps I could find a wizard."

Tsoraz stirred the air with his hand, encouraging her on. The Ring helped her to see, it brought clarity. She could pick out the finest detail of Tsoraz's clothing, even the fresh pollen caught in the hem of his colourful cloak. She had seen footprints in the Dovecote, footprints on stone. Maybe the Ring would allow her to see magic, once her talent to use it had grown enough. Maybe there was something in what Tsoraz had said.

What I said, she realised. Tsoraz was being very sly.

"Why does the Ring grow warm?" he asked, repeating her second question in doing so.

"It does that when I'm discovering something, when I do something new which I feel is right. I've taken it to be encouragement, though I don't know why it responds."

It grows warm when I follow the truth.

"Why does it grow cold?" he prompted.

"When I'm doing something which leads me away from the wizard?" It was a guess, but even as she spoke the words, the Ring warmed.

"Why is it invisible to most, but not to you?"

"It is made of a kind of magic, and I can see it. I can see magic?"

The guessing game was fun, but Tabitha was losing her footing. Tsoraz was turning everything upside down. She had asked him all these questions, now he had tricked her into answering them herself. She wished Zarost was here, to make up for his son's ignorance. The Ring was as warm as ever, though.

"What does it do to you?" he asked.

"It allows me to see things clearly. It allows me to think clearly. It allows me to be clear."

"Will the wizard be able to take it from you, do you think?"

"Only if I am finished with it," she said, with utmost certainty. It was her ring, and while she was learning from it, she did not want to give it away to anyone, even a wizard.

"So you are committed to learning from the Ring, then?"

She nodded.

"Well, then you shall find the wizard!" he exclaimed. "That's what I was told. At the end of the path of knowledge is the wizard."

So he was not totally ignorant of the Ring's ways.

"When did you learn about the Ring?" she asked.

Tsoraz hopped from foot to foot. "Forgive me," he said, "if I do not answer that. Forgive me too, if I answer not another personal question. A man likes to retain a bit of his mystery."

A bit of his mystery? He was already worse than Twardy Zarost, and that was saying a lot. The Riddler's son, more of a riddle than the Riddler.

"Did Twardy Zarost say when he'd be back?"

"He said nothing of his return, but I am sure he shall. He did say to remind you that you have a gift, and that you should use it."

"What gift?"

Tsoraz shrugged, and offered her lyre back to her. The wood had warmed in the bard's grip, the fine grain of the strangle-oak was smooth under her fingers. Tabitha followed the curve of the instrument. She had been unable to use the lyre for days—she'd had no heart to sing. Yet Tsoraz the Bard had changed how she felt. He was like a burst of sunlight through her cloudy day. She appreciated what he had done, despite his intrusive manner. He had brought music to her, and brought her back to music. He deserved a good performance.

She began her first stanza of the Lifesong gently. The clear essence on the floor shimmered under her influence, and Tsoraz stepped warily away, though by his expression he was fascinated as well.

Colours danced in the liquid as the spirit of the Lifesong surged through Tabitha. The lyre added so much power to the singing. She was aware of a greater resonance surrounding her. The perfect notes released by the strings gave her a foundation upon which to build her song.

She remembered the butterfly she had created in the Dovecote, but she was sure that more was possible. She had more clear essence under her influence, and she knew it worked, now.

Her voice resounded off the walls. A thrill passed down her spine. As the stanza drew to a close, she visualised her creation. A beautiful wildcat with fierce green eyes and a sleek black coat. But at the last moment, she changed her mind. She couldn't risk having such a feral creature in the room. Something more innocent and gentle would be better.

The rabbit was as white as the snow upon Fynn's Tooth, its long ears pink and fluffy on the inside. It looked at her with soft eyes wide with surprise. A button-nose twitched briefly at her scent. Then it made a high-pitched mewling squeal and fell over on the floor. It writhed, turning as it did so.

Tabitha gasped.

Where there should have been a cotton puff tail, angry feline eyes glared at her above a snarl of teeth. The cat thrashed, using two clawed feet, and so the creature turned upon the floor, a double-headed swirl of fear and fury. The remnants of her first visualisation, not fully abandoned when she had thought of the second.

Tabitha cried out as she recognised the implications of her mistake. She had created a cruelly deformed creature.

Tsoraz was beside her in an instant, a firm hand on her shoulder. He pressed down harder when she tried to rise.

"You must not go to it, Tabitha. It will maul you, you cannot heal that kind of thing."

Tabitha fought his grip. Terror rose in her throat.

"What can I do?" she asked, in a constricted voice. "I can't leave it. Oh, mercy, what have I done?" A wave of nausea washed over her. She shook with revulsion.

"Is that all you know of the Lifesong?" Tsoraz demanded. "One little stanza? Zarost said you were a great singer, you must surely know more."

His tone was so uncompromising, so unsympathetic, that Tabitha found anger rising within her despite the overwhelming shock.

"There is a second stanza," she cried, "but it brings death! I have brought enough wrong to this day." She hunched over sharply away from the awful sight which thrashed against the wall.

"How can you stop there?" he argued, forcing her head up, directing her gaze to the freak. The cat was clawing at its own body, the rabbit's body. It was drawing blood. Something was chittering, an awful lonely terrified sound.

"What is life, without death?" Tsoraz demanded. "To have balance, both must exist. What if every person that ever lived were never allowed to die? How would they fit into the world? If you create life, you must bring death, also. It is time to accept that balance, Seeker. Accept the balance of being a creator."

When the rabbit tried to scrabble up the wall to escape its tormentor, she knew Tsoraz was right. She had to end what she had created.

He couldn't know how the Dark gripped her heart then. She had created an abomination, and now she was to kill it. She was truly tainted with evil. She hadn't realised she had whispered her thoughts aloud until Tsoraz answered her. He squatted down in front of her, his expression earnest.

"Is it evil to show mercy to a thing which should not be?"

No. It would be evil to leave the creature to the terror of its existence.

"The Lifesong is your path," he urged. "You shall not find the wizard if you walk backwards."

It required only the gentlest aid from the Ring to clear her recollection of her mother's scrolls. Just as the spell patterns were burned into her memory, so too were the words and tune of the second stanza. She was sure she could remember everything that had happened to her since she had donned the Ring—everything stood clear in her mind, waiting for her attention.

She stroked the lyre with the first bar of music, and tried to keep the quavering from her voice when she sang, but she couldn't stop the tears. The creature was held as soon as she began—it ceased its struggling, and sat still. The rabbit watched her with soft, round eyes.

Sing low from your heart with grieving,
and sing back the faults you have cast,
Undo the hurt in the words never meant;
for hate can return from the past.
All Death is an end to a circle,
all circles must close to be tight,
better the truth than the lies of before,
when wrong was held to be right.
Better the truth than the falseness before,
when you hold the Creation in sight.

Tabitha knew that it was not the words that held the magic. It was the music, the interplay of notes and their timing which created a compelling resonance. The words helped to bind the spell. Tsoraz squatted beside her all the time, watching her. At one point, he leaned close, and whispered in such a manner as to not disturb her singing.

"Keep your focus tight, do not let your attention wander, or many will be touched by what you do. Sing only to what you would affect."

And then it was done. The white fur flickered with sudden colours, turned transparent, and washed outwards on the floor. The poor creature that had lived such a short, terrible life, was dead.

A pool of clear essence. It was difficult to see.

Tabitha stared at the floorboards. Her heart was heavy with the burden of what she had just done. Tsoraz had said her path was forwards with the Lifesong, but that last step had frightened her more than she was willing to admit. Killing brought her too close to the darkness, too near to the depression she had been fighting so hard. It threatened to drown her once again.

Tsoraz's voice was distant. "You need the death, sometimes. It is the balance in life. In the same way that the darkness is so important, when you can only see light. Especially true for one like you."

The Darkstone. He knew about it. He toyed with her just as the Riddler had. She suddenly hated him, both of them, for their Riddler's ways.

"Out! Get out! I wish to be alone."

He did obey this time, but he poked his head into the room one last time before closing the door.

"It is important to learn, but keep the curtains open, so that the light can get in too."

36. KING'S CROSS

"If I spoke through my hat,
would my words be simpler to understand?"—*Zarost*

Ashley shifted the cord on his waist, and tried to clear the rumples from his robe. It was hopelessly stained, even torn in places. The road from Ravenscroft had been hard. There was no way to appear more presentable before the King of Eyri than to stand up straight and deliver his news. He waited as silence descended in the throne room.

At least he had found Sister Grace, and she stood beside him in her clean Gifter's white. She added both credibility and support to his story. Grace hadn't needed much convincing, she had read the truth in his eyes. The young Sword who had brought him from Fendwarrow stood to his left; one of the new swords Glavenor had posted to seal the base of the Black River pass. Without the Sword's aid he would still have been walking. His legs shook with fatigue as it was.

It had not been easy getting past the indignant Court Official, but the King had allowed an immediate audience as soon as he had heard where Ashley had come from. Petitioners and nobles alike were politely cleared from the throne room, and only a few pages were retained in attendance. The Official stood to one side of the throne, shifting in his yellow robe as if standing on hot coals. Terrik, or Tarrok, if Ashley's memory of the last audience served him correctly. He ignored the Official's indolent glare, and addressed King Mellar on his raised throne directly.

"The Lightgifters walked into a trap in Ravenscroft, your Highness. We lost almost all of the Light essence we have to command. The Rector sent every able Gifter to the vale, because we received word that the Sword had conquered the Shadowcasters. We were sorely misled."

"I was never told of the Sword's victory," the King stated. "We have heard nothing of the Swordmaster's campaign. Did it fail so completely?"

"The Swords sealed the trap we walked into, your Highness. There are Swords in Ravenscroft who have been turned to serve the Darkmaster."

King Mellar took the news in silence. The only reaction Ashley noticed was the clenched muscles in Mellar's jaw. The King scrutinised Ashley as if he searched for evidence of dishonesty. Mellar found none.

"What of Glavenor. What of my Swordmaster?"

"I did not see him, your Highness." Ashley paused. "He is a strong man."

He left it at that. He could not believe the Swordmaster could be turned. If Glavenor had been turned, they would all fall. Every captive of Ravenscroft would serve the Darkmaster, and a terrible army that would be. But he could not be sure that it was not true.

"You did not see him," repeated King Mellar, "and yet did any come down from the Black River pass?" The question was directed at the young Sword. The man stood to attention.

"No, Highness. This young man was the first to return. I have been there for over a week."

The King seemed to grow smaller in his throne. "You did not see him, and yet he must still be in that vale."

"I witnessed—a turning." Ashley didn't know how else to describe the seduction of Father Keegan. "One of the Gifters, converted to serve the Dark. I believe it is the fate of all who have been captured in Ravenscroft. They are being held, and those who can be, are turned."

"And yet you escaped?"

"I was lucky, your Highness. And I had warning, of a kind."

"How so?"

"Tabitha Serannon, the singer. She caught wind of the plot. She sent me a messenger, though it arrived too late to save anyone but me. She suspected the Rector Shamgar as an ally of the Darkmaster. I would not have believed it, but I saw enough in Ravenscroft to be sure. He sent us there with all our essence deliberately."

"That is a great accusation!" Tarrok interjected. "The leader of the Lightgifters, a traitor to your cause? He must have been misled by this false news you spoke of."

Ashley shook his head tiredly. "We were herded into Ravenscroft, we were crippled by their wine, we were guarded by Swords who spoke of the Darkmaster as their lord, and I saw our sprites being turned to create the motes of Dark. I have no doubt that it was a trap, and that Tabitha was correct."

Sister Grace spoke up for the first time. "Again, she is the pivot around which strange events turn."

King Mellar turned to Grace. "Could she be summoned as well? Maybelle told me that she is in Stormhaven."

Sister Grace looked reluctant. "She is in a poor way. Something happened to her in the Dovecote, and she will not speak of it. I have sought her out, but was refused each time. But she would surely not refuse a royal summons—" Her voice trailed away.

King Mellar considered it briefly, then nodded his head. "Yes, I need to know why she believes the Rector a traitor. Have Tabitha Serannon summoned, in my name," he announced, pointing to a young page amongst the few close at hand. "She is in the Boarding." The page left the throne room with tassels flapping. King Mellar didn't rebuke him, though Ashley knew it was forbidden to run in the palace.

"However, our present dilemma is the Sword, not the Dovecote."

The King's observation brought Ashley up short. He had not considered how priorities would differ in Mellar's eyes. But there was something that might change his mind.

"They plan to assault the Dovecote, your Highness. We have the Source, the crystal which creates Light essence. They wish to turn that to their way, and I believe they can. I have seen one of these," he lifted his Lightstone on its short chain, "turned as black as midnight. Once they have the Source, they will have a constant supply of essence, and no Gifters to oppose them. Then they plan to come to Stormhaven."

The Shadowcasters had the means to achieve their goal. If they could capture the Swords and the Gifters who had been sent to Ravenscroft, they were halfway there already.

"How do you know so much of their plans?" King Mellar asked.

"I heard it spoken by a Shadowcaster."

"Hearsay! And heresy!" Tarrok declared. "One Shadowcaster speaks out, and you take that as fact. Your Highness, we know how they lie."

"Enough, nephew," King Mellar chided. "Keep your observations until we hold council, or you will lose your value in my court today."

Tarrok looked partially humbled. King Mellar steepled his fingers.

"How many of these traitorous Swords did you see?" King Mellar asked.

"Fifteen acted as escort to us. There may be more."

"Is it possible to do such a thing, to turn a man's mind against his own King?" Mellar asked the question of the air.

It was Sister Grace who took the opportunity to answer. "Your Highness, you know that the Shadowcaster who was killed on the Kingsbridge left a woman in his wake. She was used by Arkell as a decoy, on the last day, and—for other things—before. I have been trying to heal her. She was of a strong mind. The Shadowcaster has left her a wreck. She does not remember her own name, she just repeats his. It may be different with those captured in Ravenscroft, but I believe the effect of some Dark spells can be devastating."

There was a pause, in which the King held his hand up to forestall any further comment.

"To act with prudence, I must fear the worst. I will take your word on what you report, young Logán. We shall know of the truth of it soon enough. If the Darkmaster plans to take the Dovecote, then he shall have to move through Fendwarrow, and we shall meet him there with steel. Summon the Sword Captains!" He sent another page from the throne room at a run. King Mellar covered his eyes briefly with his hand.

"Would that Glavenor were here. Oh, my friend! You are a most grievous loss."

When Mellar looked up again, he had regained his composure.

"Maps!" he commanded, selecting another pageboy. "But first, take Logán that he might eat and wash, and regain some strength."

"I can stand," said Ashley, swaying on his feet, but the comment of bathing warmed his cheeks. He was a dishevelled beggar in the presence of the King.

"And I can see the toll your speed has taken. I would have you strong, for your retelling. I want every Captain to know what they shall be up against. I shall convene the council in a quarter hour."

Ashley bowed, and was thankful for the page's hand, which steadied him suddenly. He allowed the page to lead him away. He needed food desperately. Besides, they had to wait for both Tabitha and the Captains to make their way to the palace before any decisions would be taken. He caught Sister Grace watching him as he left, an approving look in her eye. He gave her a wan smile, though he meant it to be more.

Mercy, I am tired.

Ashley caught a final wisp of conversation from within the throne room.

"What of the Houses of Rule, my lord?"

"This is a war council, Tarrok, not governance. War!"

Ashley wondered why the King used such a toad in his Court. Maybe there was some benefit to the man he could not see. There was surely more to being a King than being a Lightgifter.

The page led him along a corridor that never seemed to end, but finally there was a wash-room, with hot water and towels and soap. It took him much longer than he'd expected to clear the grime from his body. The page found a clean white robe for him in the meantime, and a servant brought a tray from the kitchens. It was more food than he could possibly eat in the time he had left, but he did his best.

Tabitha stared at the marbled floor. The clamour of arguing voices filled the throne room. The page had been in a hurry to fetch her, but now they all seemed to be waiting. The Sword Captains were using the time to pore over a large map of Eyri. They argued about military tactics. The King was among them. She didn't care enough to listen. The world was crumbling in around her.

There was a momentary dip in the volume. Some of the Sword Captains turned towards the door, and the King paused in mid-sentence to announce the newcomer.

"Ah, welcome Logán. People! Behold the only one to escape from the treachery of Ravenscroft."

The news had been cruel enough, without that reminder. Tabitha wished to be locked in her room again, yet here she was, amongst the war council, where those in armour only reminded her more painfully of the man who was missing. Garyll Glavenor had not returned from Ravenscroft. She had suspected part of that truth, but these men seemed to accept it as a fact. The Swords had fallen into a trap, and the Lightgifters had followed. The Swordmaster would not be coming back. She wished for the world to end.

She realised Ashley had greeted her some moments past. She nodded, woodenly; her mind had been vacant. Ashley looked gaunt. She wondered if she looked any better in his eyes. Not that it mattered.

Why didn't you save Garyll?

But she didn't give voice to the thought. It was unfair. She knew she was hopelessly depressed. The King urged them to be seated, and she took a place in the semicircle around the throne, because she had to.

"The news is most dire, and I'll not waste a moment," said King Mellar, "but I'd like you all to hear the full reports, and then I shall take council on how to best respond. First, let me introduce Miss Serannon. You all know her, the singer on the Kingsbridge who faced down the Morgloth with Glavenor." The mention of the last name cut Tabitha like a harvester's scythe, right through her heart. "She knows something of the beginning of this treachery, learned when she was serving as apprentice Lightgifter."

At least the black scarf hid both the stones at her neck. She didn't wish to answer one more question than was absolutely necessary.

King Mellar faced her.

"Tabitha, we need to know why you suspected the Rector."

It was a question she had expected, for the page had told her as much. She had already decided what she would say, and what she would not. Her voice came from far away.

"When the Gifters were sent to Ravenscroft, he turned me over to a Shadowcaster."

Sister Grace was incredulous. "There was a Shadowcaster? In the Dovecote?"

"The same one we faced on the Kingsbridge. Kirjath Arkell. He lives still." A murmur passed through the gathered Captains.

"I can confirm that," said Ashley. "I saw him as well."

"And you are certain that the Rector knew this?" the King enquired, turning back to Tabitha.

"He closed the door on us. He guarded the door so the Shadowcaster could have his way with me."

That stung them to silence; even the King. His gaze was full of sympathy, and outrage.

Let them think what they will. It was as bad.

"Then it is settled. He shall be arrested, and brought for questioning."

"What of the Source, your Highness?" Ashley asked, his voice somewhat tremulous. "The Dovecote must be protected."

King Mellar nodded, slowly. "Captains, a squadron must be sent to Levin. Our Swords may have fallen in the trap of Ravenscroft, but we can surely hold our own ground against these Shadowcasters, and we can cut out the rot before it fails us. Sister Grace, could you advise them where to look, should the Rector choose to hide in the Dovecote?"

"I'll do better, I shall go with the Swords to Levin. You may well need someone who can defend against a malignant spell of Light. The Rector Shamgar shall not get away with this." Sister Grace had a cold fire in her eyes.

They were missing the point. Garyll Glavenor had not returned from Ravenscroft. That was all that really mattered. She would learn nothing by remaining in Stormhaven, she would only strengthen the clutches of her spiralling depression by living in doubt. Levin would be a step closer to the truth, a step closer to Ravenscroft.

"I wish to accompany them as well," Tabitha declared.

"That is very brave," King Mellar said, "but you have surely exposed yourself to enough danger, Miss Serannon. You do not need to do so again."

"Saving the Source is important to me, your Highness. Without Light, there will be no more hope."

"Yet you would be safe, here in Stormhaven."

"Safe from the dark, but not from despair."

"You are wise beyond your years, Truthsayer." King Mellar nodded to her. "Very well."

He turned to face Ashley. "Time for our second report, then. Do not spare the detail, young Logán, the Captains shall need every scrap to prepare our defence."

Ashley began his recount with the Gifters' departure from the Dovecote. As his tale progressed through the Black River mists, across the fearsome bridge of ice, to the possessed Swords and the trapping of the Lightgifters, Tabitha wondered if her despair would indeed be any less at the Dovecote. The distraction of a purpose, even a dangerous one, might not be enough to escape the cruel fingers of doubt. She might have to go further than Levin to discover the truth about Garyll.

Her intuition would not reveal his present fate. She wanted him to be alive so badly that her inner voice whispered only that he would return, be it truth, or lie.

◆ ——————— ◆

Ashley was glad for the open carriage. The Swords set a pace which would have unsaddled him had he been expected to ride. Their driver kept the pair of horses at a gallop, and the Kingsbridge flew by under the wheels. The thunder of hooves discouraged conversation. Overhead, high clouds scurried across the afternoon sky. It was a fine day for the month of Furrow, but it was fast paling.

He returned his attention to the new member of their party—the bald man who had introduced himself as Tsoraz. The bard's fire-coloured cloak whipped around his square shoulders. Something about the man made Ashley wary. But if Tabitha Serannon accepted his friendship, Tsoraz must be on their side.

Yet the uncertainty lingered. The man was odd, somehow. Ashley considered snooping in his mind, despite his promises to the contrary. Just a moment, to see what the man was thinking behind those shifting golden-brown eyes.

He had regained some of his strength during the second meal at the palace, enough to concentrate for the task. He had a sense that his own ability to reach out in thought had grown. He had gained something from his extended link with Father Keegan's mind. He probed gently into the thoughts of the strange bard Tsoraz.

He encountered something altogether terrifying, complex and vast. He understood nothing of what he heard or saw in that instant. If each thought was a star, he was looking at a galaxy.

The bard's eyes widened, then went stony-cold. Ashley recoiled from a sting that originated in his own mind. It was as brief as a slap as one would give a midge, yet it took his breath away.

He didn't know what to say. He had never considered what would happen if someone became aware of his snooping. He knew his cheeks had reddened.

"Ah. Sorry," he said, too quiet to be heard, but Tsoraz nodded, a smile already on his lips. The man's swift mood change just added to Ashley's distress. Tsoraz beckoned to him, and hunched forwards on his knees so that they might exchange words in the space between their seats. Ashley didn't want to get any closer to the man, but he couldn't refuse. He had begun the trouble.

"Talent demands to be used," said Tsoraz, his raised voice barely audible over the thunder of their escort. It would be too faint for Tabitha and Sister Grace to hear, even though the women were in the carriage beside them.

"I didn't mean to—that is—I don't know you very well, and –"

"You do well to be suspicious, in these times."

"I wasn't going to –"

"Be very careful who you watch. When you stare so hard, you are easy to sense, and easy to capture. Those with a dark nature might decide to use you."

Tsoraz sat back, but he continued to watch Ashley with those glittering eyes, as if considering what use he could be put to.

Those with a dark nature? He's not talking about himself, is he?

Tsoraz smiled again, and Ashley decided his statement had been a clever way of referring to the Darkmaster. Tsoraz was strange, but he was on their side. He was no Shadowcaster.

When they began to climb through the winding streets of Levin, the horses slackened their pace enough for those in the carriage to talk over the clatter of hooves. Ashley turned to Tabitha, if only to avoid the bard's intense attention. He could still feel the man's gaze on him. Tsoraz had made his point well. If you stared too hard, even an idiot would become aware of being watched. Likewise with the mind's eye.

"I wanted to thank you, for the warning," Ashley said.

Tabitha's wooden expression didn't change. She was in a place far away. "I am sorry it came too late," she said. "I sent it as soon as—I knew."

"It came in time," he said, remembering the little dove which had tracked him from Fendwarrow. "Only, your Courier was too much a bird. It was frightened to land."

Tabitha nodded. She made no effort to keep the conversation alive. He tried again.

"Where were you, the day we left for Ravenscroft? I thought you would have joined us."

"The Rector already had me isolated."

"Isolated? When were you isolated?" asked Ashley.

"The night we were—out. I was caught. I believed it was my punishment to be locked away, to atone. In truth, it was so the Rector could keep me for the Shadowcaster, when the cote had been cleared."

And I was angry with her for holding out on me.

She had been punished, and he had escaped. It had been his idea in the first place, to seek out the inner sanctum, and Tabitha had been made to pay for it.

He reached out a hand. "Sorry, Tabitha. I didn't know. I should have checked that you made it back."

"It's all right. I knew the consequences before we began."

It was a brave thing to say, but she had surely not expected the Shadowcaster. While she had been isolated, the Rector must have questioned her, yet she hadn't told him much, or Ashley would have been snared as well.

He had nothing to give her, besides a hug.

"Thank you for keeping silent," he said, holding her close. "I hope I can repay your friendship."

When he pulled away, he noticed the scarf tied high on her neck. He had seen it at the King's council. The question still begged asking.

"Why do you hide your Lightstone?"

Her hand flew to her throat. Her alarm was the first expression she had displayed in their journey.

"The Rector had planned to banish me. I was never going to be a Lightgifter. I should not pretend to be one."

"Nonsense!" Sister Grace cut in. She had not intruded before, though she had been close enough to hear most of it. "We now know the Rector is not true to the Light. I think he would not raise you because you would be too great a Lightgifter, not too poor. You should wear the Lightstone with pride. That you cast a Courier spell for Ashley with the Light is proof enough that you have the talent for gifting."

Tabitha did not seem to be comforted by Grace's praise. If anything, she appeared more panicked.

"I wish to follow the traditions of the Lightgifters. I'll only be of age at Yearsend."

"The traditions of the Lightgifters won't mean a thing if they succeed in taking the Source," Grace said. "We shall have little to gift."

"That is why I come to fight beside you."

It was Grace's turn to look alarmed. "I pray it does not come to that. What do you hope to do, if you'll not use the Light?"

"I have other ways of fighting than with sprites."

She had a solid-looking lyre with her, and he supposed that was what she meant. Ashley remembered the shrill power of her voice, the sheer volume which had crippled the Morgloth. Other ways indeed. The more Ashley considered what he knew of her, the more unique she seemed.

"It is good to have you with us," he said, bringing to an end a conversation that was obviously troubling her. Tabitha dipped her head. He didn't try to coax her into conversation after that.

The bald bard was still watching him. Ashley twisted slowly in his seat, but even when his back was to Tsoraz, his ears still burned with an awareness of the bard's attention. He pretended to take interest in the tall buildings of Levin. Townsfolk peered down from high balconies and windows, merchants and customers alike gathered in doorways to watch them pass. The squadron drew much interest, especially the higher they rode through the narrow streets. The Swords seldom had any business in the higher quarters of Levin. It was unheard of for Swords to be needed at the high Lightgifter's monastery.

Ashley's stomach churned as they neared the Dovecote grounds. It was one thing to agree that the Rector was a traitor. It was quite another thing to stand up to him. They had a full squadron of fifty Swords with them, but it was small comfort. Ravenscroft had swallowed more than twice that number.

They won't be here yet. They can't be here yet. Just the Rector.

They came to the Dovecote building. The Swords dismounted, and divided into units, some taking strategic positions close to the main doors, some forming into a wedge around the Lightgifters. Tsoraz the Bard joined them, a staff in hand. They climbed the wide steps, and the Captain swung the great East-door open.

The Hall of Sky was filled with the salmon glow of sunset. The marble floor glistened like the surface of a still pool. The Source towered on its mount, throwing gentle caresses of light to the walls. The channel at the edge of the Scribbillarre was a dry, empty rut. No Light had been drawn from the Source since Ashley had departed. There was little movement within the building, even the clatter of pots and the hiss of boiling water from the kitchens was subdued.

Had it not been for the servant, who shuffled into the Hall with head downcast, Ashley would have taken the Dovecote for deserted. The woman took such fright at seeing the force of Swords in the Hall that Ashley didn't think she even noticed him, or Sister Grace and Tabitha at his side. The woman ran toward the kitchen, shouting for the matron.

"Mistress Wyniss! There's Swords here! Mistress Wyniss!"

The Matron arrived with the important bustle she always exhibited. She greeted Sister Grace with a bow to her head, as was proper.

"Wyniss, what has happened to everyone?"

"When you were in Stormhaven, Sister Grace, most of all the Gifters went to help the Swords at that dark place. Oh, you would know that—hullo, 'prentice Logán. Well I was thinking they should be coming back around now, but the Rector said it would be a while longer. He was in a funny way today, said they should be celebrating the victory at Ravenscroft, and a ride to heal the country folk around Fig Tree would be the way they would do it. He ordered everyone out, even old Sister Sherry. They took the last few sprites. He even hired a carriage and some horses, seeing as how all the others were gone to that dark place. He said I was to just look after the ghosts while he was gone, keep things running as normal, that I was not to worry, the cote would be full soon enough."

The Rector had deserted the Dovecote. He must have been forewarned of their arrival. For some reason Ashley couldn't help thinking of a small, sweaty Court Official in a yellow robe.

Sister Grace was quick to recover. "Well, the Dovecote is full tonight. The Swords are here under the King's business, and they shall lodge here until it is done. They can bed in the men's wing. Would that suit you, Captain Jorge?" she asked, swivelling to include the commander of the squadron in her question. Jorge, a hard-faced veteran with a distant manner, looked around the Hall and finished on the Source.

After a moment's consideration, the Captain nodded. "If this is the rock they're coming for, then we'd best be close to it."

Mistress Wyniss gave the man a puzzled glance.

"Wyniss, could you prepare a meal for us all?" asked Sister Grace. "There are fifty Swords, and the four of us. Are there—enough of the servants left for the task?"

"Oh yes, Sister Grace. He left all of the ghosts here."

In the path of the Shadowcasters.

The Rector had a lot to answer for.

37. THE BURDEN OF BETRAYAL

"Is it easier to sacrifice life,
or love?"—*Zarost*

The flickering play of the torches had long since rubbed Garyll Glavenor's nerves raw. Light was worse than darkness. It felt as if hot sand lined his eye sockets. He had lost track of how long he had been tied over the altar in the torture chamber, how long they had worked on him. They had hooked his eyelids back, and his eyes streamed and smarted, even in what dull light there was. He had been tied with his head so far back for so long, that images did not appear upside down anymore. A distant part of him supposed that if he were to ever stand upright again, the world would appear reversed. He had not been able to close his eyes for days. Or nights. He couldn't tell—in the heart of Ravenscroft, it was just time, never-ending.

His left hand was a mess. So many nails had been driven into the fingers, that he had lost count. It would never heal, he knew that much. He wished they would just cut it off at the wrist, and burn the stump with one of the torches. But even with that wish, came a sudden flood of pain. He must not think about what they had done to him. He must only be in the Inferno, the raging mental fire that was his only refuge. The image of the Inferno sputtered, a pale remnant of the strength which had once protected him as the Swordmaster.

No matter how much he tried to forget, the memories of the screams plagued his mind. His screams, and those of the others who had been brought to the torture chamber. The weakest Lightgifters had been turned easily, sometimes with only a trade to seal their treachery. He had been forced to watch, tied and hook-lidded he could not help but see the exchange of jurrum, or gold, or other goods. Sometimes a Shadowcaster seductress worked the men over, until they screamed out the words he sometimes longed to scream himself. The Devotion to the Darkmaster was always the result of the visitor's time in the torture chamber.

He set his lips in a grim, hard line. He might cry the words inside, but his lips would remain sealed, to death. He would not betray his King. He would not betray Eyri. Therefore they worked on him, as they worked on the others. He was forced to bear witness to every turning, as if watching would teach him the futility of his ways.

The strongest Gifters had not wished to be turned, even with the most attractive of offers, even in this place where the screams of tortured flesh echoed off the walls. Those who refused, knew the consequences, and yet still they refused. Garyll took strength from them, for a while, until he learned that every one of them was broken in the end, under the many tortures the Shadowcasters could design. Every one that was taken away left as a Shadowcaster.

He knew then that he was going to die.

Yet he was still alive.

A man was laughing at him. Long, wheezing exhalations washed against his face; air that was full of rotten odours. The newcomer bobbed up and down beside him like a frog. He had a frog's protruding eyes. The visitor's Darkstone was a jagged tooth, rather than a full orb. Garyll wondered what that meant, and how the tortures which this pasty-skinned cretin would dole out would differ from those he had already endured. The man's robe was not as dark as the others, maybe a dull red rather than black, though it was hard to tell in the smoky half-light. The man came close, and stroked the stone at Garyll's neck.

In an awful moment, he recognised the Shadowcaster. A split-lipped grin spread across Kirjath Arkell's face.

"Ooh, isn't it lovely?" Kirjath crooned, in a voice distressing by its lack of sanity. "Hullo Swordmaster, I've come back to play, today, flay, nay, pay, way, hay!" Spittle flew with his nonsense rhyme, then he doubled over with a great, wheezing laugh. When he recovered, he brought his whisper close to Garyll.

"You never expected me to live, did you now, you swaggering butcher. You should not have murdered my beast."

A tongue flickered into his ear. The lobe was sucked past sharp teeth. There was a crunch, and a fresh bloom of pain in Garyll's ear. Something warm trickled over his cheek.

"Just like the girl, so sure I was dead, dead, dead, so surprised to be caught in my hands again, again, again." Arkell hopped away with sudden jerking movements.

Every restraint strained to its limit on the altar. Garyll arched his back as strength tore through his body, strength that should have long since abandoned him. He couldn't get any closer to Arkell.

"What girl?" he demanded.

"Ooh, it talks, the Master said it wouldn't, but Kirjath can make it talk, hahaa! Kirjath made it talk."

"What girl!" Garyll shouted.

Arkell danced away in tight circles.

"The little slut from the farmyard, the be-titted singing thief. The bitch from the Kingsbridge, the one who broke my stone. Kirjath's got his own back now. Ah, yes, Kirjath's got his own back!"

Pain told Garyll he shouldn't have clenched his left fist, but he didn't care. "Tell me her name!" he demanded.

"I sealed her Darkstone, she wears the Darkstone, and a good little Shadowcaster she shall be. The Darkmaster will summon her. You'll see how pretty she looks as a Darkwhore. We might even let you have Tabitha Serannon yourself, if you promise to behave."

A roar sounded in Garyll's ears.

"Singing—slut!" Arkell shouted, spinning to face the walls. "Rude—rut! Pert—piece! Vulgar—virgin!"

No. Nothing could be worse than Tabitha, in this place. Garyll's jaw ached from clenching. If she wore the Darkstone already, she was bound into the web. The only hope was that she might manage to hold out against the coercion, somehow, as he had done. It was small hope, considering the people he had seen turned. She must not come to this place.

"Call your master!" he shouted at the Shadowcaster. "Call him here!"

Arkell did not seem to hear him. He was sitting on the floor, crying or laughing into his lap.

"Darkmaster!" Garyll's shout boomed off the walls. "Cabal! Come to me! I will talk to you!"

He had expected to wait, but it was not a moment later that the rustle of robes announced the Darkmaster's presence; he had been watching Garyll all along. A creeping sensation ran through Garyll's body, radiating from the stone at his throat. Cabal regarded him with cold eyes.

"So it is the young Serannon girl who lives in your heart. I had wondered what gave you the strength, all these days. Tell me, what is it like, when your last hope is snuffed?" Pale teeth glistened in the dark.

"She must not come here."

"But she is orbed, just as you are. She is mine now." The certainty in the Darkmaster's voice settled any doubt. Arkell had not been lying.

"I will trade with you." Garyll had to force the words past his lips.

"What could you have, that I could want?" The Darkmaster chuckled, and turned to leave, but Garyll knew he feigned his disinterest. They hadn't tortured him for so many days, for nothing.

"I shall say the words you wish, in exchange for her."

Cabal did not turn, but he stopped pacing away. "The Darkstone is sealed, but I might leave her to her own devices, if I knew a certain man served in her stead."

"You will leave her alone then, for every day that I live."

"Then every day that you live, you shall serve me."

Those words held a sickening finality. He was throwing his life over the edge of a deep, dark pit. But if he did not, Tabitha would be pulled into it herself. He had to be sure his sacrifice would last.

"What guarantee do I have that you shall keep your word?"

"If I don't keep my word, you shall fail to serve me. That is all. You had best be certain that you are useful to me."

It was the slim end of the bargain he held, but it was all he was being offered. It was the only way to save her from the Dark.

I am the shadow and he is my master.

He is the shadow and I am his caster.

The echoes of his words lasted forever.

38. WALKING ON SUNLIGHT
"Is there a shadow cast, under your feet?"—*Zarost*

The night crawled around the Dovecote, waiting, watching. The Swords did their best to light the Hall with torches, but they could do nothing to quell the paranoia induced by staring into the dark, not knowing where or when the enemy would approach. The tension crept into Tabitha's shoulders and wound her as tight as a harp-string.

She couldn't sleep, neither could Ashley, though the exhaustion was plain on his face. Sister Grace paced the marble apron of the Scribbillarre, keeping herself close to the steps of the Source where Tabitha and Ashley sat. Tsoraz snored behind them, upon the highest step of the dais, as if declaring that their vigil was a foolish one, for sure. Without sprites, the Gifters had no defence. Their only hope rested on the Swords' broad shoulders.

Captain Jorge kept half of his squadron inside the Hall, in case any of the tall doors should be breached. The other half endured the fearsome duty outside, keeping a ring of constant patrol around the main building.

A dark shape appeared on one of the high windows, but when Tabitha blinked, it was not there. She couldn't be sure if it was a Morrigán or her tiredness. She said nothing, and it did not come again.

Slowly, the eastern sky grew pale. If she could have woken the sun any faster by shouting at it, she would have tried. It seemed to take the night forever to fade, but finally there was a Sword's call from the far side of the East-door, and Captain Jorge opened it to a crimson dawn.

"Captain, what would you have us do?"

"It's unlikely the Dark will attack in daylight," Jorge answered the Sword outside. "I don't believe they'll get past Fendwarrow, but never mind that. I'd rather the men were fresh, in case something happens tonight." He turned. "Aw'right! You lot in the Hall get to patrol the grounds for a while. You can tell the bounders outside they're dismissed for breakfast, and bed."

Tabitha stretched, and knuckled the small of her back. The men trooped out, the others trooped in with a crisper air. When the last dismissed Sword strode in, something flitted in his wake. A small pale butterfly came into the Hall, dancing with an errant motion. It flew a few loops around Ashley, passed low over Grace's head, then settled on Tsoraz, where he slept on the dais. When its wings spread wide, Tabitha recognised the rainbow markings. Her Lifesong butterfly, sent to Twardy Zarost.

Yet it rested on Tsoraz's nose, quite undisturbed by his snoring breaths. It was a flying question mark. Why, if it was bonded to Zarost, was it with the man who claimed to be his son?

Tsoraz startled awake at that moment, as if aware of Tabitha's attention. The butterfly fluttered, but didn't go far. He noticed it at once, and shooed it away with waving hands. He shot a hurried glance at Tabitha, then shooed the butterfly again. It gambolled beyond his reach, and circled his bald head.

"What a pretty butterfly!" exclaimed Sister Grace. She watched the air above Tsoraz.

"Yes, it is," he agreed, looking at Tabitha instead, with not a trace of sleepiness in his eyes. "The most unique in Eyri. If the egg makes the caterpillar, and it the cocoon, how does the butterfly learn flight so soon?"

The question generated enough of a pause around the bard for him to hop to his feet and patter down the stairs. Before Tabitha could compose the question she wanted to ask, he was through the East-door, with his butterfly flitting after his colourful cloak. Tsoraz had cleverly avoided the question he must have seen in her eyes. He was every bit as tricky as the Riddler before him.

"That is a strange man," commented Sister Grace, following Tabitha's gaze. "I hope he has only your best interests at heart."

"So do I," said Tabitha.

Ashley came up and stood beside them. "Ladies, I think I might catch a wink of sleep now that it's light."

Sister Grace laid a hand on his arm.

"Before you go, Ashley, I thought we might sing the Morningsong."

"But there's only three of us. Will it be any good?"

Tabitha knew it needed an Assembly of thirty, at least, to spark the sprites from the Source.

"It was not the sprites I was thinking of," replied Grace, "it was our spirits." The two exchanged an understanding glance.

"The singing might do me good," he agreed. "Do you know the

Morningsong, Tabitha?"

He wasn't to know that she had sung it every morning with her mother, hoping that one day she would sing the full song in the hallowed Dovecote. At the time, she had never imagined it would be to an empty Hall of Sky, in the face of impending doom. She nodded.

On a whim, Tabitha lifted her lyre from her bag on the stairs. They spaced themselves around the Source. The first verse faltered along, while Tabitha tried to find her voice and pluck the strings in time, but she knew at once that Grace was correct—the Morningsong did lift her spirits.

They sang, and Tabitha strived to find perfection. She drew on the Ring, and became aware of the hollows and holes in the pattern of sound, just as she had once before, when her singing in the Hall had been illicit. There were places where her voice needed to fill the harmony, and notes she could alter, ever so slightly, to bring completeness to the music. Their voices seemed to fill the Hall as they sang. The sun touched the Source, gentle as an artist's brush, a luminous wash upon clear crystal.

The first sprite sparked within the Source, and shot to the wall. Ashley took a step back, and Sister Grace raised her hands in surprise, but they continued to sing.

Tabitha gave it her all. The spell of the Morningsong surged through her. She noticed how it was clear essence which was drawn to the Source, a steady flow of barely visible particles which shimmered through the door. Once within the crystal obelisk, they were energised by the Light, and spun away as sprites. More and more sprites struck the high walls of the Hall, where they slipped to the floor and trickled into the channel scribed around the rim of the Scribbillarre. Tabitha was jubilant. They were creating Light essence. They sang until the flare of sprites from the Source reduced to a flicker, an intermittent flash, finally nothing at all. The sun had climbed clear of the jagged Zunskar mountains, and they had created Light essence.

The other two wore dazed expressions. They watched Tabitha.

"And the Rector did not want to have you as a Gifter," said Sister Grace, shaking her head. "You sing like Ethea."

"I have seen many days when a full assembly has not produced as much," added Ashley. "Thanks to you, we are Lightgifters again."

"You sang as well, both of you," Tabitha answered. The praise was an awkward thing to bear, especially from a full Gifter like Sister

Grace. She had just sung what she had felt was right.

"That was you, far more than it was us, Tabitha."

"Didn't you see the sprites pouring from the distant side of the Source, as if you drove them?" Ashley asked.

Tabitha used the pretence of putting the lyre back in her bag to avoid the awkward praise. But they were still watching her expectantly when she straightened.

"Thank you," she said. "It felt good to sing the Morningsong with you."

Ashley smiled. He pointed to the channel at the rim of the Scribbillarre, where the sprites had collected. "Thanks to you, we can help the Swords, if the Shadowcasters come tonight. We should decide on a plan."

"Couldn't we just throw Light at the Dark? It fizzles out, becomes clear essence."

"Really? I was thinking more of the forbidden spells, the Flameburst and Spriteblind. They might have enough power."

"Ashley!" exclaimed Sister Grace. "We can't use those, they are too dangerous, they were forbidden for good reason. And Tabitha might be right, we might only need to mix the essences. I have heard of it being done. But how do you know of that, Tabitha?"

"I—came across a few motes, recently."

She couldn't tell them the motes had been summoned by her hand, controlled by her Darkstone.

Sister Grace looked puzzled, but she didn't pry. "It might work, but if they have a greater number of motes, we would lose all of our Light essence and still be found wanting."

"Then we must try the Morningsong again," said Ashley. "Build our strength."

"Not for a while yet," Grace disagreed. "We have taken what sprites we can from the Source for this morning, and far more than I expected."

Tsoraz came running in through the East-door, cloak flapping. "Morrigán!" he announced, halting on the threshold. "Morrigán all around!"

They ran to look. It was true. Black ravens dived and swooped around a distant patrol of few Swords. The Swords had their weapons drawn, but the birds dodged the blades with ease, flapping and mocking the men from above their heads. The hoarse cries of the birds set Tabitha's teeth on edge. She knew a sudden alarm. Where there were Morrigán, there were Shadowcasters.

Ashley raced down the stairs, and hauled the mighty East-door closed. It swung ponderously on giant hinges, and slammed against the frame. Tabitha helped him set the bar in place, though her hands shook.

We should rouse the Swords within the Dovecote.

She turned on this thought, only to see the door to the men's corridor being closed. The rotund man who set the bar in place wore a purple robe. When he turned and summoned the Light essence to his hand in the same motion, she recognised him, in one dreadful moment.

The Rector Shamgar.

A broad smile was stretched across his face, a forced expression which did not suit him.

"Welcome back, welcome back," the Rector said, "I was not expecting you back so soon. What a wonderful surprise." His eyes said it wasn't. Sprites massed around his hands—most of what they had created. Tabitha was too surprised to act.

"Have you forgotten your manners, Gifters? You will kneel before your Rector. If you are quick, I may forgive your transgression."

No one moved. Shamgar's face gained a shade of red.

"By your Vow I compel you. You shall kneel before your Rector!"

He wove a pattern in the sprites, and sent some of them flickering through the air towards them. Tabitha's Lightstone bloomed warmth against her throat. She felt a compulsion to obey the Rector's command, but it was faint enough to ignore. But for Ashley and Sister Grace, it did not seem to go so easy. They sank to the floor, and Ashley pressed his head to the stone at his knees.

"If you had taken the Vow, Miss Serannon, you would understand what it is to be a Lightgifter, to be sworn to serve the Light and your Rector. A pity that you are so untrained, what? The Vow is quite compelling."

The Rector advanced across the Hall, his gaze steady. He passed a gap in the Scribbillarre, a dark trapdoor, similar to the one Tabitha had used to reach the Inner Sanctum. She stared at it with growing dread. It must have been how the Rector had sneaked up on them. There was something else down there, besides darkness. She could feel its advance like the coming of a cold wind.

"My friends shared an old secret with me, a wonder of architecture," the Rector commented. "Could you believe that there is a doorway in the floor? Quite amazing what the essence can be used for."

"You can come up!" he shouted, facing the trapdoor. "The Swords are out, at last. There is nobody here but two useless Gifters, a commoner, and an unskilled girl who has already been given to the Dark. The Morrigán have done their task well—we have the Hall."

Ashley and Grace were still held by the Vow. Tsoraz looked uncertain, and shifted from foot to foot. His staff was at hand, but he didn't look inclined to use it.

Tabitha edged close to him. "Will you help me?" she whispered.

"This is not my fight," he muttered, to himself as much as to her.

"What is your fight, then?"

"Guiding you. Not leading you."

"Guide me then!" she hissed. The Rector was closing on them.

"You are promised to neither, so can use both."

A riddle, in the face of adversity. She could have screamed at him in frustration. She backed away from the Rector, and Tsoraz stepped easily beside her.

Tabitha tried to summon the Light to her hand, but all the sprites were bound to the Rector, and his command was stronger than hers. He sneered at her as he tightened his grip on the essence. He had it all.

"You believe you can make a difference, against the coming of the Master?" She backed away. Shamgar snorted. "Behold, what you are up against."

The Dark entered the Hall of Sky.

At first it was just a tendril, like a black snake, curling out of the trapdoor, writhing across the marble floor. A gust carried motes in a low, roiling cloud. Tabitha stumbled away from it, and found herself running for the dais with Tsoraz. Dark essence flooded the Hall at her heels. She could do nothing for Ashley and Grace. When she had mounted the stairs beneath the Source, she turned, and saw the Gifters writhing against the cold touch of Dark. The Rector remained beside them, holding them with the compulsion of their Vow, but he laughed at Tabitha. Beyond the kneeling Gifters, a dark figure pulled itself up to the Scribbillarre.

The cowled Shadowcaster was wreathed in motes, a funnel of Dark centred on her body like a whirlwind blasting through ash. It was a woman, Tabitha was sure, from the way her robe hung. The call of the Dark, which had driven her to despair in Stormhaven, whispered all around the Hall, urging her to reach out and draw the motes to her own hand. But she also wanted to gather all the Light from the Rector, and destroy the Dark.

While Tabitha's emotions warred, the other Shadowcasters climbed from the secret passage. Those who followed the woman were bigger, and they moved like men. A final rush of motes followed the sixth man from the open hole. The Shadowcasters arranged themselves in a circle around the Source. Tabitha could retreat no further—the crystal obelisk pressed against her back.

The lead Shadowcaster shielded her eyes with a hand held close to her cowl, as if the sunlight pouring in the windows of the Hall was painful. After a few moments she turned, and scanned the rest of the Hall. She laughed then, a sound of honeyed seduction. The Shadowcasters joined her, though their voices were rough by comparison.

"This is the last resistance of the Light, Rector Shamgar? What a sweet way to end it—with two Gifters, two commoners, and a cupful of sprites."

"Be done with it, woman. The Swords will not be fooled for long."

"Then we shall deal with them," she answered. But Tabitha noticed that the Shadowcaster began immediately with a spell pattern, guiding the motes into a smooth current around the Hall. The other Shadowcasters joined her, building the large, unified spell. It was a great circle, but imperfect, like one made from a twisted ribbon. The air was thick with motes.

"Link with me," the woman ordered, and the current of motes became denser, changing from black mist to vitriol. The Shadowcasters chanted in unison, a slow, deep dirge.

"Are you ready for me?" Rector Shamgar asked. He strode into the circle without awaiting the reply. He held a cloud of sprites high, clear of the Dark essence. The motes rippled where he broke their current with his legs, but the flow resumed at once. He sent the Light outward in a flow which mirrored that of the Dark, joining it in the design of the twisted circle. The Rector approached Tabitha, Tsoraz, and the Source.

"Step away, commoners, I have work to do."

"The work of treachery," accused Tabitha.

The Rector shook his head sadly. "In time, you will learn that treachery fetches a higher price than honesty. Now begone!"

Tabitha had less strength in her legs than a new-born lamb, yet she refused to move. Before her stood the man who should have led the Lightgifters against the evil of Ravenscroft. Instead, he had planned their downfall. As a Lightgifter, she had to defy him. Everything he had done, had been to weaken the Dovecote.

They must have paid him dearly, made it worth his while. She whispered the words of a summoning, holding the double-looped pattern in mind, focusing on her Lightstone. But the Rector's will was stronger, and his command of the sprites remained. He stepped close, and reached for her. Tsoraz blocked his hand.

"A traitor has no right to compel the faithful."

"Who are you? How dare you insult me, you miserable common filth! Step aside!" He came up close to Tsoraz. "Or would you prefer the Dark in your ear?" His breath must have upset the butterfly, for it took flight from somewhere upon the bard's cloak.

"You would know what it is like to have the Dark in your ear," Tsoraz mocked. "Do you really believe Cabal will keep his word, when your use has passed?"

"What we do is no concern to you! Stand aside!"

The delicate coloured butterfly came between them, but the Rector reached up suddenly, and caught it with a sharp clap of his hands.

"Bloody spring plague." He released the dead butterfly.

Tsoraz stared at the fallen, squashed creature. His face was unreadable.

"Close the circle, let us be done," announced the Rector. He stepped around Tsoraz, pushed Tabitha aside, and placed his hands on the Source. The seven Shadowcasters paced inwards, bringing the twisted circle closer.

The staff was a whistling blur. It caught the Rector flat on the temple, and broke upon his skull, sending a splintered shaft spinning away into the air. Tsoraz was possessed with fury. The power of it was more terrifying than anything Tabitha had witnessed, it washed over her with raw force, setting her hair on end.

"The first of the Lifesong! That was my butterfly! A living sign!" Tsoraz shouted at the falling Rector. "Thus you pay, for taking what was."

He turned to Tabitha. An ultimate rage burned in his eyes. His power shimmered around him. "Now act, Tabitha, or all is lost! This is not my test!"

The command jolted Tabitha from her stunned reverie. The

Shadowcasters were all around, their circle fast closing. The Light essence followed the pattern, following the last command of the Rector. But he lay at her feet, beside a dead butterfly.

Tabitha summoned the sprites. They pulled away from the Turning spell without resistance, speeding for their new master. Her Ring was a band of heat. There was one pattern Tabitha held clearly in mind, a spell she suspected would be magnified by the Source. She spoke the words her mother had sought to preserve.

◆ ———————————— ◆

Ashley didn't know why he reached out to Tabitha at that moment, but the briefest touch of minds allowed him to see the pattern of the spell she intended. He warned Grace of the Spriteblind not an instant too soon.

Even with his eyes closed, kneeling on the far limit of the Scribbillarre, Ashley was blinded by the brilliance of the flash. A blast of heat scorched his skin. Sister Grace groaned beside him. The Shadowcasters screamed.

He opened his eyes to swirling spots of brightness. He jumped to his feet as his vision cleared. The Dark circle had collapsed, and the motes washed to the walls, unbounded. They stung his legs with cold. All around, Shadowcasters were clutching their heads, or crawling on their hands and knees, roaring in agony. He ran for the nearest, then stopped short.

The Shadowcaster showed no sign of having noticed him. Ashley remembered only too well the agony of the Spriteblind. He raised his fist indecisively.

Someone pounded on the East-door, and there were shouts. The Swords had noticed the commotion. All he needed to do was raise the bar on the door, and the Swords could deal with the Shadowcasters. He took one last glance around the Hall.

Unbounded motes rushed about like smoke from a burning field, hiding Shadowcasters where they summoned motes in defence. Two figures were locked in a struggle, but it was not the black-robed man who made Ashley's breath catch in his throat. Sister Grace was straining with all her might against the Shadowcaster's powerful stranglehold.

"Move, and I snap her neck!" the man shouted. "Nobody move!"

Ashley was paralysed with fear. Even though he knew the Shadowcaster was blinded, he dared not take another step toward the door or the struggling figures.

"Well done," commended a honeyed voice.

A wave of motes washed past, collecting on the strangler's head. The man seemed to gain some benefit from it. Someone had command of the Dark; Ashley's hope died a quick death. Motes struck him before he was even fully turned. A black figure approached him, one of the shorter Shadowcasters. A wisp of black essence curled upwards from the floor, and wrapped itself around the Shadowcaster's slim waist. Ashley steeled himself for the effect of the spell. Something about the approaching Shadowcaster was terribly familiar.

He reached out with his mind, and dived into the thoughts of the Shadowcaster. The Shadowcaster stopped suddenly, reached up slender hands, and pushed the cowl back. Ashley gasped. He should have guessed that it was a woman, by the way her robe clung to the body beneath it. The honeyed voice, the body movement. He looked into the Shadowcaster's dark eyes, took in her cascading black hair, the sensuous lips, and was paralysed.

Gabrielle.

The dream woman, the seducer, the lover. Her power fell on him, and he understood why Tsoraz had warned him of his mind games. He knew why Father Keegan had been turned. He was caught by her seduction again, but so completely he couldn't bring his attention back under his command.

He could not resist her urgency. He forgot that he had meant to strike her with his fists. She was so lovely. Dark essence rose in whirlwind patterns up Gabrielle's body, caressing her, exploring her. Her hungry gaze stopped his heart beating.

Mercy! She is the most beautiful woman I've ever known.

The memory of her lovemaking with Keegan bloomed in his mind, but it was he who fell into her arms, he who cried out the words of the Turning. Pain seared through the fantasy. Cold claimed his body. Every muscle clenched as the Dark poured through him. He stared at Gabrielle. It was too late. He could not move.

A flicker of a smile crossed Gabrielle's lips, and she reached out a hand to caress Ashley's paralysed face. If anything, the gesture made him colder, for he felt his own desire even though the Shadowcaster had struck him helpless.

Gabrielle!

She moved past him, and was gone from view. The edges of his vision were eaten by gnawing dark. He could see only a narrowing circle, wherein the Source stood upon its dais, and beside it, Tabitha Serannon. Then even that was lost. His heart sounded slow pulses in his ears. His rigid legs forced him to remain upright, staring into the darkness of his mind. There was no Light.

♦ ———————— ♦

Tabitha's eyes smarted. It had been like standing in the centre of the sun. She knew most of the Light must have been drained from the essence with the casting of the Spriteblind spell. Even before her vision returned in full, she could sense the Dark surging through the Hall again. At least one of the Shadowcasters had escaped the effect of the Spriteblind. She had done her best, and it had not been enough. Something cold grabbed her ankles and held her. She didn't bother to look down. She knew what it was.

She looked instead for some sprites, and caught sight of them through a haze of receding blindness. They were high on the walls, and only a glimmer remained in them. She summoned them all to her hand; a weak haze of Light.

"Move, and I snap her neck!" a man shouted. "Nobody move!"

Sister Grace, held hostage by a big Shadowcaster. She saw their struggle in an instant, and knew she could not dare to do anything.

The Dark whispered to her, called to her, urged her to let go. She wanted to. She knew she must. Very soon, she would be accepted into the family.

I am the shadow and he is my master.
He is the shadow and I am his caster.

Then she saw the woman watching her. The deep cowl hid her features, but it felt as if her eyes touched Tabitha, a caress as intimate as a lover's. Then the touch was gone, and the Shadowcaster turned towards Ashley.

Tabitha watched in mute horror as the Shadowcaster bound Ashley in motes. At the same time, it was fascinating. She drew on the Ring to see the fine details of the Dark spell pattern. The woman wove a second pattern atop the first, and when it struck Ashley, he went rigid.

She wanted to have that power, and yet she was repulsed by the thought. The sprites faltered in her hand, and some hissed to extinction against the motes which swirled at her feet. She supposed she should be cold, but she didn't feel it.

"Keep command of your Light, my dear," commanded the lead

Shadowcaster, her voice raised to carry from the floor. "We need you to complete the Turning spell." She came closer, her movements as sinuous as a cat. "You will join us, now that you can see who shall win in the end?"

When Tabitha did not answer, the Shadowcaster wove a brief pattern in the Dark, and sent it rippling through the air. The last tatters of hope were torn away in the current of motes. Tabitha tasted the spell of Despair once again. The Shadowcaster's order became compelling.

"Keep hold of the sprites. I shall instruct you when we are ready."

Tabitha obeyed. It was useless to resist.

The Shadowcaster moved around the Hall, guiding motes to her fallen comrades. Soon, all six had regained their feet, if not all of their sight. They dragged Sister Grace to beside Ashley, and bound her in the same Freeze. Tabitha noticed that Tsoraz had disappeared. He must have fled up the stairs to a higher level of the Dovecote under the cover of the Spriteblind spell. How he had endured the spell better than the others she couldn't guess. He had left her, abandoned her to her doom.

The Swords pounded on the doors, both the East-door and the one to the men's corridor, but the doors were well-barred from the inside.

The Shadowcasters spaced themselves around the Source, and the twisted circle of motes took shape within their slow advance. The woman was watching her again.

"You can see the pattern, girl. Guide your sprites to run alongside the motes, but do not let them touch."

Despite her fear, Tabitha hesitated. To work with the Shadowcasters, in this spell of Turning, would mean her own turning as well. She would be aiding those whom she had fought, and would become one of them. The Light would be taken from Eyri forever, and there would be only Dark. She felt herself teetering on the brink of ruin.

She thought of her mother, the way she had given everything in the fight. She thought of Ashley, of all the hardships he had endured to bring warning. She thought of Garyll Glavenor. He would not have given in to the Dark. But even as she denied it, the Dark fed upon her anger and built a towering rage within her, a rage at the Shadowcasters gathered before her. She knew that if she used the Dark, she would become one of them herself. She hated herself for that, and it only made the rage swell, constricted in her clenched heart.

She could find no release for her fury—she couldn't beat the Shadowcasters in a contest of magic. They had too much Dark essence; she had a faint memory of Light in her command.

"Come, join with us, let the Dark be your master."

A cold hand reached into her heart, and she was compelled to do as the woman asked. The hidden Darkstone Tabitha wore linked her to the woman in a bond that was stronger than blood. The sprites left her hand, and flowed to the twisted circle of essence, where the Light formed a skin upon the Dark, guided by Tabitha's will and the pattern she held in mind.

The Shadowcasters closed.

"Now, hold your hands to the Source, and speak with us."

Tabitha mouthed the words as they became clear. Motes circled the dais in a hush. The air was chill.

"Hold the pattern, round, and round,
in the hidden turn, to the stronger will be bound."

The Source was smooth under her hands, so tall and clear, the true heart of the Dovecote. Without it, there would be no essence of either kind, Light or Dark; only clear essence, and peace.

The Shadowcasters reached the first step of the dais.

Her reflection was faint, and warped by the curved surface of the Source. A wide face, with sad eyes, above a neckerchief, under which lay the Darkstone that compelled her so. And a Lightstone which would soon lose its meaning. She supposed she would still have the Ring, even if she became a Shadowcaster. The Sage had warned her of the inevitable path to Darkness. But she had known the Light, for a time.

The twisted circle of the Turning spell disturbed the air around her. The Shadowcasters were so close she could smell their stale body odour. She suspected that when their hands joined hers on the surface of the Source, the Turning would be done.

Her reflection watched her, with deep eyes. The eyes of the Truthsayer, the eyes of the Seeker. She found a moment of clarity in her thoughts. She bore both orbs, but had spoken neither of the vows. She could be a Shadowcaster without betraying anyone, so long as she was not only a Shadowcaster. She leapt at the chance and accepted the Dark, took command of the motes that were binding her, let them slip from her body. The others were so intent on turning the Source that none of them noticed her release. Maybe they thought she had already been Turned. The twisted circle of motes and sprites closed on the Source, a hair's-breadth from the surface.

With the hold of the Dark released, she knew clarity. There was one path to freedom, one power the others could not fight. The Lifesong. There was time only for one note, that first note which had split the Sphere of the Universe, the note of beginnings, and endings. She knew her skill had grown since the Kingsbridge. There was no time for doubt.

She sang the Shiver with all her heart.

The Shadowcasters reached to the Source, their hands touched the crystal. Tabitha's hands were already upon it. Her voice reached into it. She held only the Source in mind; there was nothing else. The Source, and the Shiver. The note found perfection, and Tabitha was drawn into a timeless moment where all that was, was song. Nothing was solid, there was nothing to contain the power which ran through her, a vibration which could undo everything, pull the universe apart, or set it aright.

She opened herself to the power. She knew she was the channel, her mind formed the guiding banks of a torrent which was far greater than she would ever be. The Shiver flowed through her, and she was a part of the Lifesong. She heard a thousand voices, and yet sang with one. She heard a thousand stanzas, yet knew only the moment of the Shiver. She promised that some day, she would explore the knowledge that she could sense was hidden deeper in the music. It all happened in the space of a heartbeat, and then the Source shattered, in a storm of crystal boulders, shards, splinters and dust.

Tabitha jumped away from the tumbling debris, but she tripped at the edge of the dais, and took the stairs in a fall. Her feet were still numb from the Dark. When she regained her bearings, she saw that many of the Shadowcasters lay amongst the debris. Many, but not all. She had only enough time to scrabble to her feet before the black-cloaked figure was upon her. The woman tripped her again, and had her boot upon Tabitha's chest before she could take a breath.

"You little bitch!" The woman kicked at her head, and did not miss. Tabitha was blinded with pain and dizziness.

Voices. She could hear, but could see nothing.

There was a splintering of wood.

"The Swords!" shouted a man.

"To the tunnel!" shouted another. "To the docks!"

"Take her!" shouted the woman, close by.

Tabitha was grabbed by a rough arm around her neck, and dragged a short way. She was dropped down a level onto her feet, but she collapsed in a heap against somebody's legs. Heavy boots landed beside her, then a second, lighter pair.

"What about the others?"

"They failed!" replied the woman. "To hell with them!"

There was a clamour of shouts, and running feet, but it became distant, as if sealed off behind a closing door. There was a grating of stone, then a click, and near silence, except for muffled murmurs and thumps from afar.

"But they can't open it. They have no Light, and we have the Dark."

"I don't care! We run. I want this one to learn the torture room in Ravenscroft. I want her to regret living. Rat spawn! We have lost the Source! And now I must report that to the Master."

Something struck Tabitha's head again. Then there truly was nothing to hear or see.

39. WHISPERS OF WAR

"Darkness to itself does draw,
the kind that makes the darkness more."—*Zarost*

It was cold. The Darkmaster savoured the chill breeze which swirled through his Cavern. He liked to see the new subjects stamp and shiver. Their bodies still fought the cold, even though their hearts had long since been turned to his service. It would do them no good to resist, for their moment of trial had come and gone, and they were given to the Dark. Resistance only gave them pain. That was good as well, he supposed. Yes, let them learn of pain, in all its many flavours.

The Cavern was fuller than it had ever been. Men of the Sword lined the walls, his Sword, the Darksword, all sworn to his service. Then there were the fallen Lightgifters, like a flock of dirty sheep in the wolves lair. Their white robes were stained with the fine dust of Ravenscroft, but they were not yet turned fully to black. Unlike their Lightstones—that Turning had been all too easy. Yet now that their conquest was over, he despised them for their weakness. They had none of the toughness of his matured Shadowcasters, who numbered most in the Cavern.

It was a strange time to summon them all—noon, from the middle of their sleep—but it was a momentous occasion, and it could not wait. They would hear the words of victory, and they would be bonded to him tighter than ever. The converts' last hopes would be crushed. Once they heard the news that the Source of the Light had been turned, they would belong to the Dark completely. Their robes would be dyed to black, and they would be named Shadowcasters. For his loyal followers, the news would bring strength to their faith. It was to be the final boon before they marched to war.

They had spent days preparing, strengthening the new heights of the dam in the Black River, gathering essence from every corner of Ravenscroft vale, rehearsing the strikes and counters. Years of planning, culminating in this day. His people were prepared. Now he would give them the confidence to march on Stormhaven, and take it.

The raven croaked loudly. It was agitated by the long wait, eager to deliver its message and reach the culmination of its brief life. It flapped its wings where it stood, then cocked its head to the side to question the Darkmaster with a glassy eye. Still Cabal did not say the word. He watched the crowd, waited while the feet shifted and scraped on the floor, while those nervous of his gaze coughed or looked away.

The moment came at last, when all was quiet in the chamber, and all eyes were on the Darkmaster.

"Alight, Morrigán, and deliver your word." The eager flurry of wings became an explosion of motes, and the words sounded loud in the silence. It was the voice of Gabrielle, as he knew it would be.

"Master, the Light has been conquered." Cabal smiled with victorious satisfaction. "But—the Source is shattered," the voice continued, "the crystal was broken by a girl they call Tabitha. I don't know what art she uses, but her voice is like a thunderbolt. Four of our seven are in the hands of the King's Swords. I return with the girl. She shall sing a different tune in Ravenscroft."

Dead silence.

Cabal's rage swelled to the walls. No one drew a breath in the Cavern—it was as if there was suddenly no air at all. Cabal gripped his sceptre tighter, to hide the shaking of his hands. He roared, and sent a wind of motes shrieking across the crowd. The torches guttered, and Dark filled the hall. He wasn't even aware of the spell he had cast until a woman's scream came from somewhere amongst the crowd. The cracking of bone cut the second scream short. He abandoned the Breaking, and turned his attention to casting his own Morrigán.

"Failure! You shall not return to Ravenscroft. You shall never return to Ravenscroft! Await our march on Stormhaven. If you secure that victory, you shall be allowed to live there."

He would kill her anyway. Her failure was unforgivable. If the Source was broken, there would be no new essence. It was terrible. His power would be limited to what he had amassed in Ravenscroft, and much of that would have to be used, in the storming of Stormhaven.

He did not release the raven. There was more to his message.

The girl! Becursed girl!

He had to. She was the only piece that kept the Swordmaster in play. He needed the Swordmaster. At this stage in the game. Revenge could be taken, in time.

"The girl—must be released. Let her find her way to Stormhaven. Do not fail me in that."

He hoisted the messenger. The Morrigán flapped over the stunned crowd, and left the Cavern, bound for the higher passages.

He turned on his subjects. He didn't think anyone had breathed yet.

"It is time, we shall wait no longer! We have *all* the essence in Eyri, and all of it is Dark. We march tomorrow, at nightfall. We march to war."

The ancient word of power rippled through the crowd.

"War!" he said again. The awe of the crowd was broken, and was replaced with the hunger he had instilled in them, a lust they touched whenever they slept, whenever they heard the Darkmaster's whispering suggestions—the desire for domination and conquest. War.

The Darkmaster strode from the Cavern to the sound of wild cheers, the beating of fists and stamping of feet. His people were hungry for victory. They had been hidden for too long.

Losing the Source was enraging and unfortunate, but he would not allow it to change his plans to march on Stormhaven. The death-stroke was the Swordmaster, and he had already been placed at the heart of the realm. One more day, and Glavenor should have done what was needed to be done. Then it would be time for night to fall on Eyri. King Mellar didn't know that he had already lost.

"War!" he whispered, to himself. He slammed the sceptre into the rock. It gave him focus.

One pathetic girl, and she defied him at every turn. For the last time, he vowed. The Swordmaster expected her to be left alone, and that would be what he would see. But there were things that were possible with a Darkstone that neither could anticipate.

◆ ——— ◆

A shoulder dug into Tabitha's stomach, again and again in the incessant rhythm of walking. Blood pounded in her head. She was slung over a large man's shoulder, and he walked down stairs, with little care to how she was jolted.

The Shadowcasters!

She knew they had taken her into the tunnel beneath the Dovecote, but she had no idea whether they were still in that, or in another secret way. If they were under Levin, they were a long way under, for the stairs were steeply angled, and disappeared into darkness at the limit of the flickering light someone carried. Tabitha was at the back of the group, and could see little apart from rough stone, and the boots of the man who carried her.

His shoulder thumped into her again, hard enough to bruise. She cried out and discovered that she could make only a muffled moan through her tight gag. She struggled in the Shadowcaster's grip, and learned that her hands were tied as well. The man halted.

"So, it lives. I'll be glad to get rid of your dead-weight," he announced, tipping her from his shoulders onto her feet. He steadied her, then turned her to face down the stairway. "Walk," he ordered, pushing her with a rough hand.

It took all of her attention to avoid falling on the stairs. Without the use of her hands, there was nothing to help her balance. The steps were not altogether dry, for a stream rushed beside the walkway. It was damp and cold in this place. The torch, in the hand of one of the Shadowcasters ahead, cast only a dim light. She stumbled on. The two figures ahead of her didn't turn, they walked with brisk urgency, and another rough push told her that she was expected to do the same. Thankfully the stairs became a sloping ramp, which was easier to negotiate, but the Shadowcasters increased the pace, until she was heaving breaths through the stifling fabric in her mouth.

She thought of removing the gag only once. A vicious rap on her knuckles from behind convinced her otherwise.

After a time, the tunnel began to grow lighter. Tabitha caught a murmur of activity above the rush of the stream, though it was so muted as to be unrecognisable. They rounded a bend in the tunnel, and came upon a chamber filled with a grey-green light. The stream became a pool, and it was from within the depths that the light came. The walkway came to an end against a sheer wall.

The torch-bearer doused the brand, and dropped it on a pile of similar faggots. He climbed the wall. Tabitha noticed the iron rungs for the first time. The woman took the iron rungs next.

"Up!" commanded a gruff voice behind her. The rope which bound her wrists was untied roughly. Her fingertips stung with the sudden return of blood. She didn't have long to relish the sensation.

At the top of the ladder there was a landing, just wide enough for all four of them. A rusted iron door sealed an exit. When one of the Shadowcasters rapped on it, it issued a hollow note, like a dead gong.

A strong hand gripped her neck from behind. Soft fabric was pulled over her head, and everything went dark. It smelled of damp leaves inside the bag. Then her wrists were bound again.

"Who is it?" came a muffled voice.

"Gabrielle."

A bolt was shot with a squeal. The door groaned away.

"Your captive. Can she hear?"

"Yes. I wouldn't worry, she won't be coming back from Ravenscroft."

The doorman muttered something, but Tabitha suspected it was supposed to be unintelligible, even to the Shadowcasters.

"The tariff," stated the doorman.

A faint rustling of hands.

"We need a boat, and some cloaks to hide these," Gabrielle said. "We must travel in daylight."

"More jurrum. Another ten leaves."

"Eight."

The whisper of hands again, then a grunt, and they began to move. Someone kept a hand on her shoulder, and steered her by twisting the joint. There were many doors—she heard them closing softly behind them. They walked upon thick carpets, then wood, and finally down some stairs to bare stone. The smell of fish crept through the fabric of her hood, and the shouts of men at work. They walked along a level area, and water lapped nearby. There was a flurry of wings, and a croaking cry she recognised as a raven. Her guide paused, and the woman spoke.

"Alight, messenger, and deliver your word."

The Morrígan released a voice as dry and scaly as a dead snake, yet for all its emptiness, there was fury in the words as well.

"Failure! You shall not return to Ravenscroft. You shall never return to Ravenscroft! Await our march on Stormhaven. If you secure that victory, you shall be allowed to live there."

The only sound was the lapping of water against the pier.

"The girl—must be released. Let her find her way to Stormhaven. Do not fail me in that."

A curdled scream and a fast step was all the warning she got. A hard, blinding slap left Tabitha's left ear ringing. She fell to her side, but she was dragged to her feet again, then slapped the other way. She fell against a wall.

"Gabrielle!" said a gruff voice. "We are in enough trouble after what happened at the Dovecote."

"And what happened there is her fault, this miserable brat!"

"Come aside!" the man urged. When his voice resumed, it was from further away, yet not far enough to evade Tabitha's ears. The Ring brought great detail, including the glowing pain in her cheek.

"I heard the Master's words as well as you. She must be released."

"She cannot be released here," answered Gabrielle. "By the balls of Krakus! She knows too much already. She should not be let free."

"The Master has spoken."

"Yet he will blame us if the secret of this way is breached! Be damned if he won't. And they will be forewarned of our march as well, if this wretched girl speaks of it."

"So be it. The Master must know these things; it is not our place to question his wisdom. We can have a dock-hand take her to the lower market, let her go in the crowd. She'll not know how to follow."

Tabitha didn't hear Gabrielle's answer to that, but footsteps soon approached. A strong hand gripped her at the nape of her neck.

Gabrielle's voice was terribly calm.

"Never imagine that you are any more than a servant to the Master's plans. When you find your legs, you little tart, you run. Run away, and do not try to find me or this place, or I shall have you killed! Greater crimes have been committed in the service of the Dark."

Heavy sacking fell about her. She was sealed in a bag, of sorts, when it was tied beneath her feet. They set her upon a barrow, and someone wheeled her from the building into the open, through what she guessed were the alleys of Levin waterfront, with many twists and turns and double-backs. They could have let her free with no blindfold or restraints—Tabitha felt like a rabbit, about to be released from a fox hole. She would have run a long way before turning around to see where it was she had come from. Freedom was too great a prize to squander.

As the barrow bumped along, she wondered at her change in fortunes, but the more she considered it, the more unsettling it became. The Darkmaster wished her released, that much was plain from the Morrigáns missive. Yet he knew that she bore the Ring, and he had sent Kirjath Arkell after her, once to kill her, the second time to orb her with the Darkstone.

Every day since that awful moment in the Dovecote chapel, something like a disease had grown inside her, spreading in secrecy. The hunger to use the Dark, the lust for its spells, the anger at her own desire, and the compelling whispered presence from afar. She had learned to live with it all, and still find a place in her heart for hope. But she could not understand why the Darkmaster had released her.

They had spoken of a march upon Stormhaven. If that were true, it meant bringing the war to the heart of Eyri. If the Darkmaster came with his forces, closer to her, his presence would grow within her Darkstone.

He must be very sure of his power, to release me.

Sure that she would be turned. Sure that she would serve him, and with her, his old Ring would again be used by someone who was loyal to the Dark.

That thought alone chilled her blood. The Darkmaster might be many things, but she doubted that he was a fool.

The barrow tipped, and she slid to the ground. There was a hubbub of activity around her; the busy sounds of trade. The sacking which covered her was cut, and a knife worked at the rope on her bonded wrists. Just as suddenly, she was left alone.

By the time she had worked her hands free of the loosened rope, torn her way out of the sacking, and lifted her blindfold from her eyes, there was no barrow-man in sight. The sunlight was blinding, the colours of tents and traders' clothes all too bright. She was seated in a muddy corner amongst broken pallets and discarded canvas, behind a line of stalls. The passers-by disregarded her, as if she were just another beggar, of which Levin had many. She attracted no attention when she loosened the gag and hobbled out to join the flow of people. In the hard trading of the Levin waterfront, folk knew not to take too close an interest in the affairs of others.

Tabitha found her way through the streets, south toward the Kingsbridge. She intended to run the length of the causeway, if she could not beg a ride of a carriage or cart. News of the planned march on Stormhaven would shake the King's Isle to its roots.

There was a war coming upon Eyri.

40. ONE STRONG MAN
"How easily we see
that which we wish to see."—*Zarost*

"They plan to march on Stormhaven," announced Garyll Glavenor, over the heads in the throne room. A startled hush fell upon the audience as one after the other turned, and took his presence in with shocked recognition.

"Swordmaster!" exclaimed King Mellar. "We thought you were lost at Ravenscroft. We have all but mourned your death."

"And I almost found that death," he replied, striding through the parting people. All eight of the House Rulers were present, Garyll noted. The Sword Captains saluted him with right fists against their chests, surprised, but without displaying wariness. He trusted that his confident air would wash any doubts from their minds. It had worked thus far. People saw the Swordmaster, regardless of how heart-sore or damaged the man beneath that facade was. His left arm hung in a sling, secured at his neck. His ruined hand was hidden in the folds of that fabric, the bandages pressed snugly against his throat.

Garyll reached the foot of the throne, and dropped to one knee. King Mellar was already out of his seat though, and bade him rise. Mellar took his right arm in the double-handed grip of comradeship.

"It is good to have you back, Glavenor! How I have wished for your counsel. We have agonised over the little we know of our foe and his methods. But tell us of your escape! We heard a terrible treachery took place in Ravenscroft."

Mellar's eyes searched him. He would have to tread carefully if he hoped to lead the King astray. The subterfuge struck revulsion into his heart, but the Darkstone reminded him of his pact—there was a path away from Tabitha's ruin, and a path towards it. He was already too far down the first path to back out, and he would not choose the second. Yet with every lie he spoke, he killed a part of the man who had been the Swordmaster of Eyri.

He would kill all of that man, rather than allow the Darkmaster a chance at Tabitha.

"There is nothing great to tell, your Highness. I was taken prisoner, along with my men. We spent days in their Keep. I worked a weakness

into my chains, and tore my left arm through a shackle to win freedom.
I found a way out of their stronghold, and stole down the river-course
until Fendwarrow."

"And the men?"

Garyll didn't need to feign the bitter expression which came over
him.

"Lost. To a man, they were either slain, or taken prisoner. The
Shadowcasters worked them over in a torture chamber, driving their
will from them until they succumbed to the Darkmaster. Few Swords
remain alive. Many more of the Lightgifters chose life, and were
turned. I was too late to save any of them."

"Yet you escaped."

Mellar held him with an unwavering gaze. The set of the King's
brows told him that this was the crucial moment. He would convince
the King of his loyalty now, or he would die here in the throne room,
upon the point of one of his Captain's swords. They would not refuse
a royal command, they must not.

He prayed it would not come to that, for his orders from the
Darkmaster were terrible, in that instance. Nevertheless, he primed
himself for a rapid draw of Felltang. He had loosened his sheath
at the City Gates. He considered the cost of failure, and found the
determination that he needed.

"I have a strong will, your Highness."

King Mellar continued to regard him with a steady eye, but at last
he nodded, and smiled broadly.

"Yes, indeed," he said, returning to his throne. "So tell me,
Swordmaster of Eyri, what must we do with these Shadowcasters?"

Garyll didn't allow himself to sigh with relief, but he heard a
few members of the audience do so nearby. "They plan to march on
Stormhaven," he stated.

"We know, that is why the Captains are assembled."

"How does this news come ahead of me? I swear I rode harder
than I have ever, and when I escaped, the rumours of the march had
just begun."

"Tabitha Serannon brought word. She was caught by the
Shadowcasters in Levin. She heard words they didn't expect her to
hear."

Every drop of blood in Garyll's body went cold. "Tabitha! Is she
taken?"

"Like you, she escaped. She arrived late yesterday, she's here in

Stormhaven."

"Thank the Creator!" It was like the sun coming out in the dark sky. Realising he might have let his mask of strength slip, he turned away from the King for a moment, to speak to those in the audience.

"Might there be no more innocents risked in this conflict." His words settled on the assembly, and he faced the King once more, with the calm expected of a Swordmaster. "What did she tell you of their march?"

"Little, in fact. Only that they intend to march, and that it would be soon."

"What has been done?" As military commander, it was not out of place to expect the King to brief him on the decisions made in his absence.

"I have sent word to withdraw the men from Fendwarrow," replied Mellar. "If they have bypassed our guard there once, to strike at the Dovecote in Levin, they can do so again, with more Shadowcasters. I thought to bring the men back within the walls of Stormhaven, and the Captains agree –"

"Your Highness –"

"- though not without some argument," the King added, raising his hand to forestall the protest from behind Garyll. "I have always felt Stormhaven to be impregnable. Let them come to our Gate, and we can sweep them from the Isle with a hail of arrows. I see you disagree as well, Swordmaster. What would you advise?"

"We cannot give so much ground, with no cost to them. They will use the Morgloth, sire, that much I know from what I overheard in Ravenscroft. No man can stand on the battlements, for they are exposed to the sky. Arrows will have little effect against the Morgloth, only against the men on the ground. And arrows last only so long, after which we have to release men to engage the besiegers with blades. Which means opening the City Gate, and endangering all of the folk of Stormhaven to a counter-attack. No, we must weaken their charge before they reach the Isle. We must meet their assault with all of our force, at the head of the Kingsbridge. With a tight front to the battle, we can face the Morgloth as well, for we have the whistles Yzell devised, and if we have a narrow target, we have a chance."

"What of the castle defences?" a Captain cut in. "With respect, Swordmaster," the Captain added hastily, when Garyll turned upon him.

"We shall have little need to defend the castle, if we have good enough men on the Kingsbridge."

The Captain stepped back a pace, without appearing to do so.

"Swordmaster, when do you think they will strike?" another Captain asked.

"Very soon," answered Garyll. "By the look of the preparations they were amassing in the vale, they were ready to march. It seemed as if the Darkmaster was waiting for something."

"The fall of the Dovecote, no doubt?" said the King.

Garyll had not stopped for news on the way to the palace. "The Dovecote, highness?"

The King shook his head, his expression bemused. "How hard did you ride, Glavenor? Too fast to hear the talk on everyone's lips in the entire city? The Shadowcasters attacked the Dovecote yesterday. They attempted to claim the giant crystal that is the Lightgifters' source of essence. Were it not for three brave Gifters, they would have achieved that. As it is, the Source is a shattered relic, of use to neither."

"This is grave news," Garyll said. "The Dark will be marching then, if that was the event for which the Darkmaster waited. Which brave Gifters stood up to the assault?"

"You know them well. Sister Grace, Ashley Logán, and the young woman who is woven into everything, it seems. Tabitha Serannon."

They had said she was orbed with the Darkstone, and he had believed it. For the first time he felt true hope for her. Maybe she hadn't been tainted at all. His pact would ensure that things remained that way.

"Where can I find them?"

King Mellar looked puzzled. It was a strange question for the King to answer, Garyll supposed. His calm shield had slipped once more. He had to be more careful. It was one of the House Rulers, the Lady of Ceremony, who answered.

"They have a room in the Boarding."

"I must talk to them. There is something I must know, on which our strategy depends. Your Highness, with your leave, I need to brief and dispatch a squadron to hold the head of the Kingsbridge, while I ready the others for the construction of what we shall need to hold the Dark at bay."

"Heaven's sake, man, rest awhile!" said the King. "Find a mirror, and look in it, Glavenor. You are as haggard as a wayworn crone, the agony of Ravenscroft is etched on your face. Rest, and let your Captains set things in motion."

The King's words struck dangerously close to the truth. It would do no good for anyone to think any further on his experience in Ravenscroft. Garyll shook his head. "The man who rests in the path of the war must surely lose. I must prepare the defence of Stormhaven, and I must do it well."

The King gave him a hard stare. "It is good to see you haven't changed, my friend. Very well, you may go. I know you shall only sleep when you fall down, and nothing I can say shall change your diligence."

"Thank you, your Highness." He bowed by way of leave. "My apology for my brisk manner—I will admit to being strained, but it is a taut bow that shoots the farthest."

"And a sharp blade that cuts the quickest," answered the King. "Be sure you keep your blade sharp, Glavenor. I can't use a Swordmaster who draws a blunted blade on our foes."

Garyll left the throne room as fast as he could whilst still walking, but he couldn't outpace the echoes of King Mellar's final words. Drawing a blunted blade on Eyri's foes. It was exactly what he had to do, to keep Tabitha alive.

Revulsion at his duplicity seethed in his chest. He had to find her, if only to remind himself why he had made the pact. He could never allow her to love him, not the way he was, not ever, for he was a traitor to everything that was good and true. He didn't expect her to ever understand, and he hoped she never found out what he had sacrificed. All he wanted was to know that she would be kept from what he had endured, and to see her once more, before the end.

◆ ———————◆

When he found the Lightgifters in the Boarding, Tabitha Serannon was there, tending Sister Grace on a bed. She wasn't seated for long.

"Garyll! You're back!" she cried with delight. Her soft arms encircled him, and the warmth of her spirit penetrated his heart. He returned her embrace as strongly as he could with his one free hand, wishing he could forget what he was for only a moment, wishing he could accept her love. It was heavenly, to hold Tabitha after believing that he would never see her again.

"Sister Grace, Ashley," Garyll acknowledged the other Lightgifters over the head pressed close to his chest. Sister Grace looked too weary to talk. Ashley looked none too strong himself.

"I feared you were lost with the rest of the Sword at Ravenscroft," said Ashley.

"I almost was," Garyll replied, running a hand over Tabitha's hair. It felt good, so clean and pure beneath his fingers. He drew the purity into the great thirst of his soul. "It is not an easy place to escape from unscathed."

Tabitha pulled away slightly, her face a joy to behold, but Garyll noticed a wide bruise on her cheek. On her neck, a white orb glistened on a fine chain, all the more dramatic because of the dark neckerchief it lay upon. His relief at seeing the lone Lightstone overwhelmed him for an instant, and left a chink in his armour. Her question flew true as an arrow.

"What scars do you bear from that place?" she asked.

Garyll choked off his reply. He had forgotten the compelling honesty Tabitha wore like a robe. He had almost damned himself with his answer. He had been away from her too long, forgotten her touch. He could not lie, not now, not so close—he knew that she would know it. But there were many ways of phrasing the truth.

"I watched my comrades fall. I watched men and women tortured. That has left a heaviness upon my heart that I'll not forget."

"What happened to your hand?"

"I damaged it, just before I escaped. I had to pull it free of a shackle."

Once the lie was out, he knew it would not endure inspection. If Tabitha ever saw his ruined fingers, she would know it. The bones were shattered at impossible angles by the nails they tortured him with. The only reason it had not driven him to madness in its current state, was the deep Freeze that had been cast into the flesh before his departure from Ravenscroft. They had told him it would last two days.

"Let me heal it for you," she said. She looked suddenly forlorn. "I can't promise much though—we haven't found many sprites on the Isle."

He couldn't risk any of the questions that would come with healing. He intended another solution to that problem, and Felltang would be his only witness.

"It is a small thing, and I've had it seen to already. Save your Light for more important healing to come." Tabitha nodded, though her eyes were reluctant to leave his bandaged hand, tucked up in the sling beneath his chin. He had to get away, before she began to peel the layers of armour from his heart. He had received what he had come for.

"You have heard of the fall of the Dovecote?" asked Ashley.

Garyll nodded. "The King told me, and I came to congratulate you all on your strength, to stand up to the Dark. There are so many who haven't."

"It was mostly Tabitha," said Ashley. "We were so glad to see her here in Stormhaven, when we came back. We thought she'd been taken to Ravenscroft."

"I got away," she said. "They'll not catch me again."

He prayed that was true. Everything was worth it, if he could believe that she would be safe. "Be careful," he said. "The Dark is unscrupulous. Be very, very careful."

"I will be," she said, and stood on tiptoes to kiss his cheek. Her lips left a tingling warmth on his skin, the only warmth he had felt for days.

"They march, and the head of the Kingsbridge will be their target." Garyll released Tabitha. He bent in a brief bow. "Forgive me, I cannot stay. I must prepare the defences."

His eyes lingered on Tabitha for a long moment, then he stepped close and kissed her on the cheek. He hoped that felt even a fraction as warming as her kiss had.

He regretted having done so almost at once. He had no right to her heart. He should be gone from her.

◆ ———————◆

"He was in a hurry to leave," Sister Grace commented, her voice no more than a whisper.

"He's got a battle looming," Tabitha offered in his defence.

Sister Grace was silent for a while. "There is something ailing that man, Tabitha, something more than weariness of body. You should go to him tonight, he needs you more than he will say."

It took Tabitha a while to react to the inflection in Grace's comment. "*Go* to him? You mean in his rooms?"

"Do you love him?" Grace asked.

"Of course I do. I love him, deeply."

"Heed my words then. I have healed many men with the Light, and seen also those men who could not be healed. I know of only one hope for those with doom in their eyes. Love has powers we can only guess at."

"But you can't give your love to a man as a healing!" Tabitha objected. "As if it were a potent brew or soothing balm." It was her mother speaking now, she knew. She had been raised on conservative values. It was wrong to be with a man before the marriage bed.

Darkness surged through her blood, and roared suggestions in her ears. She fought the wild fantasies. *It's just the Darkstone. Not my thoughts. Something the Dark is doing to me.* The more she fought to ignore them, the more the dark fantasies filled her mind.

"You will lose that man to despair, and only physical love will bring you close enough to change his world now," Grace warned. "You saw how he pushed you away. He has endured more than he tells."

"How can you give such advice as a Lightgifter?"

"I do not speak as a Lightgifter now. There is much I have learned in the last few days, lessons I should have learned years before. Goodness is not something you learn, or attain by dispensing Light, it is something you feel. If you do something with goodness in your heart, then it is good. All our codes, rules, and restrictions of the Dovecote, all were used to control us, to act in ways to help the Dark, though most of us were unaware. Shamgar hid behind the shield of holiness for years. Yet his every action was with a bad heart, for his own gain, for riches through treachery. He has tainted everything the Dovecote did, and because of our Vow to him, we did not see it. Because we believed the rule. So don't think of what is right and what is wrong, according to the rules. Think of what is good, in your heart. There is only that."

Her grey eyes were penetrating. "Isn't Garyll Glavenor the most important man in the world to you?"

Tabitha bit down on her lip, and nodded. His abrupt visit had only served to re-awaken her longing for him. She had feared him lost. How could he leave her again, after announcing his return? She ached to be close to him. He had tried to shield her from the depth of his pain; she knew that some of his answers hadn't been entirely truthful. He hadn't even let her see to his wound.

Sister Grace called to her, in a fading voice. "Love should not be denied. Close your heart, and you have dark. Open, and there is light. The longer a man's heart has to grow hard, the darker it will become inside. I am sorry, I have said too much. I must rest."

Sister Grace lay back on the bed. She was almost as pale as the sheets. Her ordeal at the Dovecote had left her weaker than a babe. Her throat was still an angry purple from where the Shadowcaster had strangled her. But her advice had been filled with strength and truth.

Go to him tonight. Tabitha's pulse raced. It was an outrageous suggestion, full of risk, full of excitement. There was one question she couldn't leave unasked.

"How would this be any different from a Shadowcaster seducing one of the weak to their way?"

A ghost of a smile touched Sister Grace's lips. "You're a woman. You'll be able to tell the difference between sex and love, and it's love I'm talking about. Sex would drive him further into despair in the morning."

"What's being a woman got to do with it?" Ashley interjected, with an impish grin. He took a seat on the bed beside Grace, and set a gentle hand on her forehead. "We can be sensitive, too."

"Men have more difficulty discerning the difference," said Sister Grace, reaching up, and tweaking his ear.

"You wouldn't do too badly though," she added.

Ashley turned the colour of a fresh rose.

"For a man," Grace finished, shooting a knowing glance to Tabitha. Tabitha nearly managed to stifle the giggle.

A heady rush of romantic visions coursed through her veins.

◆ ———————— ◆

The Swordhouse was filled with an air of tense expectancy, like dry grass awaiting the flame. News of his return had run ahead of Garyll, and there he was watched, wherever he walked. When he returned their attention they saluted hastily. He strode on, cloaked in his anger.

Let them fear me now, and they will not dare to ask.

None of them had been to Ravenscroft, none of them knew what was possible with the Darkstone. All he had to do was to be the Swordmaster they had always seen. But it was not an easy act, for honesty and treachery warred within his heart like two dogs with a scrap of meat between them. The burden from Ravenscroft grew heavier with every step that he had taken away from it. Every Sword that he passed, he saw as a man whom he had betrayed. Every citizen of Stormhaven, every woman and child, even his King. All betrayed, to save the life of one.

It isn't fair, it isn't just. She should be sacrificed.

Every time he came upon that thought, the cold crawled through his chest, and gripped his heart. The smell of the torture room came sharply to his nostrils, the sound of the screams never-ending filled his ears. If he gave Tabitha to that nightmare, he knew he would fall upon his own sword. She was the only thread that kept him from the abyss. Everything else had been picked clean from his soul by the ravens. Everything else had been committed to the Dark. There was no going back. Only, forward.

His voice was harsh even to his own ears when he ordered a young Sword away from the upper corridors.

"Assemble all of the men. I shall address them in half an hour."

His quarters were as he had left them, as severe and spotless as ever. He pulled the bath tub out from the corner. He stripped, and laid each item of armour in a row upon the floor. There was water in the pail beside the tub. He began with his body, scrubbing with brush and soap until his skin was pink and raw, and his rank smell was gone. He knew he could never clean the memory of it from inside his head. His ruined hand he kept bandaged. It would have to wait. The pain within it was a monotonous roar.

He polished the breastplate until it gleamed again. The shoulder-pieces were bent, and he beat them into shape as well he could with the hilt of Felltang. The helm rolled away when he tried to clean it, so he gripped it between his knees, and rubbed until even the nosepiece shone. He set the light-mail hauberk into the sand barrel, and rolled it with his foot. It made a rhythmic grinding sound as it moved around on the floor. Some of the blood which had rusted the fine iron rings was removed.

He dressed with precision. Clean garments beneath the padded tunic, high black boots with steel tips and calf-ribs, designed for close-quarter fighting, not for riding. The armour he had cleaned was awkward to don with one hand, but he would not call for the assistance of a junior Sword to act as squire. The sling he tied tighter than before, hiding the damning Darkstone beneath the lump of white fabric which bound his left hand.

Finally he drew the ceremonial blue Swordmaster's cloak from a chest, and set it about his shoulders. The less he was Swordmaster on the inside, the more he must appear it, on the outside. He was ready.

The men were restless when he arrived in the training hall, but they soon grew as still as mice in the presence of a cat. Many had just returned, after being recalled from Fendwarrow. He had passed them there, and commended their strategy of blocking the base of the Black River pass. He would have to explain to them why he had countermanded the King's strategy of retreat. It was not a good precedent. He had to command the Sword, as was his right as Swordmaster. The men should look to no other for guidance.

"Swords of Eyri!" he greeted the three hundred men, one and all. He saluted with his right fist across his chest. Most of the Swords returned the salute immediately, a greeting of the dedicated soldier to his commander, unquestioning.

A few hesitated before the salute. It was barely noticeable, just a fraction of delay, but Garyll marked their faces. They would form the front-line, the furthest from Stormhaven. He could not afford to have those close to him uncertain of his command.

"We face an enemy who is both treacherous and deadly. You know that of the double-squadron I took to Ravenscroft, no one but I returned. The men went down fighting, and let it never be said that they were not the best of the Sword. That is a measure of our adversary. The Lightgifters stood not a chance—I saw them tortured, or killed. We have one chance against this foe, one place we know they shall have to pass. The head of the Kingsbridge is where we shall fight. We have at most a day to prepare our battle ground."

A Captain raised his fist, indicating his desire to question—Vance, a soldier with less sense than he thought he had, and with a weedy moustache to prove it. Only the Captains had the right to question the Swordmaster, and Garyll intended them to have a limited use of that privilege. He gave Vance a stern look, to let him know as much. Garyll's accepting nod was curt.

"Swordmaster, we heard that the Shadowcasters have a way of turning some to serve their purpose. How will we know if a man is turned against us?" A hush fell upon the Swords. The question was a double-edged blade. He marked Captain Vance as one of the front-line as well. There was an intense eagerness for the answer in Vance's eye, an eagerness reflected in those men who had hesitated in their earlier salute.

"You shall see them raising their blades against you, Captain. Only where the Darkmaster finds a weakness, can he work his evil."

Garyll bored into the Captain with the glare of a hawk. The silent battle of wills lasted only a moment. Vance averted his gaze, and looked all the more uncomfortable about it when he realised that he had.

Leather creaked, and someone in the ranks coughed, quietly. No one else dared to suggest Garyll Glavenor might have a weakness. It was unthinkable. Garyll intended to show them just how unthinkable it was.

He selected his special group of Swords, and set them apart in the hall.

"This is the front line, the first squadron to guard the head of the bridge," Garyll announced, "and they shall be unarmed. Let it be a test of their strength of character that they are not turned."

"But unarmed, Swordmaster!" exclaimed Vance, at the head of the group. "How can we defend the Kingsbridge, how can we defend ourselves, without our swords?"

"Do you mean to tell me, Captain, that you do not have the skill to take down an unarmed adversary? The Shadowcasters bear no weapons. Or is it that you lack the courage you were chosen for?"

"No, Swordmaster." Vance looked distraught. "But they have magic. What are we to do against that?"

"And how do you think your sword is going to defend you against magic?"

Vance opened and closed his mouth like a beached fish, and finally found a question to save himself with. "What about the Morgloth?"

"Every man shall be equipped with the whistle we devised. It is protection against the Morgloth, and it shall repel them. That is all the front line need do—repel the Morgloth, and break the Shadowcasters advance with their fists."

Mutters broke out all through the crowd, but Garyll took no special heed of it. It was to be expected that a Sword would be uncomfortable with the idea of setting his namesake aside, in the face of a deadly foe.

"Silence." Garyll said it quietly, but the effect was immediate. "I have been to their lair, I know how these Shadowcasters work their ways. There is reason to my commands. You are not gathered here to think, you are gathered to act, in defence of Eyri. I will not see the second and third squadron fall under the blades of the first, if the front line is turned to the Dark. We will break their assault with the fist, or you men shall bring little back against the loyal Swords remaining."

The faces amongst the hand-picked squadron were pale. Garyll ploughed on, before any questions could brew to the surface of Captain Vance's small mind.

"The blades will be in the second wave. Their task is to take the Morgloth down, and the Morgloth shall concentrate there when they hear that none in the second wave bear the whistles. Archers shall be in the third wave, and shall be kept to take down the Shadowcasters who escape the front line. Any man who ceases to move toward the front shall be taken by arrow as well, for that means you have been turned by the Darkmaster, and we cannot have such traitors in our midst. If you know the men at your back have drawn bows, you will fight harder away from Stormhaven, than toward it.

"There can be no retreat. I will not risk a siege of Stormhaven, for the Morgloth will devastate the city." His eyes roamed the hall, challenging every man present. There was surprise, and fear, but no defiance. Some merely nodded, with the grim acceptance of their Swordmaster's superior judgement. Their loyalty was hard to bear.

"The Shadowcasters shall attack tomorrow night, and try to gain the head of the Kingsbridge. We must build a barricade to prevent their access there, which the archers shall hold during our battle." Garyll swept his hand across the right third of the ranks. "Tonight, you shall row to Southwind to collect timber." He indicated the left third of the assembled Swords. "You shall begin the preparations, collecting the ropes, pitch, tools and supplies we shall need. Those remaining, shall form the rear-guard. Your task for now is to prepare the citizens of Stormhaven for the war, and to allocate strongholds as defence against the Morgloth."

All that remained was the order for Captain Vance's squadron. Garyll turned toward the cluster of men.

"You brave Swords of the front line had best be ready to march within the hour. I want you stationed at the head of the Kingsbridge tonight, in case I have underestimated the speed of the Shadowcasters approach. Keep signal fires burning. If they cease to burn, I shall bring what men I can to your aid at once."

Captain Vance clenched and unclenched his fists at his side. "It would be better to keep all the men inside the walls of Stormhaven. No force could breach the City Gates, and we could endure a siege for months."

Garyll would have been angered by his defiance even without the effect of the Darkstone. As it was, his blood seethed with a rage he could barely contain.

"Do you challenge my command as Swordmaster? I would be glad to accept you now, for the testing."

Garyll waited long enough for beads of sweat to form on the man's brow. Vance knew he had not the skill to win Felltang from Glavenor, let alone survive the testing before it.

560

"You only bring attention to your weakness of mind, Captain. You would leave the entire realm of Eyri open to whatever designs the Darkmaster wished to exercise, while our strength is trapped here in the city, while we are besieged for months? No! I will have no further dissent. We are at war, and I am the Swordmaster. The time for questions is over. Dismissed, Swords! Strength to your hearts!" He punched the air, and brought his fist to his chest in the Sword's salute.

"Strength to your heart," they repeated, as one, returning his salute. They couldn't know how much he needed it.

41. THE WINDING OF PASSION

"In darkness, the line of virtue
becomes a smudgéd thing."—*Zarost*

Cabal took a last look around his private chamber. He wouldn't miss it. The raised bed with the four stone posts, the floor covered with obsidian chips, the lounge pit with the deep hearth of coals in the centre—all seemed unusually plain and poorly. Nothing short of the throne would do. Nothing short of the royal rooms in the palace would replace his chambers. Conquered noblemen would serve him on their knees, and noblewomen would be his for the taking. No, he wouldn't miss Ravenscroft at all.

"Out! Out!" he shouted. The apprentice slipped from the deeper shadows, and walked straight to Cabal. He was brave, this one.

"Is it time, Master?"

Cabal ran a hand over the boy's fiery red hair.

"Yes, we shall both pay a visit to the old King. Now go!"

The apprentice skipped out of the door. Conquered noblemen indeed. Though he was only a boy, he had all the signs of arrogance and ruthlessness of the royal line, and a natural hunger for power. He had learned fast, at the Darkmaster's side.

It was only an hour short of sunset, and the Keep bustled like an ant-heap before the storm. One hour, and the great march would begin. They would be close to Fendwarrow by dawn, where the caves would hide them through the day, before the final assault on Stormhaven. He wet his lips.

All was well, except for the persistent problem of the girl. A night of dream-weaving should have claimed her, even from such a distance, but no matter how he had bent his will, no matter how he had called to her Darkstone, all through the night, she had not spoken the Devotion. It seemed that she had lost her fear of being a Shadowcaster, and without the fear, she was not as pliable as he had anticipated.

Tabitha Serannon was the one element he could not afford to have loose on the eve of his victory. She must be turned, or killed. Yet he couldn't risk the consequences of her death, not yet. He would lose his hold on the Swordmaster.

And so the solution presented itself.

If Glavenor could be made to couple with the girl, she would be easy to turn. The Devotion spell spread like an infection between Darkstones. That was why female initiates were brought to the Darkmaster's bed on their first night—when they left, they were so devoted they would do anything, if they thought it would please him. The Dark spread like a bloodstain, and no act could spread it quicker than a good rut.

Cabal chuckled. Their own love would be used against them. He cursed himself for not having seen the solution sooner. Glavenor had drawn strength from her name. She must care for him. It was poetic. The one woman who Glavenor had wanted to save, he would help to turn, and he wouldn't even know he was responsible for it. He would think her safe, in Stormhaven, at his side.

Cabal summoned motes to his hand while his shoulders shook with mirth. He spun the Seduction spell, but did not release it. Using a modified form of the Morrigán pattern, he created a messenger more suited to the task at hand, then linked the Seduction spell to its tiny body.

"First, to Glavenor. Then to Tabitha Serannon," he whispered.

The words were not needed, but they always helped to focus the mind on the target intended for the spell. The messenger would have no trouble finding them—both wore Darkstones.

The black mosquito whined away.

Blood could be relied upon to create a most compelling bond.

◆ ──────── ◆

Tabitha sat at her window in the Boarding. There were lights burning in many windows, but no one in the street. Doubtless the taverns were doing a good trade tonight, with all the fearsome news of war.

Her thoughts were of Garyll. She had had some time to cool off since her discussion with Sister Grace. She wasn't so sure it was a good idea to visit the Swordmaster. She knew the wisdom of what Grace had suggested, but she couldn't pluck up the courage to go. In truth, she was terrified. What if he rejected her, or worse, was angered by her wilfulness?

It would drive him further away, and as it was, the distance between them was tearing her heart. He hadn't called for her. Since his abrupt departure, he had given no sign that he wanted to see her at all.

A high-pitched whine passed close to her ear. It would be better to have the window closed, and keep the night pests out. Even as she hauled the sash down, she felt the bite on her arm. A small black mosquito, its proboscis deep in her skin. She slapped, and caught it before it could fly away.

"Hah! Sucker!"

There was a large smear of blood where the mosquito had been; a lot of blood for such a brief visit. Maybe it had fed on someone else before her. There was no sign of the squashed critter.

She walked to the washroom, to clean her arm. A curious sensation ran along the inside of her thighs. She reached the basins, but had to steady herself on the wall, as a shiver thrilled up her spine. With it, came the vision of Garyll Glavenor, alone in his quarters, sharpening his sword, preparing for war. He needed her, he wanted her, and their union would be glorious.

She drew a shuddering breath. She would consume all his hurt in the fire of their loving. It might be their last night together. She had been wrong to be afraid. She could feel his need for her, and her desire for him. She ran from the washroom. She had to get ready.

No matter how many times she brushed her hair, tangles remained. She despaired of the unruly brown curls. Then there were her trousers. No amount of pressing and smoothing could hide the fact that they were plain, and made for a woodsman, not a young woman. It would not do.

She had underclothes, but there was need to cover herself more modestly than that. One did not go to a loved man in a grubby ghost's robe either, she was sure. Borrowing? The only woman she knew well enough in Stormhaven was Maybelle Westerbrook, and she laughed out loud when she contemplated how alluring she would look in a dress borrowed from the stout Lady of Ceremony. May would disapprove, at any rate, and she couldn't risk her finding out. Through all these thoughts, was the pounding excitement of anticipation.

She counted out her small reserve of coins. After the theft in the Dovecote, she had been left with one gold, and little else. The gold had long since been broken into its exchange of thirteen silvers, and less than half remained. When she had carried the full weight of her inheritance of coins, she had been scared of not using the wealth wisely. Now she owned a fraction, and the need for wisdom was even more pressing.

She knew she didn't *need* new clothes. She *wanted* new clothes.

But in a few days it might not matter at all what she had done with her wealth. Considering the man, the extravagance would be worth it.

Garyll.

Just the whisper of his name decided the matter. She hastened to the cutters shop in the merchants quarter.

◆ ─────── ◆

The front door was closed when she reached it, but when she called out to the windows above the street, a sharp-eyed woman poked her head above the sill almost at once.

"We're closed, luvvy. What're you looking for?"

"A good-looking dress, ma'am."

"Humph! If I open, you understand there'll be a premium on my prices, for being so late and all."

Tabitha nodded. She suspected the dress-maker would squeeze her purse for all it was worth, but her need was greater than her reason, and she knew it. She hoped the dress-maker didn't recognise the flush of excitement in her cheeks, at that distance.

Five silvers, I'll not spend more than five.

The upstairs window closed, and soon enough, the front door was pulled just wide enough for Tabitha to slip in. The dressmaker was a little woman, too broad to be called shapely, yet dressed in a sheer, green gown whose fine tailoring created the impression that she was both tall and elegant. She closed and bolted the door behind Tabitha.

"Can't be too careful now, what with the talk of war coming. Why, the Swords came through earlier, warning us to keep the windows and doors barred against Morgloth. There've been all sorts of girls in here, buying dresses, hoping to make a catch in the last hour before our doom. Silly people, there's not been a war in Eyri for five hundred years. It's all rumours, spread by those unwholesome folk from Fendwarrow, and not a few of the Swords are involved in that, I'm sure."

She winked knowingly, then, perhaps realising she might be talking her customer out of buying a dress rather than fattening her own purse, changed her direction in mid-stride. "But what do I know of wars? We may all be fighting the Shadowcasters in the streets come Saturday. I always say you've got to take your opportunities while they are there. I know just the kind of dress you'll be wanting. Just the thing." She waved Tabitha into a dim interior, full of soft fabrics and fine garments.

The dress-maker fitted Tabitha into the most shapely, expensive and revealing velvet dress of deep red she had ever seen. When she was guided to stand before the candle-lit mirror, Tabitha gasped, and caught the dressmaker's knowing smile in the corner of the mirror. She looked ravishing, even without the added effect of the strategic lighting and subtle hint of soft incense.

"Hhh—how much is it?" Tabitha asked, her voice unsteady.

"Eight silvers, and fifteen," the dressmaker replied. "You deserve to wear something like this, you look beautiful in it."

"Really?" Tabitha asked, feeling both thrilled, and tearful. "Oh but I can't afford that! I haven't got near enough."

The dressmaker came closer, and held a brazier of candles to the side, an angle which served to outline Tabitha's breasts with deep shadows, and caress her legs to a golden brown. There was a good portion of leg, before the firm line of the hem.

"How much do you have?"

"Five silvers, maybe twenty blackmetals."

The candles flickered and burned. The incense trailed delicately through the air. The dressmaker was close, her voice soothing.

"Do you have any special skills, apart from Gifting?"

Tabitha nodded, staring at her reflection. "I can sing. I was a tavern-singer in First Light. Yzell the instrument-maker said I could sing with him, should I need to."

The dress-maker seemed delighted. "Such work would earn you a good wage. I can see you really want it, and the dress was made for you. It would be a shame to see it on any other woman, for she would never be as alluring. I will let you pay it off as you earn the coin, though it will cost you ten silvers that way."

Ten! It would take her weeks of work to make up the shortfall. Maybe there was hope to get the stolen money returned, now that Garyll was back. Maybe money wouldn't matter at all, when the Dark fell upon Stormhaven. She gazed at her reflection.

"Come, let us remove this scrap of a scarf," said the dressmaker, "and see how you look in your new dress."

"No!" Tabitha's hand shot to her throat, restraining the dressmaker's pull on the loosed knot.

"Forgive me, my beauty, I didn't mean to alarm you. It is a nice enough scarf. A fine scarf."

Tabitha's looked forlornly at her reflection. Now that the offending neckerchief had been identified, it stood out like mud on a jewelled necklace. Yet without it, her Darkstone would be revealed beside the Lightstone, for all to see.

"You wouldn't happen to have a more slender scarf, in red, perhaps?"

The dressmaker smiled. She had just the thing. It was expensive, though.

◆ ——————◆

Only in the privacy of her bedroom in the Boarding did she undo the offensive neckerchief. The Darkstone fell free of its restraint, and pressed cold against her throat. The Lightstone looked out of place beside it, so she slid the white orb around to the back of her neck, and tucked it underneath her hair.

The dress had lost none of its appeal. Even the inside of the velvet fabric was soft, touching her skin with sensuous weave. It made her want to run her hands down her body, to feel the smoothness of the contours. The Darkstone added its own allure to her reflection, its hard, cold surface only made her realise how soft and warm she was.

She stroked the Darkstone absently. It whispered to her, in an intimate, companionable way—a far cry from the relentless pestering of the night before. Maybe the Darkmaster had finally realised she was not going to take the Devotion, no matter what he did.

She hid the Darkstone beneath the red silk scarf.

"Goodnight, Matron," she called through the open door, pretending to turn in for the night.

A voice answered from some distance within the Boarding.

She blew out the single candle. She descended the stairs in silence, and slipped through the shadows to the front door and the street beyond. A heady urgency thudded through her veins.

The cold night air was welcome, touching her in delicate caress.

Garyll Glavenor had quarters high in the Swordhouse. The various Swords who directed her there were extremely reluctant, but Tabitha's insistence that Garyll had invited her made them unsure. Her dress was effective. Even the most dour of the escorts feigned a faltered step to gain a better view along the way.

At last she was shown to a solid oak door at the end of a top-floor passage. "He'll be none too happy if you have no appointment," the escort warned. "I'll not be around to receive his displeasure—you just come on down to the front door, you know the way."

With those words, the Sword left her, as fast as he could.

She straightened her dress and hair, and raised her hand to knock on the door. She hesitated, then she rapped once on the hard wood.

There was no answer for a long time, and she was about to knock again, when the door was wrenched open, sucking the air from the corridor past her legs. She stood frozen before him.

Garyll was still dressed in armour. His breastplate reflected the light of the hall-brand. His helm shone from under his arm. Even his high black boots gleamed.

Tabitha's alluring dress offered her no defence. Garyll bristled with hard steel. He was bigger than she remembered him, the set of his jaw harder. The only softness about him was the sling, which held his left arm against his chest.

He said nothing, but at last he stepped back to allow her in, and closed the door behind her. The room was simply furnished. A fire burned in the hearth. Garyll's sword, Felltang, lay upon the near edge of the hearth, the blade red-hot for half its length.

"I didn't think you were allowed from the Boarding so late," he said. He would not meet her eye, he preferred a point somewhere above her head.

"Nobody knows I'm gone," she answered, regaining a little of her boldness. Her legs had steadied, at least, but she still felt small. "I can leave if you don't wish me to stay."

"No!" Garyll's eyes found hers. There was depth of pain to them. For just an instant, she saw the man beneath the steel.

"You may stay, if you wish," he said.

He motioned her toward the wide couch, but he chose the hard-backed chair opposite her for himself. Fear and doubt thudded in Tabitha's chest again. She couldn't force herself on him, she had to seduce him.

She didn't know where to start—most of her nights in the Tooth-and-Tale had been spent learning how to fend men off, not to entice them. There followed a most awkward silence, while Tabitha blushed furiously. Garyll watched the flames flickering in the hearth, and the slowly cooling blade.

Tabitha tried to cross her legs in such a way that didn't reveal so much of her thighs, but the slinky dress had a way of creeping upwards. There was nothing to say, every topic she could think of seemed lame and girlish before Garyll's blunt silence. Finally she could bear it no longer.

"So how goes the preparation for the battle?"

He answered her quickly, as if he too had been waiting to escape the impasse. "As well as can be expected for such short notice. Some of the timber has already returned from Southwind, and is being iron-bound at the forge. We shall have a firm barricade to protect the Kingsbridge tomorrow. The Swords shall be well-placed for the battle which is to come."

Tabitha smiled. She did not really want to talk of the war, but it was good to hear his deep, resonant voice. She didn't care what he said, so long as he talked to her, kept his eyes on her, and not on the blade beside the fire. She was grateful that he spoke before the silence could be repeated.

"How goes the recovery of the Lightgifters?"

"Sister Grace will find her strength, in time. There is little we can do, without Light essence. The sprites that answer our summoning calls are fewer every time. Soon we won't even be able to raise a Courier with what meagre Light there is."

"Why do you hide your Gifter's orb now?" His eyes were on the red silk at her throat. She cringed, and tried to control her panic. He took the bulge in her scarf to be the Lightstone. With the way she had dressed, the Gifter's orb was hiding under her hair. The stone at her throat was one he must not see.

"I—wish to keep it hidden." Tabitha's mind spun. It would be the end of her chances, if he saw the Darkstone. He would reject her, as would everyone. She would be branded a Shadowcaster, regardless of what she said in her defence.

"I am scared to be a target for any traitors who find their way into Stormhaven."

"And what kind of traitors would those be?"

"Ones who serve the Dark," she answered, without thinking.

"The ones who bear the other kind of orb?" he asked rhetorically.

She nodded, aghast at what she had actually said. He must never find out.

"I see." He braced himself on his chair, as if accepting a great burden. He stood, abruptly. "Forgive me, Tabitha. I have many duties tonight, with the approach of the Dark. I forgot myself for a while. Please excuse me."

She wished he would take off his armour. The loneliness in his eyes had deepened. Her need for him pulsed through her veins. She couldn't let him banish her from his rooms, not now, not when he was so close. When he offered her his hand, to lift her from her seat, she took his fingers to her lips instead.

He froze, but he did not pull away.

"Why do you live so alone?" she asked. She kissed his palm.

He jerked his hand away. "I have never found reason not to be –"

It was a slap across the face for Tabitha. She had been too daring. She could feel the tears rising to her eyes.

"- until you," he whispered, as if not meaning to admit it.

The world turned around that moment.

He stepped close, and lifted her from the chair, his powerful arm around her. He hugged her close, lifting his sling over her shoulder to do so. His breastplate was cold against her cheek, but Tabitha didn't care. It felt so good to be held. He kissed her forehead, then spoke over her head, to the room behind her.

"I wish I could love you as I should."

"Why can you not love me?"

He pulled away, just enough for her to watch his lips when he spoke.

"I am a cold stone in the shadows, you are the flower in the sunlight. There is no place in your world of beauty for one as harsh as me."

The fire's glow played over his strong jaw. His eyes were dark. He smelled of clean strength. He smelled like a man.

"What if I say there is place, what if I want you in my world?"

She could get nearer to him if she stood astride his leg. She moved in close. She wasn't sure if it was his body, or hers, that was quivering.

"I am a rough man," said Garyll, a catch in his voice, "I know only the life of the Sword. I can offer nothing to you."

"Maybe I want to give you something, and not take something from you."

"I have many burdens. There are things I don't wish to expose you to."

"Would you share them with a lover?"

Some of the earlier discipline returned to his features.

"No, Tabitha." He seemed to force the words out. His hand caressed her hair, then her ear. "Maybe with my wife, but I would not take one now." He closed his eyes, as if to hide some inner turmoil.

"If you were not the Swordmaster, would you love me?"

He smiled, a wry, sad smile. He kissed her cheek. His breath was warm.

"I love you, even as the Swordmaster," he whispered. "I shall always love you, but because of my position, I dare not act on that love. I dare not."

Desire raged through her. She knew what she wanted, she knew what he wanted, he just wouldn't allow the passion to rule him. He had been inside his armour for too long. She knew how she could push him over the edge. She would not lose the man she loved to a misguided sense of duty. Loving her would not compromise his duty to the King, she would never let that happen. She held him close again, close enough that he was looking over her head and could not see how she summoned the motes behind his back.

She whispered the words of the Seduction, so quietly he couldn't possibly hear. She had seen the pattern used by Gabrielle, when she had snared Ashley in the Dovecote. She had not forgotten one curve of it. The Dark essence touched his back, the motes were absorbed by his body.

Garyll stiffened in her arms. She stood on tip-toe, and kissed his cheek. Strangely enough, he grabbed at his own throat, where his bandaged hand was held high in the sling. Now was no time for him to be thinking of his wounds. She would take his mind from all of that. She reached for the back of his head, ran her fingers through his hair.

"Tabitha, what are you doing?" His voice was husky, his eyes never left her face. He did not pull away.

"Daring to act on love. You deserve to be loved."

She pulled his head down to her, and kissed him on the mouth. His lips were full and warm. In that moment, the spell she had cast exploded into a raging tempest of lust within her as well. She felt his tongue on hers. She knew Garyll felt the ecstasy of it himself, for his back arched, and he lifted her clear of the floor with his arm suddenly around her waist, holding her close. The power of attraction overwhelmed them both.

Suddenly, there was another presence in the room, an almost-familiar voice, a faint touch against her intuition that begged to be answered, and yet urged her to kiss Garyll harder. She tried to clear her thoughts by drawing on the Ring, but it was a half-hearted attempt. She wanted to ignore the warning, to abandon herself to the tight web of hunger which gripped Garyll to her, but something, somewhere, was wrong.

The whisper of the Darkmaster had returned in her stone.

Her dress fell from her shoulders, exposing her breasts. Her breath came in short gasps, her heart beat in a wild tumble.

It should not be like this.

She had cast a spell on Garyll, and it was devastating. The Darkmaster was calling to her, whispering at the edge of hearing.

Garyll lifted her on his knee against the wall. His tongue explored her throat, his hand searched her breasts. His touch was fierce, insanely erotic. There was something in his eyes, a hunger within that would never be sated, not by her body alone.

The Dark would tear their love to shreds.

"Stop. Stop!" she cried. "This is wrong."

Garyll threw her onto the couch. He unbuckled his breast-plate in a frenzy, and cast it aside. His chest heaved inside his padded tunic. She was defenceless against his strength, he was defenceless against her spell. His free hand found her naked breasts again.

She knew then, with certainty, what had been done. The Ring showed her the truth, she only had to look. She had been seduced, herself; tricked into using the Dark. There was Dark in her blood, and dark in her mind. The Darkmaster was whispering a mantra, one she had to only say once, to consummate the spell of the Devotion.

"This is the way the Shadowcasters would do it," she cried.

Garyll froze. The fire crackled in the hearth, the light flickered.

"This is the way the Dark would do it," she repeated, in a whisper.

Garyll's face fell. He stumbled backward. The full shock hit Tabitha with all the force of a charging bull. She choked upon her first cry, and fled the rooms of the Swordmaster of Eyri, drawing her dress up as she ran. She heard Garyll fall to his knees behind her.

She was through the doors and beyond before the flood of tears caught her. Panic swept her through the worn stone corridors of the Swordhouse. No matter how fast she ran, she could not escape the burden of the Darkstone, or the way it struck against her heart with every step.

◆ —————— ◆

Garyll's room filled with silence. He remained on his knees. He wanted to jump up, to scream and tear something apart, break furniture with his fists. But it was more of a torture to remain still, to allow himself no vent to the rage within. And so he sat.

He rose, at last, to close the door. When he reached for the latch, his hand shook. It was a peculiar affliction. He closed the door softly.

The deep coals were red in the hearth, but Felltang had cooled to its former silver. He thrust the blade deep into the fire, and sat on his haunches. The heat only warmed the surface of his skin. He doubted he would be warmed even if he threw himself into the coals. His darkness was absolute. He had proved that beyond doubt, upon the pure innocence of Tabitha Serannon. A more final step into damnation he could not imagine. He had ravaged his own love.

He worked the knot of his sling free, and threw the fabric into the hearth in his place. It flared to flame, and burned away. The ligaments in his elbow protested at bearing the weight of his arm, but that was a minor call when compared to the return of blood to his lowered left hand. The ruined fingers each had a unique scream.

Garyll kept his hand low, at his side.

He wrenched the bandage clear, exposing the horror of shattered digits, the reminder of the tortures he had passed, and the consequences of defying the Darkmaster. He had hoped, once, that the twisted flesh could be healed, that he could be restored. He knew at last that there could be no forgiveness, no healing, for what he had become.

Where before, the path ahead had been clouded by his hope, it was now clear. He would guarantee Tabitha's safety during the invasion by following the terms of his pact to the letter, and then, when he was beside the Darkmaster on his new throne, he would end first Cabal's life, and then his own. It was the only way to be sure Tabitha Serannon would be left alone.

There was never going to be a repeat of the crime committed in his chambers, before the witness of Felltang.

The blade was hot enough—he drew it from the fire. He set his left hand on the edge of the hearth. The sword shrieked with its unique note, and cut clean into the stone. His past was severed, and with it, the hope of any future. The stump of his wrist was cauterised on the blade. A vile smoke issued briefly from the end, and left an unwholesome smell in the air. Felltang was streaked with black. Garyll endured the spasms with clenched teeth.

He allowed himself no time to contemplate what burned in the coals. He retrieved the work of the armourer, where it was placed beside the hearth. Four curved blades were worked like claws into the end of a long steel gauntlet. It gripped tightly to his arm, and he rammed the blades into the stone to force his stump all the way to the stop inside. He tied the leather binding as tight as he could. The armourer had made good work of the savage blades—they were thick and strong. And sharp.

Garyll grunted in satisfaction. There was one purpose to any weapon, one purpose alone—to bring death to one's foes. He could only hope to get close enough by becoming a trusted servant. The Darkmaster would taste his clawed hand in the end.

42. BURDENS AND BARDSONG
"None so torn, as lovers, apart."—*Zarost*

Tabitha woke on a wet pillow.

Tap. Tap-tap, it came again, like a fingernail knocking on glass. It was an insistent, small sound. Her curtains were drawn, but the pale dawn light crept around the edges.

Then the weight of the world fell upon her. The memory of the night before was thick with the taint of the Dark. Tabitha found the Ring, drew in the clarity which had saved her from ruin. She had been a Shadowcaster, for a while.

Garyll! Oh, Garyll, what have I done?

She donned her simple grey robe with shaking hands. She approached the window, and pulled the curtains wide. A sudden explosion of feathers against the glass left her gasping for breath. A glossy bird beat its wings, then fell to perch on the windowsill once more. She covered her face with her hands as her heartbeat resumed.

A Morrigán. The Master calls.

The Dark was insistent, ever-present.

"Go away!" she cried at the harbinger. "Go away! Just leave me alone!"

The bird flapped out over the street, but circled, and returned to its perch. Nausea crept into her stomach. The Master was watching her. The Dark would soon be in Stormhaven.

Eyri's hope rested on the shoulders of one man, and she had burdened him with a terrible thing. She had stopped him with unfair words. She had accused him of acting like a Shadowcaster, when it had been she who had cast the spell of Seduction. The dishonesty demanded to be set aright.

The Morrigán cocked its head, tapped its beak on the window.

She had to be honest with Garyll, let him know what hung at her neck, and what she had done to him. She had to know if there was a chance that he could ever forgive her. She had to know if the passionate words he had spoken were true, or forced from his lips by the seductive grip of the Dark she had inflicted upon him.

The longer you left a lie, the more damage it did. She had learned that much, as Truthsayer.

She closed the curtains.

He had said that he loved her. She hoped that was still true.

Tabitha made her way down into the street, and set off for the Swordhouse. The Morrigán swooped low over her, but had to find a perch again, for the one who received a messenger commanded its delivery. She did not intend to offer the raven so much as a glance. Yet she was aware of it, lurching from rooftop to road to rooftop, calling out its croaking frustrations.

She was directed to the practice hall of the Sword, but when she reached it, a Captain blocked her access.

"He's not likely to want visitors this morning, Miss Serannon."

She couldn't stop her lip from trembling. Rejection. She should have expected it. She bit down on her rising tears, and hoped against hope. She had to know.

"I just need a word with him, sir. A minute is all."

The Captain measured her with a foreboding gaze. She hoped that her tears weren't showing.

"All right," he finally said, "it might be what he needs. But if he refuses, you'll leave at once."

The Captain ushered her into the practice hall of the Swordhouse. The clang of steel and the harsh grunts of men in mock-battle filled the hall, though only a few combatants sparred. Most of the men were crowded at the far end of the hall, where a weaving swordsman was stripped to the waist.

His lean body was covered in sweat, and not a little blood. He worked his great blade with furious power against a many-armed mannequin, a contraption which rotated with every blow struck against it, causing it to swing its deadly-looking weapons at its assailant. The swordsman wore a savage gauntlet with blades on his left hand, which he used as often as the sword, though not as swiftly. He ducked to avoid a flail, revealing his face for an instant. Garyll. His body was so much thinner than she had expected; lean, wiry. He had been scraped to the bone by his time in Ravenscroft.

"What is he doing?" Tabitha whispered.

The Captain's voice was gruff. "That is the Dumbfist. It's made of stonewood. Nobody stands against it for more than a few minutes. No one has ever caused it damage."

She followed the Sword's gaze. Chips of stonewood exploded from the mannequin. Already its head seemed to have been crushed, and a severed mechanical arm lay amongst the circle of dust and debris beneath Garyll's boots.

"He's been at it for over an hour, my Lady. I've never seen anything like it. We have tried to calm his rage, but –" He looked away. "We're afraid to, my lady. He has the battle fury upon him. We need his reason in this war, not madness! He is our Swordmaster."

"I—I should go," she stammered. Her reasons for wanting to see Garyll seemed suddenly foolish, in the face of his power. He would not forgive her. His rage infused the hall.

"No, it may break his fugue. Sit here." He indicated a plain wooden bench against the wall.

Dread filled her as the knot of men parted to allow the Captain through. He leant in toward the sphere of destruction which whirled around the Swordmaster. Garyll continued in an unbroken rhythm, though the Captain must have spoken to him. Tabitha watched in mute shock, feeling the renewed rage tear through the hall. Chips of stone flew from the Dumbfist. A severed part crashed to the floor. The Dumbfist whirled.

The Captain bent in toward Garyll once more, and Tabitha could see his lips move, though the words were lost in the harsh ring of steel. All other movement ceased, the men stood with weapons laid aside as the tension gathered and focused on Garyll.

The Dumbfist became a blur. The raw strength of the blows which Garyll delivered boomed through the hall. Within seconds, the Dumbfist had lost all of its remaining limbs. It spun naked and crippled before the onslaught. Garyll's blade shrieked, and he roared. The Dumbfist exploded as the final terrifying blow struck home.

Tabitha trembled. It felt as if she had been assaulted directly by the deathblow. The hardened veterans and strong recruits in the hall looked just as stunned.

At last Garyll turned on his knee. He was bleeding from many cuts, and his chest heaved. At his throat, a studded collar was buckled tight over multiple wounds, flesh torn as if a cat had raked his neck. The world disappeared around Tabitha, there was only Garyll's face, and the deep pools of his eyes in which malignant creatures swam. He looked away, and stood, his back straight. The men retreated from his path. He strode toward the exit, then he was gone.

Someone whistled as they let out their breath.

The prospect of meeting his rage head-on was terrifying, but the Ring warmed on her finger when she considered Glavenor, and she knew that she couldn't abandon the path to truth. Her legs wouldn't support her weight though, and she sat down abruptly upon standing.

Take it as rejection, girl. He doesn't want a woman like you.

She would not believe it. She had to find him. At least to apologise, if nothing else. This time her legs retained a semblance of stability.

She worked her way through the dispersing men. She had almost reached the exit when an iron grip stopped her in her tracks. Captain Steed, the veteran of First Light, wore a look of concerned determination.

"No, Miss Serannon, I'll not be letting you go after him. He is a dangerous man today, more so than ever before."

Her will was set. She was going to the Swordmaster. She took a gamble.

"Captain Steed, how delightful to see you. Don't I get a greeting any more?" She curtsied, smiled her broadest smile, and offered him her right hand, because he had not released the left. If he was half the gentleman she knew him to be, he would kiss her fingers.

Captain Steed looked mildly abashed, or amused. He raised her hand to his lips. When they touched the Ring, his eyes rolled back in their sockets. He sank to the floor like a felled ox.

She gave a little theatrical scream, to bring the men running. They soon huddled around the unconscious Captain. A Sword bent to check his pulse, and nodded.

"His heart is strong, and he's breathing. The blight must have struck his mind. What happened?"

"I was—just talking to him, then he fell. He was Captain in my village. I've seen this happen to him before. He just needs some water." She backed away from the knot of men. "I'll get some."

She ran for the exit, hoping there was indeed water in that direction. No one called out after her, so she supposed her ruse would hold.

She drew on the Ring to refine her sight, and used the skill she had learned of in the Dovecote. She became aware of the faint traces of feet which had passed through the corridor, the ghostly footprints of recent traffic. If she kept her attention vague, the most fresh of those prints stood out. Big prints with an angry stride. Garyll's tread led her through the corridors of the Swordhouse to a staircase.

She slowed in the ascent, taking care not to scrape her boots against stone. She emerged to the battlement, where the palisade curved away along the eastern walls of Stormhaven. It was bitterly cold, yet no wind blew.

A lone figure stood with his back to her, his upper torso naked, his trousers sweat-stained. Garyll spoke before she had reached him, even though she had made no sound.

"Get as far away from me as you can."

The distance in his voice drove the tears into her eyes before she could resist them. The precipice loomed before her.

"Garyll, I am sorry, I didn't mean—"

"Last night proved how different we are. I am not the kind of man you need. I am the worst man for you to love."

She laid a hand on his shoulder. He brushed it away gently, and yet an ache passed through her fingers and up her arm.

"Garyll! Look at me. Tell me that your words were true. I know I did wrong, but was it true that you love me?" She managed to push her way between his body and the outer rampart, forcing him to face her.

Only then did she realise that there was fresh blood running from a wound in his neck, where his skin was torn in scrapes around the studded collar. The savage gauntlet which had made those marks was terrifying, up close, not because of the curved blades, but because there didn't seem to be any place within it for Garyll's left hand.

"You did no wrong," he said, in an empty voice. "It was I who ravaged a Lightgifter last night. I am no man for you, for anyone."

"Garyll, I am not ravaged. I am sorry for what I did. I still love you."

He turned aside as if struck across the face.

"Tabitha, go."

"No! Garyll, you must let me explain." Honesty compelled her forward, despite her fear. As the Swordmaster, he might choose to imprison her as a traitor.

She could not live the lie any longer. She drew her scarf away. Both orbs were free at her neck. "I bear the Darkstone, as well as the Light. I used the Dark to seduce you. It is I who was at fault last night."

Garyll just stared at her, struck as mute as stone.

"Which is stronger in you?" he whispered, at length. "The Dark, or the Light?"

"The Light," she answered, too quickly. "I can use both. I am sworn to neither. The Dark—plagues me, but I can resist its call. Most of the time."

"Then there is more reason than ever for you to stay away from me."

He could not accept her with the Darkstone on her throat. After what he must have gone through, she couldn't blame him. The Dark was the enemy.

"Garyll, forgive me," she pleaded, her voice catching in her throat. "I didn't mean to use the Dark on you. I promise I'll never do it again."

"No! There is nothing to forgive." Though he was close enough to touch, he seemed far away. "I wish to protect you. That is why you must go."

"Let me help you fight the battle against the Darkmaster."

"It is too late for that now."

"I am not ruled by this Dark stone! It does not control me!"

"Go, Tabitha!"

"Garyll, please don't shut me out. I want to fight on your side. I love you."

"And I cannot love you. I can never love you. Find another."

Those words were too powerful to bear. Her heart shattered against the cold, hard stone of Garyll's glare. The palisade tipped underfoot, the world spun. She turned away from Garyll, to hide her face. She could have fallen, yet she didn't care where she ran, so long as it was away.

She found the stairs.

She was not challenged on her way out of the Swordhouse, but when she reached the street, a hoarse cry announced the return of the raven. Its threat was insignificant, beside the deadly pain of what she ran from. Yet both followed her.

A long time later, she found her way into the garden of the Leaf of Merrick. How long she had stumbled through the streets of Stormhaven, she couldn't remember. Only that she had needed refuge from the staring citizens. But from one presence she could find no escape.

The Morrigán waited, in the tallest tree of her grove.

◆ ———— ◆

Tabitha cried dry tears. She lay on her stomach. The world was cold beneath a leaden sky, the sun's pale disc was hidden somewhere overhead. The Amberlake was a curve of rust-coloured liquid beyond the city walls. A gathering wind from the east sighed through the trees nearby. A poorly, dark grass grew beneath her. It seemed there was not going to be a summer in Eyri at all, this year.

She did not care. Eyri did not matter. She did not matter.

Garyll loved her no more. At least during the night, she had been able to cry herself to sleep.

There was no refuge from this daytime misery.

She had driven him away, because she had used the Dark.

What was worse, was knowing that the Dark was part of her. She could resist its effect, but she could not remove it. The Dark was strong, and hour by hour, the Darkmaster's presence seemed to grow, his pull grew stronger, even though she hated it. It could not be much longer before his army marched upon them. Maybe that night.

If the Swords lost the battle, she would lose Garyll. If the Swords won, she would still lose him, because of the Darkstone she wore. She might as well accept the Darkmaster, take his damned Devotion. Violence, evil, mourning, loss—her life was an endless trail of woe, because she resisted the Darkmaster's will, because she fought. There was no light left in the world. There was no way out, but to accept the Dark.

She waited for the end to come.

It came too slowly.

Birdsong broke the silence with careless disregard for Tabitha's mood. It was a small chirruping sound, joyous, bright, and alive, not the ugly call of the Morrigán.

What did it matter? She didn't care. Her thoughts sank and darkened, with the great inertia of despair.

The bird sang again. It was an unfamiliar call. Like a nightingale or a starling, it was endlessly inventive. She searched the grove half-heartedly. The bird moved before she could find it. It repeated its tune elsewhere. Then again, close by. It slipped from one tree to another as if by magic, for it never exposed itself.

Tabitha rose and brushed the dirt from her robe. Something about the birdsong was intriguing. She shouldn't care what it was, but finding the bird gave her something to do while she waited for the end.

She walked to where she had heard the last call. When she peered around the bole of the tree, chirruping erupted from behind her. She retraced her steps on tiptoe. The bird chose another tree. She chased, careful to avoid the sticks and leaves on the grass. The bird flew on, unseen. She raced toward its call. There was nothing there. When she halted, breathless, it called from the tree where the whole pantomime had begun. Tabitha suspected the bird's intelligence was sharper than its song.

She grudgingly drew on the Ring to augment her awareness. If the bird was never where she looked for it, maybe her ears were at fault. The call came again, and she spun on her heels, away from the sound.

The bird emerged from the trees, running hunched over. It was as tall as Tabitha, and wearing a patchwork cloak. Its bald head bobbed as it ran on light feet towards a new location in the grove. The grin it wore stretched wide across white teeth. The figure froze in mid-stride when he spotted her watching him. Tsoraz, the Bard.

"Do you take me completely for a fool, sir?" she challenged.

Tsoraz erupted into laughter. It was a familiar laugh. The sense of humour was familiar too. The art of the Riddler certainly ran strong in that family.

Damn him and his games.

"I refuse to be cheered up! My life is in no state for laughter."

Tsoraz came close. He bowed respectfully. "Your advisor apologises for his absence. I wasted my time searching in Levin, when in fact you were here."

"You searched for me? You abandoned me, in the Dovecote."

Tsoraz raised his hands, as if to fend off Tabitha's glare. "So quickly you forget that I slapped the Rector with my staff. Quite hard, too. I could do no more, without ruining the balance around you. I must not protect you from your rivals."

"Balance? There is no balance around me. You can see for yourself. It is all dark," she said, waving her hand at the bleak day.

"All Dark? Then it seems I need to sing you another song."

"If it's 'where does the river end?' I'll stuff that coloured cloak down your throat," she snapped.

Damn him if he isn't making me feel better.

She turned her face to hide the hint of a smile, and yet she desperately needed to smile. The day was too dark to endure without a spark of light. She had been close to ending it all, too close. She drew heavily on the bard's goodwill.

I wanted to bow to the Darkmaster? What was I thinking?

Tsoraz's voice filled the glade, his notes vibrated in the leaves overhead. He sang a beautiful song, in a strange language. The words sounded musical in themselves, in the way a chuckling brook holds a tune of the high mountain peaks, and a bird speaks of spring. The music was reminiscent of the Lifesong stanzas she knew. The Ring warmed on her finger, and she watched the way the air shimmered around Tsoraz, like clear essence. It was a trick of the diffused sunlight, she was sure. Tsoraz looked so familiar as he sang. Tabitha could well imagine that with the passage of many years, the bard would grow to look just like his father, the Riddler.

Then he began the stanza again, using words she could understand.

The heart that loved shall be broken,
the heart that is broken shall sing,
the old man who smiles, has wept long ago;
the Winter shall melt into Spring.
All things must have their own balance,
all balance is made from these things,
for we live in the centre of circles,
where the ending's end begins.
We shall live in the centre of circles,
when the true Lifesinger sings.

The last note of the bard's song lingered in the grove, and was drawn softly away amongst the trees. She spoke quickly against the return of silence.

"Where does that come from? Where did you learn that?"

Tsoraz had a distant gaze, and he took his time before answering, "My sister Syonya."

"Where is she? Is she the wizard?"

"O no! Not a wizard, they didn't let her get that far. No, she is dead now, died a long long time ago." A shadow passed across his face, and for a moment he looked inconsolably sad, but when he looked up again his eyes were bright. "She sang like you, she sang anew. I can only remember what has been sung in my time, but you can hear Ethea!"

He was right, she had been foolish to think her life was only dark. Even if the Darkmaster won, she still had the Lifesong, and it had the power to heal all the pain, to take her away, to create life afresh. She remembered the butterfly she had made, and all its rainbow colours. Twardy's butterfly, though it had followed Tsoraz.

"Why were you so angry when the Rector killed my butterfly?"

Tsoraz sat down on the grass beside her. "I must be losing my art, if a young woman has been waiting for nothing but for my song to end, to drown me in questions."

"Oh. I'm sorry, Tsoraz. I'm really sorry, your song was beautiful. It was beautiful, thank you. I didn't mean—I—"

"Your butterfly was beautiful, too," he said. "Beauty is a rare thing."

They were both silent for a time.

"You saw the shattering of the Source?" Tabitha asked.

"Saw it? Heard it as well. Very wise, to thwart their plans so. The less Dark essence there is in Eyri, the greater chance you have of surviving this war."

"You think we have a chance of beating the Darkmaster?"

"Only if you find the wizard in time."

She rotated her Ring absently. The wizard's Ring. She still wasn't sure where to look, or what she was looking for.

"What is a wizard?" she asked.

He barked with quick laughter. "I've never been too sure myself," he replied, "but I know there may be someone in Eyri who has been called by that name."

He knew who the wizard was! Tabitha tried to interrupt, but Tsoraz continued with his answer. "From what I've heard, wizards keep themselves well-hidden. You would have to discover the wizard yourself, to enlist the wizard's aid."

"Where is the wizard, Tsoraz, where do I look?"

"Point in any direction, and you shall point three times at the wizard."

As obtuse as ever—Tabitha could make no sense of the riddled answer.

"If you stood where I did, which way would you walk?"

"I would sit down!" Tsoraz exclaimed, grinning like a madcap.

Tabitha gritted her teeth. She had been spared the frustrations of riddling for some days.

"Are you saying I have the means to find the wizard right here?"

"That depends on how you look."

When Tabitha just looked at him blankly, Tsoraz said, "Zarost left you this note. He said it was a clue, to be used if you were at wit's end."

Tsoraz handed her a scrap of paper, which bore a few words scribbled in black ink.

Use your gift. ZAROST.

When she shot a questioning glance at Tsoraz, his eyebrows danced a jig, but he said nothing. Tabitha remembered that he had offered similar advice, at their first meeting. At the time, she had taken his words to mean her gift for singing. There was another meaning she had not considered. The Riddler had given her a gift once, in the boathouse in Southwind. She had used it once or twice, but it had lived in the pocket of her grey robe ever since. Her searching fingers found the little circular mirror, and she drew it out.

"You haven't used it much, have you?" Tsoraz asked.

"I'm not one to pamper."

"Then you are different from Zarost's idea of most women!" He laughed. "It explains why you have not questioned the riddle, why you have not recognised the changes in the Mirror of Self-Reflection. You should use it now."

She traced her fingers over the delicate script carved in the wooden backing. *See thyself as thyself see.* She raised the mirror. The coiled serpent on its edge framed an image of a tired young woman sitting beneath a tall tree. There was something about her eyes she had never noticed before—there were tiny flecks of gold in the brown irises, fine fibres that were almost invisible, yet when she held the mirror closer, they were still there. The mirror was a plain enough glass, she was sure. Yet she was seeing things she had never seen before. *Things I never looked for.*

There was another thing—trails of disturbance wreathed her head, like lazy currents of mirage. Clear essence, she realised, when she drew on the Ring to achieve greater clarity. She had an aura of clear essence. Where the trails of her aura passed over things, they appeared in vivid colour. Her scarf was scarlet, her robe was intense grey, the grass was bright green. In her lap, a note was written in curving script.

Tabitha gave a start. She tilted the mirror, and looked more closely at the image. TSORAZ. The word was unmistakable, though some of the letters were misshapen. On the note in her lap, it was signed in capitals—ZAROST. In the mirror, the script was reversed. A smile crept across her lips.

Tsoraz, Zarost; two sides of the same word. Suddenly a whole number of things fell into place. Her butterfly, sent to find Zarost, had plagued Tsoraz, though it should not have recognised him at all. The young bard knew too many of the things the old Riddler knew. He always became unsettled when she questioned him about Zarost. He spoke the same, he acted the same, he only looked younger, fresher, *rejuvenated*; a change which was impossible. He had appeared only when the other was gone.

There was only one explanation for such a riddle. The bard was just a disguise for the Riddler. There was a wizard in the realm of Eyri, and she had just discovered his name.

Twardy Zarost.

She rose and turned to face the wizard.

The power that emanated from him was plain, once she looked for it. He filled more than the space his body occupied, his presence extended in shields of vibration, or colourless waves of force. It *was* clear essence, and not a trick of the light. She must have been blind not to have noticed. Blind, or not ready to see.

"You are Twardy Zarost. You are the wizard!" she declared.

The broadest smile she had ever seen split his face.

"A wizard maybe, but not *the* wizard," he answered.

"There's another?"

"The wizard you seek, the one who can save Eyri."

"Then why are you here, if not to fight against the Dark?"

"To help you find the one who can, if that is what you wish to do."

Hope flared in her heart. There might be a chance, despite the gloom.

"How am I to find the wizard?"

"Find one, and you find two, for it takes one to know another."

Tabitha stamped her foot. He was laughing at her, and twisting her words. She would make him speak the truth, even if she had to beat every crooked word straight.

"Damn it, you know who it is, Zarost!" she exclaimed. "Tell me where I can find the wizard I seek. Tell me!"

"*You* must tell you, or you cannot be what matters to me."

"I am the wizard?" She paused. "I am the wizard!"

"Yes!" he exclaimed, dancing into the air. "Yes! Young Tabitha, at last you see! I've watched your presence, it grows like a gown, yet until you see and know that yourself, you are not wise, or fit to be free. You have searched through the Light, and through the fierce Dark, but until your clear vision comes, you will miss the true mark. It is the balance which matters, the power between, the art of discerning the patterns unseen."

"What about the Ring, then? I was supposed to take it to the wizard.

Must I give it to you?"

He raised the middle digit of his right hand. It was a considerably rude gesture, the way he did it. He roared with laughter at her expression.

"No, look closer," he urged.

A glint outlined an edge, then she saw the whole of the ring. A clear ring, just like hers, set on his middle finger. It was difficult to see, even when she concentrated on it.

"I already have mine," he said. "That one is yours."

"So the path to the wizard is ended?"

"The path *to* the wizard is ended, but the path *of* the wizard has just begun! You have come a long way in a very short time, but you have much further to run. One hill of a mountain-range climbed, one day of a season done."

Like the serpent on the rim of the Riddler's mirror that ate its own tail, finding the end of the path to the wizard was not the end, it was the beginning instead. The Ring was exceptionally warm. The truth was within her.

"What if I don't wish to be a wizard?"

Zarost laughed. "O, you have little choice now, little at all. Take the Ring off and see what happens."

She tested its grip, and was surprised when it moved easily. For the first time since she had taken the Ring, it seemed loose on her finger, comfortably so. She pulled it free. Her view of the world didn't change at all. Zarost was still wreathed in his mighty aura. All around her the world seemed connected by clear essence—it flowed through the air, it pulsed in the earth, it shimmered in the trees. There was clear essence in everything. If she chose to, she could summon that essence. Her augmented senses remained—she could bring items that were far away into her sight, and hear the sounds of distant people moving in the city. Her mind was clear, and in the background of her refined awareness, a hundred voices were joined in song.

"You have developed the sight, you have no need for the assistance of the Ring," Zarost explained. "The Ring is a test, to see if a Seeker can bear the burden of their catalysed magical ability. You're not going to keep the Ring on if you've got no talent. It gives daring, it will lead you into danger, into places where you are forced to practise your talent. It has subtle Order-benefits, the clear thinking, the clear remembering, the increased sensitivity to everything, but it doesn't make you a wizard. It is only by seeing clearly yourself that you see the clear essence and begin to imagine uses for it.

"You can turn your back on the path ahead and hide from what you see, but think of what it has cost you to reach the end of your apprenticeship. You don't really have a choice. Wizard Serannon."

Tabitha rolled the Ring between her fingers. It had cost her everything. She slipped it on again.

"But if I am a wizard, then why am I so helpless against the tide of Dark which sweeps toward Stormhaven? Wizards have power! They are capable of magnificent things. The wizards of legend created stonewood and the Kingsbridge. They shielded Eyri from harm."

"Which do you think is more wonderful—a run of rock, or a living butterfly? We each have talent in our own particular lore. Clear essence is what carries the magic, but the lore is your own, and you wield a great power."

"But Twardy! When I sing the Lifesong, it does wonderful things, but when I am silent, I am just a girl. Not a wizard."

Zarost grinned, and clapped his hands together. "You have true wisdom already! That is the way of all magic. It flows through us, we can guide it, but we do not create it ourselves. The sooner you know that, the stronger you can be."

"I am the wizard?" She sat down heavily, so strong was the sensation of truth. "I am the wizard."

"And so the battle within Eyri is your responsibility, for you have the greatest power," Zarost said, stretching as if a great burden had been released from his shoulders. "It is the test which has developed around you and your Ring. Your success shall be the final proof."

"I have to save the realm?"

"If you so choose. You've left yourself precious little time, Wizard Serannon, but then there's a lot more in that mirror than you thought."

Within the coil of the carved serpent, a determined face looked out at her, a woman with a red scarf, concealing two orbs—one of fading Light, the other of the deepest Dark. She had hidden them for long enough. If she was to be the wizard, she had to be clear and honest. She pulled her scarf aside. The stones hung free; the darker one seemed more ominous than its pale cousin.

"How can I stand against the Darkmaster, my Riddler?"

"Build on the knowledge you have gathered." He was suddenly serious, his eyes intent. "A wizard can see truth in a tangled web of facts. You have knowledge of the Dark and the Light."

"But the Darkmaster –"

"Cabal is dangerous, but never confuse him for a wizard! He failed to keep the Ring, he did not attain the sight. He cannot wield the clear essence, he is capable of doing only that which uses the Dark, and then only the spells which he has deduced. Most of those have their equal in the Light."

What Zarost had proclaimed brought little comfort. With the shattered Source, Dark was the only thing left. Cabal had all the power, as far as Tabitha could see. Singing clear essence into butterflies wasn't going to stop an army of Shadowcasters.

"How am I to change anything, when I know so little magic?"

"I believe the best magic is discovered within your own knowledge—not taught. You've seen something of the power of a mirror, not so? Well, there are many truths to be learned by reflection. For now, reflect on what it is you wish to change."

"I don't want –"

"No-no!" he exclaimed, raising a hand and turning his head away. "You are a wizard, now. You should begin to act like one. That means you can stare into the distance, and say nothing, and it is not considered strange. Think first. Speak only later."

She bit back a retort. She had been about to say she didn't want to become a servant to the Darkmaster. But Zarost was right—it demanded more than an impulsive answer. She might be deciding the fate of the realm. All Eyri would fall under Cabal's rule, if nothing was done. The Sword would fight, but what hope was there when the previous battle had been such a disaster? The Darkmaster had amassed so much power, he had worked for years to turn the Light to Dark. There was no defence against so much dark essence. What was Zarost expecting of her? How was she supposed to use reflection?

"I don't see it, Twardy. What do you expect me to do?"

Zarost hopped from one foot to the other. "If the Light can become Dark, why not the other way?"

A ray of sunlight touched the trees. The air didn't seem so cold anymore. A world of possibility opened before Tabitha. She had been looking in only one direction, along the inevitable descent from Light to Dark.

Reflection!

Zarost was right—if sprites could be turned to motes, they might be turned back into sprites again, if the spell was reversed. There was hope, in the Turning spell. But just as that hope bloomed in her heart, it was crushed again.

"We'll never find a Shadowcaster willing to give the Dark away," she said. "The Turning spell needs a Lightgifter and a Shadowcaster."

"Look in the mirror," Zarost answered, dancing in tight circles. "You shall find both, and more."

She understood at last. She was a Lightgifter, and a Shadowcaster. There was only one way to find out if she could be both, and yet be neither.

"Motes. I'll need motes."

"Ask the big bad bird," Zarost offered, with a twinkle of mischief in his eye. "It has followed you well enough today."

As if aware of their attention, the raven gave a hoarse caw from the tree above. The Darkmaster's messenger waited. She needed it only for the motes it held, but it would bring more than just the Dark essence.

The grey sky was darkening again. The east wind had become icy, and it blew in fitful gusts. Tabitha stood, and steeled herself for what was to come. She reminded herself that she was a wizard, and that the Darkmaster was not. The path ahead was clear—the Darkmaster had taken everything, and she had nothing left to lose. A calm filled her as she found a place of strength beyond emotion. It was time.

She raised her arm.

"Alight, Morrigán, and deliver your word."

There was a terrible moment where the bird looked too real to be a spell, and its swooping advance seemed to be the dive of a predator. The raven was ugly, with a heavy, sharp beak. It reached eagerly for Tabitha's soft arm with gnarled taloned feet. As it landed, the Morrigán exploded into the motes of its spell, and the slippery voice of the Darkmaster Cabal was released.

"Tabitha Serannon, how good of you to acknowledge what you are. As a Shadowcaster you have a duty to speak the Devotion to me. You must know that the Dark shall win, and you shall see that victory, before a full day has turned.

"You choose to resist my service, so I must warn you. If you use your strange singing against me, I shall send all of the Morgloth. But not against you; against the Swordmaster. Ask yourself if you believe your precious Glavenor can hold twenty beasts with his sword, or thirty. Ask yourself if his life is worth your selfish defiance. Not one note of your song, or he will surely die. If you are silent, I shall use only the Dark essence in my claiming of Stormhaven, and you shall be spared the responsibility of many deaths."

The motes showered to the ground, staining the grass black.

Tabitha tried to hold her purpose firmly in mind, but the planned experiment of the reversed Turning was swept aside by the dread which the Darkmaster's announcement brought.

Morgloth. She had always hoped it was impossible to summon more than one, and that they had already killed it. A horrific image burst into focus—Garyll, holding three Morgloth at bay with desperate lunges of his sword, and behind him, a fourth beast descending from the sky, unseen. It was too real to forget.

She looked at the black stain of motes in the grass, like a dried pool of blood.

Selfish. It would be selfish, to resist the Darkmaster now, knowing what she did. To sacrifice Garyll would be too terrible to endure. She could not use the Lifesong.

Yet the Ring burned on her finger, urging her on, and she knew it was her duty to defy the Darkmaster. She could not abandon Eyri to the Dark. She was sure Garyll would feel the same, and there was something which the Darkmaster had not considered. The Turning spell was not part of the magic of the Lifesong. She did not have to sing, to turn the essence. She only had to perfect the spell which could take the power away from the Darkmaster.

She would meet his power with her own. She summoned all of the motes to her hand, and guided them into the twisted circle of the Turning. The Dark essence flowed, following the pattern in her mind. One of the orbs was cold against her throat. She was a Shadowcaster, in command of her small share of Dark power.

She reached for the memory of an innocent girl, the one who had sung the Morningsong with pure devotion, the part of her that was a Lightgifter. She reversed the current of the motes, guiding them the other way around the twisted circle. She guessed the spell's words would reflect her intentions.

"Hold the pattern, round, and round, in the hidden turn, to the stronger Will be bound."

There was a pulse of heat in the air before her, and a burst of brightness. Sprites glittered to the ground, a puff of radiant seeds upon the previously dark earth.

"Bejigerred if that isn't a fine beginning!" exclaimed Twardy Zarost. "With reflection, you can achieve great things. Beware, Wizard Serannon, you have just become the Darkmaster's biggest threat! Take care to keep that a secret, until you are sure of what you do."

Tabitha summoned the Light to her hand. The sprites shimmered around her fingers. A haze of essence, barely enough to make a Courier. Or a Morrigán. Enough to stop an individual spell, maybe, but against the flood of Dark which was coming to Stormhaven?

She would hold the advantage of surprise once only. The spell had to be perfect the first time. It had to take all of the power from the Darkmaster, in such a way that he did not suspect what was happening, and could not stop it in time.

Tabitha turned to Zarost. "Is there any hope of turning even half of the motes the Darkmaster will bring?"

"The greater the darkness, the brighter the light can burn within it. I suppose we could build a better spell from what you hold in knowledge, if you've the mind for some riddling."

43. ΠIGHT OΠ THE KIΠGSBRIDGE
"A hole can always become deeper."—*Zarost*

They stood alert, an armoured wall against the dark night. The half-moon had abandoned the sky to the shredded clouds, and yet that lack did not fully account for the darkness which approached on the Fendwarrow road. The scouts had already retreated. Some of them had not returned.

The Dark was coming, in a viscous low cloud that hid whatever was beneath it. No villagers from Wendelnip or Vinmorgen farmers ran ahead of the advancing threat—not even a dog or stray pony—it had crept upon them silently, it had passed over the people undetected, and done its foul work in the secret of its own shroud. The blight crept towards the Swords with an agonising pace. The wind was cold, and bitter with fear.

Garyll noted how the men around him reached for their swords every time the Dark pushed closer, but their hands returned empty from their sides. He had ensured that the front line followed his orders to the letter. The second wave, massed against the barricade and one-hundred strong, would be the ones to use their swords. They watched the sky for the Morgloth that Garyll knew would never come. He was sure that many of the Swords wished to be with the archers on the other side of the barricade that held the Kingsbridge at their backs.

Garyll was without Felltang himself, to convince the men of his commitment. The other weapon, no one had questioned. He raised his bladed false hand before his face. It reminded him of his task. He prayed that the battle would soon be over, with as little killing as possible. Only two deaths were important. All the others could be spared. He wondered what the four blades would taste like, when drawn across his own throat. Bittersweet, he expected, if they were already coated with the Darkmaster's blood.

He had to behave as Cabal expected, or his defiance would be recognised too early. Some men would have to be sacrificed in the subterfuge. He consoled himself by remembering that their deaths would not be for nothing. They would save Stormhaven. They would save Tabitha Serannon.

"Be ready for the charge!" he barked at the front line. "Make sure your restraints are at hand." He had issued them all with strips of fabric, looped over their belts. Some of the men even believed they would be of use to gag and bind the Shadowcasters, and thus deny them access to their spells. They could not suspect the true purpose of those bindings.

The wall of Dark crept closer, yet it spread out as well, curving across the head of the Kingsbridge to form its own front line. Garyll felt a compulsion to lie down on the ground and surrender right away. Only his experience at Ravenscroft told him that it was the Darkmaster's whispers which brought despair on the wind. There was so much Dark.

One by one, the stars went out.

Torches flared quickly along the front line. Every fifth man held his flaming brand high. Blinded by their own light, they could see even less of what was beyond the glistening blackness. Another aspect of an intricately laid plan.

"Front line, advance to engage!" Garyll ordered. The men moved, spreading out to cover the broader front. It would have been wiser to form a wedge and engage the front in one place. It would have been wiser to bring the second wave in closer, and not leave them stationed against the barricade. Garyll was thankful that soldiers did not question, once in battle.

"Charge!"

He ran with them at the implacable face of darkness. The night became colder. The wall of motes towered overhead, blocking out all of the sky. He knew he should not fear what was to come, and yet the tension corded his muscles. The moment of contact was a shock of cold, then complete darkness. The air was thick with motes, then partially clear again as he broke through the far side of the Dark wall. He came to an abrupt halt. He was not alone, and the sharp point of a sword pressed up against his throat.

He was about to swipe the sword away with his clawed hand, and slash the man's stomach open, when he recognised the surge of Dark bloodlust in his own veins, and saw his opponent for who he was. He eased his blades down and away, and knelt in submission. The swordsman stayed close, his deadly blade held firm. Just another one of the men Garyll had led to disaster in Ravenscroft, turned to serve the Darkmaster. Garyll could not strike the man down. They were too much alike.

A woman stepped around the Darksword, and stooped to gather

the strips of fabric from Garyll's belt. She was cloaked in a dark robe, and she had a scent of wild spice. Garyll recognised her. Gabrielle had gone too deeply under his skin in Ravenscroft for him to ever forget.

She gagged him tightly, then bound his wrists behind his back, while the Darksword held Garyll on the blade.

"For appearances," she whispered in his ear. "They mustn't know your secret yet."

Garyll noticed that two men of the front line knelt nearby on either side, held on the point of Darksword blades. Without weapons, their struggle had been brief. Beyond them, darkness swallowed the night, but the clash of swords told Garyll that not all of the men had been caught as easily. Some would die, if they fought. He doubted that any of the front line would escape from their charge. The second wave had been ordered to wait for the Morgloth, or a direct assault. They would watch the sky, and would not follow their comrades, not yet.

"Up!" ordered Gabrielle, then she breathed against his face. "The Master wishes to see you. When we are done with all of this, I shall wish to see you as well."

He tried to ignore the strange anticipation she awoke within him. He concentrated instead on his plan. If he could get close enough to Cabal, much would be saved.

A tendril of motes stung his Darkstone through his collar, and Garyll lurched as pain raked through his nerves. The Shadowcaster's grip was too compelling to refuse. She drew him after her.

"I have him!" she announced to the nearest Darksword. "Assist where you are needed, then ready the turned Gifters for the blind-run." The man sprinted for the dying sounds of battle, and Gabrielle led Garyll away.

The air filled with motes again. The maddening whispers and gusty wind faded to a silence thicker than treacle. His skin crawled. Garyll knew what that meant. The Darkmaster was near.

It was so dark he could see nothing, not even his own shoulders. He was brought to a halt by a rough hand against his chest, then a sharp kick behind his knees took him to the ground.

"Always kneel before our Master," Gabrielle rebuked. She knelt beside him, Garyll presumed, because he heard the crick of her joints and the swish of fabric there. Her voice sounded on a level with him.

"The front line is captured, Master. We are ready for the

flanking."

"Thank you, Gabrielle." Cabal's voice slithered through the air, coming from many directions at once. Garyll couldn't discern the source. He guessed he wasn't supposed to. He just needed one chance, to sink his talons into that heart. Garyll worked at his bonds, but his wrists were tied firmly. He tried to judge where Gabrielle faced, by the sound of her voice.

"Shall I give the signal for the turned Gifters and Darkswords?"

"A moment, Gabrielle. Their charge is—a diversion. If they die, I want it to be of use to us. The shroud has not spread enough to cover the flanking yet."

The source of Cabal's voice wandered, but Garyll discerned a soft footfall to his right, close by. He needed just one more utterance from Gabrielle to confirm the Master's new location.

"I shall deepen the Despair spell then," said Gabrielle, "while those at the barricade realise their comrades are not coming back."

Garyll leapt. He crashed into somebody's chest, and threw the figure off-balance. With a quick sweep, he hooked the figure behind his legs, and tripped him to the ground. He just had to twist and fall on the Darkmaster himself, and his bladed hand would burst through that chest and find the twisted heart.

"Stop."

The single word compelled him to failure. Garyll was unable to move. He stood over his enemy, poised to fall, and cried out against the paralysis. Not one muscle responded to his efforts to regain control.

The Darkmaster scuffled away, then laughed.

"Do you think I would be so feeble-minded to let you go if you could turn on me, Glavenor? No, you cannot turn on me. The Devotion you spoke is the seal on a powerful spell. Wonderful, really, for it is your own mind that holds that seal, in the terms we agreed upon. That you tried to break the pact, will be remembered. I see I was right to refresh our bond, before the final day."

Cabal came close. Cold fingers worked the buckle of Garyll's collar free, and took his Darkstone in hand. Doom sank into Garyll's body.

I am the shadow and he is my master.
He is the shadow and I am his caster.

"Good. I am glad to see you have not forgotten too much of what you were taught. Now, say it again."

The devotion to save Tabitha. He could not defy it. The pact was like a barbed arrow, it worked deeper into him with every struggling word. Only by accepting, could he spare Tabitha from harm. He could not go backwards, against the teeth set in his heart. He had overestimated his free will. He had forgotten some of the raw agony of the torture chamber. It filled him now, layer upon layer of pain, depth upon depth of Darkness. His strength was taken from him, until he found abandon in the words.

"Again," the Darkmaster ordered.

Some time later, a second Shadowcaster announced the completion of the shroud, whatever that was. Garyll didn't care. He only wanted the Darkmaster to release him.

"Gabrielle, signal the turned Gifters, and see to it that they throw themselves against the defenders with good vigour. See that they find blindness themselves, when they have cast that spell amongst the defenders. Use the Darkswords to dispatch whatever remains."

"All of the turned Gifters are to be—executed?" There was a catch in Gabrielle's voice.

"None of those recently turned can be trusted. Our friend the Swordmaster has shown us that. I want only the loyal Shadowcasters to join the final taking of Stormhaven. The spells are too complex to risk tampering."

"Am I to join the final assault?" Gabrielle asked, in a small voice.

"If your task is complete," said the Darkmaster.

"But it shall be slaughter, Master! The turned Gifters swore allegiance. Can we not simply overpower the defenders, and leave it at that?"

"You think to lecture me on what is best? You have forgotten your failure with the Source quicker than I. See that you follow my command, if you wish to find a place in the Eyri of tomorrow. I want the Kingsbridge anointed with blood."

An angry, animal lust for savagery swept through Garyll, then the Darkmaster finally withdrew his hand from Garyll's throat, and the bloodlust lessened. Garyll guessed he had felt the intent of a spell sent Gabrielle's way. She had departed at a run.

"Come, Glavenor. It is time we progressed towards the end."

Garyll's collar was tied again, hiding the Darkstone. He was pushed from behind, and he staggered through the unbroken darkness. After a few steps, the motes thinned, and a pale mist replaced the murk with ghostly luminescence. Robed figures waited on the shore of the

Amberlake.

"Begin," commanded the Darkmaster, close behind him.

The Shadowcasters began to chant, and motes flickered outwards to lace the mist with tendrils. Garyll wondered absently how they were going to flank a battle which occupied the entire head of the Kingsbridge. The barricade had been constructed to span the causeway from waterline to waterline. There was no way around it.

A baleful horn sounded off to the right.

The Shadowcasters united their Dark essence into a coiled mass, and threw it outwards, as if wasting it upon the Amberlake.

"Freeze!"

For as far as Garyll could see into the shroud of mist, the water had turned to ice, in a broad swath wide enough to walk upon. The Shadowcasters moved, and he was compelled to move with them by the hand on his back. Garyll walked with care. If the ice cracked, he knew his armour would take him to the bottom. With his arms tied, there would be no escape. They walked out onto the Amberlake a way, and the Shadowcasters repeated the spell. The ice was slick and unsteady underfoot.

Screams, confused shouts, and the clash of metal came over the water from the right. The mists hid the head of the Kingsbridge, but Garyll could imagine what was taking place. Turned Gifters darting in amongst the defenders, under the cover of darkness, and blinding the Swords with motes. Darkswords coming in their wake, and hacking down the sightless. The archers would be intent on the front, but wouldn't know where to fire. The turned Gifters would fight desperately to win their prey without being injured, though they wouldn't suspect it was all for nought. They would find the blades of the Darkswords through their backs, once the defenders had been massacred. Swords against Swords, Eyrians on Eyrians. It was all happening again. The bile Garyll tasted was worse than before.

A chunk of ice broke underfoot, and drifted on the water. Garyll skirted the hole, but the ice cracked further under his weight. A hand steadied him, and the Shadowcasters chanted the spell again in unison, thickening the floating bridge in the mist. The sounds of battle were still to the right, though the screams had begun to drown out the clash and clamour of weapons.

The sloping bank of the Kingsbridge thrust across their path. Shadowcasters sent runners of mist to cover the places that were bare. When Garyll reached the road level, the gag was torn from his head, and his restraints were severed. He felt hopelessly crushed. The Darkmaster remained close behind him, and whispered a final directive.

"You will be silent until you reach the Isle. Run along now. We have to surprise a few archers, and pin them to a barricade with their own arrows. Tell your King we are coming to claim his crown. You know what must be done, in the end. Be ready for my command."

A lash of cold stung Garyll's back, and he lurched into a run. He didn't ease his stride when the mist thinned, or when he finally gagged upon the horror of what was taking place behind him. He ran faster. Things were only made worse, when one fought the Darkmaster.

He would ensure that those within Stormhaven suffered as little as possible.

He knew the Kingsbridge was perfectly level, but his sense of balance denied it with every step. The road led ever downward, into a deep pit of despair.

44. ALLIES AND TRAITORS

"How small a light is needed
to illuminate the dark?"—*Zarost*

Ashley Logán ducked into a doorway just in time. The man whom he tailed cast a furtive glance over his shoulder, then continued down the narrow alley.

Mind-reading had distinct advantages. Every time his quarry thought of checking for pursuit, Ashley was forewarned. Even so, he had only a second to react. The man was moving fast, which made hiding all the more difficult. He couldn't rely on the night to conceal his white robe completely. Ashley slipped into the street, and loped after the fleeting back of Lethin Tarrok.

The man's mind was as soft as a rotten fruit, and as unsavoury. Ashley had learned a lot in the short time he had trailed him. There was much awry with the preparation of the Isle for the coming battle, and each shortfall was the work of Lethin Tarrok, work much gloated over.

Rats had found a way into the food stores. A strange madness was spreading amongst the horses. The Sword would soon suffer from weak bowels. Ashley intended to warn the Swordmaster of all these plots, but first he had to catch Tarrok in the act or he would be in hot water himself. His only proof thus far was that Tarrok thought these things, and that was no proof at all. He wanted to keep the wandering ability of his mind a secret. So the trail of treachery drew him on.

He hadn't been able to sleep at any rate. The impending battle was common knowledge. Ashley had loitered near the Gatehouse for most of the night, but when the news had been cried out from the battlements that the signal fires had been lost to mists at the head of the Kingsbridge, he had been ready to hide in the Boarding. That was when Tarrok had slunk past. The thoughts that lingered in his wake were too dangerous to ignore.

Tarrok ducked into the mouth of a descending stairwell. Ashley hesitated for a moment when he reached it, then followed into the dank passage. The few stairs ended in a solid-looking door. Tarrok was gone. Ashley pressed his ear to the door, and heard a voice on the far side.

"Shatter the sun! Catch alight, you damned thing!"

A faint rasp came through the oak panel—the scrape of steel on flint, Ashley guessed. It wouldn't do to enter the room at the wrong moment. He reached out with his thoughts instead of his hand. As before, Tarrok's unsavoury mind was easy to penetrate.

Ach! I can leave it open, it'll make for a quicker return, Tarrok thought. Ashley lost contact for a few moments. When he regained the link, the thoughts were weaker.

Bloody dark! Curses! This tunnel is as filthy as a Fendwarren brothel. The Master will pay for this chore.

Then the mental link became fainter and slipped from his grasp. Ashley hoped it meant that Tarrok had simply moved out of range. He guessed it was safe to enter, and pulled tentatively on the door-ring. The door opened as quietly as it had for Tarrok.

He was in a wine cellar, and a single torch was alight nearby. Racks of wine bottles, and a great many casks, were stacked all around. Against the wall on the far side of the room was a large cask, lain on its side, different from the others in that its end gaped wide. When he got close enough, he could see that it was not a barrel after all, but a cleverly concealed entrance to a tunnel.

A good way into the tunnel, a figure worked a key in a lock. His kneeling posterior was towards Ashley. With a grinding of aged hinges, something was moved, and then the figure and his torch slipped out of a circular exit. Ashley prayed over his Lightstone for courage, then followed.

It was dark, and dusty. When he reached the end of the tunnel, his suspicions were confirmed.

So much for the impenetrable walls of Stormhaven.

The legend was disproved by the scent of fish. Ashley wondered how many citizens knew of the back door to the harbour. By the rusty sound of the hinges, very few.

The boats lay still, floating like sleeping water-fowl. There was no sign of the Sword around the harbour. It raised Ashley's hackles, but he supposed they had not considered the harbour a target—their attention was likely concentrated around the City Gates and upon the battlements. Better defence of the harbour could have been maintained with a minimum of men. Strange things were happening tonight.

Tarrok's torch bobbed along the pier to the left. The flame suddenly flew up in an arc, and disappeared into the hull of a nearby vessel. The *whump!* of immolation accompanied a flare as tall as the mast.

The boat must have been prepared with pitch or oil. Within moments, the flames licked across the surface of the harbour waters, bleeding toward other vessels. Oil had been leaked across the surface of the entire harbour.

Tarrok must have an accomplice, or three.

There was nothing Ashley could do to halt the spread of the fire, but there was something he could do about the traitor who ran toward him, heading for the tunnel. Ashley backed up as fast as he could, and reached the wine cellar just in time. He recoiled from the exit, in case his body blocked the torchlight and gave him away. But he needn't have worried—he could hear Tarrok fretting with the lock at the far end of the tunnel.

Got to get out of the dark! No light! No bloody light! There was a significant edge of panic to Tarrok's thoughts.

Ashley's hand found the neck of a heavy wine bottle on the rack nearby. He was beside the mouth of the open barrel when Tarrok's head emerged. The bottle made quite a mess when it broke. It stained the traitor's yellow robe red. Tarrok hit the ground with a thump.

Three keys on a ring fell from Tarrok's slack hand. Ashley retrieved them from the pool of wine and glass. He shoved Tarrok back into the barrel. Tarrok didn't object. Tarrok didn't even have anything to say when Ashley closed the heavy lid which acted as the door. Ashley found the correct key, and turned it in the lock.

Ashley guessed that when Tarrok came to, he would be screaming at the top of his lungs. The little arsonist was afraid of the dark.

Considering the side which he had chosen, it was hopelessly ironic. Ashley quenched the torch in its holder on the way out. The third key turned smoothly in the cellar door behind him. It was quite a thick door, really. No sound would carry through all that wood.

He set off to find the Swordmaster. He hoped Glavenor had remained in Stormhaven, and had not gone to hold the head of the Kingsbridge. The thought of the darkened signal fires had begun to bring a queer nausea to his stomach.

◆ ——————— ◆

The Swordmaster was not easy to find. He seemed always two reports ahead of Ashley. Although the guards had admitted Glavenor at the City Gates, he had moved fast, collecting Swords and sending them to the Gatehouse. The news was alarming. The Kingsbridge defence had failed, and a final attack was expected to come at dawn.

Few men were placed upon the battlements, for fear of the Morgloth, yet it was there that Ashley found Glavenor, gripping a cornice as if intending to rip the stone from its place and cast it against the last vestiges of the night. The tall flames of the watch tower cast an angry light against the roiling clouds of smoke which poured from the harbour.

"Swordmaster?"

Glavenor didn't turn, but the tightening of his jaw-muscles suggested that he was aware of Ashley's presence. Losing the head of the Kingsbridge must have taken a heavy toll, in lives as well as strategy. Ashley could guess how embittered the Swordmaster felt.

"Glavenor, sir, I have discovered a traitor in the city."

The Swordmaster whirled in an instant. His eyes were as fierce as a hawk's, and as predatory. Ashley faltered in his approach. He couldn't miss the fact that Glavenor's hand gripped the hilt of his sheathed sword.

"What do you know?" demanded the Swordmaster. A chill ran down Ashley's spine upon Glavenor's advance.

"I know who it was who set fire to the harbour."

"Who might that be?" demanded Glavenor. He was extremely angry, Ashley decided.

"Lethin Tarrok," Ashley answered. He backed away a pace from the Swordmaster.

This is crazy. He's the Swordmaster, you can trust him.

"Who else knows about this?" Glavenor asked, catching his wrist and arresting his retreat. Ashley wanted to squeak. The only good thing he could see about the hold was it meant Glavenor had released his grip on the sword-hilt to achieve it. The Swordmaster was terrifying, so close.

"N-no one," Ashley stammered. "I came straight to you. I thought you would know what to do."

"Where is Tarrok now?"

"I locked him away, in the tunnel he used to reach the harbour."

"Do you have the keys?"

"I –"

There was a something very wrong about the Swordmaster's eyes. They weren't as fierce as a hawk's, Ashley decided. Rather, they were as cold as stone. Dark, midnight stone, devoid of all feeling. Ashley pushed out to touch the Swordmaster's mind in desperation. In a flickering instant of thought, he found the horror that was there.

"I left them in my room," he lied.

Ashley reeled. Glavenor's mind was dark, so dark, and only one thought was clear, a voice which echoed a devotion against the bare walls of his soul.

Garyll tightened his grip. There was a wicked contraption of four blades affixed to the Swordmaster's left hand. His raised the blades.

"Well, get them, and bring the keys to me. I must find out what else he knows."

Ashley almost fell from the palisade when Garyll released his arm. His legs buckled with relief, but he fled the stairs three at time, and did not tumble. It was terrifying to consider what might have happened if the Swordmaster had not believed his lie. He ran. There was only one person in Stormhaven who had a chance of reaching the Swordmaster. He prayed that there was enough time to find her.

45. THE COMING OF DARKNESS

"Of all the engines of war,
fear is the most powerful."—*Zarost*

Cabal was furious. They had come through the covering smoke of the harbour, only to find the secret way closed. No one would answer his coded knocking on the iron door. Each of four Morrigáns stared at him, baleful reminders that they had failed to reach their target. Lethin Tarrok could not be found. It was well past the time when they should be inside the city walls. Dawn would soon begin to stain the sky. The plan had been perfect, his instructions had been explicit.

But the way was closed.

The Shadowcasters recoiled from him when his gaze flicked over the assembled figures. The best of Ravenscroft, and yet none of the sixty had power enough to break the stonewood walls of Stormhaven.

A sudden croak and flurry of wings announced the return of his fifth Morrigán. Cabal accepted the messenger, which collapsed to a thousand motes.

The Swordmaster's voice was clipped. "Your Tarrok was locked in a room, by a boy. The boy took fright, and has gone into hiding. The keys cannot be retrieved. We might break the doors in, but not without alerting the men of it."

Cabal closed his eyes. His grip tightened on his sceptre. He stood quite still. Then he threw the sceptre, hard. The metal-worked staff whirled through the air, and struck the nearest Shadowcasters with a satisfactory smack. Two of them went down. They would never mention it, if they valued their positions in the new order. Someone went to retrieve the sceptre.

Cabal summoned motes to his hand, and cast a second Morrigán for the Swordmaster.

"We shall present a target for your forces at dawn. See to it that all your men charge from the City Gates toward it. And see to it also that the Gates are not closed, afterward."

◆ ———— ◆

Kirjath Arkell worked in darkness. There was a creature inside his skull that banged a hammer against the bone with every heartbeat. There was a fluid coming from his ears that was not blood. He had forgotten what it meant, only that he must hide in the bowels of Ravenscroft, where none of the painful light of day could find his eyes, where it was cold.

It was quiet since they had all gone, but often the silence was filled with hoarse shouts and screams that came from somewhere inside him. They had left him, he remembered that much. He had stolen Dark essence. He needed it. It was the only thing which numbed the pain. It was the only way to call his friends. But he could not remember the pattern.

Things had been getting worse, he knew. How much worse, he couldn't guess, only that there had been a time, once, when the thousand needles had not resided in his flesh, a time when he hadn't crooned and jabbered without being able to stop himself. Gone, now. Gone. Only, forward. His task. He must complete the task.

He scratched suddenly on the rock between his knees, using his bloodied fingers to find where he had left off in the pattern. He cackled, and dried the tears from his cheeks. He knew. A triangle, within a circle, that was what he should draw. He remembered it now. Or was it the circle within the triangle? He lifted the rock from his design, uncertain. The flickering lights came again, and he gritted his teeth against the rolling cycle of madness.

He pulled a jurrum leaf from his pouch. There had been many in the store, so many, but fewer now. He chewed absently. The juice leaked into his throat. The mind-splinters were numbed, and the kaleidoscope of thoughts resolved slowly into one, clear objective.

The Morgloth. That was how it would be done. He would bring them all, and set them upon those who had wronged him. He remembered part of the spell. Half of a chanted verse escaped his lips. He ran his fingers over the incomplete outline, where his rock had scored the floor at his knees.

The flickering lights returned and swept all else aside. He pounded his fist on the stone while he twitched and gibbered. After a time, the twitching slowed, and he could summon the Dark to numb his bloodied knuckles. There was a good store left. At least there was that. Enough Dark to raise hell.

He worked at the task of remembering. In every lucid moment, he scored more of the pattern into the floor. Little by little, it began to build.

His first Morgloth was dead. The girl had caused that to happen. He added that crime to his list. The girl and the Swordmaster, they would die. His first Morgloth had been but one of many behind the Gateway. There had been others, lurking deeper in the Underworld. He had summoned only the one because he had been afraid of the others. They were too strong, too immense to contain.

What was fear, when he had survived everything? He had survived! He licked his dry lips, and began to chant. The pattern was clear in his mind. But he could not remember how to summon the Dark essence this time. His shattered Darkstone didn't help. He roared in frustration, but that only reduced him to a fit of coughing.

Then it came to him, all of it, in a clear drop of sanity; the pattern, the words, the summoning spell. He visualised the Gateway, and guided the Dark essence to take that shape. He felt the air suck past his ears, as the portal to the Underworld was opened.

"Step through the Gate!" he shouted to the void, "and enter my mind!" He didn't know what name to call, or which presence to channel. Instead, he welcomed them all. He could sense the madness rushing back.

They came as swift as snakes. He felt the force of their presence, heard the sound of many wings. Within moments, the screech of their strange hunger filled the chamber. Kirjath's thoughts were scattered to the far walls as an alien mind invaded his and burst through every shrivelled thread of his brain. Kirjath had a new master, who emerged from the Gateway last of all.

The Morgloth's bulk pushed Kirjath back. His foul odour brought Kirjath to his knees. His raw strength left Kirjath weak. Kirjath was glad it was dark. He didn't want to see the horror before him, and yet he knew every aspect of the horror already, for the Great Morgloth was his master, and commanded his mind. A taloned hand gripped him by his neck, and he was lifted from the floor and set upon the creature's back as if he weighed no more than a rat.

They crawled from the catacombs of Ravenscroft as the dawn broke the eastern sky. They took to the wing. Kirjath's eyes smarted, and he could see nothing. He clung to the foul flesh of the Morgloth's neck, and shivered in the shrieking wind.

◆ ——————— ◆

Dawn was a weak affair. A red-streaked overcast sagged across the sky. Dark essence swirled about the buttresses of Stormhaven, bringing a chill which pulled warmth from the bones, worse than a winter storm. Garyll allowed the numbness to spread, but King Mellar tucked his hands under his armpits, and stamped on the battlement beside him.

They surveyed the gathered forces. Stormhaven was besieged, by only sixty figures, or so it seemed. It was difficult to count the Shadowcasters in the midst of their writhing mass of motes, a mass which spilled across all of the island between the city walls and the lake.

None of the loyal defenders had returned from the head of the Kingsbridge, where the night mists swirled still. That knowledge only made the waiting worse. Garyll just wanted it all to end.

He considered setting a foot on the edge, and leaping. That might save Stormhaven and his King. But it might not, and the horror of what might be done to Tabitha thereafter kept his feet where they were. He was the only reason she was safe. He wasn't sure he believed that, any more.

"You are strained, Glavenor."

"The Darkmaster has taken too much already. I fear he shall take it all."

"Stormhaven is secure inside these high walls of stonewood. We can wait, and consider what is to be done."

"While we are trapped in place, your Highness?"

"No man would march to the door of his enemy with such a small force if he were not supremely confident. There is some fact about this siege I have missed. I am loath to order the counter-strike until I know what it is."

Although he fought the words, Garyll knew he had to speak them. "We should attack them now, while they are gathered before us. We have enough men for the task."

Down behind the Gates, the rear-guard were assembled in readiness. A double line of cavalry, their chargers stamping, and snorting steam. Behind them, foot-soldiers glinted dully in their armour. Garyll had been about to command their charge, when the King had demanded this meeting, to survey the battleground, and review the tactic. Mellar could not have chosen a worse moment to question his Swordmaster's judgement. Garyll tried to keep the rancour from his voice, but failed.

"Waiting breeds fear and weakness."

"There is something amiss, and I will know what it is, first."

Garyll shifted on his feet, but remained tight-lipped. Out in front of the Gates, a circle was clearing in the blackness. It became evident that the Shadowcasters were not the only ones assembled there. As the Dark drained from the road to collect in a ridge on either side, kneeling men emerged, strung in a line. Men in armour, but bound hand and foot. Swords. Near to one hundred of them, bloodied and weapon-less.

Another Sword walked stiffly into position at the end of the line of captives. Garyll knew it was not the same kind of man who readied his blade, as those who knelt before him. The Darksword pointed his blade at the sky, for a long moment. Then he brought it down, with wicked precision, on the neck of the man at his feet.

The head of the first captive fell, struck the hard-packed road, and rolled. The other men cried out, and thrashed against their restraints. The Darksword took a position at the second in line.

A great number of the Shadowcasters turned and marched away then, heading through the tide of motes toward Levin. They disturbed the essence like moles running a head of earth, but their figures were unmistakable. Fewer than ten Shadowcasters were left to control the kneeling captives.

"Where do you think they are going?" asked the King.

"To collect more sacrifices."

The executioner's blade fell, and this time, the dull thump of its prize was carried on the wind. King Mellar tensed, as if struck himself.

Garyll allowed a few moments for the words to sink in. The King paled visibly as the next victim was lined up. Garyll drove another wedge into Mellar's vulnerability.

"They could do this with every man, woman and child in Eyri, until we surrender. There are no Swords remaining beyond the Isle, to defend the people."

King Mellar turned his head quickly away from the scene before them. "What do you suggest?"

"We must try, your Highness. It is a short way to fight, to reach them. There shall be more men to fight their way out. We shall outnumber them nearly four to one, when we free our men. The longer we wait, the fewer there shall be."

The sound of another head falling upon the road was unmistakable.

"And if you fail?"

"You shall be within the walls of Stormhaven. I shall see to it that the Gates are closed at the first sign of the Shadowcasters returning in force. If the men are still outside at that point, then they must fight."

"This is a brave charge you propose, Glavenor."

Garyll grimaced at the lie, and hoped the King took his expression as trepidation. Somewhere out beyond the rim of the battlements, a long scream was cut suddenly short. Mellar was haggard.

"Do it."

◆ ─────────── ◆

The crank handle turned, and the ropes tensed against the strain. Two men worked the winch, another shot the bolt free. Dark essence seeped through the widening crack of the drawbridge. The Gate creaked against its hinges, and resumed its ponderous descent. The horses balked at the touch of Dark, but their riders held them firm. The foot-soldiers stood tensed and ready in the gloom.

As the rope unwound, the tension wound tighter.

"This is a dash and rescue!" shouted Garyll, over the glinting helms. "Be quick about it. Reclaim our men, and return, do not haver for a battle. We have lost too many to the Dark already."

"Swordmaster!" challenged a Captain, "Will you not lead the charge?"

"I shall hold the Gate. Make sure you get back before the approach of the Shadowcasters, or you will find it closed." He turned to the winch operators. "Enough! Let it go!"

The two men released the handle, and the wheels and pulleys of the mechanism rattled and spun. The mighty Gate fell through its final angle to strike the ground with a thunderous boom.

Despair swept in with the wind, and the cries of those wretches who still lived, out on the road. Only the ten Shadowcasters were visible beyond them, though the ridges of Dark essence on the roadside had swollen and come close to either side of the end of the drawbridge. The distant executioner raised his blood-stained sword again.

"Ride!" shouted Garyll.

The chargers galloped over the hard planking of the open drawbridge, and the infantry followed on their heels. The rear-guard of Stormhaven poured from the Gates, and rushed between the two arms of slick essence. One rider streaked ahead of the others, and was the first to fall upon the acting headsman. The Darksword put up a brief fight, but he was soon outnumbered. Another rider reached the first of the Shadowcasters, and swung his blade. The black robe became a swirling dirty mist, before the motes sank to join the essence at his horse's knees. Illusions, one and all.

The real Shadowcasters were far closer, and they flowed into the Gate of Stormhaven, bringing their cover of Dark with them. Motes choked the giant archway, and poured past Garyll into the city.

The men at the winch had only enough time to cry out in alarm, before they were engulfed with Dark, and silenced. A moment later, the winch handles ran under the guidance of two Shadowcasters. The rope sprang taut, and the drawbridge climbed into the blood-red dawn. With every crank of the handle, the Gatehouse became darker.

Garyll did not move, or draw his sword. He wished for the end, more than ever. The Shadowcasters arrayed themselves around him. One figure came closest, and Garyll recognised him by the way he made his skin crawl with cold.

"The King?" wheezed the Darkmaster.

"The battlement overhead," Garyll answered.

Cabal turned to his Shadowcasters. "Bring Mellar to the forecourt. Round up all the citizens you can, and bring them to witness. Today is the day when history will change."

◆ ———— ◆

The King cried out, his voice full of rage and righteousness.

"Enough! Show yourself, let us see who dares challenge the rule of Eyri! You will be denied the crown. You will be denied!"

It never ceased to amuse Cabal how witless men became in the grip of a proper disaster. He guided the motes so that Mellar's words were drawn away, as if by a wind. He kept himself shrouded in darkness, and cast a spell of Silence, which he laid thickly upon the people. No one but his Shadowcasters knew where he stood. He watched the shivers and nervous glances run through the crowd. They were like sheep, the citizens of Stormhaven, gathered into the forecourt with his wolves all around. The web of motes encircled them, and the approach of dawn had been reversed.

Cabal savoured every moment of the theatrics. He had waited so long for this, and now it was all before him, handed to him on a plate borne by the Swordmaster. He kept a hand on Glavenor's shoulder, to strengthen the bond. There was one final task he had planned for the mighty man. For the moment, it would do to keep him at his side, like a faithful dog, hidden in the dark.

King Mellar turned in the centre of the forecourt, not knowing which way to face to receive the answer he expected. The coveted crown glinted on his head, even in the gloom. Cabal watched it turn.

Cabal modified his Messenger spell so that it would spread his words out wide. The voice produced was mighty, booming, vibrating, it resonated in their bones. Women clapped their hands over their ears, children cried, dogs barked.

"This is the day when history will change."

History will change. Will change. The words echoed off the walls of the taller buildings.

"The crown shall be raised by a more powerful hand."

More powerful hand. Powerful hand.

"This is the day when you shall witness your new king, and the Dark shall finally be complete."

The Shadowcasters had done well to weave the motes so densely for him. Now, when he separated them to form an outline, the contrast of the light beyond was startling.

"Behold! I am your Master!"

Though the citizens shut their eyes and turned their heads away, Cabal knew that the image was burned in their minds, a figure created of the dark, outlined by light, a man, huge and terrible, standing astride the northern edge of the forecourt on legs which were each the size of tall trees. His arms spread out to embrace them all.

Then the illusion was gone, with only the sharp sting of a Despair spell in its wake. Cabal allowed the hope to drain away into the walls of Stormhaven before he spoke again. This time the words were a deafening hiss, sharpened by the whine of a sudden wind.

"You shall surrender your crown, Mellar. For every minute you hesitate, a citizen shall lose a life."

People wailed throughout the forecourt.

"No more killing," Glavenor whispered, but the Darkmaster knew he had not intended to speak aloud. He ignored the man and his misery.

"I deny you the crown!" shouted Mellar, a pitiful sound in the face of the booming volume which had addressed him. The King spun stupidly, talking to the wind.

Cabal sent a vortex spinning up to the ceiling of the Dark web, and spread the motes apart. Sunlight lanced down and cut a circle from the gloomy forecourt. He nudged Glavenor on, with the boy in his charge.

"There is the place of your surrender, where all can see," Cabal announced. "In exchange for your crown, the life of this first sacrifice!"

Two figures moved across the flagstones and into the circle of light. The big Swordmaster held the end of a noose which was tied around the smaller figure's neck. A youth with red hair, and a pale face, and an unmistakable bearing—his father would recognise him, no doubt. Mellar would not realise at first how much the Prince had changed during his confinement at Ravenscroft.

The King staggered visibly. He stood on the one edge of the illuminated circle; his son and the Swordmaster on the other.

Cabal kept the motes circling in a sickening gyre, all around the forecourt. He spoke from everywhere at once, all-powerful, all-mighty.

"I expect a decision within the minute. The entire realm expects your decision, Mellar. Surrender, or defiance. Life, or death. Which do you choose for your people? Which do you choose for your son?"

Mellar called out to his boy, and approached him with arms outstretched. The Swordmaster followed his briefing, by blocking the King's passage with the point of his sword. Mellar looked even more distraught than ever. Cabal shifted closer to hear their discourse. The crowd needed no urging to back away from his aura of Dark essence.

"Your son, or your crown, which do you wish to keep?" asked Glavenor.

Mellar swayed on his feet, disbelief in his eyes. He looked from the sword at his throat, to his son, to the Swordmaster's impassive face. His expression hardened then.

"Why? Why did you do it, Glavenor?"

The Swordmaster fretted at a buckle behind his head. He pulled the studded collar away, revealing what lay beneath. The obsidian crystal was perfectly smooth, as dark as midnight.

"It was the only way I could save what I loved."

The two men locked eyes. The silence had little to do with the work of the motes. Cabal used the time to gather more essence to his hand, in case he needed a Despair spell to aid Mellar's decision.

"Then I must do the same," said Mellar, at length. He knelt, and took the crown from his head. He placed the golden Kingsrim gently on the stone before his knees. From somewhere within the spectators, a woman sobbed.

Cabal rejoiced. So long the wait, so sweet the victory.

The crowd shifted nervously as the currents of Dark essence spun tighter at the edges of the forecourt. It would seem to them that they were within a dark cave, and that the walls had begun to move inwards. Devotion and Despair, his Shadowcasters blended the spells with seamless integrity. The words became a mantra as more and more of the people fell to their knees, and joined the chanted dedication to their new master.

Cabal presented himself at last to the sunlight. It was wan enough not to be a bother, but by contrast to the surrounding gloom, his black robes glistened in splendour.

"Give me my son." Mellar's voice was thick with grief and anger, amidst the chanting of the affected crowd.

Cabal waved a negligent hand in Glavenor's direction, and the Swordmaster sheathed his sword and stepped away. Father and son faced each other. Tears wet Mellar's cheeks. Prince Bevn started forward, but instead of walking to his father's embrace, he stooped to pick up the crown and then backed away. The young man's words brought laughter to Cabal's lips. His apprentice had learned so much in Ravenscroft.

"You old fool. You've just thrown your crown away, for nothing." The young prince fondled the Darkstone which dangled close to his throat. "This is true power. The kind of power you never had, the kind of power I will have forever, at the side of the Master."

He backed away from Mellar, crossed the circle, and brought the Kingsrim to Cabal's hand.

"I'm on the winning side now," Bevn finished, looking up into Cabal's face, his devotion shining bright and hungry in his eyes.

"He has even more wisdom than his father," Cabal announced, then shook with dry laughter. It was a glorious moment. He threw his cowl back, raised the Kingsrim, and placed it upon his head. The Devotion spell quickened as he had expected it to—every Eyrian was sworn to serve the crown. His link to the cowed citizens of Stormhaven was stronger than ever.

Mellar stared across the sunlit paving to where his son stood beside the new King of Eyri. At last, the words he managed were barely more than a whisper, but he repeated them, and Cabal caught them the second time.

"What have you done to my son?"

"Look to the one who shall execute you, and you shall truly

understand my power. Glavenor!" He cast a swift Devotion spell on the Swordmaster, when he noted his hesitation and anguish. "Obey your King, and your Master." Cabal signalled to his Shadowcasters to draw all the motes inwards. The web tightened until it cut off the sunlight once more, plunging the forecourt into cold, crushing gloom.

The ring of a sword being drawn again from its scabbard was loud and clear.

"Now do you understand, Mellar?" crowed Cabal. "Do you see my power? Your best man, and he can offer you no aid. Once I have his allegiance, he can never take it back. My power is absolute, my rule shall endure forever."

The Swordmaster of Eyri raised his sword.

46. WIZARD OF EYRI

"If magic did not surprise,
would it be magic?"—*Zarost*

Tabitha broke inwards from the cover of the crowd, and ran. The Darkstone on Garyll's throat confirmed everything which Ashley had told her. His raised sword settled her indecision—Garyll did not struggle against his oppressor, he had taken the Devotion. He had been turned.

She refused to believe that all of him was Dark.

"Garyll, wait!" she cried. Her strapped lyre beat against her back as she ran.

It took a terribly long moment to reach the King, a moment in which Felltang glistened at the high point of its arc, but did not fall. She threw herself over the King's back, shielding Mellar's bowed head with her own.

"If you will kill the King, you must take my life first."

The depth of horror in Garyll's eyes was immense. The weight of the realm rested on their love.

"Tabitha, don't do this," he whispered.

Cold stung her from behind, from where the Darkmaster stood. She endured the sudden pain of it, and clung to the King. The air was thick with motes.

"Be true to your heart," she cried weakly to Garyll, against the grip of what she presumed was a Silence spell working its way through her chest. It was not yet the moment to reveal her own skill to the Darkmaster. She had to know Garyll would be on her side when she did.

"Kill them both!" roared the Darkmaster, from close behind. "I am the King!"

Garyll tensed. His jaw shook, and he jerked Felltang downward, but halted the strike just as suddenly. The blade was inches from Tabitha's neck. Something cracked—she couldn't tell if it was the hilt of the sword, or a bone in his hand. Then he raised Felltang again. There was a turmoil behind his gaze, but then his eyes grew wide, as if he had come upon some awesome realisation. A sudden resolve spread across his features as if a mask had been lifted from his face, and the true Glavenor was revealed at last.

"By the terms of our pact, I am released," he shouted, and flung the sword after his words. "You promised her no harm. You have breached the pact!"

Felltang screeched through the air over Tabitha's head. There was a sudden wet impact behind her. A choking, gurgling cry, then something soft and heavy struck the stone. The Kingsrim tumbled past her feet.

She released King Mellar, and turned. A figure writhed, facedown. A wide blade protruded from his back. The Darkmaster flipped over with a convulsion. The movement drove the exposed sword into the forecourt. Metal scraped. He clutched at his chest, then jerked a knee to support himself. His eyes locked onto Tabitha.

The Darkmaster was dying. But he was not dead yet.

"You die with me," he said, no more than a wheeze. In the shocked silence of the crowd, his words were sharp. Despite the blood frothing from his mouth, he gestured a command, and whispered a spell. The motes of sixty Shadowcasters combined, and flew at Tabitha as a wall of Dark, coming from all sides at once.

There was no time for fear. Tabitha found the clarity of the wizard's attention through the Ring. She had known Cabal would assault her when she declared her defiance, but she had not expected to face the reckless fury of a dying man. Tabitha formed the pattern of the reversed Turning in an instant, yet it was still not quick enough. The first of the motes struck. If Zarost had not insisted she meditate on her spell for the entire night, she knew she would have lost the form under the assault.

She extended her spell. One twisted circle, reflected to form two, and reflected again to four, all within a flickering of thought. She reached through sudden pain. Four circles became eight, eight sixteen. A deathly cold gripped her legs, tore at her back. Sixteen circles reflected to form thirty-two, a wavering net of scales, like a coat of mail. Her arms were in agony. She drew everything from the Ring— all the awareness she could bear, all the enhanced concentration she could demand. Time stretched out, every fraction of every second gave her a moment within which she could act, and yet she needed more time to save herself.

Thirty-two, sixty-four, one-hundred-and-twenty-eight. The reflections doubled her pattern with frantic growth. Something was grinding into her spine, threatening to break her bones.

Then she had it, as she had practised—a net of fine circles, so fine they caught each mote at the moment it struck, so numerous they surrounded her like the shell of an egg. It did nothing to protect her as it was, it only afforded her a moment of control over the motes, before they pierced the pattern and struck to her core.

The entire web of Dark under the Master's control was aimed inwards, a thousand arrow-points, driving to the centre. Tabitha stood with her hands outstretched. She could never have summoned so much of the Dark to her command. She could not have summoned any while holding the full complexity of the twisted circles in mind at the same time, but the Darkmaster's assault offered thousands upon thousands of motes. She was entombed in essence. She did not have to escape the Dark, she embraced it, accepted it. She was a Shadowcaster. The Dark was hers to command for the instant it was within her pattern.

"Hold the pattern, round and round, in the hidden turn, to the stronger Will be bound."

She was a Lightgifter.

It was as if a thousand lightning flashes ignited in one brilliant instant. The motes that were in her sphere of influence became sprites, the cold became heat.

As the wave of Dark washed against her spell from all sides, it was returned, as if it had washed against a wall, or a mirror. Tabitha strained to hold the spell as a unified whole. The Dark was reflected as Light, upon the advance of its kind. Sprites struck motes. The essence was neutralised around her.

The Darkmaster's fury did not abate, if anything the motes came faster as the Light bloomed around Tabitha. The Shadowcasters threw all of the Dark essence against her spell. The intense concentration was too much to maintain, it drained her strength faster than ever, but she held on. Tabitha bowed her head.

The final wave of Light around her met the Dark. The air was filled with the cacophony, as a thousand particles of essence met their nemesis. Flagstones shattered, and chips of masonry stung her legs. People cried out against a sudden clap of booming thunder.

Then there was nothing, just silence, and the returning breeze.

She looked up.

It was not Light that filled Stormhaven, though the citizens probably thought so, for the Dark that stained the air was removed, and the daylight had returned. It was clarity, more than anything else, which had taken the place of the Dark. Victory had been snatched from the Darkmaster's grasp, and in its place was left the empty air. All the spells that had wrapped Stormhaven in gloom, all the cold and grinding fear, all the despair and might of the Dark was dissolved. The motes were gone. The sprites were no more. Something new had taken their place.

Only one man could see what she saw. Tabitha knew that somewhere in the crowd, Twardy Zarost watched the flux of fusion, the clear liquid power filling the space that others saw as empty.

She had reached it all. Half of the Dark essence had been turned to create Light, and had in turn neutralised the remaining motes in the final clash. Clear essence filled Stormhaven.

Some of the Shadowcasters realised what had been done, for they broke from the rear of the crowd, and fled toward the City Gates. They were the wisest. Without Dark essence, they had no power at all. The crowd milled in confused awe.

Tabitha felt a strange tingling at her throat. She found the orbs upon their chains and held them close to her chin. Two spheres of pure crystal hung there. In the intensity of her crisis and triumph, she had transformed the stones as well.

"Ring user," came a faint, gurgling voice.

The Darkmaster had a pale cast to his face, and blood streaked his chin. The hilt of Felltang still protruded from his chest. His eyes sought Tabitha's with the appeal of the dying. A feeble presence pulled at her like the touch of clinging weed in the lake shallows.

"A—word."

Garyll moved before her. He stooped to grip Felltang, and the Darkmaster arched in agony. Garyll did not pull the sword clear. He turned on his knee, to face Tabitha.

"I'll stay my hand, only if you wish to hear him."

"I'll hear him." Cabal was so close to death's door, and his power was gone. With Garyll positioned as he was, the Darkmaster presented no threat. She came up close beside Garyll. The Darkmaster gurgled twice, before finding the breath for his voice amidst the bubbles of his own blood.

"Did you—find—the wizard?"

She nodded.

"Was—this spell—his secret work?"

Tabitha could see the Darkmaster's question would lead to another, but she did not wish to lie, in the presence of the Swordmaster and the

King. She could not lie, with the Ring so much a part of her now.

"Yes."

"Who is the wizard?"

King Mellar was close to her on the one side, Garyll on the other.

"You are looking at her."

Blood dripped from Cabal's chin, and disappeared into the spreading wetness of his black robe.

"Ah." He coughed, and grimaced. "The riddle—find the wizard. The wizard within." He coughed blood again.

"Ahh." He closed his eyes. His voice was a fading whisper.

"– time, the Dark shall return."

His eyes fluttered open. His gaze wandered over them, then he displayed a sudden focus, as if seeing something far away.

And then he laughed. It was chilling, for it was plain to Tabitha that each convulsion brought immense pain around Garyll's blade. Yet the Darkmaster laughed.

"You have won nothing!" he shouted, his voice suddenly shrill. "Look upon your doom!"

"Enough!" Garyll shouted. He wrenched his sword free as he stood, taking Felltang on an arc through the Darkmaster's chest. Even as the Darkmaster's body went rigid with death, Tabitha thought he laughed. She recoiled from the gory spectacle.

The delusions brought by the moment of death, it had to be. Still she turned, and looked off into the distance, where the Darkmaster had looked at the last.

There was nothing but the distant jagged teeth of the Zunskar. It was a strangely ordinary day. The air was cool, the sun was warm. The storm clouds still loomed in the north, but to the east they were tattered. Great rents had been blown in the mantle of grey, and through these the sky showed blue.

The sun poured down in golden falls. Large birds crossed the blue gaps, coming from the east. She drew on her Ring to refine her sight. Upon that moment, Tabitha's heart fell.

The birds sped toward Stormhaven, growing larger all the time, holding a ragged formation. They were too big, bigger than eagles, and their flight was ungainly. Tabitha stifled a cry. There were so many of them, black and deadly, airborne beasts that would never be birds. Wicked, barbed wings swept back against slick bodies. Giant malformed beaks issued horrid cries.

Garyll turned, to follow her gaze. He said nothing for a time, then stiffened beside her.

"Run!" he shouted. "Run for cover! The Morgloth come!"

The crowd erupted in chaos, voices raised in argument, people pushing against angry resistance, some escaping in different directions.

Tabitha was transfixed with horror. A company of Swords came at a run from the distant City Gates. Their armour jingled. The first Morgloth swooped past the outer battlements. The Swords slowed at the edge of the forecourt, as they considered the chaotic crowd. They had probably expected to battle Shadowcasters. Instead, the forecourt boiled with panicked citizens. The Morgloth dived from the sky behind them.

The first victim was a young Sword at the rear of the company. The Morgloth landed hard against his back. With a sickening thump, the man was driven to the ground. The Morgloth squatted, and removed the Sword's head with one swift bite. The nauseating thump of another strike sounded. Three more.

Garyll gripped her by the arm, and wrenched her around to face him.

"The palace!" he shouted. "Come!"

They ran, the King a few steps ahead of them, amongst those of the crowd who had heard Garyll's cry. Around them, citizens fled for their lives. The Morgloth seemed to have no preference. They hungered for life, and any head would do.

A Shadowcaster stood helplessly in the open, summoning the Dark over and over. But no magic came to his aid. A Morgloth took the Shadowcaster as a bird takes a fly, swooping down from behind and snapping the life from him with its vicious jaws.

A woman ran with her child. Then the child ran alone. It was too horrifying to react to. Tabitha ran, and noticed how their company had grown. Swords joined their desperate bid for the safety of the palace. A woman in a tattered, dirty-red robe ran close beside her. Tabitha was surprised to see a Lightstone at her throat. Before she could think on it, the woman was lost in a sudden crush of screaming people. The palace gates were too narrow for the rush of the crowd, and the blockage backed up all around Tabitha.

Five Morgloth swooped down upon the head of the blockage. The forecourt was too far from anywhere safe. It was terribly open to the sky, but they were forced to take a stand where they were. Within the press of bodies, she couldn't move.

Garyll was close. He called out to the Swords, and some rallied to his side. A hysterical woman almost pulled him under before Garyll pushed himself clear.

A Morgloth dived from above. A man fell, screaming, with the evil beast gripping his chest. Swords hacked at the demon, but their blades seemed to have little effect on its glistening hide.

Garyll leapt forward, and his sword whined through the air before finding the Morgloth. The Morgloth screeched and dropped its prey. Again, Felltang described a vicious arc. The beast lashed out with its talons. Two Swords were lifted from the ground and thrown deeper into the crowd. Garyll's blade found its mark, driving deep into the Morgloth's neck. When he withdrew his blade, the Morgloth slumped from view, lifeless.

Tabitha was too shocked to feel anything for Garyll's triumph. It was truly hopeless. There had to be close to a hundred Morgloth swooping and screeching through Stormhaven. Those citizens who made it to shelter might live a while longer. Those who didn't, would die.

A familiar figure with a bald head appeared at her side. Twardy Zarost's eyes were wide with fear, or anger.

"Tabitha. Tabitha! Have you forgotten everything so soon?"

She stared at him.

"Use your song! Use the Lifesong!"

"Why don't you do something yourself!" she cried. "You can save us!"

"If I take your challenge, you lose the Ring. You must be the wizard!"

"I don't care! The people must be saved!"

"Then use your song!" he shouted. He slapped her so hard, and so quickly, she only realised what he had done when heat bloomed in her cheek with the return of blood. "Your second stanza. Sing!"

Anger burst through her petrified stupor, and she lunged for Zarost, her hands claws. He caught her by the wrists.

"The people must be saved!" he said.

The echo of her own words rang with truth. The accusation brought her to an abrupt halt. Her terror had kept her from her task. It was not easy to admit that Zarost was right, but as she found the clarity of her Ring again, it became clear that he was. She had been paralysed by fear. The battle against the Darkmaster had left her drained, vulnerable. The panic of the crowd had infected her.

She swung her lyre around from her back on its strap. The second stanza, the song of death. She turned to the sky.

The moment she sang her first note, three Morgloth swerved to converge on their company. The Swords were close to the edge of the crowd, the panicked people fought to stay within their weak defence. Tabitha raised her voice to its limit to even hear herself above the roaring, wailing noise of the crowd.

A Sword screamed as another Morgloth struck. Tabitha sang, and her throat burned with the strain. Her eyes stung with sudden tears. She couldn't hear the notes she plucked, but she could feel them as her awareness widened, and the power of the Lifesong flooded her. More glossy wings veered to find her sound, and struck at the edge of the mass of people, aiming inwards. The wailing of the crowd became a piercing howl, as the Morgloth focused their attack.

Not the wailing of the crowd. She recognised the sound even as she sang—the Shiver note. The few Swords she could see had whistles between their lips, and they blew wild, shrieking notes. Yzell had made his instruments well, and at last the men had remembered them. Those Morgloth close enough to the Swords, crashed to the ground, momentarily stunned.

Tabitha reached deeper into the Lifesong, drawing the ancient power through the channel of her awareness. The clear essence swirled through the crowd, disturbed and restless, as her will gathered within it.

Garyll fought like a wild man, his sword holding the Shiver note in a continual howl, broken by regular impacts. His men survived, but as soon as one Morgloth was downed, two appeared in its place, drawn ever faster by Tabitha's song. The crippled Morgloth rose as soon as the whistlers drew breath. Tabitha realised that even Garyll's possessed fighting was not going to be enough. The ragged ring of Swords surrounding her would not stand against the assault for much longer.

She tried to hold all of the Morgloth in mind as she brought the stanza of death to a close. Her throat was raw, and her notes strained to find their mark. The clear essence shimmered through the air, wrapped itself around her targets. As her voice broke on the final note, she knew she had not reached them all, but it was the best she could do.

The power of the Lifesong was released through the clear essence. Forty Morgloth screeched. Their black bodies imploded, collapsing as if crushed in a mighty hand. In an instant, they became the raw substance of the universe. Flesh and life was transformed to clear essence. The wizard of Eyri had pronounced their doom.

Tabitha had only a heartbeat to consider her spell's effect, and wonder at the power which had flowed through her.

"Another one!" shouted a Sword, to her right. A giant beast shadowed the sky, an ugly brute who was bigger than any demons they had faced. Hunger, power and a terrible kind of awareness radiated from the dread eyes above the massive jaw. The wind shrieked over glossy skin as it swooped upon the company. The Swords braced themselves, and drew breath for their whistles. Garyll swung his sword, a weary circle, barely bringing the Shiver note from the blade.

But the giant Morgloth did not strike as the others had. It shot over their heads, brushing them only with the wind of its passing. It landed heavily in a clear space beyond the company, a tower of feral strength, poised beyond the range of attack. There was a calculating look to its eye. On its back, a figure clung, in the tattered remains of a blood-coloured robe. The figure's head was obscured by the mass of the giant Morgloth's neck.

Another Morgloth dived from the sky.

It swept over the company as well, and took a place beside the giant Morgloth, facing them. It gave a quick turn of its head to one side, as if it sought confirmation from the bigger leader.

Another Morgloth swooped to the ground, then another. They landed rapidly, and more came to encircle the crowd. The company had thinned, but not because any citizens had run; the dead lay strewn like boulders around the failing pool of humanity. A terrible fatalism settled on Tabitha's shoulders. There were nearly twenty Morgloth, all told. All stood beyond the immediate range of the Swords and their whistles. Tabitha did not waste her voice, she knew there was no time to complete the full death-stanza again, and her throat burned too painfully to trust it.

They faced their end.

"Are we tired of dying yet?" a voice shouted across the distance.

It was a mocking familiar voice. The speaker leered from behind the Morgloth's neck. The burned scalp and cruel face was unmistakable.

Kirjath Arkell. He appeared to be badly wasted.

"Send me the girl. I want the thief of the Ring to die first."

"Arkell!" shouted Garyll. "You'll pass through my sword first."

"I'm not Arkell any more."

The circle of Morgloth flapped their wings in unison, ducking and weaving their ghastly heads. A sharp screech from the giant leader brought instant order again. The deep, black eyes watched the prey.

"Then who are you?" Garyll shouted.

"I am the Gatekeeper! I shall live forever!"

The Morgloth screeched then, a horrific, tearing sound. Kirjath stared blankly from the Morgloth's back.

"Creator save us!" whispered Zarost, suddenly close to Tabitha again. "I think they're trying to laugh. He's an open gateway."

"What do you mean?" Tabitha asked, her eyes never leaving the giant Morgloth and its passenger.

"Arkell is their gatekeeper. Unless he is killed, it shall remain open, and there will be no end to their feeding. And I think he has lost his mind. They control him."

Garyll broke from the tight rank of Swords, running for the beast.

"Garyll! That's suicide!" she cried out.

Tabitha caught movement on the far side of Kirjath and the giant Morgloth. A tattered, dirty-red robe. A woman with close-cropped hair. A dagger glinted in her hand. She approached Kirjath from his blind side, but she was not going to reach him in time. Already the Morgloths to either side of the giant had caught the movement, and were turning to face the threat.

The dagger needed just a moment to reach Arkell. The woman wore a white orb, and Tabitha knew suddenly who it was. Hosanna, the Gifter who had suffered so grossly under Arkell's hand. She was sure the blade would find its mark, if given the chance.

Tabitha sang out, and ran for the Morgloth. The Shiver took effect, and for a few moments, the great Morgloth and its companions were immobile.

The tender parts in her throat exploded in pain. Her vocal cords were already raw and pushed beyond their limit from singing above the roar of the crowd. Her note wavered into something between a screech and a shriek. The giant Morgloth crouched.

Garyll reached the giant, but it blocked his advance. He struck once, twice, and then Tabitha's voice broke completely. She could taste blood in her mouth. She could make no sound. Garyll was raked clear by one huge talon. He flew through the air. The Morgloth reared, huge and hideous before Tabitha.

Through its legs, Tabitha saw the woman backing away. There

was blood on her hands. Then Kirjath fell from the back of the giant Morgloth.

He tumbled on the stone, then sprang at Hosanna like a spider. Instead of retreating, Hosanna met his charge with her dagger raised. Arkell doubled over, but his body-weight took her down. They wrestled desperately on the ground, then Hosanna's blade flashed wetly behind his back. She struck, once, twice, then twisted the handle hard.

Kirjath flailed his arms, then clawed at her face, but still she held him in the fatal embrace. Hosanna jerked the knife one last time. Arkell's head dropped. When she rolled his body away, he dropped to the stone, as slack as a bag of sand. He was dead.

The howl that issued from the giant Morgloth was deafening. It launched straight upwards. A lesser Morgloth took to the air with a screech, abandoning the crowds with a frantic flutter of wings. All around the street, Morgloth screeched, and lurched into the air. They wheeled, and flew east.

"They must go back through their closing gateway, or die," said Zarost.

The Morgloth were leaving. It seemed that they might be spared their death. But in a terrible moment, Tabitha felt a returning presence. The sky became the black wings of the giant Morgloth, its talons outstretched, its intent clear. Garyll cried out a warning, but he was too far away to save her. The giant Morgloth would kill one last time before it left this world, she knew. There was no time to run.

She spread her arms wide, took a last breath of everything. Her eyes met Garyll's, across the space, across the last moment, across the divide between life and death. He ran with his sword raised, but he would be too late.

"The oath be damned!" someone cursed nearby, and a hand touched the back of her neck.

The giant Morgloth fell upon Tabitha. His huge form enveloped her, his roared fury crushed her. The pain was absolute. Stormhaven ended in a sudden flash.

She must have died in that moment, for a terrible force wrenched her apart, as if she had been stretched in an instant to cover the whole universe.

"Infinity," someone whispered.

◆ ———————◆

It was strangely painless, to be dead. It was mostly dark, and full of stars. She lost all sense of who she was. There was no up, nor down, no breathing, no being, only the flickering currents of the Lifesong, which ran through all of her. There was no Tabitha Serannon, only clear essence.

47. A WIZARD'S END
"Death does strange things to people."—*Zarost*

The world turned fast around Garyll Glavenor, where he knelt on the slick stone. His eyes were filled with the sweat and blood of battle, and yet he saw the same scene clearly, over and over again. The giant Morgloth dived on Tabitha. Its wings enveloped both her and the bald young man who tried in vain to pull her away. Garyll screamed his rage at the beast as he jumped astride its back and struck Felltang deep into the glossy neck. The giant only tossed its head back to give a chilling screech. The suddenness of its launch threw Garyll from its back.

Then he watched the beast lurch away through the air, carrying its final prize. A coloured cloak flapped in its talons. The bald man had worn that. The thickness of the Morgloth's curled legs hid the rest of its prey.

It had taken them both. The force of its strike left cracked flagstones where they had stood. Tabitha's lyre lay abandoned on the stone— there was nothing else. She had been so close he could almost have kissed her outstretched arms. The Morgloth had not even left him the body to mourn. Tabitha Serannon was gone.

It was ended. The scattering people in the forecourt were a blur, a noisome rush of yammering wounded folk and twittering survivors.

Some time later, carts came to bear the dead away. He ignored the hands which shook his shoulders. The death-wains could find him later. His eyes smarted as he saw the giant Morgloth dive down again.

Wetness coursed down his cheeks. Sweat and blood, he told himself. A distant group of fool heralds trumpeted the victory call. They were wrong; it was utter, crushing defeat. The Dark may have been ended, the Morgloth might have fled, the King might live to continue his rule, but Eyri had lost Tabitha Serannon.

All of his sacrifice had been in vain. He should have just defied the Darkmaster, and died in the torture chambers in Ravenscroft.

Tabitha. Sweet Tabitha. She had done things with the essence he had never thought possible. She had saved him from killing his own King. She had sung like Ethea, and worked true magic upon the

Morgloth. She was a wonder.

She was dead.

It must end. He had made the pact. First the Darkmaster's death, then his own. His betrayal was too deep to be forgiven. While the Morgloth threatened Tabitha, there had been reason to postpone the moment of judgement.

Now there was nothing, save that he felt it would be fitting if he died at night. The sun oozed towards the western horizon. The stained blades of his battle-gauntlet held a dark red. He wondered if his own blood would stain them darker. If the slash was deep enough through his throat, he wouldn't have to see.

♦ ———————— ♦

Everything was made of threads. Darkness woven through short strands of light. Light wrapped around darkness. No, not threads, rather strings of vibration, places of music, or songs without words. Or a liquid, like clear essence, yet taking many forms wherever the currents converged. If this was Death, it was an impossible dimension. She was stretched across the firmament. The legends of the Passage of the Soul were all wrong; nothing could have prepared her for this. To be nowhere, yet everything. To be made of nothing, yet be all the essence of the Universe.

More than anything, she felt wide, immense beyond her greatest fantasies of freedom. It was weird to have no boundary, in any direction. Direction didn't even exist here. She drifted with the currents between the stars, going neither fast, nor slow. She was in a great place of silence, and yet there was sound, if she thought of listening.

"T-a-b-i-t-h-a."

A song, or a single voice, or a hundred; she struggled to identify the source. There were stars, millions of stars, and even more space between them, yet she could see them all. She knew them all.

"T-a-b-i-t-h-a."

The voice came from all over her, within her, or without.

"Where am I?" she tried to ask, yet had no voice to speak with.

"Everywhere," came the answer, resonant, as much a part of the stars as she was.

"Zarost!" she thought, recognising his presence, but not seeing his body anywhere.

"At last, you find your wit," came the answer.

"Where are you?"

"Everywhere." Another voice, the same voice, at the same time, but from another place. "This is infinity." Zarost was all around her. "Now you must learn how to get back."

"I'm not dead?"

"No," Zarost answered, with the impossible laughter which spread like ripples on a pond, around her, within her. "I hope not, or I've broken my oath to the Gyre for nothing."

"But where? What happened?"

"There will be time, when your skill has grown enough, to learn of the Transference. For now, think of where you wish to be. I cannot guide you to a place you cannot hold in mind."

A place. Stormhaven. She felt herself surge through the dimension of bewilderment which she had become.

"Is it—over?"

"It is never over, for a wizard. No, it has just begun."

"The Morgloth—?"

"You did well, Wizard Serannon. They have left, and the sun shines again in Eyri. But in one place, there is enough darkness to drown in."

"Where is it so dark?"

"A man grieves for your death more than he needs to."

Garyll.

"Find him in your mind, if you wish to save him. See the place clearly, and you shall return there."

His presence faded, as if he had been pulled away by something.

Then she was alone amongst the stars, and it felt like she was falling.

◆ ———————— ◆

Twardy Zarost found his own destination in the crossing-point of infinity. He wished he didn't have to visit the Chambers of the Gyre, but the wizards needed him, and he needed the wizards. The Writhe was still bearing down on Eyri, he suspected. They had said seven days, and six had passed. It must be drawing close; they would have little time to devise a counter-spell, but Zarost had not been idle since the meeting. He had a plan, something to feed to the worm which it would not like to eat, no, not at all.

He anticipated his empty place on the stonewood bench. All seven wizards would notice him at once, seated as they would be around the pool in their centre. He released his intent gently to arrive as slowly as he could manage, but he appeared with a jolt which made the Cosmologer jump nonetheless.

The atmosphere within the chambers of the Gyre was as welcoming as ever, which was to say, not at all. An unsavoury smell filled the air, an almost acrid odour of something unwashed, something like old bacon. Yes, like a lightning-struck boar. They had been using too much magic, the ozone scent of burned auric essence lingered around all of them.

"You're too late!" the Cosmologer accused from her place opposite him. "Too late, too late, too late!" She looked frightful, her skin had an unhealthy pallor to it and blue veins showed at her temples. Her hair looked as dead as the summer sedge-grasses of Rostkaan. Zarost hurriedly took them all in. The Warlock glared at him with bloodshot eyes. The Mentalist's hair, usually a radiant shock, lay down upon his shoulders in clumps. The Senior looked beyond the time of his own death—he sat with his head down, his back hunched, clutching onto a staff set between his knees as if that were the only thing preventing him from falling. He wore the sensitive magesilk vestment of old Moral kingdom, a garment which altered colour to reflect the vitality of its bearer. It clung to him like a shroud, almost as transparent as it would be if it were merely hanging over a chair. The greying Spiritist had a haunted look about her too; she didn't see him, she saw something else. And the Lorewarden! The Lorewarden was comatose, his head thrown back against a pillar, his jaw slack. The Mystery watched him with a steady gaze, but her presence was no more than a thin shimmer around her and she was shaking with small erratic jerks, an affliction which Zarost recognised as extreme fatigue.

"My time was well spent in Eyri," he answered the Cosmologer's initial challenge.

"You believe your time more valuable than ours?" she snapped.

Zarost turned away from her to address the Warlock. "The Seeker was in the centre of a war."

The Warlock kept on glaring at him, his eyebrows forming a threatening V. "She should have stood or fallen with what she had learned," the Warlock replied at last. "A battle was no reason to linger. We needed you here, Riddler, and you knew it. You have been a fool."

"But I could not leave any earlier! A gateway had to be closed!" Zarost exclaimed, facing the Spiritist.

"A gateway," she repeated.

"A gateway, to the Morgloth!" Zarost exclaimed.

She looked distracted. "How many came through?" she asked, though her tone said she didn't care.

"All of them, I think, including one of the Greater Morgloth."

"Oh."

"Sweet mother of all creation! What is wrong with you, Spiritist? The channeller became an open gateway, he was insane."

"Yes, if that had not been contained –" She gestured vaguely with one hand, and let it fall to her lap again.

"—we could have lost all of Eyri," Zarost finished for her.

He had expected the Spiritist to be wide-eyed at such an announcement—she could understand the horror of what could have been—but her attention had disengaged from the present once again.

"We have lost all of Eyri," the Mentalist explained. "So sad, Riddler. So sad. What happened to the Seeker, the girl? How far did she progress, before you left?"

"What do you mean we have lost Eyri? It was there, when I left! The Writhe is not upon it yet, is it?" He turned to the Mystery. "Is it? You said seven days, I have returned in six! There must still be time! Where is the Writhe now? Where is it?"

The Mystery shook her head. "You were wise to save her," she stated, holding Zarost with her twitching green eyes. "You were foolish to send her back."

"Six days was too long, Riddler," the Senior explained.

Zarost's blood ran cold.

"Whatever you think you have achieved in Eyri is for naught," the Warlock added. "It shall end, today, Riddler. We have lost the battle."

"No! That cannot be!" cried Zarost. "No, oh no, tell me it isn't true! It isn't! The Seeker has solved the riddle of the Ring, she sees with the wizard's eye! We have a ninth wizard, and her lore is the Lifesong. Eyri can not be gone!"

The Senior closed his eyes and pressed his forehead to his staff. "Ahh. That is too terrible, Riddler!" he croaked. "The fruit of four hundred years! Wasted."

"Why do you all speak as if the battle is already lost? I am here, our octad is complete! We can fight the Writhe. Eyri is not yet gone!"

"No, Eyri is finished, Zarost," replied the Senior. "The Writhe is upon it. We sensed the moment of your Transference—it was too late for us to come into Eyri to find you, and we thought you were lost to us. You escaped at the last possible moment. You can not return, none of us can, the Writhe has claimed Eyri as its own, it has grown enormous, and it wrangles at the head of the White River, below the falls of River's End. It is so powerful now that if you tried to Transfer inwards to anywhere in Eyri you would be drawn into the Writhe first. So we cannot reach the ninth wizard, and we cannot save her."

"No! How can this be?" he cried. "Why did it move so fast?"

"It caught us by surprise, Riddler, we lost its track when it dived at Rek. It ate well underground, it gained mass, and travelled more quickly than we expected."

"If it is below River's End, it must be upon the Shield! We must go there, we must go there at once!" shouted Zarost.

The Warlock looked into him with his angry red eyes. "Do you wish to die?"

"And do you wish our hope of fighting Chaos to be dead? Do you forget what the Seeker represents?" Zarost cried out. "Why do you think I stayed to fight beside her?"

"Fight beside her? Did you cast something in Eyri, did you break your oath?" the Cosmologer snapped.

Her challenge was too direct to be avoided, and it revealed an awkward truth. "Only at the very end, I, ah, demonstrated a spell to her, yes, one she shall come to learn on the path she walks."

"How much of your own magic did you release in Eyri?" demanded the Warlock.

"A guiding hand was all she did need, to avoid the Great Morgloth's final feed."

"Where did you guide her?" asked the Senior tiredly.

"I took her away with the Transference, and returned her again."

"So you did break the Oath!" exclaimed the Cosmologer triumphantly. "We have lost nothing, because the Riddler failed."

"Confound you, Riddler, you had me hoping for a while there!" exclaimed the Senior. "You have affected what the apprentice learns with magic of your own! You really did waste your time. Not that it really matters any more," he ended, the brief hope dimming from his lined face.

"No, she was already a wizard!" Zarost objected. "She walked the path of apprenticeship impeccably! She has balanced the light and dark of the first axis. She sings the Lifesong, by the sun and stars, she sings like Ethea! You can't deny her right to wear the Wizard's Ring.

She is everything we hoped for!"

At this news an electric interest ran through the Gyre. The Spiritist held a hand to her mouth. The Senior's eyes were alight once more. "So we do have a ninth!" he said.

"We must save her! If we cannot reach her, then we must face the Writhe."

The Warlock slammed his fist into his palm. "By the blood of the scythe! how do you propose we do that, Riddler? Look at us. You can see we have tried, we haven't slept since you saw us last, we have cast every pattern we can devise against it, and nothing slows its course! We tried to divert the Writhe with a mighty windstorm, mightier even than the winds that ran across the west of Huntersland when Ametheus sought to drown their city of Highbough in sand. Trees were ripped from the ground, boulders flew before that wind, but the Writhe carried on, unperturbed. As soon as our stormwind ceased, the waters of the Linner Lake were sucked up even though it was five leagues from the shore. As the Writhe passed further south from Jho, the woven road between Koom and Rek was stripped from the soil. We tried to bind the people of Rek into one mind with a spell of Fortitude, so that they might resist the Writhe's pull by drawing strength from each other, but the Lûk in that down were reamed out like termites from rotten wood. We shifted our attention far ahead of it, to the southern border of the Lûk's Six Sided land, where the willow-camps are placed beside the White River at the edge of the Evernon Forest. Around the willow-camps we wove a shield similar to that which shelters Eyri, albeit smaller, but the camp was scoured out as if we had not been there. The white-willows went up like frantic ghosts, despite being fortified with seventh-level Forbidding spells and their roots being bound in stone. We watched it eat across the wastes like a toppled whirlwind—even the Chaos in the wildfire did nothing to change the worm. No, Riddler, we have fought hard, and for too long. Don't make us watch any more, don't force us to see our Eyri fall. Join us quietly in our grieving, if you would, but don't expect us to fight, for we are already beaten. There is no way to oppose this faceless foe. Everything we feed it only makes it stronger."

The Warlock had epitomized their problem. They always thought in terms of what had been learned before, seldom of what could be devised with what was known. They really did need a Riddler in their circle, to put the pieces of the puzzle together. It was time to reveal his solution. He rose to take the floor.

"What if we feed it nothing?" he said.

"Don't play your games with us," growled the Warlock. "I'll rip your clever head off."

"Nothingness," Zarost said quickly. "A gap in space and time, a hole where the fabric of the tapestry was stretched until it separated. The seven of you have tried and tried, but every time you give it something. What if we gave it Nothing?"

"Impossible!" the Cosmologer objected. "That would be Chaos, Riddler! What kind of ordered Universe has a hole in it?"

He offered her the rind of a smile. "Not true, Cosmologer, not true, I don't believe you have thought it through. It would be a temporary change, the Nothingness would disappear as soon as the Writhe was defeated. The overall Order would be maintained—it would be improved, for the Writhe would be gone."

"I don't understand," said the Mystery. "How can Nothing be of any use?"

"I see it so: the Writhe gains speed as it gathers flesh and feed, it rolls upon the movement in its mouth. If it were to be fed a space, with a great enough face, it would pass into that void; there would be nothing to continue its current with. It would be like a wave encountering a headland; the wave could not continue in the sheltered water beyond, if it were not connected."

Now they were listening. Almost all of them.

"Would you wake up the Lorewarden, Spiritist?"

He waited while the balding man chewed the air, spluttered and finally opened his eyes. "Hhrr. Hhere here," the Lorewarden said. But he promptly fell asleep again, and had to be nudged by the Spiritist until he had risen from his seat to avoid her prodding. "Go on, go on," he muttered to Zarost, "I've been here all the time."

A riddled answer. Zarost smiled, the Lorewarden was more lucid than he appeared to be. "It would be an eighth-level weave, it would need all of us. We shall begin with a singular point, we shall anchor to that place, and then we move apart, each of us drawing that same anchored point in eight directions, and so we shall have the corners of Nothingness gripped in our hands. We shall form a cube, or rather there will be a cube in the Nothingness between our eight positions. The Writhe shall draw itself onwards, its own hunger shall defeat it. It shall eat nothing, and so become nothing."

"We need to be ahead of the Writhe to do this? You mean to Transfer into its course, and remain there as it advances upon us? Are you mad?" demanded the Warlock.

"No, Riddler, no," said the Mentalist, "not after what happened to the Warlock in Kah. It will draw us into the maw, we shall not escape!"

"If you think of escape, then surely are you thinking of failure. There will be no Writhe to escape from, we shall bear its deathstroke into its jaws."

The Mentalist was not convinced. "But what if we are not strong enough to hold apart? Why can't we cast our spell from afar, and see what happens!"

"Because it is not a spell which can be projected, we are the corners of an Unweaving. We cannot project Nothing through the pool," answered Zarost. "We must be there, at the Shield."

"NO!" cried the Cosmologer. "No! It is folly! Eight, to save one? The ninth wizard is not so precious. If we are all consumed, then who shall fight Ametheus? Who shall be left to resist?"

"Yet if we don't fight him now, will we fight him later? Will we be able to?"

The Lorewarden raised a heavy hand. "I am too tired to calculate the permutations," he said, "but I feel there is a good chance this might work. This is a cunning plan. The odds might be in our favour."

"And the evens as well," added Zarost.

"I'll not risk my hide to a chance!" boomed the Warlock. "We must know it will work, and we don't."

"But this *is* the moment to defeat it," announced the Mystery. "We cannot wait until Eyri is consumed. How great will the Writhe be after drawing Eyri's Shield into its spin? We have but one chance for this to work, and it is now!"

"I don't cast my spells on chance either!" objected the Spiritist.

"We face an escalating spell, there is no time to delay, certainty is a luxury we cannot afford!" the Senior asserted.

"Chaos!" screeched the Cosmologer. "You would bring Chaos into being! I won't let you."

The Senior stamped the end of his staff upon the floor. "Wizards!" he shouted. "The Riddler is right. We have a means to save the ninth wizard, and we must use it. This is a test of the Gyre's strength. Let us be strong enough to meet an eighth-level spell, let us be wise enough to cast our own."

"Then I want to call a vote!" objected the Cosmologer. "We—"

"There shall be no vote! As the Senior I overrule your objection, and yours, Warlock. We unite in this. We unite! The Gyre will face the Writhe with Nothing. Prepare yourself, and join upon my finger for our Transferance. We must save the ninth wizard, we must save Eyri." He stood with his right forefinger raised, waiting upon them, his magesilk vestment shimmering with resplendent viridian patterns. "If the Nothingness is contained by the strict pattern of our positions, it shall be an Order spell. Come and join your power with mine. We face it now!"

Zarost lived for moments like these, when the power of one wizard rose from dormancy to rush through everything. The Senior's might filled the room and infused them all. The Lorewarden shed the worst of his fatigue. The Mystery's twitching calmed. The Mentalist's hair even rose off his shoulders a bit.

Zarost strode to join the Senior. The Gyre was a strange organisation; they could spend days discussing trivialities, but when it came to important issues, they could find direction in a flash. He reached into his pocket, retrieved a flattened piece of bristly fabric, and slapped the brim against his wrist. The hat popped into shape. He spun it into the air, and caught it upon his bald dome. It sat lower than usual on his head, but the brim was tight. He was ready to face their nemesis.

The Cosmologer came to them last. There were fresh tears in her eyes. "Blast you, Riddler! You are dirty, devious and despicable. I hope you are right."

"Hold onto your corner, whatever happens," he said to her. "If one of our positions is lost, we might allow some of the Writhe to escape the trap. The worm must find Nothing, it must not find us."

"I am terrified by it," she admitted in a hollow voice. "It has more power than I."

She brought her shaking finger to the tower of seven nonetheless. The brown chamber spun around them with their combined empowered essence. Zarost took a last breath of the dry desert air. He closed his eyes.

"We are one. Let us pray we have enough strength together," said the Senior.

They reached for infinity. They Transferred together.

◆ —————— ◆

They were at the pool at the head of the White River, just beyond the northern boundary of Eyri's Shield. They stood with their backs to the great cliff below River's End, and they faced an advancing wall of Chaos. The world churned in the sky. A terrible wind howled at them, an immense hollow moan punctuated with the clacking of debris, backed by continuous rolling thunder. The dark and boiling clouds which grew ahead of the Writhe were ripped inwards at their trailing edge as the air was sucked into the choking hunger of its mouth. Silver lightning tore across the gloom in jagged forks. Amber rain stung their backs, and when Zarost looked back he saw that the falls were bent at their base. The water never reached the ground, it was sucked horizontally towards the Writhe. Some of the smaller rocks were coming by too. The boulders would be next.

They were dragged towards the Writhe at once, dragged though they dug their heels into the barren dirt. This was wildfire land, the wastes caused by the centuries of Chaos spilled from Eyri's Shield. The grey soil was dead, but safe. The silvered seams within it were not.

"Hold together!" shouted the Senior. "Anchor to this point."

Zarost concentrated on his fingertip, and watched the air grow bright as they claimed the same position. But they slipped towards the Writhe nonetheless, space bent inwards like stretched dough.

"Now, work the spell of Centrifuge, throw us outwards, and hard," the Senior commanded.

"We won't get far enough!" cried the Cosmologer. "We can't spin that fast!"

"Turn us!"

The Warlock began the Centrifuge pattern, being the most adept at second-axis spells, particularly matter-magic. They turned upon the tower of fingers in their centre, turned around the axis of the single point they held. The Writhe dragged them faster over the grey soil. Zarost combined his essence with the Warlock's pattern, as did the others, and the world became a blur as they gained speed around their centre. Their track towards the Writhe began to increase, and yet they had not separated the point as Zarost had hoped. An immense force bound the point together, a force of nature which resisted their attempt to split the fabric of space. Their fingers were bound together. Zarost could see nothing of the Writhe now, they were spinning so fast upon their own spell that he had to shut his eyes tight to prevent them from flying out of his head. He groaned against the force of his own inertia, and the horrible tension in his arm.

The Mystery cried out with sudden inspiration, "Release

yourselves from the Gyre. We must do this as individuals, or we shall stay bonded."

Zarost withdrew from the union of minds. The point split.

He was thrown like a hammer, far into the air, across the turbulent face of the Writhe, outwards to the edge of the overhanging clouds. A great rend followed him, drawn by his hand, a black emptiness, as if the day around him was a picture painted on the lit canvas of a tent, and he tore it now to reveal the vacant night beyond. He used all of his intent to hold onto the bright fire of the leading point, which still resisted their manipulation fiercely. The others had separated with just as much energy, tearing the gap of Nothingness between them. It was going to be a race now, between those who had been thrown up high falling to the ground, or the Writhe reaching the edge of the void they held open for it.

The Writhe drew them in ever faster. Being in the air was a blessing at first, because there was nothing to hit, and since he could not resist the inwards current, he moved at the same speed as the airborne debris. The four on the ground had it hard. They had been thrown to the sides by the Centrifuge spell, now they raced over the earth again through lifting soil and rocks and Chaos-dust. The Mentalist lost command of his warding spell, and hit a boulder. The Mystery was downed by a flying tree. Two corners of the Nothingness flapped free, and the void became more like a stretched pyramid than a cube.

Zarost passed the jutting cloud and fell through air thick with moisture, stone chips, and electricity. He hoped that the outer material orbiting the maw was not the governing pattern of the Writhe. The six of them were falling inwards now, ever faster. If they could just hold their void open over the inner vortex, the Writhe should end. He threw a spell of Repulsion against all of the five conscious Gyre members in turn, and felt similar spells buffet him, but the Writhe was beating them. They were drawing closer to each other as they sped into the gloom of its wreckage-filled throat.

The air was like soup in his lungs. Gravity pressed on him like a rolling mountain. This was far worse than the pressure of the Shield, far worse than he'd expected. Zarost held onto his awareness only—his body was going to take horrendous damage, but he could use the Restitution spell when this was all over, so long as he maintained his sanity. His chest and arms exploded with pain. He held onto the corner of the torn Gap, and fired like an arrow into the maelstrom.

Zarost passed through water and ice, and through rock and fire.

Time slowed the deeper he went, and he seemed to have hours to contemplate his pain and misery. And when he believed that he had truly misjudged the spell of the Writhe, when he believed they were all going to die, he entered at last a clear place, right in the heart of the destruction, like a secret chamber of peace, and as he did, so the others emerged too, including the unconscious Mystery and Mentalist, their bodies all as devastated as his, but most of their hands still holding the ends of the black tear in space. The Writhe had drawn them together through all of its detritus, and the Nothingness between them had closed, almost to a point.

Ahead of them, in the clear place, the fundamental of the Writhe turned. A small circle of silver, like a polished steel ring, too small to fit upon a child's finger, yet its density was immense, it had gathered so much matter around it and into itself. This was the pattern that drove the monster.

They rushed together, drawn by its gravity to become pulverised.

But their fingers had not touched when they passed the silver band, something of Nothing remained. In the fraction of an instant that the black emptiness between them was drawn over the pattern of the Writhe, Zarost saw how the silvered essence lost its rhythm, then scattered like a puff of dust. The tons and tons of matter orbiting the dead heart would fall to the ground now, and crush them all.

Then their fingers touched, all eight at once, and they Transferred.

They lingered in the crossing-point of infinity, amidst the stars. Zarost wasn't sure how long it would take them to recover. Even with their Restitution spells, to undo what they had endured would take much pain and patience. But he was certain of one thing.

They had conquered the spell of Ametheus.

They had killed the Writhe.

As he prepared for his time of great silence and rest, his thoughts lingered at last on Eyri. He was glad he had motivated the Gyre to save Eyri and so grant Tabitha the gift of life again. She was a rare kind of wizard, the kind liable to surprise them all. She would draw more upon herself, while the Gyre recovered, for she had a volatile combination of one cup of knowledge with five cups talent. Whatever she drew now, she would have to face herself. The Gyre would be still for a while.

"Use your gift well, Tabitha Serannon," he whispered through the stars. "Use your gift well."

◆ ———————◆

"Garyll?"

Tabitha dared not take another step closer. He was so still, so alone, kneeling in the midst of the carnage on the forecourt, his back to her. The slain Morgloth lay where they had fallen, but the people had been borne away, all except Garyll. He was wounded, yet he had done nothing to seal the deep gash in his leg, or to tend the flesh where his armour had been torn open against his ribs, or to remove the dented helm from his head. He turned his wickedly bladed gauntlet slowly before his face, as if lost in the contemplation of what it was, what it was made for, what it had done. The gold of the late afternoon sun flickered over the dirty metal talons. He did not react to her voice, but he seemed to come to some resolution in his own time, for he laid the blades against the side of his neck, and hunched his shoulders, drawing a deep breath.

"Garyll?"

He became as still as stone. She stepped closer, fearing to intrude into the tension of his reverie, fearing what might happen if she didn't. His blades quivered.

She laced her fingers between the blades, touched his neck. She kept the touch as she walked around him, and knelt on the stone before him. His eyes danced over her, touching everywhere but upon her gaze. Then they jerked away.

"You are a vision, created by my hope. Leave me! I must find my death."

The desperation in his voice was almost worse than the words he had spoken.

"I am real. Feel me!" She gripped his rough hand in hers, drew it to her face. He did not help, but he did not resist. "Am I not warm?" she asked.

His gaze flicked to his hand on her chin, then his attention crept slowly upwards. The depth of anguish in Garyll's eyes was the worst of all.

"Tabitha?"

"Oh, Garyll!" She threw her arms around him. The dented breastplate was cold between them, but Tabitha just hugged him tighter.

"How is it that you live?" he asked, to the air behind her shoulder. "I saw you taken by the Morgloth."

There was only one honest answer, though it made no sense at all. The wonder of Zarost's spell left little understanding in its wake.

"I had the help of a wizard," she said.

"The bald man?"

"You know him as an older man, but he is still Twardy Zarost."

"The Riddler," he said, then was silent for a long time. Tabitha didn't think she could explain it all, and she didn't try. It was good to feel his arms return the embrace at last, even if it was weakly.

"The Morgloth," Garyll said. "You sang, and they became empty air."

"The Lifesong passes through me. I have accepted it as my power. I am a wizard now, Garyll. That was the riddle that the Darkmaster couldn't solve."

Garyll dropped his hands and pulled away.

"And I am a traitor," he said.

She reached for him, but he brushed her hands gently away from his shoulders, and stood. "I must face the justice of that," he said. Despite his injuries, he stood with a straight back, a pillar of armour. Tabitha cried for what that armour held inside.

"No, Garyll! We were all wounded by the Darkmaster. He found a weakness within each of us."

"That he did," he whispered, and nodded, as if that confirmed his purpose. "Goodbye, Miss Serannon. To know you live, is all I need." He brushed past her.

"Garyll, no!" Tabitha ran beyond him, and met his chest with both of her hands, yet he strode on, as if she were not there. She looked pleading into his eyes, but found nothing besides the stony gaze he hid behind.

"What was your weakness?" she cried. "What was your weakness?"

That stopped him. He did not look at her, but off into the distance, for a long time. A tear, as delicate as a pearl, traced a line through the dried blood on his cheek.

"To love you," he said. The tear caught the light of the setting sun, on the angle of his chin.

"Then let it become a strength," Tabitha said. "Whatever else you believe, you were never a traitor to me."

"I have failed the duty of Swordmaster. I am not the same man you knew."

"I don't care if you've changed! I still love you!"

"The Swordmaster deserves justice."

"Let the Swordmaster die then, if you must!" Tabitha clenched her fists against the sudden alarm at her own words. The statement had come from a deep place within, the place of truth; the Truthsayer's heart.

"But let Garyll live," she finished, "that I might love him."

Some people passed them, a woman and a child supporting a limping man between them. Garyll waited for them to pass, but the woman recognised him, and brought the trio closer.

"Bless you, Swordmaster. You saved our little girl."

The limping man nodded, his lips set grimly against his own pain. He didn't need to speak—his gratitude was plain.

Garyll closed his eyes. The woman seemed to realise he was going to say nothing, for she blessed him again, quietly. The little girl threw her arms around the Swordmaster's leg. Then her mother drew her back, and the trio moved away.

Something had changed in Garyll when he looked at Tabitha again. He drew a long, ragged breath. Suddenly his cheeks were wet with tears, though he kept his gaze firmly on Tabitha.

"I don't deserve such love."

"Yet it is here," she answered, extending her hand to him. "Come with me, Garyll, come away from this battle. It is over."

He almost took her hand. Tabitha searched his face for the reason that he jerked his hand away. His brow was furrowed with determination.

"No. There is one thing left to do."

He raised his left hand. The day had ended, and the four blades were now dark fingers in the gathering dusk. He turned the blades towards his face. They were not quite steady.

Tabitha held her breath.

He fretted with something on his arm, then he lowered the gauntlet, stepped on it, and pulled his left arm free. The stump where his hand had been was an angry, livid scar.

He straightened, and met Tabitha's gaze.

"Help me with this," he said, indicating a buckle against his ribs.

She helped him work free of the armour, first the breastplate and shoulder-guards, then the dented helm, and the blood-stained coat of mail. He even pulled his heavy fighting boots off, and set them on the pile.

He waited a long while, with his sheathed sword resting across his knees. Then at last he pressed the hilt to his forehead, and set Felltang upon the discarded symbols of his life.

"Let the King decide who shall carry that blade," he said.

When Tabitha extended her hand this time, he took it.

A great roll of thunder sounded from off to the north, where a mass of dark cloud dispersed on great winds beyond River's End. The earth shook under their feet, just the once. Then Eyri was calm.

Want more? Send an email to lifesong@eternitypress.co.za and you'll get a personal notification from the author when the Second Tale of the Lifesong is released, as well as news and special offers.

Visit www.eternitypress.co.za to submit your own review of The Riddler's Gift and stand a chance to win a free copy of The Wizard's Way.